Omnibus

Gothic Blue
Portia Da Costa

Aria Appassionata
Juliet Hastings

Ace of Hearts
Lisette Allen

Doubleday Direct, Inc.

GARDEN CITY, NEW YORK

Black Lace novels are sexual fantasies.
In real life, make sure you practice safe sex.

This omnibus edition published 1996
by BCA
by arrangement with Black Lace

ISBN 1-56865-659-9

Printed in the United States of America

CONTENTS

Gothic Blue

Portia Da Costa

Prologue

*I*t had all begun at the archduke's reception, André recalled. Among the sparkling smiles, the dazzling wit and brilliant music. André had been standing on the sidelines, waiting for his beloved Arabelle to make her entrance, when an unexpected chill had cooled his blood.

Looking up, he had seen a woman passing by, her white hand on her attentive partner's arm. He had thought nothing of it at first; the room was full of such sumptuously-dressed women, and a great many of them were also very beautiful. But then she had turned around and looked straight in his direction and his shivers had changed instantly to a fever. Her luminous green-eyed gaze had cut right through him to his vitals, warming his body in exact proportion to its previous peculiar coolness.

The unknown woman was breathtaking, and her manner more imperious than that of a queen. In a swagged and tiered gown of red velvet with gold embroidery, her shape was delicate yet magnificently voluptuous. Her richly-coiled black hair had a heavy bluish lustre that caught the lamplight as she nodded slightly to him.

Who are you? he thought, then felt bereft as she began

1

to move away from him, her crimson dress like a vivid banner among the crowds.

A few minutes later, after questioning a passing acquaintance, André had discovered the name of his raven-haired enchantress. She was Isidora, Countess Katori, and her reputation was as dangerous as her beauty. Rumour had it that she practised the magic arts.

This is wrong, he told himself, as his eyes hunted for her across the ballroom, then followed her through the dance's complex figures. This is wrong, he thought, gritting his teeth and trying to ignore his suddenly aching loins.

I should not want her. I must not want her. I'm in love and in a week I'll be betrothed. It was only a matter of moments before his exquisite Arabelle would be here. Witty, radiant Belle, to whom he would gladly pledge his mortal soul.

And yet still the flamboyant countess ruled his flesh. His guilty heart hammered when, from out of nowhere, she appeared like a djinni before him, her full red lips forming a smile that left him speechless.

'Sir, do we not know each other?' she enquired, her voice low and teasing as she doffed a minute curtsey.

'I . . . I do not think so,' he answered, bending over her hand to kiss it, and discovering that her skin was fine as silk. 'Count André von Kastel, madam. At your service,' he said, releasing her, but reluctant to let her go.

'Isidora, Countess Katori,' she replied, her faint accent making her name a long caress. With a small graceful gesture, she nodded towards the nearby dancers, then turned from him and walked away towards them, apparently confident that he would simply up and follow her.

Vaguely ashamed of himself, André fell in step behind her, feeling like a callow boy in his first pursuit of love's wild passion. This daring, handsome countess had effortlessly made a youth of him, but to his chagrin, she had also made him hard. His state of high arousal was surely visible to all around him, but though it bothered him,

2

there was nothing he could do about it. And as they began the measure, he soon forgot to care.

Why me? he thought as they danced. His attire, a plain but well-cut coat and breeches, was subdued compared to most around him, and his title was just one among many others. His looks, though pleasant, he admitted, were not what he would have called outstanding or remarkable. Why on earth had the countess chosen him, a grey-eyed, brown-haired minor aristocrat of somewhat modest height, when the room was awash with dashing dukes and elegant princes?

As the dance progressed, he longed to press himself against her. His swollen member seemed to seek her female heat. From time to time, as the countess found a score of sly ways to insinuate herself against him, he tried to clear his mind of his lust for her and think of Arabelle. He imagined the shock and sadness on his dear one's face as she found him like this with another; he pictured the distress in her lovely eyes as he betrayed her. It appalled him, and yet still he felt helpless. Each time her image came to him, like a vision of grace and salvation, the woman on his arm appeared to sense it, and re-double her sinuous efforts to addle his wits.

Countess Isidora's perfume was like a dense musky cloud that hung around them, and when he thought of Arabelle, the odour subtly thickened. It filtered into his brain like a rich miasmic mist and charged his mind with exciting images that shocked him. Debauchery. Unnatural acts. Frenzied, bestial couplings. He imagined himself naked and stretched out over the countess's smooth white body, her firm breasts jutting upward against his chest. And when, under cover of the fast-moving dance, her lips touched his throat for just one second, he moaned and fought for breath, his senses reeling.

It had been but one brief contact, yet incredibly he felt her serpent tongue all over him. She was tasting him; savouring his skin and its hot, manly flavour. No part

3

of his anatomy escaped her, no secret was left unexamined. Her proximity overpowered him and sapped his will.

Half out of his mind, and unable to resist her, he imagined her lapping his belly and his privates. Her long devious tongue would wind seductively around his member, finding new areas of near-painful sensitivity.

Giddy with desire, André could not believe the messages of his senses. It was difficult to believe that they were still only on the dancefloor. In his dreams they were in a huge bed somewhere, their limbs thrashing, their mouths mating like rabid dogs. When his knees betrayed him, he stumbled towards her and half fell.

'Shall we take the air, my lord? You seem a little uncomfortable,' the countess murmured. Then, without further consultation, she led him towards a long, shadowed balcony.

Within seconds, all André's lustful prayers were answered. Her red mouth plundered his, her tongue darting into it and exploring, while her sure hands led his beneath her skirt. Through swathe after swathe of heavy lace and crumpled silk, he was drawn, ever upward and ever inward, until finally his shaking fingers met her treasure. He felt a nest of crisp, wiry curls, then folded flesh rendered slippery by her juices. She was a furnace, a pool of liquid satin, and her soft membranes flickered salaciously beneath his touch.

Almost numb with delight, André described a small movement with his fingertip, and was rewarded by a savage growl of pleasure. His elegant, high-born countess was twisting her hips like a harlot, and grinding her sex against the fulcrum of his hand. Her churning, scissoring thighs caressed his wrist.

'Pleasure me, my lord,' she demanded, rocking and swaying. 'Put your fingers inside me, before I faint.'

Delirious, André obeyed her, his nose and mouth filled with her spicy, rising vapours. Through what appeared to be a haze, an inexplicable thin blue nimbus, he saw her beautiful face slackened by lust. Somehow – by sleight of hand or by sheer force of will – she had released her breasts from her constricting velvet bodice, and their unfettered fullness gleamed like two pale fruits in the cool night air. Her teats were dark, the brownish-purple of drying blood, and he swore he could see them harden before his eyes.

'My lord!' she cried, her voice slurring as her nectar wet his hand. 'Enter me! I crave it!'

He pushed first one fingertip, then a second, inside her, and her whole body shuddered, then bore down. Her weight and the force of her made his wrist begin to ache, and to brace himself he set his feet apart. But still she was unsatisfied by his efforts.

'Fill me, my lord,' she moaned, her white teeth nipping at his neck. 'Give me more!'

He bore in with three fingers, then with four, and the countess keened like a she-wolf in full heat. Her long, perfumed thighs opened wider to give him access, then closed and locked unyieldingly around his arm.

'I spend, my lord! I spend!' she shrieked, untroubled at being heard by nearby dancers. The silky product of her rapture drenched his palm.

Only seconds later, she was down on her knees before him, her nails ripping at his breeches to free his member. As soon as he was liberated, she laughed wildly and plunged forward, wrapping her crimson lips around his tortured rod.

Never in all his days had André experienced an enclosure so sublime. The throat he was buried in seemed to undulate around him as if each muscle had a distinct and separate life of its own. She was almost swallowing him whole, he realised, and her sharp teeth were pressing perilously against his shaft.

'Madam, I beg of you,' he groaned, half in terror, half in ecstasy, his body thrilled to greater hardness by the danger.

Her only answer was to reach in and grip his ball-sac,

5

adding another layer of jeopardy to his predicament. He buried his fingers in the coils of her hair, trying desperately to control her, but he couldn't prevent her from engulfing him even deeper.

Abruptly, in the heart of his pleasure, André felt an icy surge of revulsion, of shame and betrayal, and at the moment of release, he thought of Belle, mouthing her name and picturing her perfect jewel-like smile. How could he have done this? How could he deceive her, damage her, break her faith? As he reached his peak, he despised himself profoundly.

He had little awareness of what happened in the next quarter of an hour or so, and of how they made their escape from the reception. All he remembered was a racing carriage and a moonless night. The countess's witch-like presence was like a drug to him, speeding up time and throwing a veil across his vision.

When they reached her luxurious apartments, she turned and surprised him. Instead of leading him straight to her bed and stripping him, she paused, smiled obliquely, and made the gesture of an accomplished hostess.

'A glass of wine, my lord?' she queried. 'The pleasures of the flesh are prone to make me thirsty, and I am sure they must do the same for you.'

'Yes, thank you, Countess,' replied André, feeling as profoundly out of his depth as he had done earlier. He accepted a goblet-like wine glass that was as large and ornately decorated as a liturgical chalice, even though a panicked inner voice entreated him not to.

The wine had a heavy, unusual taste – somewhat bitter and vaguely alkaline on the tongue – but he was, he realised, just as thirsty as she had suggested, so he drank it down despite its strange flavour.

When he put aside the glass, composed his thoughts and turned around, his companion was naked. Catching his breath, André looked back towards his goblet in confusion. At the reception, their dealings had been so hurried and so fumbled that he could almost believe he had only dreamed what had happened, but now he knew it was all true, and that the pale, curvaceous body before him was a prize he had won; his to enjoy, ripe and ready for the taking.

Yet he still hesitated.

'The wine ... It tastes – ' He swirled the pungent residue around his mouth ' – tainted.'

Isidora looked at him, her green eyes level and unblinking. 'I did add a little tincture to it, my lord, something of my own devising.' She smiled narrowly as he thrust the goblet along the sideboard and away from him. 'But do not worry, it is simply to increase your pleasure.' She paused delicately. 'It will enable you to endure.' Her tongue darted out, more serpent-like than ever, it seemed to André, as the room began to tilt ever so slightly. 'With this in your veins you will last for ever, my dear Count.' She began to laugh in a wild and odd way.

André felt unsteady now, and as they had at the reception, his knees began to buckle precariously. Isidora flew to his side, then helped him towards a couch, one firm breast brushing his arm as he leant on her.

'Who are you?' he asked again, his head spinning as she deftly undressed him.

'I am Isidora Katori,' she said archly, flinging away his shirt then attacking his already torn breeches. 'And very soon I will be your lover for all time.'

'I ... I do not understand,' he stammered, suddenly longing to get away from her but not able to. His brain was sending messages that he should throw her off, grab his clothes and flee these apartments immediately; but bizarrely, his body was helping her disrobe him. And as his breeches came off and were tossed away after the shirt, his penis bounced up in a lewd salute.

'You will,' she said softly, her hands gliding fleetingly over his body before she turned away and poured him more wine. 'Drink,' she ordered, pressing the newly-filled goblet to his lips.

André experienced again that strange phenomenon – his mind issuing instructions while his body ignored them and did the opposite. Silently screaming 'No!', he drank the wine.

When the goblet was empty, Isidora took it from his lips and hurled it to the floor, where it smashed into a thousand glinting shards.

'Now, my lord, you are mine,' she cried, her voice strident as she flung herself across him. 'We need only one final element to complete the process.' With an animal groan, she sank down on to his penis.

The pleasure he felt inside her tight, wanton channel was even greater than that he had experienced in her mouth. Against his will, he writhed beneath her, bucking upward to increase his penetration, while Isidora worked his body without mercy. Her flawless white skin was streaked with shining sweat, and her face was a twisted mask of dark hunger. As he looked up at her, André felt his strength begin to ebb. His manhood was still rigid inside her, but elsewhere he felt a great and surging weakness, like a torrent of tidal water rushing through him. Somewhere in his very innermost centre, he experienced the sensation that every cell in his body was beginning to melt. He was expiring, being snuffed out, his life extinguished; and as he realised it his member leapt and shivered.

A weird, singing light began to rise through every deliquescing part of him, and when it reached his brain, Isidora crowed in triumph, riding his release like a giant foaming wave.

I'm dying, André thought with an odd detachment, and knew that there was nothing he could do to stop it. With his seed still spurting, and his body still jerking, he breathed his last to the sound of Isidora's laughter and the evil pulse of her unholy, gripping flesh.

But as blackness fell and his eyes closed, a stark cold

replaced the fiery heat of sex and he saw an image of poignant horror in his mind.

It was Arabelle, his precious love, and she was calling to him. Her lovely face was glistening with a river of doleful tears and though she was nearby, he could barely hear her voice. There was a barrier of solid crystal set between them.

She's gone too, André realised as it ended.

Arabelle is gone and we never were as one.

Chapter One
Folly

'*B*loody thing! Bloody bloody bloody thing!' Belinda Seward kicked out viciously at the bumper of Jonathan Sumner's car and wished the whole damned thing in hell. 'What on earth are we going to do now?' she demanded, wiping the rain off her face, and looking up into the glowering black sky.

At that moment the darkness above seemed to split in two, as if a giant hand had torn a velvet curtain. Forked blue lightning sheared wildly across the heavens in a bolt that seemed far closer than the last one had been. Belinda felt suddenly convinced that the elements themselves were after them, or at least after Jonathan's ancient yellow Mini.

'We could shelter in the car,' offered Jonathan Sumner, pushing his wet, brown hair out of his eyes. It was a hopeless gesture because his hair, his clothes and every inch of his skin were all completely saturated. It had only been raining ten minutes but the pair of them were already soaked through to the bone.

'Oh yeah? And get struck by lightning?' enquired Belinda, knowing that all this wasn't really Jonathan's fault, but still needing to blame someone. The anger of the storm was getting to her, she realised; creating a tension that had to be released.

They had been lost for an hour or so now, and thunderbolts and torrential rain just seemed to put the cap on things, especially as the Mini – which Jonathan had assured her was reliable – had just broken down and was leaking like a sieve. Their plight wasn't all Jonathan's fault, Belinda had to admit, but somehow she couldn't seem to keep herself from blaming him anyway – something she had told herself she would try not to do.

'Well, I'm not staying here!' she said, reaching into the car for her shoulder bag, then staring first one way down the narrow road they were on, then the other. In both directions the vista was grim, wet and unpromising, so with a shrug, she set off along the route they had been planning to travel.

'What are you doing?' demanded Jonathan, catching her up. 'We can't just leave the car – '

'We bloody well can! I'm not standing around waiting for that pile of scrap to be struck by lightning. I'm going to find us a place to shelter.'

'There's shelter there!' Jonathan grabbed her arm then pointed to the heavy, mournful-looking trees that flanked the road on either side. At that moment, another great thunderflash came, making the trunks glisten momentarily in the teeming water, the knotty bark appearing silver and blue.

'Don't be a prat, Jonathan,' snapped Belinda, shaking him off and spraying water across him in the process. 'Trees are just as likely to be struck as a car is. I'm going to find a building of some kind. Maybe a house or a barn we can shelter in.'

'I suppose you're right,' said Jonathan, falling into step beside her and automatically taking the bag. 'But there doesn't seem to be much life around here, does there? That is, wherever "here" actually is.'

They had lost their bearings quite a while ago, about the same time as the storm had started brewing. It was weird, really; they had been doing quite well up until then, finding all their planned stops and keeping to their pre-arranged itinerary.

As they trudged along the ever narrowing road, chances of finding suitable shelter seemed to narrow too. The trees on either side loomed over them, moving in like tall, battle-blasted soldiers closing ranks around a helpless enemy. Whenever it was possible to see beyond the lines of trunks, there seemed to be very little to see – just desolate fields and scrubby sodden bushes. It seemed so different from the pleasant farming vale they had been travelling through just a couple of short hours ago.

Belinda flinched as another crack of thunder broke right over them, and the lightning seemed to fork both in front of them and behind. She could almost imagine that the little yellow car had just been blasted, and up ahead, the as yet unknown shelter they sought had also taken a bolt of white flame.

'Don't worry, Lindi,' said Jonathan in her ear, as he slid a wet but warm arm around her waist, 'the odds of being struck are astronomical. And if it gets us, at least we go together.'

Funnily enough, the inane remark soothed her, as did the strong male arm. There was something comfortingly solid about it; a safeness and reality that had an unexpected but not unwanted effect. They were both soaked through, but Jonathan's body, close as it was and moving against hers to the rhythm of his stride, seemed filled with an exceptional heat and vibrancy that filtered clean through the wetness of their clothes.

Saying nothing, Belinda let her own body lean in a little closer, and for the first time became aware of strange feelings. The sort of feelings that thunderstorms didn't usually engender.

The beating of the rain on her skin was insidious, and her wet clothes, pressing close against her, created the sensation of a sly but continuing caress. She could feel the water flowing everywhere; teasing her, cascading down across her breasts and dribbling between her legs, soaking a furrow that was already damp with a wetness of its own.

She was acutely aware, too, of the presence of a man beside her. Her brain said it was only Jonathan – her familiar Jonathan, her workmate and sometime lover – but her blood simply sensed him as a male. A strong, lean, muscular form with the pure power of sex between his legs.

Oh God, I'm aroused ... It's insane, but I am! I'm turned on, without trying, just for Jonathan!

There was nothing she could do about it at the moment, but the realisation of her desire almost scared her. She hadn't felt this aroused for many weeks.

As the lightning flashed again, she snuggled a little closer to him, adjusting her stride to fit his as the side of her breast rubbed lightly against his ribcage.

'OK, love?' he enquired, giving her a squeeze.

Belinda nodded, smiling up at him, then laughed as she swallowed a mouthful of warm rain.

'I'm sorry about this,' he went on, glancing up at the blackness of the sky as if it really was his fault. 'I mean ... I serviced the car, and it's in good nick for its age. It must be all the rain on the carburettor or something.'

'Don't worry, Jonathan,' Belinda shouted, competing with another roar of thunder. 'We did say we wanted a change of routine, didn't we?'

Jonathan grinned down at her, then nodded his head towards hers. 'At least it won't spoil your hair.'

'Bastard,' replied Belinda without rancour. They were both still deciding whether they liked her new look or not. After years with long hair, a mad, out-of-the-blue impulse had made her have her red-brown waves shorn to a short crop. It had been a shock to the system, and she still got a surprise sometimes when she looked in a mirror, but on a night like this she blessed her decision. The neat, elfin style shaped sleekly to her skull, and felt

14

far, far better than a dank, unmanageable mass trailing down over her neck and her shoulders.

And her new haircut didn't make her feel any the less feminine. In fact, she felt supremely female at the moment, as if the raving elements had transformed her into a nymph of the storm. She looked up again at Jonathan, just as he turned to look down at her. He seemed puzzled for a second by the heat of her glance, then he smiled, his grey eyes slowly widening in delight. Neither of them said anything, but Jonathan's arm tightened and he gave her a rakish wink.

It was more imperative than ever they find shelter.

After a few minutes more of splashing along the streaming road, it seemed as if some kind spirit in the tempest had been watching out for them. They found themselves by a wall that ran parallel to the road. It was dark and moss-grown, but a wall none the less; a high grey stone boundary that indicated an estate of some kind within, which would be sure to have somewhere they could shelter in, even if it were only a stable or outhouse.

Withdrawing his arm from around her shoulders with obvious reluctance, Jonathan took hold of her hand and by consensus they quickened their pace. Belinda wasn't sure if she was imagining things or not, but the road seemed to wind more now, and the wall with it. A little way on, after a particularly tortuous twist, an imposing set of gates interrupted the seemingly impenetrable stone barrier.

'Looks a bit dodgy,' observed Jonathan. The gateposts were somewhat broken down and the masonry crumbling, although the shape of two heraldic beasts atop each one was still quite clear, especially when the lightning lit them up. Belinda shuddered. The two statues looked like cats of some kind; not the usual lions but some sort of giant domestic cat made grotesquely malformed and ferocious.

'Here, pussy pussy,' said Jonathan with a grin.

'Don't be daft,' Belinda said shortly, a bit shaken by the peculiar stone animals.

The gates themselves were iron, and rusted here and there. They would have been as impenetrable as the wall itself was, but a broken hinge made one of them sag. Where the gate lolled lopsidedly towards the path beyond, there was a gap that could easily be squeezed though.

'What do you think, shall we try it?' asked Jonathan. As he spoke, another huge flash of blue light silhouetted his lean body in his clinging shorts and top, and Belinda felt an answering flash inside her. The strange desire that had kindled while they trudged seemed to flare up again with all the violence of the disorder above them. The sinuous forms of the cats on their pedestals appeared to writhe as if they too were consumed by lust, and though their eyes were only suggested by the stone, Belinda had a notion they were real and watching her. Or something was watching her. Maybe it was the storm itself; like a discarnate intelligence observing its own effects on her body.

'Yes, let's go for it!' she said, her voice rising to match the increasing loudness of the wind and rain. As she moved closer to one of the gateposts, she noticed something she hadn't seen before – the words 'Sedgewick Priory' cut into the stained grey stone.

Five minutes walk up an overgrown gravelled drive brought them out of the trees and face to face with the priory itself.

'It looks a bit grim, doesn't it?' said Jonathan with a resigned shrug. 'I don't think it's lived in.'

Belinda supposed the priory was built in what was termed the Gothic style; all tall brooding turrets and long narrow windows with a multitude of tiny diamond-leaded panes. The walls were dark, dark grey and sternly secretive, and had the same run-down quality as the perimeter wall and its gateposts, a decrepitude that masked a lasting strength. It looked far more like a warrior's fortified residence than it did an ecclesiastical structure, although there did appear to be what looked like a ruined chapel standing a short distance from the house, overgrown with greenery and half in the trees.

'There're no lights,' Belinda began doubtfully, 'but then again it must be the wee small hours of the morning. We were driving for ages, weren't we?'

Indecisive, they stood on the path in front of the house, kept from it by a soggy, forlorn-looking formal garden gone wild; and a series of low but straggling hedges. The house itself seemed to be staring at them, glowering and forbidding their entrance, its windows like lifeless blank eyes.

'I don't think I want to go in there,' said Belinda, pushing the shaggy wisps of her fringe from her brow and flicking away the water running into her eyes. 'I somehow don't think we'd be welcome.'

'But there's nobody in there, I'm sure,' murmured Jonathan, stepping forward and escaping her restraining hand. Belinda was impressed by his sudden boldness but still couldn't ignore the house's bleakness.

'We could break in, I'm sure. At least it'd be dry,' Jonathan said reasonably.

'No! Don't!' cried Belinda, cringing inside at a great wave of strange diffuse emotion. Something in the house had cried out at the thought of violation; it sounded crazy in her mind as she thought it, but nevertheless, it was what she had felt.

'Are you OK, Lindi?' said Jonathan, returning to her and sliding his arm around her waist again. The casual embrace was comforting and very welcome. The dour grey priory had spooked her, and Jonathan's arm was a touch of human warmth.

'Yes, I'm fine,' she murmured in a moment of quiet as the winds seemed to still. 'I just seemed to have a funny feeling about the house . . . the priory. It was almost as if there *was* someone in it . . . and they didn't want *us* in

17

it.' She paused, feeling the quality of her awareness changing. 'Well, not now at least.'

Jonathan looked bemused but seemed to accept her explanation, as he did so often in his easy-going way. 'Maybe you're right. It's probably dangerous anyway. Broken floorboards, rotted beams and such. We might be safer looking for an outbuilding or a shed of some kind.'

'What's that over there?' said Belinda, turning her back on the priory, the hairs on the nape of her neck prickling. Well, as much as they could when they were slicked to her skin with rain. As she squinted through the downpour, the lightning came again in its brightest flash yet, seeming to split the sky with a slice of blue flame. She was at once aware of seeing a small, pale structure that she hadn't seen before, about a hundred yards away across the lawn; and at the same time feeling the thick, almost tangible presence of the greater house behind her, watching her back with its dead, leaded eyes.

'I dunno . . . I didn't notice it before,' said Jonathan, turning in the direction of the little building away across the grass. 'It looks like a summer house or something.' His arm tightened and he gave Belinda a reassuring hug. 'Shall we try it? It looks in better condition than the house.'

The grass was waterlogged and squelched beneath their feet, and by the time they reached the summer house their trainers were soaked.

'I wonder if it's locked,' said Jonathan as they surveyed the odd, circular building that stood before them. It looked like a pseudo-Greek temple complete with tall, fluted columns, and its windows were narrow and shuttered. The white painted door was closed and looked as solid as the priory looked shambolic.

'Let's see.' Feeling her own rush of boldness and a determined desire to get out of view of the main house, Belinda tried the door handle, a great globular chunk of cut crystal. After a few abortive twists, it suddenly seemed to click from within, and the white door swung slowly open.

The room inside was circular, naturally, and as Belinda stepped over the threshold the lightning lit it up, bouncing jagged radiance off the pale, painted walls. There was no furniture of any kind, except a low circular divan, upholstered in a faded grey velour, but a second flash of light showed what looked like an ornamental drinking fountain set into a niche at the far side of the room.

'Weird,' whispered Jonathan, following her in.

'But dry,' pointed out Belinda, surprised that the room should be so, given the quality of the torrent outside. 'And there's a bed,' she added softly, feeling a return of the heat that the eerie house had cooled. 'A real bed. Isn't that better than being squashed up in the Mini?'

'Mmm . . .' Jonathan moved closer, as if catching her drift, then looked down at her, nibbling on his lip in a way that she always found appealing, particularly at special times like these. 'Are you tired?'

The logical answer was, 'Yes, of course I'm tired, I've been slogging up and down country lanes in a thunderstorm in the middle of the night', but Belinda found that she wasn't tired at all. She felt exhilarated, fired up by the storm, and strangest of all, aroused by her vague, formless fear of the priory. She felt its presence again, all around her; reaching out from the tall, grey building across the grass and enveloping her in a dark sensuality. Making a low sound of need, a moan in her throat, she pressed her wet body close against Jonathan's.

'Yes . . . oh yes, love,' he whispered as if he'd only been waiting for her signal. His lean, wiry arms snaked tightly around her, and his hands clasped her bottom through her shorts, pressing her loins against a hard, lively erection that she was surprised she hadn't noticed a lot sooner. She felt his breath warm and sweet on her face, then he was kissing her cheeks and her jaw and her lips and licking the trickling drops of rain from her face.

'I don't get this,' he said against her lips as they parted in readiness, 'thunder used to scare me witless as a kid – ' He ground his hot crotch emphatically against hers ' – and feel what it's done to me now.'

Belinda felt, and rejoiced in what the thunder had done. Her mouth was open now, sucking in his tongue, feeding on it. Jonathan's body felt harder than it had ever done; more manly, more appetising. Their moisture-soaked clothing was only the flimsiest of barriers between them and she fancied she could see steam rising as the heat of their bodies evaporated the wetness of the rain. Her nipples were like stones against his chest and she felt shameless, wanton. She rubbed herself against him, deliberately pleasuring herself, then parted her thighs, opening them around one of his to massage the demanding centre of her need. She was putting on a show, she knew, but didn't know for whom – it didn't seem to be for her familiar old Jonathan, no matter how much he was enjoying it.

'Oh, Lindi, you're so lovely,' he moaned when she released his mouth, his voice hoarse with surprise. She had sometimes been unenthusiastic lately, but now she felt eager, almost frantic, for sex.

Running her hands around his narrow male waist, she pushed her fingers into the backs of his shorts and slid them down over his rump, caressing the muscles and dipping into his furrow. He was tender there, as most men were, and he cried out loudly when she flexed her wrist, drove in deeper, and rubbed the tiny ring of his anus.

'Please ... Ooh, love, that's too nice,' he chanted, wriggling against her. 'Stop a minute, please ... Oh God, I need to pee before we go any further.'

'Ever the romantic,' crowed Belinda, pressing harder and massaging her pelvis against Jonathan's ready groin.

'Little bitch,' he answered, groaning but obviously

loving what she was doing. He squeezed her buttocks in return, then brought his wet lips down on hers again in a comprehensive, jaw-stretching kiss.

Belinda felt exultation surge through her. Her Jonathan was never like this; never so animal, so uninhibited. It was as if the tumult of the night had seeped into them as the pounding rain had soaked through their clothes.

'Go on then!' she almost shouted to be heard over the rolling of thunder in the air. 'Go and have your pee, then come back to me. I want you!' She abused his body once more – with a squeeze and a press – and felt her belly quiver as he groaned and twisted his wet face.

'Witch!' he hissed, then whirled away and almost ran from the folly, presumably into the undergrowth nearby, to relieve himself.

You're a wimp, Jonathan, she thought, half-fondly, half-despairingly, her head filled with a lewd, enticing picture of Jonathan's stiff, reddened penis and the long, twinkling torrent of his golden water.

What's happened to me? she thought suddenly, banishing the image, yet still feeling its forbidden fascination. She realised that she too needed to urinate, and without thinking she crushed her fingers to her crotch.

The pressure both eased and exacerbated her discomfort, and the sensation was so intense she let out a startled yelp. Pressing herself again and feeling both pleasure and pain and relishing them equally, she almost imagined she heard laughter within the thunder. Someone laughing at her antics and encouraging her; someone feeding off her hunger and erotic wildness. Still holding herself, she whirled around expecting to see Jonathan, but found the folly still empty but for herself.

'Who is it?' she whispered, rolling her hips and feeling hot darts shooting through her belly. 'Who is it?' she said, louder, then bit down abruptly on the question when the closed door of the folly flew open, and the wind seemed to fling Jonathan into the room.

'My turn now,' she said as he reached for her. In her

somewhere was the urge to do something outrageous: to drop her knickers and pee in front of him – she knew that he would love it – but the fact that this was somebody else's property cooled her madness. It was enough just to break in and shelter there.

'Hurry then,' urged Jonathan, his penis already rising up.

Out among the trees the blackness was bordering on total. By the light of the flashes, Belinda picked her way to a clearing a short distance from the folly and started unfastening the buttons of her shorts. As she peeled them down her thighs then hitched down her panties and squatted, the incongruity of what she was doing made her laugh.

God, she was wet through in the middle of a rainstorm – why was she so delicately tugging her knickers out of the way and only exposing her bum to the elements? In a few quick movements, she stripped off all her clothes: trainers, socks, T-shirt and shorts, pants and bra. Naked, she stretched her fingertips towards the raging sky, then parted her legs and angled her hips.

The release of her water was a relief so intense she almost climaxed. Whooping with manic joy, she felt the hot golden flood cascade down her smooth, shining thighs and blend with the rain on the grass.

'There! Are you satisfied?' she cried to no one in particular, then almost immediately felt a sense of being watched again. During the next lightning flash, she looked down at her own body and saw it lit weirdly, as if by a strobe, with streaks of blue radiance glancing off her wet skin. Her erect nipples shone like a pair of black jewels, and her pubis was a dark, eldritch smudge. 'Watch this!' she called out to the lightning-filled sky, then pushed her fingertips inward through her sodden female curls to seek out the tiny treasure within.

Gasping, she worried her clitoris roughly until she came, beating her hips to and fro through the downpour and the storm, then rising up on her toes as she peaked.

'Yes!' she called triumphantly. 'Yes, yes, yes!' As her pleasure swooped and spiralled, the black sky seemed to answer, as if roaring out a climax of its own.

'Who were you yelling at?' enquired Jonathan as she re-entered the folly. He was lying on the divan and his hand was near his crotch, so Belinda guessed he had been caressing his penis. He snatched away his fingers as she approached him across the tiles, as if not wanting her to think he needed manual stimulation.

Belinda knew she didn't need it. Her climax in the forest had primed her erotic spirit, and her sex felt empty and in need of male possession. Half throwing herself on to the divan beside Jonathan, she crawled on to her hands and her knees and offered him her body in the most enticing way she knew. Poised on all fours, she undulated her hips, her thighs wide apart and her vulva bare and gaping. Her whole body was wet but her female flesh was wetter still, and she knew that with the next bolt of lightning, he would see that.

Right on cue, the sky opened and pealed, and with a hoarse cry, Jonathan hurled himself upon her.

He slid in with such speed and to such a depth that Belinda was pushed forward and squashed under him. As he pounded her and pushed her, she gnawed the old velour beneath her and gouged it into bunches with her fists.

Gentle Jonathan seemed possessed with the same storm demon that she was, and his thrusts were savage and unfocused. He was hurting her but she was loving it. In seconds, she was soaring back to a climax. Rotating her hips, she shoved her bottom hard against him, then reached in between her legs to rub her centre. As his belly slapped her buttocks, she felt a flash of inner lightning, and as she climaxed, she stifled her screams in the soft grey cover.

'Lindi!' she heard Jonathan sob, then felt him lunge, then lunge again, as he jerked inside her. She was squashed like a star as he shuddered out his pleasure, but in her ecstasy there was no awareness of discomfort.

Floating in stillness and contentment, she felt Jonathan soften and slide out of her channel then roll over to lay his body down beside her. Remotely, she perceived the brutal storm was over.

The sky was quiet and the air was dark, and she and Jonathan were alone in their round, white folly. The night was all peace, and half gone, but to her surprise, she still felt that she was being watched; scrutinised in intense detail, by a pair of eyes that seemed to observe her from within. Brilliant blue eyes that were both hot and icy cold.

Chapter Two
The Eyes of the Night

'*B*elle,' the sleeper murmured. 'Arabelle, my love ...
Where are you?' he asked softly, as in his still chest
his heart began to beat.

It had been so long, so very long, but suddenly and
inexplicably she was alive again, her pleasure like a
brightly-burning flame.

How could this happen? he thought as his ribcage rose
once, then fell, then rose again, and in his veins the
sluggish blood began its flow. It seemed an ocean of
time since he had last felt this power, and never, in all
the many years of his existence, had he felt it from his
sweet Arabelle.

'Oh, Belle, how can this be?' whispered André, sitting
up with caution in his ancient, draped bed and gazing
across the room through the filter of a dozen silken veils.
He couldn't see its outline clearly, but he knew that on
the marble top of an antique sideboard stood the intri-
cately-carved rosewood casket that was the repository of
all that he had ever loved. He reached his hand out
weakly towards it, then gasped and slumped back on
the pillows. His energy was dim, and already drained
after only the slightest exertion.

Hardly able to keep his eyelids open, André stared

25

across the room through the veils. There, in the shifting darkness, he saw a thin, blue radiance that surrounded the rectangular box. It seemed to be seeping out through the very veining of the wood and forming a faint aura, an inch-wide cerulean halo.

But if you are still in there, my beloved, thought André in confusion, who is it that I am sensing outside? He turned his head on the soft lawn pillow-case, and looked now towards the window and its heavy velvet drapery. The thick, silk-lined curtains presented no barrier to his acute, inner vision, and he gazed out across the rain-lashed parkland and fixed his attention on the round white folly.

Immediately, he felt life in his lifelessness; the primal force of sex that never failed to revive him. Beyond the pale, columned walls of the little white building, there was someone on the point of making love, and against reason that someone was his Belle.

Fighting disbelief, hope and confusion, he struggled to focus and see her. In his mind there formed the image of how she had looked all those years ago, her lovely face at a very special moment. He saw her fine, harmonious beauty, the soft smile, and the delicate, almost tremulous sensuality of the first time she had permitted him a liberty.

Embarrassed, yet somehow eager, she had unfastened the lacings of her gown and her chemise, then opened them to show him her bosom. Lying in his bed now, a thousand miles and two hundred years away, André could still remember his euphoria, his delight, his instant rousing at the sublime young beauty of her breasts. How perfect her shape had been: how dainty, how pointed, how fresh. He could still hear her sigh as she allowed him to touch her, and his own groan as his passion overcame him.

He had loved her so much, and so much wanted to express that love with his body. He had been angry with himself for the brutishness of his lust, but had been unable to suppress or ignore it. Night after night, he had kissed her gently and decorously, his loins racked with craving. Night after night, he had retired to his bed and jerked his flesh to a long, solitary release with her sweet name and the word 'love' on his lips. They had been close, so close, to the night of their joining, when a dark, seductive evil had claimed him.

'No!' he cried, straining ineffectually and stretching out with his living mind towards the unexplained cause of his revival. Concentrating with difficulty, he retuned his vision on the interior of the folly, then gasped at the sight that assailed him.

Belle, but not Belle. His lost betrothed, his precious flower, on the point of being possessed by another.

Against his will, the image aroused him. Beneath his narrow, resting hand, his flesh stirred as it had not done in a long time. Like the miracle of life itself, his member stiffened and rose, far more vital than the rest of his body.

Arabelle had changed over the centuries, he saw now. Her body was boldly naked and more fully formed, and where once her burnished hair had tumbled in a wave to her hips, it was now shorn to a close, roughly-cut cap that hugged the graceful contours of her scalp. In the very centre of the circular, velvet-covered divan, she was crouched like a bitch before her master, her sex offered to a slim, dark-haired youth.

'Arabelle?' André whispered, his doubts growing stronger. He sent his mind circling the divan, and looked down into the young woman's face.

Yes, the features were the same, but seemed more defiant and a little less fine. The woman who was about to be taken looked much as his beloved might have done a few years after he had last physically seen her, when she had grown and tasted love's invigorating pleasures. This woman had experienced the richness and ecstasy of the flesh that Belle had never savoured, the consummation that Isidora had denied her.

27

'Witch! Foul devil! She-demon!' he hissed, his anger spurring him as sex had done. That black-haired monster had taken away two lives and condemned two souls to two separate kinds of torment. 'Get back to hell. I will not think of you,' he said coldly to his nemesis, and resumed his observation of the lovers. 'Who are you?' he said, as the young woman thrust out her hindquarters and the man behind her took advantage. The slim youth was rough as he thrust into his paramour's lush haven, but even so, André still sensed a mood of great tenderness. This was a joyous consensual act, just as it would have been if it were really Arabelle on the bed, and he himself were the lusty naked lover. The affection between the distant pair seemed to goad him like a new spark of dynamism. Strength returned fully to his hands and his fingers just as stiffness returned to his penis.

Clasping himself, he cried out, 'Yes!' And as if hearing him, the lovers convulsed, their meshed bodies lunging in the so-familiar throes.

'Oh dear God . . . Dear God,' André moaned, joining them in their pleasure, his own spasm so intense it felt like pain. After years spent in the half-life, his sudden release was much too much for him, and with a stifled sigh, he sank back to oblivion. His last awareness was cool fluid on his fingers.

Belinda woke to soft golden light. She smiled at a pleasant warmth on her naked body, and began to stretch and curl her toes and generally wake up slowly and luxuriantly, when suddenly awareness poured into her. With a gasp, she sat up and looked around her, panicked. Where the devil was she, and why was she naked?

Calm down, calm down, she told herself, drawing in deep breaths and trying to work out what had happened. Jonathan's presence beside her and the reassuring familiarity of his body quickly settled her, and as she touched his bare back, he grunted sleepily and stirred a little.

'Trust you,' she whispered, leaning over to kiss the nape of his neck. 'Here we are, stranded in the back of beyond, probably camping out illegally on somebody's property, and are you worried?' She watched him as he mumbled, licked his lips and then buried his face in the grey velour of the couch they had bedded down on. 'No. You just sleep like a baby. As usual . . .'

Yet somehow she couldn't find it in her to be cross with him. For one thing they must have trudged miles through the rain-soaked countryside last night, and that was enough to exhaust anyone. And on top of that, when they had found this, their haven, he had made love to her with all the power of a stallion, and given her a pleasure she hadn't felt for some time. Quite some time . . .

'It's OK, Mr Sleepy,' she whispered, ruffling his dark hair and knowing that nothing short of slapping or kicking him would wake him yet. Then, rising carefully from his side, she stood up and looked around again, hardly recognising the white folly in the morning sun. She couldn't remember whether it was she or Jonathan who had opened the shutters, but whoever had done it had changed the place entirely.

The small circular building was filled with light, and its design, with windows all the way around and going right up to the ceiling, seemed to capture and amplify the sun's radiance. It was like being trapped inside the golden, idyllic essence of summer, and it was easy to imagine the picnics and parties that might have been centred around this charming little structure.

But why have what was so patently a pleasure pavilion in the grounds of a priory? An ecclesiastical establishment? It seemed incongruous.

'Weird,' muttered Belinda, running her fingers through her hair in lieu of a comb and beginning to wonder what had happened to her clothes. Jonathan's shorts, trainers, T-shirt and briefs were strewn across the floor, clearly exactly where each item had been removed, but of her own clothing there was no sign at all.

'Uh oh,' she said to herself, as more memories of last night began to surface. Despite their solitude and Jonathan's complete insensibility, she felt the blood rise into her face in a vivid blush.

Last night, right in the middle of the storm, she had stripped naked in a woodland clearing, then peed herself and masturbated. She could still almost hear her shriek of pleasure.

Good Lord, what got into me? she thought, her fingertips brushing her throat nervously as if trying to twitch up a non-existent collar and hide the pinkness that was rising across her chest and up her neck into her face. She remembered feeling wild and exhibitionistic, and being filled with a strange sensation of being watched. And then, when she had returned to the folly and to Jonathan, she had offered him her body and they had rutted like a pair of animals.

But animals that care about each other, she thought, looking down at him fondly as he turned over in his sleep and began to scratch and fondle at the very member that had so pleasured her last night.

'That's right, get it ready for me,' she whispered to him, feeling naughty, then tip-toed away from him towards the door of the folly.

Outside, the beauty of the day took her breath away. Everything that had been harsh and turbulent last night was pacific and gently sun-kissed now. The grass was vigorously, almost preternaturally, green, and hung with drops of moisture like tiny diamonds. The sky was a delicate eggshell blue tinged with pink, and thin streamers of gauze-like mist were slowly dissipating. Even the grey priory across the park looked quite benign, and not a bit like the derelict hulk of the previous night. Belinda decided to make her way there as soon as she found her clothes.

Retracing her former steps into the woods, looking this way and that and on alert for possible company despite the apparent desertedness of the priory's spacious park, Belinda soon found the little clearing she had encountered last night. Her clothes were there, just where she had abandoned them, the pattern of their falling not dissimilar to that of Jonathan's. She could feel her blood stir again at the thought of how she had shed them and at her own crude and strangely pagan behaviour. And when she had to squat again, she was almost too embarrassed to perform.

Having been taken off in the shade, and sopping wet, her clothes were still in that condition. She shuddered at the touch of the clammy, ice-cold fabric against her skin, but consoled herself that they were at least clean again. She had never liked putting on once-worn clothes for a second time, especially after she had indulged in hectic sex. The vision of a steaming bath full of scented water suddenly presented itself, and Belinda wondered if there was a stream or something nearby so she could have a quick wash before she set off on her exploration.

Better not get lost though, she told herself, turning in a circle on the spot and squelching in her trainers. On all sides the trees were numerous and the woods deep and thick; it was only in the direction of the folly that she caught sight of bright light and open ground.

Back in their circular white refuge, Jonathan was still fast asleep, and much as she would have liked to discuss their situation, Belinda didn't have the heart to wake him. During her absence, he had turned again on the couch, and now lay in a foetal position with his two hands folded so sweetly beneath his sleeping face that he looked a perfect innocent. She decided to walk to the priory and back and give him time to come to wakefulness naturally.

As she set off across the grass, sheer pleasure to be alive made her less aware of her wet clothes and the fact that she and Jonathan were lost. The sun was surprisingly high now, and a light breeze made the bejewelled grass ripple. There were birds singing cheerfully in the woods and she caught sight of a rabbit, or a hare perhaps, sprinting ecstatically along the edge of the treeline. And now, closer up, the priory looked even less like its midnight incarnation.

The building appeared both larger and somehow smaller than it had done last night, spreading out far further than had previously been apparent, with numerous wings, buttresses and even a crenellated turret. But it no longer seemed to claw the sky and loom.

It was still not an 'easy'-looking residence however, and its tall leaded windows with their rounded Gothic arches and tiny lozenge-like panes had a curious and watchful air of latency, as if a presence beyond them lay waiting.

'Don't be an idiot,' Belinda told herself, still studying the priory and frowning. It took her just a few seconds more to realise what it was about the house that had really changed, or seemed different. Last night the priory had seemed deserted, desolate, a blasted ruin; but now, in the brilliant day, although it still wasn't a well-kept building by any means, it certainly looked sound enough to live in.

Pausing to slip off her squelchy trainers, which were taking the edge off her appreciation of the view, Belinda continued to study the priory, her eyes zeroing in on an upper window, where for a moment she thought she saw movement. What if there was actually someone in residence there; someone with a phone, who could help them in their predicament? Barefoot, she began to stride faster.

As she neared the house, Belinda soon found herself in a jungle of flowers and greenery which must have once been a garden. If there were inhabitants at the priory, they evidently weren't keen horticulturists, as both wild and cultivated plants and flowers were growing in a tangled but strangely pleasing jumble. She saw and smelt roses, as well as delphiniums and hollyhocks, but among them were deadly weeds like belladonna.

Reaching a gravel path, she slipped her trainers back on and made her way towards what seemed to be the priory's front door; a massive, weather-beaten oaken affair which stood beneath its own entrance porch. Just as she reached a set of shallow steps, the heavy studded door swung open and a handsome man greeted Belinda with a smile.

'Er . . . hello,' she said, suddenly at a loss and able to do nothing but simply stand and stare. The man standing in the doorway was remarkable; a towering, bronzed giant dressed in blue jeans and skimpy white vest. 'My friend and I are lost,' she managed to say at last. 'We spent the night in your folly.' She glanced over her shoulder towards the distant white building. 'I hope you don't mind. We haven't made any mess.' The tall man just smiled. 'I . . . I . . . um . . . I wonder if you have a telephone I could use? Our car's broken down. We need to call a garage and the battery in our mobile phone is flat . . . We're supposed to be meeting up with someone soon and we've got to let her know that we've fallen behind schedule.'

The tall man continued to smile, nodding his close-cropped head encouragingly.

Belinda felt uneasy. Why didn't the man answer instead of just standing there like a silent, living statue?

'We can pay for the call,' she offered doubtfully, remembering her shoulder bag was back at the folly.

The handsome giant continued to smile, his large white teeth almost twinkling in the sunlight, his muscled arms gleaming, his eyes –

His eyes. Fighting her growing bemusement, Belinda looked the stranger directly in the eye.

Was this the man she had sensed last night? The watching male presence? There was certainly a mythic quality about him. With his ultra-short blond hair he looked like a Teutonic god just returned from Valhalla in modern dress.

After a few seconds Belinda knew that this wasn't her night watcher. His eyes were a soft brown, and mild, and his expression was gentle and welcoming, despite the fact that he still wouldn't speak to her. The eyes she had seemed to see last night had been blue, a piercing electric blue, and while they had not seemed particularly malevolent, they had possessed a power that could frighten and inspire awe.

Still the man continued to smile, but after a moment, however, he stepped back into the house behind him, waving Belinda through with a gesture of welcome. Feeling she might be making a big mistake, Belinda ventured inside.

The hall in which she found herself was cool, quiet, and rather dark, and looking around she was surprised by its opulence. From outside, the priory looked run-down, even after this morning's improvement, but inside it was well maintained, almost sumptuous. All around her was panelling, in oak or some other rich wood, the carved patterns forming tall arches with curvaceous mouldings. A few pieces of heavyish but gleaming furniture were placed against the walls, and in inset niches hung a number of sombre paintings.

Unfortunately there wasn't a telephone in sight.

'Do you have a telephone I could use?' repeated Belinda as her golden giant closed the door behind them. As she turned round to face him he made his first recognisable response: a slow shake of his head and another smile, this time regretful. He shrugged his huge shoulders, making his taut muscles bunch and surge.

Belinda tried desperately to contain her irritation. How on earth did people survive out here in the back end of nowhere with no telephone? It was almost unheard of.

'We're stuck then,' she said glumly. They would have to see if they could start the car or get directions to the nearest village, then walk there and arrange a tow. And find a phone so they could get in touch with Paula, who wouldn't be too pleased if they didn't phone her soon.

'Could you give me directions then, please?' she asked. She was tempted to ask if the blond giant had a car and could drive them to the next village, but the request seemed a little premature.

The man shook his head again, still smiling the smile that was now getting on Belinda's nerves. Under other circumstances, she would have found the silent blond very attractive – his golden body was as magnificently hewn and solid as the wooden furniture and panels around them – but his lack of co-operation was fast becoming irksome.

'Oh, come on!' she cried, exasperated. 'Surely you can tell me which direction to set off in!'

The blond giant continued to smile but there was a strangely wistful expression in his eyes, and suddenly, as Belinda stared at him, hoping to elicit a response, he made a short chopping gesture, just beneath his chin and in front of his sinewy neck. He did it a second time and slowly shook his head.

Oh dear God, he's dumb! thought Belinda as realisation dawned, and she felt an instant wave of sympathy. Poor man, how awful. What a handicap . . .

'I'm terribly sorry,' she said quickly, 'I didn't realise you couldn't speak.'

The blond man shrugged again, and his immense shoulders rippled.

What the hell do we do? thought Belinda, wishing again that she had brought her holdall, because in it was a biro and a notepad. Presumably her blighted Adonis could write?

As she thought this, her silent companion made a swift gesture that seemed to indicate 'hang on a minute' and strode over to an elaborately-carved table. From a drawer in it, he took a thick sheaf of creamy white paper and a pencil, and grinned at Belinda as if to say he had read her mind. As she moved towards him, he leant over the table and began writing quickly.

My name is Oren, she read, when he handed over the top sheet of paper. His letters were spare and rounded but his writing was beautifully clear. *I am sorry that we have no telephone,* he went on, *but we have little need of one. If you would like something to eat, a bath, and a place to rest a while, my master offers you the hospitality of his home.*

How can he offer hospitality if he doesn't even know we're here? was Belinda's first thought. Unless the movement she had seen earlier at the upper window actually had been somebody watching her?

Her next thoughts were more basic, as she looked up and found Oren watching her expectantly. She had slept well last night, but the prospect of a bath – preferably a long, long soak in flower-scented water – seemed like a mirage in the desert. And she suddenly realised she was ravenous. The last thing she had eaten had been a bag of crisps at about seven o'clock yesterday evening. The vision of a completely wicked and calorie-laden plate of croissants, curls of butter and strawberry preserve became a second mirage, just as vivid and equally as tantalising.

'That's very kind, Oren,' she said, smiling up at him, still feeling a little uneasy, and surprised at such a generous offer made so soon. She wanted to refuse as graciously as she could, but heard herself say instead, 'I'd love a bath, and I'm absolutely starving! I just need to go back to the folly and fetch Jonathan – '

Oren turned to the table and wrote again on a fresh sheet of paper.

Please do not worry. Someone will bring your friend to you. Let me show you to a place where you can bathe.

As soon as Belinda had read the few short sentences, Oren gestured towards the imposing staircase at the far end of the hall, indicating that she should follow him.

Belinda hesitated. This was crazy . . . She didn't know this man from Adam, and she hadn't even met his mysterious master. The pair of them could be serial killers for all she knew. Yet still she found herself walking beside Oren towards the stairs.

'My name's Belinda, by the way. Belinda Seward,' she said as they reached the first step.

Oren nodded and smiled again, and Belinda suddenly felt herself goose-bumping, in spite of the morning's sultry warmth.

It was impossible – but she suddenly had the queerest feeling that Oren had already known her name before she told him. Swallowing nervously, she followed him up the stairs.

Jonathan stretched, then turned over, patting the velour beside him in a blind sleepy search for Belinda.

'Lindi?' he muttered, opening his eyes when his fingers didn't find her. 'Lindi, love, where are you?' Sitting up, he glanced worriedly around the folly.

There was no sign of her, except her bag, a few feet away from the couch, and that reassured him. She was around somewhere; probably slipped away for the same reason she had left the folly last night. Shoving his hand through his tousled hair, he grinned to himself, remembering her return.

Even now, in retrospect, her passion astounded him. And not only hers. Not for a long time had he felt so full of desire, so strong. His own forcefulness had increased his physical pleasure, and it had seemed to have had the same effect on Belinda. Never before had she responded with such wantonness, so wildly and with so few inhibitions.

'We ought to get caught in thunderstorms more often,' he said aloud to himself, reaching down to touch what memory had stirred. But as he handled himself lazily and felt his flesh swell and harden, he was suddenly surprised by the sound of a female laugh.

Snatching his fingers away from his penis, Jonathan looked around again. The soft laughter had definitely been female and for a moment had seemed to sound quite close, but it hadn't been Belinda's throaty chuckle. As he was pulling on his shorts and underpants, it rang out again, and this time he was able to discern that it came from outside, among the trees, and that it had a curious tone to it – an odd muffled quality, as if the amused person were trying to suppress her own giggling.

Jonathan wriggled into his T-shirt, stepped into his trainers, then made his way quickly to the door of the folly, bent on finding the unknown laughter's source.

Outside, he could see no one, but he heard the laugh again, and it seemed to be coming from the woodlands to the rear of the folly. Following what looked like a faint and overgrown path, he set off along it as stealthily as he could. The air among the trees was moist and fresh, and the atmosphere pleasantly cool for what seemed already to be a scorchingly hot day. Jonathan breathed deeply as he walked, enjoying the green, mossy scent of the woods.

After about a minute, he caught sight of something pale flashing among the sturdy trunks of the mature trees around him, and guessing it was the origin of the laughter he speeded up, while still taking care to proceed quietly.

All of a sudden, he found himself almost on top of the woman he sought. As he crouched behind a tree, hidden by the tall grass and weeds that grew around it, he saw that what he had thought was one woman was really two.

They were hardly more than girls, actually: two slender blondes – a little alike, cousins possibly – who appeared to be a few years younger than he was, possibly about eighteen, or perhaps nineteen or twenty.

Both were clad in thin white dresses and they were sitting on a patch of soft turf at the side of a slowly-flowing stream, kicking their bare feet playfully in the water. They were each as beautiful as wood nymphs, both in their faces and in their lightly-covered bodies, and Jonathan's penis rose again to salute them. And though their actions and their naturalness made it seem as if they weren't aware of his presence, Jonathan's sixth sense seemed to tell him a different story. Why else would they suddenly abandon their innocent splashing and lean towards each other for a kiss? A prolonged and very sensuous one on the lips . . .

Jonathan clapped his left hand across his mouth to keep in his exclamation, and with the other he reached down and touched his groin. He had often dreamed about watching two women making love, but never before had he really seen it happen. His cock stiffened and strained until it ached beneath his fingers, while on the riverbank a magical tableau was enacted.

Although in many ways the two blondes looked alike, as they kissed, distinctions became apparent. One was clearly a little older and more confident, and she controlled both the kiss and her companion. The younger girl – who wore her hair loose as opposed to her friend who wore hers in a soft ponytail – was more acquiescent, and the way she used her hands and her lips was more tentative. Her touch was cautious, almost subservient, and she allowed her mouth to be forced open by her friend's bold tongue.

To his surprise, Jonathan found himself wishing that it was he who was being kissed so forcefully. He suddenly felt a profound need to surrender somehow. He wanted to be taken, made to accept caresses rather than give them, and to perform solely for another person's pleasure. He wanted to be rolled on to his back, on the turf, as the younger blonde was being made to, and he wanted to lie there and be kissed and touched and stripped. Then be ridden until he cried out in wild release.

At the thought of that, his penis leapt and almost unmanned him, but by an effort of will he staved off ejaculation. He bit his lip, clenched his fists at his sides and tensed every muscle in his suddenly burning body. He closed his eyes as if to banish temptation, but behind his eyelids he still saw the two blonde beauties.

I'm sorry, Lindi, he thought to his absent lover. She had only left him for a little while. She might only be a matter of yards away, exploring. Yet already he was as good as being unfaithful.

But wasn't it almost Belinda's fault? he reflected suddenly. He hadn't felt this hungry for sex in ages, and thinking back to last night, and the storm, he hadn't really felt amorous then until Belinda had suddenly sidled up close and pressed her body against his. It was she who had changed the parameters, she who had set his mind to thoughts of lust.

An indistinct cry brought him back from the storm-tossed night.

The two blondes were gazing at each other intently now, as if passing messages with their eyes, the older one looming over the younger. As Jonathan watched them, hardly breathing, the older girl unbuttoned the front of her lover's cotton dress and drew apart the bodice like a pair of white wings.

The younger, more submissive girl's breasts were exquisite. Not large, but firm and unsagging, even when lying down. They seemed to challenge the very air with their fresh and perfect curves and the twin cherry-coloured peaks that delicately crowned them. And the older girl did exactly what Jonathan wanted to do. She leant over her partner and began to suck hard on one nipple while plaguing the other with her swiftly moving fingers.

Jonathan had sensitive nipples himself, and his own tiny teats seemed to stiffen and tingle in sympathy. Still clutching one hand to his groin, he used the other to tweak his small, brown crest.

As the blonde woman rolled her friend's nipple between her finger and thumb, Jonathan aped her action. Delicious darts of feeling shot down to his belly as he

40

pinched himself, and seemed to increase the building pressure in his groin. He found himself shifting his bottom slightly where he crouched, and he prayed that his two love-nymphs wouldn't hear him. He felt his penis jerking dangerously in the cage of his underpants, and he knew that at any moment he would have to set it free.

And still he could do nothing but watch the show.

The girl beneath was writhing now, her slender legs scissoring, her hands travelling rabidly over the hair, the back and the shoulders of her busy companion. The two were completely intimate but – Jonathan realised with surprise – quite unspeaking. They both made odd little muffled groans and gasps, but there were no endearments, no questions, no words of praise. Not even when the older woman sat up, lifted the other's skirt, and without pause or warning jammed her hand between her squirming lover's legs.

The assaulted one gasped as if someone had knocked all the wind out of her, and it was no wonder, Jonathan realised. Not one, not two, but three fingers had been pushed inside her vagina; very quickly, in one untempered thrust. He could see the penetration perfectly from his hidden point of vantage; the young woman's smooth legs were as widely spread as she could get them, and her body arranged as if especially for him to see.

Unable to help himself, Jonathan pushed his hand inside his shorts and underpants and began rubbing at his stiff and aching penis. The sight before him on the riverside was so raw, so real and so erotic that he knew now he would experience agony without release.

What the two blonde girls were doing before him was not a bit like his preconceptions of lesbian pleasure. What he had imagined was a slow, ritualistic build up. Love-making that was stately and gracious; prolonged; almost dream-like. But instead the older one was ... well, she was fucking her friend – there was no other

41

word that could adequately describe it. She was using her whole arm and hand in a powerful sawing motion, working her wedged fingers inside her partner and crudely stretching her.

And her partner was loving it. She didn't say so, but her movements spoke for her. Jonathan watched, rapt, and with his fingers tightly clamped around his member, as the younger girl lifted herself on her hands and feet, and began to swing her body to and fro, almost forcing herself on to her lover's stiffened hand. She was strong and limber, and she reciprocated the action of the other woman's shoves as if trying to take the entire marauding limb inside her. She seemed intent on immolation; on being entirely and comprehensively possessed.

Although neither woman spoke or even cried out, other than the most formless of grunts, it was obvious when the younger of them climaxed. Her body went rigid and her beautiful face contorted as she lurched forward in one final frantic jerk. As Jonathan watched her, almost hypnotised, her smooth belly rippled and her bare toes gouged the earth.

It was too much. He had already seen far more than he should have. Slumping to the ground, he began working his own hips back and forth in a motion that echoed the blonde girl's thrustings. His cock was a rod of iron now and he had to give it easement; swivelling awkwardly, he revealed it to the air, then groaned as a vagrant breeze caressed his glans.

His need to climax was urgent, more pressing than he could remember in a long time, and as he pumped himself, he almost forgot his wanton wood-nymphs. Jerking his hips in ungainly circles, he pushed his penis through his fingers, focusing solely on the sensations he created.

It wasn't until the perfect moment, when his rushing semen jetted out in long white strings, that he thought again of his two companions in the forest. And opening his eyes, he looked up and suddenly saw them.

42

Like two mysterious blonde phantasms, they were standing over him and watching, their slender bodies naked, their pretty faces wreathed in smiles.

Chapter Three
The Magic Interior

When they reached the landing, Belinda stopped in her tracks. At the head of the stairs was a large and quite arresting oil painting; a picture of a man in period dress who had eyes that were the bluest she had ever seen. As she stared up at the image, half-entranced by both the eyes and the commanding image that the subject presented, she became aware that Oren was beside her, also – seemingly – transfixed.

'Is he one of your master's ancestors?' she enquired, turning her attention to the equally eye-catching man at her side, the tall sculpture in living golden flesh.

To her surprise, the mute shook his head, his own warm brown eyes twinkling as if he were privy to some private joke.

'Well, it's a fabulous picture anyway,' she said, taking a step forward for a closer look. Although she was no costume expert, Belinda guessed the man to be wearing eighteenth-century clothing. His expression was both solemn and challenging, and his hair was long, caught into a tail at the back, and had a strange whitish look to it, as if it were dusted with narrow streaks of fine powder. He had on a coat of navy blue velvet, with a high stand-up collar and sloping away tails, and he cut a dashing figure in pale breeches and high boots.

He was a handsome man, in both face and body, yet it was his eyes that drew Belinda's attention. They seemed to bore right into her, directly from the canvas, their colour brilliant and their intensity astounding. There was sadness in those eyes but they also made her feel profoundly vulnerable, so much so that she was forced to turn away. Almost as if he had read her mind and her fears, Oren smiled back at her reassuringly, then gestured that they move on along a corridor to their left.

Still disturbed by the portrait, Belinda followed her guide.

Who is he? she wondered, still captivated by the blue-eyed man. She was aware that the house around her was unexpectedly well-maintained and exquisite, but she felt too fazed to note its decor's more subtle features.

The man in the painting, she realised, had exactly the same blue eyes that she had seen last night in her dream or whatever it was. They were the eyes that had watched her making love with Jonathan.

Don't be crazy, Seward, she told herself, almost running to keep up with Oren's long stride. As they turned a corner and started down a spacious oak-panelled corridor, she saw that a whole row of portraits hung there, and all, it seemed, of either descendants or antecedents of the man at the head of the stairs.

The family likeness was uncanny. The nobleman in eighteenth-century breeches and boots was the very image of the one who now wore the garb of an Edwardian dandy. Strong genes, thought Belinda, pausing before a painting of yet another family member, dressed in a morning suit from the turn of the century. This man had much shorter hair but it still had the same almost dusted look to it, and he carried a top hat, suede gloves and a cane. There was the same arrogant melancholy in his blue eyes.

I'd love to have been able to meet you, thought Belinda

45

as she tore herself away from the picture to follow Oren. Any one of you. Your eyes, they're out of this world somehow. So beautiful, so brilliant, so alive, even if only in a painting.

At last, she and Oren seemed to have reached their destination, and he pushed open a door then ushered her through into a bedroom.

Belinda gasped. The room was breathtakingly sump-tuous and about as far away from last night's impressions of the house as it was possible to get. Everything around her was luxuriously ornate and made no excuses for being so. She was in a pleasure chamber, a temple of sensuality, a retreat created to please and be pleased in.

Wherever Belinda looked she saw velvet, brocade, rich carpeting and the choicest of rare antique furniture, every piece softly gleaming with polish. The colour scheme was womb-like reds, ruddy pinks and vibrant corals, with ornamentation – wherever possible – in gold leaf.

'Wow!' she said, at a loss at the sight of such magnificence.

Oren just smiled and made an expansive gesture which seemed to indicate 'enjoy'. Then, while Belinda stood and stared, still unable take it all in, he retreated, leaving the red room with only a pause for a shallow bow.

What now? thought Belinda, staring around at the chamber that contained her, then walking over to the bed and sitting down.

This wasn't the sort of guest accommodation she would have expected for someone who had literally wandered in unannounced. No, this was the sort of setting a wealthy man would commission for a loved one, either a wife or a treasured mistress. It was a place for trysts and the long, lazy rituals of passion; it seemed to echo with the cries of past desire.

Rolling on to her back, Belinda kicked off her trainers,

stretched out on the crushed velvet bedcover and studied the elaborate mouldings of the ceiling. What would Jonathan think of all this when he arrived? she wondered. If he arrived ... Oren had implied that someone would fetch him. But who? The whole priory had an odd sense of desertedness about it, even here in its magic interior which was so different from the way it looked outside.

Something unusual caught her eye as she tilted her head back, and sitting up and twisting round she looked more closely at what appeared to be a set of velvet curtains, a couple of yards deep, that hung against the wall over the carved head of the bed. It seemed strange for them to be there as the windows were all on the other side of the room, and immediately her curiosity was piqued.

Shuffling up to the pillows, she reached for the gold tasselled pull-cord that hung by the curtains and gave it a slow, steady yank. Immediately, as if on a well-oiled modern track, the curtains parted to reveal what was behind them.

It was another portrait. Another handsome man of the same blue-eyed lineage.

The pose this time was far more casual and naturalistic, fusing a modern look with an antique background and clothing. The man in the picture appeared to be half-sitting, half-lying on the same bed that Belinda was on, or one very like it. He was leaning back languorously against a mound of crimson pillows, his expression vaguely sleepy. And though his eyes had the same hint of sorrow that pervaded the portraits of his relations, he was also smiling a smile of satisfaction. His hair was long, loose and slightly tousled, and he wore just breeches, stockings and a voluminous cloud-white shirt that lay open to show his slightly hairy chest.

It was the most erotic image of a man that Belinda had ever seen.

A woman painted this, she thought suddenly. A

woman he was involved with. He looks almost as if he's just been making love.

Turning around again, Belinda slid down to the bed's wooden footboard, and leant back against it to stare up at the unknown man.

He really was exceptionally good-looking, and would have been so as much today as in any age. His features were strong and candid, with a slightly snub nose and a generous, sensual mouth. As ever his eyes were an electric, lightning blue, only this time they were hazed, as if with passion.

'God, you're beautiful!' whispered Belinda, noting the way the pale *déshabillé* clothing only accentuated the fine structure of the man's body. He was well built – athletically 'chunky', she would have called him – although the contemporary term seemed inappropriate somehow. And there was no denying the promise of his virility; a substantial bulge deformed the smooth line of his breeches . . .

On this bed, she thought, feeling a faint stirring of lust in her belly. At some time in the past, her unknown blue-eyed paramour had made love to a woman on this bed. Closing her eyes, Belinda imagined him first smiling, then stretching, and then rising up from his resting place among the pillows and beginning to strip off his few items of clothing.

It was the ultimate romantic fantasy. To be taken in these magnificent surroundings by a powerful, courteous lover from a bygone age. She pictured him naked, his hair loose, looming over her, his strong body primed and ready for sex.

'Mademoiselle, I must possess you,' he might whisper as his elegant hands peeled the clothes from her body. When she was as bare as nature intended, he would probably kiss her all over, touching his lips and his tongue to her every sensitive zone. Modern men thought they knew it all where sex was concerned, but something told Belinda that this nobleman from the past possessed more knowledge and erotic skill than all her small band of contemporary lovers put together.

It was the eyes that made her think that way, she supposed, sliding down to lie flat on the bed, her own eyes still locked with the blue ones in the portrait. The man in the picture had a gaze that was full of experience. She knew beyond a shadow of a doubt that he had a whole gamut of poignant memories to draw on: passion, love, excess; conquest, loss, sorrow. There were lifetimes of wisdom in that look.

'Who are you?' she whispered again, as in her fantasy he began to caress her. Pushing up her T-shirt, she cupped her bare breasts, imagining that her hands were those of the man on the wall above her.

As she squeezed gently, she caught her breath. Her palms and her fingers felt suddenly and inexplicably cool. Not cool within, but simply cool against the skin of her breasts. Her nipples puckered at the sensation, tingling deliciously. The coldness seemed to spread, even as she acknowledged it, moving down over her midriff towards her belly. Opening her eyes, she looked to see if one of the long casement windows was open and letting in a draught.

One window was open, but the day was calm and the curtains hung still and heavy. Belinda shuddered, not from the cold, but from a strange excited fear. With shaking fingers she unfastened her shorts and eased them down, with her panties, to her knees.

Was it wishful thinking or was there a presence in the room with her? Belinda thought of all the tales of the supernatural that she had read in her lifetime and wondered if her own close encounter had finally arrived. It was something she had always wanted to happen, something she had often hoped for, in spite of the continued opposition of her rational mind. She had never truly believed in the supernatural but what was happening to her now felt incredibly real. The coolness flowed down over the skin she had just bared and seemed to soak in through her pores and tickle her innards like chilly fire.

'It's you, isn't it?' she said accusingly to the portrait, half-expecting the man to be laughing. But still he simply smiled his teasing smile. 'Oh my God,' she croaked, twisting on the bed as she felt something almost liquid seem to flow into her vulva. The texture was honeyed, yet cool; insubstantial yet paradoxically tangible against her burning sexual membranes.

What's happening? What are you doing? she thought frantically, pushing her fingers into her furrow to try and authenticate the sensation she was feeling. Her flesh was running wet but it was warm to the touch; she could not detect the chilly unction from the outside but could only feel its strange effects from within. With a groan she began rubbing her clitoris, massaging it slowly with the silky thrilling coldness.

Helplessly aroused, Belinda circled her hips, enjoying the constriction of her tangled clothing around her knees and the thrill of a peculiar dual reality. She could see that she was alone in the room but within her mind she was convinced that she had company. The blue-eyed man from the portrait was with her. As she slicked her aching clitoris she felt his hand upon her breast, long fingers cradling it, his thumb pressing against her nipple.

'You devil ... You devil ...' she whispered as the mysterious coldness aroused her teat and her vulva. The fluid, viscous chill was overflowing between her legs now, its ghostly trickles running down across her anus. 'What are you doing to me?' she begged as her sex-flesh rippled. It felt as if someone was pouring cooled syrup directly on to her, relentlessly filling her sensitive channel until she was awash. 'Oh God, stop it!' she cried, knowing in her heart that she really wanted more.

The ectoplasmic essence was oozing inside her now, creating chills of cool sensation within her body. She could feel it in her vagina, pushing and welling, and more subversively, sneaking its way inside her anus.

The invisible substance was rising into her and filling her, creating pressure on hidden pleasure nodes in her sex.

Looking down between her legs, Belinda tried to see the flow of fluid, imagining it blue as its cool nature suggested. But all she could see was herself.

With her thighs as far apart as her makeshift shackles would allow, she had a perfect, uninterrupted view of her womanhood. She was wet and her love-juices were glinting on her sex and on her fingers, yet there was no sign of the ghostly inundation. She could feel it and feel the tension it created, but all that was visible were her genitals, pink and normal in their arousal.

'Oh please...' she groaned as the pressure still increased, and her beleaguered clitoris seemed to swell beneath her finger. It was pushed out now, like an insolently proud berry, as if there really was a volume of fluid massed behind it. Increasing her efforts, she pounded hard on the tiny organ.

'You! You bastard!' she cried, focusing again on her blue-eyed nemesis as she climaxed and the urgent forces instantly dissipated. Kicking her legs and cupping her vulva, she thrashed and moaned and rode the waves of sweet release until they mellowed.

'You...' she muttered vaguely when the tumult was over, and she sat up, still bare-bottomed, on the bed. The man in the portrait looked exactly as he had before she had begun her self-pleasuring, but somehow she sensed that a change had taken place. He still looked ever-so-vaguely unhappy, but there seemed to be a faint glow of hope about him too.

'You!' she said again, studying the painting in search of a more tangible change. 'You did something to me... You've done something. What is it?'

The handsome blue-eyed man seemed to mock her, to challenge her.

'I'm not crazy, I'm just tired,' she told herself, trying to take hold of her innate lucidity. 'It's just the novelty of this room, or hormones or something . . . Imagination.' Shaking her head to clear it, she began pulling off her clothes, then stood up, looked around the room, and wondered where the promised bathroom was.

After a moment, she realised that there was a door set into the panelling on the far side of the room, and beside it was a fine Chippendale chair with what looked like a silk robe laid across it, something she could have sworn wasn't there when she had first entered. Frowning, she crossed the room and picked the garment up.

It was a kimono, a very beautiful one with the traditional square sleeves. And on the back of it was embroidered, in fine silver thread, the design of a rearing mythic beast. Discovering a tall mirror – something else she had not noticed before – Belinda donned the robe and looked over her shoulder to admire the skilful embroidery. It was an eagle-headed gryphon most probably, she guessed, although her knowledge of mythology was somewhat sketchy.

Jonathan will know what it is, she thought, turning from the mirror and cinching the robe's belt.

Remembering her boyfriend, she wondered where he was now. Had he been brought to the priory, as Oren had so calmly informed her in his note? Or was he still fast asleep in the folly? Belinda glanced at her wrist, then remembered her watch was in her bag which she had left behind when she had set off exploring.

What on earth was the time? It seemed as if hours and hours had passed since she had first entered this house and then this elegant, red-hued room. And yet it was probably still early. She could not 'sense' the proper time as she usually could, even when she looked out of the window. The sun was shining but its radiance was diffuse, as if it were veiled. The whole sky seemed to give off a luminosity, a brilliant blue that lit the landscape and the gardens. She had the weirdest feeling that she was trapped in a bubble, and that the priory and its grounds were a place out of time. She ought to worry, but she realised that she couldn't be bothered . . .

Opening the inset door, she found, as she had expected, a private bathroom; beautifully appointed and with well-kept antique fixtures.

'What? No blue-eyed men on the wall?' she said to herself as she began to run a bath.

Bathing took quite a while, not only because Belinda had felt sweaty and grubby after twenty-four hours without a proper wash, but also because the old-world fittings in the bathroom intrigued her.

The bath, the handbasin and the lavatory pedestal were all enormous, gleaming creations made out of white porcelain; archaic in appearance but supremely efficient in function. What's more, the water had been piping hot and abundant, and Belinda had discovered a cache of luxurious but unbranded toiletries which catered for her every feminine need. The soap and body lotion had been scented with camellias, the face lotion had been rich and silky, and the toothpaste had had a faint but delicious taste of herbs. The towels had been the thickest she had ever handled in her life, and as soft as a baby's breath against her skin.

Clean, refreshed and revivified, Belinda returned to the red and gold bedroom – to find yet more surprises awaiting her.

On the bed lay a beautiful if rather old-fashioned set of clothes: a dainty calf-length shift-like garment in white cotton – which Belinda suspected was Victorian under-wear rather than a present-day dress – a pair of rather loose-legged knickers in oyster-coloured silk, and a pair of flat slippers embroidered with a mandala design on each toe. Not much, but when she had put them all on at least she was decent, or partially so. The loose shift was extraordinarily thin and her nipples were clearly visible through the cloth's fine weave. When she smoothed the shift down against her body, she felt both unsettled and delighted by its daring.

Of her own things there was no sign at all now, and she could only assume that Oren, or someone, had slipped into the room while she was bathing and taken her grimy, over-worn clothing to be washed.

She had also been left a meal: a tall glass of milk and several slices of home-baked bread, thickly spread with butter. Plain fayre, and taboo in an age of diets and cholesterol, but somehow exactly, and uncannily, what she fancied. The milk was rich and frothy and the bread still warm. The butter was creamy yellow and tasted of sun.

The only thing she wanted for now was company.

Still unsure of the time, Belinda didn't know whether the food was breakfast or lunch, or even afternoon tea, but that didn't stop it satisfying her hunger. When she had consumed every last delicious scrap, she began to feel restless and fidgety, and she went to the open window, hoping to see Jonathan as he crossed the park to join her.

There was no sign of him, or of anyone else. But what did catch her eye was the formal garden.

It was lush with flowers, a brilliant tapestry of colour, but as she sniffed the rising scents, she frowned in puzzlement.

How could she have missed all this last night? In the thundery downpour, all she had noticed was sparse shrubbery and rain-lashed bushes. The brilliant floral hues wouldn't have shown up well in the dark of course, but all she could remember was a sterile, tangled wasteland.

Must have had something else on my mind, she reflected wryly, watching a flock of chattering birds sweep across the park.

'So? What next?' she demanded of her blue-eyed companion, as if the vivid portrait had life and could advise her.

The man's image regarded her silently, his ambiguous expression a silent provocation. Belinda shook her head, realising that she had genuinely half-expected him to answer.

She certainly couldn't lurk around in this room all day though, simply waiting for Jonathan to turn up.

Feeling an amorphous sense of longing, mixed with something akin to fear, she opened the heavy door and stepped out into the oak-lined corridor. To her left was the way to the great staircase and the lower floor, which was the logical direction to take if she hoped to find Jonathan or Oren or perhaps even the owner of the priory; and to the right was uncharted territory. Her conscious mind said 'go left, get things sorted out', but to her surprise she ignored it and turned right, her footfalls silent on the thick carpet runner.

After a moment, she found herself in a long, airy gallery filled with more portraits and a vast treasury of *objets d'art* and antiques. Once again, heavy velvet drapes hung from ceiling to floor and kissed the edge of a richly-patterned carpet. Brilliant sunshine from the windows cut into the design in bright slices, but in the shadows the darkness seemed over-dense. Belinda felt the hairs on the back of her neck prickle for no apparent reason, and squaring her shoulders she headed resolutely for the first patch of light.

'Blue Eyes' – as she realised she now thought of him – was once again the principal subject of the portraiture, but there were also several likenesses of women. Or 'woman', to be correct, in the form of a slender, gentle-eyed beauty whose long, intricately-coiled titian hair and creamy skin looked peculiarly familiar.

'I don't know your boyfriend, but I do know you,' said Belinda, standing in front of one of the pictures which showed the lovely woman in a green velvet gown. 'Although I'm damned if I know where from.' The sense of recognition was at the very edge of her consciousness, and when she tried to reel it in, it became less and less accessible. The more she tried to place the woman, the less she seemed able to; and after a moment or two, the conundrum made her head ache. Rubbing her eyes, she moved further along the gallery.

The owner of the priory had some beautiful but very strange things. Statues of gods and goddesses from the Ancient Egyptian pantheon; a long series of painted wooden representations of animal-headed deities. Gilded boxes, their lids open to display the mummified creatures that lay within: cats, snakes, even a wolf. Huge crystal vessels displayed in pairs, their attenuated spouts entwined. Stuffed birds in glass cases, caught in attitudes of flight and conflict. Two half life-size human figures, male and female, cast in gold and portrayed having sex on what appeared to be an altar.

This last item made Belinda shudder and blush, even though there was no one around to make her feel embarrassed. The copulating figures had been created by a master craftsman. Every detail was perfect, ecstatic, almost alive; even down to the grimaces of pleasure on the two gilded faces, and the intricately moulded genitals, which were fully visible as the pose had caught the outstroke. The man's thick penis pierced the woman's stretched vagina.

Looking more closely at the mating pair made Belinda's belly quiver, and she spun around when she seemed to hear laughter.

But the gallery was empty.

This is crazy, she thought. It's all the eyes in the portraits that are making me feel as if I'm being watched. There's nobody here. I'm quite alone. It's imagination –

A door creaked, and she whirled again, her heart pounding, her throat tight, her mouth dry.

'Who's there?' she called out, noticing for the first time that a previously-concealed door at the very end of the gallery was now gaping open a little. 'Who is it?' she asked, then a thought occurred to her. 'I'm sorry if I shouldn't be here . . . I couldn't find anybody . . .'

There was no answer and the open door moved no further. Belinda crept apprehensively towards it, then stopped dead when she heard a second sound.

It was a faint cry; the sort of indecipherable moan one might make while having a nightmare. Belinda's hand froze on the edge of the door as she wondered what lay beyond it in the dark.

Screwing up her courage, she pushed the door a little further open and discovered that the area behind it wasn't in total blackness. From somewhere up above, a faint shaft of sunlight illuminated a vestibule and the steps of a steeply-rising staircase that doubled back on itself again and again and again. Belinda made her way to the foot of it, then paused, listening carefully for more sound. None came, so she put her foot on the first worn step.

'Here goes,' she whispered, beginning to ascend, and knowing that both the cry and the situation had made her nervous. More than nervous. She felt genuinely fearful, but also, inexplicably, quite aroused. Beneath the flimsy shift, her bare nipples were hard and puckered.

Still straining to hear any faint sound, Belinda climbed the stairs as slowly and carefully as she could. The switchback construction of the staircase made her feel giddy, and she clung on for dear life to its rather insubstantial handrail. Beneath her, the stone steps struck a chill through the thin soles of her slippers.

Halfway to the top, judging by the quantity of steps that remained when she looked upward, there was a small landing and an anonymous panelled door. She considered turning the handle and looking into the room beyond, but instinct told her it wasn't her goal.

It took her a further minute of vertigo to get to the top, and when she did she had to stand for a few minutes breathing deeply and still clutching the thin iron rail. She was in the turret she had observed from outside the priory, she presumed, and which seemed to consist of two storeys and two large rooms. When she could at last catch her breath and her heart rate had settled, she realised she was standing on a second small landing and that the door before her must lead to the upper room.

It's just like a fairy-tale, thought Belinda, placing her hand on the massive iron ring that opened the door. Still not sure she was doing the right thing, she turned it and the door swung open silently and smoothly.

The chamber beyond was also stone lined, but its walls were hung with huge tapestries. Between these, more of the omnipresent deep-pile velvet curtains were drawn across the windows, and several thick candles in elaborate stanchions lit the room. Belinda absorbed all these facts in the space of a couple of seconds, before she focused her attention on the centre of the chamber, where there stood a great bed, all swathed around in what seemed like dozens of thin gauze draperies.

A naked man lay on the bed. A perfectly naked man with long, tousled hair and a face that she already knew too well.

Blue Eyes! thought Belinda, biting her lips so she didn't exclaim aloud. With slow, silent steps, she crossed the room then pushed her way carefully through the many layers of gauze.

In the flesh, the slumbering man – who was obviously the latest of his line – was much more striking than any of his painted forebears, even though the family likeness was still incredibly strong. His skin was very pale and his hair rather oddly coloured in that it appeared to be quite dark but thinly streaked with blond. His powerful limbs and torso were classically formed. Unable to help herself, Belinda centred her attention on his genitals, and was shocked when she saw his penis was half erect. Even as she watched, it twitched disturbingly and rose up further.

Although she couldn't see the sun now and didn't know the time, it suddenly seemed strange to Belinda that the man before her should be asleep during the day. Was he ill? she wondered. Was that why he had not been around to greet her? She peered more closely at his queer, unnatural pallor.

The sleeper looked almost as if he had spent many years indoors. There was no hint of tan about him anywhere, although paradoxically, he did not look unhealthy. His body was muscular and appeared to be in a hard and well-toned condition; it was only his unweathered skin that made him look like an invalid.

And there was certainly nothing fragile about his penis, which seemed to grow ever more rampant by the second. Belinda caught her breath when the man stirred slowly, then touched himself.

Standing at the foot of the bed, she almost swayed with excitement and arousal. The sleeper was a supremely attractive man, and the way he handled his genitals made her own sex twitch and weep. Longing to reach into her borrowed panties and caress herself, she felt weak with desire as she watched the drowsy man masturbate; fondling his hard length in extended, graceful strokes. Belinda felt a real need to hang on to the bedpost to stop herself falling, but she dare not do it for fear of disturbing her companion. As he began to writhe among the sheets, she heard him mutter; a string of foreign words and then what sounded like a name – 'Belle' – which he cried out with increasing force and anguish.

Belinda expected the man to wake at any moment; to open his eyes – which she had no doubt at all were brilliantly blue – and find her standing there watching him. The sensible thing was to sneak away; now, while he was still too far from consciousness to perceive her. But she was so bewitched by the sight of him that she stayed.

He was squirming now, twisting his powerful-looking body against the mattress as his clasping fingers continued their steady work. Unable to stop herself, Belinda reached down and pressed the heel of her hand against her pubis, trying to stanch the sweet ache of mounting lust.

'Belle! Oh, Belle!' cried the tormented figure on the bed, before launching into yet another frantic, impenetrable chant. He was lifting his bottom now, pushing his penis through his gripping fist, as his heels gouged and scrabbled against the bedlinen. When his cries and exhortations became one long strangled groan, Belinda looked away; not embarrassed, but too moved by his beauty to watch his climax.

Eyes tightly closed, and with her hand at her crotch, she waited in frozen immobility to be discovered. But when discovery didn't come, she opened her eyes again, but still felt unable to face the figure on the bed. Ignoring the heavy frustration in the pit of her belly, she darted glances around the peculiar gloomy chamber, then stopped dead, her breath caught yet again.

On top of a massive mahogany sideboard, a little way from the bed, there was a small carved box made from a lighter, more rosy-toned wood. It was an unremarkable thing, and Belinda probably wouldn't have noticed it save for the fact that it was glowing in the dark. It was pulsing with an unearthly blue radiance that – when she turned again to the sleeper – she realised was synchronised exactly with his breathing.

Her desire almost forgotten, she could do nothing but observe the weird phenomenon. What the hell was happening? Was it a trick of some kind or her imagination going crazy again? The box was definitely radiating in some way, the rhythm of its pulses uncannily regular. Half of her wanted to move closer and investigate but the other half knew better and held back. There was a special, personal bond between the sleeping man and the delicate blue light, and Belinda suddenly had the feeling she was intruding. Turning silently on her heel, she moved away towards the door, feeling an odd mix of enchantment and true terror. Once through the door, she closed it as quietly as she could, and – her earlier vertiginous feelings forgotten – raced down the round staircase at breakneck speed. She was gasping for breath as she almost burst into the gallery.

Collapsing on to an oak settle, she took in deep lungfuls of air and tried to think clearly and calmly.

What had she got herself into here? Who was the handsome, sleeping man, the one she had just seen masturbate to orgasm? And what the devil was in that luminescent box?

Suddenly Belinda felt very frightened and out of her depth. She really needed to see Jonathan's dear and rather ordinary face and to hear his pleasant, sensible voice outlining a reasoned explanation for what she had just seen.

Beginning to think more clearly, she realised that if someone really had been sent to fetch Jonathan at the time she had encountered Oren – what felt like many hours ago now – then surely her boyfriend must be here in the priory? Somewhere in the labyrinth of rooms and corridors?

Squaring her shoulders, Belinda set off determinedly along the gallery, not looking up at the blue-eyed portraits that seemed to watch her.

What she needed now, she told herself, was normality and reassurance. A bit of comfort from a man whose eyes weren't blue.

Chapter Four

Reassurance

'Where have you been?' demanded Jonathan, as Belinda strode into the opulent crimson sanctum that she supposed she could now call 'her' room.

'I might ask the same of you,' she snapped back, thrown off balance by terseness when she had hoped for understanding.

Jonathan was lying on the lush red counterpane. His feet were bare, and he was wearing a rather baggy white T-shirt and khaki shorts. His dark hair was slicked back and wet, as if he had just that minute stepped out of a shower. As she approached him he swung himself up so he was sitting on the edge of the bed. He appeared fazed by her belligerent response.

'I'm sorry,' Belinda said, relenting. Jonathan looked as confused as she felt, and they were both at sea in a strange situation. It seemed stupid to fall out over nothing. 'I was having a look around while I waited for you to turn up. Oren told me he'd sent someone to fetch you.'

'Who's Oren?' enquired Jonathan as she sat down beside him.

Alerted by something odd in her boyfriend's voice, Belinda studied him more closely, and noted that his expression was guarded.

'Well, it's hard to say,' she began, watching Jonathan start to blush, and wondering what had caused it. Last night, perhaps? What they had done in the folly had been fairly wild. 'I don't really know who he is,' she continued, keeping her own expression neutral while she considered reasons for Jonathan's embarrassment. 'He seems to be a servant of some kind, although he's not what you'd expect as a butler. He met me at the front door when I first arrived. It was weird, really, he almost seemed to be expecting me,' she said, realising as she spoke that it had been true. Her appearance had caused the big mute no surprise. 'Anyway, he welcomed me on behalf of his master, and showed me to this room. Which was pretty clever of him, considering that he doesn't seem able to speak.'

'You mean he's dumb too?'

'What do you mean, "too"?'

'The two girls who came to fetch me can't speak either.' He was pinker than ever now. 'But ... Well, it just seemed the simplest thing to come with them.' His eyes slid away from Belinda's, and he began picking at an invisible thread in the bedcover.

Something had obviously happened between Jonathan and these unknown, unspeaking 'girls'. Belinda could tell that, but own feelings rather surprised her. Her natural response should have been suspicion and anger, but somehow the idea of Jonathan with other women was exciting. She experienced a peculiar inner surge at his undisguised guilt; a superiority that, to her surprise, was quite arousing.

'Did they bring you to this room too?' she enquired in neutral tones. 'I assume you managed to tell them we're together?'

'I told them ...' he began, then paused, making a track on the velvet bedspread with his finger. 'But I'm not sure they understood me. I seem to have been given a room further along the corridor. They insisted and it was easier not to argue.' He looked up, frowning. 'So when

I'd taken a shower, I did a little exploring of my own and found *this* room . . . And it just "felt" as if you'd been here, I don't know why.' He shrugged his shoulders and looked around. 'This is some weird set-up here, isn't it?' Belinda nodded, still watching him. 'I mean,' he continued, 'last night it looked like a total run-down heap . . . and it still looks a bit dumpish on the outside. But inside – ' He gestured roundly, as if to take in the whole of the priory ' – well, it's like a palace. The furniture alone must be worth millions.'

'You're right there,' observed Belinda. 'I've done a little exploring myself and the whole place is just crammed with paintings and antiques and all sorts of weird and wonderful treasures.'

'You know . . .' Jonathan hesitated, taking her hand. 'It might be rather nice to stay here a while. We certainly seem welcome.'

Belinda examined the idea, realising she had unconsciously been feeling the same way herself. It was tempting, but there were some practicalities to be considered. 'What about the car? We've got to get it fixed. And we can't just forget about Paula, you know,' she said, referring to the friend they had agreed to meet. 'She'll be wondering what's happened to us.'

'She could come here,' suggested Jonathan.

Belinda shook her head. 'We can't just invite someone *else* to stay. It isn't our house. And whoever owns it might want *us* out today.'

Even as she said it, Belinda knew she was wrong. She didn't know why or how she felt it, but she had a weird instinct that the priory's 'master' – the sleeping man in the tower – desperately wanted them, or maybe just her, to stay in his house. A wave of desperation swept through her; not her own but emanating from elsewhere. She felt cold, very suddenly, and shivered.

'Are you OK, love?' said Jonathan, shuffling closer and sliding his arm around her. 'You haven't caught a chill, have you?' He touched a hand solicitously to her brow.

'No, it's all right. I'm fine,' she answered, despite the fact that she was experiencing a weird mix of emotions. Puzzlement; foreboding; excitement; arousal. They were all swirling around inside her, and she couldn't understand where such a medley was coming from. Especially the huge rush of desire, which had just arrived, like a cyclone, out of nowhere. She had gone from a state of being mildly turned on by Jonathan to wanting him passionately, all in the space of a few seconds. Twisting in his hold, she slid a hand around the back of his neck and drew his face towards hers for a kiss.

Jonathan balked, his eyes filled with questions, then succumbed as Belinda tightened her grip. She could almost taste his confusion as his willing mouth opened, but he accepted the strong probe of her darting tongue. She felt him sigh as she pushed him back on to the bed.

In the tower, André von Kastel opened his eyes and smiled, feeling vital energy begin to flood through his body. 'I am in your debt,' he said, thanking his distant guests.

Stretching, he tested his capabilities. He was limber, and physically more powerful now, but not back to his full, normal strength. Though the curtains were tightly closed, he sensed that it was afternoon, so there was still some way to go in his restoration. When night fell, he would be all that he had ever been, thanks to a pair of stranded lovers beneath his roof.

Slowly, cautiously, he sat up, feeling a little fragile at first but after a moment gaining control of his equilibrium. Pushing his fingers though his hair, he untousled it a little, suddenly longing to bathe and refresh himself, and to dress again in newly-laundered clothing and to feel it crisp and clean against his skin. For all his peculiar affliction, he was still, in baser matters, completely human, and during his long sleeps he perspired like any man. What's more, there were splashes of dried semen on his belly and his thighs, and its lacquer-like consistency tugged at him minutely.

Can I stand? he wondered, swinging his bare legs over the side of the bed. Leaning heavily on the carved oak bedpost, he put his weight on his feet and pushed his shaking body up to a standing posture.

His head spun and his knees felt like jelly, but reaching out from within, he drew more strength from his unknowing guests. They were inducing great pleasure in each other now, with their caresses and their strokings, and their growing rapture was a well-spring he could draw on. Bracing his legs, he stood straight, just swaying slightly.

André was just about to take his first step when there was a soft knock at the door. After a moment it swung open to reveal Feltris, the youngest and shyest of his three silent servants. She was carrying a silver tray with some small objects on it, and she bobbed a curtsey before stepping across the threshold. The blonde girl's footsteps were feather-light and perfectly noiseless on the carpet, and as she advanced she smiled sweetly and seemed to glide. André smiled too. On the tray were a number of china trinket boxes, and he already knew what they contained.

Placing the tray reverently on the sideboard beside the rosewood box with its enchanted blue glow, Feltris went straight to André and knelt down to kiss his feet.

'You are as clever as you are lovely, Feltris my sweet,' he said quietly, urging her to rise again. 'Thank you very much for anticipating what I need.' Then, feeling weak again, he sank back down on to the bed, bringing a look of sharp concern to the mute girl's face. 'Do not worry,' he said, drawing her down beside him, then accepting her supporting arm around his shoulders. 'Our new friends will soon make me feel better.' He looked at her steadily, then winked to reassure her. 'They are very passionate. They will suit me very well.'

Glancing across at the blue-glowing box, André wondered whether to tell Feltris of his suspicions about the newly-arrived young woman, then thought better of it. He could be mistaken or it could all be wishful thinking – a figment of his desperate hope. And it was likely that Oren had already described to Feltris the special significance of their new visitor, and that the servant too was aware of what might very well soon be possible.

Against his will, André's hopes surged wildly inside him, and with them came his reborn libido. His cool blood raced and his penis began to harden.

'Caress me,' he whispered urgently to Feltris.

Making a wordless murmur of assent, Feltris reached down and took his member in her fingers, delicately strumming him with all her considerable skill. As she fondled and stroked him, André slumped back among the bedclothes, his body arched and his bare feet kicking against the carpet. Hazed by pleasure, his thoughts flew irresistibly back across the years ...

He remembered a night in summer, on a bench in a rose arbour, when he and Arabelle had eluded her hawkish chaperone. Her beauty and her freshness, and her innocent, open-mouthed kisses had inflamed him to a point where he had lost his reason. Unable to stop himself, he had released his manhood from its constrictions. He could still hear her startled squeak of horrified wonder.

'What is it, André? What's the matter with you?' she had demanded, her lovely eyes agape as she stared down towards his penis. 'Are you ill?'

'No ... There's nothing wrong,' he had gasped. 'This is what happens when a man loves a woman in the way I love you.'

'But I don't understand,' Arabelle whispered, still absorbed by his towering, aching member. 'Are you in pain?'

'No ... Yes ...' he stammered, as confused by his intense feelings as she was. 'It's difficult to explain, my darling,' he continued, feeling the blood pound in his heart and in his penis. 'It does hurt, in a way, but it's a pleasant kind of pain.'

Arabelle frowned and bit her lip, regarding his uncovered staff as if it were a serpent. Not an ugly beast, but a snake that was as beautiful and hypnotic as it was deadly. Despite his extreme discomfort, André watched her, fascinated, as she lifted up her slender hand towards him.

'Is there anything I can do to help you, my love?' she said, her eyes never leaving his erection.

A thousand things, thought André, imagining a scene where he swept up her perfect young form in his arms, then lowered her gently to the greensward before them. A scene where he lifted her skirts and petticoats, parted her smooth thighs, then plunged his tortured flesh deep into her softness. A scene where he rode her body until they soared in mutual ecstasy.

'Just this,' he whispered, taking her narrow white hand and folding it around his stiffness.

'It's so warm,' he had heard her whisper. 'So warm . . .'

And suddenly her words came to him across the echoing void of history, as his body rushed to pleasure in the here and now. Even as he ejaculated, he was aware of the poignant irony of certain contrasts. His coldness that had once been so warm; Feltris's dexterity compared to the hesitant innocence of Belle. Waves of sensation poured up through him as his essence pumped and spattered, but in his heart, he was weeping for what was lost.

'Oh, Lindi, yes . . .' moaned Jonathan as she ground her crotch against him. 'God, that's wonderful! Please do it to me! Oh God!'

Belinda looked down dreamily and smiled. They were both still dressed but she was squatting astride Jonathan's hips in a far from elegant crouch, massaging her clitoris on his erection through layers of cloth.

You're just using him, she thought, closing her eyes,

throwing back her head and swirling her pelvis. He's just an object, something hard to get off on. You're a slut, girl. A nymphomaniac. Try to be kind.

As if privy to her inner debate, Jonathan cried out plaintively. 'Please, Lindi, please!' he begged, bucking up against her, his hands on her thighs. 'Take your knickers off. Let me get inside you.'

About to comply, Belinda froze. She didn't so much hear a second voice in the room with them as much as just feel a presence. Her eyes snapped open and she looked up towards the wall.

They were closed! she thought wildly. When I came in, those curtains were closed!

The red velvet curtains were wide open now, and maybe always had been, but the portrait that they flanked drew her attention. The blue-eyed man seemed to be challenging her again, the subtle curve of his sculpted mouth a mocking quirk.

'Who's in charge here?' she almost heard him say, his eyes glittering like shards of aquamarine beneath his lashes. 'Are you going to obey him, indulge him like the perfect obedient little servant? Or seize the moment, be a goddess . . . impose your will?'

You devil! she cried inside. Who are you? The cool, languid figure in the painting was most definitely the sensuously sleeping man in the tower. She knew that now, and realised that she had known it since the moment she had seen him on that great curtained bed.

Yet how could they be the same? This was the twentieth century, the 1990s, and above her, in the portrait, her nemesis wore the garb of yesteryear – an authentic costume from well over a hundred years past.

Was he in fancy dress?

It was an explanation, but not an adequate one. The condition of the paint itself suggested that both the picture and the clothing it portrayed were contemporaneous.

So how could 'Blue Eyes' still be alive and look so young?

'Please, Lindi!' came Jonathan's pleading voice again, breaking into her muddled thoughts and eccentric fancies. She felt his searching hand find the edge of her knickers and suddenly felt a great upsurge of anger – a rage that seemed to double her sexual need.

'Shut up!' she shouted, fetching Jonathan a hard slap across his cheek. 'Just shut up!' she hissed, feeling his hands drop uncertainly from her body. Looking down, she saw his eyes were bright and staring.

Is that better? she thought, circling her pelvis as she looked up again at the enigmatic, blue-eyed figure in the portrait.

There was no answer. The paint was simply paint again, formed into an image that was handsome but inanimate. 'To hell with you,' she whispered, then leant forward to concentrate on subduing Jonathan. 'So, tell me about these girls you met,' she whispered into his ear. 'Were they pretty?'

'No ... Yes ... Sort of,' he answered, moving guiltily beneath her, his hands disempowered and fluttering helplessly against the counterpane.

'Pretty enough to fuck?' she purred, putting her face close to his cheek, then catching the lobe of his ear between her teeth. Their bodies were contiguous now; her bare arms were resting on either side of his head and her breasts were pressed against his torso. Shimmying, she massaged her nipples against him, rubbing their tips over the muscularity of his chest.

'Well?' she persisted, not sure why she was asking, but asking anyway. Perhaps it was to vindicate certain feelings she had experienced in the tower – her instant desire for that naked, sleeping man.

'I didn't mean to, really I didn't,' faltered Jonathan. Belinda felt his penis twitch and lurch as he stuttered out the words, the tiny movements a subtle stimulation. Spreading her thighs wider, she bore down harder, loving the fact that her actions reversed their roles. She was the protagonist, the instigator; she was taking advantage of the man who lay beneath her, employing his desire and his hardness like a toy.

'But you did, didn't you?' she taunted him. 'I leave you for a moment and all you can do is stick your worthless dick into the nearest female body that's available.' She jammed her own female body down on to him. 'You didn't even have the decency to wait for me.'

'It ... it wasn't like that,' Jonathan gasped, half-whimpering and half-groaning as she tilted her vulva against him.

'Then what was it like?' She wriggled, making a minute adjustment to her awkward position that sent a wave of sweet sensation racing through her. Her teeth closed carefully on Jonathan's vulnerable earlobe, and his body shook with concentrated tension. He was just a second away from losing all control. 'Jonathan!' she prompted, pulling delicately with her teeth as she pushed down firmly with her crotch.

Jonathan's 'Oh God!' transformed itself into a long, falling moan, and through their clothing, Belinda felt his trapped sex pulsating. As he throbbed, she felt a sudden rush of warmth.

Afterwards, it took several minutes for Jonathan to compose himself, and knowing his sensitivity at such times, Belinda remained motionless on top of him. When he stirred again, she resumed her line of questioning.

'Tell me what happened, Jonathan,' she persisted, kissing his neck.

'I heard a noise. Someone laughing ... It woke me up.' His voice was slower now, more mellow, but still sounded just a little shell-shocked. 'I thought it was you at first, but after a minute or two, I realised it wasn't.' He paused a moment, then moved his hips, pressing his soft and sated member up against her. He shuddered as if enjoying his own stickiness. 'Anyway, I got up and followed the sound until I found myself at the side of a stream ... or a river ... Anyway, whatever it was, there were two girls there sitting on the bank. They were laughing and kissing each other.'

'Was that all?' asked Belinda, feeling an unexpected frisson of emotion. She would have liked to have been there to see those girls.

'No. No, it wasn't. They did other things too.'

'Such as?' Belinda asked, even though she was now several steps ahead of him. She had an inner picture of the two women caressing each other's bodies wantonly, their fingers probing and exploring. Her sex fluttered uncontrollably as she imagined them.

'Well, one of them – the older one, I think – she put her hand up the other one's dress and started touching her.'

'Just touching?'

'No, it was more than that ... a lot more.' As Belinda straightened up, she saw Jonathan was smiling, his face slack and dreamy. Between her legs, she felt his flesh return to life. 'She was really ... really working her,' he continued, his breathing quickening. 'Shoving her fingers right into the other one's vagina. Fast. Hard. It was just as if she was fucking her with her hand.'

Belinda made a sudden decision. 'Show me!' she commanded, rolling off Jonathan and lying down beside him. 'Show me what they were doing.'

'I could see her fingers going in and out,' murmured Jonathan, still shifting slowly and sleepily on the bed.

'Show me!' Belinda reiterated, dragging her skirt up to her waist and pulling at Jonathan's hand until it was lying against the crotch of her panties. 'Did she have knickers on?'

'No, she was bare beneath her skirt.'

'Do it for me, Jonathan,' said Belinda, jiggling her lower body so his hand moved on her sex. 'Take my pants off and do the same to me. I want it. I'm aching ... Just do it!'

Galvanised, Jonathan sat up, his expression intent.

With unsteady fingers he grasped the waistband of Belinda's borrowed French knickers, then – while she lifted her bottom to make things easier – he pulled them down over her warm, perspiring thighs.

'That's enough,' she said when they were bundled at her knees. 'I can't wait any longer. Push your fingers inside me.' The panties hampered her, but she opened her legs as wide as she could for him, then leant on her elbows, craning forward, to see her own sex and the fingers that approached it.

Jonathan looked nervous. He glanced from her face down to his hand and then at her vulva. Belinda saw his fingers flex as he lifted them towards her body, then he seemed to stare at his own hand as if didn't belong to him, as if it was someone else's hand entirely. Frowning slightly, he blinked once or twice, giving the impression that he was wondering if he was seeing things.

'How many fingers did the woman by the river use?' Belinda asked crisply, to bring Jonathan out of his fugue. She couldn't wait any longer. If he didn't act now, she would have to do the deed herself.

'Th-three,' whispered Jonathan.

'Then you use three,' she decreed, lifting her hips with an imperious little jerk.

Still appearing confused, Jonathan touched his fingers to her entrance, his actions diffident, unassertive, unsure.

'For crying out loud!'

Belinda almost snarled with frustration, feeling a contact so faint it was almost ghostly; a tantalising tingle when what she required was brute male force. Jonathan's fingertips were pale against the orchid pink of her sex-flesh. She looked fiery and his pallor looked like ice.

Suddenly, another wave of empathy washed over her. She was burning between her legs, and she longed for the cool, cool touch she had imagined earlier in this room, the liquid chilliness she had so associated with Blue Eyes. She couldn't see him any more, but she could well believe that the portrait was 'alive' again, and watching closely as she gave her body to her boyfriend. She felt her innards jump impatiently with need and defiance, and with a hungry moan she thrust her sex towards its goal.

Jonathan's fingers slid into her. First one, then two, and finally, with a wiggle, three. Ignoring the discomfort, she dug her heels in and pushed down harder.

'So, what else did they do?' she asked hoarsely, gripping Jonathan's wrist for dear life, denying him the ability to move. She wanted him to be still for a few moments, perfectly still, so she could savour the sensation of being stretched.

'I-I don't know,' said Jonathan, his voice edgy with the sound of new arousal. 'I sort of lost track of them for a minute – '

'How so?'

'I was turned on . . . really hard. I-I had to do something about it . . .' Embarrassment made him stutter again, and his fine trembling passed right into Belinda, through the medium of the fingers inside her sex.

'And was that all?' she probed, already beginning to feel she wanted more.

'No . . . Not exactly.'

Tugging his hand away from her and letting it drop, Belinda moved up on to her knees again, so that she was beside him. Feeling sure of herself, she pushed Jonathan backwards until he was once more lying down.

'And what does that mean?' she enquired, slithering her knickers down her calves and off over her ankles, while trying to avoid looking up towards the wall – towards those blue eyes that followed her every move.

'Well, I was recovering. Getting my breath back and all,' continued Jonathan, watching her closely now. 'I was just lying there and suddenly they pounced on me.'

'They what?' Belinda laughed, genuinely amused by the idea. If Jonathan had looked as helpless yet at the same time as virile as he did now, she couldn't imagine a woman who wouldn't attack him. He was sprawled on the red counterpane, looking every inch her abject victim, while his penis tried to bore out through his shorts. Suppressing her smile, Belinda reached for the elastic at his waistband.

As she pulled down first his loose, cotton shorts, and then the briefs beneath them, she wondered who the clothing belonged to. All Jonathan's own clothes were presumably still in the boot of the Mini, and she didn't recognise anything that he was wearing.

Had Oren lent him some clothes? It was possible, but unlikely. The silent servant was well over six feet tall, and in proportion to that his build was broad shouldered and massive. Jonathan was no wimp – in fact he had a rather good if somewhat wiry body – but beside the golden Oren he appeared boyishly puny.

This lot must belong to Blue Eyes, she thought, pulling the borrowed shorts and underpants down to Jonathan's trainer-clad feet and leaving them there, bunched untidily around his ankles. The two men were very similar in size, she realised, even down to the dimensions of their genitals. Both were sturdy and carried the promise of satisfaction.

'They pounced on me,' Jonathan repeated, wriggling his bottom and making his penis sway. He had his eyes closed as if trying to improve his memory. 'I was lying on the grass . . . A bit like this . . . I had my cock out.' He reached down, his fingers brushing his risen flesh, but Belinda caught his hand and replaced it with her own.

'And then what did they do?' she said, exploring the oiled silk texture of his fine, penile skin, and working it very slowly up and down.

Jonathan made an odd little hiccuping sound and grabbed a couple of loose handfuls of the bedcover in his fists.

'They did what you're doing . . . and other things,' he whispered, his voice thin and breaking. 'They kept stroking me. Touching me. Everywhere.' As Belinda slid her gripping fingers down him towards the pit of his belly, he went rigid and rose upward, his body arched. 'Oh God . . . Oh God . . .'

'And what else?' She kept him stretched, taut. His swollen glans crowned his straining shaft like a hard red fruit.

Jonathan made several unintelligible noises, then passed his tongue around his lips as if hunting for words to express his feelings. 'One of them kissed me – it was the older one, I think. She kissed my lips and forced me to open my mouth – ' Belinda blew on the tip of his penis, and his heels kicked and dragged against the coverlet. 'And the other one got on top of me and fucked me.' His body bowed again, raising his member towards her.

'You mean like this?'

With speed and a nimbleness she had never realised was part of her, Belinda released his erection then neatly leapt astride it. Her thin, borrowed dress billowed around her like a boat-sail, and at the last second she reached beneath herself to place him. She was so wet he plunged in easily and sweetly.

Oh yes!

She didn't speak the words, she didn't even think them, and Jonathan seemed beyond speaking them entirely. Yet still the exultation rang around her, and she couldn't avoid looking upwards.

The portrait looked exactly the same as it had done when she had first revealed it. The same, yet unspecifiably different. She didn't know how to describe it, but Blue Eyes was watchful again, and she got the impression he was well pleased by her pleasure. A rush of energy flushed through her like a rolling bolt of lightning, and she could almost believe the portrait was its source. She was Blue Eyes' instrument, the living wielder of his power.

Laughing, she shook her hips and felt incredible sensations at her centre. Jonathan whimpered and reached for her, but she swept his hands away and drove down harder on his penis. When she was settled, she whipped her dress off over her head.

There! she thought in triumph, arching her back, cupping her breasts and circling her pelvis. How do you like me now? she demanded silently of her watcher, meeting his painted gaze just as the euphoric spasms sparked.

I like you very well, he seemed to answer inside her mind.

'Yes, I like you very well indeed,' repeated André. He smiled into the smoke as it rose towards the ceiling, stirring the thurible's contents with his narrow black-handled dagger.

Creating an enchantment had been easy, the words and actions as natural as breathing, despite the length of time that had passed without chance to practise. Selecting a perfectly-dried rose petal from a heaped pile on a silver salver, he crumbled it slowly and added the fragments to the flames.

A single strand of hair from each of the lovers – culled by the observant Oren when he laundered their dirty clothing; several desiccated rose petals; one drop of mercury; one of blood, his own; and a little water from a stream that crossed hallowed ground. These were the constituents, the simple, easily-obtainable substances, which he burnt together to create the desired objective – unprecedented lust and sexual pleasure for his new young house guests.

As he stirred, André considered Belinda's ruminations on power. He heard her thoughts perhaps more clearly than she did, but her misconceptions brought a new smile to his lips.

'It is not *my* power you feel inside you, Belinda,' he whispered to the orgasming girl, as – in another part of the house – she cried out plaintively at her peak. 'The power is yours, my dear. It is simply *I* who feed on *you*.'

Fresh smoke ascended from the tiny pyre in the

thurible, and breathing it in André felt a dizzying rush of vigour. His body, naked but for the embroidered silk mantle around his shoulders, was suddenly imbued with a rising, reborn strength. His skin prickled; his penis stiffened. Every sinew, every muscle, every nerve-end – even the individual hairs on his head – seemed to snap with a vivid life and health. In the darkness, his limbs and torso appeared to glow.

It was purely temporary, this state of revivification, he knew that. The effects would persist in him for the duration of the lovers' current sex act, then linger on for the couple of hours that followed it. The experience was transient at this stage, but while it lasted it was as heady as vintage wine. And in character, it was infinitely more delicious.

Laughing softly, André prepared to slake his thirst. There were more enchantments to be cast if he were to grasp this opportunity, and certain circumstances must be biased in his favour. Using his dagger, he swept the contents of the thurible into an alabaster bowl, and after murmuring an oath of purification, he set up a second enchantment in the shallow bronze dish. The first constituent was another strand of young Jonathan's dark hair.

'Forgive me, my friend,' he said, as he first coiled the hair then dropped it on to the vessel. 'You must sleep. I need your companion all to myself for a while.'

Humming softly to himself, he began his second arcane task. It was good to wield his gifts again at last.

Chapter Five
An Audience with the Count

A knock on the door roused Belinda from a light doze. She was not so much asleep as resting her eyes – letting herself drift and just not thinking – and in consequence she was fully awake in half an instant. Sitting up, she grabbed Jonathan's shoulder and gave him a shake.

The knock came again, but despite her best efforts, Jonathan would not wake up. Belinda was used to his ability to sleep on a rail almost and snatch impromptu naps whenever time permitted, but this deep, near coma-like slumber was frightening. She grabbed both his shoulders and shook him as hard as she was able.

No effect.

'Miss Seward?'

At the sound of her name, Belinda grabbed the sheet and pulled it up across her breasts. What could she do? She and Jonathan were naked, their clothes were all over the floor, and the black kimono she had worn earlier was across a chair at the far side of the room. She opened her mouth to call out, 'Just a minute' but instead, to her horror, she cried, 'Come in!'

Before she had time to call out a second time, the heavy oaken door swung open, and a familiar figure stepped across the threshold into the room.

Belinda's heart raced. She supposed, in a way, that her visitor was the one she had been expecting; but it was still a shock to see him standing there, smiling.

Her visitor had his streaked blond hair caught back in a ponytail, and he was wearing clothes now – a white shirt, blue jeans and black boots – but he was definitely her naked dreamer from the tower, the latest representative of a line of blue-eyed men. And he seemed filled with male amusement at her plight.

'I am sorry. I appear to have disturbed you,' the newcomer said softly, his distinctive eyes glinting. 'But I could have sworn I heard you call out for me to enter.' He grinned, his expression keen and knowing, as if he was perfectly aware of what had happened and had probably even caused it.

'I-I did. Call out, that is,' Belinda stammered, feeling both alarm and excitement in equal measures. Blue Eyes was just as impressive awake as he had been sleeping, but his mischievous smile was completely unexpected. All the ancestral portraits had looked pensive and melancholy, and even if they had been smiling, it was a smile tinged with palpable sadness.

And not one of the portraits had done justice to his family's remarkable eyes, which in the living, present day individual were a blue so intense it was borderline unnatural. They were ultramarine, cerulean, lapis-lazuli; every vivid shade of blueness in one colour. They seemed to flash as if fired by an inner electicity, and they were certainly the ones that had haunted her dreams.

Feeling panicked, Belinda looked down at her body, and realised another disturbing fact. The sheet that covered her had slipped somehow, in spite of the fact that she had been gripping it as if her life depended on it. Her rounded left breast was now completely on show again, its nipple noticeably hardened and dark. When she looked up again, her blue-eyed host did too.

Belinda tugged up the sheet. 'I-I – ' she began, then bit

her lip. What could she say? What could she do? She was trapped.

'Perhaps this is what you require,' he said, lifting the black robe from the chair and bringing it across to her. His booted tread was inaudible on the thick Persian carpet as he wended his way among the tangle of discarded clothing.

Belinda began to reach out for the robe, but her host stopped a couple of yards away, a guileless expression on his manly but strangely pallid face.

The bastard! He wants me to get out of bed for it! thought Belinda furiously. Well, all right then, she proclaimed with inward defiance, thinking of the moment a while earlier when she had boldly abandoned her dress. Whoever you are, you've asked for it!

With as much grace as she could muster, she slid from between the sheets then turned around and held out her arms behind her, inviting her host to slip the silk robe on her. Without touching her once he complied, but he was smirking when she turned back to face him, having knotted the sash in a doubly secure bow.

'The robe becomes you,' he commented, taking a step back as if to appraise her appearance. Belinda got the impression he was a shrewd judge of beauty. Or at least that he considered himself as such. Arrogant beast! she thought, cursing him again.

'Thank you,' she said tightly. It was difficult to know where to start in a situation like this, and ludicrously, she found herself holding out her hand. 'We haven't been properly introduced, have we?' she said, feeling an insane urge to laugh. 'I'm Belinda Seward. And this – ' She nodded over her shoulder at the still comatose Jonathan ' – is my . . . my boyfriend Jonathan Sumner. We're both indebted to you for taking us in,' she added as an afterthought, wondering if the master of the house had even realised he had guests.

A second or two later, another thought occurred to her, one that shook her even more than her host himself did. He had called out to her from the landing by name, but how on earth could he know it? The only way Oren could have told him was by means of a written report.

Full of doubts now, she hesitated with her hand, then experienced a peculiar phenomenon. She had been going to withdraw it, but suddenly, and as if her whole arm had a life of its own, she lifted her hand again and held it out towards her host.

As he took it he made a movement that was entirely European; a tiny, barely perceptible heel click as he lifted her fingertips and conveyed them to his lips. When mouth met flesh, he looked up at her through his thick, dark lashes, his wicked eyes as bright as blue stars.

'André von Kastel. At your service,' he murmured, his mouth still hovering over her hand. His breath felt strangely cool against her skin. 'Welcome to my home,' he added as he straightened, releasing her fingers with an unfeigned reluctance. 'Or perhaps I should say my latest home. I have travelled considerably throughout my life, and this house is just the latest of many.'

This was his longest speech so far, and for the first time she became aware of his accent. It was delicate, very slight; a mere twisting around the edges of the words that made her insides clench and quiver. Like many women, she had always had a penchant for continental men – whether actors, singers or politicians. There was something worldly about them – a quality that was both polished and vaguely savage – which this André von Kastel clearly possessed in abundance. He was one of the most impressive men she had ever encountered, even though he was casually dressed, and appeared – on closer inspection – to still be a little fatigued.

Sleeping Beauty, she thought, grinning at him and knowing she was probably making a complete fool of herself. Did I wake him? Am I the first woman he's seen for a hundred years?

'Have I missed a joke?' he asked, returning the grin

and looking even more devastating as a set of laughter lines bracketed his blue eyes.

'No, it's just me being silly,' she replied, twisting the sash of her robe.

'In what way?' He was still smiling, still challenging her.

'Well, what with your accent, and the name, and the boots and all – ' The way his jeans were tucked into his soft, calf-high, black leather boots lent his appearance a vaguely cavalier quality ' – you're a bit like a prince in a fairy story. Especially with the long hair too,' she finished lamely.

And that was another thing, she thought, in the split second during which his smile broadened and he seemed to be preparing to respond. When she had seen him in the tower, his hair had been darker, she was sure of it. More brown, less blond. It was drawn back sleekly from his face now, but it was clearly a good deal streakier, almost platinum in places, as if he had spent day after day in hot sun. Maybe he's bleached it? she mused, recognising the thought, when it came, as bizarre.

'I am flattered,' he replied, making that tiny, almost Prussian bow again, 'but I am merely a rather poorly-connected count. Perhaps not even as much as that any more. My home country no longer exists.'

'What do you mean?' asked Belinda, silently upbraiding herself for a curiosity which could well alienate him. She and Jonathan had blundered their way into this house uninvited. They were here on this man's sufferance alone. Puerile remarks and personal questions weren't appropriate.

Count André appeared unperturbed. 'Merely that it is gone now,' he said with a shrug. 'A casualty of the redrawing of Eastern Europe, I am afraid. Which probably leaves me as simply "*Mr* von Kastel".'

'"Count" sounds much better,' Belinda said impulsively. 'Much more glamorous – '

'Why thank you,' he said. 'I shall endeavour to live up

to my title.' He reached out for her hand again, then kissed it, the application of his lips far more determined this time, pressing the print of them like a brand into her skin.

Belinda was nonplussed. The touch and the kiss were intensely erotic, even though the contact not much more than minimal. While he was bent over her hand, she seemed to see him back in his tower again, sprawled naked on his bed and caressing himself, and when he straightened up, she found herself glancing at his crotch.

As if he had noticed her ogling him, Count André gave her another of his impish white smiles. 'May I offer you a glass of wine?' he asked. 'We could retire to the library and get to know each other a little, and leave your young friend – ' He nodded to Jonathan, who, as if he had heard, turned over in his sleep and nuzzled his pillow ' – to his rest.'

'Yes. I'd like that,' replied Belinda, very aware that he was still holding her hand and that his thumb was gently stroking her knuckle. It almost felt as if he were rubbing her sex.

'Come then,' he said, giving her hand a last squeeze before releasing it. Spinning on his heel, he led the way to the door.

As she accompanied her host along the corridor to the big double staircase, Belinda was torn between studying him and taking another look at his forebears. Seeing the living man, awake now, made her realise how strong the family resemblance really was. The von Kastels of yester-year were almost identical to her handsome companion; so much so that the portraits could well all have been of him. The likeness was so exact it was uncanny.

Count André's good looks were also puzzling in another way. What made him beautiful to the female eye was difficult to quantify. Taken individually, his features were pleasantly formed, almost ordinary apart from his eyes, but the whole sum of him was nothing short of devastating. He wasn't tall, but his body looked strong and sturdy, and his way of moving was as aristocratic as his title.

'Are these all your ancestors then?' she enquired, gesturing to one of the portraits.

André turned as he walked, and gave her an oblique glance; a strange, assessing look that she didn't quite understand. 'Yes, they are all von Kastels,' he affirmed, but there was something as undecipherable in his voice as there had been in his eyes. It was almost as if he were telling a minor lie.

It was the first time Belinda had entered Sedgewick Priory's vast library, her previous explorations having been upward through the house, not downward. The room was quintessentially Gothic, decorated in a heavy ornate style which should have seemed sepulchral, but which in fact felt unexpectedly welcoming. Also a surprise, given that it was summer, was the large fire that was burning in the hearth. The bright, orange flames gave off a cheerful dancing light that flickered across the wealth of gleaming wood panelling and the glass panes in the front of the tall bookcases. A full suit of armour stood in one corner of the room, and dotted around on various tables and sideboards were mementoes and knick-knacks that must have been gathered by all the family over the centuries. Some of them were stranger than others. On a mahogany brass-bound secretaire stood a glass jar containing a stuffed and mounted animal, but not one that Belinda could recognise. It seemed to be half-lizard and half-wolf, and completely and utterly fearsome, and she couldn't understand why anyone would want it around them. She supposed that one of those blue-eyed von Kastels must have hunted it and shot it at one time.

Above the fireplace were two beautiful swords, suspended in a cross shape. They weren't the rapiers or fencing foils that one might have expected from a continental heritage, but what appeared to be Japanese fighting swords, a pair of immensely long and sharp *katana*.

Some previous von Kastel had obviously been a daring world traveller and brought back these death-dealing souvenirs of Japan.

'Do you prefer red wine or white wine?' enquired the present von Kastel, moving across to a beautifully-inlaid, bow-fronted sideboard and indicating an extensive selection of bottles.

'White, please,' answered Belinda, wishing that somewhere in the opulent beauty of the library was a concealed wine cooler. She wasn't a connoisseur, but she hated warm wine.

'A good choice,' Count André responded, giving her another of his curious looks, almost as if he were listening to something that she herself couldn't hear.

As he turned away and applied his attention and a corkscrew to the wine bottle, Belinda took advantage of the opportunity to observe him, out of range of those piercing blue eyes.

His bearing was elegant and his small movements as he eased out the cork were spare and effortlessly economical. He reminded her very much of the best type of character she had seen in costume dramas – a confident courtly man, but not a fop or a libertine. There was something very classical about him, despite the modernity of his boots and blue jeans. Jeans that fit him superbly, she noticed, admiring the firm, tight contours of his buttocks beneath them, and the way they formed faithfully to the musculature of his thighs.

It was a bit strange to be analysing his body now, in clothes, when she had already seen it stark naked, but in some ways she was seeing a different person. The André on the bed had appeared feverish, almost weak, as if suffering from some debilitating long-term disease, while this one was radiant with disgustingly good health. The tiredness she had noticed a few minutes ago had dissipated now, and she could almost feel waves of strength pouring off him. It was as if he had an aura of some kind, and it was provoking her. She squeezed her eyes almost closed and tried to see it, but there was nothing there but a fit, handsome man.

From where she had chosen to sit, on a vast brocade covered sofa, Belinda could see her host in profile, and as she watched him, he suddenly touched his fingertip to the bottle and frowned.

Yes, it's warm, she thought, isn't it? I would have thought someone like you would have had a cooler around somewhere.

As she thought those words, André turned towards her, regarded her thoughtfully for a second, then returned his attention to the bottle, first clasping it in both hands, then running his tapered fingers up and down it. After a moment, he smiled and poured out wine into two glasses.

'Here, try this,' he said, as he joined her on the sofa, holding one of the glasses out towards her. 'The grapes are grown in a region quite near to where I originally come from, I believe. It is quite sweet but I think you will enjoy it.'

Belinda nearly dropped the glass when she took it from him. It was cold, as if the wine inside had indeed been sitting in an ice bucket.

Count André grinned again and spoke a brief, unintelligible toast, presumably something from his own language. The word sounded a little like *prosit*, but with a curious part-gutteral part-musical inflection that Belinda didn't think she could have mimicked if she had tried.

'Cheers!' she said, then put her glass to her lips.

The wine was chilled to exactly the right temperature. Belinda was so surprised that she drank half of it at one swallow, hardly noticing that it was also sublimely delicious.

'It's cool,' she said, staring at the pellucid golden fluid.

'So it is,' replied Count André, lifting his own glass and staring at her intently over the top of it as he took the minutest of sips.

Suddenly Belinda desperately wanted to ask him how that was. She was prepared to swear that the various bottles had all been in the room for quite some time, and yet this wine was at the perfect low temperature for its character. The word 'how' formed on her lips, but she found herself unable to utter it. Her tongue felt unwieldy and locked in place somehow, and all she could do was see again that strange double-handed pass that André had made up and down the wine bottle.

The man's a magician, she thought, then told herself not to be ridiculous. He was just a good host who thought ahead. He had probably had the wine brought up from the cellar a few minutes before he had come to her bedroom.

'So, Belinda, are you and Jonathan betrothed?'

'What a quaint expression. You mean engaged, don't you?' she countered. 'No, we're not. But we have known each other a long time.'

'A long time,' he murmured ruminatively. 'Hmm. And what would you call a long time?' His dark brows lifted, and Belinda noticed that unlike his hair, they were not beginning to grow blonder, but remained dramatically dark.

'Three years.'

'That's not a long time,' he said lightly, swirling his wine in his glass. 'How long have you been lovers?'

It was a radical enquiry from someone she had only met a few minutes ago, and the Belinda of last week might have resented it and perceived her bumpy relationship with Jonathan threatened. But now, to her surprise, she faced the intimate question with equanimity.

'Three years,' she said evenly, then took a long sip of her wine as the man beside her digested her admission.

'And does he please you?'

'Most of the time.'

'Only most? A woman like you should be pleased all the time . . .'

88

'I don't know what you mean by "a woman like me", but I live in the real world, Count, and I don't expect miracles.'

'Perhaps you should,' he said, still rocking his glass, still watching the way the wine clung to its rounded inner contours.

Belinda was watching his hands. She seemed to see that pass again. Up and down the bottle. Lingering over the glass and subtly changing its contents. Involuntarily she imagined a similar gesture performed over her body, and this time it was the induction of heat, not cold.

She looked up into his eyes and actually saw the heat burning in their depths like a volcanic blue flame.

He's a mind reader, she thought, then admonished herself again for abject foolishness. This was the twentieth century, the age of hard science and rationality. Zoroastrian magic powers didn't exist, even if you desperately wanted them to.

Count André was still looking at her, his eyes alight with a peculiar, dark-toned excitement.

'What?' she demanded, feeling shaken.

'I was just wondering what you would look like naked.'

'But you've already seen me naked,' she pointed out, feeling mildy insulted. He had seen her body a few minutes ago in the bedroom. Was it so unmemorable that he had already forgotten it?

He shook his head, as if he was confused and trying to clear his thoughts, then gave her a curious and endearingly crooked smile.

'Ah yes, of course I have,' he conceded, 'and you are indeed very beautiful.' He frowned for a moment, and something sombre seemed to enter his expression, a cloud of fleeting sorrow that dulled every part of him. 'Your Jonathan is a very lucky man. Blessed, I would say . . .'

His eyes went unfocused for a moment, as if he were looking straight through her body to another reality; to another Belinda. He put aside his glass, then slowly, oh so slowly, he reached out his hand towards the knot of her sash, touched it, and seemed to make it unfasten. The overlapping panels of black silk slid apart, and there was a ponderous, eternal-seeming silence.

'So beautiful,' whispered the count at length, his fingertips hovering an inch or so above her navel. Belinda felt the skin there begin to flutter, and the nerves in it grow excited and sensitive. Her vulva, so near, became moist. She saw his nostrils flare and knew he could scent her.

The moment was volatile and precarious, as if they were both in violent, agitated motion even while their two bodies remained still. Then Count André's hand moved, infinitesimally, and he was touching the tender curve of her belly and sending an instantaneous jolt of pleasure to her sex.

Belinda gasped, and the count snatched back his fingers.

'Forgive me,' he muttered, reaching for her robe, as if to close it. 'I have gone too far. I am sorry.'

Belinda was too shocked to speak, but her alarm was because the caress had ended, not begun. The sensation she had experienced from just a single fleeting touch had taken her breath away. It had moved her and beguiled her in a way that would have normally taken long minutes of industrious love-making. And its cessation was instantly unbearable.

She realised she was still holding her glass, so she put it down on the carpet at her feet. Then, without thinking, or even trying to, she simply lunged forward towards him, putting her half naked body directly into his arms so there was no way he could withdraw or reject her.

For a moment, Count André remained passive, accepting first her kiss, then her embrace, as she slid her arms around his waist. His mouth tasted very sweet to Belinda's hungry lips, and the scent of his body was like roses. She felt his arms move up and grip her, then

90

effortlessly and with grace, he swivelled her body, disengaging her hold on him, and turned her until she was sitting on his lap. Belinda could not work out quite how he had achieved this, all without breaking the kiss, but the position made her feel tiny and vulnerable. The whole of her naked torso, as well as her thighs and belly, were now displayed and accessible to his touch.

'You are a very forthright woman,' he whispered, lifting his mouth away from hers momentarily.

Belinda looked up into his face, then was forced to drop her gaze again. His eyes were too brilliant to bear so close up. She felt mesmerised, and quite weak, and her mouth opened when his touched it once again.

His tongue immediately slid inside the soft cavity, tracing her teeth then plunging deeper to duel with her tongue. He tasted of wine and almonds and something else hard to define yet tantalisingly delicious, and she moaned under her breath as he kissed her. Her body had never felt more alive.

As he continued to kiss, playing and exploring, she felt his hand settle once again on her belly, his long fingers splaying out across her skin. She felt him rubbing, gently circling and fondling the curve of her with his slightly bent fingers. He was nowhere near her sex yet it was affected, the delicate folds becoming swollen and very wet.

'Do you wish me to touch you?' he enquired, making the words a part of the kiss. His hand stilled, waiting in readiness for her permission.

Belinda could hardly believe what she had done. She had leapt straight from being in bed with one man to surrendering her body to another. There was no way she could resist this fascinating aristocrat, this stranger who was so honest yet so mysterious. She whispered 'yes' under his lips, then eased her thighs apart to give him access. As his hand slid lower, she heard him sigh so poignantly it was almost a sob.

'It has been so long,' he murmured, his mouth straying

across her cheek and settling just below her ear. 'So many, many years . . .' His fingertip began gently inveigling its way through her pubic curls, moving cautiously as if her flesh were made of crystal and might shatter with rough treatment.

The approach was far too cautious for Belinda's liking. She suddenly felt ravenous for his caress. She wanted this strange, strange man to lay his hands on her so she could come to know him through the contact. She wanted to absorb him, drink him in, understand how he could seem to know her so well; even though they had only met a few minutes ago. She surged on his knee, lifting her pelvis and circling it to encourage him, and pushing herself upward against his hand.

'Hush!' he said into her ear, his breath a cool wind against her brow. 'Not so hasty. I will pleasure you, my sweet Belle, but we must go slowly. Bide our time. We have waited far too long to rush our joy and waste it.'

Belinda didn't really understand what he was whispering about. Who had been waiting? And why had he suddenly called her 'Belle'? Her mother had called her that many years ago in her childhood, but she was dead now and no one had used the name since. Not even her boyfriends. To Jonathan, she was always 'Lindi' at times like these.

The thought of Jonathan shocked her back into the reality of her situation. She was sprawled half-naked across the knee of a man she had met less than thirty minutes ago. She was about to let him touch her sex.

Oh no, oh dear God, he had closed the final gap and he was touching her! She wanted to struggle away, apologise and grab her belongings, then get out of this house as fast as she was able.

How could she do this? How could she betray her dear, patient, long-suffering Jonathan just when everything was starting to look up for them?

But the count's clever fingertips were too artful to resist, flickering over her, both hot and cool at once, and invoking shallow ripples of ethereal stimulation. Belinda moaned hoarsely when he stroked the pulsing heart of her, then buried her face against his white shirt as she came.

It had all happened with so little warning that she was barely prepared for the intensity of her pleasure. She felt tears on her face as her body throbbed and glowed, and she clung to the count, to André, as if the safety of her very soul depended on him. The release, and the feelings it roused in her, seemed out of proportion to the relationship they shared.

What relationship? she thought as she regained her equilibrium. Snuggling against his chest, she felt almost giddy from the scent of his cologne, an intense and voluptuous essence of rose that suited him despite its feminine sweetness. I have no relationship with this man, she told herself, and I don't know him. At all. I must be insane to have allowed him to touch me.

'I'm sorry – '

'Forgive me – '

The apologies, hers and his, came out simultaneously, and suddenly Belinda could see if not broad humour in the situation, then at least a lighter side to it. She sat up, drew back a little way along André's knee, and looked him rather shamefacedly in the eye.

'What on earth must you think of me?' she said, plucking at the satin robe and managing to close it. 'It must seem very "loose" of me, allowing you to touch me like that when we've only just met. I really can't believe myself. I-I threw myself at you.'

He touched her face, smiling wryly, then took the ends of the robe's sash and fastened it for her.

'No, Belinda, the fault is mine,' he said, his face shadowed with some indefinable, yet clearly painful emotion. 'You reminded me of someone. Someone I miss desperately . . . And for a moment, I thought you were she, and I lost control of myself.' He was looking down, staring at the loose black bow he had formed, but Belinda could almost swear she had seen tears. Then he looked up again, and his blue eyes were pacific and untroubled. 'I must ask you again to forgive me.' Without warning, he slid his hands around her waist, and rising himself, lifted her effortlessly on to her feet. 'Will you do that? Shall we forget what just happened? And begin again . . . as good friends?' He held out his hand again, the same hand that had touched her so beautifully. 'I promise I will try to behave myself from now on.'

Once again, the transition from one dynamic to another was staggeringly fast. Belinda had a strong urge to shake her head in an attempt to clear it. Had she imagined what had just happened? Perhaps it was a fantasy? A dream of some kind. She was tired and confused, what with the breakdown and the storm and all. Maybe what she thought had just happened had really occurred only in her mind?

At a loss to frame a reply, Belinda allowed her hand to be taken and this time squeezed in affirmation instead of kissed.

'And now, I believe it is time to dress for dinner,' the count said briskly, offering his arm. 'May I escort you to your room?'

'Yes. Of course,' she answered, still feeling befuddled by the change from intimacy to courtesy. She took his arm, as indicated, and allowed herself to be led back the way they had come earlier.

'You are free, and welcome, to stay here as long as you wish, Belinda,' he said as they began to ascend the stairs. 'The storm last night was unusual, I believe. Apart from it, we have been enjoying a spell of quite clement weather. I am sure that you will find the priory very restful.' He turned to her, his smile slight, but latent with unexpected significance. 'As I do.'

'That's very kind of you, but – ' The words died on her lips. For a moment, she seemed to see the places she and Jonathan had planned to visit, their itinerary mapped out before them, and Paula, waiting in puzzlement for their call. Then, inexplicably, none of it interested her any more. She looked around her: at the polished panels of the landing, the rare furnishings, the lavish pictures, then finally back to her smiling enigma of a host. 'I'd love to stay,' she heard herself say, 'and I'm sure Jonathan will too. He said only yesterday that he was getting fed up of driving. It's very kind of you to ask us.'

'It is my pleasure,' replied André quietly, stepping back and making another of his minute bows. 'It is a long time since I had such – ' He paused as he straightened, and his blue eyes seemed to flare even brighter ' – such compatible company.' He stepped back, still looking at her intently. 'Until dinner then. The dining room is to be found directly across the hall from the library. *A bientôt!*'

French as well now, thought Belinda as her host turned on his heel like a cavalry officer and strode away down the landing in the direction of the stairs that led up to the long gallery and his tower. And just what other talents and accomplishments does he possess? she pondered, turning the huge cut-glass door knob and opening the door to her room.

Fool! You damned fool!

André cursed himself as he ascended the stairs to his eyrie, taking them two at a time in his impatience, and making the most of his current strength and vigour.

The temptation of Belinda Seward had been too great for him to resist in his newly-wakened and not yet fully-adjusted state. The girl was so much like Arabelle, her body so sweet and so gently rounded at breast and hip, that it had been almost like caressing his beloved again. As he entered his chamber he gasped aloud with yearning, praying with all his heart that he had not gone too far and too fast and ruined everything. As ever, for reassurance, he glanced towards Belle's rosewood casket, but its blue glow was subdued and quiescent.

Could Belinda Seward really be the one? he thought, drawing aside the veils around his bed and tying them back. Had he finally found a woman who was fully compatible? He flung himself on the bed and considered the prospect.

They had been close from time to time, he and Arabelle, and enjoyed a few all-too-brief interludes of stolen communion. But these episodes were almost as painful as they were comforting. To hold Belle in his arms again and touch her and give her pleasure meant everything to him; but on each occasion they had known their happiness was transient. There was always the knowledge that in a few moments it would all be over again, and she would lose her hold on her host and have to leave. It seemed cruel to even attempt being together under such circumstances, but the state of missing her hurt him so hideously that he couldn't forgo even the slightest chance of happiness.

Should he wake Belle? Tell her what he had found? He turned again towards the box and the crystal vial that lay within it, but his mind was still full of doubt. It would be too cruel to inspire her hopes just yet. Perhaps it would be better to wait until he was sure. Sure that Belinda Seward was the woman who could help them, and also certain that he wasn't going to spoil everything by snatching too greedily for the sustaining pleasure he so needed. Covering his face with his hands, he tried to relax his taut body and find the stillness and composure to think clearly.

But such quietude was difficult to achieve and his mind remained active, pondering and ruminating incessantly in the blackness behind his fingers. Once again, he felt the urge to reach for Belle.

Suddenly, he sensed a change in the room's solemn ambience. He dropped his hands from his face, sat up, and stared towards the casket, his hopes rising as the fey blue light intensified and into the silence came the answer to his invocation.

My love, you are awake. Are you troubled?

Her voice was as gentle and animated as it had been in life, and it soothed his anxious spirit with a sense of peacefulness and stoicism he could barely credit given the parameters of her existence.

'Yes, I am troubled,' he answered, speaking aloud as seemed natural when her voice sounded so real to him. 'I think I may have found her, my love. The one who can help us. She seems a perfect match but I cannot help but be afraid.'

Afraid to die? Arabelle asked, her voice soft and steady in his mind.

'No, never that,' he answered. 'I shall be glad of it when the time comes ... No, what I am afraid of is that I may harm her. This Belinda. She is so much like you, my darling. I could be fond of her, perhaps, had you never existed, and I have to question my right to risk her life.'

Arabelle remained silent but he sensed that she was listening patiently, letting him take his time.

'And yet if I do not try, you can never be released, my love!' he cried out, feeling torn a thousand ways by his emotions.

Hush, my André, do not fret, Arabelle soothed. *If this thing is meant to happen, it will. Perhaps, if you are open with her ... if you tell her of our plight, and let her choose, she will help us of her own free will.*

'Perhaps you are right,' murmured André, lifting his hands away from his face and staring at them. Those fingers had touched Belinda Seward a little while ago, but many decades in the past they had once caressed Arabelle. He could still remember the superlative softness of her skin, the way she would sigh when he stroked her and blush when he pushed and took liberties. Her erotic soul had just been stirring and growing when they were parted, and each time they had been together he had sensed her wanting him and becoming more daring. The fact that they had so nearly been one

97

flesh, yet never been allowed to achieve that precious goal, was like someone plunging his black-handled dagger into his chest again and again, in blows that hurt and bled and went on hurting, yet which could never give the release he so craved.

Do not torture yourself, my love. Remember what we shared with pleasure, not sadness. Arabelle's voice echoed in his mind like a clear, high bell, a sound so lovely that he started feeling better. *Look forward with hope, my André, and take comfort where you can ... I truly believe that all may yet be well.*

André still had his doubts, and he knew that his wise, all-perceiving beloved was fully aware of them, but as he sent his mind across the years and imagined her sweet body in his arms, his heart grew calmer and he closed his eyes and smiled.

Chapter Six
Nemesis

*L*eaning back against the fragrant, kid-skin upholstery of her chauffeur-driven limousine, Isidora Katori closed her painted eyes and smiled in satisfaction. Her narrow, gloved hand stole momentarily to her cleavage, where beneath her clothes rested her talisman of Astarte.

To an observer, she appeared completely tranquil, as she always did, but on the inside she was a mass of swirling passions.

She had found him again! Her fallen angel. Her object of desire and hate. Tapping the precious medallion with her finger, she considered him: the only man who had ever defied her, and who had obsessed her for decade after decade. André von Kastel, who she had changed and damned for ever.

Drowsing in the opulent comfort of the long black car after a tiresome flight and an exhausting stay in Paris, she had sent her mind roaming through the aether, and suddenly hit the mental signature she sought. André was awake somewhere, in this country of England, and quite close; his consciousness a beacon she could follow.

Sending her imagination back over the years, she could still see his face as she had last seen it, in every beautiful, graven detail. She could taste the rage in his newly-blue eyes; savour his sorrow and his desperate confusion. He had still desired her while he hated her utterly. And that, to Isidora, had been her purest, most gratifying triumph.

'Are you OK?' enquired a voice beside her, snapping her reverie and banishing André's tortured countenance.

Isidora opened her eyes and viewed her companion with momentary annoyance.

Who was this worm? What was his name? She couldn't even recall it. He was just a handsome face on the plane, a clean-cut yuppie – fresh from successful business no doubt – who had made a pass at her after too much champagne. Isidora had felt wasted after the debauch of Paris, but even so his gauche advances had amused her. And his expression, on seeing her limousine, had been a picture.

'Yes, thank you – ' She paused, trying to remember ' – Miles. I'm just a little tired, that's all. Paris was ... fatiguing. Delicious but fatiguing. But don't worry – ' She hesitated again, then laid her gloved hand delicately on his thigh, quite high up ' – I'm very resilient. I have a strong constitution.'

'Oh ... er ... great,' Miles replied, his eyes bright and eager but bemused. He really had no idea what she was doing to him, she realised; no inkling of how controllable he was.

Withdrawing her hand, Isidora lounged back again and studied her prey through her long black lashes.

He was presentable enough, she supposed, although with André in her mind he appeared bland and characterless. Miles was slim, smooth and well groomed, and under normal circumstances she would imagine him to be the acme of masculine self-confidence. But these weren't normal circumstances, she thought creamily, picturing him naked, vulnerable and afraid. At her mercy, as André should have remained instead of cursing her, tricking her, and taking flight.

Enough of negativism, though. André was near, far

nearer than she could have hoped for, and as she knew she was a psychic blank to him, there was no way he could be aware she had located him. She could bide her time, then strike out and reclaim him as and when she chose. Having waited so long, she could approach with stealth, then reveal herself when it was too late for him to flee.

And in the meantime, she had her handsome yuppie. A connoisseur of ever-changing fashion, Isidora admired Miles's loosely-tailored designer suit and the way it hung on his well-toned body. She imagined him working out in some exclusive gym or health club; sweating designer sweat, no doubt. He would be sweating for her too, soon enough, she thought, relishing the scenario she was beginning to have in mind. He would sweat, he would cry out, he would lose the mastery of his own body. She would enjoy him, and when it was over he would adore her.

'So, is there anyone waiting at home for you, Miles?' she enquired, sitting up again and turning to him, giving him the full force of her brilliant green eyes.

'Yes, there is actually,' he replied, a little cockily.

Isidora felt like laughing out loud at the rather smug way he said it, as if he were boasting that he was a man of the world and fully accustomed to cheating on his partner. In a little while, he wouldn't be feeling quite so full of himself.

'Then why not ring her?' she suggested. 'Let her know that you won't be rushing to her side.'

Miles frowned, clearly affected by some of the guilt Isidora had intended him to feel. He took a minute mobile phone out of his briefcase and quickly punched a number. Isidora kept her eyes on him as he spoke into the mouthpiece, enjoying the charge of his discomfort and sexual confusion. She continued to watch him closely while he concocted a garbled and implausible reason for not hurrying home. Faint but sharp words indicated that the other party was not happy with the delay, and Isidora sensed Miles's ambivalence.

'It's OK. All sorted now,' he said, snapping the phone shut jauntily in a vain effort to show her he was his own master.

'I never said you could stay the night with me,' she pointed out, watching the words bring a blush to Miles's cheeks.

'But – '

'We'll have to see, won't we?' she said, cutting him off. 'If you please me, I may want to keep you a lot longer.'

He opened his mouth to protest, but Isidora was on him before he could speak, taking control of his lips and pushing her tongue between them. In shock, he allowed her to plunder him, his own tongue retreating as she kissed him aggressively. He tasted of the champagne they had both consumed.

When they broke apart, Isidora pulled away, still smiling, and took out a lace-trimmed handkerchief from her bag. With it, she blotted all trace of him from her red-painted but completely unsmeared mouth.

'We're here,' she said expressionlessly, placing the handkerchief in his hand as the limousine pulled up outside her building. He was still holding it when the chauffeur opened her door and helped her to alight.

The fact that she possessed a prestigious penthouse in a prestigious building in a prestigious part of London clearly impressed Miles. As they ascended in the bubble-like lift, he glanced around him, grinning with excitement and drinking in the sight of one of the city's most exclusive views, as well as the understated symbols of wealth all around him.

Once they were inside her living room, he attempted to kiss her, but much as she relished his untutored mouth, Isidora swung away and left him standing alone, briefcase in hand, like a pupil on his first morning at the 'big school'.

'A drink, perhaps?' she enquired, moving across to her varied selection of alcohol and drugs.

'Oh . . . Yes! Great!' he answered, shifting the briefcase from hand to hand, as if not sure what to do with it. Isidora refrained from offering to take it, and after a few moments he put it down beside a chair.

'Wine?' she enquired, reaching for a bottle of red from the wine rack and picking up a corkscrew before he had a chance to express a preference.

'Can I do that for you?' he asked, as she set the device against the bottle's neck. He was attempting to appear suave now and gain an advantage. Isidora was amused. Couldn't he tell that he had never had a chance?

'No,' she said, watching him, her eyes level as she deftly relieved the bottle of its cork.

Turning away to pour the wine, she could sense him fidgeting behind her. What would he do if I put a drop of one of these in his glass? she thought, eyeing the row of tiny vials that stood on a low shelf out of sight of the rest of the room. They contained her own devised potions: aphrodisiacs, mood-altering compounds, preparations to aid sexual performance or to make a victim sleep. As she considered a mixture to increase Miles's suggestibility, Isidora couldn't prevent herself from thinking about another of her alchemical creations; one she had employed long, long ago, before he was born.

No! She needed no esoteric assistance to master this young cavalier of the 1990s, and she would not think of that blue fluid she had once made use of.

'Here,' she said, turning to Miles and holding out a large crystal goblet full of wine.

Miles accepted it, sipped gratefully, then seemed to realise he should have waited and made a toast. Isidora said nothing, took one sip from her own wine, and put it aside. Then, with neither modesty nor flourish, she began, very calmly, to remove her clothes.

First went her gloves, then her chic veiled hat, then her jacket, revealing the draped black moiré blouse she wore beneath. She held Miles's gaze as her fingers sought its row of black pearl buttons.

'Oh yeah ... Great!' he burbled, gulping down his wine and abandoning the empty glass before plucking at the lapels of his jacket.

'Wait,' commanded Isidora, her voice soft yet threatening.

Miles licked his lips, still grinning broadly. The fact that she appeared to be doing a strip was clearly a treat for him, and he made as if to sit down in one of her low, leather-covered chairs to enjoy it.

'I said "wait",' she reiterated. 'Exactly where you are,' she continued, savouring his gasp as her blouse slid down her arms.

Isidora was wearing an ice-grey basque beneath her outer clothing, a sleek but sumptuous creation that most women would have found uncomfortable to wear for any length of time. She, however, enjoyed the fierce embrace of its tightly-laced panels and the way her breasts were displayed by its flimsy quarter cups. More pleasurable even than that, though, was the secondary effect of its rigid, relentless boning. Her internal organs were constricted, and bore down heavily on her pleasure zones from within. Her vulva felt like a ripe fruit, constantly pouting open, and her clitoris was an aching pushed-out stud. Her swollen bladder, from the in-flight champagne, only enhanced the dark, erotic tension.

'Wow!' said Miles, as she retrieved her gloves and pulled them back on again, smoothing the thin hide very carefully over her fingers.

'I'd prefer it if you didn't speak,' Isidora said conversationally, sliding a gloved hand beneath each bulging breast to cup herself, then rolling each nipple between a leather-clad thumb and finger. 'I require concentration and quiet, Miles. Your undivided attention.' As the sensations built inside her, she closed her eyes and swirled her hips, gyrating elegantly on her narrow-tipped high heels.

Although she could no longer see him, Isidora studied her young admirer with her inner eye. He was gaping at her; ogling like that schoolboy she had likened him to earlier. At his groin, his fashionable trousers had begun to tent. She could almost feel the nerves twitching along the medians in his fingers. He was longing to touch her, or failing that, touch himself.

'I wouldn't do that if I were you,' she said as he lifted his hand, about to press it to his crotch. Her eyes snapped open, and she fixed her gaze on him.

'Isidora?' he began querulously. 'What's going on? I don't – '

'Silence!' She cut him off, his thunderstruck expression exciting her.

'But – '

This time she silenced him with a look using the full force of her sparkling eyes and her fierce beauty. His hands dropped to his sides and he looked shame-faced.

'That's better,' she said, giving her nipples one last pinch, then beginning work on her narrow pencil skirt. She unhitched the placket, slid down the zip, then let the whole thing slither down to her ankles.

Once again, she silenced Miles with a chilling look, and saw him bite his lips to keep in his exclamations.

Standing in a crumpled pool of linen and satin lining, she knew she looked the very rising goddess. The steely-coloured basque ended just above her navel and her long legs were encased in hold-up stockings, but between these two she wore no other garment. She could feel Miles staring hard at her luxuriant pubic bush and the shimmering ooze of juice that was already trickling through it. She saw him lick his lips as if imagining her flavour.

Ah yes, my dear naïve little Miles, you will get to taste me, mark my words, she thought, stepping neatly out of her skirt and shoes, then slipping her feet back into the slender high heels. You'll use that soft mouth in my service until your jaw aches.

'Stay there,' she ordered softly, realising he was once again about to move. Retrieving her wine from the drinks table, she took a long refreshing swallow, then removed a glove and dipped her fingers into the glass. When they were sufficiently moistened, she opened her legs a little and rubbed her throbbing clitoris.

The weakish alcohol tingled only a little but the pressure alone was enough to make her climax. She groaned gutturally as waves of pleasure passed right through her. Her distended bladder edged each one with a delicious pain.

'Thank you, goddess,' she murmured to the deity whose image rested between her breasts, as self-possession returned from out of chaos. Withdrawing her scented fingers from the niche between her legs, she lifted the talisman and pressed it to her lips. 'For everything,' she added, thinking of a blue-eyed nemesis whose soul would soon be hers.

Opening her eyes, she surveyed her pleasant if rather nondescript diversion. Ah well, he would pass a little time.

'Come,' she murmured, holding out her left hand to Miles and smiling narrowly.

And like a willing lamb for the sacrifice, he walked towards her.

Where on earth has he gone? thought Belinda as she stepped into her bedroom. Jonathan was nowhere to be seen, the bed had been made, and her clothes had been picked up and spirited away out of sight. The casement window stood open to the sepia-toned twilight and there was a strong scent of pot-pourri in the air. The room no longer smelled of sweaty sex.

'I suppose I'd better get ready for dinner then,' she muttered, wondering just who had been in and tidied up. One of Jonathan's blonde friends, she presumed, or perhaps the silent but strangely friendly Oren.

She was just about to shuck off the black robe and see

if she could find anything suitable to wear for taking formal dinner with a continental blue-blood, when there was a soft rap on the door.

Not again! thought Belinda, tempted not to answer. Who was it this time?

'Come in!' she called out resignedly.

The door opened and two young women entered. Two beautiful blonde women who smiled at her warmly but didn't speak a word. One was carrying a notebook and a pencil, and the other had her arms full of clothing.

These were Jonathan's silent paramours, Belinda realised, the wood-nymphs with whom he had frolicked by the river.

'Er . . . hello,' said Belinda doubtfully, unsure of what to say to them. Could they even hear, given that they were mute? Oren had perfect hearing but that didn't mean to say that these two could also hear. 'My name's Belinda,' she offered tentatively, patting her chest, then felt awfully self-conscious. What if they both understood her perfectly and were insulted?

To her relief, the smiles of both the young women broadened, and the taller one, whose flaxen hair was tied back in a ponytail, gestured gracefully with the pencil and notebook, then quickly wrote a few words on the first blank page. Holding out the notebook, she showed them to Belinda.

My name is Elisa, the girl had written. *And my cousin's name is Feltris. Our master has sent us to assist you in any way you require. We have brought fresh clothing, so you may bathe and change for dinner.*

As Elisa took back the notebook and placed it to one side, the younger girl, her cousin Feltris, stepped shyly forward with her burden. As she must have done with the shift and the French knickers Belinda had worn earlier, the graceful blonde began to lay out the clothing on the bed. This time there was more though, and Feltris arranged each item with tender care. Belinda was astounded at the sight of such beauty.

The first garment was a dress; an ethereal shimmering thing that Belinda was instantly compelled to touch. Constructed from layer upon layer of embroidered silk gauze, it was a glorious blend of peach and orange in colour, and cut in a low-waisted Roaring Twenties style with a straight bodice and an intricately-scalloped hemline. The dress was lined in satin and when Belinda bent to examine it more closely, she discovered it was hand sewn, every facet of it individually crafted. There was no label and no indication of either a designer or a brand name, and something told Belinda that the dress was an original, deriving from the Jazz Age itself. What she was being given to wear was a genuine haute couture antique, and was probably worth hundreds if not thousands of pounds.

'I can't wear this,' she protested, itching to stroke her fingers over the exquisite fabric but afraid to. 'It's too precious. It should be in a museum.'

But the girls just nodded their heads and smiled, encouraging her to examine the dress more closely. Elisa took Belinda's hand and put it gently against the shining silk.

'OK. If you say so,' Belinda conceded, her senses thrilling to the delicate smoothness of the rare and feather-light fabric.

The lingerie was a match for the dress: elaborate, fabulously fragile and so lovely it made Belinda gasp with pleasure. An ivory chemise and long knickers in crêpe-de-chine were both encrusted with soft flounces of lace and tiny embroidered roses. There was a suspender belt too, which was just as pretty, and stockings in off-white woven silk. For her feet there was a pair of satin ballet pumps the same colour as the dress, and beside them lay a tiny matching bag, a lace hankie and a scented corsage.

'And you shall go to the ball, Cinders,' murmured Belinda, transfixed by the beautiful clothes and accessories. So much opulence for one simple dinner.

But what if the count had guests? What if his melancholy solitude was just something she herself had conjured up? Despite the initial image it projected, he had a lovely home; it was a perfect venue for entertaining and parties.

And yet somehow she still knew he was lonely and that all this finery was purely to please him. Maybe not Cinders after all? she thought, lifting the chemise's shoulder strap and discovering it was as light as the very air around it. I'm being decked out and adorned to suit his taste and his fancy, like a concubine being prepared for her master.

Strangely enough, the idea didn't repulse her. Instead she felt an electric anticipation; an excitement that flowed and flowered between her legs. Clutching the black robe closer around her, as if her arousal might be visible, she turned around to face the two waiting cousins.

'OK. I'm ready. What's next?'

Elisa's answer was to take her by the hand and lead her to the bathroom, with Feltris following silently behind them.

Once inside, the two worked as a team, setting out fresh towels and apparently unopened toiletries that seemed to have replaced the ones used earlier. Belinda frowned at the evidence of such efficiency. So far she had encountered only Oren and these two, but the count's establishment seemed to function as if there were scores of household staff in attendance. It was yet another mystery to add to a lengthening list, and as she pondered it, she realised Elisa was reaching for her robe.

Belinda hadn't really thought about what the other woman had written in the notebook, but now she panicked and clutched the thin black silk around her. She had shared communal showers often enough, but she had never actually been bathed by a woman, at least not since the days of her earliest childhood. And judging by what Jonathan had said, the cousins were lesbians: they would not look at her nakedness with cool detachment.

'It's OK, I can manage from here,' she said nervously, trying to snatch back her sash from Elisa's grasp. 'Thanks very much, but I'm used to looking after myself ... Really.'

But the blonde girl would not be gainsaid. With great deftness and determination, she teased the sash back out of Belinda's hold, then handed it to Feltris, who was standing close beside them. Smiling, she reached forward and touched Belinda's face, then leaned towards her and kissed her on the cheek. It was a very soft kiss, but full of reassurance.

Confused, Belinda released her grip on the robe and allowed Feltris and Elisa to peel it from her, revealing her body bare and flushed from their little tussle. She felt an overpowering urge to try and cover herself – with an arm across her breasts and a hand shielding her pubis – but she realised that would only make things worse. Acting like a shrinking violet would only emphasise the fact that their sexual nature scared her. If she behaved nonchalantly, they wouldn't realise she felt threatened.

Yet as she stepped forward, trying to smile, she felt dizzy. Something seemed to rush through her like a wind, and she had a sense of being transformed, transmuted, utterly changed. For a moment she could have sworn she saw Count André's blue eyes – not outwardly but within her mind – and a smile that was kind but gently mocking.

'Oh dear,' she gasped, swaying in the trailing edge of the experience, and almost immediately two pairs of arms were confidently supporting her. In a moment, they had her sitting on a chair.

Pressing her hands over her face, Belinda tried to analyse what had just happened. Something *had* happened, but the more she tried to think, the less she seemed to know. She only knew that now it was over, she felt much better, and lowering her fingers, she looked out and down into a pale and lovely face.

Feltris was kneeling in front of her, an expression of concern across her fine-boned elfin features.

Oh God, she's gorgeous! thought Belinda, astounded at the revelation. The younger girl was so pretty, so sensuous. So desirable.

Desirable?

But why not?

Trembling, Belinda reached out and touched Feltris's silky hair, then slid her fingers through it to cradle the back of the girl's head. Their gazes locked, and in Feltris's grey eyes Belinda saw tenderness and a kindly, encouraging lust. Without a second thought, she leant forward and began to kiss her.

I'm kissing a woman, thought Belinda, savouring the delicately fresh flavour of her companion's minty breath. The girl's lips were soft, almost the texture of rose petals, and they seemed to melt and flex beneath the contact of her own. Belinda felt Feltris's tongue dart into her mouth, flick around playfully, then seek out her own tongue. Automatically, she engaged it in a duel, and felt the young woman's slender arms come up around her.

Without the slightest awkwardness or need to consider her actions, Belinda slid forward, her mouth still pressed to Feltris's, and allowed herself to be guided to the bathroom floor. The embrace seemed so much easier in a horizontal position, and as she went on to her back, she felt Feltris rise up over her and continue the kiss in a dominant, man-like style.

Belinda was acutely aware of her nakedness – and that it gave her joy. She wrapped her arms around Feltris and pressed her bare breasts tight against her, then wriggled her bottom on the bathroom floor as she opened her legs. Feltris made a crooning, happy sound.

What's happened to me? thought Belinda dreamily, feeling her vulva open up like a sun-kissed flower. I'm lying on the floor without any clothes on, and I'm kissing and being kissed by another girl. It's wonderful . . . but what do we do next?

As if she had heard the question, Feltris answered it by shifting her body sideways and making Belinda groan a protest into her mouth. She felt doubly exposed without the mute girl's warm presence lying over her, and the fact that they were still kissing seemed to exacerbate her nudity. Feeling profoundly lewd, she stretched her thighs wider and swung her hips.

After a moment, she felt Elisa move in between her legs, a warm presence with experience and gentle hands. Belinda quivered as the older woman kissed her thigh, then kissed it again, but this time closer to her quim.

Oh no . . . Oh dear God, oh dear God, she's going to lick me, thought Belinda, as Feltris began sucking on her tongue. The two clever cousins were working as a team now, each conspiring with the other to give her pleasure.

Belinda tried to cry out as Elisa prised her open, delicately folding back the fleshy petals of her womanhood; but her protest was absorbed by Feltris's lips.

I can't . . . I can't bear it . . . The words rang in Belinda's brain because there was no way she could utter them. She tried to kick out with her legs but Elisa held them easily, then sank her soft mouth into Belinda's tender sex.

Cunnilingus felt just the same as it did when Jonathan used his mouth there; just the same, yet as different as night from day. Elisa's tongue was smaller, slyer, and supremely nimble. It seemed to find areas of responsiveness that neither Jonathan nor Belinda – with her own fingers – had ever encountered. Roving the entire length and breadth of her sexual landscape, it lingered here and there, and in other places made quick and darting forays. Within just moments it was far too much and Belinda climaxed.

The women held her tightly through the waves of

sweet sensation; gentling her body with their wordless sounds of comfort.

I can't believe what just happened to me, thought Belinda, as the spasms faded and she was able to relax. Utterly content, she was aware of her two companions sitting by her, one on either side, and she almost purred when Feltris stroked her brow. It felt so right, and so appropriate, and the more she thought about it, the more she wondered why she had never had a female lover before.

Perhaps it was just that she had never met the right woman? Or never met that woman when she was feeling so receptive? As she was now, in this weird but lovely place.

All of a sudden, she sat up and laughed out loud. Elisa and Feltris looked puzzled for a moment, then joined in, their laughter a little muffled but still sexy. They smiled and touched her, as if they too had been struck by a revelation.

'André von Kastel . . . you devil!' cried Belinda, throwing her head back and gazing up at the moulded ceiling. 'It's you, isn't it?' she demanded of the absent nobleman, having not the slightest doubt that in some way he could hear her. 'You've changed me. Made me like –' She looked from one beautiful face to the other '– making love with women. I've never had the slightest inclination before, but suddenly I-I'm different.'

At that moment, Elisa rose fluidly to her feet and reached down to draw Belinda to hers too. Beside them, graceful Feltris stood up also.

'What is it?' asked Belinda of the silent Elisa, looking her straight in the eye. 'Has your master called? Told you to hurry?'

The blonde woman smiled placidly, her eyes lambent and slightly teasing. With a lovely dance-like gesture, she pointed towards the bath, and as she did so, Feltris sprang forward and turned on the taps.

'OK, I get the message,' said Belinda, moving forward,

aware that there was no way she was going to be allowed to bathe herself now. Even if she had wanted to. She smiled with pleasure as she realised her friends would be joining her, and as she tested the water, they were pulling off their dresses.

Forty-five minutes later, Belinda stood before the looking glass in the bedroom next door, studying the image of a woman she had never seen before. A new woman, transformed by antique magic.

In theory, the orangey-peach dress should have been hideous with her titian colouring, but in practice it was just the reverse. The strong, fruity shade seemed to light up her hair, her eyes and her lips and give her pale complexion an almost ghostly glow. In her flapper's gown, she looked every inch the Jazz Baby, just as if she too – like her mysterious host – had stepped straight out of a portrait. It was a portrait she hadn't seen, but she was sure it existed somewhere.

'Boo doo pee doo,' she murmured to her reflection, and touched the strands of hair that were curled forward across her cheeks, emphasising her bone structure. Behind her, Elisa frowned, then reached around and made a minute adjustment to the same curl.

If she looked special, Belinda realised, it was because she owed much to the efforts of Elisa and Feltris. They had bathed her, perfumed her and preened her; assisted her with every last ritual of a woman's intimate toilette, including some that had been more intimate than others. She had balked and blushed to the roots of her hair several times during the process, but always, within a moment or two, she had unwound. Until today she would have found it difficult to understand how she could communicate with someone who didn't speak, but she found it easy to get on with the two young women. Not only were they friendly, they were also amusing, and their silence had a sly and jaunty humour. They were incredibly sensual too, and attuned to the erotic possibilities of even the simplest task. There had been slight delays, more than once, while they were getting her ready.

Turning from the mirror, Belinda glanced at each of her friends and asked, 'There! Will I do?'

Elisa smiled and nodded, her eyes dark and expressive, while Feltris, who Belinda had discovered was the more demonstrative of the two, stepped forward and pressed an airy kiss to her powdered cheek. Elisa wagged a warning finger at her cousin, but Feltris had been careful. Neither Belinda's gleaming hair nor her delicate make-up had been disturbed.

'So?' she queried again, and both girls kissed the tips of their fingers as a sign of approval.

Belinda turned again to the mirror.

But will *he* be impressed? she wondered, studying the sleek straight lines of the exquisite embroidered dress and the way it suggested rather than clung to her body. She smiled. Of course he will. How can he resist? she thought, remembering that intriguing mix of impishness and courtesy. The way he had kissed her hand, then later touched her body –

He?

'Good God,' whispered Belinda, amazed at her own thoughts. It was Count André she was daydreaming about, not Jonathan, her own boyfriend. It seemed disloyal, but there it was. Her thinking mind wanted to abhor the idea, but her instincts – and her subconscious – had suddenly overpowered her intellect. She was far more concerned about the opinion of a rather evasive stranger than the approval of a man she had been close to for years.

This place is changing us, she thought, glancing at the two beautiful women who stood to either side of her. Me and Jonathan, the pair of us; we're no better than each other. We've both been led astray.

Whatever next? she thought, turning around as a loud knock at the door surprised her. Another seduction?

André? Oren, perhaps? Someone I haven't even met yet?

But what puzzled her most was how little guilt she felt.

Chapter Seven
Curiouser and Curiouser

When the door opened she discovered her visitor was Oren and not Count André as her subconscious had hoped for and expected.

The tall, blond servant clearly didn't sense her disappointment though, because his smile was broad and cheerful. Nodding respectfully, he then glanced behind her to Feltris and Elisa and an unmistakable glint lit his eyes.

They're lovers! Curiouser and curiouser, thought Belinda, imagining the three of them together. They would make quite a sight, she was sure it; all blond, good to look at, and uninhibitedly full of life's joys. She could just picture their three golden bodies, meshed and contorted in pleasure. Who did what to whom? she wondered, speculating helplessly. Oren was so immense, so tall and broad – what would it be like with a lover so strong and huge?

Although the good-natured subject of her musings seemed prepared to wait indefinitely while she daydreamed, Belinda gave herself a mental shake.

'Have you come to escort me to dinner?' she enquired of Oren, who made an expressive sweeping gesture, indicating that she should follow him.

Enjoying the swish of the shimmering antique dress against her silk-stockinged calves, Belinda stepped out into the corridor, then turned to bid farewell to her beautiful new friends. Elisa and Feltris smiled back at her, then each blew kisses, their dark eyes full of what had happened in the bathroom. It isn't over, they seemed to be saying. And the next time will be even more delicious.

'Oh boy,' Belinda whispered almost silently, as she and Oren made their way along the corridor. The tall, Nordic servant was a pace or two ahead of her, and she got a shock when he turned and eyed her knowingly.

'Are you their – ' What could she say that didn't sound intrusive? 'Are you their friend?' she finished lamely.

Oren glanced at her, his eyes mocking her naiveté.

'Their cousin, then?' She couldn't bring herself to be any more explicit.

He nodded, then made an odd little circling gesture with his fingers, which seemed to say 'a bit more than that'.

'Oh ... Yes, I see,' Belinda murmured, wondering again what it would be like to make love with him. He was a colossus but he was obviously considerate and gentle. And he looked good enough to eat in the clothes he wore this evening: white denims and a white piqué polo shirt, both of which enhanced the bronze-like sheen of his skin.

Goddamnit, Seward, get a hold of yourself, she castigated silently. What on earth had got into her since she had arrived here? She could think of nothing but sex and bodies. Bodies and sex. Shouldn't she be worrying about Jonathan? Finding out where he had so suddenly disappeared to?

'Excuse me,' she said, touching Oren's massive golden arm. 'I was wondering what happened to my friend? We were together earlier, but then he sort of vanished.'

Oren paused in his stride and nodded, and when they reached the top of the stairs, he steered her towards another long landing instead. Halfway along it, they stopped before another heavy oak door – much like the one to her room – where he knocked softly, then opened it for her to enter.

Jonathan's bedroom was luxurious – perhaps not quite as much so as her own red and gold room, but still strikingly opulent and comfortable. The predominant colours were rich, masculine greens, and significantly there were no portraits of the distinctive von Kastels. The only pictures were one still life and one landscape.

The bed Jonathan lay in was like a woodland bower hung with greenery. He was fast asleep and his face looked angelic against the snow-white lawn pillow-case.

'Johnny?' Belinda called out softly as she approached the bed. 'Johnny, are you all right?'

Jonathan stirred slightly and muttered something indecipherable, but he didn't wake up. Belinda turned to Oren, who had followed her into the room.

'What's the matter with him?' she asked, feeling concerned. Jonathan was a great one for taking a nap whenever he got the chance, but she had never seen him sleep quite this deeply. What was more, it was well into the evening now, she realised, judging by the twilight she could see descending beyond the window. And Jonathan was a night person; he usually perked up about this time.

Oren smiled calmly. Launching into another of his eloquent mimes, he described meeting Jonathan on the landing a short while ago and then discovering that the young man felt dizzy.

'And you asked Count André to see him?' said Belinda, understanding the account but feeling puzzled. 'What could *he* do?'

Oren made a stirring motion and a few slow, flowing passes with his fingers, then pointed to a white beaker that stood on the bedside table. Frowning, Belinda remembered André's strange performance with the wine bottle, and she picked up the white mug with real alarm.

119

There was a strong smell of herbs clinging to the interior of the beaker, a scent that was quite pleasant and minty. Belinda guessed it had contained a tisane.

'Was it a medicine of some kind?' she asked.

Oren nodded.

'Something Count André made?'

He nodded again.

Whatever next? she thought, reaching down to touch Jonathan's brow. The man's a doctor now, as well as a magician.

And obviously a good one, she decided. Jonathan's temperature felt perfectly normal, and he seemed to be sleeping contentedly. It was a shame to wake him up just for the sake of it.

'He must need the rest,' she observed, then leant over and kissed her boyfriend's smooth cheek.

As Oren led the way back to the head of the stairs, Belinda felt guilty that she hadn't noticed Jonathan's weariness herself. He had done most of the driving so far on their trip, and obviously the strain had tired him out.

When they reached the ground floor, she was ushered once again into the great library – where the sight of the leather sofa made her blush. It seemed only a moment since she had sat there half-naked on André von Kastel's lap.

The count was waiting for her. Standing before one of the tall bookcases, he had an open leather-covered volume in his hand, and appeared deep in thought. He frowned suddenly, then flicked over several pages. Belinda cleared her throat to attract his attention.

When André looked up, the first thing she noticed was that his blue eyes were serious. The teasing quality she had seen earlier was conspicuous by its absence, and there was again an obscure aura of sorrow about him – something intense that came from deep in his psyche. He smiled to welcome her but still the sadness lingered.

'Good evening, Belinda,' he murmured, closing his

book, setting it aside and coming towards her. 'How lovely you look. You truly are a sight to fire the spirits.'

When he reached her, he bowed over her hand again, clicking his heels. Belinda's heart pounded as his lips caressed her fingers.

André too had changed for dinner, and was now clothed from head to toe in black. Black silk shirt, black trousers and black shoes. Surprisingly, he was tie-less, but he was wearing the most elegant of antiquated dinner jackets, which suited him so beautifully that Belinda caught her breath. His weird, striated hair was hanging loose around his shoulders, but despite its bleached look it appeared glossy and well kept. Belinda could have sworn it was even blonder than before.

'Thank you,' she said in answer to his compliment, feeling disturbed that he clung on to her hand.

'You are worried about your friend, are you not?' he said, giving her fingers a small squeeze before finally letting them go.

He's reading my mind again, thought Belinda, still feeling his firm, cool grip. 'Yes, I am rather. Johnny's usually so fit. It's not like him to come down with something.'

'Do not worry,' said André, his eyes hypnotic and soothing. 'I have examined him and basically he seems quite healthy. He is simply a little over-tired.' His mouth quirked very slightly, as if he was suggesting that *she* was the cause of Jonathan's tiredness. 'I gave him a herbal tonic. Something that will make him sleep deeply and renew his strength and vigour.'

'Thank you,' murmured Belinda again, her eyes sliding away from André's, unable to cope with the intensity of his look. She glanced around at the massed ranks of books. 'I didn't realise you were a doctor.'

He shrugged and somehow managed to capture her eyes again. 'I am not one.' He smiled, a little crookedly. 'I have a little medical knowledge but I am by no means a physician. Simply a dabbler in certain – ' he paused, his brilliant eyes dancing ' – therapies that have stood the test of time.'

'I'm very interested in alternative medicine – herbalism and aromatherapy and suchlike,' said Belinda quickly. It wasn't a lie. Standing here with André, she suddenly *was* interested. 'Do you have any good recipes and potions you can pass on?'

As she spoke, that strange shadow seemed to pass across his face again, but it disappeared just as swiftly when he replied.

'I would not exactly call them recipes,' he said, smiling, 'but there may be one or two things I can teach you. After dinner, that is.' He looked across to Oren, who seemed to be waiting for his orders. 'And now, I think, we shall have some champagne.'

This time, funnily enough, the wine was in an ice bucket. Belinda hadn't seen it when she had entered the library, but she noticed it now on the sideboard, coolly embracing a familiar, shapely bottle. With characteristic efficiency, Oren uncorked the frothing wine and filled two glasses without spilling the tiniest drop.

André took the two crystal flutes and handed one to Belinda, dismissing his servant with a slight nod as he did so. 'Not from my own country this time, alas,' he said, as he clinked his glass to hers, 'but delicious nevertheless. To your health, Belinda,' he murmured, 'and happiness.'

'What about long life?' she asked, as they sat down together. She felt intoxicated on just one sip of wine. 'Isn't that usually a part of the toast?'

André looked away then put his glass down by his feet. When he looked back at her, he seemed a mass of mixed emotions. His cultured face bore traces of irony, thoughtfulness and humour, as well as his slight but ever-present melancholy.

'Would you really want it?' he asked, his voice low and intent.

'What? You mean long life?' she countered, surprised

by the sudden fire in the question. 'Well, yes, I suppose I do. Doesn't everybody?'

For a moment, André didn't answer, and Belinda got the impression that she had lost him somehow. Or somewhere. He was sitting right next to her – handsome, charismatic and desirable – but it felt as if she were seeing him across a huge gulf, a division of time and space it was impossible to quantify.

Belinda felt frightened. In spite of what had happened here on this very couch, she did not know this man at all. She also had a feeling that if and when she came to know him fully, her present fears would seem as nothing by comparison.

'There are some to whom long life is a curse,' he said quietly. Then he reached down to retrieve his wine and downed it in one long swallow, his throat undulating sensuously as he drank. 'More champagne?' he enquired, on his feet again so fast it made her jump.

Belinda looked at her glass. She had hardly tasted the wine at all. She took a quick sip, then held it out. 'Yes, please,' she said, smiling as brightly as she could in an attempt to lift the suddenly sombre atmosphere.

'I'm sorry,' she said, when André returned with the wine, 'I think I've said something to upset you ... but I'm not quite sure what.'

'It is I who should be asking forgiveness,' he replied, his smile returned and his blue eyes unclouded and brilliant. 'I am being a poor host. I allow my worries to intrude at the most inopportune moments.'

'If you want to talk, it's OK, you know,' Belinda suddenly heard herself say. 'I know I'm a stranger ...' Colour flushed in her cheeks. She hadn't acted like a stranger earlier, when she had allowed him – and encouraged him – to touch her. 'But sometimes it's easier to tell your troubles to someone you don't know than it is to tell them to a friend or a loved one.'

For several seconds André stared at her unblinkingly. Belinda felt he was studying everything about her; her every thought, her every memory, her every hope and desire. 'You are a very kind and sensitive woman, Belinda,' he said softly. 'Perhaps I will confide in you. In a little while.' He smiled again, his eyes cheerful and full of promises. 'But first, we should enjoy our dinner, I think.' Draining his champagne, he put aside the glass, then rose to his feet, extending his hand to her like the courtier he most probably once had been.

He's like a prince in hiding, thought Belinda as she accompanied André to the dining room. A dissolute prince, banished for some unspeakable crime of passion and doomed to solitude for the rest of his days. It was a desperately glamorous image, she knew, and made him utterly fatal to women, especially imaginative ones like her, who loved tales of high romance and gothic mystery.

She was laughing by the time they reached their destination, and André gave her an amused look, as if once again he knew her thoughts exactly.

'OK, I admit it,' she said, as André drew her chair out and waited until she was comfortable before taking his own seat. 'You ... and this place ... I hate to admit it, but it really gets to me. I've got an ordinary life, an ordinary job, and I meet ordinary people. All this is like something from a book,' she said, gesturing around her. 'A foreign nobleman. A crumbling but fabulous house. Antiques. Gorgeous pictures.' She paused, realising she was gushing, and appalled by it. 'You've got me at a bit of a disadvantage. Really.'

André laughed, a merry, husky sound that seemed to dispel the last echoes of his sadness. 'It is *I* who is at a disadvantage,' he said, laying his hand across his chest. 'I am at the mercy of your beauty, your compassion ... and your open-mindedness.' He hesitated, as if debating some thorny inner point. He seemed on the very edge of revealing something, something which Belinda sensed was crucial. 'You have much that I want, Belinda, and much that I need,' he said at last. 'I am your servant, believe me.' He bowed his head momentarily. 'And I would do anything to keep you here in my company. Anything.'

He spoke with such emphasis that Belinda felt chilled. The words 'do anything' seemed to chime around the room and envelop her, despite the fact that he had spoken only quietly. It was a relief when Oren entered the room, bearing their first course on a large chased silver tray.

The meal was light and delicious but Belinda scarcely noticed the fine cuisine. It was as if André had put a spell on her; she could do nothing, really, but watch him and listen to his voice, and answer every question he asked about her. Revealing virtually nothing about himself, he seemed to effortlessly coax everything from her. Her past history; her present thoughts; her future hopes and dreams. Almost the whole of her life – even down to some of the most intimate details she had never told anyone about, ever – was described over the perfect food and heady wine. And when they were finished, she could hardly believe what she had disclosed.

Has he hypnotised me? she wondered as she studied the tiny coffee cup before her and smelt the divine aroma it exuded. It certainly seemed that way. She had just talked and talked and talked, while André had remained enigmatic, and listened.

He had also, she noticed, eaten very little of his excellent dinner. Just a few morsels here and there, and then only taken for her benefit, it seemed. As the strong but sublime coffee began to clear her fuddled head a little, Belinda had the most extraordinary idea ever.

He's not human, she thought, watching André push away his plate and fold his table napkin.

Suddenly, all the books she had read and the films and television shows she had seen seemed to conspire and produce an extraordinary conclusion – Count André von Kastel was a vampire, a ghost, or some other nether being who possessed strange powers and did not take ordinary nourishment.

Everything seemed to point to it. He slept during the day, he barely ate, and she was almost convinced that he had done some kind of magic trick with the wine that afternoon in the library. Plus the fact that he lived alone, in seclusion, with only three dumb servants to attend him, in a house that was crammed with peculiar arte-facts. He even came from the appropriate part of Europe.

Belinda began to shake when André rose to his feet and walked around the table towards her. She felt foolish, letting her fancies control her, but when he stood over her, smiling slightly, she couldn't move a muscle and she couldn't seem to speak.

'What is it?' he asked softly, putting out his hand to her. 'Are you afraid of me?'

Belinda licked her lips. She was caught in the thrall of a being who had the combined sexual magnetism of a dozen cinematic Draculas, and even if he were just a man after all, she was sure that wouldn't lessen her growing fear of him.

'Belinda?' he prompted, making a tiny gesture of encouragement with his fingertips.

'I-I'm sorry, I think I've had too much wine,' she said, finally finding the strength to take his hand. 'I started imagining the silliest of things just then.' She stood up, half-expecting to swoon or something, but found herself quite steady on her feet.

'Tell me about them,' said André, tucking her hand beneath his arm and leading her to the door. 'Entertain me while we stroll on the terrace. I always enjoy a walk after dinner.' He patted her hand, his fingers cool but corporeal.

'It's too stupid. I couldn't tell you, really,' she insisted, as he led her along yet another corridor she hadn't been along before, that seemed to lead right through the centre of the priory.

'Try me,' he urged, as they reached an iron-studded door that surely only a man the size of Oren could master. 'I have heard many a tall tale in my time ...

And told my fair share too.' He grinned and released her arm. Then he opened the huge door without effort.

The terrace that lay beyond was broad, stone flagged, and lit by a string of what appeared to be oil-burning lanterns. The sky was dark now, a rich shade of indigo, and the brightest of the stars were breaking through. A three-quarter moon rode above them like a sail. Belinda breathed in and smelt the perfume of many flowers, a rich fragrance that seemed to blend with André's cologne.

'This is so lovely,' she murmured, then hurried forward towards the elaborately-carved stone parapet so she could look out over the gardens beyond.

Why didn't I see this earlier today? she wondered, discovering that in the distance and to her left was the folly. She had approached the priory in broad daylight this morning and seen no evidence whatsoever of this long terrace. The whole house seemed to be remaking itself by the hour.

As she leaned over the parapet, she sensed rather than heard André join her. 'You were going to tell me what you had been thinking about,' he said, sliding his arm around her waist as if it were a perfectly natural thing to do with a near stranger, and as if they were about to take up where they had left off in the library. She felt his mouth brush the hot skin of her neck.

'I . . .' Feeling almost faint, she swayed against him. His lips were still against her throat, and filled with her insane notions of earlier, she expected him to attack at any second.

'Why do you fear me, Belinda?' he whispered, feathering a soft kiss against the line of her jaw. 'I am not what you think I am, believe me. I am just a man who is entranced by your beauty.'

He knows! thought Belinda as André turned her expertly and put his arms around her body to embrace her. He knows I thought he was a vampire. That I still think he might be one.

127

Cradling her head, André pressed his mouth to hers, probing for entrance with his tongue as she yielded. Belinda tried to keep her mouth closed and her brain sent the message to her lips, but with half a sigh and half a groan, she felt them open, admitting him to explore and taste her moistness.

The kiss went on for a long, long time, and as she enjoyed it, Belinda seemed to see a stream of inner pictures. Erotic images of herself and the man who held her.

First, she saw the way she must have appeared this afternoon: half-naked and sprawled across André's lap, moaning and crooning while he stroked her. Then, a second later, she seemed to be kneeling before him, on this very terrace, taking his strong, erect penis into her mouth. She could almost feel his fingers clasping her head as he thrust savagely, seeking the back of her throat, and she could almost taste the salt-sharp tang of come. The vision of fellatio melted then and changed to a picture of her leaning over a bed somewhere, possibly the red and gold one in her room, while André caressed her naked buttocks. He was teasing her, playing with her; dipping his fingers into her slit from behind, then drawing them up and back to fondle her pouting anus. To her horror the tiny portal seemed to welcome him, relaxing lewdly as a single digit entered.

The fantasy images were so real and so vivid that her body couldn't help but react to them. She groaned around André's intruding tongue and rubbed herself involuntarily against him. In response, his long, graceful hands sank immediately to her bottom, moulding her cheeks through the glistening dress, and pressing her to him.

Whatever his nature or strangeness, he was possessed of a living man's erection, and Belinda felt it bore into her belly. There were several layers of fabric between them, yet it was one of the most exciting sensations she had ever felt. He was like rock against her – like steel, like diamond – and despite the masking barriers, she seemed to feel his shape.

Massaging him with her body and feeling his fingers caress her buttocks in return, she began to see another set of pictures. But this time they were all of André only, in his tower room, fondling his penis until he came. She saw again, in every detail, the way he had arched with pleasure and squirmed like a wild man against the sheets. She almost seemed to hear his incoherent outcries, his mutterings and exclamations in his own language. She saw him rising towards his climax, his body growing more and more tense as he strained to reach it, but at the instant he seemed to get there, the image faded. As she gasped in disappointment, he broke the kiss.

Panting for air, Belinda slumped against André's straight body, feeling grateful for his strength in her own weakness. She almost felt as if she had just had an orgasm herself, the rush had been so huge. She had certainly never been kissed like that before, and to her dismay, she felt a sudden urge to weep.

Confused, Belinda snuggled closer than ever, and as she buried her face in the hollow of André's shoulder, his hand came up and stroked her hair to soothe her. She heard him whisper something, his voice sounding vaguely Germanic but nevertheless flowing, and she realised he was speaking in his mother tongue to calm her.

'What are you doing to me?' she pleaded, drawing a little way away so she could look at him.

André looked at her steadily, his face appearing chiselled in the uneven radiance from the oil lamps and his eyes glowing with a fire both light and dark.

'I do not want to hurt you,' he said at length, using his thumb to brush away her tears. 'Only to arouse you, and enlighten you – ' he paused, a hint of a plea forming in the brilliance of his gaze ' – so you can help me.'

Belinda sniffed and he produced an immaculate white

cotton handkerchief from his pocket and put it into her hand. Dabbing her eyes, she tried to think straight and ponder the significance of the words 'help me'.

It was the second time he had intimated that he needed her in some way, but Belinda couldn't begin to see why. She crumpled his snowy handkerchief, then frowned and tried to straighten it, knowing that there was no way she could put off asking the question.

'What are you, André? And why on earth would you need *me* for anything?'

He looked away towards the distant woods, as if seeking the right way to approach a difficult answer in their depths.

'I am just a man, Belinda,' he said eventually, still staring out across the gardens and the park, 'but I need you because – ' He paused, then turned fully away from her to face in the direction he was looking. His hands settled on the parapet, his fingers first splayed then gripping the stone tightly. 'You are beautiful. Desirable. Exquisite. I need your pleasure in order to be strong.'

It was Belinda's turn to seek an answer in the beautiful darkness. What did he mean by 'your pleasure in order to be strong'?

'I don't understand,' she said in a small voice, studying the shadows. 'You say you need my pleasure. Does that mean you are a – ' She couldn't say the word. It sounded ridiculous. Such things only existed in books and on celluloid.

'A vampire?' he asked, moving close behind her, his mouth brushing her neck just like the blackest Nosferatu's.

'Yes.' She was trembling again and gripping the parapet just as André had. She could feel his breath ruffling the fronds of hair at the nape of her neck, and the beating of his heart where his chest lay against her back. Both of these seemed to deny her mad suspicions.

'No, I am not a vampire,' he said, pressing a brief kiss

to the lobe of her ear, 'although I can well imagine what it must be like to be one.'

Belinda could not speak. Her shudders doubled and re-doubled. He was skirting the issue. There *was* something wrong with him. Something different. She felt herself about to fall, to crumple face down over the parapet, but André's arms were around her again, holding her tightly against his body. His strangely cool body and his so very human erection.

He was still as hard as ever as he pressed himself against her, massaging his stiffness into the crease between her buttocks. 'Oh, Belle,' he whispered, 'I need you so much.' His hands moved away from her waist where he had held her, one sliding up to cup her breast, the other going downwards.

The fear Belinda felt seemed to have aphrodisiac qualities. She was still terrified but her body began to rouse. Her nipples stiffened, peaking beneath the fragile fabric of her dress and her chemise, and between her legs the silken moisture welled. When André pressed his palm against her pubis, she jerked and whimpered.

'I c-can't,' she sobbed, not knowing why she was trying to resist. What was the point in defending a barrier he had already breached? Hadn't he 'fed' this afternoon, when he had touched and stroked her; hadn't he been nourished by the orgasm she had then experienced?

'But you can,' he told her, his hands moving guilefully to squeeze and massage. 'It is so easy. I would never hurt you.'

Belinda went limp in his grasp, her body seeming to melt as the sensations quickly mounted. Her breasts were aching now, swelling inside the silk of her bodice, and her vulva was a pool of simmering heat.

'Oh André! André!' Moulded against him, she no longer cared who or what he was. He was simply caressing hands and a male body, superbly strong and fragrant.

Suddenly there were too many layers of clothing between them. Still held, she struggled in his grip, trying to reach the fastenings of the priceless period dress.

'Hush,' he murmured. 'Let me. It will be easier.' He took his hands from her body in an instant and set to work, deftly undoing the tiny buttons at the back of her dress.

Without André's hands on her, Belinda felt feverish, and she moaned for the return of his fabulous touch.

'Patience,' he said into her ear as the dress fluttered down on to the stone flags beneath them, forming a pale, fluid pool around her ankles. Too impatient even to step out of it, Belinda pressed her thinly-clad body back against him and circled her hips to work her buttocks against his penis.

'Touch me,' she begged, tugging at the cobweb-like chemise and knickers. 'I want you to touch me. Please. Like you did before ... I want to feel your fingers between my legs.'

Somewhere far back in her mind, Belinda was appalled. She was pleading and grovelling like some helpless nymphomaniac, calling out for a virtual stranger to lay his hands upon her sex. It wasn't like her, but it didn't seem to matter. She was another person here, transformed by André, her magician, into a thing of pleasure, pledged only to serve his whim. As his fingers slithered beneath the chemise, she grunted, 'Yes!'

Hunting among the layers of delicate silk, André soon had his hand inside her knickers, and with unerring efficiency, he worked it down to find her quim. One finger wiggled its way through the sodden curls of her pubic forest, and when it found her, Belinda crowed with lust and triumph.

'Oh God! Oh God!' Her cries rang out loudly in the mystical blue-black night, her bottom jerking as André flicked her clitoris. She was a breath away from orgasm, a heartbeat from coming gloriously and freely, but he kept her hovering, his touch wicked and as light as swan's down.

'Oh please,' she begged again, kicking her legs, heedless that she might tear the priceless gown around her feet. 'Oh please, André, please, I need to come. I can't wait. I'll go mad if I don't!'

One arm held her tight around her waist while the other slid loosely to her side. 'Don't worry, my beautiful Belinda,' he purred into her ear. 'You will have your release. But it will be all the sweeter for a little wait. A little craving.'

Belinda kicked again, sending the peach-orange dress flying across the flags. 'You beast! You bastard! You really are a monster!' she howled, squirming and squirreling against him. Her sex was on fire and so engorged it seemed to hurt. She hissed 'I hate you' as he draped her forward against the parapet.

'Be still,' he ordered her, his voice soft yet seeming to resonate with command. She felt his hand lie flat against the small of her back, and though he held her lightly, she seemed to lose the will to move.

Belinda quivered finely as she lay prone across the parapet, toweringly furious yet more aroused than she could measure. She bit her lip as André stood behind her, and she sensed him studying her bottom. After a short pause, she felt him plucking gently at her knickers, then easing the fine, slippery fabric slowly downward.

When her drawers were around her ankles, he lifted the pretty embroidered chemise up to just beneath her shoulders and with a few deft tucks and twists, he secured it there. When that was done, she heard him step back to admire the view.

'Oh God,' Belinda moaned again, as she imagined the shocking vista before his eyes.

Her bottom and her thighs were completely on show, while her suspenders and her stockings enhanced their bareness. She could feel the fragrant night air flowing playfully across her vulva, its cool caress a blessed balm to her burning heat.

'What are you going to do to me?' she asked defiantly, fighting hard to keep the quaver from her voice. 'Beat me or something? Smack my bottom ... I'm sure that's just what you decadent aristocrats live for – a chance to humiliate the lower orders.'

'How wrong you are,' said André, his voice soft and far closer than she had realised. 'I only want to give you pleasure.' She could swear she felt his breath upon her back. 'Although if to be beaten *is* your pleasure, I would be far more than delighted to oblige you.'

'Don't be ridiculous!' she cried, yet at the same time she imagined his hand crashing down upon her buttocks. The idea should have been horrendous; revolting. But suddenly, against her will, she seemed to want it. She felt her sex-flesh pulse and flutter at the thought of André smacking her bottom, and her hips began to weave of their own accord. She pursed her lips to prevent her voicing her wayward urges.

'I know ... I know ...' His voice was soothing and she felt the brush of his dinner jacket against her thighs. 'Perhaps I should beat you?' He seemed to reflect for a moment. 'But not just yet. Tonight we will enjoy a simpler pleasure.'

He *does* know, she thought, feeling herself sink to a delicious nadir of shame. He understands what I want before I do. He anticipates the way I think and what I feel. How will I ever keep a secret while he's near?

Chapter Eight
Indigo Secrets

'*R*elax ... relax...' murmured André, his long hair tickling her back as he sank to his knees at her side. 'There is no need to keep secrets from me. I have no wish to harm you.'

Belinda stiffened involuntarily. The more André confirmed his strangeness, the more her fear of him increased. And as the fear grew, so did her arousal.

He must be able to see how much I want him, she thought, unable to prevent her thighs from shaking. She could feel his breath on her now, his cool breath, like a breeze that teased her naked bottom. His face was just inches from her vulva. She imagined him flaring his nostrils and drawing her scent; her strong female odour. She could smell it herself, so André must be drowning in it. She pictured him studying the engorged folds of her sex then putting out his tongue, pointed and mobile, to taste and lick her. The idea made her cringe with shame, and yet, with all her might, she craved it. And in acknowledging that need, she knew that he too knew what she wanted.

But still he kept his distance. Inches seemed like feet or yards. His breath and his masculine aura seemed to tantalise and caress her, but his fingers and his tongue remained aloof.

'Well, do something if you're going to!' she cried, unable to bear the waiting any longer. She felt like an exhibit in a gallery or some infernal experiment in responsiveness. Was he waiting to see how wet she would get without the benefit of contact? Was he waiting for her to crack and reach to touch herself? Or perhaps to have an orgasm, just from need?

'Patience,' he whispered, laying his fingers on her flank. 'You are so beautiful. Let me admire you a moment, before I pleasure you.'

Belinda let out a low, frustrated cry. Her swollen sex was calling to him, begging for him. She kicked her legs and felt her knickers at first constrain her then slide off over her shiny satin ballet pumps, one foot after the other. Kicking them away, she edged closer to the parapet, trying to press her pubis against the stone and get relief.

The hand on her thigh moved inward, fingers splaying, thumb beginning a rhythmic stroke. It moved back and forth, less than an inch from her anus, sliding over the sensitive skin with ineffable lightness. As she groaned, his left hand mirrored his right, and then both his thumbs were working in concert, stroking the area around her rosy entrance with the greatest care.

Belinda pushed back towards him, feeling both her sex and her rear portal pout rudely. Her body seemed to speak of its own accord. Choose! it demanded of him. Take me! Take whatever you want . . . it's yours . . . take everything!

The thumbs edged closer together, right into the channel, their soft pads brushing the forbidden opening. Liquid gathered in her vulva, pooling as it never had before, then became too much to be contained and overflowed. She could feel her sexual juice trickling down her inner thigh and landing in a sticky puddle on the stone. Shame made her whole body flush, but it

136

made no difference. The fluid only ran faster than ever, oozing out of her like honey from a jar.

'Oh please! Oh please!' she begged again, unable to bear being touched yet not touched, being viewed but not allowed to come, being so wet and needy she was running like a river. 'Oh please,' she grunted, shoving her whole body towards him and tilting up her hips.

His answer was to dig into the flesh of her bottom with his thumbs, exert a measured, devilish pressure, then slide them outwards again, parting her lobes like a ripe peach. Her sense of being exposed increased exponentially as the entrances to her body were stretched wide, but she urged him on by pressing backwards and stretching them wider –

When his tongue touched her sex, she almost fainted.

It was just the very lightest contact at first. His tongue-tip was furled, extended, probing like a dart into her sacred inner sanctum. Moving like a hovering, nectar drinking bird, it circled the snug mouth of her vagina, then seemed to flatten and lap at her welling fluids. The feeling was so sublime and so longed for, she began to come.

As the pulsations lashed her vulva, she felt André grip her tightly and his tongue point again and dive inside her. Squirming, she reached beneath herself and rubbed her clitoris.

'Yes!' encouraged André, his cultured voice muffled against her bottom.

Belinda rubbed harder, her whole body in manic, jerking motion as the sensations spiralled up to a new intensity. She could hear herself sobbing, shouting, grunting; her sex seemed to be a mile wide, a vast landscape of pure, lewd pleasure; every inch of it beating like a misplaced heart.

The next moment, she felt André withdraw his tongue from her vagina then slither it backwards until it rested against her anus.

Oh no! screamed a scared little voice inside her; then

suddenly the same voice was howling out anew in perfect ecstasy. Furled again, and as stiff and determined as before, his tongue breached the puckered aperture between her buttocks.

'Oh no! Oh no! Oh no!' she crooned, appalled by the power of what she was experiencing. This was an unthinkable taboo. It couldn't be happening. She couldn't be feeling such pleasure because he was doing *that* to her. She couldn't be coming even harder than she had before . . .

After a while, Belinda seemed to wake up from a dream of sobbing and disorientation. She was aware of what had just happened, but her mind was trying to stop her from believing it. No man had ever done such a thing to her before, and the strength of her own responses confused and confounded her. Shame and horror vied with delicious wonder. She didn't know what to think, but she couldn't deny what she had felt. The pinnacle of pleasure from the basest kiss of all.

As her shoulders heaved and her teardrops fell down into the garden below, she sensed André rise behind her. What he had just done should by rights have abased him, and yet it dawned on Belinda that precisely the opposite had happened. If anything, her awe of him had increased. He was remarkable. Uninhibited beyond belief. A sexual prize she was unworthy of and had not earned.

'Do not weep,' he whispered, leaning over her. 'There is no shame in enjoying the *feuille de rose*.' His arms slid around her and lifted her from the stone, and when she was standing, he gently turned her to face him, using the very tips of his fingers to erase her tears. 'And it pleased me to kiss you there. Your *cul* is enchanting. I cannot imagine a man who could resist its tender beauty and its tightness.'

Belinda buried her face in the lapel of his dinner jacket, very aware of her own vulnerability. Her pretty chemise had slid down over her back but her buttocks were still naked. She could feel herself blushing again, thinking of André's cool aristocratic face pressed tight between the cheeks of her bottom.

'Hush ... hush ...' A long, graceful hand settled on the back of her head, ruffling and smoothing her short hair. Belinda felt a great calm flow over her, a feeling of being exactly in the right place in the world. What André had done had been wonderful. How could she possibly have perceived it as wrong?

'That's a pretty name for it,' she said at last, looking up into his lambent blue eyes.

'*Feuille de rose*?'

'Yes. Trust the French.' She suddenly found herself laughing.

André chuckled too. 'Yes, as a nation they have an aptitude for the *bon mot*,' he observed, smiling at her. 'But the description is valid. Have you never taken a glass and studied yourself?' His eyes twinkled. 'The entrance is soft and a dark, dark pink, and it is ruffled like the petals of a rosebud.'

'I-I've never looked,' she said nervously. Would he think her less of a woman if she wasn't fully familiar with her own sexual anatomy? She had taken her body for granted until now; perhaps not revelled in it as much as she should have.

'Never?'

'Never.'

'Then why not begin tonight?' He eyed her intently, his expression indicating an order rather than a question.

'I – ' Belinda began, then she fell silent as André slid his fingers beneath the hem of her thin chemise and whisked it up over her head.

'But how can I look at myself here?' she protested when it too fluttered down on to the flags of the terrace. She fought the urge to cover herself, especially her nipples, which were as hard and dark as plum stones.

'You cannot,' he replied, reaching gently for her breasts and cupping them, 'but I can.' He bent down,

139

kissed each delicately pointed crest, then met her eyes again. 'And I have been promising myself this privilege all night.' He reached out and enfolded her in his arms, crushing her near-naked form to his fully-clothed body.

If Belinda had felt vulnerable before, she felt doubly so now. She was standing on an open terrace, at night, virtually nude. Her flimsy suspender belt, her stockings and her ballet shoes were no protection, especially from the mysterious, audacious man who held her. Any second now, he might bend her over the parapet and perform whatever outrage he so desired on her unprotected body. It might be more than his tongue that entered her this time – and yet, snuggling closer, she longed for the deepest of debasement.

For a while he just kissed her and held her, his mouth quite circumspect as it roved across her face, exploring briefly but always returning to her lips. Occasionally, he would mutter a scrap of a sentence against her skin, something unintelligible in his own language that nevertheless made her quiver.

Presently, his mouth settled firmly on hers again, his tongue pressing for entrance then possessing her completely the instant her lips yielded. At the same time, his hands began to range across her body, visiting her breasts, her thighs and her buttocks. In sliding circles, he rubbed and aroused her and his fingers delved repeatedly into the grove between her legs, touching her sex and the sensitive 'rosebud' of her bottom. Aflame anew, she couldn't stop herself from moaning, uttering her muffled entreaties around his tongue.

'You want me,' he said, releasing her mouth and looking down at her. It was a statement of fact, not a question.

Belinda tried to look away, but he cupped her jaw in his fingers and prevented her.

'You want me . . . I know that,' he said again, with a strange expression on his face that puzzled her. She watched him bite his lip in perplexion, then heard him sigh.

Sensing the sudden return of his melancholy, Belinda moved her body against his invitingly. She found it difficult to say the words, but actions were easy enough. She shimmied sinuously, rocking her belly against the bulge of his erection.

'Would that things were different . . .' he said quietly, his eyes on her face, their brilliant blue suddenly darkened to indigo. He was aroused, she could tell. There was no denying the truth of his hard, swollen cock against her. But the very fact of it seemed to cause him sorrow instead of joy.

'What's wrong?' asked Belinda, thoroughly puzzled by the contradictions. She suddenly realised that she had perhaps never wanted a man this much ever in her life, and she couldn't bear the idea of being thwarted now. A second ago, she had been sure he desired her.

'I *will* tell you,' he said, placing a cool hand on either side of her face and making her look at him. 'But first we will share pleasure as best we can.' Releasing her, he stepped back a pace, then reached for her hand. 'Come. We will go to your bedroom. We can be more comfortable there.' He gave her a small, almost nervous smile, and began to lead her across the terrace towards the house.

'But my clothes – ' She looked back towards the pools of pale silk that were the dress and the lingerie. 'And I left my bag and my flower in the dining room.' Why was she protesting? The things were André's so what did it matter?

'You do not need clothes,' he said, urging her forward, his playfulness returned. 'Come, I want you to walk naked through my house. I want to see your breasts and your bottom sway as you move. Indulge an old man, Belinda. Please be kind.'

More confused than ever, she obeyed him, very conscious of the bounce of her breasts with each step and

141

the way her bottom rolled voluptuously from side to side. And what on earth had he meant by 'indulge an old man'? He had been flirting with her as he had said it, yet the words themselves had seemed to carry an odd significance.

He wasn't old, not by any means. Not really. Yet as she thought about it, Belinda wondered exactly how old her intriguing host was. It was hard to put a precise age on him. His features were peculiarly ageless; neither old nor young. He could have been anywhere between his early twenties to his late thirties, and his streaky hair made him even more of an enigma.

'Why are you frowning?' André asked suddenly as he stepped aside to let her pass into the main hall. 'Please do not spoil a masterpiece with such a worried look.'

Wondering what he was referring to, Belinda spun around and saw herself and André reflected in a long mirror which she hadn't noticed before.

The contrast between them was stunning: André was a dramatic and ominous figure in his sombre black clothing, while she was a pale, gleaming vision of delicate curves. The minimal scrap of lace around her hips and her gossamer fine stockings only appeared to increase her nakedness rather than cover it, and the glossy amber of her pubic curls was a brilliant splash. Once again, she felt an overpowering urge to try and cover herself, but before thought could become deed, André grasped her arms.

'Do not hide, Belinda,' he whispered, drawing her arms back and making her straighten her shoulders. Her breasts lifted proudly as if displayed. 'Your bare body is sublime. A treasure. You should exhibit it as often as you are able.' Starting to blush again, Belinda looked away, but André released her and made her turn her head. 'Look . . . Look into the glass,' he murmured. 'See your own beauty.' His hand passed across her breasts, then down over her belly to rest briefly against her pubis, the dark sleeve of his coat making her skin look

142

white and pearly. There seemed no trace left of her holiday tan. 'Would you like to watch while I caress you?' His voice was low, like velvet in her ear, and the expression on his face was almost predatory. 'Would you like to see your own face when you are in the throes of ecstasy? See it grow savage as you reach the peak of pleasure?' His mouth was against her neck; she could feel his teeth. 'Would you, Belinda, would you?'

'No! I can't! I don't want to!' She jerked away from him, aware that she was lying but also frightened. Her body was moistening at the thought – the image of her naked hips bucking, her face twisting. Her thighs spread wide while a strong hand worked ruthlessly between them. 'Please, no,' she whispered, turning in towards him then almost collapsing against the dark-clad column of his body.

He held her again, soothingly. 'Do not worry,' he said into her hair, 'there is no compulsion. You need only do what you want to do, Belinda. I would never force you to do anything against your will.'

Belinda snuggled against him, breathing in great lungfuls of his heady rose cologne. Within her, she could already feel her fears transforming into desires. It was on the tip of her tongue to tell him she had changed her mind and that she would be glad to fulfil his wishes, when he patted her back and then released her from his arms.

'Come along, to your room. We can relax there and feel comfortable.'

Belinda nodded and gave him a small shy smile, wondering how it was that she could suddenly change from a self-possessed and rather bossy young woman into a creature so pliant and submissive. It was less than a day since she had first set eyes on André von Kastel, and already she was obeying his every word.

The strangest thing, she thought, as they ascended the staircase together, arm in arm, her breast brushing the fine cloth of his dinner jacket, was how easily it had happened. André was a puzzle to her, and mysterious sexually, as well as on every other level. Yet despite this, she somehow felt strangely safe with him. She sensed he was keeping secrets from her – probably a good many of them – but she also knew, without knowing how, that he wouldn't harm her. At least not intentionally.

Turning to him, she smiled again, and as they reached the top of the stairs, he returned her smile and nodded infinitesimally.

Belinda shrugged her shoulders. How long would it take her to remember that while André could hide his secrets effortlessly, hers were an open book to him?

When they reached her door, he opened it, then stepped back, executing a slight bow to let her pass.

The room was filled with candles and their flickering casting a moving veil of light. Some were in elaborate candelabra, wrought out of iron and bronze and more precious metals; while other, thinner candles stood in a variety of small, individual holders of porcelain, crystal and brass, scattered on every flat surface to be seen. The result of all this was eerie but also welcoming, and Belinda gasped, feeling sheer delight at the magical effect.

'How lovely!' she cried.

'My servants know their duties well,' said André from behind her, a note of satisfaction in his voice.

Belinda moved forward into the room, looking around at the array of dancing lights, then down at her own body where the radiance played on it. It was something of a cliché that candlelight flattered the human body, but this was the first time she had seen the phenomenon for herself. The shimmering glow seemed to lend a soft peachy radiance to her skin, as well sleekening her curves and creating a subtle mystic shading. Without thinking, she ran her hands down her flanks and watched the shadows of her fingers leap and race. From behind her she heard a male sigh of appreciation.

When she turned around, she found André staring at

her fixedly, his eyes filled with both excitement and what appeared for all the world to be exquisite nostalgia. Seeing her body by candlelight obviously brought back a memory of some kind, a recollection that was both erotic and deeply poignant. His face shining, he held out his arms, then fiercely embraced her.

What is it? she wanted to ask as they were kissing. Who does this remind you of? The questions faded as André's kiss bewitched her senses.

Belinda had never been a great one for kissing on its own, but with André the simple act brought a ravishing pleasure. His mouth was soft, yet active and strong; as cold as ice-cream, and figuratively, just as sweet. She found herself swaying again, almost swooning; quite lost in the experience. And it was André, with a sigh of regret, who at last drew back.

'Do you need a moment to yourself?' he asked, nodding towards the bathroom.

Belinda felt confused for a second, then realised what he was asking, and was thankful.

'Yes. Just a minute,' she said, breaking from his arms. 'I won't be long.' Conscious of his scrutiny, she walked as smoothly and gracefully as she could into the adjoining room.

What am I letting myself in for? she thought, doing what she had to as quickly as possible. He scares me, and yet I let him do exactly what he wants with me.

Why is that? she asked her reflection in the mirror, studying the wild eyes and passion-flushed face she saw before her. She was in unknown territory, the realm of the imagination. After having read so many tales of the supernatural – and half-believing them at the time – she was now in the presence of a real 'phenomenon', a man who could very well not be human. And yet she trusted him.

So, what *do* you think he is? she mused as she sprayed on a little scent, then ran her fingers through her hair to smooth it. He says he isn't a vampire, but he is *something*.

No normal man can do what he does and feel how he feels.

Standing with her hand on the door handle, she had a last irrational urge to pull back, to lock the bathroom door, and shout for André to go away. But then she remembered his kisses, and his touch, and she could no longer wait a single minute to be near him. She flung open the door and strode back into the bedroom, her heart pounding madly.

André was waiting in bed for her, his clothes flung everywhere on the floor. His smile was almost shy as she approached him, and he held up the blood-red coverlet to reveal the crisp, lace-trimmed linens that lay beneath it. She caught a fleeting glimpse of his long bare flank as she slid in beside him.

'Belinda ... The beautiful one,' he murmured, as they lay facing one another, propped up on a mound of pillows. He reached out to touch her cheek, but otherwise kept his distance, as if reluctant to press his unclothed body against hers. His face bore an expression of disbelief, an almost boyish befuddlement at the simple fact that they were together, sharing a bed.

'Why are you staring at me like that?' she asked, feeling the hairs on the back of her neck rise. André looked stunned, yet extraordinarily focused. 'You said I reminded you of someone. Is that what it is? Do I look like a woman you once made love to? Someone you've slept with already?'

'I never made love to her,' he said quietly, his mouth twisted in a quirky sorrowful little smile. 'At least, not the way I would have liked to.'

'What happened?' asked Belinda, moving closer, then clasping his arm so he couldn't retreat. As her thigh touched his, she felt the coolness of his skin, but suppressed her flinch of shock. It seemed that his entire body had the same unnaturally low temperature that his lips and his hands did.

'Did . . . did she die?' She felt compelled to ask, even though she suspected his answer would cause him pain.

André looked away, and for a long time he didn't speak. His cold body felt so still against her that he might just as well have been carved out of stone. 'Not exactly,' he said eventually, 'although sometimes I wonder if it might have been better if she had died. And that I had died also.'

The wistful expression on his face was so affecting that Belinda surged forward, wrapped her arms around him, and kissed his cheek, his throat and his cool chest. Now that she was accustomed to his chilliness, she began to find it exciting. She pressed even closer, forcing him back against the pillows, gasping with relief as his body moved against her. His penis was no warmer than any of the rest of him was, but at least it was imposingly erect.

'You must have loved her very much,' she whispered, rising up over him and looking down into his face. His eyes were closed; his expression was unreadable.

'I love her still,' he said, his lashes flicking up. His eyes were clear and frank, their blueness like the light of a distant star.

'And you want me because I look like her,' stated Belinda, swirling her pelvis and stimulating his engorged sex with her belly. She couldn't understand why she wasn't feeling jealous. Under any other circumstances she would have felt so.

'Yes – ' He paused. 'And no.' He grinned, then grasped her hips, pulling her down, hard, against him. 'It is difficult to explain . . . I know in my heart that you are not Belle, and yet you seem so much like her.' He frowned, as if his own emotions were hard to comprehend. 'To hold you like this is to experience something I thought was forever lost to me. And yet . . . and yet at the same time I know you are Belinda Seward, a new friend whose intelligence and beauty enchant me, and whose naked body excites me beyond measure.' He

147

shrugged, making his penis slip and slide against her hip. 'I am at a loss to know what I feel, and what I *should* feel. You must bear with me, Belinda. I find this very strange.'

'So do I,' said Belinda, wanting to touch him and feel his hardness – to explore flesh that by any normal standards should be hot. 'Everything's strange here. The house is strange. Your servants are strange. Even time itself is strange. I know I should be scared to death – ' She paused, holding his brilliant, unnatural gaze, and fighting not to look away ' – but I'm not. Even though the strangest thing of all here is you!'

'You are right, Belinda,' he said, staring up at her, his eyes unblinking. 'So right. The source of all that is strange here *is* me.' He moved again beneath her, inveigling his thigh between hers; opening her and letting her feel the strangeness, right there, against her sex. 'And yet still you lie with me.' His mouth surged up towards hers just as his hand gripped her head, and he overwhelmed her with a long, demanding kiss. His cool tongue subdued hers, and as it did so, he slid an arm around her and rolled her effortlessly on to her back, pressing her down with great force against the mattress.

A million fragmentary thoughts and impressions rushed through her. She did feel fear, and it made a lie of her earlier statement. But she also felt a bigger, wilder excitement than she had ever felt before. The fear and the excitement were mirrored emotions, and both stirred her heart and her body profoundly. She became aware that this man – this being – who was caressing her, could probably kill her or worse at any second, and yet her body still burnt with desire. Her essence was flowing; she was open; she was ready.

Struggling to manoeuvre herself into position without their mouths breaking contact, she moaned in her throat when André wouldn't allow it. Exerting what Belinda sensed was only a fraction of his strength, he held her motionless beneath him, her womanhood spread by his cool, firm thigh, her throbbing clitoris pressed hard up against it. His hands slid to her buttocks and he began to rock her – at first slowly, then faster and faster and faster – against the unyielding column of muscle and sinew.

'No! Oh no!' she protested into his mouth, feeling the wave of her orgasm break and her unfilled vagina contract and pulse. The pleasure was blinding, like a white light imploding in the core of her; yet it was spiked with a vein of dark denial. She had so wanted to have him inside her as she came.

'Why – ' she began as he lifted away from her, only to have the question suppressed by his mouth. The kiss was quick and peremptory, and she understood that it meant 'don't ask'.

'Caress me!' he commanded, sliding on to his side next to her. His penis was still stone hard, and he took her hand and folded it around himself. 'Please ... oh please,' he said, sounding less sure of himself as he moved her fingers with his own. 'Grant me pleasure, I beg of you,' he gasped, his hips lifting as their nested hands slid.

'But – '

'Please. Do it my way,' he groaned, gripping her tighter when she tried to release him so she could straddle his body.

Confused, she reseated her hold on him and began her task, creating a rhythm as best she could.

Why is he so reluctant to penetrate me? she wondered as he seemed to swell in her hand, his cold flesh juddering as if he was already about to ejaculate. Does he think he'll hurt me? Or is it me that might hurt *him*?

But how could she hurt such magnificence? His penis was thick. Long. Covered in skin that was as fine as oiled velvet. Even its very coolness was a turn-on. Warm was normal; any man could be warm. But cool was exotic and forbidden. She imagined pressing her hot mouth against his glans.

149

'Soon,' he gasped, as he arched and thrust himself through her fingers. 'But not yet.'

Oh God, thought Belinda. He can even read my mind when he's almost coming!

'Yes ... oh yes ... yes!' André murmured, his body jerking, his penis pushing, pushing, pushing.

Was he answering her? she wondered. Or just crying out with pleasure? It didn't matter as she swirled her hand around his shaft.

After a few moments more, André cried out loudly and froze against her, his member a rod of crystal in her fingers. The sound was inarticulate at first, then he let forth a string of tangled words in his own language, and at the same time jerked violently sideways – making her lose her hold on his sex as he came. Belinda got a momentary impression of a cold, silvery slipperiness – a thin, silk-like fluid that almost evaporated as it splashed across her wrist – then he had swivelled away, the tangled sheet around his loins.

'What are you?' whispered Belinda into the silence that settled over them afterwards. She remembered asking the question earlier – what seemed like a lifetime ago – and getting no satisfactory answer. Would he still continue to evade her, even now?

André rolled over in bed and sat up. Turning to face her, he tucked his bare legs into a yoga-like position, then let his arms rest loosely on his thighs. His gaze was gentle, resigned and utterly human, and Belinda began to wonder if she had been imagining things. Even his soft, subsiding penis looked exactly like a normal man's.

Abruptly, he looked up towards the portrait that hung over the bed. Belinda had barely noticed it when they had first entered the room, but now the candlelight seemed to be shining on it more powerfully, and showing every detail of the figure it depicted.

'That is what I am, or should I say, *who* I am.'

Belinda stared at the image, acknowledging the likeness but confused by the antiquated clothing.

'I thought he was your ancestor, like the rest of the pictures,' she said.

'All the portraits are of me,' said André softly, a little smile playing around his lips – a rather sad little smile.

'I d-don't suppose you were in fancy dress?' said Belinda, smiling herself, with trepidation, as an inkling of the truth began to come to her.

'No, I am afraid not,' answered André, shrugging. 'Just in clothes that rather appealed to me at the time . . . or times.'

'Then you *are* a vampire?' Belinda said, knowing the issue had to be faced sometime, especially now, after what had just happened between them. They hadn't had sex as such, but it was close enough. Would she slip beneath a hypnotic spell any minute?

'No, as I told you before, I am not,' he said, reaching out to take her hand and squeeze it reassuringly. 'Vampires do exist, believe me, but I am not one of them. I endure a similar plight, but my needs are slightly different. Far less dangerous.' He paused for a moment, frowning, and Belinda felt a moment of doubt. Was he lying to her, trying to lull her into a false sense of security? 'To the best of my knowledge, I am still human,' he went on, rubbing his thumb across her knuckle in a way that did seem very much the action of a tender, human lover. 'Changed, but still a man. Still flesh and blood.' He smiled, more brightly this time, as if the fact that he was still mortal cheered him up.

'How old are you?'

André appeared to think carefully. 'I was born in 1760, so that would make me – ' He counted silently ' – well, over two hundred years old.' His thumb stilled and his gaze levelled to meet hers.

Belinda swallowed. Her head felt light and she experienced a sudden detachment from reality, as if she had been dreaming and had woken up too quickly. What André had just told her was more or less the secret she

151

had been expecting, but when framed in actual words, it seemed preposterous.

'Will you live for ever?'

'I do not think so,' he said matter-of-factly. 'I am extremely long-lived, yes, but as I have aged slightly since my misfortune – perhaps four or five years – I believe that I will grow old and die eventually. But it will not be for several centuries yet.'

Belinda was lost for words, yet from somewhere deep inside she found a question.

'You said you weren't a vampire, and that your needs weren't dangerous – '

André forestalled her. 'Were you not listening to me when we spoke on the terrace?' He turned her hand in his grip, then kissed her palm, licking her skin slowly and sensually.

Belinda remembered the terrace. She remembered being befuddled by shame and sensation. He had told her something, but she had desired him too much to be able to think straight. It was a miracle she remembered her own name.

'My need is very simple,' he said, drawing her towards him by kissing his way up her arm. 'And exactly as I described to you.' Rearranging his limbs, he was suddenly looming over her, his mouth swooping to brush her shoulders, then her breasts. 'I feed on your senses, Belinda. Your ecstasy, your bliss, your gratification.' His lips grazed her nipple as his tongue laved it softly. 'The erotic pleasure that you experience while making love.'

Chapter Nine
Japanese Whispers

*H*as she understood me? thought André, arranging his star-strewn cloak around him as he lay down among the books and parchments tumbled across his bed. It was close to dawn, and soon he would be compelled to go to sleep again, but until that happened he could nurture his hopes and dreams.

To his great relief, Belinda Seward had expressed no horror at his unusual longevity and shown very little fear of him, but he did sense that she harboured many questions. Questions, and an instinctive awareness of her own importance in the scheme of things; an importance that transcended simple dalliance.

Not that the love they had made had been insignificant, he realised. Far from it. Abandoning himself to memory, he lay back and hugged his silken cloak around him, thinking of the pleasure he had experienced just hours ago.

Touching and caressing Belinda Seward had been frighteningly like his recurring dreams of Arabelle. Their bodies and faces were so similar, or at least alike in the fact that Belinda was his Arabelle matured to womanhood. If Belle had not been taken from him before she had even achieved her twentieth birthday, she would have looked very much as Belinda looked now. He smiled, wondering if Belle would ever have considered cutting off her lustrous titian hair and sporting the short, elfin crop that Belinda favoured. He would have to ask her. What he was sure of though, was that she would certainly have had the same sensual nature; the same sweet blend of naïveté and daring. A rich amalgam of the pure and the profane.

As his penis began to rise again, stirred both by recent acts and by long-lost dreams, André sat up, squared his shoulders, and reached for a book. It had always seemed odd to him, but he had discovered that he did his best and clearest thinking while he was aroused. Whenever he cast an enchantment, he incited a state of desire for the process – either by stimulating thoughts or by touching himself – and he ascribed much of his magic prowess to the powers of lust.

And he would need every last scrap of that prowess if he were to achieve the difficult goal that lay ahead of him. Opening the grimoire, he turned quickly to the relevant pages, to a ritual that he already knew by heart yet which was so hazardous it had never been given a name.

Would it work? he wondered, wrinkling his nose as a familiar but hated perfume rose up from the age-darkened paper. This grimoire might be the only means by which he could achieve what he wanted for himself and Arabelle, but its origins inspired a deep revulsion. It seemed like only yesterday that he had snatched it up from among the clutter on Isidora's work table, then fled into the night, taking only it and Arabelle's crystal vial.

The book of enchantments had not come to Isidora by fair means though, he knew that. She had probably stolen it, most likely from the esoteric collection of one of her previous victims; it was a treasure that had already been antique two hundred years ago. Within its weathered pages was the lore of more than a dozen revered mages – alchemist wizards who had sought eternal life and the secret of creating gold – and even to them the knowledge had been a received wisdom. It contained lore from the Orient, from the Middle East and from Ancient Egypt; where death and rebirth and allegorical erotic ritual had been central to their complex pharaonic cult.

Where would he and Arabelle go if the rite described in the grimoire was successful? he wondered. To the stellar heavens – as the Egyptian kings had believed – or to another world entirely? To nothingness even? There was no way to tell in advance exactly what would happen, but he knew that in some form at least they would be together, freed at last from their state of separation.

There were many hazards though. The ritual might fail and condemn him to live on even longer, his mind affected, his body weakened. He might even lose the spirit of Arabelle, setting her adrift in some dark and unknown void. The greatest danger was that Belinda, as his beloved's mortal host, might be extinguished too; many ingredients of the elixir were deadly poison when taken under normal circumstances. Belladonna; mercury; azarnet, or·arsenic as it was more commonly known. All these were fatal in their unenchanted forms.

Did he have the right to risk Belinda's life? And if he explained the dangers to her, could she still care for him as the ritual also demanded?

There was no way he could avoid telling her. He already felt a particular fondness for her after just one day's acquaintance, and besides which, any deception would void the magic. The host had to be aware and completely willing.

Putting aside his qualms for the moment, André considered what other elements he must assemble for his endeavour. Sacred ground was easily found – the priory's ruined chapel was the perfect site. Candles; incense; bindings? Yes, he had all those in abundance. They had been prepared for decades, in anticipation of a suitable host's arrival. The one facet he did not have to hand was an attendant sorceress to preside over the final stages of the spell.

This was a most critical requirement indeed. Michiko, his dear friend and comforter, had told him once that she was always awaiting his call, but was he yet sufficiently strong enough to summon her? Their mind-link was tenuous across great distance. And if he could contact her, how quickly would she be able to reach him?

'Michiko,' he murmured, closing the grimoire and putting it aside. 'Michiko-*chan* . . . Where are you? I need you . . . Come to me . . .'

Almost immediately, a vivid image appeared to him, not of the present but of many decades past. It was Michiko clad in the gorgeous formal kimono she had been wearing when he had first met her, back in Japan, in a period when he had been relatively strong, and travelling extensively to escape detection by Isidora.

In need of his particular kind of 'sustenance', he had arranged to be introduced to a famous courtesan, Madame Michiko, a great lady from the elite of her profession. When she had ushered him into her boudoir and they were sitting cross-legged, facing each other across the tatami mat, it had taken him only a second to discover what she really was; a Miko, or white sorceress, who was blessed – or cursed – with the same long life as he.

'I perceive your dilemma, my lord,' she had said to him from behind her fluttering fan, in his native tongue. André had been impressed by her superb command of language, although her mental gift meant she had little need to speak. 'Please accept my humble assistance in this matter. I will do everything within my power to aid your success.' And with that she had snapped shut her fan, risen to her feet and shuffled gracefully towards him, then begun, with fastidious fingers, to unfasten his clothes.

'Michiko,' he whispered now, remembering her imagination and her gentle, arcane skill. Her poise, above all things, was a wonder to experience, and she created art in the realm of sensual dealings.

Each garment she had removed from him she had meticulously folded and placed on a low cedarwood table. Each accessory she had arranged with reverent flair. His stiff collar had encircled his silver collar studs, and his cufflinks had been positioned one on either side. It had seemed, at first, that she was taking more care of his clothing than she was prepared to lavish on his body, but André soon realised that that was not the case at all.

'Be at your ease, my lord,' she had murmured, when at last he stood naked before her. 'I am here to serve you and to bring relief to your hungering flesh.'

Though he had a hundred years of dealing with women behind him, André felt nervous with this bright exotic creature. That she was a sorceress, possessing the same longevity that he did and most probably far greater powers, put him at a disadvantage in her presence; something he had not experienced since his seduction by Isidora. Michiko's beauty, too, condemned him as her slave.

Her oval face was painted chalk-white in the traditional geisha style, but the heavy make-up wasn't in the slightest mask-like; on the contrary, it seemed to enhance the exquisite bone structure that lay beneath it, much in the way that a glaze increased the loveliness of precious porcelain. A vivid, blood-red lip paint outlined a mouth of glorious symmetry, and her long dark eyes were boldly outlined by jet-black kohl. Her hair was hidden by an elaborate traditional wig, adorned with carved ivory combs and paper flowers, but André knew instinctively that it would be long and black and glossy. Similarly, though her body was concealed beneath her ornate many-layered kimono and its huge folded obi, he was certain she would be the very acme of slender shapeliness.

157

As he watched her, his penis already erect, she took a thin padded futon from a cupboard, then unrolled it on to the mat, bidding him to lie on it.

'You are very vigorous, my lord,' she said softly, sinking down in a cloud of silk beside him, her painted gaze settling intently on his penis.

'My name is André,' he told her, conscious of his own flesh swaying as she studied it, 'and you are the most beautiful woman I have ever seen.'

'I think not,' Michiko observed, her smile oblique but her eyes full of sympathy. 'There is another . . . You love her, yet she resides in a place that is neither earth nor heaven. I believe that *she* is the true beauty that you treasure.'

Unmanned for a moment, André turned away, conscious – as he often was at times like these – that he had never been fully naked for Arabelle; never given her the gift of his rampant body. She was aware of his unclothed appearance, of course, and was present in his chamber each night while he undressed, but she had never looked upon his nakedness with corporeal eyes; only 'seen' him with her strangely powerful psyche.

When Michiko's narrow hand settled on his thigh, André flinched.

'I know your pain, André-*chan*,' she said, her voice like a bell lilting in the breeze, 'and I know too, what it is that soothes it.' Her fingers drifted upward. 'Fear not for the sensibilities of your beloved. My mind has touched hers. I sense her, and she urges me to minister to your needs.'

With a great, relieved sigh, André rolled over on to his back, knowing that his clever, exotic companion spoke the truth. He too could feel Arabelle's approval, her tender urging that he empower himself through sex.

Expecting Michiko to disrobe, as he had, André was surprised when she continued to caress him, her fingers fluttering across his skin with nimble purpose. She did not touch his penis straight away, although it was standing up proudly to tempt her, but instead stroked the tender creases of his groin. Her touch was so light yet so effective, and the contact was so near to the seat of his arousal that he experienced it almost as pain instead of pleasure. He groaned, wanting her long, slender fingers to strum his aching hardness and their dainty tips to titillate his glans.

But still Michiko denied him, exploring his belly and his flanks with a studied thoroughness. André tried to reach for her, but with a strength and swiftness that astounded him, she dashed his hands away then deftly snared them in her own. In a rare feat of legerdemain, she took both his wrists in a single-handed, long-fingered grip and pressed them down against the futon at his side, leaving him helplessly pinned and at her mercy.

'Remember what I am, my lord,' she said quietly, her near-black eyes narrowing inscrutably as she surveyed him. 'I have all the power that you possess, and much more that is different and unknown to you. I am your equal, and I will have my way in this.'

Her determination suddenly reminded him of Isidora, and he shuddered.

'I am not like she, either,' said Michiko immediately, demonstrating again her undeniable mental gift. 'I wish to control you for a time, André. To play with you and give pleasure to us both.' She touched his cheek with her free hand. 'But when that is over, you are sovereign. And I serve you.'

Relieved, André relaxed against the futon, expecting Michiko to instantly release him. She did not however, and set about fondling as much of his body as she could reach with her one roving hand. André was constricted, his torso twisted awkwardly to one side, but the feeling of being bound was insidiously delicious. In the past, he had always had supremacy in such matters, and the sensation of being controlled was a piquant thrill.

As she touched him, Michiko stared deeply into his eyes, making a lie of the Japanese woman's reputation

159

for submissiveness. She had pledged to serve him but there was nothing soft or pliant about her nature. Her fierce dark eyes were filled with an almost warrior-like zeal, and André felt a great relief that she had taken to him. With powers like hers, and her indomitable personality, she would be an enemy who made even Isidora seem weak.

'You are quite right, my lord *gaijin*,' she murmured, her crimson mouth an inch from his throat. 'I could destroy you . . . or make your constant anguish a thousand times more frightful.' Her lips came within a hair's breadth of the line of his jaw, and at the same time her fingernails skimmed his twitching penis. 'But I like you . . . and I offer you my help.'

André moaned, his body in thrall to his slender Nippon goddess, while his intellect, riding above it, blessed her name. She would be as awesome an ally in his cause.

Thrashing ineffectually, he tried to brush himself against her silk kimono. The pressure building in his sex was almost agonising now, and he was at the point of begging for her touch; pleading for it, crying out for any kind of friction.

'Oh no, my lord!' cried Michiko gaily, flirting her brightly-clad body away from him. The solemn herons on her kimono seemed to mock his captivity, the shimmer of silk creating the impression that they were taking flight. From out of nowhere, Michiko produced a length of woven white cord, and before André could really absorb the fact that his hands were free, they were restrained again, caught behind his back this time, the cord wound around his wrists. Jerking against his captivity, André found the simple bonds unyielding, and taking a ragged breath, he subsided sideways on to the futon. Michiko inclined over him and trussed his ankles with the same uncompromising cord.

'What are you going to do to me?' he asked, as she

knelt beside him, a speculative expression on her regal, pearl-white face.

'What if I do not do anything at all?' she said, her eyes glittering and her red mouth curving wryly. 'What if I ignore you now ... and go about my toilette?' She slid her hand into the layered folds of her kimono's bodice and quite clearly cupped the curve of one pert breast. A tiny gasp escaped her lips and her head tipped back gracefully on her slender neck, as if weighed down by her heavy, formal wig. Her narrow eyes closed and crumpled as if she were enduring some intense sensation, and André saw little movements beneath the thick brocaded silk.

The pure sensuality of her action made his own state of arousal increase alarmingly. She was blatantly pleasuring herself, manipulating the sensitive tip of her breast, and he was left immobile and unable to ease his growing torment.

'What if I bring myself to orgasm, my lord? Finger my own body, coax it slowly to the pinnacle of pleasure? Could you endure that, and expect nothing for yourself?' Michiko's low, soft voice was slurred, and the movements within her kimono grew faster, more frenzied, as if some small animal was trapped against her bosom and struggling to get free. The rest of her body was quiescent, a placid statue clad in robes of coloured silk.

'I ... I do not know.' André's teeth were gritted as he imagined what he might have to go through. The idea of seeing Michiko masturbate, again and again, while he grew increasingly engorged, was horrific, not to be dwelt upon. And yet he did dwell on it, savouring the build-up of denial, the ever-increasing stiffness of his flesh, the slow throb of blood gathering in his shaft. The condition of his groin was taxing him to his limits; he felt dizzy with need. It was pure torture, but something dark in him exulted.

'Perhaps we sh-should try to discover what your limits are?' Although her telepathy was obviously unimpaired,

Michiko was having trouble with her voice now. The words seemed to catch in her throat, as if clogged by sensation, and beneath her kimono her action was small but rhythmic. Against his will, André imagined her pinching her nipple; squashing the nub of flesh time after time, using acute pain to trigger her rise to joy.

'Amida ... Amida ...' she murmured, her free hand fluttering in a gesture that appeared peculiarly liturgical. It stilled for a moment, then she clenched it into a fist, her whole body stiffening. A second later, she relaxed and breathed a sigh.

'That was most delightful,' she said, withdrawing her fingers from the depths of her kimono. 'I feel refreshed ... and I am ready to begin binding you in earnest.' Performing another exquisite sleight of hand, she produced a further length of the finely-plaited cord, which she twirled evocatively in tight coils around her fingers.

As she shuffled towards him, her sharp eyes were focused upon his penis –

Returning suddenly to the present, André groaned, ejaculating heavily between his fingers, his cool essence splattering the bed and the gathered books and papers. As always, his recollection had been so real that he had become totally absorbed in it, and he felt a vague disappointment that his orgasm had brought matters to a halt.

Back in Japan, in the previous century, he had not come nearly so quickly. Michiko had almost covered his body in her infernal white ropes, then used a finer cord to firmly bind his penis. After that she had ridden him. With his hips raised by a hard cylindrical cushion, and his tethered arms wedged uncomfortably beneath him, she had ridden him for what had seemed like the whole night, forcing him to suffer while she had countless orgasms.

When, finally, to the accompaniment of his tears and wails of blissful agony, she had released him and rubbed his member briskly, the resulting climax had rendered him unconscious, so concentrated was the surge of his deliverance.

'Michiko,' he whispered, sending his thoughts across the aether to try and find her.

To his astonishment, within just seconds he heard her mind-voice. It seemed incredible but she was nearby somewhere, within the watery frontier, on this same English soil –

'My lord *gaijin*,' came the soft, exotic tones of her sensuous spirit, 'I am close by. In what manner may I serve you?'

'Oh, Michiko,' he answered thankfully, then told her quickly of his dreams, and of his hope.

He's not telling me everything, thought Belinda as she opened her eyes the next morning. She felt as if she had been dreaming of her near-immortal lover since the moment she had gone to sleep, and he was still in her mind now she was awake.

He had 'fed' on her again, if that was what one called it. Exciting her with his fingers and his lips, and the weight and force of his body, he had brought her effortlessly to several more orgasms, then held her in his arms until an exhausted sleep had claimed her. He had not come again himself throughout all this, and whether he had pleasured himself afterwards was something she had no way of knowing.

She had so many questions in her brain it seemed to buzz.

Principal among them was: how had André come to be the way he was? It must have taken quite a trauma to change him so thoroughly.

Furthermore, why was it that he considered himself unfortunate? Long or never-ending life wasn't something Belinda had ever given much serious thought to. She had read about it often enough, in horror stories and fantasies, but now, with the perfumed presence of a 200-

year-old man all around her, the impact of his longevity really hit her.

All those years! Did he remember it all? Every place he had ever lived, every person he had ever met? Every woman or girl he had made love to? There must have been plenty of them over the decades, she deduced, if sexual pleasure was the prime source of his nourishment.

Stretching, Belinda became aware that she was now wearing a nightgown: an exquisite, pin-tucked Victorian affair that covered her chastely from throat to ankle, and had long sleeves that ended in ruffled cuffs.

'Did you put this on me?' she asked, turning to the portrait above the bed – the painting of André in eighteenth-century dress, at the time of his mysterious and undefined changing. 'I suppose you must have . . . but I swear I don't remember you doing it.'

The idea of him handling her inert body made her quiver. It was one thing to participate consensually in love-making and permit him to touch her and fondle; but to be unconscious and have him do exactly what he wished without her knowledge? That was scary, but it was also exciting.

Running her finger over the fine smocking and embroidery at the nightgown's yoke, Belinda wondered if it had belonged to a former lover of his. Perhaps even the one he had loved and lost.

That was something else she would have liked to have asked him about. The woman she looked like, the one he was obviously still devoted to; had he known her before his 'changing' or after?

The biggest puzzle of all was his peculiar reluctance to penetrate her. Once he had brought all her senses to life and primed her desire, there had seemed to Belinda nothing more fulfilling than to finally join their bodies. It seemed unnatural not to.

But that, she supposed, was the kernel of the matter. Nothing about André von Kastel was natural. Or normal. Or commonplace. There had been a definite reason for him not entering her, something critically important. But whether to him or to her, she couldn't tell.

What a shame, she thought, remembering the erect majesty of his penis as he pressed against her. There had clearly been nothing wrong with his sexual anatomy, no physical impediment to the penetration she had so wanted. And still wanted, she admitted ruefully. If André were to come to her this moment, she was ready.

Suddenly, as if thought could summon deed, there was a knock at the door.

'Come in!' Belinda called, her heart racing, her body reacting.

Her visitor was Jonathan, however, and her rush of disappointment brought guilt in its wake. Jonathan looked handsome and well rested and she should have been glad to see him so, not irritated because he wasn't someone else.

'Hey, you! How are you feeling?' To make amends, she sprang out of bed and hurried towards him to give him a hug. 'You were out like a light last night. I came to your room to see you and you were sleeping like a baby.' She slid her arms round him, enjoying the sure, familiar feel of him and his warm body beneath his T-shirt and shorts. 'I was just going to get up and come and see whether you were awake yet.'

Jonathan reciprocated with an embrace of his own, a strangely heartfelt one, then a quick, hard kiss. 'I'm fine now,' he said, giving her a quirky smile. 'But I feel such a fool. I must have been more tired than I realised. I keep thinking of how it must have looked. I sort of flaked out, and that great big bloke just picked me up like a doll – ' He shuddered in her arms, an odd expression on his pleasant, open face.

'So the mighty Oren put you to bed, did he?' Belinda enquired lightly. The image that Jonathan had just conjured had a strange effect on her. Without thinking, she suddenly saw a picture of the two men together: Oren masterful and silent, and Jonathan in his arms, naked and pliant.

'Yes,' Jonathan continued, as together they walked over to the bed and sat down, side by side. 'And I think I've met the guy in charge here too ... The owner or whatever he is. It must be him, because he's a dead ringer for that guy over there.' He paused and nodded towards André's portrait. 'He must be his descendant or something – '

'André?'

'Is that what his name is?' Jonathan looked at her with a hint of suspicion, and Belinda immediately blushed, realising as it happened that she was giving herself away.

'Yes ... He's Count André von Kastel, to give him his full title. He owns the priory, and Oren, and Elisa and Feltris, your two girls, they're all his servants.' She took Jonathan's hand and began to stroke his palm with her thumb, the way he liked her to, hoping to distract him from asking awkward questions. 'When did you meet him?'

'It was sometime after our big blond friend put me to bed.' It was Jonathan's turn to blush, as if he too was experiencing ambiguous thoughts. 'I felt very weird, sort of spaced out. I closed my eyes, then the next time I opened them, there was this other guy there. Long hair, sort of aristocratic looking, bright blue eyes. He said, "Here, drink this. It will make you feel better", and he gave me this herbal drink in a fancy china goblet. Funny-tasting stuff, but quite pleasant really, after the first sip or two.'

'And did it make you feel better?'

'Yeah, I think it did,' replied Jonathan thoughtfully, studying their clasped hands. 'I felt a sort of instant sense of well-being ... and then I went straight to sleep. A really good deep sleep, not the sort of dozy feeling I had before.' He brought her hand up to his lips and gave it a shy little kiss. 'I slept right through ... I only woke up about quarter of an hour ago, and the first thing I wanted to do was find you.' His grey eyes brightened as he kissed her hand again.

I want him, thought Belinda, experiencing a weird sense of detachment. After all I've done and felt since I got here – I've had more sex in the last forty-eight hours than I've had for months, but I still want more.

It's you, isn't it? she accused André in her mind. You've done this. You've increased my libido to make me of more use to you. She would have looked up at the portrait, but it seemed important right now to lavish her whole attention on Jonathan. He was a good man, a sweet, sexy man; and she owed him for her recent infidelities – the ones she was certain beyond all doubt that he suspected.

'You look lovely in this,' said Jonathan suddenly, touching her shoulder through the fine cotton of her nightgown. 'It's sort of ... innocent. You look like a Victorian maiden, all untouched and naïve.' He trailed his fingers downward, across the smocking and the lace trim, until they were resting very lightly on her breast. He turned his hand and cupped the firm curve through the delicately-woven fabric. 'As pure as a nun, but inside simply dying for it!'

How true, thought Belinda, her nipple tensing beneath his touch. Because of André and the magic he seemed to weave around her, she *was* dying for it – dying for anything. She had roused in a matter of seconds at the first hint of impending eroticism. Her particular need was for penetration – for straightforward, unelaborate sex – with the familiar body of a man she was fond of. Moaning softly, she twisted towards Jonathan, hoping he would caress her other breast too.

'You're a naughty girl, aren't you?' said Jonathan, entering into the spirit of the thing as he held both her breasts and flicked at her hardened nipples with his thumbs. 'You're thinking about rude things, I can tell. That's what makes *this* happen – ' He pinched each teat, pulling them out slightly, creating a small but delicious jolt of pain.

Her eyes closing, Belinda gasped, sensing the presence of a new facet to Jonathan's sexual persona. Was André at work on him too? she thought, wriggling her bottom against the mattress. She could feel her vulva responding to the tugging sensation on her nipples; she was flowing wantonly, wetting her nightgown where it was bunched up beneath her.

'And I'll bet you're not wearing any panties either, you little slut.' Jonathan continued his pinching, giving a little jerk which made Belinda's eyes snap open. In the eyes of her partner, she saw no malice or cruelty, but just a teasing streak of humour. He was only paying her back for her own actions earlier, but his masquerade severity was a goad to her senses. She thought back to being with André last night on the terrace, and how, for a moment, she had wanted him to hit her, to spank her bare bottom and infuse her with shame. Was this a new twist to her own sexual persona? she wondered, unable to keep still as her thighs scissored and her sex pulsed. Was she a secret masochist? Would she get off on pain? Real pain; not just her breasts being nipped?

'Come on, I think we'd better have a look, hadn't we?' Abandoning her breasts, Jonathan placed his palm on her midriff and tipped her back on to the bed. With one hand, and a dexterity she had not realised he possessed, he snagged both of her wrists and held them tightly, while with the other hand he swiftly raised her skirt.

'Just as I thought,' he crowed, when the soft white cotton was bunched at her waist and her belly, and thighs and pubis were exposed. 'You're a wicked little thing, Belinda Seward, going to bed without your panties ... I bet that was so you could diddle yourself in the night, wasn't it?'

Belinda nodded, sinking happily into the fantasy of being a 'naughty little girl'. 'Yes, that is why I did it,' she whispered. 'I'm very sorry.'

'I should think so,' replied Jonathan, clearly relishing the shadowplay too, 'and you know how I feel about that, don't you? I'm going to have to inspect you now. To see how far this wickedness has gone.' He hesitated, and Belinda guessed he was either working out where to go next or trying to suppress his laughter. 'Assume the position, please.'

Belinda had no idea what the position was, but she improvised, her body shaking as she shifted on the bed. Hitching her bottom to the edge of the mattress, she slid her hands beneath her thighs, then hauled them up, at the same parting her legs. With her knees squashed against her breasts, she was in the most revealing position she could imagine for 'inspection' purposes, and Jonathan's low, delighted growl confirmed her instincts. Giddy with arousal, she lifted herself higher.

'So eager to show off, aren't we?' commented Jonathan, his voice revealingly husky as he leant over to get a better view. 'That's it, open right up. Let's see everything.'

Belinda pulled harder on her thighs, straining every muscle to expose herself completely and lifting her bottom up from the bed so he could see the dark crinkled portal of her anus. For an instant she imagined André seeing the same view, but from a different perspective, and the image made her weeping sex contract.

'This is an inspection,' said Jonathan gruffly, his breathing uneven. 'You're not supposed to be enjoying it. Come on – open wider!'

Belinda did her best, but she was beginning to climb now, to ascend towards pleasure, and her mind filled with rude, inflaming images.

Behind her closed eyes, she pictured the whole household assembled in the room, all watching the proceedings with great interest; all observing her vulgar struggles to display her sex.

She seemed to see André, sitting in one of the beautiful gilded chairs, his eyes languorous, his cool penis clasped

169

loosely in his fingers. Before him knelt Elisa and Feltris, their golden bodies naked, their bare nipples hard and dark and rosy, while in the foreground, imposing Oren advanced towards her. He too was nude, and his huge erection pointed straight towards her vulva. She seemed to feel it touch her, and the imagined impact made her squeal.

In reality, the contact was with Jonathan's fingers, two of them, which curved slightly as they entered her vagina.

'Hmmm . . . Just as I thought,' he muttered, waggling the intruding digits inside her. 'Extremely wet.' He pressed determinedly, finding her G-spot and making her cry out again as she felt the phantom urge to urinate. Her inner muscles grabbed greedily at her assailant.

'I think this calls for the special treatment,' Jonathan observed thoughtfully, his fingers still exerting the teasing pressure. 'Don't you?'

'Yes! Oh yes!' Belinda croaked, not knowing what he meant but wanting it anyway.

Jonathan quickly slid his fingers from her body, and with a speed and assurance that she blessed high heaven for, he took her by one thigh and lowered the tilt of her body with one hand, while the other rummaged urgently in his clothing. Within seconds, the head of his penis was nudging at her entrance, and a heartbeat later he was pushing it inside her.

'Oh God, yes!' Belinda's cry was strangled but joyous. How many hours now had she been longing for penetration? It seemed like a lifetime . . . no, much longer . . . an eternity.

As Jonathan began to thrust, she matched his rhythm with her thankful sobs.

Chapter Ten
Inertia

*B*elinda felt as if she were pinned to the mattress by inertia. She couldn't get up because her limbs were too relaxed and too glowing to function. It was ten o'clock, but she simply couldn't stir.

Beside her Jonathan was equally still, although his even breathing told her he was sound asleep.

'You deserve the rest, sweetheart,' whispered Belinda, rousing herself just enough to sit up and look down on his peaceful, boyish face. It wasn't all that long ago since he had made love to her like a veritable demon, deploying a strength and authority that she had never previously seen in him – a dominant aura that seemed to suit him very nicely.

After he had given her 'a good seeing to' – while she was folded awkwardly on the edge of the bed – he had pulled out, still erect, and bade her move. Then, once she was lying in a more comfortable, less contrived position, he had pushed into her hungry body for a second time, his thrusts longer, less staccato, and more gentle. This considerate lover had been the Jonathan she was used to; the one who fucked her as an equal and made no attempt whatsoever to bend her will.

'And I like *both* of you,' she said, smiling fondly down

171

at him. 'Mr Discipline *and* my dear old Johnny.' She touched his face but he just mumbled and hugged his pillow.

The temptation to do the same; to lie down, snuggle up to Jonathan's bare warm back, and go to sleep again, was enormous. She felt as if she were floating in a delicious pool of lethargy, her limbs bathed in a glowing sexual silkiness. She knew that if she did lie down again, she would be sleeping within seconds; but at the back of her mind there were questions that needed answering. As she accepted that, she woke up once and for all.

The biggest question was, 'What the devil are we still doing here?' It was well over twenty-four hours since she and Jonathan had abandoned the Mini in the rain, and yet neither of them had made the slightest effort to go back and see if it would start, or to check on their belongings. This sort of behaviour was fairly typical of Jonathan – he was rather happy-go-lucky over things like possessions and time-keeping – but she was a compulsive organiser and it was not like her at all. Under normal circumstances, she would have had them back on their way by now, if the car was functional, or at least made some arrangements to get it fixed.

But somehow, most of her business-like qualities seemed to have been washed away by the storm, and all she wanted to do was drift around this peculiar, brooding house, and have sex in a variety of novel forms. And she had a strong suspicion as to how this had come about.

'What are you doing to me, André?'

As she spoke the words, she made a concentrated mental effort to project their meaning outward. It seemed a rather esoteric thing to do, but she was almost certain that their strange host could sense her thoughts.

Just what powers did he possess, this handsome young 200-year-old nobleman? His claims of abnormal longevity should have seemed a complete cock-and-bull story, but somehow, right at the heart of her, she believed him.

He was still withholding part of his story from her, she sensed, but she was certain what he had told her was true.

André? she probed again, then shook her head, laughing softly to herself. What was she expecting? An instant telepathic answer or a knock at the door in response to her summons? Or even that he materialise in the centre of the room from a cloud of blue mist? She smiled again, deciding she had read far too many spooky stories.

The count's extrasensory radio clearly wasn't switched on this morning, however, because nothing happened. Did he sleep during the day? she wondered. She had accused him of being a vampire, and though he had denied it, he had admitted to sharing some of their characteristics. Resting during the hours of daylight could well be one of those. He had been asleep yesterday, when she had first seen him in the tower room, and by the time she met the conscious André, it had already been the early hours of evening.

Rising cautiously from the bed, she held her hand to her head. All this deliberation over matters 'fantastic' was giving her a headache. She decided to wash her face and get a drink of water.

Proceeding languidly across the room, she bent down to pick up the Victorian nightdress which Jonathan had flung triumphantly on the floor during the course of their love-making – another symptom of his brand new sexual dynamism.

Fifteen minutes later, a slightly refreshed Belinda discovered that there was no other female clothing to be had in the room. All the things she had worn last night had disappeared, as had the shift she had been supplied with yesterday. Of her own shorts and T-shirt there was no sign at all. Neither was there any underwear of any kind.

I'm trapped, thought Belinda, recalling her presentiments that André had some secret purpose in mind for her. He's stolen all my clothes so I can't escape from

173

him. 'Well, we'll see about that,' she muttered grimly, unfolding the nightdress again and pulling it on over her head. Giving Jonathan a kiss – to which the only response was a drowsy snuffle into the pillow – she set out to find some life in the silent vastness of the priory.

The upper corridor was completely deserted, as she had expected, and she debated making her way through the gallery towards the high tower where André 'slept'. One part of her wanted to confront him immediately and voice her suspicions, while another part told her to be wary. She had to be sure of her facts first – and find out more about him, if she could. A deeper study of his house and his possessions might help, and the library in particular had been crammed with books and documents. There was bound to be something there that could enlighten her.

Descending the stairs barefoot, Belinda felt conspicuous despite the absence of any company. The house was very still, yet there was a teasing breeze coming from somewhere. It seemed to creep beneath the hem of her nightdress and remind her that her bottom and sex were bare, and as she moved, it did too, making balmy air flow across her naked skin.

On the landing, a particularly striking portrait of André in some kind of antique military uniform seemed to smirk down at her, as if its blue eyes could see straight through the thin lawn that covered her. Pausing to frown up at him, Belinda ground her teeth in mortification. The damn thing was ogling her! And the body it perused was responding. She felt her nipples stiffen, coming to their hard, erect state so fast it was almost painful, while between her legs, her female groove began to moisten.

'Leave me alone!' she cried to the smiling portrait. 'I can't take this! It's not natural to be aroused all the time!'

Shocked by her outburst, she looked around, fearing that someone might have heard her, which was ridiculous because Jonathan was fast asleep, André was probably the same, and there was no sign whatsoever of the three blond mutes. All this weirdness is getting to me, she thought, smoothing the inadequate cotton of her nightdress against her. I'm talking to the bloody pictures now!

Fired with new determination, she hurried down the rest of the stairs, trying to ignore her sudden feeling of sharp arousal. She could even smell herself now; she caught a strong, disturbing hint of her own sexual musk as the thin nightgown billowed and flapped around her.

'Stop it!' she snapped, not sure whether it was the absent André she was castigating or herself. 'It takes two to tango,' she muttered, pausing in the lofty hall, the stone floor pleasantly cool beneath her feet. She had to be just as interested in André von Kastel as he was in her, or she wouldn't have responded to him. She had let him make love to her. Let him coax liberties out of her that her boyfriend never had. It was quite outrageous when she really stopped to think about it.

The terrace . . . As if falling through time, she imagined herself suddenly back there, lying prone across the parapet while André assaulted her with his fingers and his mouth. The way her senses recreated the incident was uncanny, and stunned to a halt in the middle of the hall, she seemed to feel again the wet intrusion of André's tongue: first into her vagina and then into her anus. As she relived it, her swollen clitoris began to ache.

'No! Oh no!' she cried, the sound almost pitiful. Her sex felt so heavy with blood that it was difficult to stand straight. Her thighs were parted of their own accord, in an attempt to ease the sudden pressure, and clenching her fists, she resisted the urge to do what her sex was silently screaming for – to reach down, where she stood, and wildly masturbate.

Around her all the portraits seemed to whisper. A dozen Andrés murmured, 'Do it! Do it! Do it!'

'No! Oh please, no!' keened Belinda, while her body betrayed her and she shifted her feet further apart, widening her stance. She tossed her head, her eyes

175

closed, refusing to see the portraits but pinned to the spot by their seditious blue gazes. Her hips tilted and her vulva twitched and rippled. Liquid began to ooze between her labia, escape her pubic hair and crawl in a single stream down her inner thigh.

'Go on,' the heard but unheard voices urged her. 'Amuse me ... Surrender to your lust and caress your dripping jewel ...'

The line between engorgement and real pain beginning to blur, Belinda took a step forward, biting her lips at the resulting jolt of pleasure. Her nipples were so tensed they were tugging on the sensitive tissues of her breast and creating friction against the thin stuff of her nightdress. It was woven cotton lawn of the finest, lightest texture, but she might as well have been wearing a hair shirt.

Beyond words now, she whimpered, wrapping her arm about her chest and squeezing tightly to assuage the subtle torment. She was just about to clutch her vulva when a creaking door froze her actions. Spinning around, almost coming, she expected to see André walking purposefully towards her, his brilliant eyes glinting sapphire in his triumph.

'Who's there?' called Belinda, her fingers creeping, of their own volition, towards her sex. She almost didn't care any longer if there was anyone there; they could watch her as far as she was concerned; she was too deep in her own desire to hold back now.

A door on her left swung a little way, but no one came through it. The shadows offered up no hidden voyeur. There was no one. She was alone, as she had been all along, but the interruption, she realised, had thwarted her. Suspicion had drawn her just far enough back from the brink of orgasm to return control of her actions to her brain, her thinking mind.

She still felt aroused and she still yearned for relief, but she was no longer a mindless animal led by lust. She wanted to masturbate, but she couldn't stand here and do it.

'I hate you, you bastard!' she cried out, her every instinct pointing accusingly at André. Even when he wasn't with her, he *was* with her, taunting her. He had control of her while he probably wasn't even conscious.

Belinda could feel fury welling. There was nothing she hated more than to be a man's puppet. At least, not when she didn't want to be. The games she had enjoyed last night had been consensual, inspired by delicious wine and the magic, brooding darkness. Even the little 'performance' this morning with Jonathan had been tempered by a sense of fun and their mutual familiarity.

But right now she was being used – relentlessly manipulated – and all to serve a man's unnatural needs.

She was just about to storm back up the stairs, along the convoluted corridors and galleries and then round and round the circular staircase to André's eyrie, when an irresistible aroma tickled her nostrils.

Coffee. Sublime, strong, revivifying coffee. Healer of psychic ills and restorer of lost tempers. Belinda immediately began to salivate and to long for a steaming cupful. A mugful. Several mugfuls. Suppressing her inner complaints against André – but not forgetting them – she turned in the direction of the fabulous smell. It was Blue Mountain, her favourite; she would put good money on it.

Her nose led her to the terrace, and she hesitated in the doorway from the house, recalling fragments of last night's alfresco debauch.

There was no sign of the peach-coloured dress or her abandoned underwear, and in the hazy sunlight, the long, stone-flagged expanse didn't look in the least bit gloomy and ominous. The terrace was like the rest of the priory: its character seemed infinitely mutable. On a pleasant, normal, holiday morning like this it was difficult to remember what this house had looked like in a thunderstorm.

At the far end of the terrace, a white, circular patio table had been set up, and over it a large sunshade was inclined. Belinda could see that this table and its contents were the source of the delightful smells, because it was set for breakfast, with a tall insulated coffee pot in pride of place.

Plucking at the thin fabric of her nightdress, and weighing its flimsiness against her craving for coffee, Belinda continued to hover a little longer.

'Oh, bugger it!' she exclaimed to herself, when the aromatic lure finally became too much for her and she traversed the warm stone towards the table. Virtually everyone in the house had seen her naked already anyway, so what did it matter if she took breakfast in her nightie?

Alongside the jug, she found a basket covered with a thick blue linen napkin, and once she had helped herself to her first hit of coffee, she investigated it. Her mouth began to water all over again.

Croissants. Thick, light, sinfully and outrageously buttery, they were the exact breakfast she had hankered after yesterday. Like a starving child, she grabbed the nearest one and bit into it, sighing with pleasure as it seemed to melt on her tongue. The pastry was still warm and flakes of it fluttered down over her front and on to the table, but the flavour was so exquisite that she just didn't care.

Belinda hadn't realised she was so hungry, and could have gobbled down several of the delicious croissants without a pause, but she forced herself to be more civilised with her second, breaking it open and applying a little conserve from the lidded dish that had thoughtfully been provided. Taking smaller bites, and chewing each one properly in between sips of the glorious coffee, she surveyed her surroundings from her idyllic vantage point.

Although the gardens and the grounds beyond were overgrown, they did not appear derelict or sterile.

Whereas in the thrashing rain and sky-splitting thunderstorm everything had taken on shades of black and grey and midnight blue, they now appeared green and gold and mellow. It was difficult to believe she was staying in the same place.

Looking out along the terrace to her right, she espied an additional building she hadn't taken much notice of before. Beyond a rioting and unruly rose garden, there appeared to be a small chapel, complete with more or less intact stained-glass windows and a solemn liturgical aura. This must have been the place of worship for the religious community that had originally inhabited Sedgewick Priory, Belinda decided, feeling a sudden curiosity. Perhaps after breakfast a walk that way would be in order.

'Better get dressed first, I suppose,' she muttered. The heat of the morning was gathering itself now, and though the sunshade had created a cooler area and a slight breeze played across the terrace, Belinda still found herself sweating. Her sexual tenor had calmed a little since those almost insane moments in the main hall, but she still felt a remnant of lingering desire, like the pilot light for a greater, fiercer flame. Concentrating solely on her coffee, she tried to ignore it.

I'll try and keep a clear head from now on, she pledged. And I'll get organised. As soon as I'm dressed I'll set off to find the car, then I'll see if there's somewhere to charge the mobile, and failing that I'll find out if there's a public phone box anywhere nearby.

Belinda knew that she should have done – or at least tried to do – these things yesterday, but for the life of her she couldn't recall where the time had gone. But today would be different, a day of achievement. Hopefully, before nightfall they would have made contact with the world beyond the priory.

More determined now, she sipped more coffee and nibbled the last of her croissant. She was just about to rise and make her way back to her room, when a light tread behind her interrupted her thoughts. Turning in her seat, her heart pounding, she expected to see André, but once again, the newcomer was Oren. In one hand he was carrying a fresh pot of coffee and in the other a slim notebook and a pencil. He was almost naked, his only garment a pair of frayed denim cut-offs.

'Hello,' said Belinda quickly. 'It's a lovely morning, isn't it?'

Oren put down his burdens and favoured her with a smile that was more than a replacement for his unfortunate lack of speech. He gestured to the fresh coffee and Belinda accepted a top-up. Then, to her surprise, he sat down in another chair. The expression on his face was both open and attentive, and it dawned on her that he was waiting for instructions.

'I'm glad you're here, Oren,' said Belinda, leaning forward. 'I really need to go back to our car today, to see if it'll start and that our things are OK.'

Oren's grin widened and he shook his head.

What on earth was he on about? 'No, really, we have to get to our car and get it started again,' she insisted, feeling anxious. Was she being obstructed again? Had André given orders that she mustn't leave? 'It's important. We're supposed to meet someone.'

Oren shook his head again but this time reached for the notebook and pencil.

Please do not worry, said the note he handed to her a few seconds later. *Your car is here, and all your possessions are safe.*

'But how?' she demanded, looking up at him. 'It wouldn't start the other night.' And what was more, she realised, Jonathan had brought the keys with him, in his shorts pocket.

Oren gave her a shrug and a modest look which seemed to indicate he was a man of many talents.

'Well, thank you,' said Belinda, a little shaken. This gentle giant had just hot-wired their car. 'I'd better get dressed and then go and check it out.'

Oren's warm brown eyes seemed to assess her body beneath the inadequate protection of the nightgown, and after a second or two his blond eyebrows quirked in a way that seemed to suggest that he rather liked her in what she was wearing now. Belinda felt herself colouring as she remembered the sheer nature of the cotton lawn. The mute was observant – he could probably see everything!

After sipping the last of her coffee, Belinda stood up. 'Right, I'll go and get dressed, then,' she said firmly, ignoring the merriment in Oren's expression. 'See you later!' Flipping her fingers at him in a cursory salute, she set off towards the house –

Then stopped almost immediately, yelping and hopping.

In the time she had taken over her breakfast, the sun had climbed quite high in the sky overhead and had been beating down consistently on the terrace. Consequently, the stone flags were now baking hot, and Belinda's bare feet felt partially fried.

'Ouch! Oh God,' she squeaked, hitching up her skirt and preparing to make a run for it.

She got no further than a couple of steps before she sensed a swift, feline movement behind her, then felt herself being literally swept off her feet. Scooping her up in his arms, Oren carried her effortlessly across the remaining portion of the terrace, his own bare feet presumably too weathered to feel the burning heat.

'Thanks. Thanks very much,' Belinda said, breathless with shock as Oren made a neat sideways twist to negotiate the door.

Once inside, she expected him to let her down, but instead, Oren continued to carry her through the much cooler house. Her female form seemed to make no impact whatsoever on his giant, muscular body, and he was able to walk quite quickly with her in his arms.

The sensation of such perfection of strength and vitality against her was so exciting that Belinda forgot to protest. The wall of Oren's chest, which she was cuddled against, was like a slab of living stone, but she could feel his heart beating beneath it. His body smelt very fresh and clean, though not of any particular cologne. He was just man, pure and simple, freshly showered. And so powerful that even the long staircase didn't agitate his steady breathing.

'It's OK, I can manage from here,' Belinda announced when they reached the top of the steps, although she was aware that she was still clinging to him tightly. Her arms seemed to be ignoring her dictate, and instead of loosening her hold on him, they gripped steadfastly around his strong neck.

She felt a little worried when they reached her room and Oren switched her weight to one arm to negotiate the door. What would Jonathan think if she was carried in by Oren?

But her room was empty, with only a scribbled note on her pillow to indicate a man had shared her bed. Belinda picked it up when Oren set her on her feet, then sat down on the disordered bed to read its contents.

Gone for a quick shower. Something made me all sweaty. Love you lots. Jonathan. Short and sweet and underlined with a long row of 'X's, it made her smile and think fondly of him. It had been a bit of an adventure ending up here, what with the thunderstorm, Feltris and Elisa, and André and everything. But in a bizarre twist it had also drawn her and Jonathan closer, when by all that was logical it should have pushed them apart. Impulsively, she showed the note to Oren, and he smiled and nodded as if he too endorsed Jonathan's show of sentiment.

Strange, she thought, eyeing the tall, magnificent blond. A moment ago, she had felt herself beginning to want him, and had sensed – very definitely – that he wanted her. Yet he showed no animosity over Jonathan's note, and seemed to approve of the relationship it implied. Count André wasn't the only unusual and unfathomable person here at Sedgewick Priory. In their own ways, his servants were special too.

I should have asked him to stay and wash my back for me, thought Belinda a little while later as she was dressing.

It had been an odd little 'blip' of feeling that had passed between her and Oren – a hovering on the edge of something. If he had stayed to help her with her toilette, she was certain she would have allowed him to make love to her, and though she had desired him, she was still in two minds about it. It was just too much that she should have sex with everyone in the house. It felt like a kind of 'rampage' somehow; yet each encounter so far had seemed inevitable – a natural event at the time. And she now she was regretting that she had missed her chance with Oren.

She imagined him stepping into the curiously antique yet fully-functional shower with her. There would not have been much room for the both of them in the shallow china tub together, but for her purposes that would have been an advantage. Oren's massive body would have been pressed against hers. Hugely strong, he would probably have picked her up again as they stood in the teeming water, and mounted her effortlessly on the thick shaft of his sturdy prick.

Although she had not yet seen him naked, Belinda could well imagine that Oren was phenomenal. If he were all in proportion, as the bulge in his shorts had suggested, his magnificent penis would stretch a woman in all directions.

'For crying out loud!' she exclaimed, wishing she could temper her thoughts and think of something other than sex. Concentrating on her clothing instead, she tied the drawstring at her waist in a bow. The skirt she had been left while she was in the bathroom looked suspiciously like an Edwardian petticoat. Just as yesterday, today's clothes were really lingerie in disguise. Lingerie from past times, but perfectly cared for and preserved.

Her camisole top had tiny sleeves and an embroidered front, and both it and the full petticoat were made of ivory cambric. Her knickers were loose-legged and French style, made from the same very fine pale cloth.

Staring at her reflection in the mirror, she fancied herself as a nymphet from a continental movie, her gamine hairstyle completing the impression to perfection. She remembered seeing a picture of Brigitte Bardot, wearing a wig probably, but dressed similarly in thin white clothes. Pouting for an unseen cameraman, Belinda flicked her fringe into pixie-like points.

'This is getting me nowhere!' she chastised herself, slipping a pair of flat canvas shoes on to her feet. 'I'd better make a move and check out the car.'

Striding past the many portraits of André, Belinda hurried downstairs, across the hall and out of the front door, wondering if what Oren had written about the Mini was true. Apparently it was, she discovered almost immediately, espying Jonathan's cheerful yellow vehicle parked in the gravel drive where it curved out around the gardens. The car appeared so ordinary, so unremarkable and so much a part of the normal life she had led two days ago, that she laughed out loud in relief.

The Mini was open and the keys now in the ignition, but when she tried to start it, the engine was completely dead. 'You stupid thing!' she cried, leaping out of the car and feeling a strong urge to kick it. 'Why did you work for them, but not for me?'

Striding to the boot to check that their bags and belongings were intact, it occurred to Belinda to wonder who had driven the car this far.

Certainly not André. Instinct told her he was asleep now, resting during the day as she suspected his strange nature demanded. So that left Feltris, Elisa and Oren. The two blonde girls looked as if they wouldn't know what a car was, let alone be able to fix a wonky one and drive. Belinda imagined them being pulled by unicorns in a fairy chariot made of diamonds.

Too weird, she thought, rummaging among the luggage and finding – to her relief – that nothing was missing. She and Jonathan would have to get away from here soon because she could not believe some of the notions she was having.

'Bingo!' she cried, fishing out Jonathan's mobile phone. But her sense of satisfaction was short-lived. On pressing the usual buttons, she got a display of peculiar symbols she had never seen before, and no sound that in any way resembled a dialling tone. The battery needed charging, obviously, but even so the compact gadget was behaving oddly.

'Like everything and everybody else,' she muttered grimly, retrieving the charger from Jonathan's bag, then hurrying up the stairs towards the house. She would come back for their clothes and sundries later; the first priority was to make contact with real life!

In the hall, she met Jonathan, looking bleary-eyed and munching a piece of toast.

'I keep asking you this, love, but where have you been?' he said amiably. 'There's all sorts of breakfast stuff on the terrace if you're hungry.'

'I'm fine. I had something earlier,' replied Belinda, a little perturbed by Jonathan's vagueness. 'First I was having a shower and then I came down to get this.' She gestured with the mobile phone. 'Would you believe it, the Mini's parked outside! I've no idea how it got here because the engine's dead as a doornail now.'

Jonathan frowned, chewing his last bit of toast. 'Maybe we should ring the AA?' he suggested, rubbing his eyes then passing his fingers through his dishevelled hair. He looked as if he had only just crawled out of bed that very minute – his T-shirt was crumpled and his trainers weren't laced.

'Are you all right, Johnny?' Belinda asked, moving closer.

'Yes, it's nothing, I just feel a bit zonked again, that's all.' He gave her a crooked grin. 'It must be you, you're wearing me out. I can't resist you.'

Belinda smiled at him. He had been pretty impressive back in her bedroom, she thought fondly. Strong and intuitive; the best he had ever been for her. But now, on top of the growing heat and the lingering exhaustion he seemed to have sustained with the driving, his fine, lusty performance had taken its toll on him.

'You were wonderful. You deserve to be tired,' she said, sliding her free arm around his waist. 'Let's go to the library where it's cooler, and sit down while we decide what to do.'

'Good idea,' replied Jonathan, giving her a squeeze that proved there was still life in him. 'Now lead me to this library of yours. I'm totally lost around here.'

'We ought to move on,' said Belinda, when they were in the library, with Jonathan stretched out on one of the leather sofas while she looked for an electric socket for the mobile phone's charger. She had ascertained that the house did have electric power – there were bulbs in the light fittings and something must be providing the abundance of hot water and firing the stove that cooked all the delicious food. She couldn't imagine Oren or the girls tending an Aga. But she couldn't seem to locate anywhere to plug in the charger. Abandoning the idea, she sat down beside Jonathan and savoured the cool, shady atmosphere of the huge room.

'We can't stay here,' she said, then noticed Jonathan was already dozing. 'Hey! Did you hear what I said?' She gave him a gentle poke in his middle.

'Yes,' he sighed, 'I heard you.' He opened his eyes and gave her his most boyish, appealing grin. 'But why can't we stay here? It's comfortable, it's restful. His lordship or whatever seems to want us to stay.' He slithered across the leather and slipped his arm around her. 'And it's very romantic,' he whispered, leaning closer. 'Exactly what we hoped for.' He kissed her neck, and almost before she realised, he had the lower edge of her camisole eased out of her skirt waistband.

'But what about Paula? She'll be wondering what's

happened to us,' Belinda insisted, wanting to sort things out but feeling distracted by Jonathan's roving hands. One was stroking her back, the other sneaking upward across her ribs.

'Phone her,' said Jonathan reasonably, cupping her breast and beginning to flick the nipple. 'I'm sure your André won't mind another guest. We can try and get her off with Oren. She is on the look-out and she always did like big men.'

It was preposterous and also so rational. Despite her protests, Belinda knew she did want to remain at the priory. It was beautiful and strange and its very mysteriousness seemed to seduce her in to staying. And she had to find out more about André. She had to discover *exactly* what he was.

'Don't be silly,' she said to Jonathan, knowing as she said it that her resistance was empty. The touch of his fingers, moving expertly in circles around the hardening peaks of her breasts, seemed only to increase her returning sense of inertia. She wanted to stay here for this, too. For the pleasure that seemed to stalk her from all directions; from every last corner of this house and its environs. She groaned, her earlier frustration reactivated, and began to shift her bottom on the slippery leather couch. The vivid memory of being masturbated in this very same place by André excited her, and she opened her legs to invite a repeat performance – only this time from a more familiar lover.

'Oh Lindi,' gasped Jonathan, getting her message. 'You're so beautiful.' She felt him raising her skirt then sliding his hand inside the loose cotton of her knickers. 'And so wet,' he went on, his middle finger finding the core of her.

As he palpated her delicately, and she kicked her legs and climaxed, the mobile phone slid off the settee, unnoticed.

Chapter Eleven
Open House

Some time later, a familiar beeping roused Belinda from drifting, non-thinking sensual stupor.

The mobile! Good grief! Someone was ringing them! It ought to have been impossible – the batteries were flat – but a call had come through anyway. Rolling to the edge of the settee, away from Jonathan's dozing form, Belinda slithered inelegantly on to the floor and picked up the phone.

'Hello?' she said cautiously, tugging at her French knickers which were tangled around her knees.

'Belinda?' queried the caller. 'It's Paula. Where the devil are you? I've been trying to call you but getting the "not switched on" message. What's happened to you? Have you fallen off the edge of the earth?'

What *has* happened to us? thought Belinda, at the sound of her friend's pleasant, extraordinarily normal voice. How do you describe to someone that you're shacked up in a weird old priory with a 200-year-old Middle European nobleman, and you've had enough sex in two days to last six months?

'Well, it's a long story,' she began, lifting her hips so she could pull the knickers up over her bottom. 'But basically, we broke down in the middle of the night and took shelter in the grounds of this old priory ... and now the owner's asked us to stay with him for a while. As his house guests.'

Why am I telling her that? Belinda mused, instead of making arrangements to meet.

'You jammy things!' exclaimed the distant Paula, sounding so clear she could have been right there in the room. 'Does this mean the rendezvous is off? I can go to Aunt Lizzie's for a few extra days instead, if you like?'

'No! Don't do that!' Belinda said quickly, as behind her Jonathan yawned and stretched. 'Why not come here – to Sedgewick Priory. It's fantastic and there's loads of room. I'm sure Count André won't mind. It's open house here. And there's a fabulous garden. A river. A folly, even.'

'Wow! It sounds amazing,' replied Paula, audibly impressed. 'Who's this Count André? He sounds a bit exotic to me ... Is he a hunk?'

Belinda considered the question. Was André a hunk? Sort of, perhaps, though certainly not by conventional standards.

'He's very nice, actually. A perfect gentleman.'

'Obviously not too much of a gentleman, from the sound of your voice.' Paula laughed. 'What's he look like? How old is he?'

'An angel' and 'about two hundred and thirty' were the answers, but instead Belinda simply said, 'He's very good-looking. Sort of thoughtful ... with blue eyes and streaky, blondish hair.' She thought hard. 'I've no idea how old he is really, but he looks around the thirty-something mark.'

'He sounds divine!' said Paula. 'Are you sure he wouldn't mind if I just turned up?'

'Not in the slightest, I'm sure of it,' answered Belinda, realising that she was sure. She had a feeling that André would grant her whatever she desired, possibly without her even having to ask him.

'OK then,' said Paula, sounding pleased and excited.

'Gimme directions, and I'll be with you as soon as I can. This is far too good an opportunity to miss.' She paused and made a little 'mmmm' of satisfaction. 'Count André, eh? Good grief, I can hardly wait!'

Belinda was instantly aware of a dilemma. How could she give directions if she didn't know where she was? They had been entirely lost the other night, even before they had abandoned the car. And there had certainly been no Sedgewick Priory on the map.

'Give me the phone,' said a voice behind her, making her nearly drop the mobile. It had been Jonathan, yet he had sounded quite peculiar. Expressionless, almost robotic. And when she turned to him, Belinda saw a face that matched the spaced-out voice. Jonathan was reaching for the phone, but he was not looking at it, or at her, or at anything else. He looked as if he was in a trance, but at a loss for anything better to do, she handed him the mobile.

What followed was the most eerie thing Belinda had ever seen – and that was saying something, given the weirdness of the last two days.

Jonathan delivered a set of clear and very detailed instructions on how to get to the priory from the last town they had passed through. And throughout them he neither moved a muscle nor blinked his eyes once. Belinda heard Paula ask a question, and he replied, 'Just a guess . . .', continuing to stare into some inner middle distance. Without another word, he handed the phone back to Belinda.

'Is Jonathan OK?' queried Paula. 'He sounds a bit out of it.'

'He's just tired,' said Belinda, watching in perfect astonishment as Jonathan lay back again and promptly went to sleep. 'It's the driving and the heat. That's one of the reasons I want to stay here. So he can have a nice relaxing time.'

'Sounds great to me,' said Paula cheerfully.

They chatted for a few minutes more, then said

goodbye, the plan being that Paula would join them after visiting her aunt.

The instant the call was over, the mobile phone went completely dead in Belinda's hand. No ready signal, no dial tone, no nothing. She gave it a shake then dropped it on the settee, feeling vaguely scared of it. Turning to Jonathan, she found him still fast asleep.

This is creepy, she thought, reaching out to brush a love-lick of hair that was dangling on his forehead. Just who the hell was it that had given those directions? It certainly hadn't been Jonathan, she was quite sure of it.

Isidora Katori was shaking with excitement, although she strongly doubted that the average observer would have noticed.

Her powers serving her as well as ever, she had taken a route south from the city, letting her instincts choose the roads and the turnings. After an hour or two behind the wheel, she had felt an urge to pull off for a while, take refreshment and consider her next move, and a pleasant country pub with a beer garden had beckoned.

Not one for bucolic pursuits at the best of times, she had nevertheless experienced a growing anticipation as she sat in the shade with a cool drink and a light lunch. Her psychic awareness had sharpened to a degree that was almost painful when a young woman, carrying a lunch and a drink of her own, had asked politely if she could share the same table as there was nowhere else available in the sun.

Hiding her interest, Isidora had said, 'Of course', and after a few moments her new companion had taken a mobile phone from her bag.

The conversation that followed had been exactly the set of clues Isidora had been waiting for, and it had taken all her considerable self-control not to shout out in triumph as she had listened with her enhanced hearing to its contents.

He was here! Less than thirty miles away! And this

rather ordinary young woman, with her phone and her shoulder bag, was expected as a guest in his house. It was high time to make some introductions.

'Isn't it a beautiful day?' said Isidora to her dining companion, gracing the woman with her most brilliant of smiles. 'I do so love this part of the country, don't you?' She edged a little closer, along the wooden seat, towards her victim. 'By the way, my name is Isidora ... . What's yours?'

Jonathan had slept for half an hour after the strange phone call, and it was only when Oren entered the library, carrying sandwiches and a jug of juice, that he woke up and looked around, his face puzzled.

Belinda – who had been nosing around the library and discovering erotic literature which made her own recent exploits seem profoundly naïve – moved to sit down beside him as Oren served their lunch.

'I had the weirdest dream,' said Jonathan, when the blond servant had discreetly made his exit. 'It was really vivid ... Gives me the shakes just to think about it, although there nothing much actually happened.'

'What do you remember?' Belinda reached for a sandwich, and, taking a bite, realised they were smoked salmon, a delicacy she had only very rarely indulged in.

'Well, I was in this stone-lined room, sort of round – ' He paused to sample his own sandwich, and his eyebrows shot up in appreciative surprise. 'Anyway, it was dark, but there were candles burning all around. And there were draperies of some sort.' He finished the sandwich. 'These are brilliant!'

'But what happened in the dream?' prompted Belinda, recognising an uncannily accurate description of André's tower room.

'Someone held this card up, with blue writing on it. And I had to read it out aloud. That's all I remember.' He took another sandwich, put it on his plate, then added a couple more.

192

'What did it say? The blue writing?'

'No idea!' said Jonathan blithely between bites. 'I don't remember a single word.'

I do, thought Belinda, eating her own sandwich but too preoccupied to appreciate its deliciousness. She herself could remember those directions almost perfectly, and the ghostly way they had been issued from Jonathan's lips.

After their lunch, Belinda and Jonathan ventured out into the park for a walk.

Belinda said nothing to Jonathan, but the incident in the library had spooked her. André had intervened in their lives again and prevented them from leaving his house, but there didn't seem to be any way to go back on their decision and leave. The mobile phone was dead again and there seemed to be nowhere to charge it, so they couldn't contact Paula and make a new plan. They were trapped here until she turned up to release them.

Jonathan took his sketching gear from the Mini and Belinda had a book from the library – one of the risqué ones she had been looking at earlier – and they set off in the direction of the river. No one appeared on the steps to stop them as they left, so it seemed it was all right that they explore.

'How old do you think André is?' asked Belinda, a while later. They had walked all the way across the park and found a path through the woods, and were now settled on the bank beside the stream. Belinda had a suspicion that this was the very site where Jonathan had watched Feltris and Elisa make love, but she didn't say anything. She just smiled at the way his gaze darted to one particular spot, and his expression became both dreamy and excited.

'I dunno . . . Thirty. Thirty-five. Something like that,' he said after a while. 'I only saw him for a few minutes, And I was half-asleep anyway.' He gave her a puzzled look. 'Why do you ask?'

'No particular reason,' she said quickly, opening her book. 'I just wondered.'

'Well, he's definitely older than us,' observed Jonathan, as if that was the end of the matter. Holding up his pencil, he closed his left eye and measured the size of an object on the far side of the river, already deeply absorbed in his drawing.

You can say that again, thought Belinda, turning her attention to what lay on the page before her. She had discovered this treasure of perversion while Jonathan had been dozing, and been so intrigued – and shocked – by it that she had been compelled to bring the outrageous thing with her.

Not an entirely unsophisticated woman, Belinda was aware of some of the weirder practices people indulged in for pleasure. She and Jonathan had experimented a little when they had first got together, but they had never tried what was depicted in this lavishly-produced volume – the dark, cryptic delights of erotic punishment. It was all new to her, but the images were affecting.

The content consisted almost entirely of photographs of women being spanked. Some were from the very earliest days of photographic art, before the turn of the century, and some were from far more recent eras.

Paradoxically, it was the older, fuzzier prints that were most exciting. The women in them were swathed in voluminous layers of frilly underwear, much like the garments she was wearing now, and often trussed into tight corsets too. But in every case, their pale bottoms were exposed. Rounded cheeks appeared out of peep-holes in the most decorous of knee-length drawers, or were visible only between rolled-up petticoats and the dark tops of snugly-gartered stockings.

Other girls and women were more lewdly presented, with legs raised or stretched apart in a variety of uncomfortable-looking poses, suggesting it was not only their bottoms that were being smacked. Seeing these willing victims – for almost all the faces visible were smiling, and others were clearly only feigning distress – Belinda found herself thinking again of last night on the terrace. Suddenly she wished André had spanked her when he could have done – when her bare bottom was pushed rudely out towards him.

She had never been punished for pleasure, but now she wanted to be, desperately. She glanced at Jonathan but he was engrossed in his drawing.

Returning to the book, she found that each successive page made her more and more excited, but one photo made her jaw drop in astonishment.

It was a picture of André – André chastising the bottom of a half-dressed, dark-haired girl. He was laying about her vigorously with what looked like a strip of leather; his face stern yet his eyes bright and lusty. The girl appeared to be sobbing, and her pretty mouth was twisted in an exaggerated moué of suffering, but between her legs there was a clearly visible glint. She was wet because her buttocks were being lashed.

Belinda came to a quick decision. 'I'm going for a bit of a wander,' she said casually to Jonathan. 'I won't be long.' She paused, watching to see how he would react. 'You don't mind, do you?'

'No, not at all,' he replied, looking up and giving her a quick grin, then looking down again. 'I'll be fine.' His pencil moved across the paper with a swift fluidic purpose, and Belinda knew he was totally absorbed.

Striking off down a path that paralleled the riverbank, Belinda walked as quickly as was practicable. She felt hyped-up, manic, and extremely naughty; and the leather-covered book seemed to burn her where it was tucked beneath her arm.

After five minutes, she found a little hollow just a few yards from the river. The mossy turf underfoot was soft and rather dry, and bushes around her provided a semblance of secluded privacy. A shaft of sunlight shining down through the canopy of trees provided just the right degree of illumination.

When she lay down, on her side, Belinda suddenly felt shy. Her actions felt calculated, sneaky, rather grubby. Why did masturbation always seem unsavoury when it was planned?

It didn't bother you the other night out here, did it? she demanded of herself, as she opened the book at the photograph of André. She thought again of the way she had wet herself in the clearing and of how the forbidden act had felt so voluptuous, then she grinned as her qualms dissolved like mist.

André looked extraordinarily handsome in the antique photograph. His long tied-back hair seemed a little anomalous for the date in the corner of the picture – 1899 – but his striped trousers, double-breasted waistcoat and high starched collar made him very much the fashionable gentleman of that age. And his rolled-up shirtsleeves showed he obviously meant business. His arm was a poem of grace; a raised arc of readiness. Belinda could almost hear the leather swishing through the air.

When she turned her attention to the girl in the picture, she suddenly felt a wash of disorientating giddiness. She rubbed her eyes, then looked again, not believing what she saw.

The clothes and the pose were the same as they had been earlier; the flounces, the lace, the exposed buttocks, the flexed, entreating body. But the long dark hair and the slightly Latin face were gone, and in their place was a short, anachronistically elfin hairstyle and features that were impossibly familiar.

How? How on earth? Rolling on to her back, Belinda felt the book slip from her fingers, the pages rustle, and the covers clop shut and conceal the picture that couldn't exist.

Suddenly, she felt herself falling, when there was physically nowhere to fall, and she realised that she needed to see more than just an image.

* * *

196

A knock on the door woke her.

Had she been dreaming? She felt very strange. Very peculiar. For a moment she didn't know where she was, but then she remembered. She was at Count André's house, the home of her handsome new benefactor. The exquisite continental nobleman for whom she would do anything: because he was kind and she simply adored him.

Belinda looked down at her booted feet, her stockinged calves and the hem of the most dainty and frilly petticoat she had ever seen. She had never been able to afford anything so pretty for herself, but Count André had lavished her with a positive mountain of expensive lingerie: chemises, bodices, corsets, petticoats, drawers – every extravagant frippery of lace, embroidery, and ribbonwork she could imagine. His only stipulation was that she wore them to be seen in – that she wore them at his special, private parties.

Thinking of the evening ahead, Belinda quivered.

'Just one or two friends who might appreciate you,' he had said, stroking her face as she sat on his lap. 'You are a jewel, my darling. You know how I love to flaunt you.' His gentle hand had begun to stray downward then. 'I feel like a king when I see the envy in their eyes.' Still descending, his hand had settled on her breast, squeezing it through the delicate lawn of her chemise, then sliding downward across the firm, unyielding panels of her corset before dipping into the open drawers she wore below. 'I love to watch them covet you. Your magnificent breasts, your pearly bottom, your beautiful quim . . . I love their jealousy. The way they wish themselves in my place, so they could have use of you every day and every night.'

And yet Count André did permit his friends certain liberties. Belinda supposed he only did it to increase their envy, but he often allowed them to touch her. To play with her; intimately. To chastise her bottom and to cause her pain and shame. The idea was, she deduced, that what they could have for only a short time, they were bound to desire even more.

Tonight, Count André was holding open house for several of his most valued friends. They would have good wine, fine food, and entertainment. An erotic diversion of which she was the chief ingredient.

'Come in,' she called, responding at last to the rapping on her door. It was typical of Count André – even though he had rescued her from poverty, and to all intents and purposes owned her – that he should have the courtesy to knock before entering her room.

The door swung open and he took a step inside – a perfect picture of male sartorial splendour in his dark cutaway, his striped trousers and his dashing neckwear.

'My dearest,' he said softly, walking towards her, taking her hand and bidding her rise. 'Let me look at you.' He led her towards the mirror. 'Let *us* look at you,' he amended, as they stood before the glass.

Belinda saw herself as a fairy-tale figure, clad all in white. She wore an almost transparent white muslin chemise trimmed with embroidered lace flowers and ribbons, a fierce white silk tricot corset that made her breasts bulge and oppressed her already tiny waist, and a white cotton petticoat adorned with flounces, frills and bows of pure silk ribbon. Hidden by this, but to be seen eventually, were her drawers – also white, also frilly, and conveniently open – and her white stockings with their frivolous lacy garters.

'You are a vision,' murmured Count André, so elegant yet so predatory behind her. He was caressing her throat slowly with the fingers of one hand while with the other he was cupping her womanhood through her undies. 'A perfect plaything.' Nipping her ear, he pressed harder against her mons.

'My lord,' gasped Belinda, beginning to wriggle. The constriction of her corset was making her sex doubly sensitive at the moment. All her lower organs were bearing down on it from within. 'Oh please . . . Oh please –

'Later, my sweet,' he said, squeezing harder, just once, then releasing her. 'You must contain yourself and give up your pleasure to amuse my guests.' He stepped away from her, then took a length of soft white ribbon from her dresser. 'Let me tie your hands so you do not touch yourself until we are ready – '

'Oh, please, don't do that!' she cried, begging for a different boon this time. She felt so vulnerable when she was bound; so frightened. The sense of being quite helpless was almost too exciting, and even though she would never dash away exploring hands for fear of offending Count André, at least when she was free, the opportunity was there in theory. When she was secured, she could do nothing, and her body was available –

'But I wish it,' he said softly, his voice as kind as ever but shot through with a thrilling steeliness.

Bowing her head, Belinda held out her hands at an angle behind her and meekly let her slender wrists be tied.

It was difficult to descend the stairs in high-heeled boots when your hands were bound, but Belinda managed it, with Count André's guiding help. He supported her elbow solicitously, letting her lean on him if she needed, his attention as courtly as if she had been a royal princess.

'Do not be frightened,' he said, when she balked on the lower landing after hearing convivial voices in the parlour. 'Remember how proud I am of you ... How I prize you above all others ... Now hold your head up, and show them your perfect, graceful posture.'

'Oh, well done, André old chap,' said an English voice as they entered the room. A hearty-looking fellow gave Belinda a long appraising glance.

'She's divine,' said a woman, her tones aristocratic, her eyes filled with lust.

'You lucky thing, André,' said another, older woman. 'What I wouldn't give for a tender morsel like that – '

'Is she as good a looker underneath all those fancy

clothes?' said a second male, this one florid and rather coarse in appearance. 'What about her tits, her arse and her fanny?'

'She is perfect in every aspect,' said Count André evenly. 'And you may inspect any part of her you wish in a little while.'

There were one or two others in the small appreciative group, but for the time being they confined themselves to looking at her.

'Come along, Belinda,' said Count André, leading her forward into the centre of the room. 'Stand here and let my friends admire your charms.'

While the count attended to the needs of his guests, refilling their glasses and making idle smalltalk, Belinda stood still where he had left her, blushing furiously. She knew the fragile material of her chemise barely hid her breasts at all, and she could feel the heat of many eyes upon her nipples. Her maid had rouged her there, in preparation for just such eager scrutiny.

'André darling,' said the woman who had called Belinda 'divine', a handsome brunette with a small and petulant mouth. 'May I uncover her breasts? They look so delightful. I'd rather like to hold them.'

'Of course, Mabel,' said Count André genially. 'Please proceed.' He took a sip of champagne and winked at Belinda over the glass.

Mabel hurried forward and began unfastening the buttons of Belinda's chemise. 'Oh, she is just the prettiest thing,' she exclaimed, folding aside the thin muslin and easing Belinda's aching breasts forward. 'And rouged nipples too. How droll! André, you are so naughty! I do so love that, especially when they're firm and pink to start with.'

Belinda clenched her jaw as Mabel began to handle her. Pinching, rolling, pulling, inflicting little pains that did diabolical things down below. She felt desperate to move her hips, to work them to and fro a little; to do anything that might assuage her growing tension.

'Do you whip them?' enquired Mabel, cupping both Belinda's breasts and pushing the nipples inward until they touched. 'I'm sure they'd look absolutely glorious if they were wealed.'

'No, I do not,' replied Count André, coming across to where they were standing and touching each of Belinda's nipples with one forefinger. 'I prefer to see her breasts unmarked. It is more aesthetic, in my opinion.'

'A pity,' said Mabel, sounding slightly thwarted. 'What about clips? Have you tried them on her? Apparently the best ones can be quite excruciating.'

'Oh yes, clips can be very becoming,' said Count André thoughtfully. 'If you wish to experiment, you will find a selection of appropriate ornaments in the usual drawer.'

'Wonderful!' cried Mabel, releasing Belinda and nearly skipping across to the secretaire. 'Oh yes, these are just the thing,' she said, reaching in and bringing out some tiny silver objects, then returning to stand in front of Belinda. 'The very thing. These will look so pretty.'

Taking each breast in turn, Mabel screwed on the wicked silver clips, tightening each one to a terrible, crushing pitch. Belinda felt tears trickling down her face as they were adjusted, as much from shame as from the clips' fierce effect. The horrid pressure on the tips of her breasts only increased the arousal that surged within her. She bit her lip in a hopeless effort to keep still.

'Does it hurt, my dear?' enquired Mabel, brushing away Belinda's tears, then kissing her on the mouth. When Belinda nodded, she gave each clip an additional turn. 'Don't worry. We'll take them off in a minute or two.' She grinned devilishly. 'And that will hurt more than having them on.'

'Courage, my darling,' whispered Count André, when Mabel had retreated in search of more wine. 'See how beautiful you look,' he said, directing Belinda's attention to the large mirror that had been set up at one side of the room for the express purpose of letting her see her own humiliation.

Belinda observed her flushed face, her glowing skin and her maltreated nipples, and knew that she was indeed beautiful; the very picture of submissive, erotic suffering. She wanted to lift her petticoat and open her knickers too, so she could show all the party how aroused the pain made her.

Like a white-clad living ornament, she stood waiting while Count André and his friends drank their wine and discussed her appearance. Some of the observations they made and some of the things they proposed to do to her made her blood run cold. If she were to belong to any one of the others, she knew she would suffer unimaginably, but at least she felt safe in Count André's possession. He respected her and his limits were hers too.

'Let's see her arse then!' said the crude man after a while, breaking away from the others. 'It's high time she felt a taste of the lash.'

'Yes, perhaps you are right, Henri,' Count André said pleasantly, obviously humouring the man. 'Come along, my sweet,' he said to Belinda. 'Let me undo your hands so you can pose more comfortably to receive your punishment.'

'You're too soft with her,' said Henri, licking his lips. 'If she were mine, I would have thrashed her by now, bonds or no bonds.' He moved closer, then grabbed her cruelly, his fingers digging into the softness of one buttock. 'And I'd have sodomised her too. It's plain as day that she needs it. She's got a loose, wanton look about her, André old man. She needs a proper taming.'

'You're probably correct, Henri,' murmured Count André as he unfastened the ribbon around Belinda's wrists.

Belinda trembled as she looked into her beloved's eyes. If he wanted his friend to possess her backside, she would endure it, but only because it was his – her master's – wish. And if Count André would hold her hands and kiss her lips while his friend took his pleasure, she could almost believe she would enjoy it too.

'Now, my dear, perhaps you would kneel on the chaise-longue?' said André encouragingly, as if she were a nervous fawn to be coaxed out of hiding. Taking her elbow, he helped her up on to the padded, velvet-covered chaise, and then pressed down on her back so she assumed the right position – resting on her elbows with her rump up in the air.

The pose was difficult to hold, especially with her clipped breasts dangling down like pears and throbbing cruelly. Belinda swayed a little, then felt her spirits lift as André touched her cheek.

'Would you assist me, Pierre?' she heard him ask another of his friends, one who had not yet spoken. 'Perhaps you would be so good as to uncover Belinda's bottom?'

'Of course, *mon ami*,' replied Pierre, his voice refined and pleasant. Belinda felt happy that it was he who was uncovering her. Monsieur Pierre was dark and handsome, his features exotic and Eastern, and he had always been a little kinder than the others. He would enjoy her punishment, certainly, and the spectacle of her red and fiery bottom; but she sensed finer feelings beneath the surface of his lechery.

Even so, she flinched as she felt him deftly adjust her clothing; lifting her flounced petticoat, then dividing her loose, open knickers.

A gasp of approval went up around the room, and all those assembled moved in a little closer to improve their view.

'That's a sumptuous arse, André,' observed Mabel, her voice slightly breathy. 'What I wouldn't give to have one like that to beat whenever I wanted.' Belinda heard the swish of silk as Mabel sidled close, then felt feminine fingers touch the furrow of her bottom. 'She's so sensitive too. Ooh, how lovely! Like velvet to the touch.'

Despite the awkwardness of her position, Belinda bit

her knuckle and tried not to respond. Mabel's drifting fingertips were as light as a feather, and they seemed intent on lingering. Belinda felt the whole of her bottom groove being explored, her anus being palpated, her sex-lips being patted and pushed very gently. Where she had been rough with Belinda's breasts, Mabel was tenderness itself with her nether regions; but in the pit of shame, the woman's cruelty was easier to bear. Suddenly, Belinda yearned with all her heart for the lash – the blessed instrument that would both elevate and focus her.

Surprisingly, or perhaps unsurprisingly, it was Henri who came to her aid.

'I've had enough of this shilly-shallying about,' he said, pacing the room grumpily. 'When is she to be beaten? It *is* what you invited us here to see.'

'Of course,' said Count André courteously. 'We will begin in a moment. But first perhaps another drink for you all?'

Belinda remained motionless on the chaise while Count André dispensed hospitality. For a few moments, she perceived herself as they might – not really a person but just a human entertainment. She pictured herself as such – a study in still life. A mass of white linen, a creamy rounded bottom, a set of stockinged legs, and feet in buttoned boots. And at the centre of it all, her wet, blushing pudenda and her shadowed anal crevice. The image in her own mind made her sex pulse and quiver, and she felt a great urge to gyrate her naked buttocks.

If only one of them would touch her again. Rub her. Insert something into her. Her unfulfilled need for stimulation was intolerable; she was almost beside herself. And yet she knew that if she touched herself, she would be dismissed and found wanting.

After what seemed like an interminable wait, Count André spoke up. 'And now it is time,' he said solemnly. 'Henri, will you take the strap from the drawer?'

Belinda heard the slight squeak of the drawer being opened, but there was no other sound. Breaths were bated and she sensed lips being licked all around her.

'I will beat her myself first.' The leather strap hissed experimentally through the air. 'And then, perhaps, someone else would care to take over?'

There was a chorus of heartfelt 'yeses', 'absolutelies' and 'with pleasures'; there seemed no shortage of candidates to torment her.

The next thing Belinda heard was a series of tiny rustling sounds – her beloved count removing and folding his jacket, then rolling up his sleeves.

'Mabel. Pierre. Perhaps you would be kind enough to hold her in position?' Belinda sensed her master moving into place somewhere close behind her. 'Henri, I think you will find that the seat by the secretaire will give you the best view.' The strap swished again. 'Julian and Madame Clermont, perhaps if you stood a little to your right you too would be better able to see.'

Unable to stop herself, Belinda whimpered when Mabel sat down beside her on the chaise and took hold of her hands. At the same time, Pierre took her by the hips, raising them higher and making her part her thighs further. 'That's it, Mademoiselle,' he whispered to her. 'Spread yourself a little more.' Belinda felt him sit down beside her, then felt one arm slide over her and secure her around her waist, while his free hand settled snugly on her vulva, middle finger crooked so it compressed her swollen clitoris.

'Oh no! Oh dear God!' keened Belinda, feeling the familiar spasms tremble beneath that fingertip.

But just as her vagina began to convulse, the leather strap lashed down heavily across her bottom. There was a moment of complete blank shock, then it was followed by a raging slice of pain.

'Oh André!' shrieked Belinda in her agony and ecstasy. At last her exaltation had begun.

Chapter Twelve
Help at Hand

'Is something wrong?' Jonathan asked Belinda, as they walked towards the priory.

'No, not really,' she replied, telling a little lie. The leather book-cover felt strangely warm beneath her fingertips, but she was quite at a loss to explain how she had suddenly found herself in one of its pictures, then lived in it like an encapsulated world with no memory whatsoever of her 'real' existence.

'We need to talk,' said Jonathan, obviously not fooled. He eyed her shrewdly. 'Let's sit down for a while.' He nodded to a stone garden seat at the edge of the overgrown formal garden, then guided Belinda towards it.

'OK, Lindi. What is it?' he said, taking her hand once they were settled on the sun-warmed stone.

Belinda decided to pitch straight in at the deep end. 'Do you believe in the supernatural?'

'I don't know,' said Jonathan thoughtfully. 'I'd like to ... I think ... But nothing's happened to me yet that would make me believe.'

Belinda felt relieved then slightly annoyed with herself. Why had she doubted him? Jonathan had always been an open-minded type, and of all the boyfriends she had ever had, the one most prepared to explore new ideas.

'What would you say if I told you that we've stumbled into a supernatural situation right now?' She paused and looked towards the house, which was beginning to look mysterious and secretive again, now that afternoon was slowly blending into evening. 'That nothing here's really what it seems.'

Jonathan followed her look. 'You mean André?' He turned and smiled. 'Yes, I have noticed that he's not exactly Mr Average. I mean, the hours he keeps, for one thing – ' He faltered, his smile looking a bit nervous at the edges. 'You're not trying to tell me he's really Count Dracula, are you?'

Belinda laughed, trying to diffuse her own nerves. Framed in words, it all sounded so preposterous. 'I did ask him if he was a vampire, but he said he isn't – ' Oh Lord, how could she phrase this? 'But he *is* two hundred years old!'

'You're kidding!' Jonathan's hand was shaking slightly where it curled around hers.

'I'm not. You know all the portraits of men with the blue eyes? They're not of his ancestors; they're all him!'

'Jesus wept!'

'It's true. He – '

Belinda was just about to explain as much as she knew about their peculiar host when she heard an insistent, roaring, thrumming noise. It sounded quite distant at first, but quickly grew louder as the source of it drew closer. Looking in the direction that it seemed to be coming from – the winding drive they stumbled along in the rain two nights ago – she saw the dark shape of a motorcycle burst violently from the tree line then charge towards the house, spewing stones and gravel from beneath the blur of its wheels. As it passed behind the building, the powerful engine note was throttled back- then abruptly killed to silence.

'Well, that certainly wasn't Paula,' observed Jonathan

mildly. 'Unless there's something she's forgotten to tell us.'

'It must be a friend of André's,' said Belinda.

'What, another two-hundred-year-old raver?'

'He's not a raver!' cried Belinda, not sure why she was springing to the defence of a man she hardly knew, especially as he was sexually exploiting her.

'Really?' Jonathan lifted an eyebrow in a way that said he either knew or suspected what had passed between Belinda and their enigmatic host.

Belinda was about to go on the defensive when she recalled Jonathan's own confessions. She quirked her own eyebrow back at him, and he had the grace to grin.

'OK, so neither of us is blameless, but – ' He hesitated, as if he couldn't find words to describe his feelings, or didn't, perhaps, quite know what those feelings were. 'I don't feel jealous and I don't really feel guilty.' He squeezed her hand. 'How do you feel? About everything, I mean?'

Well, how did she feel?

'About the same,' said Belinda, after a long pause. 'When I'm with André, it's as if I'm enchanted and he's the most important thing that ever happened to me. But when I'm away from him, I'm more sorry for him than anything – although I have to admit I still find him attractive.'

'Why do you feel sorry for him?'

Slowly, and very carefully, trying to piece together the big picture as she spoke, Belinda outlined what she knew of André's history.

'He's lonely,' she said finally. 'He adored this girl, his fiancée, and he lost her. And he's lived all these years missing her, and wanting to be with her. I mean . . . it'd be bad enough in a normal lifetime, but with him living so long, it must be a total nightmare.'

'It doesn't bear thinking about,' said Jonathan, his voice full of feeling. Belinda looked at him sharply, but he was studying their entwined hands, deep in thought.

Silence hung over them for a few minutes, until finally she said, 'I think he wants something from me.'

'Of course he does,' countered Jonathan with a wry little grin. 'He wants you to keep on having sex so he can feed on the energy.' He gave her hand another little squeeze.

'Yes. But I'm convinced there's more to it.'

'How do you mean?'

'I think the fact that I resemble his fiancée is significant.' She stared at the house, as if its darkening grey facade held an answer. But there was none. 'But I get the impression that he's frightened to tell me why.'

'Do you think it's something that might be dangerous?'

'I don't know ... but I've a sneaking feeling it could be.'

Jonathan shook his head, frowning. 'Then we better had get out of here. As fast as we can.'

'We can't ... Paula's on her way here now. We've got to wait for her,' Belinda pointed out, knowing that it was only a superficial argument.

'We could try and intercept her,' countered Jonathan. He looked up and gave her a long, appraising, sideways look. 'You want to stay, don't you?'

'Yes,' she admitted. 'I want to find out what it is André wants from me. And if it's not too awful, I'd like to help him. I'm sorry for him,' she finished, knowing that that too was a superficiality.

'Look,' said Jonathan, seriously. 'We've covered this ... I don't mind if you want to help him because you like him ... because you're attracted to him.' He hesitated, then blushed furiously in a wild red way Belinda had never seen before. 'I ... um ... I can understand that, you know. I...' He faltered again, as if what he were about to say was so strange to him that he physically could not get the words out of his mouth. 'Look, don't think I'm going queer on you, but, well ... I think he's attractive in a way too.' This last sentence came

209

tumbling out so fast it made Jonathan sound breathless. 'I only saw him for a few minutes but it was really strange ... Something I've never felt before. I wanted him to stay. To ... Oh God, I don't know what!'

Belinda put her arms around her confused boyfriend. 'Don't worry, I get the general idea ... I was with Feltris and Elisa, remember. That's just the same ... And you don't think any worse of me for that, do you?'

Jonathan shook his head, his smile returning.

'OK then, there you are!' Tugging on his hand, she urged him to get up. 'Now come on, let's get back to the house and see who was on that bike!'

'My lord! How good it is to see you!'

Michiko strode into the darkened tower room, an imposing figure in her skin-tight black leathers. André knew it was Michiko, even though her head was encased in a gleaming helmet adorned with the design of a ferocious fire-breathing dragon. Her electrifying aura was so strong he could almost taste it.

Yet he got a shock when she removed her shiny headgear and set it aside.

'Michiko! Your hair!' he cried – in English, the language in which she had addressed him – as he rose from his disordered bed, still naked. He knew he was awake but for a moment he seemed to be dreaming.

The last time he had seen his friend the sorceress, thirty years ago, her lustrous black hair had fallen in a water-straight curtain to her waist, but now there was no sign of that coiffure. Instead her hair was short – cut with a thick, wedge-like fringe and short back and sides – and all tinted a brilliant orange-toned yellow.

'My countryfolk are in an experimental phase,' she said blithely, flipping her lurid locks with her fingers. 'This is the latest thing, especially for girls who dress up as boys.' She rubbed her fingers across the cropped back of her head.

'Ah, the Takarazuka,' said André, beginning to understand the metamorphosis. For her own amusement and to bring an element of variety to her long, long life, Michiko had abandoned the life of a geisha, and instead joined the Japanese all-girl theatre, the Takarazuka. She had already become something of an idol, even when André had last encountered her, and with her commanding, imperious manner, she made a perfect male impersonator. But back in the 1960s, she had always worn a wig.

'Do you like it?' she enquired pertly, sidling closer, the ultimate predator in her shiny black carapace.

'Yes. I do,' said André, after a moment, quite beguiled by the eye-catching new style. 'It is most becoming ... even if something of a shock.' He smiled as she sat down beside him on the rumpled sheets, her gloved hands as ever straying towards his groin. 'It was a shock to find you so near to me, too,' he continued, his voice catching as she delicately touched his penis.

'We are on tour,' she told him, her slanted eyes downcast, studying the reaction of his body, 'and currently in London. Most opportune, my lord *gaijin*, is it not?' she murmured, playing her leather-clad fingers along the growing length of flesh.

'Indeed,' said André, leaning forward and inclining his mouth towards hers. At the last minute, he saw her upswept eyes dart sideways, seeking Arabelle's blue-glowing casket. 'She sleeps, my dear friend,' he said softly, placing his hand against Michiko's exquisitely-sculpted jaw, 'and even if she were awake, she would not deny us. You know full well that she is fond of you.'

'Yes, I do know it, my lord,' whispered Michiko, her brilliant mouth moving against his, 'and in a little while, when she is awakened and I have greeted you sufficiently on my own behalf, I will bring her to you.' She paused a moment, her lips perhaps a hundredth of an inch from his. 'Only briefly, I regret to say. My powers cannot sustain her all that long.'

André shuddered, relishing the hope and the expectation of that peculiar fusion, even while his spirit soared in anticipation of a greater one.

Almost against his, Michiko's eyes flew open. 'I can sense your "discovery", my lord,' she said, her normally calm voice full of excitement. 'And you are right, she *is* the one.' She cocked her head, as if listening. 'Tell me more about her, with your mind, while I pleasure you.'

And do you really think I will be able to concentrate sufficiently, while you are caressing me? observed André, obeying her even as her gloved hand moved faster on his penis. In contact like this, they could easily exchange thoughts, but it would not be long before his became disordered. *Let me pleasure you first, my dear Michiko. That way, I will still have enough of my wits to make sense of it.*

Gently removing her hand from his member, he reached for the long zip of her voluptuous leather suit, and began to describe – by means of thought transference – the arrival of the woman he hoped would help free his soul.

Michiko wore no underwear beneath the form-fitting hide that enclosed her, and the combination of the jet black suit and her honey-coloured skin made it seem as if he were unpeeling a ripe and luscious fruit. She moaned softly as he reached into the slit he had created and massaged her small, firm breasts, amazing him with the way she simultaneously assimilated what he 'told' her, even down to asking questions as she writhed with easy pleasure.

Stretching out her arms above her head, across the tangled sheets, Michiko offered both breasts to André's feverish hands. *How much does she know?* her mind asked coolly. *Is she aware that she resembles Arabelle?*

Yes, she knows that she looks like Belle, replied André, leaning down across his friend to kiss her nipples. *And she knows that I lost Belle many years ago.* He nipped first one crest, then the other, then settled down to a long, concerted suck that made Michiko lift her hips and beat the air.

But does she know the significance of that likeness? questioned Michiko, her inner voice as placid as the surface of a lake, while outwardly she was gasping and groaning and pulling André's fingers to her unattended breast. *Does she know exactly what you are?*

I have told her of my longevity, replied André, complying with Michiko's wishes and squeezing her nipple between his fingers. *And I think she does believe me*. He closed his teeth on the nipple in his mouth, carefully gauging the exact degree of pressure. *But she knows nothing of how both I, and Belle, can be released*. He glanced towards the casket, thinking of the pure spirit that slept within the vial. *She does not even know of Belle's continued existence*.

Despite the fact that he was the one doing the pleasuring, André suddenly found himself distracted. Lying over Michiko, he felt her body's leather covering against his own skin, the touch slick and clingingly sensuous. He rocked his hips slightly, making his penis slid back and forth over the smooth, almost living hide, his rough breathing matching Michiko's wild gasps.

Then you must tell her, instructed Michiko, her head tossing as he held her nipple between his teeth. *And tell her soon, in case there isn't much time*.

André well understood the need for urgency, but it made him angry. He twisted Michiko's teat cruelly between his fingers, re-directing his rage in a useful direction. He would not think of Isidora now; he would not accept the fact that she too could possibly be close by, and may already have detected his 'awakening'. It was something to discuss with Michiko later. Later, when she wasn't bouncing her hips around on the bed beneath him and trying to push her mons pubis against his midriff for stimulation.

Lifting himself and sliding himself along Michiko's body, André pressed his penis against her leather-clad thigh and at the same time crushed her parted mouth with his. Kissing her profoundly, he eased down the zip of her suit a little further, then discovered that – most conveniently – went all the way down between her legs, up her bottom crease, and to her waist. When she obligingly lifted her rump from the bed, he whipped the zip open to bare her whole genital area, revealing her sex-lips and her silky pubic bush; a tuft of hair that was far blacker than the leather.

Will you help me? he asked Michiko while he tugged apart the unzipped aperture so he could get to the sleek rounds of her buttocks. *I have everything we need. It only remains to distil the elixir.*

Of course, she concurred, wriggling furiously, almost searching for him with her hindquarters. *I am at your service, my lord,* she said, her mental voice serene as she located his fingers then jammed herself down on them, forcing him to fondle the puckered portal of her anus.

And I am always in your debt, my faithful friend, André replied, beginning to give Michiko the caress she clearly wanted. Rubbing hard at the little hole, he got a satisfyingly violent reaction. Michiko's legs flailed and her torso shook; she threw her thighs wide apart, physically knocking André off her as she bucked and heaved on the bed. Reaching down behind her back, she took hold of her own bottom cheeks and opened herself, blatantly coaxing him to breach her darkest orifice.

'Ah!' she cried, her physical and mental voices merging when finally he pushed a digit right inside her. '*Amida,*' she murmured, her arms stiffening above her head as he used his rigid middle finger to fuck her bottom. André sensed in her an almost overwhelming longing to touch herself. She wanted to squeeze her breasts or finger her clitoris, but she was tormenting her own body by denying it. He would have done either of those things for her, or he would have curled himself up and licked her between her legs, but he knew that too would defeat her prime objective – her desire to orgasm by only anal stimulation.

'My lord, my lord,' she grunted as he moved himself around, his finger still firmly lodged inside her. Kneeling, he positioned her in front of him, and brought her knees up to squash against her breasts. Then he grabbed a pillow and jammed it against the small of her back, making her lift her skewered bottom even higher.

What a sight she was, his contorted lotus flower. Her body was almost doubled, and her bottom was protruding like a split and honeyed peach from between the edges of her night-black leather suit. He twisted his finger inside her and she made an uncouth gobbling noise, the superb muscles of her buttocks bunching madly. The snug ring around his finger gripped and tensed.

'Do you remember the jade phallus, Michiko?' he whispered, leaning over her, studying the invasion of her forbidden amber rose. 'The one we played with in Paris. The one you made me suckle on before you put it in me?'

'Yes, my lord,' she said, her voice small as she trembled around him.

'Well, I wish I had it now. So I could insert it into you . . . right here, where my finger is.' He wiggled the digit he spoke of and Michiko almost choked. 'It was very big, Michiko . . . even for me.' He paused, easing out his finger a little way, playing it delicately around the inside of her sphincter. 'It was uncomfortable. Very uncomfortable. It hurt me, and yet still you pushed it into me. Right into me.' He began to push in again. 'My belly and my bowels were in turmoil. Surging. Protesting. But you were stern. You would not be denied.' His finger slid in, one joint, two, as far as it would go. 'You forced almost all of that horrid thing inside me.'

He began to pump her. Slowly, metronomically, using his finger as a miniature penis to sodomise her. Michiko's booted heels flailed dangerously near to his face, but the hazard only added to his enjoyment. She was chuntering now, yelping in Japanese as she squirmed, her Oriental reserve entirely dissipated. To squeal and struggle was an enormous loss of 'face'.

215

'You fucked me with it,' he told her, savouring the Anglo-Saxon word that somehow had more impact than its equivalent in the other tongues he spoke. 'Like this!' he exclaimed, driving his finger in and out of her like a piston and enjoying both the view and the way her bottom gripped and grabbed him. For a moment, he considered whipping out the finger and inserting his penis instead, but he knew something quite different – and almost sacred – lay ahead of him, so he concentrated his energies on pleasing Michiko.

It didn't take long for them both to reach that goal. With a cry that was softer and strangely peaceful, Michiko went rigid in every sinew of her magnificent body, while between her legs her entire vulva moved and rippled. André was torn between watching those exotic pulsations – the ones he could feel transmitted through her vitals – and observing the suddenly placid expression on her face. Within the violence of orgasm, Michiko seemed transfigured, as if she had passed over into some realm beyond his imagining, a place of rest and quiet and tranquillity which he longed to reside in himself. A haven he could share with Arabelle.

Presently, he and Michiko untangled themselves, and studying him with her clear, dark eyes, she rolled away and peeled off her disordered clothing. Nude and beautiful, she brought a scented cloth and cleansed them both, then she knelt on the bed in a pose of meditation. Observing her as she murmured some unknown sutra under her breath, André was struck again by her unexpected new hair colour. He supposed that he too should have been meditating and preparing himself, but he couldn't ignore the vivid difference in Michiko. He liked it. The brilliance of her short, sharply-cut hair matched the vivacity of her spirit and personality and negated the only thing about her that had ever troubled him – the fact that long black hair had unhappy connotations, reminding him of Isidora and the evil she had done.

'Don't think of her, my lord,' said Michiko, looking

up, her aura more powerful for her impromptu devotions. 'The lady you love is awakening.' She touched one slim hand to her bosom. 'I feel her here. She speaks to me, André.' She smiled her small inscrutable smile. 'And in a few moments, she will speak to you through me.' They both looked across to the rosewood casket and the slight increase in its weird blue nimbus.

André trembled. It had been a long time since this phenomenon had occurred, and though he yearned for it, its pleasures were bitter-sweet. The precious moments were always over almost before he had begun to relish them, leaving him lonelier and missing Belle more than ever.

And yet there was no way on earth he could refuse the chance.

Quitting the bed again, Michiko advanced on Arabelle's casket and lifted it with reverence from its resting place. Her face still, but her near-black eyes alight, she held the carved box to her naked breasts, cradling it gently and rocking it against her. André got the impression that she was already communing with his beloved somehow; that they were engaged in some intimate girlish interchange that he could never be privy to, even if Arabelle were corporeal. He smiled as he recognised a pang of jealousy.

Michiko turned after a moment, and brought the box towards the bed. Smoothing the coverlet, she placed it carefully, then fetched a length of pure silk ribbon from a drawer in the secretaire. With a swift glance towards André, she lifted the lid of the casket and waited for his sign that she could take out the vial within.

André nodded, his heart pounding far faster than it had ever done in his natural life. He swallowed, full of nerves as Michiko lifted the crystal flask and the weird blue radiance that was all that remained of the woman he loved more than life cast slowly dancing shadows across their bodies.

André? queried Arabelle, her clear discarnate voice full

of happiness. *Do not be afraid . . . Michiko has told me of the hopes you share. Perhaps next time you and I will be together always . . . And if not, let us take heart from what we are about to share now . . .*

She was always so calm, so accepting. It made him feel weak sometimes; inadequate because he could not endure his lesser torments with the same grace. But by the same token her equanimity was a solace. He remembered the early days, and her fits of manic uncomprehending terror and raging confusion, and gave thanks that she had matured and found wisdom. In truth, the way she had accepted her fate was a miracle, because never having physically aged, she was effectively still little more than a girl. The same exquisite, innocent, sensual girl he had fallen in love with over two centuries before.

Michiko put the flickering flask on the bed, then wound the silk ribbon around her wrist and arm in a complicated pattern, leaving one long end of it trailing free. She nodded to the vial, and with fumbling, shivering fingers, André unscrewed the glass lid then very carefully slid the tail of the ribbon into the opening.

'Great *Amida*,' intoned Michiko softly, 'guide the *kami* of the lady Arabelle into the shell of thy humble servant.' Crossing her free arm across her torso, she arranged her fingers into a magic symbol and pressed them against her skin, murmuring a low incantation in Japanese. Tilting her head back, she closed her eyes tightly, then her lips parted in a tiny yielding gasp.

André watched for a moment, tense with anticipation, as Michiko's breathing quickened and a droplet of sweat appeared on her suddenly furrowed brow, then he switched his attention to the vial and the ribbon.

Slowly, oh so slowly, the blue radiance that was Arabelle began to flow along the pristine white ribbon. Through sheer power of her will, Michiko had banished her own spirit, her *kami*, to some unknown nirvana, and Arabelle was passing into the vacated body by osmosis.

When the blue glow was right out of the jar and just about to slide across Michiko via the ribbon, André could observe its progress no longer. This temporary fusion was unpredictable and sometimes didn't work at all. Lying back and struggling to hope, he closed his eyes. If the process was successful, he wouldn't open them till it was over.

'André ... my love,' murmured a dear familiar voice in his ear, while a slender, female form lay down beside him.

'Belle! Oh, Belle!' he gasped, drawing her into his arms and rolling over to kiss her with more power. His eyelids still firmly shut, he seemed to see the woman he was embracing with his inner vision, and every detail of her lovely face was sweetly sacred.

Arabelle returned his kiss with a quiet, nascent passion that delighted him, pressing her body against his without shame. Even though Michiko, the vessel, was completely naked, as he held Arabelle he seemed to feel the brush of clothing. She had come to him, as she had before on these infrequent occasions, dressed in the gown she had been wearing when he had last seen her – a soft, elegant dress of the palest blue sprigged muslin, bound at the neckline and at the waist with fine blue ribbons. The bodice was low cut, as the fashion had been at that time, and he had a keen, almost painful memory of her allowing him to dip his hand inside her linen and touch her breast. He groaned, recalling the puckered texture of her nipple.

Just as he received a tactile recollection of Arabelle's pretty clothing, he also seemed to feel her silky hair; the heavy fall of her cascading auburn ringlets. As a fresh young girl, not yet tainted by the excessive pursuit of fashion, she had mostly worn her hair loose and flowing and only very lightly curled, its glossy thickness a delight to eye and hand. One day, he had made her blush profusely by describing how, when they were man and wife, he would ask her to caress him with her hair –

to rub her lustrous satin tresses against his penis. She had laughed and told him he was a wicked man to corrupt her with such an outré suggestion, but later, when he was touching her, and she was sobbing with pleasure, she had promised him he would eventually have his wish.

Too late now, he thought, feeling a little wistful as her firm, sweet lips parted under his. There were limits to how far illusion would stretch.

'Do not be sad, André,' she whispered, as if she, or Michiko, had sensed the thought. 'Let me make love to you.' Her quiet, vibrant voice was filled with humour. 'You will be surprised how much dear Michiko has taught me.'

Gentle fingers slid down over his chest, spreading deftly to create a flat caress, then closing to catch his nipple and carefully tweak it.

The sensation was so intense that André murmured, his head tossing against the pillow, his body arching. Because he loved her, even so slight a thing could thrill him.

Arabelle laughed, the husky impish chuckle that had always meant 'beware' because she had some further naughty trick laid in store for him. Pressing her slim thigh between his legs, she massaged his erect penis with the textured muslin of her skirt, pinching his teat in the same relentless rhythm.

'My lady, have a care,' he gasped, clasping her closer and locking his legs around the one that rubbed against him, 'or I will soil your handsome gown.'

'Who cares about gowns,' she answered, continuing to roll and jerk, her lips opening like rose petals against his throat.

'Minx,' he whispered, making her stop her gyrations by gripping the lobes of her bottom. How firm and trim and rounded they felt in his hands – sheer perfection! Tightening his hold on her, he quickly turned the tables and rocked her thinly-covered sex against his hip.

After a moment or two of this, Belle went deliciously limp against him, her slender shape as pliant as a reed. Her arms slid around him and he felt her panting, her breath cool and sweet, her mouth just an inch from his ear. 'Oh André,' she breathed, her pleasure evident not only in the beautiful malleability of her body but in the unguarded message he received directly from her soul. Her whole ethereal being was ablaze with love and wonder, an emotional wavefront that stunned him to silent awe. He would do anything to make her happy, he realised, and in any way. He would risk any risk and take any chance, regardless of any perils that path incurred.

An instant later, he forgot danger, he forgot the odds against success and he forgot all the moral considerations that plagued him. Uncoiling her right arm from around him, Arabelle walked her fingers down his belly, the steps as light and tiny as those of some mythic fairy, until her fingerpads were resting on his penis, just touching the root of it through his flossy pubic hair.

Moaning, he surged against her, pressing his hard length into the billows of her skirt. Her lips were at his throat again, kissing softly, whispering and encouraging, while below, her fingers curved around his shaft, gripping firmly with the exact pressure that he craved.

'My darling, my darling,' he chanted, as that snug grip began to move smoothly on him. Up and down, up and down, sliding the mobile skin over the iron-hard inner core. Stretching; pumping; tantalisingly gloving, twisting and teasing, his virgin beloved used a whore's skill upon his flesh.

'Oh God help me!' he cried out hoarsely, as his penis leapt and juddered and his spinal column seemed to melt and turn to fire. Collapsing backwards among the sheets and covers, he held his lover close, knowing that even as he climaxed, she was receding from him.

'Oh, Belle,' he whispered, as her essence fluttered and shook like a guttering candle flame, and he felt the

221

woman he was embracing twist and struggle. She was Michiko again now, reaching out for the crystal vial that lay beside her, guiding her discarnate friend towards the safety of containment.

'I am so sorry, my lord,' she said after a moment, and André realised he was sobbing like an infant.

They had been so close, he and Arabelle, but under these conditions their joy could never be more than fleeting. Michiko was an accomplished sorceress, full of sympathy and power, and using her mental skills she could temporarily be a vessel. Fundamentally however, she was incompatible with Arabelle, and even her greatest efforts couldn't furnish what they needed.

As he snuggled into Michiko's jasmine-scented embrace, he thought again of another woman who was within his orbit.

Belinda Seward – who *was* compatible, and who could, if she were willing and brave enough, sustain Belle's essence through the erotic ritual of release.

But would she help them? he pondered, his hand moving automatically over Michiko's satiny back. Would Belinda risk her very life for two people she hardly knew?

You can only ask her, said his Japanese lover, her voice clear and assertive inside his mind. 'And you must ask her,' she reiterated – as if for emphasis – by forming the words with her perfect rose-hued lips. 'You must ask her soon before it suddenly becomes too late. We both know there is only a limited period in which to act.'

He knew it only too well. It was only a matter of time before his revived state was detected – and the pursuit that never ended resumed again. 'You are right, my friend. As always,' whispered André, touching Michiko's brilliant coiffure and remembering certain long, black tresses that he had once had the misfortune to handle – a fall of hair that was *not* that of his faithful Japanese ally.

Neither one of them named the danger they feared was coming.

Chapter Thirteen
Perils and Pleasures

'*T*ell me about Arabelle,' demanded Belinda of her exotic and eye-catching new acquaintance. 'How can she live like that? Without a body?'

She and Michiko were strolling in the garden after dinner, and though the night was warm, their conversation had made her shudder. Michiko had told her all the things that André couldn't. 'And you said there were dangers. What dangers? To whom? To André? To Arabelle? To me?'

Now she knew his secret, Belinda could understand her host's strange reticence. André needed her to escape. Only she could help him leave a life she had already sensed was purgatory for him; and only through her could he take his best beloved with him.

'One thing at a time,' said the beautiful Japanese softly, slipping her arm through Belinda's as they wandered along the path. The touch of her bare skin was cool, as André's was, the sure hallmark of a being more than human. 'Arabelle is a discarnate spirit. When she was drugged and killed by the black witch Isidora, the life force was teased out of her, along a silken filament, and trapped inside a crystal vial.' The orange-haired woman spoke calmly and reasonably, as if such things were commonplace. 'And once she was sequestered inside the vial, Isidora destroyed her body so she could never return to it.' Michiko paused and turned, her near-black eyes glittering with anger. 'Her beautiful body burned to ashes ... to bones and dust. And all so that foul creature could indulge her evil passions and have André to herself for ever.'

'But André told me that he wasn't actually immortal ... just very long-lived.'

Michiko released Belinda's arm, then took her firmly by the shoulders. The Japanese woman's eyes were as glossy as chips of onyx. 'The spell was never completed, which is one of the reasons why Isidora pursues him.' Strong thumbs dug into Belinda's naked upper arms. 'She created a bond with André. Linked their fates. If he achieves his goal – if he dies – then Isidora can no longer live either.'

'I see,' said Belinda, knowing she didn't – properly – see at all.

'You see a little of it,' countered Michiko, a smile softening her fierce samurai face.

Belinda couldn't speak. Michiko's momentary gentleness was far more affecting than her dominant persona, and it spoke to something in Belinda that was new-born and unsure of itself. She found Michiko intriguing, a little frightening, and quite stunningly beautiful. It was strange to feel desire again, after all that had been revealed to her within the last hour, but she felt a strong urge to touch the Japanese woman – to repeat what she had learnt from Feltris and Elisa.

She became aware that Michiko was studying her closely – a new look in her dark, upslanted eyes.

'You have questions?' she enquired of Belinda, cocking her luridly-coiffed head to one side. *Questions about me, little one*, she seemed to add, confusing Belinda completely because the words were audible but Michiko's lips had remained still.

Can you read my mind? thought Belinda, concentrating

earnestly on the phrase, so much so that she felt the muscles of her face tense painfully.

'Yes, I can,' answered Michiko, her smile broadening, 'but if you don't like it, I can stop.' The fingers that gripped Belinda's bare arms released a little of their pressure, and the hold seemed to take on a more subtle quality.

Something about the Japanese woman seemed to dare Belinda to accept the challenge of mental communication, but she still felt slightly afraid to rise to it. Michiko was powerful, frightening. She induced in Belinda a peculiar sensation that was vaguely reminiscent of being a child cowering before a stern, omnipotent teacher – and yet not like it at all. It was fear, it was awe, and it was excitement. A physical thrill that was completely sexual in its content. She had experienced something of the feeling with André – a need to obey and to be controlled – but his haunted aura had somewhat softened its effect.

'I – ' Belinda began, then faltered. Michiko's look, and her touch, seemed to be making weakness steal up through her. She felt her knees almost buckle and she swayed in the Japanese woman's hold. She was also aware that her body was betraying her in other ways. Her nipples were hard points beneath the thin bias-cut satin dress she had been left to wear – she suspected it was a thirties nightdress rather than a real evening gown – and she could feel a tell-tale flush seeping up across her chest and throat.

'Ask your questions, Belinda,' commanded Michiko, her tone like a sheathed blade. 'I have nothing to hide from you.' For the moment, she seemed to have forgotten about telepathy.

'Are ... are you like André?' Belinda asked, still conscious of her vulnerability. Her dress was revealing, the off-white satin poured over her shape like fluid, without underwear beneath to give even a semblance of protection. In contrast, Michiko was clothed in leather,

225

which only reinforced her personal supremacy; narrow trousers and a waistcoat in a fine hide the colour of gunmetal, worn with soft, unstructured boots in the same grey shade. Around her neck was a brushed-steel pendant, suspended from a white cord, in the shape of an indecipherable ideogram.

'In some ways,' she said, answering Belinda's question, 'only my longevity derives from a different source.' She looked thoughtful, almost amused. 'A bargain with certain gods. A twist in the laws of reincarnation, you might say. I am allowed to retain the same body, and my belief is what sustains my state of youth.'

'Not sex then,' Belinda blurted out without thinking.

Michiko laughed loudly, her slanted eyes crinkling, then she kissed Belinda full on the mouth.

'No, not sex!' she said after a moment. 'I enjoy it, but I do not need it to survive.'

'Oh,' said Belinda, feeling vaguely crestfallen. She ran her tongue across the print of Michiko's lips.

'Are you disappointed?' the Japanese enquired, loosening her grip, then sliding an arm around Belinda's waist and encouraging her to continue along the path. It felt just as if they were a pair of lovers out strolling, the male suitor guiding his mate towards seclusion. 'Were you hoping that I was desperately in need of sexual stimulation, and that you were my next intended victim?'

Uncannily, that was exactly what Belinda had been hoping, and the words crystallised her muddled yearnings. She saw now that since she had first encountered André's Japanese friend in the library, where they had gathered for a pre-dinner drink, she had been wondering about the body beneath the leather. Wondering about it, wanting to explore it and caress it; and wanting to give herself to Michiko in return.

Are you still reading my thoughts? she asked silently.

You never actually said I shouldn't, came the reply, projected into her mind by Michiko's.

'Then you know what I feel,' Belinda said, swallowing. She was aware that her whole face and throat were pink now.

Michiko nodded. 'Come! I know a place which will serve our needs perfectly.'

It's too late, thought Belinda, as her new friend hurried her along the path, through the overgrown rose garden with its almost narcotic odour of night-scented blooms, and in the direction of the building she had noted earlier. The dilapidated shell of the almost ruined chapel.

As they stood in the porch and Michiko tackled the massive door with its rusted hinges, Belinda was unable to control a jumble of mental pictures. Herself, being fondled and made love to by Elisa and Feltris; herself, being exposed and studied by André, her buttocks naked to the night air of the terrace as she experienced disappointment when he didn't smack her bottom; herself, in a new scene, one that at first seemed unknown, then suddenly became familiar. She was kneeling awkwardly, with her bottom raised and completely bare, while an unknown figure stood threateningly behind her. Belinda realised that she was seeing a representation of her fantasy, the one in which, like some kind of latter-day Alice, she had fallen into the pages of a book and been a submissive who was about to take a beating. As the image grew in detail, the figure behind her raised its hand, ready to bring it down again with raw and stinging force. The figure turned and showed familiar almond eyes –

As Belinda gasped in recognition, Michiko swung open the chapel door, then whirled to face her. The Japanese woman's smile was oblique and knowing – and Belinda acknowledged the source of the final image.

'A preference of mine,' Michiko said, her voice smooth, 'and a fantasy I perceived in you when I first saw you.' Her eyes narrowed for a moment, became quintessentially inscrutable and Oriental, then she turned and led the way into the chapel. Belinda followed, watching her companion's boyish bottom sway.

Once inside, Belinda was able to forget her nerves for a moment, swept away by the high drama of their surroundings.

At one time, the roof of the chapel had been removed altogether, although there was no sign of the rubble and debris that should have resulted. Consequently, the small building was completely open to the sky and the moon that rode across it, surrounded by the tiny brilliant pin-pricks of a host of stars. Belinda knew little about church architecture, but she could see pews and what she supposed was a knave, but of an altar or an elaborate crucifix there was no sign. They had been whisked away as comprehensively as the roof. And a long time ago, too. The forces of nature clearly had no respect for hallowed ground because there were weeds and wild flowers growing here and there inside the building; springing up from pockets of silt-like earth that suggested a flood at some time in the past. In the bright moonlight the effect was strangely beautiful.

'Is this wh – '

Michiko silenced Belinda's question with a hand across her lips. *No!* came her psychic voice, commandingly. *Do not think of that now. This is our night. Let us concentrate on us!* She drew her hand laterally over Belinda's mouth, then inserted two fingers into it, touching the quiescence of her tongue. In a reflex as old as life, Belinda suckled.

'Ah yes, my little one,' the Japanese woman murmured, letting a third finger join the other two and stretch the corners of Belinda's mouth. 'My little girl, my naughty little girl. What have you been doing while you have been here, my wicked child?'

The words should have sounded twee and rather silly, like the words of a mock Victorian nanny in an indifferent and poorly-written play, yet on Michiko's lips they had the ring of true authority. Somewhere at the back of

Belinda's mind was the memory of what Michiko had described as her profession in the real world. She was an actress, a principal player in a world-famous Japanese theatre troupe, and she was a very fine one, judging by this, an impromptu performance.

'I'm s-sorry,' stammered Belinda as Michiko removed her fingers. The response was automatic; she suddenly even seemed to *feel* remorse. The submissive role had completely engulfed her just as smoothly as the mantle of dominance had been taken on by Michiko.

Belinda hung her head, unable to look her Japanese mistress in the eyes.

'Sorry for what?' A strong hand cupped her jaw, lifting her face again. 'Look at me, little one. Are you not at fault?' Belinda obeyed, meeting ebony eyes that glittered. 'Should you not be punished?'

Again, a portion of Belinda's mind remained rooted in reality and recognised the absurdity of the dynamic that was emerging. She hadn't done anything wrong. In fact, quite the reverse. She had been wanton because it was the spark that André needed –

But another part of her mind acknowledged ritual, theatrics and role-play – all key elements in Michiko's way of thinking. It was clear too that the Japanese woman enjoyed pain and power exchange as a satisfying form of eroticism, perhaps even the one that most fulfilled her, but her civilised mind demanded they be presented in a framework. Hence the sudden appearance of a 'mistress' and her 'penitent'.

Their eyes remained locked for perhaps thirty seconds, during which neither of them smiled or acknowledged any kind of covenant, yet even so Belinda sensed an agreement made. Looking down again, she slowly nodded her head.

'Good girl,' said Michiko softly, her thumb brushing across Belinda's lower lip. 'You will feel so much better.' Her free hand brushed Belinda's hair, ruffling it affectionately as a mother or a sister would. Or perhaps a teacher who was old-fashioned and lovingly stern.

The gesture was sexless, but Belinda's response to it could not have been more different. She felt a wave of delicious languor sweep through her. A melting. A soft, hot weakness that seemed to pool in the pit of her belly. It was as if she had wandered into a dream within a dream, where a new set of rules and responses held sway. Just the lightest touch of her hair could set her body and her sex a-quivering, and the thought of being punished made her heart leap with a strange dark longing.

But I don't like pain, she thought, as Michiko took her by the hand and led her across the uneven stone floor of the chapel. I hate it. I'm a baby; I cry at the slightest thing. What will I do when she actually starts to hit me?

Michiko paused when they reached the area where Belinda supposed the altar had once been, and seemed torn between two possible sites where her desires might be indulged. One was a deep, high-backed oaken pew, standing parallel to the nave; and the other was a heavy, solid-legged table – also of oak – which stood against the outer wall, behind the pew. Nodding her head, Michiko studied first the pew, then the table, then the pew again. She glanced sideways at Belinda, then squeezed her hand.

'Both, I think,' the Japanese whispered, as if she were offering not one gift, but two. Drawing Belinda's quivering hand to her crimson-stained lips, she kissed it once, then gave it another encouraging squeeze. 'Come along, my dear, it's time we got started.'

Releasing Belinda's fingers, Michiko stepped smartly towards the pew, then sat down on it, her long legs manishly spread. Lifting one elegant finger, she made a curling 'come here' gesture, then pointed to a spot a foot or so from where she sat.

Belinda hurried forward but stumbled slightly on the irregular flooring. The slip was barely noticeable and she recovered in an instant, but when she stood before Michiko she couldn't help blushing.

Michiko gave her a look which indicated she had taken note of her clumsiness but was prepared to tolerate it. Slowly, measuredly, the Japanese woman reached out and laid her left hand on Belinda's right hip, then with her right hand she touched Belinda's left nipple. The little crest was hard to start with, and embarrassingly distinct beneath the moulded satin of the dress, but when Michiko's finger settled on it, it puckered even more.

Belinda bit her lip. It was as if an encoded message was passing through the tiny contact – all the information she needed about this and other activities that loomed ahead of her. For a second, she had a wild urge to break away and take to her heels and run, but Michiko's narrow smile seemed to act as a shackle. Belinda could no sooner move than stop breathing in and out.

'This is a very revealing dress, little one,' observed Michiko, taking the nipple in her finger and thumb and twisting it. Her other hand squeezed quite hard on Belinda's hip. 'It's a whore's dress. What could you be thinking of wearing something like this?'

'I-I don't know,' gasped Belinda. Her nipple was hurting now, really hurting, from a combination of being tweaked and the crushing grip itself. Michiko's hands were so slender and graceful that it was hard to believe they could wield such painful force. What on earth else could they do to me? thought Belinda, feeling panicky. Without her being able to control it, her pelvis began to weave.

Why? Why is this happening? She was in pain now, and she still didn't like it; but down below she could feel her sex engorging. She was dripping with desire, but it was *because* she was suffering, not in spite of it. As Michiko pulled her breast outward, like a plump fleshly cone, she whimpered loudly.

Immediately, the nipple was released, though the low ache still remained. Still holding her by the hip, Michiko's warrior hand travelled downward until it hovered lightly at Belinda's pubis, then pressed on the thin satin slip and made it cling to her crisp knot of curls.

'The grove of heavenly delights,' intoned Michiko, pushing the shiny fabric inward. Belinda felt her sex-lips part and the pale satin begin to moisten with her juices. There was just a single layer of delicate cloth keeping Michiko's finger from touching her vulva, and she could feel the pad of that finger a bare inch from her clitoris.

'Take the gown off your shoulders,' said Michiko coolly. 'Come on, girl, lower the straps.'

Belinda flinched and obeyed. It felt like a miracle that she could actually move her hands and perform the simple action required of her. The situation, and Michiko's presence, seemed to inflict a paralysis upon her limbs. Flicking the thin the straps of the slip-like dress off her shoulders, she allowed the garment to slide down her body and expose her swollen breasts. With a struggle, she slid her arms out from the straps, leaving her torso naked and the satin rumpled around her hips.

Michiko just looked at her, long and hard, her pressing finger remaining quite motionless in its hazardous position. Belinda seemed to feel the Japanese woman's scrutiny like a strange, liquid ray cruising her body at a slow-motion pace. Her nipples stiffened even more and almost seemed to jump. Despite being exposed to the night air, her body began to sweat. She imagined perspiration forming in visible pools in her armpits, beneath her breasts, and in her groin. Phantom streams of it trickled over her skin and oozed down her flanks like jewelled, betraying rivers.

Suddenly, Michiko withdrew her left hand for a moment and let the bunched satin slip off Belinda's right buttock. The Japanese then grasped the naked lobe and squeezed it firmly, the tips of her fingers digging crudely and suggestively into Belinda's bottom-cleft. The whole weight of the dress now seemed to be hanging from her one probing finger.

Belinda moaned softly, desperately wanting something to happen, but afraid that it would. She no longer moved her hips; she dare not. Michiko's fingertips were so close to her most sensitive zones that the slightest of movements would bring them into contact with bunches of nerve receptors that screamed silently to be triggered.

'Oh please,' she whispered, remembering the same begging situation with André, the same state of being driven almost to madness in need of something.

'Remember what you are begging for,' warned Michiko, palpating the muscles of Belinda bottom-cheek. 'Remember what I want of you –'

'I don't care!' cried Belinda, rocking, and getting the most minuscule of half-nudges against her clitoris. She felt a brief but brilliant shard of sensation, then the hand was withdrawn and her dress slithered to the ground, leaving her bare but for the white stockings she wore gartered at her knees, the only other garments, except her shoes, that she had been provided with.

'Do anything with me! I don't care,' she repeated, waggling her bottom in the Japanese woman's hold. 'I don't care,' she sobbed, her eyes filling with childish tears of thwarted lust.

'As you wish,' said Michiko, her face a mask, her eyes as fierce as supernovae. She released Belinda's buttock. 'Step out of your dress, then let's have you across my knee.'

Belinda stepped clear of the pooled satin around her ankles, then dithered, feeling a wanton in just her stockings. Michiko gave her an intent look and she stepped to one side of the Japanese woman's braced thighs, then with as much grace as she could summon, she went across them.

The pose wasn't as easy to hold as she had expected. Though Michiko's thighs were muscular and firmly braced, Belinda still felt an alarming sense of vertigo.

She felt as if she were falling both literally and figuratively – tipping head-first off Michiko's lap and cartwheeling wildly into a new and frightening world. She was more relieved than she could have imagined when Michiko's left hand settled securingly in the small of her naked back, while the other lightly toyed with her buttocks.

'Hmm ... Nice and firm,' the Japanese murmured. 'Resilient – '

Almost while she was still speaking, the first smart slap landed unannounced.

'Oh God!' shouted Belinda, in total shock.

It felt like a slab of wood had crashed down on her bottom, a seasoned timber that had been pickled to make it harder. After a second of blank whiteness, her right buttock flamed, then almost immediately its twin caught fire too.

Michiko's rhythm was immaculate, each blow timed so that the previous one's impact was given time to fully develop. Crying within thirty seconds, Belinda could not believe how hard the smacks felt, how hard Michiko's hand felt. How stunning and painful a simple spanking could be.

Wriggling and squirming, she felt heat building and building in the muscles of her bottom, and at the same time sinking through into her quim. It was difficult to credit the way the sensations began to blend.

Michiko was really hurting her now, making her suffer far more than she had expected to, yet between her legs, Belinda was slippery and excited. Her brain seemed to be in a state of short circuit somehow, sending all the wrong responses to her breasts and her genitals. She was being hit, punished, belaboured; being made to experience excruciating pain and profound humiliation. But instead of despair, she felt jubilant, elated; her heart soaring with a wild, sweet desire.

'Oh Michiko,' she groaned, lifting her bottom high to meet a slap, then riding down on it to grind her crotch against her mistress's thigh. Each hard blow made her clitoris jump and pulse. 'Oh Michiko, I can't bear it,' she squealed, opening her flailing legs wider so her tormentor could seek out more tender targets.

When her climax finally came, she felt stunned and fought for breath, enduring pleasure waves so powerful she nearly fainted. Her throbbing, blazing bottom and the deep spasms of her vagina seemed to fuse into one huge, amorphous feeling, a fabulous sensation that transcended all description. It was ecstasy; it was pain; it was both of them and better . . . and it seemed to last for hours and hours, yet fade far too quickly.

As her senses wavered, she heard, *Well done, my little one.*

'Is Michiko a lesbian?' asked Jonathan, apropos of nothing.

Of all the questions he could have asked, having heard the bizarre story his companion had just told him, it surprised him that this was the one he had posed. What did it matter which way the Japanese woman's preferences swung? And what difference did it make to their involvement in André's future?

'Sometimes,' said André, staring back at him over the rim of a rounded crystal glass. They were in the library, drinking brandy, while the women walked in the garden. 'And sometimes not. It depends,' he continued, then took a sip of the amber-toned spirit.

Jonathan drank some brandy too, although rather more than the count had done. This was the first occasion that he had spent any length of time with their mysterious host, and the conversation alone would have been enough to drive the most abstemious puritan to the bottle, dealing as it had done with gothic magic and abnormal longevity.

It's more than that though, thought Jonathan, studying the other man. André was sitting at the other end of the leather-upholstered settee, and seemed to be lost in deep, dreamy fugue.

It's *him*, as well, Jonathan told himself. Him, and the weird effect he has on me.

Reaching for the bottle which stood before them on a low table, he sloshed a little more into his glass, then gestured towards André's glass with it.

'Why yes, I will,' said the count, his smile still a little distracted.

Jonathan poured more of the glowing fluid into his companion's glass, wondering as he did so whether it would have the same effect.

Is he still human? Can he even get drunk? he pondered, watching André's throat undulate as he sipped the warming spirit. The count was wearing a loose royal blue silk shirt with a tiny tab collar, and the vibrant colour made his smooth skin appear very pale.

'About Michiko,' he prompted, returning to the subject of the Japanese woman because his thoughts about André von Kastel were too alarming. 'You said "it depends". Depends on what?'

'On how beautiful the other woman is,' said André mildly. 'How spirited. Michiko is a great admirer of physical beauty, but if there's no spark there, no fire of individuality, she's not interested.'

Jonathan sighed. 'I suppose that means she's seducing Belinda right now, even as we speak.'

'Probably,' replied André, his blue eyes so bright that Jonathan couldn't look away. 'Does that bother you?'

Did it? He really didn't know what to say. Or to think. The idea of two women making love was a classic male fantasy, he knew, and it had worked for him well enough in the past – in general terms. But he had never visualised Belinda with another woman. Not even here, when the way she had spoken of her dealings with the two mute girls seemed to suggest that Feltris and Elisa had been as affectionate to her as they had to him.

'I detect that your feelings are ambiguous,' said André,

into the quietness of the big high-ceilinged room. The only sound, apart from the occasional creak of the leather sofa, was their breathing.

Jonathan opened his mouth, but still couldn't seem to form a word.

'The idea of Belinda with another woman is new to you, is it not?' the count continued. 'And puzzling. You wonder why you do not feel more jealous.'

'I-I'm not sure what I – ' Jonathan faltered, swirling his glass then lifting it to his lips, trying desperately to analyse his feelings. About Belinda. About Michiko. About all the strange revelations. About the man with whom he was sitting and drinking; the man who suddenly seemed far closer than he had a moment ago. So close that their thighs were almost touching. So close that he could see the toned shape of the musculature beneath André's tight, faded denims – and the size of the firm bulge at his crotch.

With brandy in his mouth, Jonathan spluttered furiously and felt himself choke and start to cough, his face turning a bright, blushing red. Eyes watering, chest heaving, he felt his brandy glass being removed deftly from his hand, and the impact of a solid, well-placed thump against his back. He coughed again, gratefully this time, and suddenly found he could breath deeply and evenly.

'I'm sorry,' he muttered, wiping his bleary eyes with the sleeve of his shirt. 'Maybe I've had too much to drink.'

'Perhaps you have not yet had enough?' countered André, and Jonathan felt the hand that had struck him stroke his back.

The caress was so light and innocuous it was almost illusory, but coming after the realisation of a moment ago, it made Jonathan start to shake and blush again.

'Here, but drink slowly this time.' André held out the refilled brandy glass. 'Sip by sip.'

When Jonathan took hold of the fat, rounded glass, he

was alarmed to feel André's hand curve around his, lifting the drink to his mouth. The count's skin was extraordinarily cool, yet its very coldness was exotic and exciting, and sent a thrill through Jonathan's shocked body.

I can't feel this! thought Jonathan helplessly, feeling it anyway. He's two hundred years old. I don't know him. Dear God in heaven, he's a man! He's a man! He's a man!

'Sip,' André urged again, his free hand returning to Jonathan's burning back.

Jonathan sipped. Far faster than was wise, but he was desperate for some kind of anaesthesia. He was experiencing something he had never felt before, and something he had never in his wildest dreams or darkest nightmares expected to feel – and the worst part was that it was ravishingly delicious. The brandy seemed to be having no effect on him whatsoever, but as he was allowed to take a breath, André's cologne made his head whirl. It was the smell of roses, and a sharp visceral musk.

'Think of Belinda and Michiko,' whispered the count in his ear. 'Imagine them together.' That long cool hand was still on his back, moving a little, rubbing him through the cotton of his shirt. 'How does that make you feel?'

'I don't know!' cried Jonathan, horrified by the strange sound of his own voice; its shrillness, its girlishness.

'Does the idea of same-sex love repel you?' André's voice was deep now, very masculine and cajoling. 'Surely not.' The final two words were not a question but an observation – and not one about Belinda and Michiko.

I'm being seduced, thought Jonathan. Just as Belinda was, here on this couch. And for all her single-mindedness, all her steadfast resistance of any kind of exploitation, she succumbed to this man within moments of meeting him.

'Jonathan?' prompted André gently, his hand still now, and so chilling through Jonathan's lightweight shirt.

'I don't know,' repeated Jonathan, feeling broken apart but somehow strangely resigned. He looked up, staring into the middle distance, intensely aware of the alluring figure beside him yet knowing it was he, himself, who had the choice.

'Look! Get it over with, if you're going to,' he said suddenly, unable to cope with the growing tension any more. If André made a move and it was thoroughly repellent, well, at least he would know. He would know, and he could leap up and flee from the room as fast as his feet would carry him. And if it wasn't? He couldn't know until the moment came.

'It is your choice,' said André quietly, as if he had viewed the brief debate in Jonathan's mind. Maybe he had?

Jonathan turned his face, and found his lips just inches from his companion's. He could smell the brandied sweetness of André's breath, and almost drowned in the aquamarine pools of his eyes.

He's so beautiful, thought Jonathan. He attracts me. I want him. But my body doesn't quite know how I want him. He shuddered, filled with thoughts and fears of buggery. 'I don't know what to do,' he said, his voice extraordinarily small.

'Do not worry,' said André, reaching up and undoing the thong that tied his striated locks back. 'I know what it is we need to know.'

Jonathan bit his lip to restrain a gasp. André's hair was soft, thick and shiny, despite its peculiar coloration. Jonathan felt a strong urge to bury his hands in it.

'Go ahead, do it,' urged André.

His breathing shallow, his heart racing, Jonathan put up his hands and slid them through André's silky tresses until he was cradling the other man's head. He watched André's lips part, almost in ecstasy, revealing the soft

239

rosy interior of his mouth. Without thinking, Jonathan lunged forward and kissed him.

It's just like kissing a woman, he thought, feeling André's strong, slender arms come around him. The sensations were the same: velvety lips under his, parting provocatively and admitting his tongue. He was so used to kissing like a man – probing strongly and taking the initiative – that he continued to do so, while André seemed perfectly happy to let him, relaxing back on to the settee and drawing him down.

'Mmmm . . .' murmured the count as they broke apart for a moment, and he reached up to touch Jonathan's chin. 'Not so bad, is it?' He smiled, then took Jonathan's hand, from where it still held his head, and turned his face so he could moistly kiss its palm.

'No . . . no, it isn't,' stammered Jonathan, disconcerted as André surged up against him, kissed him again, actively this time, and at the same time began unfastening his shirt buttons. Before he knew it, the garment was open to the waist and the loose tails pulled out, then André was shimmying along beneath him and sucking at his nipple. He felt the count's teeth close wickedly and he groaned.

Jonathan had always had sensitive nipples and loved to have them played with and nibbled. For a moment, he thought of Belinda and how beautifully she did this for him, but the next instant he was dragged back to reality, his body excited by the extra layer of piquancy that having a man's mouth on him created.

The pair of them rocked and wrestled. Jonathan on top, his hands rubbing and stroking at every bit of his partner he could reach; André beneath, holding tight, his teeth still nipping. As he wriggled and struggled and cried out in excitement, Jonathan was embarrassingly aware of his erection. It was as big and hard as it had ever been before, and it was poking André somewhere in his mid-section. The count too was erect, his organ pressed against the side of Jonathan's leg. His bulge felt enormous, even through two layers of denim, and wriggling faster, Jonathan wondered what it looked like. Would it be smooth or veined? Circumcised or uncut? Would it be long and thin, or shorter, but very thick?

Exhibiting, once again, the telepathic ability that Jonathan suspected him of, the count suddenly slithered out of the peculiar clinch and got to his feet.

'Let us make ourselves comfortable,' he said, with a playful little grin that almost reminded Jonathan of Belinda. What a conundrum the man was; one minute he was the archetypal alpha male, all effortless command, and the next, he was more feminine, more languorous. The weird contrast was confusing but still attractive. Jonathan watched, rapt, as André first unbuttoned his shirt, flicking the tails out of his waistband, and then, standing elegantly on one leg, then the other, removed his boots. He wore no socks, and when he had unbuckled his belt and unfastened his jeans, then removed them, Jonathan discovered he wore no underpants either, and his penis was both sizeable and rigidly hard.

'Now you,' said the count quietly, still wearing his lustrous blue shirt.

Nervous, embarrassed, yet excited too, Jonathan began the same procedure. He was convinced he could not get his clothes off with the same graceful ease that André had, but nevertheless he tried, and was rewarded with an encouraging smile. Off came his trainers and his socks, then his belt and his jeans, and finally he slid down his boxer shorts and kicked them away from him.

André said nothing, but regarded him steadily for a few moments, his frank gaze ultimately settling below the waist.

Jonathan felt himself blushing again, all over, and his penis growing so rigid that it hurt him. He knew his body was reasonable, and he had never had any complaints from the women he had made love to, but beside this male lover he began to feel inferior.

After what seemed like a lifetime, André spoke. 'You have a handsome body, Jonathan. Strong. Straight. And very manly. It is no wonder that a woman like Belinda chooses to be with you.'

Still speechless, Jonathan stood like a statue, too timid now to move forward. With a gentle smile, the count moved towards him.

'No need to be scared,' he whispered, wrapping Jonathan in his arms and pressing his cool, smooth body to Jonathan's warm and sweaty one. 'No need at all,' he said, guiding him back towards the couch.

Then, as they settled down on to the leather, their limbs entwining, their sexes duelling, it dawned on Jonathan that his strange new friend was right.

He sighed contentedly. He wasn't scared at all.

Chapter 14
Preparations for Departure

'*H*e didn't fuck me,' said Jonathan, his voice solemn in the shadows. 'And I didn't fuck him. I didn't seem to need to.'

Belinda touched his arm reassuringly. It must have cost Jonathan a lot to reveal what had happened between him and André. Men were touchy about their masculinity, and Jonathan was as much a man as any other. To admit to a homosexual tryst was a major catharsis.

'What did you do?' she asked quietly, glad for him that it was night and that the darkness was dense.

It had been after midnight when she had left the chapel with Michiko, and a strange cloudiness had passed across the sky. She had felt tender as they walked through the garden towards the priory; her bottom had been glowing from the spanking she had received, but she had been filled with another radiance too. A glow of satisfaction. The nurturing of a special secret. The knowledge that she had followed a hitherto untrodden path – with yet another charismatic new lover – and that despite the pain, she had loved every second of it!

She had also been hoping that Jonathan would come to her, so she could tell him about it; and here he was, with his own tale to tell, which was equally wild.

'He took me in his arms,' her boyfriend said, sliding his own arm around her shoulder and drawing her close. Belinda rested a hand on his chest and felt his heart beating furiously within. 'He kissed me and touched me and I kissed and touched him. It wasn't a lot different to the things we do together–' He paused and seemed to ponder a second '–up to a point.'

'And then?'

Belinda could feel the heat of Jonathan's blush; his chest was hot beneath her face. 'He rubbed me until I came. Then he put my hand on his . . . his cock and sort of rocked against me until he came too.' He halted again, and Belinda sensed awe in him now and not a little fear. 'It was cold, Lindi . . . Like his skin. Cold and sort of thin; not like ordinary semen at all.' Belinda reached for his hand, and squeezed it tightly. 'That was when I really believed him. About what he is. It never really sank in until I felt that weird, cold stuff trickling over me.'

She had been going to tell him about Michiko and the spanking, but now it seemed they could no longer avoid the bigger, more dangerous issue. The strange service that she alone could perform for André and Arabelle.

'Are you going to do it?' Jonathan asked, as if the tenor of his thoughts had altered too.

Although she paused for a while, as if considering her answer, Belinda had already made her decision. She had made it quite some time ago, she realised. When she had first seen André asleep in the tower room, she had felt a strange bond with him. Perhaps even before that, when she had been caught in the thunderstorm with Jonathan and had sensed another presence observing them. She wasn't sure if she believed in fate and destiny and events being mysteriously preordained, but somehow she had known right from the beginning that her life and André von Kastel's were entangled.

'Yes, I am,' she said at last.

'It's dangerous,' said Jonathan, his arm enclosing her

tighter. 'If what André told me is correct, there's a chance that you might die too.'

His voice was even, resigned, lacking argument; and Belinda was aware that Jonathan had not only accepted her decision, but was glad of it. She smiled. How clever André was. By making love with Jonathan, he had bound him to the cause too – quashed his objections with the power of affection.

'I know,' she said calmly, 'but I have no choice. I can't bear to think of them going on for centuries and centuries like that. So near, but apart. Loving each other, wanting each other, but unable to do anything about it.'

'I certainly couldn't cope with it,' said Jonathan. 'If it were you and me, I would've gone mad.'

For a moment, Belinda forgot the plight of André and Arabelle. Jonathan had spoken spontaneously, without thinking, and revealed feelings for her that were deep and all-encompassing – feelings she suddenly realised she shared. They had had their troubles – only weeks before this holiday they had even discussed splitting up – but the thought of losing him now was suddenly appalling, as much if not more than the thought of losing her life altogether.

Lost for words, she struggled in his hold, then scooted upward, pressing her lips against his jaw, then his mouth. Despite everything that had happened in the last two days, despite her still smarting bottom that reminded her of pleasure at the hands of Michiko, despite even her fear of what was to come and the very real possibility of death, she wanted desperately to express her love for Jonathan now. Right now. She wanted, no, needed to let him know, while she was still able, that she shared his deep but unarticulated emotion. That she loved him as much as he loved her.

As his tongue entered her mouth, she felt his body harden against her. Embracing him tightly, she knew that it wasn't yet too late.

*　*　*

245

'It must be tomorrow night,' said Michiko, pacing the tower room, something André had observed she always did while thinking and planning.

'So soon?' he said, feeling a frisson of jumbled anticipation.

'Yes, it is imperative,' said Michiko, smoothing the voluminous sleeve of the thin green kimono she now wore in readiness. 'I sense her. I feel her approach.'

André watched her shudder, feeling the same revulsion himself, and more than that, a blank, all-consuming rage. Time after time, he had eluded Isidora, knowing she had the power to enslave him for ever if she came close enough, but now the tables were finally beginning to turn. With the help of Belinda, Michiko, and even Jonathan, he had the power to destroy her, and to be free; but if she perceived that fact she could well unmake his plans.

'Would that my powers were as sensitive as yours,' he said, rising and wrapping his own robe around him. 'Then perhaps I would not have had so many perilous moments in the past. Do you believe she already knows what we intend to do?'

'No, I think not,' replied Michiko, pausing in her circuit and moving towards André. 'Remember, her psychic powers are incomplete.' She took his hands and smiled at him. She was reassuring him, for which he almost loved her. 'She can sense your consciousness over great distances but she cannot read your mind. Or any other.' Her dark eyes narrowed conspiratorially. 'And even if she has employed some new spell and gained the ability to read thoughts, I know a stronger spell to counteract that. I can protect all the minds beneath this roof.'

'What would we do without you, my dear friend?' said André, smiling at Michiko, then glancing towards Belle's glowing box.

'You would find ways to prevail, my lord,' replied Michiko pertly, giving his fingers a fierce squeeze that made him yelp. 'Now come, we have much work before us! And when dawn comes, you will be no help at all!'

There was a great deal of apparatus set up on his workbench – burners, flasks of various shapes, pipettes, a pestle and mortar, earthenware vessels and several thuribles. And the great black grimoire lay open at the fateful page.

'First things first,' André said, smiling at Michiko and feeling focused now the work was in hand. Picking up a white linen handkerchief, he unfolded it, then plucked from its smooth white surface a single red hair about four inches long – which Feltris had deftly retrieved from among Belinda's clothing. This André placed on a thurible, then tugged a single hair from his own scalp to join the red one.

Next he strode to the night-table beside his bed and picked up a small rosewood casket, decorated in the same style as Arabelle's refuge, but smaller, and from this he took another single hair – one strand from the long coiled lock that lay within. It was as red as Belinda's, almost exactly the same shade, but in this case approximately three feet in length. Twirling it around his finger, he pressed his lips against it with reverence. 'All that I have of you,' he murmured, letting Arabelle's strand of hair uncoil, then carrying it across and adding it to the others in the thurible. As he lit a taper, he felt Michiko touch his arm.

'Soon you will be with her, my lord,' the Japanese woman whispered, as they watched the three strands burn to minuscule ashes.

'There have been times when I believed I would never make these preparations,' he said thoughtfully, stirring the charred mixture with a small glass rod and then tipping it into a fresh vessel. Although he knew this ultimate enchantment by heart, having spent many hours – during his last wakeful period – learning it in readiness, he consulted the grimoire to affirm the next step.

247

Hallowed water from the underground stream that ran beneath the chapel, this time lovingly distilled for him by the ever-faithful Oren, was placed in an open-necked glass flask and set to heat over a burner, ready to receive the rest of the ingredients of the potion.

In other containers, Michiko was mixing components of the complex, many-faceted elixir. Herbs: bettony, agrimony, cedar. Spices; nutmeg, cloves. The magic poisons: belladonna, azarnet and mercury – the monarch among metals. Each mixture was stirred with its own particular pattern – here a square, here a triangle, here a hexagram – and as both the magicians worked, each of them chanted in accord with their beliefs. André called on the Christian trinity of his upbringing, and then on other patrons he had come to understand later. Hecate, the queen of the spirits. Hermes Trismegistus, the mediaeval god of alchemy. Beneficent Isis, the matriarchal goddess of the Ancient Egyptians. The good offices of all these would aid his cause.

As he chanted, he was aware, too, of Michiko's liturgical murmurings. André understood very little of her native language, but he knew that for her part she would be calling on the air spirits, the *kami* of the sky and the heavens beyond, who would also wield their forces to assist him.

Finally, when all the separate conglomerations were prepared, it was time for the final combining. 'Be as one,' whispered André as each vessel yielded up its contents into the flask. 'Be as one that she and I may be as one.'

The resulting melange was dark and murky, an indeterminate mud-like dark brown. André agitated it carefully with the point of his black-handled dagger, stirring in all the magic symbols that he had used with each ingredient, while repeating the appropriate chant with each separate shape. Beside him Michiko whispered in Japanese. The last step was to apply a flame to heat the flask.

Slowly, very slowly, as the contents became tepid,

then warm, then hot, a startling transformation took place within the vessel. What had been a dirty, odiferous blend of disparate constituents very gradually took on a hue of beauty, and by the time it was bubbling steadily it had changed nature completely. Within the glass now there was a clear, jewel-like liquid of the most intense lapis blue – the same brilliant colour as André's own eyes in the mirror.

'It is ready,' he said quietly to Michiko, as they both gazed at the contents of the flask. He was glad that they had achieved the transmutation so successfully, but he still felt a slight pang of uneasiness. Although it had not been precisely this mixture that Isidora had added to his wine that fateful night two hundred years ago, what he had before him now was only a variant of the potion that had damned him.

'It will not work unless you believe that it will, my lord,' said Michiko softly from beside him. 'Your faith is the most potent of all ingredients.' She slid her slender arm around his waist, beneath his robe, and gave him a squeeze.

'I hope you are right,' he replied, still gazing at the enigmatic fluid.

'Of course I'm right.' Michiko's voice was confident but tender, and her slender fingertips slid down across his hip. 'And now, my lord, I am going to make love to you.' Her hand cupped the muscled curve of his buttock. ' – because this could well be the last chance we'll ever have.'

Realising she was right, André turned to her, his throat choked at the finality of her words. He would miss his old friend – miss her spirit and her loveliness – and he would miss the closeness that their strange condition had forged in them. Opening the folds of her kimono, he pressed her naked body to him, then brought his lips down on her mouth in a long kiss.

Her face was wet, but were they her tears or his?

* * *

249

The sun was high in the sky when Belinda woke.

Shifting Jonathan's arm from across her body, she slid as quietly as she could from the bed and padded to the window, naked. The grounds and the garden looked as ordinary as they had looked at any time during their short stay at the priory, but what caught her eye was an express delivery van trundling along the drive towards the house. It was the first real sign she had seen of an interaction taking place between the inhabitants of this strange place and the outside world – but instead of reassuring her, it made her feel nervous.

The problem was, while she was completely cut off from her everyday life, with its patterns and its artefacts, she could believe in things like magic, extreme longevity and discarnate spirits trapped in bottles. But when evidence of the commonplace and the mundane presented itself, the veracity of the supernatural world wavered. And when she thought of what she had done – and what she might do – she felt ridiculous. And frightened.

As the delivery van pulled up outside the house, she saw Michiko and Oren walk down the steps to meet it. The driver opened the back and pulled out several large white cardboard cartons – which Oren took and carried back inside – then proffered a clipboard, which Michiko signed. The whole transaction was so utterly unremarkable that when the van sped away, Belinda wondered whether she had dreamed it. That was until Michiko looked upward and gave a wave.

As Belinda waved back, the Japanese smiled broadly and blew a kiss.

'Who were you waving at?' enquired the waking Jonathan, when Belinda stepped away from the window after Michiko had gone inside.

'Michiko. She was outside. Taking delivery of some packages.'

Jonathan said nothing, but climbed out of bed and wandered towards the sideboard, on which – Belinda noticed for the first time – was a tray containing their breakfast.

'This looks nice,' he said, lifting an immaculate white napkin. 'Brioches, butter, preserves.' He flipped up the lid of an insulated jug. 'Mmmm. Fresh coffee! Just what I need!'

A few moments later they were both sitting cross-legged on the bed, tucking into the food, with big white French coffee cups balanced precariously on the bed beside them.

'What do you suppose everyone is doing now?' said Jonathan, chewing. He had brioche crumbs in his sparse, dark chest hair, Belinda noticed, and she smiled. He had never looked younger or more appealing.

'Well, as I understand it, André will be sleeping,' she said thoughtfully, breaking off a piece of her own brioche and popping it in her mouth. 'But Michiko and the others could well be getting things ready for tonight. Those boxes might be something to do with it.'

'Tonight?' Jonathan looked quite shocked, and his cup trembled in his hand as he conveyed it to his lips, letting a little of his milky coffee drip on to the sheet. 'How do you know it'll be tonight?'

How *did* she know?

Belinda was surprised at the certainty of her own intuition. She had not been told when the freeing ritual would take place, but she couldn't shake the powerful feeling that it was scheduled for tonight. Had Michiko imparted the knowledge to her subconscious somehow? Anything was possible given the Japanese woman's esoteric talents.

'I just know,' she said quietly.

Jonathan studied the coffee stain, jabbing at it with his fingers. 'Oh God, I just thought of something,' he said, looking up again. 'We've told Paula to come. She'll probably arrive today. What are we going to do with her? Tonight? She'll probably expect us to stop up until

251

the small hours, drinking and talking. I mean, that's what we've always done before, isn't it?'

Belinda saw the problem, and just as quickly the answer. The coolness of her own logic astounded her. 'You'll just have to keep her occupied on your own then, Johnny, won't you?' She looked at him levelly, willing him to comprehend her.

Jonathan frowned, and she knew he had got the message.

'She's always fancied you. It'll be easy.'

'But . . . won't you mind?'

Belinda considered the idea. 'If you'd asked me a few days ago, yes, I would have minded,' she said, musing on the way she and Jonathan had progressed. 'But things have changed.' Ignoring the cups and the tray, she reached out and laid her hand on his thigh. *'We've* changed.' She squeezed his wiry but muscular flesh. 'We've both had sex with other partners, but it hasn't split us up, has it?' She saw him nod then smile sheepishly. 'And there's a higher purpose behind it this time. Something important.' She grinned back at him. 'You'll just have to close your eyes and do it for the cause!'

'I suppose I can force myself,' said Jonathan, laughing now. He leant forward to retrieve the cups and plates and all the other remnants of their breakfast, then put the lot in a semblance of tidiness on the tray. 'But I'll have to be prepared.' His eyes gleaming, he slid off the bed, scooped up the tray, then put it out of harm's way before climbing back on to the bed again. 'I might need some practice,' he said in mock-thoughtfulness, as he reached for her. 'Do you think we could have a quick run-through now?'

Opening her legs and tumbling backwards, she said, 'Of course.'

Smiling with satisfaction, Isidora Katori rose from the rumpled hotel bed and stretched the kinks from her slender, shapely limbs. It was already late in the day, and she had to move.

Walking naked to the dressing table, she spared only the briefest glance towards the figure who still lay deeply sleeping. Her victim, who would now stay in a coma for three or four days.

It had been quite easy to pick up this 'Paula' in the pub garden where she had found her, then the simplest of child's play to flatter her and seduce her. With a few drinks and a little assistance from an aphrodisiac, the poor thing had almost believed that she was a closet lesbian and that she had been waiting for Isidora all her life.

Smoothing her hands over her voluptuous curves, Isidora had to admit she had enjoyed such an innocent passion. Bewitched and rendered insatiable by a few drops of the special tincture, love-struck Paula had been touchingly grateful for her orgasms, and most anxious to repay for them in kind. They had stayed in bed together for far longer than Isidora had planned on, and now it was afternoon and high time she was leaving.

Even so, she took a moment to study her face.

Paula Beckett was pretty enough, Isidora supposed, lifting her fingers to touch the features that were now hers. The girl wasn't stunning nor really beautiful, but her face would be quite passable for a limited period. The best thing about Paula's appearance was that it was sufficiently similar-looking – in general terms – to Isidora's own, and could be copied quite well enough to fool observers.

What she was seeing now, Isidora knew, turning her head this way and that, was a clever psychic projection, a mental mask that would fool any person without special powers. And it would fool André von Kastel until it was too late for him to flee.

Isidora smiled again, watching the curve of her unfamiliar lips and finding them pleasing.

'I will have you, André von Kastel,' she whispered,

trying her borrowed voice for the first time out loud. 'And this time I'll finish what I started. This time there will be no chance for escape . . . and I'll destroy that red-haired milksop bitch of yours completely.' She laughed Paula Beckett's laugh, and found it light but acceptable. 'Before this day is out, André, you will be mine for good and all.'

It was afternoon before Belinda and Jonathan rose, and even then a strange lethargy hung over them.

At first, Belinda felt nervous, thinking she should be doing something, making preparations of some kind, or even just finding Michiko and discovering more of what might happen to her, but it wasn't long before she felt too dreamy to care. After Jonathan had gone to his room to dress, she took a long and leisurely shower, then dressed slowly in the clothing that had been left for her – another shift-like petticoat in the flounced Edwardian style.

When she left her room, she was torn between going to the library and trying to seek out background reading on the ritual that lay ahead of her, or going out on to the terrace to enjoy the sun. She knew that anyone in their right mind would choose the library and 'preparedness', yet somehow she couldn't seem to make that choice. Her head felt light but in a rather amenable way, and all she wanted to do was just relax and float along.

On the terrace, it seemed that someone had anticipated her decision, or perhaps even initiated it. In addition to the table where she had breakfasted the day before under the sunshade, there were also now two surprisingly modern loungers. And on one of these, she found Jonathan half-reclining, his attention already embroiled in a charcoal sketch. His fingers were smudgy and he was naked apart from his shorts.

'So?' she said, sinking down on to the adjoining lounger and arranging her skirt so she could get the sun on her legs. 'Is anything happening? Have you seen Michiko? Or the mutes?'

'Oren was here a minute or two ago,' Jonathan replied, setting aside his drawing pad and wiping his sooty fingers down the side of his shorts, 'and I think he asked me if I wanted a cool drink, but I'm not quite sure.' He shrugged and put up a hand to shield his eyes from the sun. 'Anyway, whatever it was I told him yes ... and make it two.'

'Lovely,' said Belinda, seeing the image of a tall cold cocktail, and feeling thirsty. 'But what about the others?'

'They seem to be busy, apart from André, that is.' He blushed a little at the name of the man he had made love with. 'I keep seeing them taking things over to that ruined building over there.' He nodded in the direction of the chapel.

'What sort of things?'

'Armfuls of flowers ... What looked like rugs or something ... Books, wooden boxes ... All sorts of stuff.' He frowned slightly, as if the list of paraphernalia troubled him. 'I suppose that's where it's all going to happen, isn't it?'

'I believe so,' she replied quietly, feeling fear stir in her mind then quickly subside again. 'It's funny, I still can't seem to get my head around it.' She paused, wondering how to explain herself. 'I know I should be worried. Scared stiff. But I'm not.'

'Perhaps there isn't anything to be scared of,' said Jonathan, touching her arm and leaving a smear of black on her skin. 'Michiko seems very capable. Very organised.' He grinned. 'I don't know. I know she looks a bit exotic, but she acts like a businesswoman. A high-powered motivator or something. She seems too real somehow to be a witch!'

'Oh, she's real all right,' murmured Belinda ruefully, her fingers settling suddenly on her flank. The soreness in her bottom had disappeared quite miraculously, but she could still remember the impact of being spanked.

Jonathan eyed her with sudden interest. 'You never did tell me what happened with her last night,' he said, his voice full of curiosity. 'I'm not the only one who learned something new, am I?'

'No, you're not,' admitted Belinda. 'I had a lesson of sorts too.'

It was on the tip of her tongue to describe the whole incident, but just then Oren appeared in the doorway to the house, and he walked towards them, carrying a loaded tray. When he reached them, he nodded politely and set it down.

'Oh Oren, this looks wonderful!' cried Belinda, with feeling. The tray contained a tall jug full of some reddish Pimms-like concoction, complete with tiny fruit pieces bobbing on the surface. There was an insulated ice container – not the bucket that she had seen in the library, she noticed – and beside it a couple of heavy crystal glasses. Also on the tray were several bowls of savoury nibbles: tiny cheese biscuits, potato chiplets, salted nuts. One final item was not immediately identifiable: an alabaster jar with a fat cork in its neck.

As Belinda sat up in anticipation, Oren poured the fruity cocktail into the two glasses, then added several rocks of ice to each one. Belinda took a sip of her drink as soon as he handed it to her, and gasped at both its deliciousness and potency.

'Phew!' she said, then sampled it again, trying to analyse what made the taste so special. It was similar to many of the kinds of fruit cup or punch she had tried before, but with a pungent aftertang that was totally unfamiliar.

It's drugged somehow, she thought, setting the glass down. It's either full of aphrodisiac or it's to prepare me for tonight. After a moment's thought she settled on the former; if the same drink was being served to both her and Jonathan, its effects weren't specifically for her.

A model of efficient service as ever, Oren set the jug and the tray of food down between the two loungers so it was in easy reach for later. He also set down the alabaster jar, and when Belinda frowned doubtfully at it, he gestured upward towards the hot afternoon sun, then made a rubbing motion along his bare arm.

'Sunscreen?' she queried, and the tall man nodded, then gestured again towards her own bare legs, and crouched down to retrieve the chunky jar. He tilted his head questioningly, then tapped his chest.

'No, it's OK, Oren, I can manage,' she said, putting her hand up for the jar.

Oren smiled amiably and gave it to her, clearly not offended that his services weren't required, then nodded briefly and turned, leaving Belinda alone once more with Jonathan.

'Tactful, isn't he?' observed Jonathan, reaching for his drink and taking a long swig. Belinda watched his eyes light up as he savoured its effects. 'Wow!' was his only comment as he set the glass down again, before picking up his sketch-pad and stick of charcoal. After drawing a line or two, and then smudging them, he looked up at Belinda and prompted, 'You were going to tell me what it was you learnt last night.'

Unable to look him in the eye, Belinda picked up the jar, twisted off the lid and stuck a finger into the soft, cream-coloured substance within. It had a slick texture and a sharp but very pleasant, vaguely citrus smell. When she daubed it on to her calf, it felt cool.

'Lindi!' shouted Jonathan playfully.

Slowly, and in as much detail as she could bring herself to go into, she described her painful tryst in the chapel with Michiko. As she spoke, she smoothed the sun balm on to her lower legs and thighs, the sensuous movement complementing the eroticism of her account. Pausing for a moment to admire the glistening sheen on her skin, Belinda seemed to remember her spanking even more vividly than she had earlier. Her bottom, although it showed no sign of what had happened, and had ceased to hurt quite some time ago, started to tingle again, as if her flesh had a separate memory of its own. She could almost feel hands gliding over it then crashing down with a remorseless, fiery force.

'It was painful,' she conceded, dipping her fingers into the jar again, and beginning to work the cream over her shoulders, 'but it was erotic too. I wouldn't have believed how much.' She paused, switched hands, began creaming her other shoulder, then spread the cream in a thin film down her arm. 'I – I had several orgasms.'

Jonathan set his glass down with a clatter and poured in more fruit cup, sploshing quite a bit of it over the side.

'Jesus,' he murmured, then took a long, long drink, his eyes unfocused as if he were seeing the picture she had just painted.

Belinda smiled, seeing the bulge in his soft jersey shorts. Men were so easily excited, and clearly he was responding to both of the two classic fantasies she had outlined for him: lesbian love-making and a girl's bottom being spanked.

Not that her account and her memories hadn't stirred her too. She felt lightly aroused, but not uncomfortably so. Her whole body felt warm and sensitised and it was a condition she did not dislike being in for its own sake, rather than a prelude to something more powerful and more passionate. As she watched Jonathan shift uncomfortably on the lounger, trying to find ease for his engorged penis, she had a sudden revelation of quite extraordinarily startling clarity.

Although it sounded rather silly when framed into words, she knew she had to 'save herself'; to conserve the sexual energy and the desire within her so that tonight she would be ready for, and want, André. The ritual demanded a willing partner, and more than that, it needed her to genuinely need and care for him. If she satisfied a simple and fairly low-key bodily itch with Jonathan now, she could destroy the last hopes of two desperate people later. It was not too much to ask of herself, she decided, letting her fingers drift dismissively across her crotch.

But that didn't mean Jonathan had to suffer.

Rising gracefully from her lounger, Belinda took the couple of steps it required to stand before him, then sank on to her knees, her floaty skirt drifting out around her. Jonathan watched her over the rim of his glass, his eyes filled half with lust, half with awe, as he sipped nervously at the ruddy fruit-filled cocktail.

With a confidence that felt new to her, Belinda took the glass from him and set it aside. He started to protest but she laid a finger across his lips and he subsided, then obediently lifted his bottom when she reached for the waistband of his shorts.

His penis sprang up bouncily as she slid down the garment; a column of hungry flesh, prime and vigorous.

'Belinda!' he moaned almost querulously as she cupped his balls in one hand and with the other delicately enclosed his straining shaft.

'Shush!' she said, then settled her lips around his glans.

Chapter 15
The Freeing

Belinda stared at her reflection in the mirror, already feeling her identity start to blur. The soft, periwinkle-blue dress she wore couldn't actually be Arabelle's, she knew that, but instinct told her it was a good facsimile.

'It's no wonder he misses her,' said Jonathan, moving up behind her and slipping his hands around her waist. 'If she looked like you she must have been very beautiful indeed.'

She met his eyes in the mirror. 'Thank you, Johnny.'

'My pleasure,' he murmured, smiling shyly. 'It's true.'

She put her hands over his. 'I'm scared.'

'I know.' His smile turned to a small frown.

'But I can't back out. He may never find anyone else who can do it. You understand that, don't you?'

'Yes. Yes, I do,' he replied, his fingers flexing against her waist. 'And I want you to help him . . . them. If there was anything I could do myself I'd do it. I just wish it wasn't so dangerous for you!'

Belinda was about to reassure him, to lie to him, but just then there was a sharp rap at the door, and before they had time to react, Michiko swept into the room, an expression of concern on her face. She was wearing what looked like a sumptuously elaborate kimono, which she

260

hadn't had time yet to fasten, and on her feet were bifurcated white socks. Her elegant Oriental face was heavily painted in purest white, her lips were crimson, and her eyes were lined with black.

'She's coming!' she cried, hurrying towards them, her steps silent in her socks. 'We must be ready. And Jonathan, you must help us!'

'What do you mean?' demanded Belinda, feeling Jonathan's embracing hands drop away. 'Who's coming? What's the matter?'

The Japanese woman reached out, took each of them by the hand, and squeezed hard. Her eyes were burning coals in her whitened face. 'Isidora is on her way here. I sensed her. I think she may well arrive within the hour.'

'Can't we just lock the gates or something? Or lock the house itself?' suggested Jonathan. 'What about Oren, can't he stop her? He's big enough.'

'Poor Oren is helpless against her powers,' said the Japanese woman. 'He would surrender his life to protect André, but it would do no good. Isidora would find some way around him.' She squeezed Belinda's hand again, then released it, taking hold of both of Jonathan's hands. 'You, on the other hand, I can protect. And you must act as a diversion while we complete the rite.'

'Why would she take any notice of me?' demanded Jonathan. Belinda saw doubt in his face, and real fear. It was clear he now believed completely in the supernatural.

'Because she is approaching in disguise. I was able to catch a glimpse of her mind without her detecting me,' said Michiko intently. 'She is using subterfuge. Hoping to get close enough to André to act, before anyone even realises she's here, and she knows her new face is welcome at the priory, because she has an invitation!'

Belinda had a horrible thought. She remembered a phone conversation, just yesterday. 'Paula!'

'Is that your friend?'

'Yes,' said Jonathan, speaking up while Belinda considered exactly what they had done. They had created a loophole for André's worst enemy to sneak up on him. 'But what has she done with our Paula, the real one?' Jonathan demanded.

'Put her to sleep for a while,' answered Michiko, her smooth brow puckering. 'I think. I didn't seem to sense anything that indicated permanent harm.'

'Dear God,' whispered Belinda, letting out the breath she hadn't realised she was holding.

'But what can I do?' demanded Jonathan. 'I don't have any special powers.'

'You have your manly charms,' observed Michiko, her fine eyebrows quirking with wry humour. 'If there's one thing that we know Isidora delights in, it's to steal another woman's lover. She simply can't resist it.'

'But how will she know?' persisted Jonathan, looking down at his hands which Michiko still held.

'She's not a mind reader,' said the Japanese, releasing him with an encouraging little shake, 'but she's an expert at making people say more than they want to. She uses her persuasive powers. Drugs. Flattery. Her body.' She smiled narrowly. 'She will know a great deal about you two and your relationship.' Suddenly, although it was well nigh impossible, Michiko seemed to blanch beneath her make-up. 'Your friend ... Would she have carried any photographs of you with her? Any image of any kind?'

Belinda considered. 'Not to my knowledge,' she said, desperately trying to remember the last time she and Jonathan had been photographed. 'Why?'

'If Isidora realises how like Arabelle you are, she will stop at nothing to destroy you, as well as Arabelle's vial.' Michiko clenched her hands together, clearly thinking and scheming. 'She knows about the ritual of the freeing. Even though André has her grimoire. It's not something she's likely to overlook.'

'Look, I'm almost certain she won't have any snaps of us,' offered Jonathan hopefully.

'And if she does,' Belinda continued for him, trying to rationalise even though it wasn't easy, 'it'll be pictures of you, Johnny boy, not me.' She flashed him a reassuring grin. '*You're* the one she fancies!'

'Really?' said Jonathan, momentarily distracted.

'Good! Excellent!' said Michiko, her voice suddenly strong and resonant. 'If Isidora knows there's a relationship to be split up, then she will be interested in you, Jonathan. Would you be prepared to have sex with her? As a distraction?'

Jonathan went very pink and Belinda didn't know whether to laugh or protest. The whole situation suddenly seemed to her like a kind of black, or deeply gothic blue, comedy, and she looked from her boyfriend to Michiko and back again.

'It seems only fair,' she observed, her lips shaping themselves without her permission into a grin. 'I get to make love with a sorcerer, and you get a sorceress.'

'I – I don't know if I'll be able to get it up,' said Jonathan, his face so serious that Belinda did laugh. Michiko too.

'Your friend, Paula, are you attracted to her?' enquired the Japanese woman frankly.

Belinda listened carefully for the answer, but Jonathan said, 'She's quite attractive, but I've never really thought of her as fanciable . . . Not really.'

'I think you will find her a good deal more "fanciable" tonight, my young friend,' said Michiko, eyeing him. 'Isidora's powers of seduction are prodigious . . . I don't even think a change of face will cramp her style.'

He's here! He's here somewhere, thought Isidora, slamming the door of the car she had purloined along with Paula Beckett's face.

Glancing towards the house before her, which seemed to brood in the soft amber twilight, she could sense the presence of André all around her. She could already feel the delicious thrill of conquest, a sensation so erotic it

263

almost made her knees go weak. Or it would have done so if she had been other than what she was. Her quarry – so long pursued – was almost hers for the taking, and if she had felt like it she could have sought him out immediately. But it was so much more satisfying to savour the dénouement, to stretch it out, and make the most of the build-up.

As she walked determinedly across the gravel, a young man appeared at the top of the steps. She had never seen him before, but all the laws of probability pointed to him being Jonathan – the one a slightly drugged and very drunk Paula had admitted she was half in love with. Totally confident, Isidora called out to him. 'Jonathan! Hello!'

The young man's smile seemed a little guarded as he came down the steps, and in the few seconds before he reached her, Isidora studied him.

Was something wrong? Did he know something?

'Hi! So you found us all right,' he said. 'I was a bit worried with it being so late.' After a moment's hesitation, he slid his arm around her. 'Boy, am I glad you're here!'

'I'm glad to be here,' replied Isidora, rather liking the feel of his arm. She had not expected much of the gullible Paula's most likely just as gullible friends, and had been prepared to simply brush them aside now she was here. But this dark, wiry youth was quite tempting. A toothsome morsel she could toy with while anticipating her triumph.

'Where's Belinda?' she asked, as Jonathan led her up the stairs, his arm still around her. 'I thought she'd be here to meet me too.'

'God knows!' he replied, sounding cross. 'She said she had a headache and she wanted to lie down. But . . . well . . .' He faltered, his face tight.

'What is it?' demanded Isidora, stopping in what was a most impressive hall, with – she noted gleefully – several portraits of her prey upon its walls. 'Something wrong between you?' She reviewed her memory for things Paula had said. 'The holiday spirit not bringing you together after all?'

The young man appeared to hesitate, then his words tumbled out in a jerky rush. 'I – I've been really exhausted since we got here ... I think I was ill or something, and I slept a lot. And I thought Lindi was taking it easy too, but it turned out she wasn't.' His expression looked set, and his rather seductive mouth was tense. 'She was ... She was ... Bloody hell, I think she's been playing around with this fucking André ... this Count Whotsit ... Our oh so gracious, oh so generous host!'

'Oh, that's awful!' exclaimed Isidora, putting her arm around him, her loins almost melting with pure delight. 'How could she? You poor thing!'

It was too delicious. Dissent in the camp. Perhaps she could set about seducing both of these delightful young things? Deprive André of his comforts, and flaunt a fresh pair of conquests in front of him, before she finally took away his freedom? The slut Belinda obviously deserved punishing rather than pleasuring, but perhaps there would be time to do both?

'Come quickly! We must hurry now,' urged Michiko, leading Belinda down a narrow back staircase. The Japanese woman was negotiating the narrow stone treads with the greatest of ease, despite the fantastically elaborate beauty of her clothing. In her traditional geisha garb she was almost unrecognisable.

Hurrying as best she could behind Michiko, Belinda knew now what had been in the boxes delivered this morning. A many-layered kimono in sumptuous brocade; a sash or obi, which fastened in an immense, folded bow of enormous complexity; a formal wig, shaped into high, stiff coils and adorned with flowers and delicately beaded combs. All these elements – combined with her white, painted face and her peculiar clog-like footwear – seemed to transform Michiko into a creature of even greater mystery, and of complete refinement and total femininity, yet they detracted not one whit from her power.

The foot of these particular stairs led out into a small courtyard at the back of the house, which was only a few strides away from the chapel. With any luck, Jonathan had already steered Isidora towards the library – luring her with his sob story and his willingness to be seduced – but it was still not wise to linger long outside.

The heavy door of the chapel was pushed to, and when Belinda opened it and entered with Michiko, she felt a frisson of cool excitement ripple through her. In the gathering twilight, the old nave looked very different to the way it had looked when she had last visited the chapel.

There were hothouse flowers everywhere; their scents heavy in the air, their brilliant colours muted in the strange light. Candles were burning in various candelabra and torches stood in wall sconces, but the radiance they all exuded was fuzzy. It seemed to hug itself unto itself; and Belinda realised she hadn't seen the slightest hint of it outside. There was nothing visible to alert the predator to their presence.

The heavy oak table had been moved – by Oren's massive strength, no doubt – and now stood more or less in the centre of the chapel. Its surface was covered with a beautifully embroidered quilt and a selection of cushions, and the very sight of it made Belinda's loins clench. It was there that she would lie entwined with André.

She did not at first see her prospective paramour; it took her a moment to notice his presence in the shadows. He was sitting on the gleaming old pew where Michiko had sat, only last night, to inflict punishment. He was wearing what appeared to be a long cloak of lustrous silk, decorated with stars picked out in silver thread, and his head was bowed as if in private contemplation. On his lap he had a small rosewood box, the one Belinda had seen in his tower chamber, and as his fingers moved across it, it seemed to glow. When Michiko called his name, he looked up slowly, his hand still possessive on the box and its intricate carvings.

'It's time,' said Michiko gently, gliding towards him. 'We must do it now, before Isidora detects our purpose.'

André rose, still cradling the box, and stepped forward in readiness, but when his eyes met Belinda's own, they mirrored her fears.

Jonathan trembled as Isidora's cool arm slipped around him. This was the most terrifying thing that had ever happened to him in his life, but what was so astounding was that the danger seemed to rouse him.

Charged with one of Michiko's spells, he seemed to be seeing things. It was Paula's familiar face before him, and for some of the time he could see nothing untoward in it; her features were the same as they had always been; pretty but to him not particularly exciting. She was just his friend. But every now and again, reality seemed to slide sideways somehow, and he would see something he could only define as a doubling. Paula was still there but behind her was a presence that was infinitely threatening. A face more beautiful – by far – yet hard and deadly as a shaman's painted mask. The face of a woman with seductive powers that made all others seem like pale impressions. Jonathan instinctively loathed her, but his penis ached like fire.

'She's been hanging around him, throwing herself at him at every opportunity,' he said, trying to make his voice poignant with complaint, 'but when *I* tried to make love to her she didn't want to know.'

Of course, some of it was true, he thought wryly, as a look of carefully crafted sympathy appeared on his companion's face. Belinda had been with André, but by the same token, so had he, as well as with Feltris and Elisa. The difference was that their various combinings

267

had been consensual and free. He didn't resent Belinda's involvement with André, but here on the front line, he had to pretend it hurt a lot.

'The bitch!' he cried, looking down at his clenched hands, then feeling Isidora tighten her hold. 'How could she do that to me?'

'I don't know,' she answered, reaching over to stroke his hands, then his arm, and then his thigh. 'I really don't – ' She paused, and Jonathan felt her fingers edge a little way towards his groin, their pressure insidious. 'Although, sometimes . . . just sometimes, I've wondered about Belinda. She's a little bit fickle. She doesn't always think. And – ' She paused again, her face drifting closer to his, her perfume somehow thickening and becoming mesmeric, ' – I've never mentioned it before, but I've seen her with other men too.'

'The bitch!' repeated Jonathan, feeling full of a peculiar unfocused resentment, as if he genuinely had been cuckolded.

'Don't let it upset you, Jonathan,' came the silkiest voice in his ear. 'You're a handsome man. Intelligent. You don't have to take such treatment. You could have any woman you wanted.'

As she kissed his neck, so delicately he almost didn't feel it, Jonathan fought to retain a hold on reality. This was the enemy, the creature who would damn his new friend, his first and possibly only male lover, for ever. He was supposed to seduce Isidora, or to allow her to seduce him, but it seemed quite wrong to feel so attracted.

'Jonathan,' she whispered, planting kisses along his jaw and across his cheeks. 'Forget her.' Her hand slid the last few inches up his thigh, out of the neutral zone, and became a positive caress against his groin. 'I've always been attracted to you. I've always wanted you. I'll make you happier than Belinda ever could.'

Her touch was so light yet so commanding that Jonathan groaned. His cock leapt in her cradling hand, as if trying to burrow out of his jeans and get at her. He felt her lips settle at the corner of his mouth.

Realising now that he would have no trouble feigning or generating desire for this woman he knew and yet didn't know, he lifted his hand, cupped her cool chin, and angled her face to his for a kiss.

Immediately, her tongue shot into his mouth, brooking no resistance as it explored and moistly probed. Even as he yielded, he could feel her deft fingers tackling his zip, whizzing it down effortlessly, then parting his fly. Within seconds his cock was in her hand.

'You don't know how long I've wanted this to happen,' murmured Isidora huskily, nibbling at his lower lip as she manipulated his penis.

'Same here!' gasped Jonathan, for a moment half-believing it was true, then almost immediately hating himself for what he was feeling. There was a sort of loathsome voluptuousness to the way she was touching and rubbing him, and he suddenly understood the sweet, sickly lure of forbidden fruit – and how bad women down the ages had been adored.

'Shall we go to my room?' he said, almost choking on the words, he felt so aroused. His sex had swollen and hardened so much that it seemed to be an iron bar dragging on his belly; a rod of engorged flesh that would explode if he didn't soon find release.

'No, why wait?' growled Isidora, sliding herself sinuously off the sofa and on to the rug, and dragging Jonathan down with her by his cock. 'Let's get comfortable right here,' she urged, and with one last provocative squeeze, set free his cock. 'You're not scared of being found out, are you?' she teased, beginning to undress for him with no apparent qualms.

Jonathan had seen Paula in a bathing suit on several occasions, but as Isidora slipped off her last garments – a thin white bra and panties – he experienced a lack of phase between image and illusion. The revealed body

269

was undeniably Paula's, but it had never seemed so irresistible until now.

'Touch me!' the sorceress ordered, lying back on the antique rug and parting her legs. Jonathan could instantly see every detail – her copious juices trickling down over her inner thighs and bottom, the swollen puffiness of her vulva and her clitoris enlarged and standing out, as if to invite the ministrations of a man.

'Jonathan, I command you to touch me!' Isidora cried hoarsely, reaching down to part her outer labia with her fingers.

Jonathan obeyed. He felt both entranced by what was so blatantly offered, and afraid of what would happen if he refused it. As he slipped the tips of his fingers into her furrow, he found that the unusual coolness of her skin did not extend to her genital organs. The wet terrain between her thighs was burning hot, and he felt it ripple as if further to entice him. When he began to rub her, her thighs trapped his hand like a vice.

'Yes!' she crooned, reaching up and wrapping her whole self around him. Her body rocked and she ground her nakedness against his still clothed torso, then she growled like a lioness in evident pleasure, her vulva tensing and relaxing beneath his touch.

Isidora's orgasm seemed to last for an eternity, exciting Jonathan beyond measure in return. He felt as if he were hovering on the edge of a brink of some kind, engaged in a dangerous sport that could kill him at any second; holding his breath, ready to soar up or descend. Adrenalin pumped and his heart was thudding wildly.

As he hesitated, Isidora ceased her writhing then sat up straight and pushed him backwards, looming over him.

When she murmured, 'Your turn,' he felt his perilous plunge begin.

Belinda suddenly felt embarrassed as well as frightened. How could she just make love like this; in cold blood, in plain sight, with no preamble? How could she even begin when she knew how it might end?

And if she had doubts, might not André have them too?

As if reading her thoughts precisely, he looked up from his contemplation of the glowing rosewood box. 'Come here,' he said softly to Belinda, his face a little eerie in the rising blue radiance.

She went to him and sat down on the pew beside him, as Michiko set about some complex, arcane task which involved muted chanting and the burning of incense.

'I know,' said André as Belinda sat down. 'This must seem so contrived to you, so strange.' He smiled, and his blue eyes twinkled in a way that was so normal and boyishly appealing that she felt the first twist of sweet desire in her belly. 'And you are right. It is the most unnatural reason to make love, under the most unnatural of circumstances. But if things were different...' He shrugged and let his breath out in a sigh.

Noticing a fluctuation in the quality of the light, Belinda looked down at the box on André's lap, resting among the folds of his luxurious silken cloak.

How could someone live in there? And that someone; how might she feel about what André had implied? That in other circumstances, he would happily have betrayed her with Belinda.

She looked up again, and saw that he had been staring at the box as well. 'You could have been friends,' he said, his voice barely audible. 'Sisters even, soul sisters. You are so alike, so akin in many ways... Here!' he said suddenly, lifting the box and offering it to Belinda.

She hesitated, her fingers pleating the thin muslin of her dress.

'She will not bite,' assured André, smiling.

Belinda took the box and immediately felt a diffuse impact. A force. A presence. The wood was cool to the touch, but her brain twisted the message in its interpretation somehow, and Belinda perceived it as warmth.

She felt a great rush of emotion, a recognition, a kindred feeling that was so powerful it was almost erotic. Without thinking she found herself stroking the box, almost petting it. She felt a great urge to open it and look inside.

'Go ahead,' said André.

Or was it André? There had been a strange almost ringing quality to the words, as if it had not only been him who had spoken.

Within the box was a stoppered crystal flask which was filled with a swirling hazy substance that could be defined as neither liquid nor gas. The colour was incredible – the simple word 'blue' was not sufficient to encompass it. It was sky; it was ocean; it was the most exquisite jewel-blue, sapphire or lapis lazuli. The substance – the 'personality' – was formless, yet Belinda's senses told her she was looking at a smile. The essence of a greeting, of a touch; the feeling of love.

'Hello,' she whispered, letting her fingertips rest on the vial, and experiencing another surge of the disembodied impression of welcome. It was the psychic equivalent of a hug. An embrace of sisterhood and all that it entailed, an emotion that dispersed her fears and doubts. She felt a sudden eagerness to know this, her strange sibling, better; to share her life and her mind, if only briefly.

'Come, it is time,' said a voice that sounded as if it came from miles away. Belinda looked up and saw Michiko standing over them, an imposing figure in her ornate wig and her layered silk finery. She was holding out her hands, ready to receive the precious container. Belinda kissed the vial, feeling its cool surface tingle on her lips like sherbet, then closed the box and passed it reverently to Michiko.

'So we begin,' said André, rising at Belinda's side and offering his hand to assist her to her feet.

As Michiko bowed, holding the box in her slender white hands, Belinda let André lead her courteously towards the table.

* * *

'Oh God!' moaned Jonathan as hot sensation surged through him in waves. Isidora was above him, astride his loins, her naked body bouncing up and down on him, her cool vagina a tight sleeve around his cock.

'It's nothing to do with him,' she growled, swivelling her hips in a way that seemed more animal than human – if that was what she was, or ever had been.

Jonathan hardly dared look up at her as she rode him. The more he saw of her in the throes of copulation, the less he could see of familiar Paula. The features above him were those of his friend and colleague, but the expression and the frenzy were dark and alien. He had never really fancied Paula, much less been to bed with her, but instinct told him she could never be like this.

Isidora was using him, engulfing him, overwhelming him. He felt as if he were being drained dry by a bottomless black void; his vital energy being siphoned from him through his cock. Yet again, she circled her pelvis, then jerked down hard.

'Caress me, Jonathan,' she urged, her voice harsh and raw with sex as she clasped his limp hands then clutched them to her breasts.

He groaned, feeling the resilient orbs of flesh against his fingers, and hating himself for the way his body reacted. His penis stiffened and lurched within the confines of her body, and his balls felt like boiling fiery stones. Without conscious thought, he began to knead her breasts.

'Yes!' she squealed, squeezing him in return, her inner muscles flexing on his shaft.

Jonathan whimpered, bucking his hips up against her and getting a low, feral grunt of appreciation. This was the wildest, darkest most breathtaking sex he had ever experienced, the whole process rendered profoundly thrilling because of the danger. He had a strong but illogical feeling that Isidora was fully aware that he knew she wasn't Paula, and was putting him through the grinder in order to drive that awareness home. She was fucking him into submission, and making him too much hers to protest. And though he didn't know how, she was keeping him hard beyond his endurance. Under treatment like this, he should have ejaculated many minutes ago.

'Oh, this is so good,' she growled, grabbing his hair and wrenching him up from the rug beneath them to kiss his gasping lips. His hands, still holding her breasts, were squashed between their bodies. 'Isn't this good?' she demanded of him, the words distorted by the mashing of their mouths and the duelling of their tongues.

Jonathan's scalp hurt furiously where she pulled at him, and his back felt ready to snap in two, but his entire groin was one pulsating well of ecstasy. It was as if his cock was about to explode in the very next second, and that when it did it would kill him, but he couldn't summon the energy to care. His pelvis juddered, and he knew his climax was imminent –

But when he hit the leading edge of it, Isidora cried out in fear.

'No!' she shrieked. 'The devil take you, no!' And even as Jonathan spurted, she was leaping up and off him, a startling transformation beginning before his pleasure-blurred eyes.

Staggering to her feet was a woman he had never seen before.

Belinda sighed. She licked her lips. André's kiss had expunged the bitterness somehow. She could no longer taste the potion's astringent flavour.

She felt weak now, too, but pleasantly so. She didn't complain when André eased her on to her back on their makeshift but comfortable couch. She simply smiled at him, then smiled again, over his shoulder, at Michiko, who was studying the huge book on the lectern before her, and murmuring softly in what sounded like Latin.

The chant was soothing, and Belinda let her eyes flutter closed. In a dreamy, pleasant cocoon, she felt André's lips roving over her throat and her chest in an arcane pattern that must have been decreed a thousand years ago by the gods. His mouth was cool but exciting, his tongue flicking out to lick her skin. After a few moments, she felt his hands slide beneath her, lift her a little way off the quilted mattress, and deftly unhitch the fastenings of her blue dress. She giggled a little as he drew it off her then just as cleverly removed her thin cotton shift. All these actions seemed to be occurring a long long way away from her, yet she still received delicious messages from her body when André's chilly fingers touched her skin.

'I want you,' she purred to him, the words slipping from her without conscious volition. Reaching for him, she tugged at the corded silk fastening of his floating blue cloak, then pushed the garment off his shoulders. She heard a swish as it fell to the chapel floor.

They were both naked now, in the balmy night air, their bodies quickly pressing and fitting together. Belinda was aware of a thick rush of moisture between her thighs, her channel flowing as if to invite André's penis. He was hard and enticing against her leg, and she put a hand on him as he pressed a finger to her sex.

Michiko turned a page, and whispered on.

After a moment, André began to rub in earnest, and Belinda heard herself laugh with delight as her vulva quivered.

'This is for you, Belinda,' he said, pressing his lips against the skin of her arching throat. 'Just for you, and you alone.' His fingers curved cleverly, pressing on either side of her clitoris and making it roll like a bearing in thick oil.

After a moment, she came – a very clear, light orgasm that was so effortless she cried out happily. Her legs scissored and she scrabbled at his back to pull him closer, feeling her quim pulsate and joyful tears run down her cheeks.

Drifting in a perfect aftermath, she felt André lift her upper body away from the mattress; but she was so loose with residual pleasure that she could do nothing to help him. As he held her, draped forward across him, Michiko was suddenly beside them, and Belinda sensed something narrow and silky being threaded around her. When she looked down she saw it was a long length of white satin ribbon, which the Japanese sorceress was winding loosely about her bare waist. When she was finished, one tail was left dangling over the side of the table and the other was run down over Belinda's belly and then drawn meticulously between the swimming folds of her still-aroused sex. She could feel its ghostly presence against her clitoris and just touching her entrance.

She did not seem to need to question the arrangement, and she was unsurprised when André positioned himself gracefully between her thighs, then pushed deeply and surely inside her, his cock brushing the trapped silk ribbon.

'Oh my dearest,' he groaned, sliding his arms around her waist.

Belinda felt her head begin to lighten strangely. She could feel him in her and feel the satisfaction of it, but the sensations were still coming from a great, great distance. Even further than before, and through time now as well as through space.

She kissed his throat, and had the sudden impression that she was watching another woman kiss him, even though she could feel his smooth skin beneath her lips. His penis was stretching her, yet seemed to be lodged in some other vagina. The condition was peculiar, but she felt no trace of fear.

As André began to move gently inside her, Belinda felt an urge to turn her head. Looking to one side, and peering through what seemed like an oscillating nimbus of light, she saw Michiko standing beside them, her lips still moving. She was not reading from the book now, but reciting something she must have known by heart. In one hand she held the silky end of the pure white ribbon, in the other the crystal vial that contained Arabelle.

Slowly, still murmuring, the Michiko tipped the vial, and the blue radiance poured out and seemed to gather in the ribbon. When the transparent vessel was empty, the shifting blueness began to flow swiftly along the inch-wide strand of white.

Belinda would have watched, but she felt André shift his position a little so he could reach up and touch her cheek. Angling her face towards his, he looked down at her, his eyes like twin blazing sapphires, his whole face transfigured.

'It is happening ... Oh dear God, it is happening!' His mouth pressed down on hers, still moving in a final kiss that stole her senses. 'Oh thank you ... Oh thank you, Belinda,' was the last thing she heard.

Epilogue

'What happened? Did it work?' cried Jonathan, bounding into the chapel, his face blanched and wild.

Belinda felt a reassuring squeeze, Michiko's strong arm supporting her and revivifying her, and with a quick glance at the Japanese woman she said, 'I think so.'

'Yes, it worked,' said Michiko quietly, her face radiant beneath its white cosmetic mask. 'Completely. My friends are free now.' Belinda saw her shoot an enquiring glance at Jonathan. 'There is nothing more to fear.'

'Are you all right?' he enquired, moving towards the table where Belinda was sitting supported by Michiko. She had André's starry cloak around her, and she felt cold and more than a little shaky, but she could not say that there was anything really wrong with her. She was suffering from mild shock, she guessed, but otherwise all felt well.

'I'm OK,' she replied, giving him a smile, but not sure it would convince him. Then, looking more closely at her boyfriend, she frowned instead. 'But what about you? You look terrible!'

Jonathan's face was still unnaturally pale, and his hair

was standing up in tufts, as if he had run his fingers through it again and again. His clothes were rumpled and half unfastened, and he was barefoot. His eyes were almost starting out of his head.

'I've never been so scared in my life,' he said, a slight quiver in his voice as he sat down beside her. 'One minute, I'm getting it on with Paula – ' He flashed Belinda a shamefaced look, but she touched his arm to reassure him ' – and the next minute, she's leaping up off me and she isn't Paula at all. And she's screeching and whirling about, almost as if she was on fire or something. Then suddenly, "poof", she disappears! I was so terrified I damn nearly wet myself!'

Belinda could feel his arm shaking beneath her fingers. She squeezed it gently. Jonathan's experience obviously hadn't been quite the lyrical one she had participated in. Not that she knew properly what had happened. She had woken up a few minutes before, cradled in Michiko's arms, but of André and his spirit lover there had been no sign at all.

'She is gone for ever now, Jonathan,' said Michiko calmly, beginning to gather up the paraphernalia of the freeing: the grimoire, the crystal flask, the limp silk ribbon. 'Her original spell bound her existence to André's. So when he went, so did she.' She shrugged her kimono-clad shoulders. 'But not, I'm afraid, to quite the same place.' Wearing a wry smile, Michiko continued her task.

Belinda looked at Jonathan and they exchanged a glance of tacit agreement, then both got to their feet to help. Belinda felt slightly rubbery at the knees at first, but after a moment, she regained enough strength to move around carefully.

'What will happen to Oren, and Feltris and Elisa?' asked Jonathan, a little while afterwards, as they were walking back towards the moonlit house. Michiko had left the accoutrements of the ritual gathered together on

279

the table for Oren to collect later, but in her arms she was carrying the great grimoire.

'I will take them into my service, if they wish it,' the Japanese sorceress said. 'I am thinking of making a home in England. Perhaps I will even settle here at the priory. That way they can continue to live here undisturbed.'

'Good,' said Belinda, 'I'm glad about that. I didn't like the idea of them suddenly being left on their own.'

When they reached the house, Michiko bade them both retire to their beds and get some sorely-needed sleep, while she went down to the servants' quarters to break the news.

Functioning with the same sense of mutual understanding that they had experienced earlier, Belinda and Jonathan both made their way to Belinda's red room. Deep in a thoughtful but companionable silence, they got ready for bed, then snuggled up together underneath the covers. They were both naked but Belinda felt no urge to make love, and neither, it soon became obvious, did Jonathan. The peculiar events of a peculiar night had taken their toll.

Although she hadn't expected to be able to sleep, Belinda soon found her thoughts losing focus. She felt loose and drowsy, and Jonathan's presence at her side was warm and calming.

The descent into refreshing sleep was more welcome than it had ever been, and she embraced rest with a relief that was almost blissful – seeing André's smiling face as she succumbed.

The next day, in the afternoon, Belinda and Jonathan left Sedgewick Priory. Not for ever, because they had promised to visit its new châtelaine in the future, but it was good to be heading back to a normal life.

A normal life where life's appliances worked as normal.

The Mini started first time, and Belinda, who had

chosen to drive, felt convinced it had never run so smoothly.

The mobile phone also functioned perfectly, even though they had never actually got round to charging it. Jonathan rang Paula's mobile number and got through on the first try. He spoke to a nurse and discovered that their friend was in hospital in the nearest big town.

Paula had been found unconscious in a hotel room, it seemed, but she had come round now, and apart from remembering nothing whatsoever about the last couple of days, she was completely unharmed and resting comfortably. It also turned out that she had been most concerned at missing her meeting with her friends, and that her car had been stolen. Belinda smiled as she listened to Jonathan instructing the nurse to tell Paula not to worry, and that it was probably just a joy-rider and the car would soon be found, most likely in a lay-by on some quiet country road.

Jonathan's sense of direction and his ability to read maps had been reinstated too. Without the slightest problem, they located the hospital where Paula was sequestered, but as it would be too late to visit by the time they got there, they made their way to the hotel instead. As luck would have it there was a room vacant for the night.

'You know, these last few days,' Jonathan said, as Belinda walked naked into the room after her shower. 'It was all so weird, so different, like a dream somehow.' He was lying on his back on the bed, wearing only his jockey shorts, staring up at the ceiling as if its tiled surface held an explanation of some kind. 'I keep wondering if any of it really happened.'

Belinda looked at him sharply and closely, and found her body reawakened by the view.

Jonathan's limbs were strong, his torso lean, and his groin full of bulging erotic promise. She experienced a jolt of yearning at the sight of his cock so snugly contained in his close-fitting briefs; and his face too, cast

281

in lines of thought, had a sweet allure. Her familiar boyfriend wasn't a patrician, mysterious André, or a massive, golden Oren, or even a Michiko, so female and exotic; but he was truly hers, he was always willing, and he loved her. In repose, he was an innocent male temptation.

'Oh, it happened all right,' she said in answer to his musings. Turning away, she stood before the mirror and studied her own shape.

Her breasts, her waist and her hips she found pleasing. It had never before occurred to her that she was beautiful, but now, with a clear new perspective, she saw she was. Or at least, she had certain possibilities. She ran a slow, searching hand over the curve of her belly until it reached the fragrant grove at her rousing crotch.

'Lindi?' Jonathan's voice held a new note, and as she turned, still touching her vulva, she discovered him watching her.

Smiling, she withdrew her fingers and looked down to see them glistening. Without conscious thought, she raised them to her lips and tasted desire.

'Oh, Lindi,' said Jonathan again, his lust undeniable as he moved up from the pillow and held out his arms.

Belinda went to him, lying down at his side then rolling towards him. His skin felt warm yet somehow invigorating where their bodies touched.

'You're cold, sweetheart,' he muttered, pressing himself lovingly against her breasts and against her belly. 'Don't worry, I'll soon warm you up.' He slid his hands around her and stroked the swell of her bottom, while between her legs he rubbed her genitals with his thigh.

Belinda moaned, grinding herself against him, humping the taut muscle and feeling a familiar pleasure bloom. Reaching around behind herself, she took Jonathan's hand and drew his fingers to her anus.

'Oh yes! Oh yes yes yes!' she shouted out joyfully, while she rode him – and he industriously stroked. Within seconds she was coming against his skin.

'Oh Lindi, you are really something special,' he crooned to her as she fell back against the pillows, slack and sated for the moment. 'I didn't think you'd be interested just yet, what with . . . I dunno . . . André and all – '

'But of course I am,' she said, smiling and opening her eyes, reaching up to touch his face and make him look at her.

Jonathan complied, his own eyes filled with affection, then suddenly, with abject puzzlement.

'Oh dear God,' he whispered, his voice almost nothing, his body trembling furiously against hers. His cock was still hard, but the strange shaking wasn't sex.

'What is it?'

'I – ' he began, 'It – ' He faltered again, then sat up, climbed across her, and slipped off the bed. Taking her hand, he drew her with him towards the mirror. Then, making her face it, he stood behind her and said 'Look!'

'What at?' she demanded, although deep inside her the answer was rapidly dawning.

Reaching around her, Jonathan brushed her fringe from her brow, then slid his hand under her chin to move her a little closer to the glass.

Belinda blinked. And blinked again.

'Oh, I see . . .' she murmured, studying the change she had half-expected with fear and wonder.

Her eyes, which had once been hazel, were now bright blue.

Aria Appassionata

Juliet Hastings

The Story of the Opera

*C*armen, *a beautiful gypsy girl, is arrested for causing an affray. She taunts her guard, the young corporal Don José, into a dangerous infatuation so that he fights his commander over her. For Carmen, José is prepared to desert the army, abandon his childhood sweetheart, the virginal Micaela, and take refuge in the mountains with Carmen and her smuggler companions.*

Carmen is becoming bored with José's jealous possessiveness. She plays at fortune telling with her friends Mercedes and Frasquita: the cards foretell nothing but death for her. Escamillo, a famous entertainer, arrives looking for Carmen. José, in a jealous fury, challenges him to fight and she intervenes to save Escamillo's life. Micaela arrives to call José away to his mother, who is dying.

When José returns Carmen refuses to accept his love and declares her passion for Escamillo. Mad with jealousy, José kills her.

Aria Appassionata

Cast of characters

TESS CHALLONER	*Carmen, Mezzo soprano*
DAN ASHBOURNE	*An actor*
JAMES JONES	*Director*
ANTONIO VARGUEZ	*Don José, Tenor*
EMMA RIDLEY	*Micaela, Soprano*
LEO HEDLEY-WHITE	*Escamillo, Baritone*
CATHERINE GIBBS	*Frasquita, Soprano*
JEANNETTE BALDWIN	*Mercedes, Soprano*
RICHARD SHAEFFER	*Escamillo #2, Baritone*
JULIAN FARQUHAR	*Répétiteur*
ADAM SOMERVILLE	*Assistant Director*
BOB	
STEFAN	*Stage hands*
CHARLIE	
SARAH CARTER	*A Tarot reader*
DEAN	*A waiter*
BENEDETTO CORIAL	*Conductor*
MICHAEL HANSON	*Tess's agent*
CHORUS, ORCHESTRA, BACK STAGE AND FRONT OF HOUSE STAFF	

Overture

Hampstead, June

*B*irdsong and traffic noise competed to wake Tess up.
She opened her eyes and looked up at the high
ceiling. A bar of sunlight had pierced the curtains and
glowed across the white plaster.

She lay breathing deeply, savouring the knowledge
that Dan was lying asleep beside her. She could smell
his warm skin and a faint trace of his expensive
fragrance. How long could she make herself wait before
she rolled over and looked at him?

The bed smelled wonderfully of sex, a salty, hot smell
that caught at the corners of Tess's nose. She shut her
eyes and swallowed. Between her legs the muscles of
her sex clenched, squeezing together, signalling
resurgence of desire.

Unable to resist a moment longer, she rolled onto her
stomach and looked at Dan. He was fast asleep, sprawled
bonelessly beneath the blue and white duvet, taking up
more than his fair share of the space as usual. Tess folded
her arms over her pillow and rested her chin on them
and gazed.

Dan was miraculously handsome. Tess had always
thought so, and since the TV drama in which he starred
began to play to massive audiences every Sunday night,

she knew that practically every woman in the country agreed with her. The reviews in the papers called him 'The new Cary Grant' and he had that look of the forties film star, that perfection of bone and skin, that sleek polished air, even when he was fast asleep with his soft hair tumbling over his forehead and his chin darkened with stubble. Seeing him lying beside her, Tess couldn't believe her luck. Every Englishwoman's fantasy was in her bed.

She had sung the title music for the TV series and had met him when visiting the set. He had just broken up with his previous girlfriend, an actress, and seemed interested in Tess and in her singing. He didn't seem quite so interested any more, but he was still the best-looking man Tess had ever seen. Quite a catch, considering he was only her second lover ever. They had been together now for three months, and the tabloids were beginning to lurk outside Tess's Hampstead flat to get pictures of *new heart throb Dan Ashbourne and his gorgeous girlfriend, aspiring diva Tess Challoner*. In three months nothing had changed for Tess. Every time she set eyes on him it was the same: she wanted him.

But he was so fast asleep. She frowned, then reached out gently and touched her fingertips to the smooth, biscuit-brown skin of his tanned shoulder. He was warm and sleek as a coiled cat. He took a deep breath when she touched him and rolled away from her, heaving the covers up and muttering. Tess very, very softly drew the duvet down again so that she could admire the perfection of his back. He had broad, strong shoulders, and the hair on the back of his neck was kept very short, almost shorn, absurdly boyish. She leant forward and drew in a deep breath. His nape always smelled wonderful, concentrated *eau de Dan*, as if two square inches of skin produced enough pheromones to fill a concert hall. Beneath the delicate, vulnerable skin of his neck his spine curved away in a fluid groove, inviting her to run her fingers down between his shoulder blades, down behind his ribs and his taut flanks, down to where the arches of his muscular buttocks lifted the duvet with their unexpected softness.

She sniffed his neck again. He murmured complainingly and fumbled for the duvet. Tess drew back a little and crossed her arms, lifting her full breasts. Her nipples were tight and erect, signalling the desire that Dan's body awoke in her. But to wake him up ... She sighed and pushed back the covers on her side of the bed and got up.

It was warm in the room. Tess stood naked before the window, letting the bar of June sunlight trickle over her pale skin. She linked her hands and stretched them high above her head, closing her eyes and breathing deeply. The muscles of her rib cage obeyed her, stretching outwards to draw in air, the singer's raw material. She let out the air slowly, playing the breath steadily through the column of her throat.

The tall mirror in the corner of the big room reflected her figure. She was a little above middle height and profoundly feminine in shape. Her breasts were splendid, high and full and lush, and her shoulders and arms deserved a Victorian evening gown to show them off. Her waist was narrow when her lungs were not full of air. Below the tuck of her waist her buttocks and thighs were rounder than was convenient. It was always hard for her to look convincing in a boy's part, which singers in her mezzo soprano range often needed to do. She had shapely calves and ankles and big, businesslike feet and hands. Catching sight of herself in the mirror, she leant over a little so that the bar of sunlight fell on her face. It illuminated a heavy dark mane of shoulder-length, tousled hair, falling in unruly waves rather than curls and sparking in the sunlight with a fiery auburn glow. Her skin was very white. She had a true redhead's porcelain skin, and sunlight brought her out into golden freckles, never a tan. She shook back the rough tendrils of fringe that hung over her high forehead and stepped a little closer to the mirror, examining her face. Striking, rather than beautiful: good in stage make-up or photographed in black and white. Unforgettable, according to her agent's blurb. She had high, sharp cheekbones, arched dark brows over heavy-lidded green eyes, a strong, narrow nose and a wide, generous, full-lipped mouth. Normally the corners of her lips were curved upwards in a faint unconscious smile. Now she tugged forward her hair to shade her face and pouted at the mirror, trying to command a sensual, smouldering look. It didn't really work, and she laughed at herself.

In the bed Dan moved, rolling over and flinging out one arm. Tess looked at him with a surge of sensual yearning and caught her breath, longing to go over and kiss him and wake him like a prince in a fairy tale. But somehow she didn't dare. Instead she stooped and picked up her silk overshirt from the floor and slipped it on as she went towards the kitchen.

Not many young singers can afford a flat next to Hampstead Heath. Nor could Tess. She had inherited the flat from her grandmother, who had also been a singer, though in music hall, not in opera. It was the top floor of a grand Victorian house. Tess's bedroom had once been the nursery and her big, high sitting room had been the children's playroom. She had a big old rocking-horse in the corner of the room, to recall its previous existence and because she liked rocking-horses. The kitchen, which looked out over the Heath, had once been the nurse's own bedroom. It was bright with sunshine, and green with the reflected light from the trees outside.

Tess pottered about in the kitchen for a few moments, making a pot of tea: Darjeeling, which Dan preferred. Left to himself he might well have started the day with a glass of wine, but Tess tried to keep his alcohol intake fairly low on the grounds that actors need to take as much care of their voices as singers do. As she filled the pot, she heard footsteps in the flat and the sound of water running in the bathroom. Dan must have surfaced.

She worked faster, pouring the tea deftly into brightly coloured mugs. With a mug in each hand, she went back through the living room and into the glowing dimness of the bedroom.

Dan was back in bed, his eyes shut. She came towards him a little hesitantly, one step at a time, wondering if he had gone back to sleep. When she was within touching distance of him he opened his eyes and raised his perfect brows at her.

'You woke me up,' he accused her. 'What are you, a bloodhound, sniffing at my neck?'

'Sorry,' Tess said guiltily, offering the tea by way of recompense. Dan looked supercilious, but accepted the mug, sniffed the fragrant steam and took a tentative sip. Tess pulled back the duvet and got into bed beside him. His body was perfectly proportioned, smooth and glossy as an ancient Greek statue. She drank a little of her own tea and put the mug down on the bedside table. Her fingers itched to stroke Dan's close-grained, silky, tanned skin. But she was shy of initiating lovemaking, uncertain where to start, unsure of herself as much as of him.

There was silence. Tess raised her eyes from the ridges of muscle on Dan's flat belly and saw that he was looking at her quizzically. He said archly, 'See anything you like?'

'You know I do,' Tess managed to say. She wanted him so much that she was beginning to tremble.

Dan quirked the corner of his mouth in a half smile and set down his mug of tea. He pushed the duvet off him, down to the end of the bed, revealing the long lean length of his muscular body. Tess's throat went dry and she swallowed convulsively. His prick was already hard, lying flat against his belly, gleaming in the glow of sunlight through the open curtains. Dan stretched out on the bed, lifting his hands above his head, and closed his eyes. He said lazily, 'You know what I like.'

A word of permission was all that Tess needed. With a little moan of suppressed excitement she leant forward and laid her cheek on the taut plane of his abdomen, staring open-mouthed at the wonderful smooth column of his cock. His masculine, subtle smell filled her nostrils. Shivers of desire crawled between her shoulder blades and made her nipples ache. Her lips felt the softness of his belly, moved a little so that her tongue could explore the shadowed hollow of his navel, then began their journey down the almost invisible seam of fine brown hairs that guided her way towards his groin. She avoided touching his penis with her lips, letting its heat strike through the skin of her cheek as she moved on to the hollow of his loins. His balls were tight and firm in their lifted pouch of skin. She brushed her nose against them and he gave a little gasp, then purred and stretched, lifting his cock towards her lips. 'Suck it,' he said. 'Tess, suck it.' His hands lifted from the sheet and found her shoulders, pulling her forward over him. She would have liked to tease herself a little longer with the anticipation of delight, but she opened her mouth obediently and allowed the hot, smooth head of his cock to slide between her full, wet lips. For a moment she sucked him as she would a stick of rock, letting her lips slide up and down the length of his shaft and shivering with pleasure. It was wonderful to hear his breathing deepen and feel his body tense and stiffen.

'Ah,' Dan murmured, 'ah, that's good, Tess.' He put one hand into her thick hair and held her head still, lifting his hips towards her face so that his cock thrust more deeply into her mouth. Tess's fingers tightened on his narrow flanks, digging into the taut tanned skin. Her bottom was lifted high into the air as she leant forward to suck him, and between her parted thighs the lips of her sex were moist and swollen with lust. For a moment she imagined herself moving, lifting herself over his body, lowering the glistening flower of her vulva towards his face for him to use his strong tongue on her. He would lap and probe at her most sensitive parts, drawing her quickly to a shuddering climax as she sucked him. But she could not move while he held her head, and besides, it was daylight. She was shy, and the thought of straddling his face so that he looked up directly into the delicate, intimate folds of her sex made her shudder with a frisson of apprehension. She couldn't, she couldn't. She tried to concentrate on the wonderful sensation of his cock moving in her mouth and the delicious friction of her engorged nipples against the fine dark hairs on his long thighs.

Between her working lips his cock was twitching and beginning to throb as he approached his climax. His breathing became hoarse and determined, harsh gasps in rhythm with the thrusts of his thick phallus in her mouth. His hand knotted in her hair. Suddenly she sensed that he was not going to stop, that he meant to come in her mouth. She wouldn't have minded, but she was desperate for release herself. Fighting against his restraining hand, she pulled back, panting.

'What's the matter?' said Dan sharply.

'Nothing.' She felt guilty and selfish. 'I just, I wanted . . .'

'Wanted to be fucked,' Dan finished brutally. 'No problem. Come here.' He fumbled in the little box on the bedside table where the condoms lived and quickly covered his eager cock in its second skin. Then he reached down and caught hold of her by the shoulders, pulling her up towards him. His lips descended onto hers and she shuddered and submitted to him, lying between his hands as limp as a rag. Her open eyes feasted on the sight of his beautiful face as he kissed her. He laid her down on the bed and pushed her thighs apart with his knee. The muscles of his arms and shoulders flexed as he took his weight. Tess sighed with delight as she felt him between her open legs. She ran her hands up his arms, shivering open-mouthed as her hungry eyes took in all the perfection of his body. His cock nudged its way between the lips of her sex, easing slowly inside her. She was wet, ready, eager. As he filled her, she drew in one deep breath after another, relishing the heat and thickness of his cock as he slid it up into the heart of her. He looked down into her eyes, frowning almost as if he was angry, and then he began to move.

Nothing special, no banquet of Eastern delights, no athletic or dramatic expertise, just the most simple, basic sex, his rigid cock sliding strongly in and out of her vagina, his body rubbing against her pulsing clitoris. But the shaft of sunlight through the curtains fell over his back and shoulders and lit his soft hair with tendrils of gold, and the sight of him transported her. He took her to orgasm with his beauty, not with his body, as if a young god had come down from Olympus and taken some humble mortal to be his bride. She cried his name, clutching him with her hands, her mouth and eyes wide open as her climax jerked through her. His eyes were closed and as he came he snarled like a beast, his body arching and twisting as his cock pulsed deep within her.

She reached up to draw him down on top of her, longing to feel the wonderful weight of him. But he shook free of her hands and rolled onto his back, breathing fast, his eyes still shut. Tess lifted herself on one elbow, suddenly anxious. Dan was usually at his most affectionate after they had made love. She wanted to ask him what the matter was, but the words would not come. Robbed of the contemplation of her pleasure, she snuggled down beside him and pressed her face to his golden arm.

The telephone rang. She would have ignored it, but as soon as he heard it Dan gave a heavy, angry sigh and rolled over away from her. She sat up and lifted the receiver and said huskily, 'Hello?'

'Tess!' said a well-known voice. 'Tess, darling, your dreams are coming true. You've got *Carmen*. Congratulations, duck. Crack open the bubbly.'

'Oh,' Tess said, hardly able to speak for surprise and amazement and delight. 'Oh, Michael, really? When did you hear?'

Nothing is as happy as an agent who has just earned himself a fat fee. Michael's voice positively dripped satisfaction. 'James just rang me. It's yours, darling. Rehearsals start in two weeks. Can you come over? They're faxing the offer through.'

'Yes,' she managed to say. 'Yes, of course, as soon as I'm up. Michael, did he tell you who else is in the cast? The other main parts?'

'Sure.' There was a rustle of paper. Tess just registered that Dan had heaved himself to his feet and stalked off towards the bathroom, but she was too excited to watch him go. 'Let's see,' said her agent's voice. 'They managed to get Antonio Varguez for Don José, how about that? This will be a classy production. For once they'll have a José who looks as good as his Carmen. Emma Ridley got Micaela, nearly as big a break for her as it is for you, duck. Frasquita, Catherine Gibbs: Mercedes, Jeannette Baldwin.'

'Oh, Jeannette!' exclaimed Tess, after a moment's hesitation. 'This will be fun. We worked on a student production of Cosi once, she's great.'

'Isn't she black?' asked Michael. He went on without waiting for an answer, which was typical of him. 'Anyway, who else is there. Oh yes, Escamillo, Leo Hedley-White. Don't you know him, too, Tess?'

'Leo?' Tess repeated, her voice almost inaudible. 'Er, yes, I do know him. Quite well.' This was the understatement of the decade. Leo was the man who had taken Tess's virginity, four years ago when she was a struggling 23-year-old singer and convinced that she was the last virgin in London. 'Gosh,' she said, suddenly eager to see Leo again.

'Look, duck, I'm up to my neck,' said Michael. 'Come round when you can, will you? I'll be there. You're a peach, you'll be a wonderful Carmen. Love you.' The phone clicked and buzzed at her. She looked at the receiver wonderingly.

'Good news?' said Dan's voice behind her.

She turned and saw him standing in the half-light of the sun through the closed curtains, glowing like a fallen angel. His face was shadowed and unreadable. 'Yes,' she said, breathless with excitement. 'Yes! I got *Carmen*, Dan. I got it.' She jumped to her feet, opening her arms as if she expected a hug. 'I've got a bottle of fizz in the fridge,' she said eagerly. 'Let's get it out and have a drink before I go over to see Michael. This is it, Dan, this is the big break. It's fame for me from now on.'

Dan looked puzzled and, she could have sworn, discontented. She wanted him to understand how important this success was to her. 'Dan,' she explained, 'I did tell you about it, didn't I? Opera in the Park? It's the biggest open-air opera festival in London – in England. People have made their names from being in it. And *Carmen* – well, it's the big show of the festival! And they've got Antonio Varguez, Dan. Women will come miles to see him. There were hundreds of women auditioning for the part. Hundreds! Women with much more experience than me.'

'Congratulations.' His voice sounded thin and acid. 'Mind you, I should think they didn't have many others at audition with tits like yours.'

Tess stared at him, astonished and hurt. Dan had touched a very raw nerve. Even at audition she had been anxious about quite how explicit the director might want this production to be. She forgot the champagne in the fridge. Unconsciously she reached out for her shirt and held it in front of her, shielding herself from his sudden hostility. She said, feeling crushed, 'I think it might have had something to do with my voice.'

She still could not see his face. He said coldly, 'I suppose this means you'll be busy for some time.'

'Rehearsals start in a couple of weeks,' she said, 'and the performance is at the beginning of July. There's never enough time to rehearse, whatever it is, you know that, Dan. I'm sorry if – '

'Don't be,' he interrupted her. He came a little closer

and pushed back his heavy hair with one hand. 'Tess, this is a good time to tell you something. I, ah, I won't be seeing you again.'

She took a step back and sat down on the bed, clutching her shirt across her so tightly that its buttons bruised her breasts. Her throat hurt. She didn't know what to say.

'You'll be cut up about it, I suppose,' Dan said callously. 'But it had to happen. I started seeing Philippa a couple of weeks ago and she's told me to finish with you now. You just can't keep my interest, Tess, darling. I'm afraid you're insipid.'

It was bad enough to be dropped, but to be dropped and criticised in one fell swoop was almost more than Tess could take. She clenched her fists, trying to regulate her breathing so that she could reply. After a moment she said in a husky, choked voice, 'Do you mean you've been seeing Philippa *at the same time* as me?' Philippa was Dan's co-star from the TV series, a very glamorous cookie indeed.

Dan nodded and shrugged. 'Can you blame me?' he asked coolly. 'Let's face it, Tess, our sex life hasn't exactly been overpowering, has it? And Pippa's an animal in bed, an absolute animal. I – '

'You've been sleeping with her?' Tess could feel tears burning behind her eyes. Her lower lip was starting to tremble. All she could think about was that she had to get him away from her, get rid of him, so that she didn't have to look at him and be reminded of how beautiful he was and how cruel. 'I think,' she managed to say, desperately trying to sound calm, 'that you'd better leave now, Dan.' She got to her feet and pulled on her shirt and went through to the sitting room. She climbed onto the rocking horse and began to rock to and fro, staring in front of her and trying to ignore the sounds of Dan moving around in the bedroom, picking up his things. What a bastard. To tell her now, just when she was feeling good about herself and successful. To have sex with her and then to tell her. What a bastard!

After a few moments Dan came into the sitting room and looked across at Tess. She set her jaw tightly and said nothing. He raised his eyebrows and went to the door. She heard his feet on the stairs and then the distant sound of the front door slamming, followed by a little jabber as of journalists converging.

Oh God, Tess thought. *Ashbourne drops singer for sexy co star.* Her failure would be in every gossip column in every tabloid for the next week. She would have to go to ground, hole herself up with her singing teacher and a score of *Carmen* and hope that nobody came after her. She should have been celebrating the biggest break of her career, the part that every mezzo dreams of playing, the part that was going to make her an international opera star: but all her pleasure and pride was gone. She felt six inches high. She leant forward until her forehead rested on the rocking-horse's silky mane and began to cry.

Act One, Scene One

Covent Garden, one week later

The rehearsal room was in the back streets of Covent Garden, one of the little quiet streets where nobody has bothered to spend any money and nothing seems to happen. No bars, no shops, just grimy brick buildings and nondescript doors with flaking paint.

Tess stood on the doorstep for a moment, breathing hard. One hand was clutching the strap of her canvas satchel, containing her score – the music to the opera – and a large bottle of mineral water. The other was unconsciously gripping at the front of her blouse, crumpling it beyond repair. She had agonised over what to wear. Michael had told her the production was to be modern, contemporary, but even so, what does Carmen look like? She had settled for a plain white linen blouse and a full denim skirt. A battered knitted jacket hung on her shoulders in case the rehearsal room proved to be an icebox. She had bought herself a new pair of shoes as a reward for getting the part, smart, flat tan loafers, and now she was shaking in them.

'Idiot,' she told herself. 'Why be nervous? You're the star! Come on. Just because Dan dropped you – '

Because Dan dropped you your self-confidence has

evaporated. She shook her head and went through the door and up the stairs.

'Tess!' screamed a shrill, raucous voice. Tess looked up and ran the rest of the way, holding out her hands. The woman who had spoken was tall, athletic-looking and black, with long hair in a myriad of tiny plaits, each tipped with a brilliant bead. She seized Tess and embraced her and kissed her sloppily on both cheeks. 'My God!' she exclaimed. 'It must be six years, is it six years? And we promised never to lose touch!' Her speaking voice sounded like a circular saw cutting through hardwood.

'Jeannette, it's wonderful to see you.' Tess squeezed the strong elegant back and drew away, smiling into Jeannette's fabulous eyes, huge and almond-shaped with smoky blue-tinged whites and dark, dark irises. 'I, I meant to keep in touch, but – ' *But the last time I saw you you tried to seduce me.*

Jeannette was being a little disingenuous. Tess vividly remembered visiting her at her awful student flat after their show was finished. They had sung through their duets, exchanging parts for a laugh, and talked into the night about men. Tess had confessed that she was still a virgin and Jeannette had first refused to believe it and then become fascinated by it. They were sitting side by side on the battered futon and Jeannette leant forward and kissed Tess on the lips. Tess could still feel the shiver of mingled horror and delight that had filled her. She hadn't known what to do. She was frightened, aroused, uncertain. Jeannette put her long hands on Tess's breasts and touched her nipples and the sensation flew through her like an electric shock. She had heard her voice moaning as if it were someone else's. Perhaps, if Jeannette had been a little more gentle, things might have gone on. But as it was Tess had fought down the feeling of spiralling excitement and jumped to her feet and fled, mumbling some ridiculous excuse, out into the cold, hostile London streets and straight into an extortionately expensive taxi.

'I'm looking forward to this so much,' said Jeannette, kissing Tess again. 'Honestly, Tess, you've deserved this break. It's marvellous. You'll be fab.'

Tess wished she felt as confident as Jeannette sounded. She was going to say something modest and unassuming. Then she saw Leo coming towards her, mousy and tousled and friendly, smiling his familiar, warm, lopsided smile, and she glanced at Jeannette apologetically and abandoned her and turned to hug him.

'Hello, darling,' Leo said, putting his arms round her. He felt the same, he smelt the same. Actually he felt a little broader than he had three years ago, but that just made him more comforting to hold. She lifted her face to his and he rubbed noses with her. 'How are you?' he asked.

When Leo asked her a question he really wanted to know the answer. 'Scared,' Tess confessed, and felt better at once.

'No need,' Leo whispered. 'You'll knock them dead.' He smiled into her eyes, then stepped back a little. 'Now,' he said, 'let me introduce some people. Tess, Emma Ridley, our Micaela.'

'Tess!' exclaimed a little blonde vision. 'I've been looking forward to meeting you *so* much. Won't this be fun?'

Tess leant down to exchange kisses with the air on either side of Emma's cheeks. Emma was a tiny thing, like a porcelain doll, pink and white and crowned with a mass of tumbling curls of light-brown hair, just shading towards gold. Her body was delicate and rounded, slight but unmistakably feminine, and her voice, unlike Jeannette's, was as sweet in speech as it was in singing. Huge blue eyes looked up with an expression so relentlessly gentle and innocent that it set Tess's teeth on edge. She detested overdone theatrical luvviness. 'I'm very pleased to meet you, Emma,' she said.

'And this is Catherine Gibbs,' said Leo. Something about the tone of his voice caught Tess's ear and she gave him a quick, acute glance. Although he was introducing Catherine, he was looking at Emma with an expression that no one could mistake, an expression of eager, hopeful desire. Tess turned to meet Catherine and said something polite without even noticing what she looked like. It was absurd to be jealous, she hadn't seen Leo for three years, but the way he looked at Emma made her insides crawl with possessive fury.

Catherine Gibbs was saying something. Tess shook herself back to the present and made herself pay attention. She saw a woman who was short, opulently built, fleshy and strong, with a handsome face and a pair of fine dark eyes under a mass of heavy brown hair. Big breasts thrust aggressively against the fabric of a cheesecloth shirt which did nothing to hide the darkness of the areolae beneath it. 'I'm sorry,' Tess said, 'I missed that.'

'I was just saying', said Catherine, 'that you'll make a great Carmen. I always imagined her with red hair. You'll look just right.'

'Do you know what the director has in mind?' asked Tess at once, interested despite herself.

'Not really. But I heard – ' Catherine launched into some operatic gossip that had recently come her way about the eccentric, exotic productions favoured by their director, James Jones. 'Both the sopranos topless,' she exclaimed, 'and covered in glitter!'

Tess listened for a while, then felt herself becoming more and more nervous. She had known when she auditioned for the part that James tended to the extreme, but the more she heard, the worse it felt. Why had she got herself involved? Why not stick to nice, safe, ordinary productions? 'I'm just, er, just going to find the loo,' she said, sidling away from the company.

'Me too,' said Jeannette quickly. 'It's out here, Tess darling.' She took Tess by the elbow and guided her out of the big, light rehearsal room into one of the cold, cruddy service corridors and down it towards the loo.

When they were inside and the door was shut Jeannette turned at once and caught hold of Tess's arms. 'Right,' she said. 'Come on, Tess, out with it. What's the matter with you?'

'It's nothing,' Tess said, shaking her head. 'It's just . . .' She felt weak and stupid. After a moment she lifted her head and looked up into Jeannette's liquid eyes and said, 'It's quite simple, really, Jeannette. Did you hear about – about me and Dan?'

'Dan Ashbourne? I heard he dumped you. Stupid bastard. Actors are all the same. Brains in their bollocks.'

'Well, it gave me a bit of a shock,' Tess admitted. 'And I – I knew Leo quite well, a few years ago, and I had hoped, and – but he – '

'All he's interested in', said Jeannette succinctly, 'is the contents of Emma Ridley's knickers. Right?'

Tess nodded hopelessly. 'So frankly, Jeannette, I'm feeling a bit – disappointed.'

'How do you come to know Leo, then?' asked Jeannette. She hitched her tight bottom onto one of the cracked basins and folded her long elegant arms, looking curious. 'You must have met him after you left college.'

'Oh yes. We were in a production together, just little parts. It was *Figaro*. I had second bridesmaid and he was gardener.'

'And?'

'And I really liked him, and after the after-show party he took me home.'

The taxi pulled up outside the big Hampstead house and the interior light came on. Leo scrambled for the door and paid the driver. 'Hang on a moment while I get her out,' he had said with a grin.

The driver leant through his window and laughed as Leo clambered back inside. 'Tess, come on,' he said. 'Come on, you're home. Up the little wooden hill.'

Tess had been more than half asleep, fuzzy with lateness and unaccustomed booze. She lifted her head with difficulty. Leo's face swam before her. She realised dizzily that Leo hardly seemed to be drunk at all. He helped her out of the taxi, put his arm tightly around her waist and half-carried her to the door.

'Keys,' he murmured. She fumbled in her bag, found the keys and promptly dropped them. Leo laughed at her, caught the keys on his toe and tossed them up to within reach of his hand. He wrestled with the door, got it open and turned on the light.

'Leo,' Tess slurred as they staggered up the stairs, 'oh Leo, I think I've had too much to drink.'

'You certainly have,' Leo agreed as he unlocked the door at the top of the stairs. 'Let's get some water down you, or you'll have a prize hangover tomorrow.'

In the kitchen Tess stood by the sink and obediently drank glass after glass of cool mineral water. Gradually the waves of muzzy drunkenness receded and she felt rather better. She looked up at Leo and managed a fairly composed smile and said, 'Leo, you are kind. However are you going to get home? It's so late. Do you want to sleep on the sofa?'

Leo's pale eyes were suddenly very intent. He came and stood in front of Tess and said softly, 'Tess, I brought you back here because I want to make love to you. If you don't want me to, you'd better say so right now, and I'll go.'

'What?' Tess swayed with shock. The thought hadn't crossed her mind. One reason she had stayed a virgin so long was that she was quite dense when it came to spotting the signals of male attraction.

'I want you,' Leo whispered. 'I've wanted you right through rehearsals.' He reached out and put his hands on her face and looked into her eyes. He had a round, cheerful, boyish face, but now it was tight with anticipation. 'You're beautiful,' he said. 'I want you so much,

Tess.' He held her face more tightly and leant forward to kiss her.

Tess stood frozen, unable to react. Alcohol still coursed through her blood and her brain. She liked Leo very much, but she didn't know if . . .

And then his lips were on hers and he was kissing her, first gently and then with suddenly increasing passion. She gasped with surprise and pleasure and let him pull her into his arms, pressing their bodies together. His warm tongue explored her mouth and his hands were strong and tight on her shoulders and buttocks. Tess's nipples were aching and she tore her lips free of Leo's and flung back her head, protesting, 'Oh God, Leo, I . . .'

Leo's warm mouth fastened tightly to the hollow of her neck. 'Tess,' he whispered into her skin, 'Tess, I want you so much. Please, please, let me.' He guided her out of the kitchen towards the big, battered, comfortable sofa in the gloom of the living room. She came unprotesting, not knowing what she wanted, but unable to resist his quick decisive movements. He lowered her onto the sofa and laid his big body on hers. For a moment the sensation was terrifying. He was heavy and hot and he pinned her down like a trapped animal. Then his lips found hers again and suddenly the fear was gone and the feel of his weight was deliriously exciting and even her helplessness was erotic. His hands moved, sliding up under her loose T-shirt, pushing it up and up until her breasts were exposed. Leo made a noise halfway between a growl and a grunt and pushed his fingers inside her bra, seeking out her nipple and squeezing it as his tongue lashed the inside of her mouth.

Tess cried out. He was pinching her nipple hard and she could not prevent her body's eager reaction. Her back arched tightly upwards, offering her breasts to his searching hands. He squeezed again. It hurt her, but the pain was delicious. She said his name and caught hold of him by his curling hair, pulling his mouth back to hers.

His penis was bulging through his trousers, hard as a piece of bone. It felt wonderful and frightening. What would they do? She didn't have any condoms, of course she didn't, why should she have any? Would Leo have one? How in God's name did you put one on? She wished she'd practised with a cucumber, or whatever it was you were supposed to use. She wanted to touch his penis, but she was afraid to.

Leo was not afraid to touch her. His other hand reached down, found the rucked hem of her skirt, moved up underneath it. Tess moaned in protest as his fingers touched the inside of her thigh, stroked the soft skin, ascended. She thought, Oh Christ, elderly M & S knickers. I wasn't ready for this!

His fingers found the edge of her panties. She stiffened, expecting him to put his hand inside, but instead he very gently stroked the taut fabric that covered her sex with his fingernail. The movement sent a shudder of pleasure through her and she cried out in shock and delight. She clung to Leo and her hips began to move in involuntary arching ripples as he put his tongue in her mouth and squeezed her breast and stroked and stroked the swelling bud of her clitoris through the damp fabric of her panties. Waves of sensation made her whimper and writhe. It was like the pleasure she could give herself when she masturbated, but with an astonishing additional dimension. She did not know what would happen next. Leo set the pace, the rhythm, like the conductor leading the orchestra, drawing her onward quickly or slowly according to his whim. She lay in his arms quite helpless, responding to his slightest movement, to his lightest touch.

Then his hand left her sex and moved to the waistband of her panties and found its way inside. He murmured, 'Tess, I want you. I want you so much. Let me have you, Tess, let me make love to you.'

Suddenly Tess was afraid again. She stiffened and tensed as his fingers wormed their way downwards, burrowing gently through the soft curls of her pubic hair, reaching for the delicate folds of her labia. Tess closed her eyes tightly. In a moment, in a moment he would know she was a virgin. He would laugh at her. She couldn't bear it. Suddenly she pushed him away and dragged herself up, saying, 'No, Leo, no.'

He clawed himself upright, gasping. 'Tess,' he protested, 'what's wrong?'

She shook her head. 'Too much to drink,' she muttered, 'I need – ' and she staggered through the bedroom and slammed the bathroom door shut behind her.

It was true that her bladder was full, though she was so tense that for long moments she couldn't empty it. When she wiped herself the paper came away gleaming with her juices. She washed herself thoroughly and splashed her face. Her heart was pounding. She looked at herself in the mirror and her green eyes looked unsteadily back.

'I want him,' she murmured to herself very quietly. 'I do, I want him. But I'm afraid.'

'Tess.' It was Leo's voice outside the door. 'Tess, are you all right?' He sounded anxious, apprehensive. 'Are you angry with me?'

Tess looked down at her hands. She couldn't stay there all night, shut in the bathroom. It was absurd. She took a deep breath and went to the door and opened it. Leo blinked at the sudden light and smiled at her. Behind him the bed loomed in the shadows.

She swallowed hard. 'Leo,' she whispered, 'Leo, I'm a virgin.'

He did not laugh. His face eased into the kindest, gentlest smile imaginable. 'Tess, darling,' he said, 'I had guessed.'

It was so late that it was almost early. The first birds were beginning to sing outside the window and the dark sky was streaked with grey. Leo led her over to the bed and turned on the bedside lamp. Tess turned it off again.

311

He said, 'No, I want to see you,' and switched the light on.

Then he began to take her clothes off. She was ashamed of the battered old bra and the comfortable knickers, and more ashamed of her nakedness beneath them, but Leo breathed deeply in wonder when he revealed her breasts and her white flanks. He stooped to draw one nipple into his mouth and Tess almost sobbed with the sharpness of the pleasure. Gently he pushed her onto the bed and with one hand stroked down the length of her body. He said, 'You're beautiful.'

Tess lay very still, watching as Leo removed his clothes. Her head was spinning. It was really going to happen, it would be now. She put her hand to her mouth as Leo pulled off his boxers and stood by the bed quite naked. The bedside light glowed on him. His skin was very pale, pink and white, and his legs and his chest were covered with golden fur. His cock was strongly erect, thrusting eagerly forward from the soft nest of his tight balls. Tess's mouth went dry as she looked at it. She found herself wondering whether it was big or small, thin or fat. Then he knelt beside her on the bed and kissed her and she didn't care.

He lay down beside her and pulled her gently into his arms. She came willingly, but she was still afraid. 'Leo,' she whispered, 'will it hurt?'

He shook his head. 'Sometimes it hurts, sometimes it doesn't. Tess, darling, don't be afraid.'

'You know what you're doing,' she said, with a little, nervous half laugh. He was only about a year older than her. How could he be so calm when she was so anxious?

'Yes. Hush.' He kissed her again and took hold of her hand and put it on his penis. It was hot, silky and dry, and so hard that it startled her. It felt lovely. She lifted her head cautiously and looked down. Her white hand was wrapped around the dark shaft. Its shining, glossy head thrust towards her, the tip dewed with transparent moisture. She very gently moved her hand and Leo smiled and murmured and closed his eyes. 'That's nice,' he said. He let her touch him for a moment. Then he put his hands on her shoulders and pushed her back to lie flat on the covers. He kissed her and arched his body over her.

No, she thought, not yet, I'm not ready. But she need not have feared. Leo kissed her mouth, her throat, her breasts. His hands rested on the insides of her thighs, pushing her legs apart. He slid down her white body, brushing his lips against her ribs, her belly, the edge of her hipbone. Tess realised what he was going to do and opened her eyes wide, breathing fast in anticipation. She was afraid, but everyone had always told her that it was . . .

Bliss, ecstasy. Leo's face was pressed close between her spread thighs and his warm hard tongue was probing gently, gently into the damp whorls of her secret flesh. Tess cried out and her body twisted. Suddenly she realised how close the tension of fear was to the tension of sexual arousal. Leo's hands moved up to her breasts and his nails scratched against her taut nipples as he licked and licked at the trembling stem of her clitoris. Tess cried out again. 'Oh God, oh God, I don't believe it. Leo, Leo.'

Leo did not cease his gentle caresses. He scarcely seemed to touch her, and yet the delicate quivering tip of his expert tongue made her writhe and moan. She sobbed with pleasure and lifted her hips towards his face. His hands clasped her buttocks and opened her to the darting thrust of his tongue and the quick nibbling of his lips. She heaved and cried out as her orgasm swelled and burst inside her like a ripe fruit, filling her with aching, shuddering pleasure.

For long moments she hardly knew where she was. Then she felt Leo's lips on hers and she kissed him eagerly. He tasted of her and she shivered with a sense of delicious lewdness. 'Leo,' she murmured.

'Has a man ever made you come before?' he asked

softly. She shook her head and saw his eyes brighten. 'Good,' he whispered. 'I'm glad. Was it good, Tess?'

'Oh – ' She pulled him close and ran her hand down his body, reaching for his cock. It seemed to have swelled even further, as if his caressing of her body had actually aroused him. It moved Tess deeply to know that Leo found it erotic to give her pleasure. She wanted to repay him somehow. She licked her lips and said shyly, 'Leo, shall I – would you like it if . . .'

He smiled at her. 'I'd love it. Just for a little, Tess, or I'll be over-excited.'

Tess couldn't have explained what she had expected him to taste like, but somehow she was surprised. Things she had read had suggested that taking a man in your mouth was more of a chore than a delight. But when she flicked her tongue experimentally over the swollen head of Leo's cock it tasted – odd, pleasant, slightly salty, warm and satisfying. And when she opened her lips and allowed the thick hot shaft to slide up between them the urgent immediacy of the sensation made her moan. This was something she would like to do for herself, not just because it was good for Leo. She timidly touched his balls with her hand and he gasped with pleasure. But then, just as she felt she was beginning to understand the rhythm of his suppressed movements, he put his hand in her hair and gently drew her head away.

'No more,' he said, when she began to protest. 'Not now. I want you, Tess.'

'Oh,' Tess whimpered, feeling helpless and stupid, 'Leo, I don't have – I'm not on the pill, and I don't – '

'Hush. I've got one.' He spirited the little packet out of the air and smiled at her. 'Know what to do with one of these?'

She shook her head, wondering why Leo's face glowed so with delight. 'I'll show you,' he said. 'Tear it open, come on.' She obeyed him. Her fingers were clumsy with alcohol, inexperience and anxiety. He showed her patiently how to find out which way out it was, how to position it over his eager penis and roll it down. 'There,' he said, when she had managed it. 'Full metal jacket.'

Tess drew back her hands and looked up into Leo's eyes. 'Leo,' she admitted miserably, 'I'm frightened.'

'Don't be,' he said softly. 'Tess, sweetheart, pretty Tess. Don't be scared. You'll love it. Trust me.'

He kissed her and laid her down on the bedcover. She closed her eyes, trying to calm herself. Leo stooped over her and kissed her lips, then parted her thighs with his hand. She expected that he would enter her at once, but although he was trembling with urgent desire he did not. He knelt between her spread legs and put his hands on her hips, drawing her closer towards him. He lifted her buttocks onto his strong thighs and put his hand gently between her legs, stimulating her sex with his fingers.

A shaft of intense pleasure pierced Tess, making her gasp. She opened her eyes and looked down the length of her body. Leo was kneeling upright, watching her with brilliant eyes. With one hand he caressed and teased her clitoris and with the other he held his penis and rubbed it against her labia, over and over again. It felt hot and smooth and slippery with her juices. The sensation was so delicious that her fear began to leave her. She flung back her arms and arched her back, moaning with delight.

Leo did not stop. With his fingers and the swollen head of his eager penis he rubbed at her moist tender flesh until she was moaning rhythmically, lifting her hips towards him, intensely aroused. He did not stop until Tess's cries and movements showed that she was almost at the point of climax. Then, smoothly and without hesitation, he put his hands under her thighs and lifted them and as he did so the stiff shaft of his cock slid between the lips of Tess's vagina and began to penetrate her.

'Oh, God,' Tess cried out as a sudden pain made her flinch. But Leo leant forward over her, her legs hooked over his arms, and thrust firmly until the whole length of his penis was sheathed inside her.

'There,' he whispered. He leant forward to kiss her, tilting up her hips towards him. Tess gave a desperate, aching cry. The feeling of his hot, hard cock filling her was like nothing she had imagined. She felt utterly helpless, utterly possessed, taken, ravished, powerless.

'Leo,' she whimpered. She didn't know what to do. She couldn't move. Every breath pressed her body against his and filled her with a sort of shivering heat. 'Leo, don't, don't.'

'Too late,' Leo murmured. 'Too late, Tess. And now I'm going to fuck you.'

She clung to him and he began to move, easing his eager cock even further into the clinging tightness of her virgin flesh. Then he withdrew and thrust. Tess's eyes opened very wide and she gasped as she felt the wonderful sensation of him sliding within her. She wrapped her ankles around his hips and moaned with delight. He thrust again, rhythmically, deeper and deeper within her spasming tunnel, and with his hands he caressed the stiff tips of her breasts. Tess closed her eyes tightly and gave herself up to the sensation of being taken. Fear was gone, replaced by surging delicious pleasure. She heard her own voice making strange animal sounds, moans, whimpers, cries, as Leo's strong, thick cock moved urgently in and out of her. He grunted and clutched at her breasts and his thrusts became more sudden, fast and deep. Tess opened her eyes and looked up at his face, tense and concentrated, his eyes tight shut, his lips drawn back from his teeth like a snarling dog's. Her body was doing that to him, was turning him from a kind gentle man into a rutting animal. His hands spasmed, gripping at her nipples, and suddenly sensation sparked in her breasts and her sex, and she flung back her head and gasped as another orgasm rushed through her.

'Yes,' Leo grunted as he felt her clutching him with

the urgency of her climax. 'Yes, yes, yes,' and with a last lunge he flung himself down on her, panting as his cock shuddered inside her. She wrapped her arms and legs around him and held him tightly. Her head was spinning and outside the window the sun was rising.

'Wow,' said Jeannette enviously, 'I wish my first time had been like that.'

Tess smiled rather ruefully. 'The trouble is, Jeannette, that's what Leo really likes doing.'

Jeannette frowned. 'What, virgins? Where does he find them?'

'He found me. We stayed together a few months, but then he – lost interest, I suppose. He likes teaching, that's what it is. It's not that he was nasty to me, he wasn't, he was always really kind. I'm very fond of him. But it was stupid to think that he might be interested in an action replay.'

'He sounds like Prince Calaf in *Turandot*,' said Jeannette with a grin. 'Making ice cold virgins tremble at his touch. But honestly, Tess, don't you think it was a good start? For you, I mean?'

Tess looked down. 'He was wonderful. But – '

'But what?'

She shook her head. 'I don't know. Jeannette, I don't know. He always knew what I wanted, he always gave me everything. I don't know how to ask, I don't know how to – ' She shrugged helplessly. 'I still feel as stupid as I did then. And then, with Dan just dropping me for that – actress – '

She was just about to confess what Dan had said, that he thought she was boring in bed: *insipid*, that was the deathly word. But then Jeannette glanced at her watch. 'Oh, Christ,' she said, 'we've been in here half an hour, Tess. What will people think? They'll have started without us.' She caught hold of Tess's hand. 'Look, tell me more about it another time, yes? They've got us a flat to share, me and Catherine and Emma. It's amazing, it's just behind Piccadilly, one of the sponsors has lent it to the company. Come round and stay one night. You can tell me all about it then.'

'You're sharing with Catherine and Emma?' Tess repeated cautiously.

'Yeah, but that's all right. I know Catherine quite well, she's great. And Emma – well, I'll just have to put up with her.'

'Why put up with her?'

'Oh, she's a little bitch. Butter wouldn't melt in her mouth, but just you try crossing her.'

'She's very pretty,' said Tess mournfully.

'Handsome is as handsome does. She's the biggest prick-teaser in the business, believe me.'

'Leo must think she's worth a try.'

'I wish him luck.' Jeannette curled her lip scornfully. The haughty expression made her look like the Queen of the Nile. 'He won't be the first man to try, but our little innocent Emma is waiting for Mr Right.' Jeannette shook her head, making her plaits bob and swirl. 'God, Tess, will you keep me talking? What will James think if we're late? Come *on*!' And she caught Tess by the wrist and pulled her back to the rehearsal room.

The room was full of people now, the whole of the cast and nearly all of the chorus. There must have been two dozen singers there. Nearly everyone was young and physically attractive. Tess saw a number of people she knew from college and from other productions and she waved at them, but there was no chance to talk. The director, James, had just arrived. He was a good-looking man in his fifties, with carefully cut receding iron-grey hair and a face that was dominated by a big, sharp, well-shaped nose. He was deep in conversation with a younger man, whose long dark hair was tied back from his pale face in a neat ponytail.

'Know who that is?' whispered Jeannette in Tess's ear.

'Adam Somerville,' Tess supplied. 'Assistant director.

I worked with him last year. He's good, but he's never done a big show like this before. He's younger than me.'

'He still seems to be quite friendly with James,' commented Jeannette archly, watching as the grey and the dark head bent together in eager discussion.

'They're – ' Tess leant close to Jeannette's ear to whisper. 'They're, well, boyfriends. And what do you mean, he *still* seems to be friendly with James?'

Jeannette smiled knowingly. Then Tess forgot her question and stared, amazed, as from behind James another man appeared. 'Oh,' she whispered, 'oh Jeannette, look: it's Antonio Varguez. Isn't he *gorgeous*?'

'Whatever turns you on,' muttered Jeannette. But Tess had not heard her. She was gazing in amazement at the smooth, olive-skinned, aquiline face of the best young tenor in Europe, the one they called the new Placido Domingo. She'd seen him before, of course, in productions here and there, but she'd never worked with him or been so close to him. He was fabulous. Not too tall, broad-shouldered and athletic, with hot, dark eyes and raven-black hair that fell in waves over his high brow. His lips were perfect, well cut with a cruel twist to them that made her feel helpless.

Unbelievably, he was coming towards her, and he was smiling. 'You must be Tess Challoner,' he said, holding out his hand. His voice was limpid as a clear stream, warm and caressing and only slightly accented. 'Antonio Varguez. Call me Tony.'

Tess took his hand and managed to say, 'I'm really pleased to meet you.'

'You look wonderful,' he said, holding her hand up and turning her around like a dancer. 'Stunning. A red-headed Carmen. What a production this will be, eh?'

'Ah hah,' said the crisp, authoritative voice of James Jones. 'I see our principals have met. Well, you look good, both of you. Let's hope you sound as impressive.'

Tony smiled as if he didn't think this would be a problem. Tess felt herself blushing. James looked at her for a moment, his eyes narrowed thoughtfully. Then he said, 'All right, gather round, everyone. Let me tell you what this production will be all about.'

Cast and chorus gathered around. 'All right,' James said. 'I'm sorry the designer couldn't be with us today, but he's provided me with all his drawings. We've been working on this for some time. Now, you all know that for an Opera in the Park production this one is going to get a lot of attention. That's primarily because we've got Tony in the cast.' He extended his hand to Tony, who smiled and inclined his head gracefully, accepting the compliment. 'But I want this to be the hottest production of Carmen that anyone has ever seen. It's going to be dripping with sex, dripping, like a workout in a steam room. If any of you feel like doing it live on stage, go ahead.'

The room filled with nervous giggles. Tess glanced apprehensively at Tony and saw to her relief that he was smiling as if this was no concern to him. He said below his breath, 'I'm game if you are, Tess, darling.'

Another blush fired Tess's cheeks. She didn't know what to say, and instead looked quickly back at James.

'Here's the setting,' said James, and Adam unrolled the first of a big clutch of drawings and held it up. 'Tacky, eh? The thing is to make it like Cuba. A crumbling, corrupt régime, coming apart at the seams, everyone out for what they can get. The soldiers are all bastards and the women in the factory are all exploited tarts. No wonder Carmen can't wait to get away.'

'What about Escamillo?' asked Leo curiously. 'Do they have bullfighters in Cuba?'

'We'll do better than that,' said James. 'He's a TV star, a big star, the star of some show like *Gladiators*.' He passed his eyes up and down Leo's thickset body. 'Better start doing your sit-ups at night, Leo.'

Leo grinned, not the least concerned. 'Costumes can do miracles,' he said.

It was an exciting concept. The cast pressed closer

around James and Adam to look at the designs, exclaiming at the overtly sexy styling of the costumes and the deliberate tawdriness of the simple sets. James took them through the main structure of the opera, explaining what he had in mind for each scene and how the rehearsals would work.

'Adam's in charge of chorus movement,' he said. 'He'll be coaching you all in how to look as if you're shagging like rabbits and carry right on singing.'

Adam grinned at James. 'Come to the expert,' he said, grasping the air and thrusting with his hips. 'You'll all be expert by the time I've finished with you.'

'All right,' said James. 'Let's do some work getting to know each other. Actor's exercises. Adam, darling, you take over.'

They didn't sing a note all afternoon, just worked on exercises to build trust and understanding of each other's physical styles. They built bridges out of each other, mimed, fell and caught each other, leant forward and back. Tess was flattered to notice that whenever they had to work in pairs Tony hurried over to claim her as his partner. His body was strong and flexible beneath his loose shirt and faded jeans. She began to think that perhaps the production wouldn't be a dead loss as far as men were concerned, after all.

Adam identified two of the chorus, a man and a woman, as guinea pigs for his live-sex-on-stage simulation. He had a good eye, because the couple he had chosen didn't seem to mind at all. He formed the remainder of the cast into a rough circle and then choreographed his chosen pair into a variety of positions chosen for maximum erotic effect.

'The thing you have to convey', he said, 'is immediacy. If I ask you to hold a position, hold one that looks as though something incredible has just happened to you. Look, Tom, on top of Gina. As if you've just entered her. Yes, that's it, that's great. See his face? See the tension? And Gina, how would you feel? Yes, fabulous. Look how her back arches, look how her breasts stick out. It's that first moment. Perfect.' He slapped the man, Tom, on the rump. 'Lovely, the pair of you. I'll have you front stage centre if you're happy with it.'

Tom and Gina got up and grinned at each other. They didn't seem the least bit embarrassed. Tess could only imagine that they had known each other before, that perhaps they had already been lovers, that Adam had known and turned the knowledge to his advantage. She hoped that was the case. The idea of simulating sex with a total stranger before an interested audience was enough to make her cringe with mortification. And yet Tom was hitching at his jeans as if they were uncomfortably tight at the crotch and Gina's nipples were pressing tautly through the fabric of her baggy T-shirt. They had actually been aroused by what Adam had asked them to do.

They had finished what James had wanted them to do and now people began to drift away. Tess stayed for some time, discussing the rehearsal schedule, and then went to the stairs. She looked around for Jeannette, but her friend was already gone.

'Tess,' said a warm voice behind her. She jumped and turned round. It was Tony, smiling at her. 'I wondered', he said, 'if you fancied going out for something to drink? Or a meal, maybe?'

Tess was taken aback. 'Oh,' she managed, 'well, thanks, Tony, but – but I really have to get home. Things to do, you know.'

He smiled. 'Fine. No problems. Another time, maybe.'

'Yes,' she stammered, 'I'd like that.'

Tony smiled at her again, then gave a little Mediterranean bow and turned to go. Tess watched him, her lip caught between her teeth, wondering why she had refused. Timid, so timid.

Suddenly she realised that she'd left her canvas bag upstairs. It had her score in it, and like many singers she was ridiculously superstitious about her score. She hurried back up the stairs for the bag, found it, drank a gulp of mineral water and thought about Tony.

Certainly one of the best-looking men she had ever met. And so smooth! His attention to her was very flattering. Still thinking about him, she went through the door at the side of the rehearsal room to find her way to the loo.

She stopped in the shadows, staring. There in the corridor, illuminated by the glow of light through a slanting loft window, stood Tom and Gina, kissing deeply. Tess began to recoil, meaning to dart back into the main room. Then she saw with a frisson of excitement that Tom's jeans were open and Gina had her hand inside them. Tess pressed her hands against the cold, hard door and stared open-mouthed. Gina drew out Tom's cock, smiling and laughing throatily as she rubbed her hand up and down its stiff scarlet length.

'Come on,' Tom hissed. He pressed Gina against the wall and lifted her skirt. She was wearing delicate lace knickers and Tom shoved his hand inside them and pulled them out of his way. He spread her legs and put the head of his cock against her body and thrust.

Gina cried out and lifted her thigh to hook it over Tom's thrusting hips. Tess gasped, because now she could see everything. She could see Tom's hot, eager penis drive deep between the soft, swollen lips of Gina's sex, lie for an infinite second deeply embedded in her, and then withdraw, glistening with her juices, to thrust again. Gina moaned and put her hands on Tom's buttocks to pull him into her harder and Tom pushed his hands up inside her T-shirt and began to pinch and pull at the distended nipples of her pouting breasts. Their mouths joined, parted, joined again, their tongues darting and thrusting as Tom's erect cock darted and thrust into Gina's willing body.

Suddenly Tess couldn't bear any more. Not caring if they heard her she jerked the door open and rushed through it, slamming it behind her. James and Adam

323

turned from the production designs to look at her in surprise and concern, but she ignored them. She ran for the stairs and tumbled down them, gasping as she felt the cool air of the street on her hot cheeks.

'Dear God,' she whispered, covering her face with her hands. 'A baptism of fire.'

Act One, Scene Two

The rehearsal studio, three days later

'*L*ook, Tess.' James's strong voice sounded suddenly impatient. 'How many times do I have to tell you? It's no use just singing. You have to act too.'

'I am,' Tess protested, bristling. 'I am acting.'

'Who are you being, then? If it's Carmen it's nothing like the Carmen I've got in my mind. You're too bloody nice.'

'Nice?' Tess's voice lifted in disbelief. 'Nice!'

'Nice. You look as if Tony's doing you a favour by looking at you. Listen, Tess, darling, Carmen thinks she's the sexiest thing on legs. Of course Don José wants her! Every man wants her! She can take him or leave him alone. The only thing that surprises her is that he doesn't fall for her straight away. Tess, I don't see any of this in what you're doing. You look more like Micaela than Carmen, and I'm sorry, dear, but you can't reach Micaela's notes.' He swung away from Tess, throwing up one hand in an irritated gesture. Tess stood looking at the ground, wishing that the planks of the rehearsal room would open and swallow her up. She glanced up at Tony. He raised his arched, dark brows at her sympathetically.

'Now,' said James, 'let's try it again from the top. And

remember, Tess, you want to screw him. You just set eyes on him, and you want to screw him. I want to see it in your face.' He tossed Tess a little plastic rose.

Tess caught the flower and held it against her breast, breathing hard. She remembered how she had looked into her mirror and tried to smoulder at it, tried to look sexy. She had failed then, in the safety of her own bedroom, with her lover lying asleep in the bed. How could she smoulder at Tony now, with James watching her with cool appraising eyes?

'Off you go,' said James, and Tony began industriously to polish an invisible weapon.

Tess took a deep breath and lifted her head. *'Hey, soldier. What are you doing there?'*

Tony glanced at her and then away again. *'Polishing my rifle.'*

'Can't you think of something better to rub, soldier?'

'No!' James shouted. 'Tess, listen to me. When he looks up at you I want your eyes to lock with an audible sound. Do you hear me? I want his face to change as he looks at you. I want the sight of you to go straight to his cock, I want him to get a hard on the moment he sets eyes on you. Do you understand me? And your face has to show it, darling, it's got to be there in your eyes. All I see at the moment is a timid English girl trying to look like a stripper.'

Tess fought tears. She couldn't bear the thought of crying in front of James and Tony, no matter how bad she felt. 'Look,' she said earnestly, 'James, I'm doing my best. I just can't do it, can I? James, give me some help. Tell me how to do it.'

'Listen, darling, I'm not a woman. What do I know about it? I want you to find out how to do it. I want you to be amoral, self-centred, just going after kicks. Get out and screw someone, darling, and find out what it feels like. There's only room for one virgin in *Carmen*, and Emma's got that part.'

There was a long silence. Then James said, 'Well,

enough for today. I've got others to work with, Emma's waiting. Tess, don't take it to heart, darling, but I think you'd better get some research under your belt. Get my drift?'

'I can't do this,' Tess whispered as James left. 'I can't do it.'

'Hey, of course you can.' Tony looked anxious and concerned. 'Come on, Tess, you'll be fine.'

If he had been callous she would have been able to cope, but his sympathy was more than she·could bear. She burst into a storm of tears. 'What does James know?' she demanded, snuffling hopelessly. 'He's gay, for God's sake. What does he know about women?'

'Tess,' said Tony, putting his hand on her arm, 'you need some tea. Come on back to my place, it's just around the corner. Couldn't you do with a cup of tea?'

Tess dashed her hand over her eyes and looked up into his face. She wasn't fooled for a moment, but his eagerness was flattering. She said, 'All right, Tony,' and picked up her bag.

She had heard that Tony's flat was a gem, and it was. Right in the middle of Covent Garden, but quietly situated. It was on the top floor of an old commercial building and it glowed with light. 'Gosh,' Tess said. By comparison her cosy little place in Hampstead looked old-fashioned and suburban. Everything in Tony's apartment was modern and chosen by someone with strong and distinct taste. The floor was bare boards, polished to a waxy gleam. There was little furniture, and what there was, was made of metal, bare wood and natural linen. It looked like the design section of a glossy magazine. The walls were hung with handsome Bokhara rugs, their warm dyes of scarlet and rose and saffron providing a welcome touch of colour. The last rays of the June sun filtered through the high windows, illuminating the whole flat with a light like liquid gold.

'Nice place, isn't it?' said Tony. 'It came like this.

Belongs to some interior designer. My agent found it for me. Right in the middle of everything, too.'

'Oh.' Tess was faintly disappointed. She had hoped that the flat reflected Tony's own taste. She wandered into the big living room, reaching out to run her fingers across the silky pile of one of the rugs. There was a big black grand piano in one corner and she went over to it and pressed down a few of the keys. She picked out the theme of Carmen's first aria, made a face and turned away.

'Now then,' said Tony, 'would you like a drink? There's some wine, if you like. Spanish, of course.'

'I shouldn't,' Tess said. Like many singers, she firmly believed that alcohol was anathema to the voice. 'I'd love some tea, if that's all right.'

'Tea. Sure, tea. I may take a little while, Tess. I don't seem to have got the kitchen quite sorted out yet.'

Tess followed him across to the long galley kitchen in one corner. Everything suited the style of the flat, elegant and minimalist. The cupboards were made of a wood so pale that it was almost the colour of milk and the work surfaces were solid granite, dark grey faintly flecked with white and shining like glass. The utensils were gleaming chrome and the kettle looked like an object from the Tate Gallery. Tony stopped by the sink and looked around. 'What's the problem?' Tess asked hesitantly.

'Oh,' said Tony, 'I just haven't really found out where everything is . . .' He stood looking helpless, and Tess smiled and began to open the cupboard doors. She soon found a packet of Earl Grey tea and a teapot, an extraordinary utensil more or less triangular in shape and glazed in very brillant colours. She made the tea and found a couple of mugs for it.

'Thanks,' said Tony, accepting the mug she handed him. He smiled at her. 'Just a plain old hopeless man, eh? Can't even make my own tea.' He put his hand familiarly on her shoulder. 'Come through and sit down,' he said. 'Let's talk about the part. James is certainly giving you a hard time.'

There was only one place to sit in the whole of the huge living room, and that was a massive sofa, big enough for half a dozen people. Tess sat down cautiously at one end of it, cupping her mug of tea in her hands. Tony went over to the sound system and chose some discs. After a second the room filled with intense, threatening chords.

'Oh,' said Tess at once, '*Tosca*. I saw you in this, Tony. I thought you were a wonderful Caravadossi. They should have made a recording.'

Tony was clearly very pleased. 'Thank you,' he said, gracefully enough. 'It's a great role. Though if I'm honest I didn't really think that my Tosca was up to it. That's a really hard part for a woman. Top class sopranos only, and in that particular production I wasn't sure – ' he stopped talking, took a deep breath and came across to the sofa. He sat down next to Tess, closer to her than felt entirely comfortable. She would have moved away, but the big padded arm of the sofa prevented it.

'Listen, Tess,' said Tony softly. 'Don't worry about what James says. You're the best-looking woman in the cast. Things will be fine.'

Tess frowned at him a little. 'Tony,' she said hesitantly, 'there seems to be a bit more to it than what I look like.' She tried to smile in a careless, cheerful way. 'You know, some acting? And singing?'

'Oh, you'll be fine,' Tony repeated, leaning a little closer. 'Listen, I know you sound great. I heard you with Julian the other day.' Julian was their répétiteur, their rehearsal pianist, note teacher and unofficial vocal coach, a callow young man fresh out of Oxford. 'You sounded wonderful. You've got a world class voice. Combine that with your other assets, and the critics are bound to love you.' He grinned admiringly at Tess's breasts.

Compliments on her physical appearance were not really what Tess ` was seeking, but when they accompanied compliments on her voice she didn't feel able to reject them. Tony was obviously doing what he could to make her feel better. She said sadly, 'Thanks, Tony,' and hid her face in her mug of tea.

Tony drank a little of his own tea, then set down the mug. He looked at Tess narrowly for a few moments, as if he were trying to think of something to say. Then he shook his head, leant forward and took her mug from her hand.

'Tony – ' Tess said, drawing back a little. But he just leant forward and put his hand behind her head and held her still so that he could kiss her. For a moment she pulled away from him, resisting. Then she thought, Oh, what the hell, and opened her mouth and succumbed.

He kissed beautifully. His lips were sensitive, his tongue strong and searching and delicate. It felt wonderful to be kissed by someone new, someone exciting and handsome and unusual. In recent weeks, before they split up, Tess and Dan had hardly kissed at all. Tony moved very close to her and wrapped his arms around her, pressing her close against his hard, muscular body, and she revelled in the novelty of it. She closed her eyes and let her hands see for her. They touched his face, his neck, his hair. Dan's hair had been very fine and soft, like a child's; Tony's was strong and glossy and springing, crackling with life. She dug her fingers into the silky harshness and breathed in deep shuddering gasps as he kissed and kissed her.

He wasn't in a hurry. It was wonderful, as if there was all the time in the world. They sat on the sofa enmeshed, mouths meeting and parting, tongues entwined, and as the sun set outside the high windows the tea grew cold. Music surrounded them, swirling and expansive, Caravadossi and Tosca singing passionately of their shared ecstasy of love. Tess felt herself melting, dribbling away into helplessness, everything within her warmed and liquified by the gentle glowing flame of Tony's expert lips.

330

Then suddenly he changed, as if the sunset had freed the beast in him. He set his lips to her throat and sucked and strained her to him. One hand released her back and cupped her breast, stroking, fondling, every movement revealing a sudden intense urgency. His touch sent an icy chill of arousal shooting from her nipple to her loins. She responded helplessly, throwing back her head to invite his lips to travel down her throat to where her pulse hammered below the delicate skin. With a sudden shock she realised that this wasn't just a snog, that Tony meant to go all the way. She didn't want to. It would look cheap. She caught hold of his hand and pushed it away and said, 'Tony, please.'

'Please?' Tony whispered. He smiled at her. His eyes narrowed into dark glittering slits and the twist of his cruel mouth made her bowels turn to water. 'Please, Tess? Please what?'

She swallowed. 'I don't – we shouldn't . . .'

Tony smiled again. 'Oh, come on,' he murmured. 'Remember what James said to you? Screw someone, darling, and find out what it feels like?' He took hold of her hand and put it on the front of his jeans. She breathed faster as beneath her fingers she felt the hot pulse of his erect cock. 'Ready to help, Tess,' Tony whispered.

Tess couldn't take her hand away. The warmth, the contained energy of his erection held her fingers as a magnet holds iron. She swallowed again, hard, looking into Tony's shadowed face. It had taken Leo eight weeks of rehearsals to bed her, and then she had been surprised. It had taken even Dan Ashbourne, the handsomest man in England, four expensive dinners and two carefully-administered bottles of champagne. How could she succumb to Antonio Varguez the first time he asked her?

Because he was gorgeous. Because he was what she so wanted to be, a happy, successful opera star. Because nothing seemed to worry him. Because she admired him. Because the wry twist of his beautiful lips made her stomach lurch. Because she knew his phenomenal reputation as a lover.

On the Puccini recording the deep menacing voice of the villain Baron Scarpia sang as he waited alone in his study for Tosca to be brought before him: *God made different wines and different women, and I will try them all.* Tess half heard the music and shivered. She couldn't say *yes*. She couldn't say *no* either. She couldn't say anything. She just sat with her hand quivering on Tony's fly and looked into his face and waited for him to make the decision for her.

Tony stroked her hand and smiled into her eyes. Then he put his fingers to the buttons on her blouse and began to unfasten them. Tess sat very still, watching as the crisp crumpled white linen parted to reveal the white skin beneath it. She was wearing a pretty bra today made of stretch lace and Tony nodded in gentle, deliberate approval at the sight of her dark, taut nipples protruding through the fabric. He muttered something incomprehensible in Spanish, then put his hands very deliberately over the swell of Tess's breasts. He leant forward to kiss her and as he did so his fingers coaxed down the tight fabric of the bra, revealing her erect nipples. He began to flicker and scratch his beautifully manicured nails across them.

'Oh,' Tess moaned into his open mouth. Her breasts felt very cold, as if his fingers were icicles. The feel of him teasing and scratching at her nipples was so intense that it was almost unbearable. She jolted helplessly as if she would pull away, but she was trapped between him and the arm of the sofa. Tony smiled and thrust his tongue deep into her mouth and began to pinch the swollen pink buds, squeezing them tightly between finger and thumb in a remorseless, driving rhythm that made her body jerk and writhe.

'Wonderful breasts,' he whispered, never ceasing to squeeze and torment her engorged nipples. 'Beautiful.' With one hand he began to push off her shirt. He reached

332

behind her back, found the fastening of her bra and deftly unhooked it. Bra followed shirt to the floor and Tess found herself naked from the waist up, feeling desperately vulnerable. The skin of her neck was flushed and her breasts were swollen and tender. Her heart was thumping.

'I bet I look like one of the sopranos in James's last production,' she joked, trying to defuse the tension that she felt. 'All I need is to have myself covered in glitter.'

Tony met her eyes. His face was quite still and burning with ferocious eagerness. 'You don't need covering in anything,' he said softly. 'You need uncovering.' And he reached out for the buttons that closed her skirt.

'Oh no,' she moaned. She didn't know why she was resisting him. She simply couldn't let him strip her, reveal her nakedness to him before he had unfastened so much as one button of his shirt. It made her feel like an object, a possession. She caught hold of his hands as he began to unbutton the skirt and jerked at them, looking pleadingly into his face. 'Tony, please.'

'Tess!' He twisted quickly in her grip so that suddenly instead of her holding his wrists he was holding hers. 'Tess, don't worry. I know what you need. Let me.'

It wasn't right, but she didn't know how to say no. How could she argue with his confidence, with his experience? She gave a little half sob of acquiescence and slumped back against the sofa and let him continue unbuttoning her skirt. At last the denim fell open and Tony sighed with pleasure and leant forward to place a kiss on the soft curve of her stomach, just above the top of her panties. As he did so he slipped one finger elegantly below the fabric and before she could move or react he was stroking delicately at the damp folds of flesh between her legs.

'Oh,' Tess moaned, taken aback by the suddenness of it. 'Oh God.'

'You're wet,' Tony hissed. He knelt over her and leant forward to explore her panting mouth again with his tongue. With his left hand he stroked and caressed her breast and with his right he squeezed her sex, all his fingers working as if he squeezed an orange. Tess moaned again and arched her back and as she did so he thrust two fingers deep inside her, twisting and coiling them within her so that she cried out sharply into his mouth. Her body tensed and clamped around his probing fingers as if it wanted to draw them into her further.

'Feel that,' he whispered. His words stirred against her lips, mingling with her moans. 'Feel that. Just my fingers fucking you, and feel how good it is. And that's just the overture, Tess.' His fingers withdrew and then lunged into her again and her hips jerked unconsciously upwards, wanting more. For a moment Tony obliged, pushing his fingers hard into her aching, slippery wetness. Then he pulled his hand away and caught at her, turning her round. She whimpered in protest but he ignored her. His black arched brows were drawn down in a tight frown of concentration. 'Like this,' he hissed, 'like this.'

He arranged her on the sofa, lying face up with her buttocks raised up on the low, soft arm, her naked body sprawled lengthways, her legs dangling helplessly. The position felt very exposed, very vulnerable, and for a moment Tess wanted to resist, to ask him to love her a little more or at least to let her touch him. But he moved with such assurance, such determination that she did not dare.

Tony got to his feet and looked down at her. His eyes shone with pleasure and anticipation as they moved up and down the length of her naked body. She lay very still, looking up at him, feeling his gaze on her skin almost like a physical touch. He had made her assume such a lewd position, the soft mound of her sex lifted and thrust towards him, that she did not know how to react. As she lay there in the twilight, breathing fast, she realised that she was almost unbearably aroused. She

334

wanted to seize him, strip his clothes from him, lick and suck his cock and balls, grapple with his tight buttocks and make him take her. But she said nothing.

Very slowly Tony began to unbutton his fly. He moved around to stand between her legs. Taking one ankle in each hand, he lifted them to rest on his shoulders and looked down with a faint smile into the open wetness of her sex. Tess closed her eyes, shuddering with mingled shame and excitement. For a moment nothing happened. Then the head of his cock nudged between her labia and she took a long, shivering breath.

The hot smoothness spread her a little way, then stopped. She opened her eyes and whimpered in puzzlement. Tony looked down at her and smiled, so callously that she could almost have wept.

'Put your hands on your nipples,' he said. 'Pinch them. I want to see you do it.'

Tess never thought of disobeying him. Obediently she slid her hands over her breasts, found the swollen peaks, began to tease them into even greater hardness. The lips of her vagina twitched and spasmed around the head of Tony's cock and she moaned.

'Now,' Tony hissed, 'now tell me what you want me to do to you.'

She stared up at him, disbelieving. He ran one hand down her leg, down her smooth calf and the silken inside of her thigh, and with one finger flicked at the engorged aching bud of her clitoris. She cried out helplessly. 'Tell me,' he repeated.

'I can't,' Tess gasped, and she truly could not make her lips say the words.

'Tell me,' Tony insisted. 'I can wait all night. Say, Tony, please fuck me. Please put your cock up me and fuck me until I come. Say it.'

She was almost in tears. She had never uttered the word in a sexual context in her life. It was a swear word, it was rude, it was an expletive, not something that she might want to be done to her. She couldn't ask. 'I can't. I can't. Please, Tony, don't.'

He touched her clitoris again. The sensation racked her. She tried to lift her hips towards him, tried to draw his penis inside her, but he laughed and held her down. 'Say it.'

'Oh, God!' She was desperate. How could he make her suffer so? 'Please, Tony, please, please do it to me.'

'Do what? What?'

'Oh!' Her voice was almost a scream now, a scream of frustration and shame. Her body's desire at last overcame her modest reluctance and the words made themselves heard. 'Please, please fuck me. Please, please, Tony, fuck me, fuck me.'

And Tony leant forward and thrust and his wonderful, hot phallus entered her. She flung back her head and actually screamed with the pleasure of feeling him inside her at last. It seemed to take forever for him to penetrate her and she opened her eyes wide as she felt herself filled to the very neck of her womb. She cried out to him, shouting encouragement, and he held her legs close against his chest and drove himself into her again and again. She writhed like an animal impaled on a spear, forgetting her modesty, forgetting that she was naked and he was clothed, forgetting everything except the sensation of his iron-hard cock plunging into her and her hands on her breasts and his fingers flickering teasingly over her clitoris, dragging her up and up to a plateau of pleasure and holding her there and then thrusting into her with such violence that she came screaming, beating her head up and down on the cushions of the sofa and fighting against his restraining hands. In the rush of her orgasm she didn't even notice whether he had come, only that he withdrew from her as soon as her spasms stopped.

After a few moments she lifted her head and said huskily, 'Tony?'

He leant over her, smiling. 'You'll ruin your voice, shouting like that.'

'What did you do to me?' she asked. She was almost afraid. Neither Leo nor Dan had drawn her into violent pleasures. She began to realise what the phrase *an animal in bed* might really mean.

'Just gave you what you wanted,' Tony said, still smiling. 'Let's have a shower. The shower's great. I'd like a shower. Come on.'

She would have liked to pull him into her arms and hold him close, but he caught hold of her hand and tugged her up from the sofa. She came obediently, though her legs were shaking, and followed him to the bathroom.

Even then, even in the bathroom, he did not let her undress him. When she reached for the buttons on his shirt he smiled at her and drew her hands away and said, 'No, Tess, darling, that's a man's job.'

Tess stepped back, rebuked, and watched as he unbuttoned his shirt. It was warm and bright in the big marble-tiled bathroom, and she stood with her arms wrapped around her, conscious of her nakedness. Tony unfastened the shirt and shrugged it off. His skin was an even olive-brown, so smooth and glossy that he looked as if he had been polished like a wooden carving, and the muscles of his chest and abdomen were perfectly defined.

It felt odd to be seeing his naked body now, when she had already felt his powerful cock ravaging her. Nervously Tess said, 'Well, Tony, if ever the voice goes, you could get a job as a Chippendale.'

He smiled at her, not the least disconcerted. Nothing remotely approaching a compliment was unpleasant to him. 'I can't bear the stereotype fat tenor,' he said, flexing the muscles of one arm for her to admire. 'I go to the gym every day when I'm not in a production. And I like other sorts of exercise, too.' His mouth twisted into a smile and he came over to her and drew her hands away from her body. 'Don't hide yourself. Let me look at you.'

Something told Tess that this assured possessiveness was less flattering than it felt. But despite her uncertainty, she felt herself stirring again into arousal as he positioned her naked before him so that he could look at her as he pushed off his jeans. I'm a sex object, she thought as his hot eyes moved up and down her body. He's treating me like a sex object. She didn't know whether it was the sexiest thing that had ever happened to her, or the most degrading.

Tony straightened, kicking his jeans aside. He was as smooth and satiny from the waist down as he was above, except for a dark, glossy triangle of curls at his crotch. His penis was not fully erect, but thick and limp between his legs. He stood before Tess for a moment, letting her look at him, then reached for her hand. 'Shower,' he said firmly.

The shower was huge, easily big enough for two, and the water sparkled around them like champagne. The tiled walls were icy cold and Tess flinched when Tony pushed her against them, but then he began to stroke her between her legs and she forgot about her goosepimples.

He brought her to another orgasm there, leaning against the wall of the shower, whimpering and shaking and almost falling as his clever fingers caressed her and the tingling water poured over her naked breasts. Then he turned off the water and yanked open the door of the cubicle, flung a towel onto the floor and pushed Tess down onto it. He dropped on top of her, his wet body sliding against hers, and she reached out eagerly for him, wanting to touch him, to explore the silkiness of his skin. But this was not what Tony had in mind. He crawled up over her, straddling her throat with his strong thighs, and with his hand guided his now swollen cock towards her lips.

Tess opened her mouth eagerly to take him in. He gave a sharp, wordless cry as her lips framed themselves into a tight O and caressed the thick wet stem of his

338

glistening penis. She lifted her hands to stroke the taut arches of his buttocks and he growled and pushed his hips forward, driving his hot shaft so deeply into her mouth that she almost choked. She had no choice, his weight was above her, pinning her down, forcing her to accept him as he thrust himself deeper and deeper, working his cock to and fro between her lips as if he was fucking her mouth. The sensation was frightening and yet oddly liberating. Even Dan, who loved more than anything else to have her suck his cock, even Dan had never sat over her face and forced her to take him in this way. She tried to make a sound and could not. Tony's penis was gagging her, and her helpless silence aroused her. When he suddenly withdrew from her mouth and flowed over her and kicked her ankles apart she knew she was ready for him and she reached up to clasp his shoulders and pull him down towards her.

'Not so shy now,' Tony hissed. 'Not so shy, Tess? Ready for me?'

'Yes,' Tess gasped, wanting him. 'Yes. Yes, Tony.'

'I'll show you,' Tony breathed through his teeth. He caught her hands from his shoulders and pulled her wrists down to the floor, holding them firmly above her head. She struggled, trying to pull free, but he laughed and leant his weight on her and pinned her down. 'Mine,' he whispered as he entered her. 'Mine, mine.'

And she was. His, all his, his possession, his slave, the captive of his body. If he had asked her to call him lord, master, she would have obeyed. He was strong and fierce and his body filled her with a furious pulsation of lust such as she had never known. Leo's gentleness, Dan's selfishness paled into insignificance beside the direct determined energy of Tony's thrusts. She could no more have resisted him than she could have lifted a cathedral. She did not climax again, but pressed her body tightly against his and tried to reach up with her teeth to bite his smooth brown shoulder as he snarled and plunged inside her. She was powerless beneath him,

339

and yet as he growled and her hips bucked up to meet his thrusts she felt power, tremendous power, as if he were the prisoner and she the captor. When he cried out and she felt his cock pulsing inside her as he came she writhed and lifted her ankles to wrap them around his quivering buttocks.

Then he hung over her for a moment, sweat trickling from his cheeks to the bridge of his aquiline nose. He pulled out of her with a little grunt and smiled into her eyes, a smile of satisfaction, not of affection. 'Time for bed,' he said.

Tess frowned anxiously. Jeannette and Catherine were coming to her flat tomorrow morning, taking advantage of a small gap in the schedule to practise one of their trios in private. It would be awful if she wasn't there. But she didn't want to get up and leave, she wanted to lie all night in bed with Tony, feeling his wonderful hard smooth body and smelling the odd complex scent of his hair. She said, feeling rather strange, 'I, I'll need to get up early.'

'Fine,' he said. 'Me too. I'll go to the gym.'

But he didn't set the alarm. Tess woke because her natural clock told her it was morning. She was lying in Tony's arms, as they had fallen asleep, her cheek resting on his shoulder, her body pressed against his, thighs entwined, close and safe. His skin was unbelievably smooth. She looked up and saw him fast asleep, his chin shaded blue with stubble, his cruel lips firmly closed.

Dan had never held her all night. It felt so secure, so protected. She took a deep breath and let it out in a long shiver of satisfaction. Yesterday she had been uncertain of the wisdom of letting Tony make love to her. Today, waking in his bed and in his embrace, it seemed like the best decision she had ever made.

The clock by the bed said quarter past eight, and Jeannette and Catherine were coming to the flat at ten. Tess reluctantly began to detach herself from Tony. He murmured and smiled as she disentangled herself, but did not wake.

Never in her life had Tess stayed overnight at a man's house without meaning to. She had no clean knickers and only yesterday's blouse. She stood by the bed for a few moments wondering what she should do about it. It felt hideously embarrassing. In the end she picked up Tony's dressing gown, a handsome affair of striped silk, and went off to find the bathroom.

Washed and feeling a little more composed, she moved through to the kitchen and put the kettle on. Morning was not morning to Tess without a cup of tea. She was a tea addict. The teapot was still on the cold, glossy work surface, full of dregs, and she busied herself washing it up, then found the mugs and washed those up too.

The kettle had just boiled when Tony appeared in the doorway, stark naked and pushing his hand through his hair. He saw her standing by the kettle and smiled. 'Tess,' he said, coming closer, 'you're wonderful. It's such a change to find a woman who doesn't mind going into the kitchen.'

Tess glanced at him and then quickly away again. He had a morning erection, hard and eager. The smooth column of his cock was dark, like the rest of his skin, glossy and inviting. She wanted to touch it, but she had a rehearsal to go to. 'Do you like tea in the morning?' she asked brightly.

'Tea second,' Tony said. He came up behind her and caught hold of the sleeves of the dressing gown, pulling them down so that Tess's breasts were bared and her arms were tugged behind her back. 'Sex first.'

'Oh,' Tess whimpered, wriggling in his strong grip, 'Tony, I don't have the time.'

But he ignored her. He pulled the dressing gown further down her arms, wrapping it around and around until she could not easily free herself. Then he reached round her and took her breasts in his hands and fastened his lips to her neck. His body was pressed up against

341

her, tight against her buttocks. The heat of his erection seared her through the thin silk of the dressing gown. So demanding, so eager. So unlike Dan. She realised now quite how much Dan had lost interest in her. Tony was muttering as he scourged her neck with kisses and his hands roamed all up and down the length of her, exploring her, touching her in places she had not dreamed could be erotic: the sides of her ribs, her collar bone, her flanks. He wanted her, and knowing that he wanted her made her feel so womanly and desirable that she stopped caring about whether he would make her late for rehearsal. She let her head fall back and sought his lips and kissed him. He smiled and with one hand he felt between her legs and began to tease the warm flesh there into willing moistness. Tess's body undulated around him, fixed at two points only, by his probing fingers and his consuming lips. Her breathing deepened.

Tony's rigid penis was trapped between the cheeks of her buttocks. He pushed himself against her like a cat wanting to be stroked. 'Hey,' he whispered in her ear, 'have you ever seen *Last Tango in Paris*?'

The question startled Tess out of her erotic haze. 'What?' she asked apprehensively.

'I've got some butter somewhere,' said Tony, smiling. 'Bend over.'

Tess hadn't actually seen the film, but she had heard of the infamous butter scene. She pulled away from Tony, wrestling her arms free of the dressing gown and trying to cover herself. She couldn't tell from his face whether he was joking or not. 'No,' she said anxiously, 'Tony, I – '

'Just joking,' he said with a smile, coming forward to grab her arms. His smile changed a little, becoming wicked. 'But I do want you to bend over. Bend over, Tess.'

He tried to make her turn around. She resisted him. 'Tony, no, I don't want to.'

'Bend over!' He had raised his voice and suddenly he spun her around and with unexpected strength forced her face down over the granite work surface. Her breasts flattened against its cold hardness. He pulled her arms above her head and held both her wrists in one hand, then leant forward until she could feel his hot breath on her ear. 'Do as I tell you,' he whispered.

She was afraid. She tried to move, but his weight prevented her. His body was warm and hard and his stiff cock was trapped between her thighs. 'Tony – '

'Just be a good girl,' he whispered. 'Do as I tell you. Just do what I say, Tess, and you'll have a good time. I promise. Now, don't struggle.' His other hand passed quickly between her spread legs, testing her wetness. 'Good,' he hissed. His hand withdrew and was replaced by the head of his cock, hot and smooth, thick and hard as stone, driving up inside her with such suddenness, such completeness, that she could do nothing but gasp. He penetrated her completely and then lay within her for a moment, quite still. Tess moaned and with a tremendous effort lifted herself a little way towards him so that his tight balls rubbed against her tender, swollen clitoris.

'Don't move,' he hissed in her ear. 'Do as I say. Lie still. I'm in charge.' Tess whimpered and tried to move and suddenly Tony's weight above her increased and he slapped her with the flat of his hand on her naked flank, hard enough to make her cry out. He repeated sternly, 'I'm in charge!'

His thick shaft was filling her, tormenting her. She wanted to writhe on it, heave her body up towards him, squirm as that smooth, hard cock slid inexorably to and fro within her eager flesh. But he was so strong, so dominant. She did not dare to disobey him. She made herself lie very still, eyes tightly shut, taut nipples chafing against the coldness of the stone, not moving a muscle. A sense of delicious freedom began to fill her. With Dan she had always felt responsible, as if failure to

343

orgasm would be her fault, her problem. Now Tony had taken that responsibility from her. She laid the weight of her pleasure between his strong hands, passive and unprotesting, shuddering as she waited for him to serve her.

'You have a beautiful arse,' Tony whispered. His weight lightened slightly and he arched his hips, slowly withdrawing the thick length of his rigid cock from her moist willing flesh. 'I want to fuck your arse, Tess. I will soon, I promise.' He was still holding her wrists against the cold stone, and now with his free hand he felt between the cheeks of her bottom. His fingers dipped into the damp flesh that clung to his penis and then slid back. Tess gave a little whimper of protest as she felt him pressing at the tightly-closed flower of her arsehole. She would have tried to wriggle away, but the head of his cock was still lodged between the lips of her sex and if she moved she might lose it. She could not bear to lose it, and so she lay still and breathed faster as his finger pressed, pressed again and at last slid into the virgin tautness of her anus.

'Oh,' she said, astonished by the extraordinary sensation, the dark fullness of pleasure. 'Oh, God.'

'I told you,' Tony hissed. He began to move his finger in and out, thrusting it into her arsehole as if it were a penis. Tess rolled her head from side to side, desperately fighting against the urge to move. Pleasure pooled around Tony's probing finger and between her legs where his thick cock lay at her entrance, parting the soft labia and just fixed within her tunnel. Her breasts ached and burned against the icy granite. Tony moved slightly behind her and the movement made his cock rub against the front of her sex, just barely touching her clitoris, and hot bright flashes of sensation like forked lightning leapt from her engorged flesh and made her jerk and cry out.

'Feel,' whispered Tony. 'Feel it.' A second finger joined the first, sliding deep into her anus and then withdrawing. Tess jerked again and he snarled behind her ear and tugged at her wrists. 'Keep still!'

'Oh God, oh God,' Tess moaned helplessly. In a moment she thought she would have to pull away, to escape from the remorseless, deliberate thrusts of his penetrating fingers. She could not bear the hybrid of pleasure and pain any longer. But just as she thought she must struggle, he withdrew his fingers and thrust into her again with his hot cock, spreading the tender lips and driving himself deep within her. His hand encircled her flank and began to rub at her pleasure bud and, as if he had set light to a pool of oil, Tess felt ecstasy like liquid fire flooding through her. She opened her mouth and cried out, possessed by the blazing spasms of orgasm.

Tony stopped touching her. He reached up and took hold of one wrist in each hand and dragged them up behind her back so that she was bent like a prisoner over the cold stone, crying out as he plunged his stiff cock into her with ferocious strength, deeper on every stroke. He went on and on, tireless, beating his body against the soft cushion of her buttocks. His breath hissed over her back. Then he said through his teeth, 'Ask me for mercy.'

Tess hardly heard him, didn't understand him. He tugged at her arms, hurting her. 'Ask for mercy!' he repeated, jerking painfully at her wrists.

The frantic lunges of his ravenous cock were drawing her into an abyss of post-orgasmic pleasure. She heard his order and could barely speak to obey him, but at last she managed to moan, 'Oh, please, mercy. Mercy.' It didn't feel foolish to beg him, to plead with him. It felt wonderful.

'No mercy,' Tony snarled. 'No mercy – ah – ' and as if her words had touched a fuse within him he gave one final frantic thrust and shuddered as he exploded into orgasm.

Tess lay very still as his spasms subsided. Her head ached and she was cold, but she had never felt so delectably wanton, so fabulously shameless, in all her life. She would have liked to free her arms, but she could not move until he permitted it.

After a few minutes Tony withdrew and let her go. He patted her on the rump and said, 'There you are, Tess darling. Get screwed, James said. Happy to oblige.'

Tess straightened, stretching her aching limbs. Tony smiled at her and went on, 'Don't worry about anything, Tess. I'll look after you. It'll be fine. Just do what I say and everything will be fine.'

A tiny voice within Tess told her that this was not what James had had in mind, and that Tony's suggestion was flawed. Had he sounded somehow deprecating? But it was such a relief to feel looked after. With Tony there to reassure her, she wouldn't have to worry, she wouldn't have to take responsibility for anything. She hesitated for a moment, but then she smiled. 'Thanks, Tony,' she said. She reached up impulsively to kiss him and he laughed with pleasure as her arms went around his neck.

Act Two, Scene One

Later the same day

'*D*ammmit, dammit, dammit,' Tess muttered as she bounced irritably up and down on the platform. Why was the Northern line always so bloody slow? At this rate she was going to be late.

At last the train came and she sat in a half-empty carriage, thinking about Tony as she jolted and rattled towards Hampstead. Mentally she ticked a variety of boxes. Handsome, yes indeed. Sexy, certainly. A good lover? Well, he had certainly given her several orgasms, which had not been Dan's strong point. And he was so refreshingly open about what he wanted, he didn't just lie there and expect her to service him. A bit demanding, perhaps, a bit dominant, but wasn't that a very erotic thing to be?

She was so wrapped in her day-dreams that she almost missed the station. She leapt from the carriage as the doors closed. They shut on her bag and she swore, wrestled it free and hared along the platform towards the lift.

It was a bright, warm summer day in Hampstead. The poseurs were already sitting sipping the first cocktail of the morning in Café Dôme and people were wandering up and down the high street languidly peering into the shop windows. Tess swerved her way between them and ran up Flask Walk towards the Heath and her house.

At the first junction she saw Jeannette and Catherine on the other side of the road, walking towards her wrapped in conversation. She called out to them, waved and dodged over the road between two taxis. 'Sorry,' she panted as she hurried up to them.

'Whatever are you wearing?' asked Catherine, her eyebrows meeting her hairline. 'That looks like – '

'One of Tony's shirts!' shouted Jeannette in her buzz-saw voice.

'Oh,' Tess said, terribly flustered. Blood rushed to her cheeks. 'Oh, it, er – '

'We already know you went back with him last night,' said Catherine. 'Don't bother to try thinking of excuses. Emma told us.'

'Emma told you?'

'She was working with James after you, remember?' Jeannette took hold of Tess's elbow and began to steer her along the street. 'When she came back to the flat last night she was only too eager to tell us that Tony had spirited you off for tea and sympathy.'

'Said she thought you were in a hurry to get a grip on him,' added Catherine, looking arch.

'Me in a hurry! The little – !' Tess broke off and walked on for a moment fast, scowling down at the pavement.

'I told you she was a prize bitch,' said Jeannette from behind her.

At this point they arrived at Tess's house and she was occupied with finding the keys, letting them in and showing them the way upstairs. Then it was time for Jeannette and Catherine to exclaim over her lovely flat. Tess explained modestly that she hadn't actually *earned* it, and she made them all a cup of tea.

They took their mugs out onto the little terrace carved from a small section of flat roof and sat in the sun, admiring the view over the Heath and the panorama of

London laid out below. 'Wow, this is the life,' said Catherine. 'What a place.'

'Tony's flat is lovely,' Tess said, and immediately wished she hadn't opened her mouth.

'Oh, Tess,' groaned Jeannette. 'What is it about him? Honestly, Tess, don't you think his ego is big enough already? You've fallen into his arms after less than a week of rehearsal! He's going to be so swollen-headed it's untrue!'

'And he's such a sexist,' said Catherine, scowling. 'I worked with him on a production last year, and – '

'Don't,' Tess said unhappily. 'Don't go on about him. He was nice to me after James said – ' She broke off abruptly and changed the subject. 'We have to practice,' she said firmly. 'I've only got till just after lunch. I have to see Julian at three for word-bashing.'

'Oh yes, Julian,' said Jeannette under her breath as she and Catherine followed Tess from the terrace. 'Now there's one it would be fun to go after.'

Tess only half heard this remark, and she didn't reply. She led the way into the living room. Julian had recorded a piano accompaniment to their trios on a cassette and she put it on now. 'Time to work,' she said.

They did work, hard, until hunger stopped them a little while after noon. Tess didn't have enough food in the fridge to feed all three of them, so they wandered out of the house to find a baguette somewhere in Hampstead.

A little coffee shop provided filled ciabatta rolls and cappucino. There was a free table on the pavement and they sat down to enjoy the sunshine. Jeannette and Catherine both looked at each other and then at Tess, who closed her eyes, knowing that more questions were on their way.

'Tess, don't get defensive,' began Jeannette. 'I just want to know what James said that upset you so much. Christ, it might be me and Catherine he decides to have a go at next. I know he can be a filthy-tempered git when the mood takes him, but what was it in particular?'

Tess took a long breath and let it out in a heavy sigh. 'Oh,' she said, 'it's just that he's absolutely obsessed with sex. That's all he thinks about.' It was harder than she expected to admit what James had said. The old sensation of fear, of inadequacy, came rushing back. 'And he was saying that I looked – that I was too nice to look sexy. That I looked like a typical English girl.'

Catherine looked equivocal. 'I wouldn't say you looked typically English,' she commented, 'but I know what he means.'

'He told me – ' tears were hovering on the edge of Tess's words. She fought them, swallowing hard. 'He told me to – to go out and screw someone. To understand Carmen better, you see? He wanted me just to find someone I fancied and do it.'

'So you went straight off and let Tony screw you,' said Jeannette callously. 'Is that really what James meant?'

'I didn't,' Tess protested, but as she spoke she knew that Jeannette was right.

Jeannette knew, too. 'Who took the initiative?' she demanded. 'Who started it?'

'Tony,' Tess admitted miserably.

'There you are, then,' said Jeannette, sitting back and folding her arms with a satisfied air.

'But – ' Tess began. Then she stopped and put her face in her hands. Had that fabulous sexual experience with Tony been for nothing? Had she learnt nothing?

'Tess,' Catherine said, quite gently, 'I know what James meant. Jeannette was right. He sees Carmen as sexually very aggressive. That's why you needed to take the initiative. Just letting a man have you might be fun, but it's not, ah, aggressive.'

'But,' Tess said, looking up with a hopeless air, 'what am I supposed to do? Go out and seduce someone?'

'Why not?' asked Jeannette bluntly.

Tess stared. 'I don't know how,' she said after a

moment. 'Or who! I mean, who on earth is around for me to seduce? Am I supposed to hang around outside a boys' school or something, like a dirty old woman?'

'Don't be daft,' said Catherine with a grin. 'There's an obvious candidate in the company.'

Jeannette laughed to herself, but Tess looked amazed. 'Who?' she asked suspiciously, after a moment's puzzled thought.

'Julian,' said Catherine simply.

Tess gasped with sudden understanding. She sat back in her chair, hugging her knees to her chest. Julian! He was young, not yet 22, and very handsome in a blond, floppy-haired, Brideshead sort of way. And he seemed very reserved, shy even, certainly not the sort to take advantage.

She would never in a million years have thought for herself of making a play for Julian. In particular she would not have dreamed of seducing one man the day after she had first made love with another. But the idea had a sort of mad appeal. Julian was so young, so callow, like a half-trained puppy. Irresistible!

She had been silent for a long time. Catherine glanced at Jeannette and smiled, then said softly, 'Like the idea, Tess?'

'Oh,' Tess shook herself back to the present. 'Well, I mean, perhaps this afternoon I could ask him round to the flat for a drink, and – '

'Hey, no, that's not what I had in mind,' Catherine interjected quickly. 'I don't mean have an affair with him, Tess. I mean fuck him. This afternoon, at rehearsal. No complications, no strings.'

'Fuck him?' Tess echoed, though her voice was barely audible. 'This afternoon? At rehearsal?' She shook her head slowly, drawing back into her chair. 'Oh no, Catherine. I couldn't. I couldn't.'

'Why not?' demanded Jeannette. 'He's cute enough. Wish I'd thought of it. I'll have him when you're finished, Tess.'

Tess still couldn't believe it. 'You mean just say to him, what about it? Then and there? In the rehearsal room?' She sounded hesitant, reluctant. And yet as she thought about it she felt a strange, warm tingling beginning in the pit of her stomach. There would be just the two of them, alone in the rehearsal room, nobody interrupting them, all the time in the world. It was like something out of a film, something that would happen to a real star. What would Julian do? How would he react? If she said, 'I want you to make love to me,' how would his face change?

Suddenly reality intruded on the fantasy. 'But,' she said, 'he probably doesn't even fancy me! He's never suggested he has.'

'He's too shy to speak a word to you,' laughed Jeannette. 'Listen, Tess, if you're prepared to give it a go, I guarantee we'll turn you into the most irresistible vamp that poor little preppie has ever seen.'

'He'll eat you up with a spoon,' added Catherine.

'Really?' Tess looked from one to the other. Excitement tingled between her shoulder blades and made the hairs on her arms stand up. She had never seduced anyone in her life. The idea frightened her and aroused her at the same time. 'Really?' she asked again, leaning forward a little.

'Really,' said Catherine. She lifted her cup and drained it. 'Come on,' she said. 'Let's get back to your place and get you ready.'

'I don't want to look like a tart,' Tess said anxiously. She was standing in her bedroom and Jeannette and Catherine were rooting through drawers and wardrobes, exclaiming over things, flinging them onto the bed or the floor for future reference.

'You won't,' Jeannette reassured her. 'Sexy, yes. A tart, no. Honestly, Tess, I don't think you possess a single garment that could be described as tarty.'

'I think we ought to start with this, don't you?' said Jeannette, holding up a black Wonderbra.

'Definitely,' said Jeannette. 'OK, Tess, strip off. Let's get started.'

Tess hesitated and pursed her lips. Then she began to unbutton Tony's shirt. It smelt of his body and hers. It was as if she was taking off her experience with him, freeing herself for something new.

'God,' Catherine said admiringly, 'you've got gorgeous tits, Tess. They'll knock poor little Julian for six.' She brought the Wonderbra over to where Tess stood naked and held it out to her. 'Gorgeous,' she said again, and with one hand reached out and touched Tess's right nipple, just fleetingly touched it. The little rose-coloured peak stiffened at once. Tess flinched and drew back, but Catherine just smiled at her, an innocent open smile, and turned away.

Jeannette and Catherine thought that ease of access was important. After the Wonderbra they handed Tess a pair of high-cut, flimsy black lace panties. It was too hot for stockings, so her legs stayed bare. Jeannette brought over a bottle of perfumed body lotion, Dune, and said, 'Rub your legs with this. Make them all silky and delicious.'

Tess obeyed. The lotion felt smooth and cool and it left the skin of her legs tingling slightly. She looked down at herself in the low-cut bra and skimpy panties and took a deep breath. She was dressing for sex, dressing for seduction, and that in itself was enough to turn her on.

'You don't want to look overdone,' said Catherine. 'How about this?' She held out a little fitted low-cut top made of cotton jersey in simple white. It fastened down the front with dozens of tiny, horn buttons. Tess took it and began to fasten the buttons from the top down.

'No,' suggested Jeannette, 'leave the top couple undone. So it looks as if more might follow?'

'But that almost shows the bra,' Tess said.

'Exactly,' said Jeannette. 'Look at that cleavage. He'll be helpless.'

'Got any short skirts?' asked Catherine.

Tess shook her head. 'I don't like them. Don't think my legs are up to them, if you want the truth.'

'This is the thing,' said Jeannette. It was a long, flared skirt in jade-green sandwashed silk, buttoned at the front and with slits in the side seams. 'This is fabulous, Tess. When did you get it?'

'Dan wanted me to buy it,' Tess admitted. 'I – I haven't actually worn it very often.'

'Wear it now,' said Jeannette, and Tess made a little face but put the skirt on. 'Perfect,' Jeannette said. 'He can see your legs, and you can unbutton the skirt to let him look at you.'

You can unbutton the skirt. She was going to offer herself to Julian. She imagined herself standing in the rehearsal room, leaning over slightly to unfasten button after button, slowly revealing her legs to the knee, to the thigh, dipping so that her full breasts were dangling before him, almost totally exposed. What would he do? Would he stare and blush and gasp? Run away? Seize her?

For a moment she closed her eyes. The flesh between her legs felt wet and warm. She imagined Julian gaping open-mouthed at her breasts, then imagined his eyes travelling down, down to the open front of her skirt, to where the negligible scrap of the panties encircled and caressed her tender mound of love. For a moment her brain just imagined that she would slip her hand down her body and gently draw aside the crotch of the panties, revealing the dark-red glossy fur and the pink folded flesh beneath them. Then she shook her head in protest at her own imagination and opened her eyes.

'Still with us?' asked Catherine, smiling. Tess's self-absorption was not lost on her. 'Good. What about these for shoes?'

Sandals, fairly high heeled, pretty but practical.

Nothing out of the way. Tess nodded gratefully and put them on.

'Make-up,' said Jeannette.

'Make-up?' Tess frowned unhappily. 'Jeannette, I don't wear make-up when I can avoid it. It's so bad for the skin, and I have to wear it on stage, and – '

'Oh, come on!' exclaimed Jeannette, whose own enormous eyes were ringed with dark kohl. 'Make an effort! Just a bit, come on.'

They frogmarched her to the bathroom and stood one at each shoulder while she put a little, dark-olive shadow on her heavy lids and thickened her bristly dark lashes with mascara. She resisted eyeliner and accepted a little neutral lipstick. Her pale skin was flushed, as if she had been running. She looked excited and eager.

'That's better,' said Catherine, looking at her face in the mirror. 'He won't have seen you dolled up before. Bound to have an effect.'

Tess's nerve was failing her. 'I can't do this,' she said. 'I don't know what to do.'

'Hush,' said Jeannette, putting her arm around Tess's shoulders. 'You'll cope. Imitate Lauren Bacall, or something. You know; *if you want me, just whistle*. Vamp him. And remember how it feels, and then Carmen will be able to do it too.'

'I tell you what,' said Catherine. 'Jeannette and I will wait for you here. Then when you get back you can tell us all about it.'

Tess went to find her bag with the score and the inevitable bottle of mineral water. When she had it over her shoulder and was ready at the door, Jeannette grinned and fished in her handbag and held out a couple of condoms. 'Here,' she said. 'You may need these!'

'Two?' squeaked Tess.

Jeannette shrugged. 'Maybe you'll get lucky.'

'We want a full report,' said Catherine. 'We'll be waiting.'

* * *

Tess emerged from the bowels of Covent Garden station, blinked at the sun and felt in her bag for her sunglasses. As always the station was surrounded by people waiting to meet their companions. She stood for a little while watching faces, wondering which of the girls were waiting to meet girlfriends, which were waiting for men, which of the men were gay. Turning her head, she saw herself reflected in the plate glass window of a fashion shop, and she narrowed her eyes thoughtfully.

I look attractive, she thought. Sexy. Somehow, as she watched her reflection, she did not feel that urge to smile. She lifted her head and put back her shoulders, watching her full breasts, thrust upwards by the Wonderbra, rising and falling with her breathing. Would Julian want to touch them? Or would he just ignore them?

That one negative thought was enough to eliminate all the impetus that had carried her through a half hour tube journey. She wrapped her arms around herself and shook her head feverishly. Seduce Julian? Forget it! She would just go and rehearse her notes and words, like a serious professional singer. She hitched her bag further up onto her shoulder and stalked away from the station and towards the rehearsal room.

Then, as she walked, she thought again. What would a serious professional singer do? A serious professional singer would do the research necessary to play the part well, as the director wanted. A method actor, she reflected, would not have any reservations about throwing herself into the role. Jeannette and Catherine were right. It wasn't enough just to let Tony take her under his wing, she had to try and put herself in a situation where she could take command.

Well and good. But how could she get up the nerve?

Ahead of her a pub stood on the corner, all engraved glass and dark wood. It looked a smart, trendy place. Tess stood on the pavement for a moment, looking into the pub's dark depths. Then she muttered, 'Dutch courage,' and walked in.

'Gin and tonic, please,' she told the barman, and fished her purse out of her bag. She looked searchingly at herself in the mirror behind the bar, then lifted the drink to her lips at once and drained half of it.

Tess rarely drank, and the alcohol delivered an immediate buzz. She rocked a little and blinked. When she looked at herself in the mirror again her eyes were very bright and there was a line of red along her cheeks. She muttered, 'Looking better already,' and drank the rest of the gin.

There was a movement at her elbow. She glanced around and saw a man standing next to her, smiling at her. He looked like a businessman, something citified in a dark, expensive suit and a florid tie. He said, 'Hi. Are you waiting for someone?'

For a moment Tess looked wonderingly into his face. He was older than her, forty perhaps, with a strong bone structure beginning to sink back into his flesh and dark, curling hair. After a second he broke eye contact and his lids flickered like a lizard's as he glanced quickly down to her breasts and then up again. His eyes narrowed slightly and he smiled.

He fancies me, Tess thought. He was not amazingly attractive or exciting, but just being approached filled her with a rush of confidence that sent the gin soaring around her bloodstream. She smiled back and tossed her head. Her hair ruffled, then settled on her neck. 'Sorry,' she said. 'I've got an appointment.'

Without waiting for his response she turned and left the bar. Her parting smile lingered on her lips. She knew that she was walking differently, with a studied poise and body-consciousness that drew glances from men as they passed her on the street. Every look, every turned head straightened her spine with a new belief in her own attractiveness. She ran up the stairs to the rehearsal room and pushed open the door without hesitation.

'Tess!' Julian got up from behind the piano, smiling at her. His face changed a little. 'Are you going out somewhere afterwards?'

'Going out?' She raised her brows. 'No. Why?'

'You look – ' Julian faltered, as if he were afraid of saying the wrong thing. 'You, er, you look as though you might be going on somewhere special. You look ...' His voice tailed off. Tess smiled at him encouragingly, but he turned away from her and went to sit down behind the piano. His eyes fastened on the score. 'Well,' he said in a businesslike way, stretching out his arms in front of him and cracking his knuckles. 'Well, what would you like to work on?'

A really confident woman, Tess thought, would say, *you*. But she hadn't got that far yet. She came over to the piano, fished her score out of her bag and leant on the glossy surface of the lid. Her folded arms framed the dark line of her cleavage. She said, looking at the music, 'The Habanera to start with, I think.' She didn't want to look up in case Julian wasn't noticing her, but in the end she made herself lift her eyes.

What she saw reassured her immensely. Julian was looking at her breasts, his lips a little parted and his china-blue eyes dark with the dilation of his pupils. He seemed not to hear her for a moment. Then he pushed back the floppy mop of his blond hair with one hand and said with a start of embarrassment, 'Right, right. Fine. Are you OK with the words?'

'Let's try,' Tess suggested. Julian nodded, looking intently at his music. Then he began to play.

Normally Tess would have stood up to sing. Now she leant on the piano like a jazz singer, watching Julian's long, elegant fingers moving over the keys. He was very aristocratic, very public school, fine-boned and delicate-looking, with slightly tanned skin that was as smooth a boy's. There were slight hollows below his cheekbones and the bridge of his nose was narrow and sharp. Tess ran her tongue around her lips as her eyes passed over

Julian's face. I am going to have you, she thought to herself. The deliberate, intense physicality of the thought shivered in her shoulders and she shifted a little from one foot to the other, feeling as she moved the wetness between her legs, warm and ready.

Julian glanced up at her to signal that it was time for her to begin and suddenly his eyes fixed on hers. Instantly Tess knew what James had meant that she should achieve in the first scene. Their gazes locked, yes, with an almost audible sound. She missed her entry entirely and Julian stopped playing. In fact he stopped breathing. Tess smiled a little, then said very softly, 'Oops.'

'Oh, good grief,' Julian said, pulling his eyes from hers. He shook his head angrily. 'Let's try it again.' He scowled at the score and played the introduction a second time, and this time he did not look up.

Tess knew this aria, the first big aria for Carmen, very well. The translation they were using was new to her, but she liked it and it was not hard to learn. Carmen sang to tease and torment all the men who watched her. Now Tess sang for Julian alone, willing him to look up again from the music and notice her.

> 'If you want me, I don't want you,
> but if you don't want me I'll take you there.
> And if I set my heart on you, sweetheart,
> if I love you, you'd best beware!'

They played it all the way through, and all the way through Julian kept his eyes firmly fixed to the music and to the keys. When they had finished he frowned and said, still not looking at her, 'That was fine, Tess, just great. One or two places I felt you didn't hold the notes to quite the right length. Benedetto is fussy about that sort of thing –'

It didn't suit Tess that he should try to continue to work. Without the drink she would probably have acquiesced, but now she was feeling contentious. She spoke straight over Julian, making him look up in surprise. 'What lovely hands you've got. Musicians' hands are so businesslike.'

'What?' Julian looked as though he hadn't understood her.

'Lovely hands,' she repeated, reaching down to lift his right hand from the keys. He flinched, but did not withdraw. 'How long your fingers are,' she breathed, examining the strong, white palm and the neat, short nails. The warm, silky feeling of her arousal began to extend from her loins to her breasts, stiffening her nipples beneath the tight cups of the bra. 'Sensitive, I bet. Are they sensitive?'

She looked up into his eyes. He was frowning, and he licked his lips quickly, like a nervous dog. There was silence. Then he said unsteadily, 'Tess, don't tease.'

'Tease?' Tess was really surprised. 'What makes you think I'm teasing?'

Julian hesitated, then said uncomfortably, 'Because you went home with Tony last night.'

Tess dropped his hand, startled and annoyed. 'Good God!' she exclaimed. 'Does the whole company know about this? How the hell did you know that, Julian?'

'I – ' Julian stammered. He looked uncertain and very young. For a moment he looked down at his hand as if he could still feel her touch. Then he muttered almost beneath his breath, 'Emma was here this morning, and she told me.'

'Emma again!' Tess was really angry that Emma was spreading gossip about her. The anger added to her determination and gave her unsuspected courage. Without another word she leant forward and caught Julian by his thick blond hair and put her lips on his.

Julian made a little sound as she thrust her tongue into his mouth. Surprise, certainly, but pleasant surprise or shock and revulsion? She didn't know and she didn't care. She shut her eyes and kissed him as if nothing else in the world existed. For a few seconds he didn't respond. Then he moaned and opened his mouth wider beneath her searching lips and his tongue tentatively touched hers. He did not attempt to hold her. Tess opened her eyes for a moment and saw his hands hanging in mid air, knotted into tight fists, squeezing until the bony knuckles were white with pressure.

She sensed that he was about to try to pull away from her. This was not part of the plan. She put her right hand on his thigh, ran it upwards and let out a little gasp of delight as she found the outline of his cock, already thick and swollen. She pressed her fingers down on it and felt it pulse with answering life. Julian moaned again into her open mouth.

Tess drew back a little and looked into his face. He sat very still and stared at her, pale to his lips, trembling slightly. His light-blue eyes with their long fringe of golden lashes were dark with arousal. Tess's diaphragm flinched and shuddered with her uneven breathing. She had become absorbed in her character, and right now she wanted Julian desperately. She wanted to see that innocent, boy's face change as he felt himself penetrate her. His cock felt splendid, long and rigid with eagerness, and she wanted to feel it inside her.

His lips moved. In a moment he would say something. That wasn't part of the plan either, and Tess tossed back her hair and spoke before he could. 'Well, Julian, what about it?'

Julian's thick blond hair stirred as he shook his head very slightly. He didn't look frightened exactly, more disbelieving. His golden brows drew down into a knot and he whispered, 'What, here?'

'Here,' Tess confirmed, nodding her head. 'Now.'

'But – ' Julian's eyes slid to the door. It was shut. 'But anyone could walk in.'

Tess shrugged, but she stepped back from him, taking her hand from the bulge of his cock, and walked swiftly to the door. There was no key, but there was an old, rusty bolt at the bottom. She forced it into the socket, smiling at the phallic symbolism of the action. She smiled at Julian, who was still sitting motionless on the piano stool, staring at her like a rabbit in the headlights. She went to her bag, found one of the condoms and tucked it into the front of her bra. Then she straightened.

'Now,' she said, 'we won't be disturbed.' She took a step towards Julian, then stooped and unfastened the bottom button of her skirt. Another step, another button. By the time she was standing within his reach the buttons were undone more than half way up, and Tess was shaking from head to foot with excitement. Why not do what she had imagined? Why not? She let the skirt fall open, disclosing the tender white flesh of her inner thigh, and then unfastened it further to show her pubis, barely covered by the delicate black lace of the panties.

Julian was gazing, dry-mouthed and wide-eyed. He was taking long, deep breaths, his slender shoulders lifting and falling. Tess hesitated, her nerve faltering for a moment. Then she put her hand to her panties and pulled them aside, revealing the soft, dark-red fur and the beginning of the moist, pink lips. Julian breathed in quickly as if someone had slapped him. The tension between them was almost tangible. Tess couldn't bear the silence. She said softly, 'Julian, kiss me.'

He took her more literally than she expected. With a little cry, of relief or desire, she didn't know, Julian flung himself from the piano stool and fell to his knees before her. He wrapped his arms around her thighs. Her buttocks fitted snugly into the crook of his elbows and his hands spread across her back. Without a word he pressed his face between her legs and licked her, whimpering as he dragged his tongue lovingly over her trembling flesh.

'Oh God,' Tess exclaimed. The rush of pleasure was so complete that she staggered and almost fell. She caught at Julian's shoulders to steady herself and thrust her hips up towards his face, moaning with ecstasy, offering her sex to his caresses. His long, clever tongue wormed its way deeper through her folds, encircling her clitoris, teasing it, quivering against it. She cried out again and put her hands in his hair, jerking against his mouth almost as if he were a woman and she were a man. Her head fell back and she stared blindly at the ceiling as the wonderful sensations swelled and coiled and mounted within her, drawing her up, up towards the distant peak of climax. Julian held her tightly, supporting her, and as her movements became more urgent he responded, pressing directly against the stiff engorged bud and flickering his tongue against it like a snake's. Tess knotted her hands in his soft hair and arched her back and gave herself up completely to pleasure, crying out as she attained her peak.

As she recovered she held him there, his face buried against her mound. His breath stirred against her moist flesh and made her shiver with renewed desire. He was on his knees before her, like a prisoner or a slave before a powerful queen, and it thrilled her. When at last she let him go he sat back, looking up at her, his mouth and face slick with her juices, and said nothing.

'Now,' she said, her voice husky, 'Julian, I want you to fuck me.'

He frowned. 'I – I don't have a . . .'

A smile twitched at the corners of Tess's lips. '*Voilà*,' she said, drawing out the little packet from her cleavage. Julian gave a nervous, helpless laugh and got to his feet. He stood for a moment irresolutely, as if uncertain of what to do next, and with a delicious sense of command Tess came to him and reached up to draw down his lips to hers.

His mouth tasted of her sex. She murmured with satisfaction and licked his face, cleaning her slippery musk from his skin. As she washed him like a cat she unfastened his shirt and felt inside for the warm smoothness of his chest. His skin was pale biscuit-gold and soft as thistledown. A pulse was beating in his neck, strong and fast. He breathed quickly and shut his eyes and his big, long-fingered hands ran down her neck, inside the soft fabric of her top, down towards the swell of her breasts. She gasped and pushed herself against him, wanting to feel him touching her nipples. For a moment he tried to unfasten some of the buttons, but they were small and his hands were shaking. He gave a stifled curse of frustration and pushed the top from her shoulder, baring her white skin and the black strap of the bra. She thrust herself towards him and he kissed her neck, her collar bone, her cleavage, and then at last he put his big delicate hand on her breast and lifted it from the cup of the bra. His fingers brushed over the stiff, swollen nipple, stroked at it, squeezed it.

She wanted to feel him inside her. The warm clutching fists of orgasm were still clenching in her belly, making her impatient to be filled. As he caressed her breast she felt for the buttons on his chinos, deftly unfastened them. The zip whined and Julian jerked with shock as she thrust her hand inside.

Boxer shorts, crisp and crumpled. She didn't bother to feel for the fly, just shoved her hand inside the elastic. His body was warm, warm, like new bread, and instantly her fingers found and fastened upon his erect penis. It was long and thicker than she had expected and slightly, charmingly curved. Julian set his teeth and gasped as she wrapped her hand around the hot, smooth column of flesh and stroked downwards, felt between his legs, probed the taut updrawn skin of his balls, weighed them, then returned to his cock. It twitched and jolted beneath her fingers. She gently drew it out of its prison of cotton and looked down, smiling dry-mouthed as she saw its swollen, scarlet head, already dewed with eagerness. It would have been nice to suck it, but her body demanded satisfaction, instantly. She pulled the condom out of her bra and tore the wrapping with her teeth.

He was ready, trembling as he looked down into her face. She realised with a delightful shiver that he was waiting, waiting for her to tell him what to do. The floor? Standing up, against a wall? Neither appealed. She put her hand on the glossy surface of the Steinway and smiled. 'Julian,' she said, 'on the piano.'

'Oh, Christ almighty,' Julian breathed. But he put his hands quickly around her waist and boosted her up to sit on the shiny black lid, then hooked the piano stool with his foot and caught it towards him to kneel on. The strings of the piano echoed faintly as Tess's weight shifted. As Julian came towards her with his cock sticking out of his open fly she eased off her panties and then opened her legs to him, slowly, deliberately. Her top was tugged off, showing one breast, and her skirt was crumpled beneath her bare buttocks. She looked like a slut and felt like Cleopatra.

He knelt before her and lowered his head to worship her breast with his mouth. For a moment she permitted it. The ministrations of his tongue, circling her nipple, flickering over it, made her set her teeth and gasp with renewed pleasure. But it was not what she wanted. She spread her thighs wide and caught hold of Julian by the shoulders and the buttocks and pulled him towards her. When she felt the heat of his cock pressing against the lips of her sex she reached down and guided him into her.

He slid up inside her in one smooth motion. She grunted and wrapped her legs over his buttocks, pulling him close. Her naked breast pressed against the bare skin of his chest. She clung to his arms, holding him to her, and looked up into his rapt, astonished face. His testicles nestled warmly against the crease of her arse. He stood very still, shuddering, and whispered again, 'Oh Christ.'

'Julian,' she hissed, low and determined. 'Julian, come on. Do it.' She tilted her pelvis, drawing away from him so that he slipped almost entirely out of her. The movement of his long smooth cock through her flesh made her snarl with pleasure. 'Come on,' she repeated. 'Julian, fuck me.'

He stared at her for a moment almost as if he were angry. His lips were parted and dry with his quick breathing and they drew slowly back, showing his teeth like a dog's. His chest lifted and fell, squeezing her breasts into fullness and then letting them sink again. His big hands slid down her back, fumbled under her skirt, found her naked buttocks and clutched them. He clenched his teeth and thrust.

'Oh yes,' Tess gasped as he forced his cock deep inside her, over and over again. 'Oh, that's so good. Oh yes, yes.' She seized him by the hair and kissed him, thrusting her tongue into his mouth as he thrust himself into her sex. They were both grunting, making low wordless sounds as he took her, as he gave her what she wanted, the simple animal pleasure of his rigid penis sliding deeply into her and withdrawing only to penetrate her again.

Tess jerked her hips towards him, wanting to take him as deeply within her as she could. The remorseless, driving rhythm built up in her loins and her brain. She arched her back, leaning away from him, lying back on the cold slippery surface of the piano and writhing as he shafted her with all his strength. 'Don't stop,' she moaned. She knew she was coming. Julian cried out and leant forward over her, his sweaty hands slipping as he held himself up, and his cock drove ever deeper into her. She tilted back her head and closed her eyes and put her hands on her breasts. She didn't care about him, she didn't give a damn, he was nothing but a moving, thrusting penis, a dildo with a brain, the necessary instrument of her selfish pleasure. She pinched her nipples hard and her climax rose up within her like a dolphin swimming out of the depths towards the bright sunlight, its whole body one great muscle, scything upwards through the chill water with strong beats of its pulsing flukes until suddenly it breaks the surface and

366

arches free of its prison, leaping for an infinite moment into the glittering, dancing air, surrounded by fountains of spray and shards of light.

Julian gave an anguished, ecstatic cry and twisted over her. Vaguely, through the sparkling aftermath of her climax, she felt his penis pulsing deep within her. She lay spread-eagled on the piano, her breasts heaving as her breathing slowed, her eyes closed, utterly pleasured and completely without shame.

Presently she sat up and pulled herself free of him. He gasped and sank down on the piano stool, fumbling at his crotch and hanging his head. He was still panting and the back of his shirt was damp with sweat. He rubbed one long hand over his face and looked up at her.

She shook back her hair. Beneath its heavy weight on the back of her neck her skin was slick and hot. She ruffled it with her fingers and then slipped down from the piano to the floor, smoothing her skirt and rebuttoning it. Her panties were some distance away. She went and picked them up, smiled ruefully at them and in the end stuffed them into her bag.

'Tess,' Julian said huskily. She turned to look at him. 'Tess, could we – would you – would you like to come out with me? Or come home?'

For a moment she didn't say anything. She was wondering what to say, how to refuse him. Then the answer came to her. She laughed and used Carmen's own words, singing them mockingly to Julian's anxious face. *'Maybe not at all, tomorrow maybe. But one thing's for sure – not today!'*

'But – ' Julian began.

She came over to him and kissed him quickly on the lips. 'You were wonderful,' she said, 'but that's it, Julian, darling. And if you breathe a word of it to anyone in the company, I'll shut your fingers in the piano lid.'

He flinched, drawing his hands protectively into his lap. He looked so distressed that Tess felt a twinge of remorse. She knew Carmen wouldn't, but she was still a long way from understanding her character. She touched Julian's face gently and asked, 'Isn't once better than never?'

He looked away. Tess straightened and stretched. 'God, I feel great,' she said. 'I could take on the world. Come on, Julian, we've got work to do. Let your fingers do the walking.'

Act Two, Scene Two

That afternoon

As Tess climbed the stairs to her flat the door opened, revealing Catherine's eager face. 'Well?' she demanded.

Tess reached the top landing and punched the air in the classic victory gesture. 'Mission accomplished!'

'Tess, that's brilliant.' Catherine reached out and took her by the arm, drawing her inside the flat. 'You know, I could have guessed just by looking at you. You're all flushed and that lovely skirt is a wreck.'

'I haven't got any knickers on, either,' Tess giggled.

'What?' shrieked Catherine. 'And you've come all the way back on the tube like that?'

'I don't believe it myself,' Tess said, shaking her head and laughing at the same time. 'Hey, this is little me! The Northern line with no knickers!' She extended her arms and whirled joyfully around. 'This demands a celebration. Come on, let's have a drink.' She went through towards the kitchen, asking, 'Where's Jeannette?'

'Gone to get some stuff in for dinner. Your cupboards are bare. She should be back soon.'

'Three glasses, then.' Tess hurried into the kitchen and opened the fridge. At the back was the bottle of champagne that she had failed to open, weeks ago, when Dan had robbed her of her triumph. 'Look,' she said, 'here's some champagne. Shall we? There's no rehearsal tomorrow.'

'Champagne!' Catherine looked surprised. 'Do you always keep bubbly in your fridge?'

'It was going to be to celebrate getting the part,' said Tess, 'but Dan was a miserable bastard and he put me off. So I think we should drink it now. I'm as proud of what I did this afternoon as I am of playing Carmen, and that's the truth.'

'I'm always game for champagne.'

They found glasses and popped the cork with shrieks and giggles. Then they carried the glasses through to the living room. Tess kicked off her sandals and flung herself onto the sofa and Catherine sat beside her.

'Now then, Tess.' Catherine's face revealed avid curiosity. 'Tell me all about it. Don't miss anything.'

Tess took a deep draught of the champagne and frowned for a moment into her glass. Then she said, 'I nearly bottled out. Very nearly. If I hadn't gone into a pub and bought myself a gin I would have done. But when I actually tried it, it – it was easy.'

'He fell for it. For you.'

'Hook, line and sinker. Men are real animals, aren't they? I mean, even a nice young sensitive boy like Julian is just an animal under the surface. He got a hard on, I swear it, he got a hard on just looking at my breasts.'

'That's understandable,' said Catherine gently. 'They are pretty much on the counter in that bra, Tess.' She leant forward a little. 'But was he good?'

'Good? Oh . . .' Tess lay back against the cushions and drank again. 'Yes,' she said, in a far away voice. 'Yes, he was good. He used his mouth on me, and it made me come. He was kneeling in front of me, like an acolyte, and I was holding his head right against me and he licked and licked at me until I came. It was amazing. Wonderful.'

370

The bubbles of the champagne seemed to fizz and sparkle in her brain, gently eroding her inhibitions. She described what had happened in a disjointed, random way, a collection of images and sensations. Julian's long fingers squeezing her breast, clutching her buttocks. His cock penetrating her completely on that first unbelievable thrust. His face, transfigured with shock and ecstasy. Sweat beading on his forehead and falling from his narrow nose to land on her breasts. Her sense of power, of manipulation, and the overwhelming response it had triggered in her.

'It was like – like masturbating with a real person. Selfish. Fabulous.' She did not speak for some time, just lay with her head tilted onto the back of the sofa looking up at the ceiling. Sunlight lay across it, turning the white paint to primrose. At last she realised that Catherine had said nothing for some time. She lifted her head to look.

Catherine had put down her glass and was lying with her head resting on her left arm. Her dark eyes were fixed on Tess's face and her full lips were slack with pleasure. Her right hand was between her legs, beneath her skirt, moving. When she saw Tess look at her she smiled dreamily and said, 'Don't stop.'

'But, I'd finished,' Tess said. Her eyes travelled down to watch Catherine's moving hand. She was fascinated and horrified at the same time. Catherine's fingers moved again between her parted thighs and she sighed, a long breathy sigh, a sigh of pleasure. Tess knew the sound well. She made it herself when she masturbated, alone in bed at night, sending herself to sleep with her fingers and her fantasies. The sound itself was a powerful erotic stimulant.

Tess hesitated, irresolute. The anxiety that had made her refuse Jeannette all those years ago was still there, but working against it was the tingling elevation of the champagne and the warm delicious echoes of her earlier orgasms. Her body heard the sound of Catherine's pleasure and demanded further pleasure for itself. If it were on offer.

Tess said after a long moment, 'Catherine.'

Catherine's opulent hips were beginning to move in the slow, swelling wave that meant that she had penetrated herself with her fingers. Her tongue showed between her parted lips. She smiled at Tess very slowly and murmured, 'Tess. You turned me on so much.' Her hand moved again and she made another sound and closed her eyes and quickly licked her dry lips. Tess shivered with sudden, direct wanting. The urge to touch herself was almost irresistible.

Catherine's eyes opened again, dark and languid. She said very softly, 'Do you want to make love?'

There was a long pause. Tess's belly and breasts were tight with tension and a spasm of lust clenched in her sex. She didn't know what she wanted. After a moment, resorting to humour as she often did to try to extricate herself from awkward situations, she said jerkily, 'I don't think that was on James's suggestion list.'

Catherine drew her hand out from between her legs. Her lips curved in a warm sensual smile. 'Oh, it is,' she said softly. 'In fact Jeannette and I discussed it with him yesterday. He would be very happy for us to suggest that Carmen and Frasquita and Mercedes are more than just good friends.'

'Seriously?' Tess breathed, hardly daring to move.

'Truly.'

Tess swallowed. She was sure that she could smell the scent of Catherine's arousal. It knotted her stomach with desire and the urge to discover the unknown. What would it be like to love another woman? She looked at Catherine and saw her still smiling, not pressuring her. No seduction: her decision. She put down her glass of champagne beside Catherine's with a definitive clink.

'Yes,' she said. 'Catherine. Yes.'

'Oh, Tess.' Catherine reached out for her. Tess moved hesitantly into her arms, waiting for the shock of that first kiss. Their lips met and pressed together and within their open mouths their tongues touched, exploring first gently, then deeply. Catherine's lips were full and incredibly soft, like satin, like the infinite feathery velvetiness of an erect cock. Her tongue was thick and short and mobile. As they kissed she put her fingers to the little buttons that fastened Tess's top and began to undo them, one after the other, quick and deft. Tess shivered with anticipation. She knew what she would have wanted if she had been Catherine and so she did it. She put her hand on Catherine's bare calf and ran it up under her dress, over the cool fullness of her smooth thighs to where her moist pubis bulged against the restraining cotton of her knickers. The fabric was already damp with need. Catherine whimpered as Tess touched her, but did not stop unfastening the blouse. Tess remembered the times that a man had put his hand inside her knickers, how sometimes they were rough and demanding and made her jump, and with infinite delicacy she insinuated herself and slid her fingers through the crisp curls of Catherine's luxurious pubic hair to the swollen wet lips of her sex.

'Ah,' Catherine moaned into her mouth. Tess explored gently, parting the soft moist labia, finding the open, grasping tunnel and slipping one finger deep into it. Catherine groaned and her soft body tautened. The sensation of giving her pleasure was incredible, so powerfully erotic that Tess thought she would come herself on the spot. She slid another finger in beside the first and with her thumb gently caressed the stiff stem of Catherine's clitoris.

'Oh God,' Catherine cried out. 'Tess.' Her hips began to undulate, lifting towards Tess's probing hand. Tess found the rhythm and began to move her fingers in and out, in and out, shutting her eyes tightly and listening with every ounce of her attention to Catherine's trembling cries. She could feel the orgasm hovering in Catherine's limbs as if it were her own. She knew instinctively what to do, where to touch, when to thrust deep, when to withdraw and tease the quivering, swollen bud of pleasure until Catherine's body stiffened and became rigid as her sex clamped and shook around Tess's plunging fingers.

She waited some time and then very, very gently withdrew her hand. Catherine shivered and moaned, then opened her eyes. 'Oh, Tess,' she said, 'you star. That was wonderful.'

Tess shifted uncomfortably. She wanted to feel Catherine's mouth on her, loving her, giving her pleasure, but she didn't know how to ask. Instead she finished unfastening the buttons on her top and pulled it off, then reached round behind her back to unfasten the bra.

'Oh, you have gorgeous tits,' Catherine breathed. She leant forward and kissed Tess's left nipple, first very gently, then harder and harder. She drew the stiff peak into her mouth and sucked on it until pleasure became pain, but such a sharp sweet pain that Tess did not want it to stop. She cried out sharply and Catherine drew back. Tess looked down and saw that her nipple was incredibly swollen, much larger than its usual size even when erect. She reached up hesitantly and touched it and flinched with the strength of sensation.

Catherine smiled at her and stripped off her clothes, revealing a firm, full body with opulent flanks and high breasts, like a Renoir nude. Then she turned her attention to Tess's other breast and as she suckled and lapped at the stiffening nipple her fingers continued to torment the left pap, flickering against the engorged point, keeping it unbearably stimulated. Tess moaned and writhed. When Catherine drew back and began to unfasten her skirt and take it off she flung up her arms in wanton abandon, longing for further pleasure.

'No knickers,' Catherine whispered smiling as she set her lips to the very gentle swell of Tess's belly. 'No knickers on the tube. Tess, you slut. You whore.'

Tess was not insulted. She arched upwards, parting her thighs and feeling the air cool on her slippery sex.

'Just getting into the part,' she said. 'Understanding my character. Catherine, Catherine, oh God.'

Catherine kissed her belly, her hipbone. She kneaded with her fingers at the tender skin of Tess's inner thighs and it fluttered in response. Tess let her head fall back and moaned with helpless longing as Catherine teased her, brushing her lips against the hollows of her loins, twisting her tongue playfully into the dark-red curls of her pubic hair and tugging at it, pursing her lips and blowing. It was torture, but blissful torture because Tess was certain that pleasure would follow it.

It did, as day follows night. Catherine drew back, waited an infinite moment and then leant forward and wrapped her mouth around the warm silken pouch of Tess's sex. Her lips and tongue were cool and firm. She thrust her tongue deep into the trembling hollow of Tess's vagina and quivered it like a butterfly's wing, titillating the outer lips until Tess's body heaved and she sighed with ecstasy. Then she began to lap gently, diligently, persistently at Tess's clitoris, teasing it into a swollen turgid peak and then tormenting it, soothing it, bathing it with her tongue and lips. Her hands left Tess's white flanks and crept up her body to find her breasts. As Catherine licked and licked at Tess's sex her fingers kneaded and squeezed her breasts, found the hard nipples and pulled at them.

Tess lay spread-eagled and open to her caresses, oblivious to everything except the wonderful sensations that were filling her. She felt an extraordinary sense of freedom. She knew she would come, she knew that Catherine was skilled and that as a woman she would understand and not settle for anything less than perfect pleasure. And then, and then, they could lie in each other's arms for a moment and then do it again, again, again, until they were exhausted and slick with sweat, drowned in sensual delight, their eyelids heavy with the weight of repeated orgasm.

And yet as she lay there, her clitoris flaming beneath

Catherine's tender caresses and her heaving breasts swollen with desire, the image that came to Tess's mind was of a man. A faceless man, a beautiful man, tall and muscular, coming to her in the night in the gloom and taking her. He came to her room and drew back the covers from her bed with one strong tug, leaving her on the sheets writhing as naked and helpless as a creature fresh from the womb. Before she could rise he flung himself on her and pinned her down, holding her wrists above her head and lowering his hard heavy body onto her. He forced his knee between her flinching thighs and drove them apart and she felt the hot glossy head of his cock between her legs, massive and smooth as marble. She tried to move beneath him and moaned in delirious assent and he laughed and rolled onto his side and pushed her head down, down to his crotch, and his strong hands were in her hair and he pulled back her head until her mouth opened and then thrust his cock into her mouth so hard that she thought she would choke. Then he used her mouth, coldly, violently, taking her with brutal force, grunting as he thrust the thick shaft between her lips so hard that he bruised them. His taut testicles brushed against her chin, cool hairy globes throbbing with the potential of his seed. He gasped and began to clench his fists in her hair and as Catherine drew her clitoris into her mouth and sucked at it and her orgasm rose spinning inside her Tess imagined this faceless man's massive cock spurting into her throat, jerking and surging with the power of his ejaculation, drowning her with his come.

She lay very still, shuddering, her eyes closed. White and red sparks danced behind her eyelids. A hand ran over her shoulders and onto her breasts. It stroked and weighed and fondled, then moved further down. A quick harsh voice said, 'Tess, I should be as jealous as hell.'

Tess's eyes flew open. Jeannette was kneeling on the sofa beside her, naked, legs spread wide, her long black limbs glistening. Her body was like an athlete's, slender and muscled, with breasts shallow as saucers tipped with long, cornelian nipples. The fur on her pubic mound was short and scanty and the pink sexual flesh between her legs glowed like a beacon. She had one hand on Tess's abdomen and the other in Catherine's hair. Tess stared upwards, speechless, and Jeannette smiled slowly. Her teeth were very white. 'Mind you,' she said, 'Catherine's good, isn't she? She had you so far away you didn't even hear me come in.'

Catherine smiled a creamy, cat-like smile of pride and satisfaction. She said, 'I don't think Tess knows that we had, er, become quite so close.'

'She knows now,' said Jeannette.

Tess was still half absorbed in her fantasy. Jeannette's sudden presence was surprising, but not threatening. She was too deep in erotic overload to feel fear now. She was filled with the urge to service, to subsume herself to someone else's pleasure. With a little whimper of submission she reached out and caught hold of Jeannette's tight buttocks and pulled at her. Jeannette quickly straddled her and pushed her hips towards her face and Tess obediently lowered her head and extended her tongue to lap. Jeannette's body perfume was intense, subtle and deep, and her sex was already wet and glistening with desire. Tess knew she would taste delicious, and she delicately and with relish slithered her tongue deep into the luxurious folds of flesh, remembering what Catherine had done to her and doing her best to do the same to Jeannette. At one stage she glanced up and saw that Catherine had got to her feet and was standing behind Jeannette with her hands beneath the slender black arms, cupping her shallow breasts, her long dark nipples tightly trapped between her fingers. Jeannette's head was turned towards Catherine and they were kissing, tongues twisting in their open mouths as Jeannette sighed and whimpered with the pleasure of what Tess was doing to her. The contrast of white and black flesh was startling and beautiful. Tess watched for a moment in rapture, then slowly closed her eyes and concentrated on the simple, delectable task of taking Jeannette to orgasm.

Jeannette climaxed with a desperate cry and subsided slowly onto the sofa between Catherine and Tess, her long limbs stretched out in delicious, abandoned weariness. She was breathing in deep, long gasps, her breasts rising and falling. 'Ah,' she said at last, 'That was wonderful, Tess.' She stroked her slender dark fingers down Tess's face, smiling with pleasure and affection. Then she turned her head. The muscles flowed on her neck as beautifully as a young boy's. To Catherine she said, 'I don't know what you did, Cath, but it must have been something right. I did my damnedest to get Tess into bed last time we met, and I didn't manage it.'

'Ah well,' said Catherine, 'perhaps she hadn't just successfully seduced a 22-year-old répétiteur.'

'That's true,' Jeannette admitted. She leant forward and poured herself a glass of champagne. 'And you've polished off half the bottle,' she commented, holding it up.

'What's for dinner?' Catherine asked, her eyes bright.

'All you think about is food. Lots of nice things. How about taking it to bed?' Jeannette suggested. 'Tess, what do you think?'

Tess stretched luxuriously. 'I'm not really hungry yet,' she said. Then she added shyly, 'But I don't mind going to bed, if – if you think we'd all fit.'

It was a slight squeeze, but they all fitted. They lay in a heap, Jeannette's dark limbs elegantly intertwined with Catherine and Tess's pale ones, and drank what was left of the champagne. It made them cheerful and giggly. Tess felt very strange. The combination of the relaxed friendliness of a girls' night out and the potential for almost infinite sensual discovery was a potent one, and it was new to her. In her experience sex hadn't really gone hand in hand with straightforward companionship, she had always been a sort of junior partner in the relationship. Jeannette questioned her about Julian and she told the story all over again, and when she had finished added cautiously, 'Jeannette, you said you wanted him when I had finished with him. You should – I mean – I mean, go ahead, if you want to.'

Jeannette smiled archly and shook her head so that the bright beads tipping her hair clashed together. 'What d'you think, Cath?' she asked languidly. 'Should we get him back to our place, just the two of us, and blow his tiny mind?'

Catherine shrugged. 'If you like. I like my men a bit more grown up.'

'Well,' said Jeannette, wrinkling her nose, 'let's face it, the chances of us managing to get him on our own in the flat are pretty small. That Emma's always hanging around like the spectre at the feast, looking disapproving whenever we have a good time.'

Tess frowned a little. 'Does she – ' she hesitated. 'Does she know? About you and Catherine?'

Catherine laughed. 'She'd have to be deaf and blind not to know,' she said. 'We've been sharing a bed for a week. Poor little maidenly Emma doesn't know where to put herself.'

'Doesn't know where to put herself? Don't make me laugh.' Jeannette put back her shoulders and stroked her fingers down over the long, taut tips of her breasts. 'She's outside our room every night with her ear to the keyhole listening. She's like all bloody prudes, absolutely fascinated by everything everybody else gets up to.'

'Is she really a prude?' asked Tess, absolutely fascinated herself.

'Certainly is.' Catherine reached over to Jeannette and began to caress her breasts. 'One hundred per cent, gilt-edged virgo intacta.'

'No wonder Leo's so taken with her,' Tess said, feeling a rather melancholy regret for the loss of her own innocence, though it was Leo himself who had taken it.

'You said,' commented Jeannette, sighing as she offered her long nipples to Catherine's enquiring fingers, 'you said he liked virgins. Well, I wish him luck with this one, but honestly I don't think he'll get anywhere. She's far too fond of her own self-image to let him tarnish it by taking her cherry.'

Tess drew down her brows, thinking. Catherine smiled and kissed Jeannette's shoulder, then said, 'James has really got himself a cast and a half, hasn't he? A tenor who thinks he's a reincarnation of Don Juan, a baritone who can't wait to deflower the soprano, a now-not-quite-so-innocent young répétiteur, a couple of second sopranos enjoying themselves amusing each other, and a mixed up mezzo just bouncing around between them all.'

'Oh,' said Jeannette, 'and don't forget the director's pretty assistant.'

'Oh, Adam,' simpered Catherine, pulling back her thick dark hair in mockery of Adam's ponytail. She mimicked his aristocratic voice. '"You'll all be expert by the time I've finished with you."'

'All be expert!' snorted Jeannette. 'All Adam knows about is how to take James's cock up his tight little arse.'

'Oh, Jeannette,' Tess exclaimed. She was trying to seem cool and sophisticated, but this was all too much. 'Do you really think so? I mean, do you think they actually *do* anything?'

'Think it? Tess, sweetie, I know it,' said Jeannette archly. 'Didn't you hear about the time I caught them at it?'

'Never mind her,' said Catherine with interest, 'I didn't hear about it, either. Come on, dish the dirt.' She sat up and snuggled closer to Jeannette, looking eagerly up into her eyes.

Jeannette smiled down at Catherine and Tess like a story-teller waiting to begin. 'Well, all right,' she said, 'here goes. It was a couple of years ago, when James was doing a sort of studio *Porgy and Bess* up at Opera North.

An all black production, apart from James and Adam of course. I was singing Clara, which means I sang "Summertime". The high spot of my career to date. Anyway, James was with Adam then, too, I think they'd not long met, and they took a place together out in the country, which is a bit shocking in Leeds! And I went out there one day to do some checking on something in the score, I can't remember exactly what now. It was a gorgeous day, the middle of July, and when I rang at the door of the house there was no reply.'

'A house?' Catherine sounded surprised. 'He was living it up, then.'

'Oh, I think it belonged to a friend of his. It wasn't a huge house, but it had a big garden and it was all on its own, no other houses nearby at all. Anyway, I rang the bell a few times and nobody came. I was a bit pissed off, because I'd borrowed a car and everything, so I thought I'd just poke about and see if there was someone in the garden. I went round the back and found it was like something out of a film, a fabulous garden, with a fountain and a little stream and drifts of flowers everywhere. The back door of the house was open and I went in and called a bit, but nobody answered.'

'And it's not as if they wouldn't hear you,' joked Catherine. 'With your hog-calling voice.'

'Gosh, Catherine, what I love about you is that you're so sweet and supportive,' said Jeannette, tugging Catherine's thick brown hair sharply. Catherine yelped and grinned. 'Do you want to hear this story or don't you?'

'Please go on,' Tess begged. She was really interested. 'Please.'

'Well, then, just for you, Tess,' said Jeannette. She turned her shoulder to Catherine in exaggerated annoyance and leant forward, setting her lips to Tess's left nipple. A quicksilver jolt of pleasure arrowed through Tess, making her shoulders tense and her heart thump. She closed her eyes and lifted her shoulders, offering her breasts to Jeannette's mouth. For a moment there was a delicate silence. Then Jeannette drew away and lay back on the bed, stretching her lean arms above her head. 'I wandered around the house for a while,' she went on, 'but I couldn't find anyone. It was obvious they were living together, though. Only one of the beds was made up. Well, I went back out into the garden and began to look for them there.'

'Did you call out?' asked Tess.

'Not in the garden. It was such a lovely afternoon, I didn't want to shout the place down and spoil it. So I walked down the lawn and into a sort of shrubbery at the bottom, all big rhododendron bushes and wild roses and stuff. It was lovely. The stream ran down through it over little rocks, you can imagine the pretty sound it made. Then I heard them.'

Tess breathed faster and swallowed. 'What?' she asked, unable to conceal her eagerness. 'What were they saying? What was happening?'

'No words,' Jeannette said. Her voice had become soft and her eyes were unfocused as she plumbed her memory. Tess was pressed close to her on one side and Catherine on the other, both of them looking up into her face. 'There weren't exactly any words, not then. Just murmurs, you know, little lovey dovey noises. So I crept closer, hiding behind bushes.' A quick, wicked grin lit up her face. 'There's an advantage to being black, if you like. I fade into shadows a lot easier than a blonde would. It wasn't long before I saw them. They were lying in the sun on a little bit of soft grass next to the stream, snogging like a pair of kids, both of them absolutely starkers. Their clothes were all in a heap on the ground.'

'Wow,' said Catherine. 'What sort of a body has James got?'

'Pretty good for his age. Quite hard, really. And a big cock. And Adam, well, he's like a wet dream if you like them thin. All bones and muscles, and a stiffy like a milk bottle. If you ask me, gay guys are a lot more hung up about big cocks than women are. They live cock-centric lives.'

'How big is Adam's?' demanded Catherine. Tess shrank down into Jeannette's side, thrilled and shocked at the same time.

'Christ, do you think I had a ruler? It looked like a double handful, anyway. And really fat. Honestly, if he wanted to have me, I'd say yes. I've always wanted to feel a really big one, just to see if it does make any difference. But I didn't get to see it for that long, because I'd only been standing there for a minute when they sort of swung together and started doing a 69.'

Tess bit her lip. Her mind filled with the image of the two men together, their faces pressed between each other's legs, lips fastened around their erect cocks, sucking. She had never thought before about what two men might do and she found the thought unexpectedly and powerfully erotic. Two hard male bodies, two stiff swollen penises, unlimited abandoned virility, concentrating on itself alone.

'What then?' asked Catherine. 'Did they fuck? Who did it to whom?'

Jeannette shivered. Looking down, Tess saw that Catherine's hand was resting on the dark crisp curls of Jeannette's mound, and her fingers were gently, diligently fondling between Jeannette's slender thighs. It was as if Catherine were thanking her for this story. Tess was grateful too, and she lowered her head and drew one of Jeannette's long cornelian nipples into her mouth and flickered her tongue across it, probing delicately into the tiny crease at its tip. Jeannette's body shuddered and tensed. 'Yes,' Jeannette whispered, and it was hard to know whether she was asking for more or continuing her story. 'Yes, they fucked. Let me tell you what they did. It was amazing, I could have stood there all day. After a while – oh, Cath, that's wonderful, don't stop – after a while they split up and James knelt over Adam and sucked and sucked at his cock. He took it really deep, I can't swallow that much of a man. I was impressed. And Adam just lay there like a young god and humped upwards towards James's mouth and you could see he was coming. He arched and the muscles in his stomach and his flanks fluttered and then James was swallowing. He looked as if he was enjoying a big ice cream cone. He loved it.'

'That's our director,' smiled Catherine. She slid her hand further between Jeannette's thighs and slipped one finger deep into her. Her other hand reached out for Tess. Tess jumped as she felt a touch on her hip, then she relaxed and let her legs part and sucked harder at Jeannette's swollen nipple as Catherine's hand brushed across her mound, wet itself with her juices, and began to stroke her swelling clitoris.

'Then,' Jeannette murmured between gasps, 'then James sat up and sort of rolled Adam over. Adam lay on his front and James kissed his back, between his shoulders and all the way down his spine to his bum. I tell you, girls, Adam's got a really gorgeous arse. I'd kiss it, too. And that's what James did, he pulled Adam's cheeks apart with the palms of his hands and then just buried his face between them and tongued his arse.'

'Eurgh,' said Tess, wrinkling her nose.

'Eurgh?' repeated Catherine. 'Tess, sweetie, just you wait. I'll roll you over in a little while and show you what it feels like. It's lovely.' And as if to illustrate her probing finger slipped backwards, teasing at the silky, sensitive membrane of Tess's anus.

'Don't,' said Tess. She remembered Tony putting one finger, two fingers inside her, and how it had made her writhe with a sort of horrified pleasure. 'Don't.'

'James liked it,' Jeannette said, 'and so did Adam. He was moaning and pushing his arse up towards James and James was eating him out, tongue-fucking him. They carried on doing that for a while, then James sat up and got a condom out of their clothes and rolled it on.

384

And Adam opened his legs and said, "Come on, James, darling, please." So James did.'

'He – ' Tess hardly knew how to express it. 'He put his cock in – in Adam's arse? Really?'

'Really,' said Jeannette, lifting her hips up towards Catherine's fingers. 'All the way in, Tess. Right in, up to the hilt. And then he fucked him, and I stood there behind a bush and watched.'

'Did it make you horny?' asked Catherine softly.

'God, it did. I'd have liked to join in, but those two really aren't interested in women at all.'

'Not like you and me, darling,' said Catherine, smiling.

A wicked thought crept into Tess's brain. She suppressed it for a moment, then suddenly laughed. Why should she hold back in front of Jeannette and Catherine, who were probably quite unshockable? They were both looking at her, a little surprised, and she grinned at them. 'Why don't we suggest to Leo that he tries that with Emma?' she said.

Catherine's face also lit with a wicked grin. 'What, having her up her arse?'

'She'd still be a virgin, wouldn't she?' said Tess.

'I heard that women used to do that years ago,' commented Jeannette, 'when it was important that you were a virgin when you married. You'd have a lover, but you'd only ever let him have you up the arse. Then who's to know?'

'I don't think Emma would like it, though,' said Catherine, still grinning wickedly. 'She'd think it was dirty, I bet. She's such a goody-two-shoes it hurts. No wonder she has so much energy left to run about being a bitch and spreading gossip.'

Suddenly the phone beside the bed rang, making all three of them jump. Jeannette said, 'Oh, Tess, let the machine take it.' But Tess had never been able to ignore a ringing phone. She lifted the receiver and said, 'Hello?'

'Tess,' said a voice at the other end. 'Hi, it's Tony. How are you?'

'Tony,' Tess breathed. She felt herself blushing, thinking of how she had spent the day. First seducing Julian, and now lying in bed with two women. 'I'm, ah, I'm fine,' she lied, and then she stifled a gasp, because Catherine's hand was back between her legs, fondling and probing. Tess swiped at her, trying to get her to move away. 'Just fine. How are you?'

'I wondered if you'd like to come over for dinner,' said Tony, 'to discuss the production, you understand.'

'Oh, I'd love to,' Tess said, 'but I'm a bit – tied up right now.' Jeannette giggled in her ear and began to fondle her breasts.

'I've got something in,' Tony said, sounding hurt. 'Don't say no.'

'Well – '

'Come straight over.' Tony's voice allowed for no disagreement. 'It shouldn't take you long, should it? I'll see you in an hour or so, yes?'

Tess wanted to say no, but wasn't quite sure how. 'I – ' she began, and then finished lamely, 'all right.'

'Great. See you then.' The phone clicked and purred into her ear.

Jeannette and Catherine were looking at her with disapproval in their faces. 'You didn't say yes, did you?' demanded Catherine.

'Well – '

'Don't go,' Jeannette told her. 'Stay here. You'll have a better time with us.'

Tess shook her head, feeling miserable. 'I ought to go. Really. He wants to discuss the production.'

'Tess,' said Catherine patiently, 'he doesn't want to discuss the production, he wants to fuck you. He's got you eating out of his hand. What's the matter with you?'

Tess scowled. Catherine's patronising tone brought her hackles up. 'I think it's up to me whether I go or not,' she said crossly. 'And if he wants to sleep with me, what's the problem with that? You two can stay here if you want. Have dinner. But I have to go.'

She got up from the bed and reached for her dressing gown. Jeannette and Catherine relaxed into each other's arms and watched her for a moment. Then Catherine said, 'Tess, be careful about what you tell Tony.'

'What? What do you mean?'

'About anything else you get up to,' Catherine explained. 'He's a real old-fashioned guy. I mean he's possessive. He thinks he owns his current woman. And he can be a real bastard, Tess. I know for a fact he hit the girl he was with the last time we worked together. Go carefully. Don't mention Julian.'

Tess looked at them, wondering if they were teasing. The black and the white faces looked back at her, sober and even a little anxious. It didn't look like teasing. She said after a moment, 'Yes. All right, I'll remember.'

Tony had bought dinner in from a caterer. He seemed almost proud of the fact that he could not cook and was domestically incompetent. Tess found herself in the kitchen, looking for plates and everything else required to serve the food. However, the meal looked delicious. It had probably been extremely expensive.

They did discuss the production, for approximately five minutes. Then Tony opened a bottle of wine and pushed a glass into Tess's hand. She said, 'I shouldn't, honestly, Tony,' but it was like trying to stop a flood. Before she knew where she was they were sitting in the living area on the huge sofa, sipping the wine, and she was listening to Tony talk. He was talking about opera. Occasionally Tess made a comment, but Tony didn't seem to need much stimulus to keep talking. When she agreed with him it was encouragement, and when she disagreed he either simply ignored her, or allowed her her opinion in a way that made it clear that he knew more than she did.

The trouble was that he *did* know more than she did. He was older, more experienced, he had sung in dozens of international productions, and in general his opinions

387

were interesting and sensible, if not particularly original. So she sat and listened, interested almost despite herself, and entranced by the way that his handsome face showed every emotion. He lit up with enthusiasm, crackled with laughter, smouldered with anger, and Tess lay back on the sofa and ate him with her eyes.

When she had arrived Puccini had been playing – a *Bohème* this time, one of Tony's own recordings – but at some point Tony went over to the sound system and changed the CD. 'Here,' he said, 'here's the role I'd love to play.'

Tess recognised the music at once. 'Mozart,' she said, puzzled, '*Don Giovanni*? But the Don's a baritone, Tony. And the tenor's a wimp.'

Tony smiled ruefully. 'It's always the way, isn't it,' he said. 'Never enough tenors to go around, all the heroic parts written for tenors, and here's me, a tenor, and the one role I'd kill to play is Don Giovanni.'

Tess sympathised. There were many days on which she wished she had been born a soprano. She said, 'So what is it about the role that you like?'

'Oh,' said Tony, stretching out his arms, 'opera's always sexy. It's so physical, you see, the actual act of singing. You sing with your body. And Don Giovanni, that's the sexiest role in the whole of opera. The man no woman can resist! I was born to play it, and what happens? I'm a tenor.'

This was the first time Tess had heard Tony admit there was anything he couldn't do. She smiled. 'I know how you feel,' she said. 'Sometimes I – '

'Did you see the production at Covent Garden a few years ago?' Tony interrupted. 'With Thomas Allen?'

Tess shook her head. 'Not live. They televised it, and I caught a bit of it. I thought it was a bit dull, in fact – '

'Do you remember the way they did the Don's final scene? His last meal? They had this great heavy table right at the front of the stage, and there was a naked woman on it. A beautiful, naked woman, spread out on the table like – like a floral decoration. And he ate his dinner off her.'

'I – I don't think I saw that scene,' Tess admitted.

'God, it was fabulous.' Tony's eyes and voice were burning with enthusiasm. 'That's the way to show Don Giovanni. What are women to him? He doesn't care about them. Get them into bed, fuck them, leave them, laugh at them. He doesn't care. He eats his dinner off them! And they're his slaves, so much his slaves that they let him do it. That's the part for me!'

'But – ' Tess began.

'Hey.' Tony's face was bright. An idea had struck him. 'Hey, Tess, how about you being that girl? Let me eat my dinner off you? What about it?'

Tess was so taken aback she hardly knew what to say. She did a double take, then shook her head. 'Ah, no thanks, Tony,' she managed. 'I really don't fancy it.'

'No, no, come on, let me.' He came across the room towards her and caught her hands, pulling her wine glass from her fingers and setting it down. 'You'll enjoy it. I promise. Listen, I can make sure you have a good time. We've got everything we need, look.' He extended one hand in a bold gesture towards the massive, heavy dining table, another piece of modern art in blond wood on sculptured metal legs. 'Table big enough for three women side by side. Delicious food. Beautiful woman' – he leant forward and kissed her – 'irresistible man. Come on, Tess, come on.'

'No,' Tess protested, trying to push him away. 'No, Tony, I don't want to.'

'You do,' he insisted. He pressed her into the sofa, resting his weight on her so that she would have had to struggle to release herself. His mouth fastened onto hers and he kissed her so deeply that she gasped. His strong hands felt for her breasts, found them, squeezed them. Tess wanted to resist him, but all day she had been in a state of intense arousal and the feel of his hard fingers tugging at her nipples threw her into a state of immediate erotic expectation. He was so eager, burning with eagerness, and his excitement communicated itself to her despite her reluctance. He unbuttoned her blouse and pushed it off, pulled her breasts from the cups of her bra and lowered his face to them, squeezing them together so that his tongue could flicker from one erect nipple to the other. Tess flung back her head and gasped and let him strip her naked, tugging her clothes from her limbs, revealing her pale skin. When he pulled off her skirt he reached down to her panties, could not at once free them, and with a snarl of impatience yanked at them so hard that the flimsy fabric tore. She tried to protest, but his eager lips gagged her.

'Come on,' Tony hissed. He caught her up in his arms and with his fingers snagged some of her clothes, the rags of her knickers, her stockings, the silk scarf she had draped around her neck. She let him carry her over to the table and lie her down on its cold, hard surface. 'Beautiful,' he hissed, 'Tess, you're my wet dream. God, you're beautiful.' He kissed her hard, his tongue exploring deeply, and she moaned. Between her legs she was wet and warm. Then she felt him spreading her wrists, holding them high above her head, and she opened her eyes and said anxiously, 'Tony, what are you doing?'

'Tying you up,' Tony said, suiting his actions to the words.

'No,' Tess said, trying to pull free. But one hand was already secured and his strong fingers were on her other wrist, wrapping one of her stockings round it, tying it quickly to the metal leg. 'No!' Tess cried, her legs thrashing as she tried to pull free. 'No, Tony, this isn't funny!'

'It's not supposed to be funny,' Tony said. He leant over her, his face over hers, and she fell still and stared up at him, her breath coming quickly. 'It's meant to be sexy. Hasn't anyone ever tied you up before? Give in to it, Tess. Trust me. You'll love it.'

You'll love it. Trust me. Leo had said exactly the same

thing to her a few moments before he took her virginity, and he had told the truth. She had loved it. And hadn't sex with Tony, the previous night and that same morning, been great? Tess stopped struggling and let Tony spread her legs and bind her ankles too. The bindings were loose, so that she could wriggle, but not so loose that she could escape.

Tony stood back and surveyed his handiwork. 'Gorgeous,' he said, in a voice that was almost a sigh of satisfaction. 'Simply gorgeous. And now for dinner.'

In a few moments he was at the table again, plates in hand. 'Here we are,' he said. 'Warm salad of duck breasts and green beans in a hazelnut oil dressing. Delicious. Now, where shall we put it.'

'Tony,' Tess whimpered, 'don't. You'll get me all sticky.'

'Sure I will. And remember how much fun we had in the shower?' Tony looked down at himself, then put down the plates on the table beside Tess's pinioned body and began to remove his clothes. He did not hurry. It seemed that Tess's flinching and whimpering, her ineffectual little protests, aroused him, because when he removed his shorts his cock sprang forward, so erect that it almost touched his flat belly, swollen and glistening and eager.

'Now then,' he said, and with one hand he reached into the plate of salad. He lifted out a sliver of duck breast and suspended it over Tess's lips. 'Try some,' he suggested.

Tess obediently reached up and ate the sliver of meat. It was, as Tony had said, delicious: rich and complex and satisfying. She swallowed eagerly and Tony smiled and fed her a little more of the salad, more duck, a few strands of the long crisp French beans, a couple of wild mushrooms, all bathed in the delicate, nutty dressing. 'Yum, yum,' he said, as she licked her lips. 'That's enough for you for the time being. Time for my dinner, table decoration.'

He picked up the dish and tilted it. Slivers of duck and a few beans and mushrooms fell from it and landed on Tess's breasts. She shrieked as she felt the warm, oily dressing trickling down her ribs, under her arms, around her areolae. 'Oh God, Tony,' she cried, 'oh God, that's awful, oh for God's sake.' She pulled at the bindings of her wrists and ankles, but she couldn't free herself.

'Be quiet,' Tony said, in a voice of monotone stillness that was so commanding that Tess closed her mouth and just stared at him. He leant over and reached with lips and teeth for a piece of meat, caught it, pulled it into his mouth and ate it. A piece of mushroom, a French bean, another piece of meat. One of the mushrooms had landed beside Tess's right nipple and as he drew it into his mouth he flickered his tongue across the coral tip of her breast. There was something so greedy, so salacious in his movements that Tess breathed quickly and arched her back in delight. It was erotic being tied there, helpless, unable to resist, used by him as if she were a piece of living furniture. She closed her eyes, giving herself up to the sensations as he ate every piece of the salad from her breasts and then began to lick off the dressing.

'More,' Tony said, putting another handful of salad on Tess's quivering body. She breathed more quickly as he reached with his lips for piece after piece. His body too was shaking, she could feel him trembling, and it aroused her to know how much he wanted her. Occasionally he fed her something and it was as if she was eating her own desire.

At last all the salad was gone. Tony looked down at her, breathing hard. The whole of her upper body glistened with oil. He took her breasts in his hands and began to squeeze and stroke them, teasing her nipples until she gasped. Then he said, 'Slippery and delicious. God, Tess, your breasts are fabulous.' And without another word he swung himself up onto the table and straddled her waist with his strong thighs, pushing her

392

breasts together into a shining mound of inviting flesh. He thrust his hard cock between them and Tess whimpered as she felt the hot shaft slide to and fro. She opened her eyes and looked down and saw the head of his penis moving towards her, scarlet with aggressive lust, the little eye at its tip weeping with eagerness. Tony held her breasts between his hands and pinched and pulled her nipples as he moved forward and back. It was an extraordinary sensation, unexpected, sensual, and Tess gave herself up to it. She could not take her eyes from the swelling tip of Tony's pulsing cock.

He thrust faster and faster, beginning to pant as he shafted the silken cleft of her oiled breasts. He grunted wordlessly, like an animal, as his pleasure grew and his surging phallus thickened and twitched as it prepared for orgasm. Tess felt frightened for a moment, helpless, vulnerable, stunned by his sudden, selfish fierceness. But although she tugged at the bonds around her wrists, she could not escape, and half of her did not want to.

Suddenly Tony began to cry out, 'Oh God, yes, that's it, yes,' and he stopped moving and Tess felt his cock between her breasts throbbing and jumping as the semen surged up the shaft and spurted out. She closed her eyes instinctively and flinched as the warm drops fell on her face, on her cheeks and lips. Tentatively she reached out with her tongue and tasted the mild saltiness of Tony's cooling seed. Then she opened her eyes and looked up.

Tony's dark face was flushed with pleasure. He was not smiling, but he looked satisfied, like a lion after the kill. With his fingers he pinched Tess's nipples until she gasped, and only then did he smile. 'I knew this was a good idea,' he said.

Tess tugged at one wrist. 'Tony, let me go,' she said. 'I'm getting stiff.'

He grinned. 'I'll soon take your mind off that. Time for dessert.'

'No,' Tess protested. But she could do nothing. Tony climbed off her. His penis was slightly deflated, like warm Plasticine, but not really soft. It was clear that he was still fiercely aroused. He picked up the bowl of fresh strawberries and the jug of cream, still cold from the fridge, and grinned fiendishly. He lifted the jug and poured a trickle of icy liquid directly onto the warm, damp flesh between Tess's legs.

'Jesus,' Tess cried, heaving her hips upwards in a vain attempt to escape. 'Oh, God, that's cold.'

'Now,' said Tony. He picked a strawberry from the bowl and without a word pushed it between Tess's sex lips, deep inside her. She cried out and he smiled and knelt between her legs and with his tongue felt within her, licking the berry, catching it, withdrawing it slowly from her and tugging it into his mouth. Then he licked the mixture of her juices and the cold cream from her and she moaned with astonished pleasure.

Tony pushed berry after berry into Tess's body and removed them with his tongue. He let her eat one or two, sometimes dipped in cream, sometimes dipped in her own juice. Time after time he drew her to the point of orgasm, then trickled icy cream directly onto her trembling clitoris, making her cry out with misery and frustration as the incredible sensations faded. It seemed to please him to torment her. She writhed in her bonds, begging him to finish her off, to let her come. He would have gone on for ever, but at last he misjudged the strength of his caresses and a massive, pulsing orgasm wracked Tess's pinioned limbs, making her forget everything that had gone before in a shuddering, heaving clench of ecstasy.

She would have begged him then to untie her, but before she had got her breath back Tony had unfastened one wrist and quickly tied it again to the other table leg, so that her hands were pinned together above her head. Then, while she still gasped and whimpered, he freed her ankles and quickly flipped her over, making her kneel with her face pressed to the cold slimy surface of the table so that her bottom was thrust up into the air.

He felt in the salad bowl for remnants of the dressing and began to anoint the cleft of her arse, rubbing the oil into her skin, pushing the tip of one finger gently into her tight anus.

Tess knew what he was going to do. She could have protested, but it would have been hopeless. Her hands were tied, she could not prevent him, and if she struggled he could always tie her legs as well. And also – also, she wanted to feel him in her arse. Jeannette's description of James and Adam making love had aroused her ferociously, and she wanted to know what it was like.

'Relax,' Tony hissed, trying to push his finger deeper. Tess began to breathe deeply and let the delicious after-effects of her orgasm bathe her in libidinous bliss. 'That's it,' said Tony, as her resistance suddenly ceased and first one finger, then two, slid into her to their full length. 'That's it.' He withdrew his fingers and replaced them with the head of his cock, again stiff and proud and ready. It felt different, sticky: he must have put on a condom. Tess drew in cold air through her swollen lips and moaned as the hot smooth shaft began to penetrate her, entering her, taking the virginity of her anus. 'Oh,' she gasped, because it was wonderful. She moaned and pushed herself up towards Tony, welcoming his thrusts. Her clitoris ached and quivered and the nipples of her dangling breasts rubbed against the table. She longed to be touched, she knew that if he would touch her she would come again, but Tony had other things on his mind. He was holding onto the swell of her hips and plunging into her, shafting her as hard as he could, grunting as his balls slapped against her body with every surge of his cock deep inside her.

'Christ,' he gasped, 'that's so tight. Oh God, it's good.' His fingers dented her white flesh, holding her still against his ferocious thrusts. 'Slave,' he growled, 'my slave, tied up for me to fuck her. Say something, slave, slave.'

Tess's hands clasped and unclasped frantically. She felt like an animal, powerless, possessed. 'Please,' she moaned, 'don't, don't,' and she did not know whether she was really begging him to stop or only saying what she knew would give him pleasure.

'I will,' Tony snarled, 'I will!' and with a final, desperate thrust he forced his throbbing penis deep into Tess's anus and as his orgasm seized him he leant forward and caught her nape between his teeth like a beast and Tess cried out with shock and pain and fell forward onto the table, crushed beneath him, panting and slippery with oil and trembling with astonishment at the irresistible power of her own response.

After a few long moments Tony leant forward and slackened the bonds round her wrists, but he did not lift his weight from her. 'There,' he whispered in her ear, 'I told you so. You loved it.'

Tess did not deny it. She moved a little, actually enjoying the feeling of him lying on top of her, crushing her against the cold wood. She pillowed her head on her hands and said sleepily, 'Tony, I'm still hungry.'

Act Two, Scene Three

The rehearsal studio, one week later

*R*ehearsals went on, and James gradually stopped shouting and began to nod approvingly when Tess sang. She had mastered the first act now, in which Carmen first falls for Don José. It was easy. When she met Tony's eyes she would imagine the moment when Julian had looked from her breasts into her face, his expression burning with sudden lust, and everything that James wanted was there – the instant desire, the audible click. So things were improving. But no sooner had she managed one thing, than another reared up to challenge her.

Tess rested her chin between her fists, staring down at her score as if it could talk. She was sitting in a corner of the rehearsal room, using a few quiet moments to study the scene in which Carmen and her friends Frasquita and Mercedes play at fortune-telling, looking for their futures in the cards. Frasquita and Mercedes are half-joking, hoping for love, for riches, for an elderly millionaire to marry them and drop dead soon after. But to Carmen the cards tell a different story.

> *Let's see what the cards say to me.*
> *Diamonds – spades –* Another card turns *– death!*

It's all true – first for me – then for him –
For both of us, it's death!

'How are you doing?' said Jeannette's screech-owl voice, pitched at a careful whisper to avoid disturbing Tony and Emma, who were busily rehearsing, under James's watchful eye, the critical moment at which Micaela tells Don José that his mother is dying and he will have to leave Carmen. As always James was giving every second his attention and making the singers work with equal intensity, insisting that Tony and Emma repeat the scene over and over until it was exactly as he wanted it. Tess had almost forgotten that she was supposed to be on stage, and so had the rest of the cast, who were standing around the room relaxing. Catherine was in the corner, leaning on the piano and looking meaningfully down at Julian, who was trying to look as if he hadn't noticed and was simply concentrating on the score. Despite her expressed preference for men a little more grown up than Julian, Catherine seemed to have decided that the young pianist was a worthy prey, and she was leaning on the piano's glossy lid watching him rather like a female tiger considering a gazelle as a possible appetizer.

Tess shook her head and looked up with a sigh. Since their afternoon in bed together Catherine and Jeannette had become rather protective of her, like older sisters, and she was beginning to rely on their interest and concern. 'It's no use,' she said. 'I'm getting closer to the character James wants, I know it. But how can someone as – as strong as the person he wants be to be, someone that sassy, how can she believe in what a pack of cards tells her?'

Jeannette sat down on the floor beside Tess, spreading her slender denim-clad legs in an inelegant sprawl. 'Ever been to a Tarot reader?' she asked.

'No,' Tess laughed scornfully. 'Why should I? It's all mumbo-jumbo.'

Jeannette raised her dark, pencil-thin brows. 'If you feel that way, no wonder you can't understand what Carmen thinks.'

'Don't tell me you believe it,' Tess said.

'I wouldn't say that I did believe it or I didn't,' Jeannette said with a shrug. 'But I certainly wouldn't write it off. A friend of mine is interested in that sort of thing, casts horoscopes, reads the Tarot, and she's got her head screwed on. She did a reading for me once and I was really surprised by how accurate it was.'

'Anyone could do something like that for a friend,' said Tess. 'She knows you anyway, doesn't she? Of course she could say the right things.'

'It wasn't just about my past,' said Jeannette. 'She – ' but then she swore and jumped to her feet. 'Come on, you're on.'

Tess had missed her cue. James shook his head disapprovingly and Tony and Emma stood looking at them expectantly. Emma drew her small mouth together in a pout, then said, 'It's not very polite to keep us waiting. Is it, Tony?'

Emma didn't really need to say anything to make Tess feel uncomfortable about missing her cue. Also she didn't need to make up to Tony quite as obviously as she was doing now. When she spoke to Tony Emma's big blue eyes looked very innocent and trusting and she stood rather closer to him than was necessary. This was not lost on Leo, who was standing at the other side of the room chewing his lip in annoyance, and Tess could see that it wasn't lost on Tony either. He smiled down at Emma with a not entirely paternal look, his dark eyes twinkling at her, and Tess felt a sudden spurt of jealousy. Emma had Leo crawling to her feet and that wasn't enough for her, she had to go fluttering her golden eyelashes at Tony as well. Little tease. Tess would have liked to go and touch Tony or in some other way show her proprietorial interest, but that wasn't possible in rehearsal. She just said, 'Sorry. I beg your pardon, James,' and carried on. It wasn't as if she actually had anything to say at this point: she just had to look as if she didn't give a damn that Don José was leaving her.

Happy now? Tony sang, his golden voice heavy with bitterness. *I'm going. But I'll be back!* He took Emma's arm, ready to lead her off stage.

Tess tossed her head and turned away. She knew it wasn't right, and she wasn't a bit surprised when James stopped Julian playing and said, 'No, Tess, no.'

Tess turned back, taking a deep breath. 'I know, James. I ought to look as if I don't care.'

'You're bored with him,' James insisted. 'You've had enough. Escamillo's the one you fancy right now. You couldn't be happier that José is off. But at the moment you look just jealous!'

That's because I am jealous, Tess thought. It had bothered her much more than she expected to see Tony touching Emma. Aloud she said, 'Don't you think Carmen might be – might be jealous, to see José with another woman?'

Emma said sweetly, 'It would be understandable,' and moved a little closer to Tony, who grinned broadly down at her. Behind Tess Leo clenched his fists and Tess thinned her lips angrily.

'In my reading,' James said, 'Carmen doesn't give a damn about José at this point. She wouldn't care if he chucked Micaela down on the stage and raped her, which, if you remember, is exactly what all the dealers want to do the moment they see her. Carmen would actually enjoy that. The one thing she wouldn't be right now, Tess, is jealous.'

They worked the scene over and over again and at last Tess managed to produce a performance that satisfied James for the time being. They moved on to the end of the act and James announced that the rehearsal was over for the day.

At once Leo swooped upon Emma and bore her off into a corner. Tess heard him saying in tones of real distress, 'Look, Emma, darling, I really *wish* you wouldn't . . .'

Tony sloped over to Tess and lifted her hand to his lips. He was always very attentive to her at rehearsal, making it clear to everyone in the cast that she was his personal property. 'I'm sorry I can't see you tonight,' he said softly. 'Or tomorrow. It's one of those things. It was arranged ages ago.'

'I know,' said Tess. 'It's all right, Tony, honestly. I'll have a quiet night in.' For a moment she wanted to tell him that she would really prefer it if he didn't play up to Emma every time they were together on stage. But she didn't think she could muster the nerve, and it wouldn't be right to criticise him in public, either. She just reached up her lips for a kiss.

'Be good,' Tony whispered. For a moment his agile tongue slipped deep into her mouth, twisting until she gasped. Then he drew back and patted her bottom and went away.

Jeannette came and stood at Tess's elbow and watched her face as she gazed after Tony's retreating back. 'You look like a Walt Disney puppy,' she said. 'What's the matter? Not got a life when he's not around?'

Tess frowned angrily, but she couldn't deny it. Tony was very demanding, and it had been easy over the last week to allow her life gradually to become subsumed into his, waiting for his calls, living for seeing him, only half herself when he was somewhere else. She looked ruefully up at Jeannette and shrugged.

'Listen,' Jeannette said, coming closer, 'Catherine managed to persuade Julian to come over tonight. Leo's taking Emma out, we'll be all alone in the house. Come on over and join in. We're going to show him what he's been missing.'

For a moment Tess was tempted, but then she shook her head. 'No,' she said, trying to smile. 'No, I think I had better just go home.'

Around them the cast were chatting, splitting into

small groups and heading out for a meal or a drink. Catherine was still leaning on the piano, smiling down into Julian's pale incredulous face like a mermaid luring a mariner. Jeannette glanced over at the two of them and then back to Tess, shaking her head. 'Listen,' she said, 'don't let him take you over. You need to stay independent, Tess. How will you ever manage the part if you don't? Keep something back. He's so greedy. Don't let him own you.'

Tess looked up into Jeannette's face. She knew that what her friend said was true, but to admit it seemed weak and disloyal to Tony. It wasn't as if he had done anything wrong, after all. He might flirt with Emma, but nobody suggested that he had been unfaithful, and his appointments that night and the following day were the sort of thing that any famous singer has to put up with: meetings with his agent, with producers, with casting directors, with someone from Channel 4 and someone from *Hello!* magazine. He was possessive, but was that so very wrong?

'Look,' Jeannette said softly, 'I'm not telling you to drop him. I just think you should do some more research, that's all. On your own. You need time on your own.'

'On my own,' Tess said slowly, 'means not with you and Catherine. Or with Julian, come to that. I told him I wouldn't see him again.'

Jeannette raised her eyebrows. 'Fine,' she said. 'Like James says, go out and screw someone. Anyone, Tess, it doesn't matter who. Tony's away tomorrow as well, isn't he? Make the most of the opportunity.'

Tess shrugged. 'Maybe,' she said. 'Maybe.'

She returned home alone and lowered her bag slowly to the floor inside the door, sighing heavily. Although it was late, the June light was still bright outside the flat, and green leaves stirred at the tops of the trees, level with her windows.

'I'm tired,' Tess told the flat. And she was, very tired.

402

For a week she had worked hard at rehearsals, gone to movement and body workshops run by Adam, visited her teacher for technical coaching through the hardest parts of the score, worked with Julian at solos and ensembles so that she understood what the conductor wanted, and each night she had gone to Tony's flat and allowed herself to be drawn into his sexual world, which each night had become more and more strange, exotic and peculiarly satisfying. There were blue bruises on the white skin of her haunches where Tony's strong fingers had gripped her tightly and pulled her violently back onto his throbbing phallus, and her wrists and ankles were red and raw where he had tied her up. She knew that he behaved as if he owned her, but she could hardly decide whether he was in love with her and eager for her to experience the whole gamut of lust, or whether he hated her and simply wanted to degrade and humiliate her. Either way, he was opening her eyes to an entirely new sensual world. But sexual discovery was time and energy consuming. Tess had hardly been in her own flat all week, and now she was so exhausted that she could hardly see it.

She walked wearily into the kitchen, thinking with pleasant anticipation of a mug of hot chocolate, and opened the fridge. An unmistakeably cheesy smell told her that the milk had gone off. She said heavily, 'Bugger.'

There wasn't much point in thinking about hot chocolate without milk, and Tess simply didn't feel up to going back into Hampstead to find some. So she slammed the fridge door, picked up an apple from the fruit bowl and stalked through to the bathroom, moodily munching.

She looked at herself in the bathroom mirror. There were rings under her eyes and her skin looked pasty. 'Early night for you,' she said to her reflection. 'Nice hot bath and an early night.'

Moving slowly, she turned on the taps and then pulled off her clothes and dumped them into the laundry basket. It was almost full, because she hadn't even had a chance to do the washing for about a week. I'll run out of clean knickers soon, she thought, and then where will I be? And then she reflected that Tony would probably approve heartily of her going without knickers, and the thought made her laugh.

Presently she was naked and the bath was almost full. Tess poured a little body oil into the water and added a few drops of tea tree oil, because her voice felt furry and she wanted to inhale the sharp, soothing steam while she soaked. She got into the bath and lay back, looking up at the ceiling.

After a while the clean, antiseptic smell of the oil cleared her head and made her feel able to sing a little. She closed her eyes and began to murmur to herself, very soft and low:

> *There's somebody here who's waiting for me,*
> *I hope that he turns out to be*
> *Someone who'll watch over me . . .*

Then she stopped and lay still, breathing deeply and frowning to herself. Why sing that song? What did it mean?

Every man Tess had known had been, in the physical sense, someone to watch over her. Leo had taught her how her body could give her pleasure and how she could give pleasure to a man. Dan had used her, but his extraordinary beauty had made her actively desire him. And Tony – Tony was possessive, physically affectionate, kinky, masterful. Certainly someone to watch over her. So why sing that song now, and why sing it in that tone of soft, aching longing?

Carmen wouldn't have wanted someone to watch over her. Tess shifted a little in the bath, letting the warm, silky water play over her floating breasts and between her legs. She thought of Carmen, her character, as she would like to portray her. Strong, beautiful, callous, doomed. Doomed because she insisted upon her passion-

404

ate independence, her freedom to love whom she chose, and a man's jealousy could not bear it.

Tess caught the chain with her toe and let a little of the water run out of the bath. Then, hardly knowing what she was doing, she picked up the shower head and turned on the shower. Hot water pulsed out onto her warm wet body. She let her head tilt back so that her hair floated around her and gently, slowly guided the spray between her legs.

She let out a long, blissful sigh as the tingling stream of water caressed her thighs, her labia, the entrance to her sex. The bobbing orbs of her breasts tensed and tautened with sudden arousal and her nipples erected, stiff symbols of desire. The beat of the water on her sensitive flesh was almost too much, and for a moment she drew the shower head away, letting the weight of the flow fall onto the furred mound of her pubis. But it wasn't enough, and after a moment she moved the spray infinitesimally, until one glittering thread of water sprang through the air and struck the swelling bud of her clitoris.

'Ah,' Tess breathed slowly. Her diaphragm rose and fell, drawing air deep into her lungs, and as she breathed her hips also lifted and fell, surging up towards the insistent touch of the spray.

She felt her body floating in the warm water as if she were the only living creature in the world, as if she were isolated and alone, seeking her solitary pleasure without compunction or shame. The ripples lapped across her breasts, stroking her tight nipples, and between her pale, parted thighs the shower beat down onto her quivering sex, pummelling the sensitive flesh with unbearable pleasure.

For a moment Tess thought of Tony, his smooth, olive skin and his dark eyes and hair, the way that when he prepared to take her his lips would curl with lustful anger as if he were the toreador and she the bull, run down, exhausted, helpless, waiting for him to plunge his spear into her shuddering body. But although she did not consciously know it, her body had had enough of being Tony's slave. She wanted variety, and of itself her brain provided the image that would accompany her pleasure.

A mermaid on a rock, silver-green tail coiled onto the slimy, cold stone. Her breasts are small and round and high and her body is white as a corpse's, starred with her coral lips and her rosy nipples like bright shells upon a beach of white sand. Her eyes are the colour of her tail, the colour of the sea, and her hair is dark red, like dried blood. It is long and thick and shining and she sits very calmly on the rock amid the foaming sea and combs her long tresses with a comb of pearl. She is beautiful, but with an unearthly beauty, a deadly beauty, and her eyes are cold as the waves and quite pitiless.

She lifts her head, never once interrupting the rhythm of her combing, like the rhythm of the waves that beat against her limpet-studded rock. In the distance she has seen a ship. It is a warriors' ship, brightly painted, and on its square sail is drawn the figure of a bull. She can see the men in it at their oars, naked for their labour, rowing with all their strength against the surging might of the contrary sea.

Men are her prey, she needs them as a beast needs meat to live. Her cold eyes brighten and she flickers her tail against the rock like a cat that sees the mouse. She combs and combs her heavy hair, and as she combs she opens her soft, red lips and begins to sing.

Her voice is like wine, like dark, soft fur, like a coil of smoke that seeps from the hearth fire to draw the man home from the hunt. She does not sing loudly, and yet that sweet dark voice carries over the crash and roar of the waves and flies straight to the ears of the young warriors rowing their ship. They hear it and stop their work, helpless, enchanted, dumbstruck and frozen by the promise of delight in the mermaid's song.

Still she sings, and now the young men tremble. Her

406

song is wordless, and each of them hears what he wishes, and each of them hears her singing of the zenith of sensual delight. Each one hears her telling him how she longs for him, how her small snowy breasts are taut with yearning, how her nipples are tight and hard as rose hips, how her soft white flesh aches for him to come to her and take her in his arms and possess her with his strong, male body, thrusting himself into her, making her cry out, her sweet voice crying out in pleasure for him alone. They see her beautiful whiteness, her breasts stirring as she combs her hair, and they forget that she is a sea creature, that where a woman has a sex she has nothing but a fish's tail, and they cannot tell that her song is no more than the web a spider spins to catch a fly. They drop their oars and begin to fight among themselves for the privilege of flinging themselves over the side into the heaving surf to swim to her.

The mermaid watches them and sings still, and now her song is more urgent. The young men fight furiously upon their shuddering ship, drawing blood, for they can hear her singing, *Draw me on to ecstasy! Make me yours! Take your pleasure in my body, spill your seed within me, ravish me, possess me!*

At last one of them flings another aside and leaps up onto the side of the ship, which is protected and bedecked with painted shields. For a moment he stands poised, splendidly naked, his beautiful body taut with eagerness, his face bright with anticipation as he hears the siren's song. He flings himself at last from the ship's gunwale and cleaves the foaming sea in a perfect dive, and the mermaid smiles and drops her pearly comb and slides from her rock to meet him in the tumbling waves.

Her song has ceased, and the other young men on the ship suddenly stop fighting and draw apart and look at each other with horror in their eyes. While she sang they were bewitched, and now they are freed they know their danger and run to their oars to try to save their foundering ship, unable to spare even a glance for their companion as he cuts through the surf towards the white body of the mermaid. But they are too late, they are doomed, the rocks are snapping their eager teeth at the ship's frail timbers and in moments they will be shivered into spars and flotsam.

In the sea the mermaid dives and swims once around the swimming youth. He is as strong and beautiful as her cold heart could wish. She swims up beside him and rubs her soft breasts against him. His body is muscular and warm and it pleases her to touch him, as it pleases a cat to rub itself against a stranger's hand. She laughs to see how his flesh reacts to her, his strange male sex stiffening despite the cold kiss of the fierce sea, and he laughs to see her laughing. She presses her chilly skin close to him and reaches up to kiss him with her mouth. Her tail locks around his thighs and her arms wrap around him, pinioning his hands to his sides, and with the tip of her tail she caresses that strange stiff rod of flesh, rubbing it, stroking the soft skin up and down until the young man groans into her open mouth and his body heaves against her and warm pearly liquid bursts from the end of his male organ and floats like froth on the surface of the waves.

He is limp in her arms, as if he has spurted his strength into the sea with his seed, and she smiles at him again and puts her lips over his. She pulls him down beneath the waves. He does not struggle, and as he drowns in her cold grasp she puts her tongue into his warm mouth and tastes his fleeing soul.

Tess arched in the warm water, her eyes tight shut, every muscle tense as the cascading liquid drew her into an orgasm that shuddered and rippled through her like the cold sea that was the mermaid's home. For an infinite second she hung there, not breathing, not thinking, a body of pure pleasure suspended in nothingness. Then she relaxed and lay back, her breath coming raggedly, her lips dry and aching.

As she made her way slowly to bed she thought about

that strange fantasy. It was new to her. Where had it come from? Why should it arouse her to think of dragging a beautiful young man to his doom? That it had aroused her was clear: her climax had been tremendous. For a moment she was afraid that Tony's dominance was making her strange. Then she realised the meaning of it. The mermaid was another personification of the character she was trying to become, of Carmen, a callous, cold, beautiful creature, binding men to her with the powerful spell of her lovely voice, sucking the strength from them and then abandoning them, limp, lifeless husks.

Tess slid down below the duvet and shivered. Such power, such control, and all springing from that extraordinary gift, her own voice. For a moment she was almost afraid. But then as sleep crept up on her the sense of fear began to fade, and when she slipped into dreams they too were dreams of strength and erotic power.

She woke very late. Fuzzy with sleep she rolled over in bed and caught hold of her alarm clock. It was quarter to eleven, and she blinked and swayed as she sat up and pushed her hands through her hair.

A day to herself. She had nothing planned, and it felt quite odd to have time to do nothing if she wanted. She got up slowly, made herself tea, sorted out a wash, showered and then put her dressing gown back on and went and sat on the sofa, still half dozing. Outside the weather was gloomy, with heavy clouds threatening rain. Tess considered the dark sky for a few moments, then went to find warm clothes and her Wellington boots.

By the time she was ready to go out the rain was coming down in sheets. She pulled the hood of her Goretex jacket securely up round her ears, galumphed down the stairs and out into the rain. Within a few minutes she was on the Heath. There was nobody else about, even the most diligent dog walkers were waiting for the weather to improve, and she splashed across the soft leaf-mould under the great oaks, breathing in the fresh, wet air. There was something about the quality of the air when it was raining that she found irresistible, healing and soothing both to her vocal chords and to her mind, and she stood in a little glade on a patch of new fresh grass and put back her hood and turned up her face to the pouring rain. The cold drops stung her eyelids and her forehead, her cheeks and chin, and she stretched out her hands and breathed deeply.

She would remember how it had felt to be the mermaid. She would remember that sense of power and strength, of sexual desire and sexual desirability combined with absolute callousness. She would infuse her portrayal of Carmen with that feeling.

Jeannette had been right, she had needed time on her own. It was so easy to allow herself just to become an adjunct of Tony, something that went along with whatever he wanted, acceding to all his demands. Not good enough.

As she turned for home another thought occurred to her. If research was what it took to play a part well, then perhaps she ought to do some research on the other point of Carmen's character that was giving her problems: her reliance on the cards.

Back at the flat Tess shed her soaking clothes and wrapped herself in a warm towel, then picked up the phone and dialled. She made a face when after three rings Emma's sweeter-than-honey voice said, 'Hello. You've reached the answering service of Emma Ridley, Catherine Gibbs and Jeannette Baldwin. Please leave a message after the beep. Thanks ever so much.' Awful woman, Tess thought. She even gushes at her answering machine.

'Jeannette,' she said after the beep, 'hi, it's Tess. It's Sunday morning and I – '

'Hi, Tess!' Jeannette's voice was breathless. Tess held

the receiver away from her ear. Talking to Jeannette on the phone was like talking to a sawmill. 'What's up?'

'How are you?' Tess asked. 'Did you have a good time last night?'

'Wow, did we! You were right about Julian, Tess. He's got a tongue like a corkscrew. Though I think the two of us must more or less have worn it out last night. And we stripped his thread, too.'

'He's not still there, is he?'

'Oh no, he went home in the small hours. He didn't want Emma to see him here this morning. Don't blame him, either. She sniffed around a bit before she went out, you could almost hear her thinking *I'm sure I smell a man*, like the witch in *Hansel and Gretel*. But Cath and I have kept mum, so Julian's secret is safe with us.'

'Listen,' Tess said hesitantly, 'I was thinking about what you said. About research. And I wondered if you would give me the number of your friend, the one who reads the Tarot? I'd like to call her.'

'Why, sure!' Jeannette sounded surprised and pleased. 'Hang on while I get my organiser. Here you go. Her name's Sarah, Sarah Carter.'

'Very ordinary name,' said Tess, surprised.

'She's just a friend of mine,' said Jeannette. 'We met at a party, years ago. She's not a singer or anything, she works in an office. But she's a good reader.' She read out the number. 'Lives in Bow. Give her a call, go and see her. Say I sent you.'

'Is she expensive?'

'She does it for fun. I doubt she'd charge you anything.'

Early in the afternoon Tess found herself at Bow station, looking at the map of the local area on the station wall and trying to find out where Sarah Carter lived.

She had sounded almost absurdly normal over the telephone. Maybe a little older than Tess, in her thirties perhaps, and quite straightforward and pragmatic. Tess had explained that she was only doing research for a role and she really just wanted to talk in principle and Sarah had said, 'Well, why not? Why not come and have tea? I've got nothing particular to do this afternoon. I'd love to meet you.'

Tess found the house quite easily and stood in the street outside, looking at it. It was a very ordinary Victorian terrace house, nicely kept. There were roses in the front garden, bowed down almost to the ground with the weight of raindrops in their tumbled flowers, and the door and the window frames were painted dark blue and white.

The door opened and a woman stood there, a nice-looking fair-haired woman. Yes, early thirties, tall and rather stately, with strong bones and deep-set grey eyes. She was smiling. 'You've found it,' she said. 'Come in. You must be Tess.'

Tess expected the house to be full of all sorts of arcane paraphernalia, but it wasn't. It was a perfectly normal house, tidy rather than not, comfortably furnished, with real fireplaces and what estate agents call 'original features'. Some of the pictures on the walls were rather odd, and the books in the drawing room bookcase revealed a very eclectic interest in all sorts of things – whale songs, folklore, herbalism, holistic remedies, aromatherapy, astrology and the occult – but there was nothing frightening about it.

Sarah brought a tray of tea and Digestive biscuits. The tea was Earl Grey, which Tess took as a good sign, and served in astrological mugs, dark blue with little golden star signs on them. It was excellent tea. Sarah smiled over her mug at Tess and said, 'So from what you told me, you're a sceptic and you want enough information to be convincing as Carmen.' Her voice was very reassuring, soft and pleasantly modulated.

'Well – ' Tess began to protest, but then she shrugged. 'No, you're right. That is right.'

'I would have thought', said Sarah, 'that the best way

to proceed is for me to do a reading for you. Then you can see the style, and even if you aren't convinced you'll understand how it comes over.'

Tess shook her head. 'No,' she said, 'I don't think that would be a good idea.' She was filled with apprehension.

'Why not?' Sarah didn't seem offended, just interested.

'Because – ' because it might be true. Tess realised that she must be looking as if she was frightened, and she was angry with herself. If it was all rubbish, why be afraid of it? 'Well,' she said, trying to look casual, 'well, what the hell? Why not?'

Sarah looked quietly at her as if she were not the least convinced by this bravado. She said simply, 'I'll get the cards.'

When Tess left the house in Bow more than two hours later she was shaken. She had expected to hear nothing but platitudes, obvious statements which anyone with any sense of the dramatic could have concocted from what they already knew about her. But Sarah, in her calm, serious voice, had laid one pattern of cards, another, and from them drawn so much that she could not possibly have known.

She had said that Tess had worked hard to achieve her current position. Well, anyone who knew anything about singing could have said that. That she was now facing a challenge: fair guess. That in order to achieve what she now sought she would need to change herself, or at least to appear to others that she had changed herself.

By this stage Tess had felt uncomfortable. She had asked Sarah about her love life, making light of it, as if it were some sort of a joke, but Sarah had seemed equally serious on this question. She laid another pattern of cards and frowned, then said, 'You haven't had a great many lovers. Two or three, perhaps. And they have dominated you. The current man especially is jealous.' She looked up into Tess's eyes, perhaps seeking confirmation, but Tess looked hunted and unconvinced. Sarah could have learnt this from Jeannette. After a little pause Sarah laid an extra card and frowned again. 'Men dominate your work life as well as love. That's not surprising, men are in such a strong position. I suppose the person you are working for at present is male and you have to seek to please him. But the pattern is very strong for love, too. You allow your man to dominate you.' She looked concerned, and after a while she said, 'In the future perhaps – perhaps you will free yourself from this dominating influence and find your own way. If you are going to develop as much as you can, if you are going to achieve everything you want, then you have to do it. You have to free yourself. You can't go on relying on your lovers as you do. But, you should be careful.'

'Careful? Why?'

'I don't quite understand this,' said Sarah. 'It's as if – as if you are two people at present. And for both of them there may be – danger, conflict, but for one it is real, for the other – potential, or imaginary, I can't tell. But if you are to progress, if you are to succeed, you will have to face the conflict and brave the danger.'

Despite herself Tess was caught up. She leant forward, studying the cards Sarah held: the Chariot, the Swords. 'Will I succeed?' she asked in a low voice. 'In – in love, I mean?'

'Are you talking about love, or sex?' Sarah asked calmly.

'Sex,' said Tess, though she meant love.

Sarah turned another card. It was a Star. She said very slowly, 'If you come through the conflict, then there is great potential. But you must take control.' She looked up. 'I can't say yes or no. It depends on you.'

This was the sort of prevarication that Tess had expected. She refrained from curling her lip and asked in a cynical voice, 'Tell me, Sarah, can you ever see death in the cards? Can you tell if someone is going to die?'

Sarah's voice was very level. 'Sometimes, yes. But I would never tell them.'

Tess didn't want to go back to the flat with all of this rocketing around inside her head. At Tottenham Court Road she got off the Central line, intending to change to the Northern, and then on impulse left the station instead and walked down Charing Cross Road towards Trafalgar Square. Her head was buzzing with possibilities. It wasn't so much what she had been told as the way Sarah had spoken. It was clear not only that she believed what she said, but that in the past her observations and predictions had been confirmed as true. And Sarah seemed like an ordinary, sensible person, not a charlatan. She hadn't charged Tess anything, she didn't make her living from it, it was just something she did.

It's as if you are two people at present . . . Yes, two people. Herself, Tess Challoner, and Carmen, her character, the character she was trying to make her own. And unless she freed herself from the dominance of the men in her life, she would fail. It was horribly persuasive. Certainly she no longer had trouble in understanding why Carmen might believe what she saw in her own cards.

A savoury, delicious smell came to Tess's nose. She lifted her head, realising suddenly that she was starving. She hadn't eaten since the morning, and now it was nearly seven o'clock. She thought of her empty fridge and the smelly milk and turned without a second thought towards Soho and a bowl of pasta cooked by someone else.

Sunday evening, and the pasta bar she settled on was fairly quiet. A waiter showed her to a table in a corner and put a menu in front of her. She looked through it absent-mindedly, still thinking hard about what Sarah had told her. If this meant that she should not continue her affair with Tony, what would she do? And what would Tony do? It was true that he was jealous and possessive. How would he react if she ended it? Could this be the danger, the conflict that Sarah had foreseen?

What should she do? With Tony in charge she never had to think for herself, never had to worry. He took care of everything, deciding where they should go out to eat, when they should stay in, where they should make love, exactly how he intended that Tess would achieve orgasm that night. It wasn't always exactly the way she might have chosen if she had been left to herself, but it happened. What was she supposed to do without him? Take Julian home to Hampstead and keep him as a pet?

'Hi, good evening,' said a male voice. 'I'm Dean. Can I take your order, or are you waiting for someone?'

Tess looked up, her mouth open to speak. But she said nothing. The young man standing in front of her met her eyes, then slowly raised his brows and smiled at her.

There it was again, that audible click of sexual attraction that James had asked her for. It was even stronger now, when she was faced with a man she didn't even know, had never seen before. It was there, undeniable. She looked at the waiter for a long moment, committing the feeling to memory.

He was very handsome in a male model sort of way, fairly tall and broad shouldered, with very clean-cut features, bright blue eyes and light brown, thick hair which should have hung on his shoulders but was tied back for his work. Like all the staff he wore black trousers, a white, open-neck shirt and a long, white apron. His face was mischievous, with a deep dimple on one cheek. He looked into Tess's eyes and smiled slightly. The dimple deepened. His smile said, *You think I'm a hunk, and by God, you're right*.

Cocky sod, Tess thought. He was a hunk, but that wasn't the point. She shook back her hair and said coolly, 'I'm not waiting for anyone, and yes, you may take my order.'

At that his expression changed. Now his eyes told her that he had enjoyed her little spark of temper and that he thought that she was very attractive too. He drew his order pad from the pocket of his apron and held his pen poised over it, looking attentive. 'What can I bring you?'

he asked. He had a deep voice tinged with East End, the voice of a bit of rough.

For one delicious moment Tess imagined herself saying, *Your cock on a plate, with a salad garnish.* She bit her lip and smiled to herself, then said, 'Spaghetti al pesto, please. And a bottle of sparkling mineral water.' She allowed herself to smile at him. *Yes,* her smile said, *I think you're a hunk.*

'Right away,' Dean said. He smiled back at her and then folded his pad and turned to go off to the kitchen. Tess watched him go. He had a really lovely bottom, high and taut, and it was framed by the ties of his white apron in a way that might have been designed to call attention to its pertness. Tess leant her chin on her folded hands and watched appreciatively as that athletic arse moved away from her, carried her order through the door and vanished into the kitchen.

A very good-looking young waiter indeed. And what, just what, did she propose to do about it?

Her mind shied away from the obvious suggestion. It made for a pleasant fantasy, but she couldn't make it reality. She moved her finger on the marble top of the small table, musing.

Somebody changed the background music from jazz to classical, the CD of the Three Tenors concert. The ringing voice of Pavarotti filled the restaurant, singing the most famous aria of all, the World Cup anthem from *Turandot. I shall conquer,* he sang, *I shall conquer.*

A movement by the table made Tess jump. She looked up and saw Dean looking down at her, smiling, a bottle of mineral water in his hand. He poured it into her glass and set down what was left on the table, then said, 'The pasta in just a few minutes.'

'Thank you,' Tess said. Their eyes met again. She thought, *He really is very good-looking indeed,* and she saw her attraction mirrored in his blue eyes. How old was he? 26, 27? He had an uncomplicated face and a splendid strong body under his waiter's uniform. She let her eyes follow him as he left the table, and before he went through into the kitchen he glanced over his shoulder at her.

She couldn't. She didn't dare. But as she sipped the cool water she imagined what she might do. She could lay her hand on top of his as he set her plate on the table or filled her glass. She could put her fingers on his thigh, on the back of his thigh where the apron did not cover him, where the skin was tender and sensitive below the fabric of his trousers. Any movement, one touch on her part would be enough. He would know what she meant – that she wanted him.

And then what? Ask him when he finished work, meet him outside, go for a drink, go back to his place or ask him back to hers? Oh come on, Tess, she thought. You're in a relationship, you don't want to start another. Why can't it just be a simple question of sexual satisfaction? You fancy him, he fancies you, you do something about it, you scratch the itch, no more to be said.

Because life's not like that, she told herself. She took a deep draught of her water and shook her head. Then she saw him coming towards her, her plate of spaghetti in his hand.

'Spaghetti al pesto,' he said, putting it in front of her. 'Enjoy it. Would you like some extra parmesan?' She shook her head mutely. 'Black pepper?'

'Yes please,' said Tess. Dean smiled and fetched the pepper mill, which was as long, thick and phallic as all its kind. He held it up and raised his eyebrows at her. 'All over?' he enquired archly.

'Please,' Tess managed to say, though she wanted to laugh.

'There you go,' said Dean, obliging. 'A couple of good screws is enough for most people.'

Tess couldn't resist it. 'Really? Only two?'

They had been joking, but suddenly he met her eyes and there was something more there, something hot and earnest. The pepper mill dangled unnoticed from his

418

hand. For a moment they didn't move, didn't speak, just looked into each other's eyes and breathed shallowly. Then Dean shook himself and said, 'Excuse me. *Buon appetito,*' and turned to leave the table.

Tess slowly addressed herself to the plate of pasta. It was delicious, but she barely tasted it. Her heart was beating fast and between her legs her sex was clenching in the way that always signified a sudden swelling of desire.

She wasn't just imagining things. She really did want to taste Dean's body. She didn't care what sort of a man he was, she just thought that he was handsome and she lusted after him. Her hand covered her mouth as if she were afraid that the other people in the restaurant would be able to read her thoughts.

Research. Take control. *I want you to be amoral,* James had told her. *Self-centred. Just going after kicks.*

Why not?

She ate a little more of the pasta, but her appetite was gone. Presently she set down her fork and leant back in her chair, turning her head to look for Dean.

There he was. She caught his eye. Her face was serious, and he came at once over to the table. 'Is something wrong?' he asked her.

'No.'

'Have you finished?' he asked, gesturing at her half-eaten pasta.

Tess took a deep breath. She was excited and nervous, but her singing training allowed her to speak without a shake in her voice. 'Dean,' she said softly and clearly, 'where can we go?'

Dean's face changed at once. His attentive, well trained waiter's expression changed, fading into a look of half suspicion, half shocked belief. 'Where can we go?' he repeated, speaking very quietly. He didn't have her control, and his voice was trembling.

Quickly Tess moistened her lips with her tongue and swallowed. 'Where can we go to make love?' she said. It wasn't as hard as she had feared. Startled lust flared in his eyes and she added quickly, 'Right now, Dean. Right now.'

His lips were parted and his chest rose and fell with his quick breathing. For a moment he didn't speak. Then he said, 'Are you joking?'

Tess shook her head. 'I'm serious. Try me.'

He was silent again. Then he said in a rush, 'The manager's office. At the bottom of the stairs, next to the Ladies loo. It's open. You go first. I'll be there in a minute.'

Tess nodded quickly and got to her feet. He stepped back to let her go past him and as she did so she let her hand trail across the front of his apron, directly over his crotch. He drew in his breath quickly and pulled away from her. She smiled to herself and went to the stairs.

As she descended she felt her heart pounding, thumping as if it would leap from her chest. Her nerves, her caution, her sense of propriety said, *Go into the Ladies, hide in there, don't do it, you're an idiot, what will Tony think of you?*

But inside her mind the character of Carmen said, *I want him. Tony doesn't need to know. I want him, and for once, tonight, I am going to have what I want. I am going to tell him what I want, and he's going to do it to me.*

Tess put her hand on the door of the manager's office and pushed it open. Inside it was dark. She didn't turn on the light, just closed the door and stood in the darkness, waiting.

Footsteps on the stairs. She tensed, but the footsteps turned aside and went into one of the toilets. She began to breathe faster and faster, her desire fighting her better judgement. More footsteps, and then the door opened.

It was Dean, eyes wide and dark in the faint light. He saw her standing just inside the room and his eyebrows drew down tight over his blue eyes. Tess realised with a shock that he was afraid too, afraid of her. The knowledge filled her with eagerness. She glanced around the room, saw a light on the desk and switched it on.

Dean closed the door and turned the key in the lock, then stood by it with his hands opening and closing by his sides. 'I can't stay long,' he said, his voice no more than a clotted whisper. 'I just asked for – for ten minutes.'

Tess wanted to say that that would be long enough, but she couldn't make herself speak. She drew in a long, deep breath and took a single step towards him.

It was enough. In two strides he crossed the room to her, stood in front of her, staring down into her face. There was a second of silent tension, and then at the same moment she reached her arms up to him and he took her face in his hands and his mouth was on hers.

His lips were softer than Tony's and his kisses were not so demanding. It seemed as natural that Tess should put her tongue into his mouth as that he should taste hers. They stood for long seconds, gasping as they kissed. Then Tess reached behind him for the ties of his apron and unfastened them.

'Christ,' he hissed into her lips, and then his arms were around her, catching her under her haunches and lifting her. He pushed her back and up until her bottom was resting on the edge of the manager's desk and he was pressing against her, pushing her legs apart, reaching up under her skirt. She gave an urgent gasp of lust and heaved her hips up towards him, inviting him to touch her. His hand was shaking and his fingers fumbled before he got hold of her panties and pulled them aside, feeling inside them. Tess knew she was wet, but even so it was a delicious shock to feel his strong thick fingers sink without hesitation into her, penetrating her so firmly that her sex clenched around them as if to keep him there.

'God, you're wet,' Dean hissed. He felt with his other hand for his fly, unbuttoned it and unfastened the zip, and in one swift motion pulled his erect penis from his underpants and advanced upon her.

'No,' Tess said, pushing against him. He looked up into her face, scowling with anger and frustration. He looked as if he thought that she was about to change her mind. She gritted her teeth and said, 'No, not yet. I want you to make me come first. Then – then you can fuck me.'

'What?' said Dean, as if she hadn't spoken English.

Tess's hand was on his arm, holding him away from her. 'Make me come,' she said. She remembered Julian falling to his knees before her. Yes, that would be good. That was what she wanted. 'Use your mouth on me,' she said. She saw refusal beginning in his eyes and went on quickly, 'You'll get what you want, won't you? You get to have me. Well, I want to be sure I get my share. Use your mouth on me, Dean. Make me come.'

Still for a second it looked as if he would refuse. His face was set in lines of reluctance. Tess held his eyes and lay back a little on the table, spreading her thighs, waiting expectantly for him to obey her.

'Selfish bitch,' Dean said through his teeth.

Her expression didn't change. She said, 'Dean.' It was odd and powerful that she knew his name and he didn't know hers. 'Dean. Make me come.'

He stood still for a moment, then hissed, 'Shit.' But it was the protest of acquiescence. Even as he spoke he was dropping to his knees, moving up between her parted thighs, ready to serve her.

Tess let her head fall back and closed her eyes. She waited, every nerve tingling, for his first touch. She expected him to be rough, to devour her and try to drag her to sudden pleasure, but she was wrong. For long moments nothing happened. Then she felt his breath on her. His mouth was hovering over her open sex and he was breathing, warm steady breaths that quivered against her trembling flesh. She gasped in response and whimpered, and only then did he touch her.

He was very tentative, very hesitant, flickering the point of his tongue along her labia, first one side, then

422

the other, gently poking it into her vagina, seeming to ignore her engorged clitoris completely. My God, Tess thought, does he know what he's doing? Has he ever done this before? He touched her everywhere but there, teasing, drawing up her expectation to the limit. And then, just as she was about to cry out *Lick me there, for God's sake, lick me there*, his warm, wet mouth clamped down over her warm, wet sex and he began to suck, burrowing into her as if he were extracting the flesh from a juicy orange, using his teeth and his lips as well as his tongue, stimulating her so unbearably that she bit her arm to prevent herself from screaming aloud. He drew the whole of her sex into his mouth and thrust his tongue deep inside her and then withdrew and tormented her quivering clitoris, lapping at it with firm deliberate strokes, lifting her to a higher and higher plateau of pleasure. His hands gripped tightly at the soft flesh of her inner thighs, pulling them wider apart, opening her to him. Tess arched her back and strained up towards him, overcome with joy and amazement that it was really happening. Her climax began in the soles of her feet and climbed slowly, rippling through her loins, cold as ice in her spine and hot as fire in the pit of her belly, building and building until it soared to her brain and exploded there and she cried out and tensed against Dean's mouth as he thrust his tongue deep inside her and she gripped frantically at it as she gave herself up to spasms of delirious pleasure.

Then he let her go, quite roughly, and stood up. He wiped his hand hard across his glistening mouth. 'Good enough for you?' he demanded fiercely, leaning over her.

Tess almost laughed. She pushed herself up from the desk and shook her head. He was holding a condom, fumbling with it as he tried to tear it open. She said, 'Let me,' and took it from him. Her deft fingers quickly opened the packet and she leant forward to where his scarlet, swollen cock stood up from his trousers. She opened her mouth and quickly drew the smooth, shining head between her lips, flicked her tongue over it and heard him gasp. Then she rolled the condom down the straining shaft and ran her hands gently over his tight updrawn balls, feeling them heavy and turgid with the weight of his seed.

'All right,' she whispered, looking up into his face. 'All right, Dean. Now.'

He moved towards her and she lifted her thighs and hooked them over his hips, opening herself to him. He did not guide his thrusting penis but prodded blindly between her legs until he found the moist notch and then groaned as he pushed himself into her, all the way up her wet, hungry vagina in one strong stroke.

'God,' Tess moaned, locking her ankles in the small of his back and lifting her hips. She wanted to feel him even more deeply inside her, filling her, penetrating her. 'Oh God, that's it. That's it.'

But Dean didn't move. He held onto her tightly, clutching at her haunches, and pressed his body closely against her. Looking down into her face, he hissed, 'I'm going to fuck you so hard.'

'Yes,' Tess moaned. She tried to move against him and a pulse of urgent pleasure radiated from her throbbing clitoris and made her sex clench around him, gripping him so tightly that he gasped. 'Yes, do it.'

'I'm going to fuck you – now – ' And Dean withdrew his whole stiff length from her and plunged it back into her with all his strength, his hips meeting her open thighs with a sharp slap. The impact made Tess groan with pleasure. Dean snarled and pounded into her again and again, harder than she thought possible, grasping her hips tightly to hold her open to his determined, ravaging thrusts. Within a dozen strokes Tess was at the point of climax again and as he continued to shaft her she knotted her fingers in his hair and clamped her mouth against his to keep in her shuddering cries. There was no end to her response, it was as if every stroke drew her up to another level of sensation. Dean's tongue lashed against hers and his hands were slippery with sweat and he grunted as he took her. Not sex, not making love, fucking. Pure animal pleasure, direct and unadorned. He didn't even know her name. Gradually he built up speed until he was pumping into her like a great engine, until the blows of his hips bruised the tender skin inside her thighs and her whole body was juddering with the power of his thrusts and she was biting his lips in the intensity of her pleasure. With what was left of her mind she thought that he couldn't do it any harder, it wasn't possible, but even as she thought it he snarled against her devouring mouth and began to move even faster, working his iron-hard penis brutally to and fro with such savage strength that pleasure and pain merged into one and sparks burst behind her eyes. And then he groaned and pulled his mouth free of hers and flung back his head, baring his teeth as his whole body shuddered with the desperate ferocity of his climax.

Tess shut her eyes and revelled in the pure physical pleasure of feeling his cock buried deep inside her and throbbing urgently as he came. She wanted to remember this feeling, the sense of uncomplicated, amoral, remorseless lust. She pulled back a little and Dean staggered and put his hands on the desk to support himself. He withdrew from her with a jerk and turned away, covering his face.

For a moment Tess stayed where she was, eyes closed, regaining control. Then she slipped down off the desk and straightened her skirt. 'Thanks,' she said. 'I needed that.' And without another word she went to the door of the office and out into the lobby.

She left a ten pound note on the table and walked straight out of the restaurant before Dean reappeared. She didn't care about him now, she had had what she wanted. Her thighs and sex ached as if she had been beaten, but her whole body was quivering with the echoes of pleasure and she felt elevated, excited by what she had done and not the least ashamed.

Well, she thought, two weeks into rehearsal and what have I achieved? I've got Tony Varguez as my lover, I've slept with two women, seduced a 22-year-old and screwed a total stranger on a restaurant desk. Carmen is certainly making some changes to my character.

Then she thought again about what Sarah had said. Other things faced her now, both in her own character and in Carmen's. Conflict, challenge. Danger. Was the danger to her, Tess, or to Carmen?

And what more could she do than she had already done?

INTERVAL

Act Three Scene One

Green Park, two weeks later

*T*ony's dark eyes were glittering with anger. 'Come on,' he said through his teeth, catching Tess by the arm. 'We're going back to my place. I want to talk to you.'

'No,' Tess protested. Her stomach coiled with the knowledge that once he was angry Tony was hard to deal with and that she couldn't control him. 'Look, Tony, they're just building the set, I need to take the time to wander about on the stage a bit.'

'Listen to me,' Tony said in a hissing undertone, leaning forward until his face was close to hers. His lips drew back from his white teeth as if he would bite her. As always when he was excited his Spanish accent became stronger, emphasising his foreignness. 'When I say I want to talk to you, you come with me. Understand?'

Tess bit her lip. The rest of the cast had already noticed Tony's annoyance and she couldn't face the idea of having an argument with him in public. She said quickly, 'All right, all right, you don't have to drag me.'

For a moment he still held her arm. She glared at him and at last he angrily released her. 'Come on.'

She followed him across the park, in between

427

deckchairs and the figures of office workers sprawling on the grass to catch some sun in their lunch hour, eating sandwiches, sitting with their noses buried in books or just watching the world go by. He was walking quickly. Occasionally he glanced behind him to reassure himself that she was following. Tess hurried at his heels, feeling like a dog in disgrace. She knew why he was angry, and she knew there was nothing to be done about it.

When they reached Piccadilly Tony hailed a taxi by the simple expedient of stepping in front of somebody else waiting for one on the kerb. Tess tried to step back and let the offended businessman take the cab, but Tony exclaimed in exasperation and crammed her into it. He snapped his address at the driver and slammed the door.

'Now, Tess,' he said at once, 'listen to me. I've had just about enough of you behaving like a – '

'Tony, don't.' Like many English people Tess hated public rows. She couldn't bear Tony's Mediterranean propensity to say whatever he thought, no matter who might be listening. 'Please.'

'Listen to me, woman,' Tony snapped. 'You know what I'm talking about. Don't try to change the subject. What do you think you're doing? Every time you're on stage with a man you behave as if you slept with him last night!'

The taxi driver cocked an interested eye over his shoulder and Tess winced with embarrassment. In a low undertone she said, 'Tony, for God's sake. You're being jealous over nothing. There's no need. You know it's acting. It's not real, it's what James wants me to do. He wants me to look as if I've slept with every one of the smugglers, not just you – not just José.' Her voice rose a little. 'It's not as if it's easy for me,' she protested. 'But James – '

'James, James, James!' Tony caught her wrist and glared at her. 'I don't agree with James. Carmen's in love with José right up to the end, she only takes Escamillo because José has to go away. It's just her pride that

428

makes her refuse him when he comes back. You understand?'

'Where's the flat, guv?' asked the driver, and Tony angrily released Tess for long enough to give instructions. He bundled her out of the cab, flung a five pound note at the startled and amused driver, and pushed her into the lift.

'I don't want you playing the whore on stage,' he said. 'People will think it's real. They'll laugh at me.'

Tess was afraid of Tony when he was angry, but this was too much. 'Don't you dare call me a whore,' she said fiercely.

At once Tony turned on her, catching her hands by the wrists and slamming her hard against the wall of the lift. 'I'll call you what I like,' he snarled into her face. 'I don't take orders from you.'

The metal wall of the lift was cold against Tess's back. She looked into Tony's eyes, which glowed with his anger, and shivered. Tony's jealousy was frightening and vicious, but it spurred him to passion. In two weeks Tess had tried three or four times to say the words that would end their affair, but she had never done it. It was as if she secretly liked his possessiveness, his dominance, his openly stated ownership of her, body and soul. He was a bastard, but still . . .

The lift door slid open. Tony held her by the wrists and dragged her across the landing, forced the key into the lock and tossed her through into the flat. She staggered backwards, watching him as he advanced on her. The outline of his erect penis showed through his tight jeans and she chewed her lip in a mixture of desire and fear.

'You pretend not to listen to me in rehearsal,' Tony said slowly. 'You know you drive me mad when you – make up to all those others. You do it to make me jealous.'

It wasn't true, but she didn't deny it. It was pointless to deny it. Once his jealousy was aroused Tony wasn't rational. 'You tease,' he hissed, 'you bitch. I'll make you know who's master.'

Tess continued to back away, her hands held up in denial. 'No,' she moaned, 'Tony, please, no.' They had played this violent game before, and Tess did not know whether her protests and struggles were real or imaginary. Perhaps they were half real and half simulated, half expressing genuine fear and revulsion and half intended to drive Tony to more ferocious heights of passion. It was like playing with fire, she never knew what he would do to her. It was dangerous and thrilling.

'Bitch,' Tony whispered, and he dived across the room and caught her. She struggled and fought and he subdued her, pushing her hands behind her back and holding them there so that her body was pressed against his. His erection throbbed against her. He forced her into the bedroom and hurled her from him to land face down on the bed. She twisted around to defy him and he stood over her, staring down. 'Strip,' he said.

'No.'

'Strip, or I'll tear the clothes off you.'

He had done that before, too. Tess didn't want an entire wardrobe composed of designer rags, so she stopped protesting and pulled her T-shirt over her head and began to unfasten her jeans. Tony stood still, his chest heaving with his panting breath, and watched her remove her clothes. At last she was kneeling on the bed entirely naked, looking up at him with a mixture of submission and defiance. What would he do? She hoped that he wouldn't whip her. Only a few days ago, when he first started to feel jealous of the other men in the cast, he had tied her down across the bed and lashed her with his belt until her backside was red, then flung himself on top of her and taken her in her arse. Although it had aroused her ferociously, it had been quite painful and she didn't really want it to happen again. But it was no use saying so. If she expressed an opinion he would do the opposite, just to spite her and put her in her place.

430

Tony looked at her kneeling naked before him and nodded slowly. He tossed back his glossy black hair from his eyes and smiled with harsh satisfaction. With one hand he unbuttoned his flies and pulled out his cock, a smooth thick column of olive flesh. He slowly drew back the foreskin, revealing the glossy, scarlet head of the glans, and then began to masturbate, ringing the thick shaft with finger and thumb and rubbing steadily to and fro. 'Touch your breasts, whore,' he said to her. 'I want to see your nipples harden.'

For a moment Tess thought of refusing, but she was already aroused and she wanted pleasure. She raised her hands obediently to her breasts and cupped them, lifting them towards Tony as if she offered them to him. He took a deep breath, staring. Tess rubbed her thumbs gently over her nipples and the little buds of flesh began to stiffen and swell. Her breath tingled with the sensation.

'Good,' said Tony, still rubbing at his cock. 'Good. Pinch them. Pinch them hard.'

Tess obeyed and closed her eyes with the sharpness of pleasure-pain. When she opened them again she saw Tony shrugging off his shirt and pushing his trousers down. He stepped out of them and stood before her naked, still tugging at his rampant cock. She gazed at him avidly. She hadn't tired of the splendour of his smooth, dark body, the close, oily texture of his skin, the glistening blue-black nest of curls at his groin. She would have liked to feel him pushing her back on the bed, lowering himself onto her, penetrating her with his thick penis. But she said nothing.

'All right,' Tony said softly. 'All right, slave. Prepare yourself.'

He walked to the bedside table, opened it, pulled out a couple of long silk scarves. Tess said, 'No,' and tried to retreat across the king-size bed, but he leapt after her and caught her and wrestled her into submission. He was very strong, and it aroused her to see the muscles

431

moving on his chest and shoulders and belly as he held her down and tied her wrists to the iron bedstead. He tied both hands together, quite loosely. Tess swallowed hard, brimming with the erotic closeness of fear and eagerness. She struggled and writhed and Tony put both hands on her body, restraining her. His fingers were warm and hard on her cool skin. She heaved up towards him and he smiled, showing his white teeth. He ran his hands down to her thighs and pulled them apart. She squealed and moaned in protest.

'Let's have a look,' Tony muttered. He released one thigh and with his fingers probed between her legs. What he found seemed to please him, because his face lit with dark gratification. 'Good,' he said through his teeth. 'I like a nice, wet hole. Shows that you want me.' He pushed two fingers deep into her, making her arch her back and cry out. He drew slipperiness from her and spread it around her labia, flickered his fingers over her clitoris, oiled her crack with her own secretions. Please, she thought to herself as she strained against her bonds, please take me now, Tony, please push your thick cock up me and make me come, please, please. But if she asked him he would refuse, just to torment her. She bit her lip and tried to pull away from his exploring hand, hoping that her struggles would arouse him to take her.

He grinned. 'Not yet,' he said. 'Not quite yet. First a little something for me.'

His strong thighs straddled her body and he came towards her face. Tess thought that he meant to plunge his stiff penis into her mouth and she gave a little moan of consent and parted her lips. But to her surprise Tony turned around and presented her with his taut smooth arse, lowering it towards her. 'Lick me,' he ordered her sternly.

This was new, and for a moment Tess felt a stir of revulsion. She flinched, trying to turn away. But her hands were fastened and Tony's thighs were on either side of her head, she could not escape him. Uncertain of what to do, she reached up a little to kiss one of the muscular cheeks of his bottom. He said thickly, 'Don't kiss it. Lick it. Lick me.'

Tess let out a little moan of protest and arousal, and very slowly extended her tongue. She touched the tip of it to the top of his crease, tasting the salt of his skin. Small, dark hairs tickled her lips. Tony drew in a whispering breath and slowly she moved the tip of her tongue, trailing it down the crease of his arse, waiting, ready to be disgusted.

It was not disgusting. It was sensual. He was clean and sweet and when she found the puckered ring of his anus the delicate skin around it was as soft as a flower, as soft as the silken covering of his cock. She hesitantly licked him and he moaned with pleasure. Delicately Tess circled the little hole with her tongue, pressed her lips to his cheeks, lapped at him almost as if she were licking a woman's sex, and above her Tony writhed in ecstasy.

He was so sensitive, so responsive. She remembered Jeannette describing how James and Adam had made love in their garden and how James had pushed his tongue deep into Adam's arse. Emboldened, she pressed the tip of her tongue directly against the tight, soft ring and thrust. Tony cried out and the taut sphincter tensed almost as if she had hurt him. She pressed her lips closer to his soft skin and tried again, keeping up a gentle, constant pressure, and at last he opened to her and the tip of her tongue slipped inside his delicate anus. Tess felt a surging rush of pleasure as she tasted the faint nuttiness of Tony's secret passage. Although she was tied and pinned down by his weight, she was using her tongue to give him pleasure, rimming the tender ring of his arse, actually penetrating him as if she were a man. Tony was a homophobe, disgusted by even the suggestion of homosexual activity, but now he was moaning and whimpering as Tess slipped her tongue deeper and deeper into the hidden channel of his body. She thrust at him eagerly, digging deep into his quivering anus, and from somewhere a rhythm emerged, steady, remorseless, building as the tempo of copulation builds to its inevitable climactic conclusion. The hairy sac of Tony's balls was taut and shivering with readiness and she thought for a moment that he would actually come, reach orgasm just with the sensation of her fucking him with her tongue. She wanted to make him come. But before he reached the point of no return he pulled away with a desperate cry and moved away from her, his breath shuddering.

'Let me go on,' she whispered. She knew the moment she had spoken that she should have kept silent. He never let her do anything that she asked for, and she wasn't surprised when he shook his head.

'No.' Tony grabbed a couple of pillows and pulled them towards her. 'No, I want your arse.'

'Not again,' Tess protested. Recently Tony seemed to have developed a fixation on anal sex, preferring it to everything else, and while Tess enjoyed it she reasoned that she was designed to receive pleasure from both orifices, not just one. She wriggled angrily as Tony caught her by the hips and turned her over, but even as she struggled she knew it was hopeless. He dumped her on top of the pillows so that her round backside was thrust up in the air, lasciviously presented to him, ready for his use. 'Please, Tony,' she begged, trying to turn back over, 'please fuck me properly.'

'Listen, slave,' Tony hissed, his mouth so close to her ear that his warm breath stirred her hair. 'I do what I want to you. And today I want your pretty little crack.' He withdrew a little and took a deep breath. 'But don't say I ignore your pleasure,' he said, and he reached again into the bedside table. He caught Tess's head by the hair and jerked it around so that she could see what he was holding.

A massive phallus made of gleaming black plastic, like something on sale in the lowest of Soho sex shops. Tess stared at it, at the same time appalled and shiver-ingly excited. 'My God,' she whispered, 'it must be nine inches long. Tony, don't – '

'And that's not all,' Tony said. He pressed something and the plastic phallus began to vibrate, making a noise like a food mixer. Tess cried out in protest and began to struggle in earnest, tugging at the scarf that held her wrists, shuffling her bottom and thighs off the pillows, trying to get away. But Tony just laughed and caught hold of her thigh and jerked her back into position.

'No,' Tess cried, flinging her head to and fro in protest. Tony laughed more loudly and pressed the cold slippery plastic against her thigh and then pushed it up between her legs and touched the engorged bead of her clitoris with the vibrating head.

'Christ.' Tess's hips jerked and arched with a sudden agony of sensation. 'Oh Christ in Heaven.' Tony circled her pleasure bud with the throbbing tip, parting her labia, lodging the massive head between the lips of her sex for a fraction of a second and then withdrawing it to buzz again against her peak, against the place where she was so sensitive that the brutal stimulation of the vibrator was almost unbearable.

Almost, but not quite. After a second Tess gave herself up to the feeling, writhing desperately on the pillows and lifting her bottom to allow the thick length of the dildo to rub against her quivering sex. Tony leant over her and whispered in her ear, 'I'm going to shove it up inside you and just leave it there while I do what I want. But first – ' he drew the vibrator away from her, making her moan with loss, and then very gently placed the tip against her clitoris and began to move it in tiny, delicate circles, stimulating every infinitesimal area of flesh to such a degree that Tess screamed and began to beat her head on the pillows, jerking from head to foot as orgasm flared from her tormented clitoris and rushed through her body like consuming flames.

'Enough,' Tony growled, and without another word he placed the massive slippery head of the vibrator between the lips of her sex and pushed. Tess screamed again as the giant rod penetrated her, throbbing right through her loins, filling her sex and her bowels with shuddering sensation so strong that it was not pleasure, making her thighs quiver with irresistible response. She tried to squirm on the pillows but Tony was on her, lying on her, nestling his hot, erect cock between the cheeks of her arse and rubbing it to and fro with eager, jerky movements that betrayed the heat of his lust. In what seemed like seconds he shouted with pleasure and convulsed over her and his warm seed spurted into the small of her back.

He lay on top of Tess like a dead thing. The vibrator hummed and shuddered within her vagina and she moaned in feeble protest. It was too much, too thick, too strong, more than she could bear. Her orgasm had been violent, but it had gone as quickly as it had appeared, leaving no afterglow to protect her from the fierce throbbing of the plastic phallus within her. She squeezed hard with the muscles of her sex, trying to eject the invading presence. 'Please,' she moaned, 'no more.'

Tony's hand moved between her thighs and pushed the vibrator a little deeper within her. 'Who is master?' he whispered in her ear.

'You are,' she whimpered, and indeed she felt entirely conquered, subdued to his will.

He nodded slowly. 'Good. Remember it.' With one swift motion he withdrew the vibrator and switched it off, and Tess's head slumped with relief. Tony reached up above her head to unfasten the scarf and release her bound wrists. He rolled away from her and lay asprawl, a cat-like expression of satisfaction on his aquiline features. Tess lay still for a moment, then reached over to the bedside table for a handful of tissues to wipe his seed from her skin.

'Well,' Tony said after a long pause in which the only sound was their panting breath, 'I'm glad that's agreed.

Now then, Tess, what are you going to make us for dinner?'

It was barely six o'clock. Tess lifted her head in exhaustion and amazement and said, 'I think I'd rather go out, actually.'

Tony didn't open his eyes, just shook his head. 'No, I fancy some real food. Make me something English. Someone at rehearsal was talking about a most peculiar thing, what did they call it? Toad in the hole. It sounds rude. Make me that.'

'Tony,' Tess said very steadily, 'I'm not your servant.'

He rolled over suddenly and caught her hands, pinning her down and grinning into her face. 'But you are my slave, aren't you? So cook me my dinner.'

Suddenly Tess felt weary and disgusted. She pushed at him and scowled and he released her, surprised. She swung her legs off the bed and got up. 'A slave in bed is one thing,' she said. 'In the kitchen it's another.' She wiped herself again and then began to dress, biting her lip nervously. Tony lay back on the bed and folded his hands behind his head and watched her with an expression of steady, cold disapproval.

When Tess was dressed she drew herself up, trying not to show that she was trembling a little. 'I want to go out for dinner,' she said, 'and if you don't want to come, I'll go on my own.'

'Rebellion!' Tony exclaimed, raising one lazy, dark eyebrow. 'Well, fine. Go ahead. I'll see you tomorrow, anyway.'

He sounded as if he didn't care, as if her pathetic attempt at independence was no more than a child's tantrum. Tess opened her mouth to argue with him, but suddenly she felt that if she once began the argument it would have to end in a break between them. She shied away from the prospect. All she said was, 'Bye.'

'Enjoy your dinner,' Tony said mockingly.

In the lift Tess closed her eyes and struck her clenched fists against the metal wall in anger and frustration. He only treated her seriously in bed, and then only as his 'slave'. Sometimes she couldn't bear it.

And yet wouldn't a lot of women be perfectly happy with Tony as a lover? He might be unreasonable, masterful, demanding, but he was handsome and virile and there was one major fault that he did not have. Nobody ever intimated that he was unfaithful. Even Emma, who seized instantly on the smallest piece of relationship-related bad news and broadcast it enthusiastically to whoever would listen, even Emma had not been able to detect the slightest tendency in Tony to stray from Tess's bed. He might flirt, but he did nothing else.

You couldn't say the same for me, could you? Tess thought. Her sexual research of the early weeks of rehearsal seemed a long time ago now, but even so she had been unfaithful and Tony hadn't. This made her feel guilty, and her guilt made her put up with him even when he was at his most unreasonable.

But even so, the research had been a challenge. And an enjoyable one. As she left the lift and walked out into the hot London streets Tess wished briefly that she could undertake some more research to deal with the latest problem that James had presented her with. Carmen was one of the band of smugglers – cocaine dealers in this production – and in several of the scenes she sang with half a dozen of them. James kept insisting, 'Listen, darling, you've slept with all of them. All of them separately and maybe sometimes a few of them together. You've done it all. So when you look at each of them there's something you remember about them, right? This one's got a big cock, this one's a fellatio freak, this one likes to come between your tits – '

'Christ, James, for God's sake, give it a rest,' she had said. But of course he hadn't. He never gave it a rest.

Now she was alone in Covent Garden, entitled, if she wished, to take herself off for dinner on her own. It didn't appeal. She wandered along to the Donmar Warehouse and amused herself for a little while poking about the boutiques, then succumbed to loneliness and sought out a phone box.

She dialled Jeannette's number, hoping her friend was in. They hadn't seen very much of each other outside rehearsals for the last couple of weeks, because Jeannette and Catherine openly disapproved of Tony and said he wasn't improving Tess's performance. Now, in a state of annoyance with Tony, she was eager to talk to them both.

The phone rang a couple of times, then Catherine's pleasant husky voice said, 'Hello?'

'Catherine, hi, it's Tess.'

'Tess? This is a surprise. To what do we owe the honour?'

'Oh – ' Tess hesitated, uncertain of what to say. 'Oh, Catherine, I just had a spat with Tony and I don't want to spend the evening on my own.' The words came out in a rush and suddenly Tess felt on the point of tears.

There was a silence. For a moment Tess was afraid that Catherine had put the phone down. Then she said slowly, 'Well, Tess, the thing is, Jeannette and I had some company coming round here already.'

Tess felt dashed. 'Oh. I'm sorry. Don't worry about it.'

'Well – ' there was another pause. 'Look, Tess, we've asked Bob and Stefan round for the evening. Emma's out with Leo again.'

'Bob and Stefan?' Tess searched her brain, then remembered the names. They were two of the stage hands who were involved in building the sets.

'Yes. Remember them? Bob's a hunk, don't you think? Anyway, look, you can come round if you like, we could always ask another one for you.'

Tess shook her head, then remembered that she was on the phone. 'No, honestly, Catherine, I couldn't – '

'Why do you always say no to everything?' Catherine demanded in irritation.

For a moment Tess didn't reply. She was thinking of what Sarah had said to her. *You have to free yourself from dominance and find your own way.* She needed to undertake some further research, didn't she? And what she had done before had been fun. And she knew that she would have to break with Tony in the end. She said at last, 'All right. I'll come.'

'Hey, brilliant! The boys won't know what's hit them. Come straight over, Tess, we'll be waiting.'

Catherine was waiting at the door of the flat to let Tess in. The three girls were lucky in their accommodation. A Friend of Opera in the Park had offered a business flat to the company for the duration of the production, and Catherine, Jeannette and Emma were living in comparative splendour in a big mansion block not far from Piccadilly. The rest of the cast called it the Cat Flat, because Emma lived in it.

'Hi!' exclaimed Catherine. Her heavy dark hair was piled up on her head and she was wearing a thin shift dress, made of white, embroidered cotton, that barely contained her full, heavy breasts. The dark shadow of her pubic hair was just discernible through the delicate fabric. She seemed very excited, and Tess thought that she might have had a drink already. 'Hi, Tess, come in. Come and see what we've thought of.' She caught Tess by the hand and pulled her through to the big main reception room. It was furnished in a very big-business way with damask-covered sofas and polished wood occasional furniture, but right now it was hardly recognisable. The sofas and chairs were draped with rugs and throws, some of brightly patterned Indian fabric, some of heavy, crunchy cotton, some of fur, real and fake. The curtains were drawn, shutting out the bright evening sunlight, and candles glowed on every flat surface. A big wine cooler stood on a low table and sensual music was playing softly in the background. Tess recognised Debussy's *Pelleas et Melisande*.

'Wow,' said Tess. 'Well, Cath, nobody would guess what you had in mind. Where's Jeannette?'

440

'Right here,' said Jeannette, emerging from the master bedroom. A blue and gold sarong was wrapped tightly around her long, slender body, and the beads that tipped her myriad tiny plaits were cobalt-blue flecked with gold. Big gold discs gleamed in her ears and her huge, liquid eyes were outlined with blue kohl. She looked like an Ethiopian queen. 'What d'you think?' She raised her arms and turned on her heel, showing herself off.

'I feel underdressed,' Tess said uncomfortably, looking down at her jeans.

'Hey, no problem.' Catherine caught her by the arm and towed her into the bedroom. 'Let's find you something. I think there's a silk slip somewhere. Jeannette, bring the wine in, will you?'

As they turned over heaps of clothes Catherine and Jeannette explained the plan. 'Last night,' said Jeannette, 'we brought Bob home with us. You know Bob, the big muscly one with long hair. I can't remember whose idea it was – '

'It was his,' put in Catherine. 'Cheeky sod, he said to me that someone had told him Jeannette and I were gay and he thought it was a waste. So I told him to come back and find out for himself. And he did.'

'All night,' Jeannette added. 'He's quite an athlete. So we suggested an action replay tonight and that he bring someone else along. He thought of Stefan.'

'Isn't Stefan the one with red hair and freckles?' Tess said, sounding confused.

'That's right. Looks like a teenager, but Bob says – well, he said he was hung like a donkey, to be honest. And you know I've always wanted to try a really big one.'

Tess smiled nervously. Catherine gave a little triumphant cry and held up the petticoat. 'Here we are,' she said, 'perfect.' It was oyster-coloured satin, with spaghetti straps and a delicately flared skirt. 'Come on, Tess, put it on.'

'So they're coming just to – ' Tess said uneasily.

441

'We're going to have a competition,' crowed Jeannette. 'Look.' She held up a handful of A4 cards with numbers on them from one to six. 'See? Like figure skating, marks for artistic impression and technical difficulty.'

'And I'm on the jury, am I?'

'Sweetheart,' said Catherine, 'you're one of the competitors. We've asked Charlie for you.'

'Which one's Charlie?' Tess asked awkwardly. She had been so taken up with Tony in recent days that she hadn't really noticed the stage hands. She tried to imagine herself making love before an interested audience, in public, if you please. Her mind recoiled from the prospect.

'The Asian one,' said Jeannette. 'Looks like a young Omar Sharif. Gorgeous.'

Tess couldn't remember Charlie at all. She slowly took off her T-shirt and jeans, letting out a nervous sigh. Jeannette hesitated, then said, 'I was a bit surprised that you agreed to come over, Tess, honestly.'

'Well,' Tess explained, 'I was mad with Tony. And I thought – I thought it might help with what James has been saying to me recently, about how he wants me to look as if I know something about each of the men in the gang.'

'Hey, good idea!' said Catherine with a grin. 'Tell you what. Tomorrow morning we'll ask you what especially you remember about each of these three guys. Good memory test.'

Tess slipped on the satin petticoat. The cool, slippery fabric caressed her skin. She took a deep draught of wine and felt the alcohol begin to work on her, eroding her inhibitions, empowering her. 'When are they coming?' she asked.

'Any minute. We have to finish early. Leo and Emma are going to the theatre and then out for dinner, but they'll be back some time after midnight.' Jeannette picked up a rather dog-eared book from the floor of the

442

room and held it out towards Tess. 'Here,' she said. 'I thought we could use this for a few ideas.'

It was a modern version of the *Kama Sutra*, attractively presented with photographs of appealing, sexy young models. Tess flicked through the pages, raising her eyebrows. 'Some of these are impossible,' she said.

'Oh, I don't know,' said Catherine. 'Jeannette's pretty limber. Me, I'm going to stick to nice simple ones.'

'How do we decide who gets whom?' Tess asked, still looking at the pictures. The sensuality of the images began to work on her. The whole situation seemed so unlikely that she couldn't even feel afraid, because she didn't really believe that it was happening. Jeannette and Catherine did this sort of thing, but not little Tess Challoner.

'Random selection,' said Jeannette. She showed Tess slips of paper with their names written on them. 'And why not.'

'I thought you wanted the really big cock,' said Catherine.

'Well, if I don't get him first time, he'll just have to get it up again,' said Jeannette, and she laughed like a kookaburra.

The doorbell rang. Tess jumped and Jeannette and Catherine both giggled at her. Catherine ran out of the bedroom and the other two followed her more slowly as she went through and opened the door. 'Hello,' she said, gesturing welcomingly. 'Bob, Stefan, Charlie, hi. Come on in.'

'We brought a bottle,' said Bob, leading the way. He was a big man, thirty perhaps, heavily built and long-haired. The open neck of his denim shirt showed fur curling across his chest. He put a bottle of wine into Catherine's hands, leant forward and kissed her without preamble.

'It's not the wine we're interested in,' said Jeannette from the doorway. Bob looked up at her and grinned, then continued to kiss Catherine with lustful diligence.

Behind him Stefan and Charlie hesitated in the doorway. Stefan was quite small, thin and pale-skinned, with a shock of carrot-coloured hair and very bright blue eyes. Freckles marched across his narrow nose. Charlie was gorgeous indeed, with smooth coffee-coloured skin shaded blue with stubble around his fine jaw and soft black hair hanging in curls to his shoulders. He wore jeans ripped at the knees and a dilapidated T-shirt. Both Stefan and Charlie looked rather like boys who have found an unattended sweet shop and can't believe their luck.

'Come in,' said Jeannette. She walked smiling across to Stefan and stroked his face with her hand as she shut the door behind them. He looked down at her for a moment in complete astonishment, then very hesitantly lifted one hand to touch the swell of her breast under the thin cotton of her sarong. She arched against his hand and with a gasp of surprised lust he caught her into his arms and kissed her hard.

Tess found herself standing alone in the hall, looking at Charlie. He looked back at her. After a moment his lips curved in a smile and he raised his eyebrows. 'Well,' he said, 'fancy meeting you here. Do you come here often?'

Thank God, a man with a sense of humour. 'Well,' Tess said, 'not that often, no. How about you?'

'I'm as surprised as you are,' Charlie said. He came close to Tess and stood looking down at her. His smile vanished. Very softly he said, 'I – I've seen you on stage, of course. I think you're marvellous. You're the sexiest Carmen I've ever seen. Do you know that all the men in the crew would like to give you one?'

Suddenly the dry tension of desire filled Tess's throat. She swallowed hard. Beyond Charlie she could just see Stefan fumbling with the knot of Jeannette's sarong, trying to free it, and Bob pulling up Catherine's dress by the hem. They had wasted no time. Jeannette was laughing breathlessly as Stefan tried to undress her and her long black fingers were deftly undoing his fly.

Charlie glanced over his shoulder, following the direction of Tess's gaze. 'Wow,' he said softly, 'no kidding, then.' He looked back at her and licked his lips. They stared into each other's eyes, each of them wondering who would make the first move. At last Charlie very gingerly put his hand on the fine strap of the silk petticoat as if he would pull it down. He didn't move it, just looked into Tess's eyes. 'Shall I?' he asked softly.

The breath was cold between Tess's lips. Her nipples tautened and stood out beneath the satin. She glanced again at her friends and frowned, then said, 'I thought – I thought Jeannette had something special in mind.'

Jeannette heard her name and pulled away from Stefan's searching mouth. Her hand was inside his trousers and she was wearing an expression of manic glee. 'You're right,' she said, 'absolutely right. Everyone into the lounge, and I'll explain. And bags me and Stefan go first.'

'Got what you want again, Jeannette?' Catherine asked with a smile as she guided Bob through into the candlelit drawing room. He noticed the small, ceramic bowls which had been filled with a variety of condoms and placed strategically around the room. Tess poured wine for everyone, sensing rather than seeing Charlie standing close behind her, so close that she could almost feel the heat of his body through the thin satin slip.

Jeannette took a gulp of wine, then said, 'OK, guys, it's like this. We take turns and the others watch, and then they can give us marks. Look, here are the score cards. Just like skating, yeah? Stefan, come on.' She turned and caught hold of Stefan's fiery hair and kissed him and as she kissed him she began to unfasten the buttons on his shirt. For a moment Tess thought that Stefan would protest or pull away, but after standing frozen for a few seconds he acceded and returned Jeannette's kisses. They were the same height to within an inch. Stefan's hands returned to the knot of Jeannette's sarong and at last he managed to open it. The bright fabric slipped down her back, crumpled above her taut high buttocks, and then fell to the floor.

'Jesus,' Charlie whispered. He picked up a pair of the score cards and glanced at Tess. 'Ah, shall we sit down?' he suggested.

Catherine and Bob were already seated on one of the big sofas, half watching Jeannette and Stefan, half engaged in pulling off each other's clothes. Tess breathed fast. Arousal was stirring strongly in her. 'All right,' she said.

She sat on one of the fur rugs. The downy soft fur caressed her thighs. Charlie sat down beside her and stared at the space in the middle of the room where Jeannette and Stefan were still kissing. Jeannette had Stefan's shirt off now and was working on his trousers, and he was devouring her and squeezing the firm orbs of her buttocks. His skin was very white, and the contrast of his clutching fingers with Jeannette's ebony rear was very pleasing.

'Oh God,' Jeannette whispered as she pushed down Stefan's trousers and underpants. 'Oh God, look at it.'

Stefan was thin and wiry, but his penis was huge. It stood up from the flaming red curls of his groin like a young tree, stiff as a piece of wood and as long and thick as the vibrator that Tony had used on Tess that afternoon. Jeannette's dark fingers wrapped around the ivory stem and she whimpered with delight as she felt its length and hardness. 'God,' she whispered again, 'oh God, I want to feel it.' She began to sink to her knees, drawing Stefan down with her, never for a second releasing the splendid pillar of his rampant cock.

'So much for artistic impression,' Charlie whispered in Tess's ear. 'I thought you couldn't hurry art.' His hand brushed against her shoulder. She turned to him in surprise and he smiled at her and trailed his long fingers across her breasts. With a startled gasp of pleasure she reached out for him and caught hold of his head by the hair and drew down his face to kiss her.

For a moment she was immersed in the sensation of his soft lips on hers. He kissed very gently and his breath tasted sweet and spicy, and his tongue was long and slender, strong and sinuous. His hand caressed the outer curve of her breast, making her whimper. Then he said, 'We don't want to miss the main attraction.'

They turned back to see Jeanette kneeling before Stefan, her lean dark thighs spread wide. She slowly leant back, back and back like a limbo dancer until her hips were arched up towards him and her garnet nipples pointed towards the ceiling. Stefan frowned in concentration and moved up between her widespread legs. For a moment his white fingers disappeared into Jeannette's sex. Then he paused to slide a condom over his massive cock, lodged it between her labia and began to push it into her.

'God almighty,' Jeannette moaned. 'Oh, oh, oh.' Her flexible spine twisted in an agony of pleasure as Stefan penetrated her, sliding his long, thick penis deep into her slender body. 'Oh, it's stretching me. Oh yes, Stefan, please.'

'My God,' Charlie whispered, and Tess gasped with soundless wonder. Watching Stefan's glistening penis appearing and disappearing from the dark cushion of Jeannette's mound was like seeing the new moon racing between banks of midnight clouds. It was beautiful. Almost without realising it Tess and Charlie moved closer together, hands searching, exploring, seeking the other's sex. Tess opened Charlie's jeans and felt for his penis. It was smooth and hot and eager. As she touched it she felt his fingers on her, slithering between her labia, settling on her clitoris and beginning to rub at it with a persistent delicacy that made her whimper.

Jeannette was crying out with eagerness. Such was her need to feel Stefan's huge member deep inside her that she changed her position, lifting her slender thighs to wrap them around his waist, clutching at his shoulders with her long fingers. Her dark red nails dug into his spine and he yelped and began to move faster, ramming into her with merciless determination. He reached under her and caught her buttocks in his hands, lifting them to open her to him even more, and she screamed. The enthralled audience watched Stefan's long, rubber-clad shaft, gleaming with Jeannette's moisture as it slid in and out of her dark juicy flesh.

'Now,' Jeannette yelled, 'now, now!' and her heels drummed against Stefan's back as he lunged into her with desperate ferocity, once, twice, three times, and on the third thrust she wailed and arched tightly against him and the scarlet softness of her sex convulsed around his plunging prick and he snarled and shuddered as his climax shook him.

There was a long silence. Stefan slumped down onto Jeanette's heaving body. Black and white limbs were glistening with sweat. Charlie took a sharp breath and his erect penis twitched in Tess's hand. He looked at her and said in a whisper, 'Who's next?'

Tess licked her lips and glanced at the other sofa. Then despite her tension she smiled. 'I think we've been forestalled,' she said.

And they had, because on the other sofa Bob and Catherine were already engaged. Catherine was bent over the arm of the sofa, her dress forced down off her shoulders and thrown up around her waist in a ruined mess of crumpled cotton. Her lush full buttocks were thrust upwards and her heavy breasts dangled, and she was moaning as Bob shafted her vigorously from behind, his thickset hips slapping hard against her with every lunge. She lifted her head as Tess spoke. Her hair was hanging around her face, swinging to and fro with the rhythm of Bob's urgent ramming, and her cheeks and lips were flushed with pleasure. She grunted as a lurch of Bob's heavy buttocks drove him even deeper into her. With one hand she reached back between her thighs and winced with pleasure as her fingers touched her swollen clitoris. 'Bob,' she gasped, 'you bastard, do it harder.'

And Bob obliged, grabbing at Catherine's full white hips with his big hands and holding her still while he screwed his cock into her with such brutal energy that she gasped as if she were being beaten. Her hand moved between her legs, faster and faster, and the dangling tips of her breasts scraped against the rough cotton of the throw. Her dark eyes widened and her lips parted in a soft triangle of delight. 'Oh,' she whispered, 'I'm coming, I'm coming,' and then a series of juddering spasms ran through her soft flesh from buttock to shoulder. Her spread thighs shook with ecstasy and she fell forward onto her face, twitching helplessly as Bob drove himself to a savage orgasm within her soft, clutching sex.

After a little pause, Jeannette said from the floor, 'Tess, your turn.' Her raw voice was husky and smothered with satisfaction.

Tess swallowed hard and turned to Charlie. He smiled at her. If he had been nervous intially, his anxiety seemed to have gone now. He said, 'Don't worry, leave it to me,' and put his dark hands to the straps of the silk slip. He coaxed them gently down over Tess's shoulders to reveal her naked breasts.

His hands touched her. Tess closed her eyes. Behind the shield of her eyelids she could forget that there were other people in the room, that every move, every turn of her head was observed. She breathed deeply and concentrated on the sensation of Charlie's gentle hands touching her, exploring her.

'You're ready for me,' he whispered, dipping one finger deep inside her and coaxing the sweet juice from her. 'You're ready.'

Tess moaned, a moan of acquiescence. Charlie drew back from her and for a moment she sat up, opening her eyes. She saw him tugging a sheepskin rug from the sofa and laying it on the floor and she closed her eyes again quickly before she saw Bob and Stefan and her friends, greedily watching.

'Come on,' said Charlie's voice in her ear, and then his strong hands were slipping under her shoulders, under her thighs, lifting her. She hung limply in his arms, the air cool on her exposed throat. He kissed her just under the line of her jaw and she shivered and turned her head helplessly. Then he swung her through the air and laid her down on the sheepskin, soft as clouds. His hands pulled down the shift to expose her breasts and pushed it up around her hips. She tightened her closed eyes and lay quivering, knowing that everyone could see the glistening flesh of her sex between her softly parted thighs.

There was movement above her and she felt Charlie lowering his body onto her. His mouth met hers and he kissed her deeply, sliding his tongue hard into her mouth. His hot, erect cock stirred against her belly and she silently spread her legs wider, accepting him.

'No,' he whispered against her lips. 'Artistic, remember?' He pulled back and knelt between her open thighs, then leant towards her. He drew one of her legs under his arm and laid the other on his chest so that her calf rested on his shoulder. Tess lay very still, breathing in quick shallow gasps. She felt helpless, exposed, possessed. Charlie's hands slid up her body, up her ribs, onto her breasts, and as he squeezed the heavy orbs his penis nudged between her labia and began to enter her.

He seemed to go on for ever. Something about the position meant that her hips were tilted up to him and he penetrated her completely, to the neck of her womb, filling her deliciously. Tess sighed with pleasure and opened her eyes, looking up into his face. His dark eyes glowed at her and he began to move, leaning gently forward, rocking back. Every move seemed to spread her wider and his hands cradled the weight of her breasts as if they were the treasures of the world. She gripped at him with the muscles of her sex, wanting to give him

450

pleasure too, and he gasped and smiled and thrust again, slow and deep and gentle.

The soft sheepskin caressed Tess's back, her neck and shoulders. Charlie pushed until his body was pressed hard against her and then he stopped moving and rested his weight on her. He teased at her breasts, stroking and kneading, and very gently his body leant against her and fractionally withdrew, leant and withdrew. His stiff penis barely stirred within her quivering tunnel, but the whole weight of his torso rubbed against her vulva with a firm inevitability that made her shudder with pleasure. She gasped and flung her head from side to side, not knowing whether she wanted him to move faster or not, and he continued the same steady, slow, pulsing pressure and his dark fingers ceaselessly fondled her swollen nipples.

Watching the others coupling had aroused Tess more than she could have imagined, and now the gentle insidious touch of Charlie's body against hers was driving her into a fever of ecstasy. She moaned and heaved, but he did not increase the speed of his movements. Very slowly, very steadily, he drew her up and up onto a plateau of pleasure and held her there, and then as her sex began to tense and clench around his deep-thrust penis he squeezed her breasts hard and began to move, lunging forward and back within her as she cried out and convulsed in the throes of a violent, consuming orgasm. She felt him shuddering inside her, himself overtaken by pleasure, and the sensation drew her back to the peak and filled her with sweetness like a cup overflowing with wine.

Tess lay beneath Charlie with blood rushing in her ears, feeling his heartbeat pulsing in his buried cock. She felt sated and yet ready for more. She arched her back lasciviously, pushing her breasts up towards Charlie's face. She was glad, yes, glad that she had done it, glad that she had offered herself. For the first time in weeks she felt free of Tony's selfish dominance.

What did Carmen say to José at the end of the opera? *I was born free, and I will die free.* Yes, that was the feeling. She tried to commit it to memory. How long would it last, after tonight? Would it survive another night in Tony's bed?

On the floor near her Jeannette stretched like a cat and grinned. 'Sod the score cards,' she said lazily, reaching out to stroke Catherine's limp hand. 'Let's just enjoy ourselves.'

Act Three, Scene Two

The Cat Flat

Just after midnight Tess and Jeannette and Catherine finished clearing up the flat. The stage hands were gone and the wine glasses were washed up, and now Catherine was crawling on hands and knees around the drawing room, scanning the patterned Persian carpet for abandoned condoms while Tess and Jeannette folded up the rugs and throws.

'Well?' said Jeannette, staggering a little. 'What d'you reckon, Tess? Remember them all?'

Tess shook her head, somewhat at a loss for a reply. After that first fabulous orgasm in Charlie's arms everything seemed to have blurred. She remembered a number of things with a remarkable combination of vividness and confusion. There was Charlie lying between her thighs and stabbing up into her with his long strong tongue while Bob pushed his sturdy prick between her lips. Charlie's tongue was exquisite, firm and sensitive, now quivering against her clitoris, now coiling deep inside her. He was gasping as he licked her, but she couldn't recall who had been pleasuring him, offering a soft mouth or a moist sex for the satisfaction of his rampant cock.

There were Catherine and Jeannette moaning in each

453

other's arms, fingers probing eagerly between their wide spread thighs as they watched while all three men occupied themselves with Tess's body. Bob was still in her mouth, thrusting his fat penis avidly between her soft lips and grunting as his hairy balls frotted against her chin. Charlie gasped as he rubbed his cock between her breasts, and she moaned as she felt him tugging at her taut nipples, pinching and pulling with the rhythm of his body's urgent movement. And then she cried out past the gag of Bob's stifling cock because she felt Stefan thrusting feverishly into her spasming vagina with his huge phallus, stretching her until she thought she would never again need to feel another man inside her, shafting her with joyful energy. Three men enjoying themselves with her, three stiff swollen penises burying themselves in her body, and an orgasm so powerful that she had actually blacked out for a minute.

And more: Jeannette whimpering with anticipation as Charlie prepared to push his taut shaft into her anus; Tess and Catherine staring in aroused amazement as big, thickset Bob knelt down in front of Stefan and moaned like a child to feel that huge, powerful cock sliding deep between his lips.

But what order it had happened in, or how, she couldn't imagine. 'Well,' she said, 'I remember Stefan's cock, of course, and Charlie's tongue, and Bob – well, Bob was so heavy, and sort of solid.'

Catherine got to her feet, grinning. 'Sounds good enough to me,' she said. 'Think of that next time you're on stage and you'll be there.'

Jeannette lowered the last rug into a heap and stretched. 'I'm cream crackered,' she said. 'Bedtime for me. You going to stop over, Tess? The little bed's made up in the boxroom.'

'Yes,' said Tess, gratefully. 'Thank you.' She knew if she went back to her flat she would start having second thoughts.

Within half an hour she was tucked up on the little

bed in the narrow boxroom beside the drawing room, gently stretching muscle after muscle, testing herself. She ached between her legs. Stefan wielded his massive penis more like a blunt instrument than anything else. But altogether she felt good. Satisfied, that was the word.

The hall door creaked open and footsteps entered the drawing room. Tess cocked her head to listen. She heard Emma's voice giggling and Leo murmuring softly, then the breathing silence of two people kissing. A pause, then a grunt of effort from Leo and a few moments later the sound of bodies landing on one of the sofas.

He's going for it tonight, Tess thought. She was tired, but the thought that she might overhear Leo taking Emma's virginity made her shiver with excitement. Stifling guilt, she got to her feet and padded silently across the room to open the door a fraction and press her ear to the crack.

'Oh,' whimpered Emma's voice. 'Oh, Leo, that's so nice. Oh, touch me there. Oh yes, yes.' Then her words stopped. Leo must have stopped them with his mouth. Tess knelt by the door, stiff with tension, listening as Emma's little whimpering cries became more urgent. At last Emma took several quick regular breaths, as if she was going to sneeze, and then let out a long, ecstatic sigh of relief and pleasure.

'Emma,' said Leo's deep voice. 'God, Emma, let me – '

'No!' Emma's little-girl voice was suddenly sharp and stern. 'No, Leo, no.'

'Please,' whispered Leo. 'I have to. I'll explode, Emma. At least touch me. Kiss it, stroke it – something – anything, Emma.'

'No,' said Emma, and you could hear the pout. 'I'm going to bed. Thank you for a lovely evening, Leo.'

And to Tess's amazement she did just that. She switched on the light, making Leo wince and Tess flinch back from the doorway in case she was seen, and flounced out of the drawing room and down the long corridor towards her bedroom, where her battered teddy bear awaited her.

Leo sat on the sofa, staring after her. When the door at the end of the corridor closed he buried his head in his hands, the picture of despair.

Tess was very fond of Leo. She hated to see him so distressed. She quickly pulled on the dressing gown that Catherine had lent her and opened the boxroom door. 'Leo,' she whispered.

Leo's head jerked up. His face was pale, with a hectic flush on his cheeks. He gazed at Tess in astonishment, then got angrily to his feet. 'Christ,' he said, pushing one hand hard through his tousled fair hair.

'Oh, Leo, I overhead,' Tess said, coming closer. 'I'm sorry. She's such a little tease.'

'No,' said Leo, shaking his head. 'I don't think she means to tease, she just – can't help it.'

Tess watched him uncomfortably adjusting his trousers, trying to take the pressure off his swollen penis. After a moment she said with a solemn look, 'Why don't you get her drunk? It worked on me.'

That made Leo smile despite himself. 'I didn't get you drunk,' he said. 'What an accusation! You got yourself drunk. I just spotted the opportunity.' Then his smile disappeared. 'Anyway,' he said, 'she won't drink. Not even a glass of wine. Mineral water, fruit juice and Aqua Libra. I used to think you were abstemious, Tess, but she takes the cake.'

He looked so unhappy that Tess came forward and stroked his face with her hand. He turned away, embarrassed at her sympathy. 'Poor Leo,' she said. 'You really want her, don't you.'

'My God,' said Leo, 'I do.' He turned back, suddenly earnest. In a very low voice he said, 'She's not putting it on, Tess, you know. She lets me – touch her. I know she's a virgin, I've felt it. Twenty-six years old and a virgin! She says she's saving herself for the right man,

456

but I know, I know she'd love it. She likes it when I kiss her hard. She just needs someone to – to master her.'

'Sounds like she would suit Tony,' Tess muttered. Leo looked puzzled and she shook her head. She wanted to do Leo a kindness, to offer him a return for the way he had led her gently by the hand into the world of sexual reality. She frowned after a moment, wondering whether an offer of some sort of physical consolation might be appropriate. But things were over between Leo and her, had been over for years, and although she was very fond of him she no longer found him as attractive as she once had. Cuddly and lovable, yes: sexy, no. She said at last, 'Look, Leo, maybe I could – we could help. Me and Jeannette and Catherine, I mean.'

'Help?' asked Leo blankly. 'How?'

Tess shook her head again. 'I'm not sure. Not sure, but I know Jeannette will have a few ideas. She always has ideas. Why don't we talk to you about it tomorrow, at rehearsal? Make plans then?'

Leo frowned at her for a moment, then laughed. 'Whatever you say,' he said. 'I need help, don't I? Good grief, look at me. I fancied myself as a seducer, and here I am, bent double while she stomps off to bed.'

'We'll talk about it tomorrow,' Tess promised, and she kissed Leo's cheek before he left.

The following day at rehearsal Tony was on stage with Emma when Tess arrived. They were deeply embroiled in the Act One duet, but she knew that he could see her lurking in the wings. He ignored her, not even turning around to acknowledge her when some technical hitch stopped Emma in mid-note for a few moments. This was unlike him, and Tess felt a stir first of guilt, then of discontent and rebellion.

Eventually Emma left the stage, looking coyly over her shoulder at Tony. It couldn't be hard, Tess thought sourly, for Emma to play Micaela. So sweet and innocent, saccharine even, the perfect little virgin, mother's choice.

457

She was born to play the part. Tess had to admit that Emma also had a lovely voice, strong and sweet and sustained on the crippling high notes of Micaela's arias, but that was almost incidental. Tess folded her lips as Emma came past her in the wings, fluttering her eyelashes at the stage manager. She wondered briefly if she disliked Emma because she was jealous of her. Was she jealous of Emma's looks, or her voice, or the fact that she was still a virgin? Was it wicked to plot that she should cease to become one?

The chorus milled past Tess onto the stage and she poised herself for her entry. Tony appeared beside her: in this scene Don José led Carmen on, under arrest. She glanced at him but he refused to look at her. 'Did you have a good meal?' he said, staring straight ahead.

Any remnants of guilt that Tess had felt about her behaviour the previous night evaporated. 'I had an extremely pleasant evening, thank you,' she said coldly, and then it was time to go on stage.

Her anger carried through into her performance. James was delighted. 'That's it!' he yelled from the middle of the area where the seats would be. 'That's it, Tess. Insolence! Impudence! You don't give a stuff! That's it!'

The scene continued. Carmen, left alone with Don José, seduces him despite the fact that he has just promised himself that he will marry Micaela. As Tess sang her aria she knew that for the first time she was reaching the core of her character, the strength, the callousness that sees what it wants in a man's body and reaches out and plucks it like a flower, only to toss it away the moment its first bloom fades.

Something was working on Tony, too. Earlier he had been angry and cold, but now he looked hungry, jealous, desperate for her. She met his eyes and saw them dark and hot with passion, and his voice when he sang had a tinge of fevered rawness that was quite new. It gave Tess great satisfaction to see Tony wanting her, and she began to think that perhaps, perhaps after all she might be able to free herself from him. It would be good if she were the one that ended it. Leave him begging for it, the way he had so often made her beg him.

The act finished to applause from chorus and stage hands. James came towards them, exclaiming enthusiastically, and Tony turned to Tess and said, 'Come round this evening. Straight after rehearsal.'

Now or never, Tess. 'Sorry,' Tess said, more evenly that she felt. 'I can't.'

'Come round!' Tony caught at her arms, holding them so tight that he hurt her. 'Tess, what's going on? I want you to come round tonight!'

She pulled away. 'I promised Jeannette and Catherine.' *And Leo*, she thought. 'Sorry, Tony. It'll have to be tomorrow.'

Then James was with them and their chance for private conversation was over. Tess managed to free herself for five minutes and found Leo standing in the wings, watching Emma discussing her costume with the designer. His pale-blue eyes were very wide and yearning and his chin was propped on his hand in an attitude of the purest melancholy.

'Cheer up, chicken,' Tess said in his ear, making him jump. He spun on his heel and looked at her in surprise. 'Got it sussed,' she said. 'Simple but effective. Bring dinner round to the Cat Flat tonight. Catherine and Jeannette and I are going out.' Emma turned towards them and Tess finished in a hasty undertone, 'I'll brief you later.'

'Why, Tess,' said Emma, coming up to Leo and taking hold of his arm with possessive speed, 'you were wonderful. Whatever made you change your performance that way? It was great. Anyone would think you had been up to something.'

'Oh,' Tess said with a bland smile, 'just thinking about it.' Did Emma suspect something about Tess's research activities? How could she know? Could one of the stage hands have blown the whistle? If she found out she

459

would run off and tell tales to Tony before you could sing two bars.

'Well, it was marvellous,' said Emma. 'You really do make a most convincing tart. I'm sure I couldn't do it.' And she looked up into Leo's face and smiled with infinite sweetness.

If Tess had had any misapprehensions about what she and the others had planned for Emma, that little remark removed them. That evening she and Jeannette and Catherine gathered giggling in the kitchen of the Cat Flat and proceeded to empty about a quarter of all the bottles of orange juice, Appletise and Emma's favourite Aqua Libra down the sink. Then they filled up the vacant space with the strongest Polish vodka the off licence could sell.

'Does it taste?' asked Catherine anxiously as Jeannette sniffed at a small glass of extremely alcoholic Aqua Libra.

'Nope.' Jeannette's plaits bobbed as she shook her head. 'No, I'm sure it doesn't. And if she never ever drinks, it should have one hell of an effect.'

'Stuff them in the fridge,' said Tess urgently. 'They'll be here any minute.'

They were ready to go out by the time that the door opened to admit Emma and Leo and a number of bags smelling of Thai food. In the doorway Jeannette called back, 'Have a nice time. Don't do anything I wouldn't do!'

'Will it work?' asked Tess in the lift.

'Up to your friend Leo now,' said Catherine. 'From what Jeannette tells me he knows what he's about. And did you pass on our suggestions?'

'Certainly did.' Tess gnawed at her lower lip. 'Gosh, I hope it works.'

They crept back into the flat at one in the morning, ostentatiously hushing each other. The drawing room was empty. Catherine pushed at Tess and said, 'You go and look in her room.'

'Forget it!' Tess hissed. 'We'd wake – '

'Them? Her?' whispered Jeannette. 'If you don't look, we'll never know.'

'You look,' protested Tess.

'He's your friend. You look.'

And Tess put her hands over her mouth and made a face and then crept down the corridor to the far end of the flat and Emma's room.

The door was shut, but the catch was not quite engaged. Tess winced, then stretched out one finger and pushed the door. It swung open a little way, silent on its well greased hinges. The light from the hall fell into the room and Tess pulled back quickly into the wall, but there was no sound from inside. She leant forward, very, very slowly, and looked into the room.

There were two bodies in the bed. Leo's big bulk was curled protectively around the little, frail figure of Emma and his hand was resting on the pillow on top of the golden-brown strands of her hair. Tess stared, then reached in to catch hold of the door and slowly pull it closed. She tiptoed down the corridor and whispered to Jeannette and Catherine's tense faces, '*Yesss!*'

They congratulated each other in undertones and then went into the kitchen to destroy the evidence in the fridge.

The following morning Tess woke in the boxroom bed quite early. She got up at once and pulled on last night's clothes. Jeannette and Catherine had offered her their bed to share for the night, but she hadn't wanted to miss the sight of Emma facing the world the morning after the night before. She went into the kitchen and put the kettle on to boil.

The tea was made and half the pot drunk before she heard a sound from the bedroom at the far end of the corridor. At first it was a low murmuring of voices. Then Emma's voice, loud and clear, shouting, 'You bastard!'

'Emma.' Leo, trying to defend himself. 'Emma, listen – '

'You bastard!' And the door burst open. Leo backed out of it, half-dressed and holding up his hands to protect himself from the tiny figure of Emma, who was wrapped in her dressing gown and battering him wherever she could reach with her fists.

'Emma,' he said between blows, 'I thought you enjoyed it!'

'Oh!' Emma exclaimed, as if words failed her. She stood for a second simmering like a pot that is about to boil over, and then she jerked up her knee and caught Leo amidships. She just missed his crotch, but her kneecap sank deep into his stomach and he let out a whistling cry and bent over.

'Emma!' Tess cried, running forward to intervene. But before she could reach them Emma had linked her little hands into a fist and hit Leo in the throat as hard as she could. He gave a strangled cry and fell forward onto his knees, gasping for breath.

'Emma, for Christ's sake!' Tess shouted, getting between Emma and her helpless prey. But Emma jerked up her head and looked down at Leo for a moment with stern disdain, then turned on her heel and stalked back into her bedroom and slammed the door. A moment later it opened again and the rest of Leo's clothes were hurled through it to land in a heap on the floor of the corridor.

'Leo,' said Tess urgently. She bent to help him up as the other bedroom door opened and Jeannette and Catherine emerged, tousled and sleepy. 'Leo, are you all right?'

'Shit,' Leo whispered. His hand was on his throat, rubbing. He looked panic-stricken. 'Shit, she got me right in the vocal cords. Shit, shit – '

'Don't talk,' Tess told him hastily. 'Don't say anything.

You'll strain it. We'll get you to casualty, come on. Come on, get your clothes on.'

A taxi whirled them to the South Bank and a hospital in no time, but then they sat among a queue of the usual denizens of the casualty department: cuts, sprains, breaks, bruises and children with saucepans stuck on their heads. Leo was obviously not an urgent case, and the waiting dragged on and on and on.

'Shit,' Leo said for the umpteenth time. He was sitting in a corner on an uncomfortable plastic chair, his head tilted back against the wall. A dark bruise was spreading across his throat. 'Shit. Fuck. Bugger.' His voice was hoarse and rough, not at all like his usual dark, velvety tones.

'Leo, please don't talk,' Tess said anxiously. 'You'll make it worse.'

He shook his head. 'I can't make it worse. It's no good, Tess, I can feel it already, the voice-box is bruised. I won't be able to sing for weeks.' He opened his mouth and made a short, strangled sound, quickly cut off. 'No. No way. The bitch, the bitch, she knew exactly what she was doing.'

There was a long pause. Then Tess said, 'No need to ask you if it worked.'

Leo laughed at that, a rueful laugh. 'Listen,' he said, getting to his feet, 'there's no point in waiting around here. Casualty is the grimmest place in the world. I'll go and see my own doctor at home. Come on, let's go along to the South Bank and have a drink and I'll tell you what happened. Then we'd better go and break the news to James that he's going to need another Escamillo with ten days before the first performance. God, what a bummer.'

It was a beautiful day, and they walked along past the Royal Festival Hall and the National Theatre to the little clutch of boutiques and restaurants in the Gabriel's Wharf development. Several of the cafés had tables outside, and Tess and Leo sat at one of them and ordered long cool drinks. 'Plenty of ice,' Leo said huskily.

'Leo,' Tess said, 'I'm so sorry. I feel responsible.'

Leo shook his head and smiled at her. 'Listen,' he said, 'to be honest, in a few weeks' time I'll probably say it was worth it. Right now my voice hurts and I'll have lost most of my fee for this show and my agent will be furious with me, but believe me, Tess, I wouldn't have done anything differently.'

The drinks came. 'Tell me about it,' Tess said, leaning forward and looking eagerly into Leo's face.

When the door closed Emma tossed her head and said, 'That Jeannette, honestly. *Don't do anything I wouldn't do.* Doesn't rule out an awful lot, then.'

'What d'you mean?' Leo asked, indecently curious.

'She'd do anything, that woman. And Catherine is just as bad. They're leading poor little Tess astray between them. I'm sure they've,' Emma's voice dropped to a prurient hiss, '*slept* together. All three of them. I mean, eww! I thought Tess was quite nice when I met her.'

'I think she's quite nice now,' Leo said reasonably.

Emma pursed her rosebud lips. 'Oh, well, she's an old friend of yours, isn't she.'

They set out the Thai food on the table and Emma sat down with an expression of satisfaction. For a very small person she had a remarkably large appetite. 'Yum,' she said happily. 'I love Thai. Where are the satays?'

'Here.' Leo passed the appropriate carton. 'I'll just get a drink. What would you like?'

'Aqua Libra, please,' said Emma. Leo raised his sandy eyebrows and went into the kitchen, found a bottle, sniffed at it, nodded appreciatively and poured a long glass of pale liquid over several ice cubes.

When he returned with the drinks Emma had unpacked the satays and was holding one gingerly by its wooden stick, dipping it into peanut sauce. 'Mmm,' she said as she lifted it to her lips, 'peanut sauce, my favourite.' The sauce dripped and she caught the drip on her tongue and licked the satay clean.

Leo stood watching her, shuddering. Her mouth was small and red and her teeth were small and white and her little tongue flickered across the satay like a cat's. He imagined that little neat tongue quivering between Emma's parted lips as he drove his cock deep inside her, imagined it moving delicately across the throbbing head of his penis as she whimpered with expectation and arousal.

'Here you are,' he said, passing her the spiked drink.

'Thanks,' said Emma. 'Gosh, that's a spicy sauce.' She gulped down half the drink in one. Leo watched her swallow, tense with apprehension. Would she notice? But she just said, 'Ah, that's better,' and dipped the satay again.

Leo sat down heavily at the table. He had meant to play it cool, but obviously the message had not reached his genitals. He could feel that beneath his trousers his cock was beginning to swell. To distract himself he opened a few more cartons and tried to concentrate on the food, but it was hard.

Tonight, it would be tonight. He would deflower her tonight. For Leo, nothing matched that moment, that first moment, when he thrust himself up inside a virgin and watched her face change, overtaken with amazement and pleasure to feel that throbbing presence moving within her, filling her, clutched between her silken walls like a sceptre in a velvet case. He knew that he was skilled, that he had never been a disappointment. Once or twice, just once or twice, he'd given a girl her first orgasm, too. Now that really was amazing. It wouldn't happen with Emma, who had shuddered her way to ecstasy practically every night they had been together, moaning in his arms as his deft fingers felt between her slender thighs. He'd had to be careful, though, since she would never let him penetrate her with his fingers, only caress her clitoris and the lips of her sex until she was running with honeyed juice and her mouth was slack with pleasure. But she had always come, trembling as she reached her climax and letting out sweet little cries of joy that made him long to show her that there was more, so much more for her to relish in the garden of earthly delight.

'Pass me the rice, would you?' asked Emma. 'And the chili beef?'

'You need another drink,' Leo said evenly. He got up from his chair and took Emma's glass out to the kitchen and refilled it with the booby-trapped Aqua Libra. What a comedown, he thought. Reduced to alcohol to get my wicked way. Oh well: candy is dandy, but liquor is quicker. He poured a beer for himself, intending to go easy on the booze in case it affected his prowess.

'Gosh,' Emma said as he returned, 'this food is great. Honestly, I don't think I've ever tasted better. Where did you get it?'

'Little place in Soho I know.' Leo looked closely at Emma and was reassured by what he saw. A hot pink flush was creeping up her porcelain cheeks and her eyes were suspiciously bright. 'If you'd come and stay with me after the production, Emma, when we have more time, I could take you round more of London than we've had time for.'

'Gosh, I'm thirsty.' Emma drained half the glass, swallowing at least three measures of vodka in the process. 'Spicy food does that to you, doesn't it.' She hiccuped unexpectedly and put her hand to her mouth, giggling. 'Oops! Leo, you're not eating.'

I'm too excited to eat, Leo thought. My prick has other things on its mind. 'Just not terribly hungry,' he said with a smile. 'Anyway, you can eat for two. I'll just put some music on.'

'It's a really weird selection,' Emma warned him as he went over to the CD player. 'Catherine listens to jazz mostly and Jeannette likes all this multi-cultural music. And pop music. Yuk.'

Leo looked at the CD on the top of the stack. It was

called *Music To Make Love To*. He smiled and shook his head and opened the CD box.

A little while later Emma said, 'Oh wow, I don't know what's wrong with me. I feel really odd.'

'Are you all right?' Leo asked with well simulated anxiety. He got to his feet and hurried round the table to catch Emma in his arms as she swayed in her chair.

'I feel giddy,' she whimpered.

'You've been working hard,' said Leo. 'You need to put your feet up.' He stooped and caught her up, holding her tightly. She was so light it was easy. She protested faintly, but he said, 'Hush,' and she closed her eyes and put her arms around his neck.

'I feel so odd,' Emma said again as Leo carried her to the sofa. 'What's the matter with me?'

Three double vodkas. Leo sat down beside her. A sudden pulse of desire beat through him from head to toes and he shuddered. She was so pretty, so delicate, like a china doll. She was no chocolate-box innocent, he knew that, but she was a virgin. A real virgin, for perhaps another half an hour. He touched her face with his fingers. His hand was trembling. 'Emma,' he said softly, 'you're so beautiful.'

She purred a little, like a young kitten, as his fingers moved gently over the downy skin of her cheek. 'You're very sweet, Leo,' she murmured.

Without another word Leo leant forward and set his lips to hers. She made a little surprised sound, then turned to him and opened her mouth. He kissed her hard, searchingly, long-drawn kisses that made his chest tighten and his loins tense with desire for her. She responded, turning her face up to his and moaning softly as his lips travelled from her mouth to her jaw, to her delicate swan-like neck, to her little pretty ears. 'Emma,' he murmured against her pale skin. 'Emma, Emma, Emma.'

'Oh,' she whispered, 'that's so nice.'

His hands found the buttons on her white blouse and

467

began to unfasten them. This would be a good sign of whether he stood a chance. She had let him touch her breasts before, but only through or beneath her clothes. He had never seen them bare. Now, though, she made a little noise of protest but did not pull away. He unfastened the last button and pushed the blouse open.

She was tiny, slender, and under the blouse she wore a little lacy bra, there for looks, since her small upturned breasts needed no support. Leo drew in a hissing breath through his teeth and put his hand on her collar bone and very slowly moved it down until he could catch hold of the stretchy fabric of the bra and push it aside.

Her breasts were like shallow snow-covered hills and her nipples were perfect, small and round, coral-pink, tipped with hardness like the stem of a succulent fruit. She said, 'Oh Leo, don't,' but she did not try to stop him as he whispered in delight and put his hand on one soft mound, squeezing it gently.

'Ah,' Emma breathed. Leo put his mouth over hers and kissed her and as he did so he caressed her breast. His hands were big, he could cup the whole tender swell in one palm, and as he softly squeezed the delicate flesh he felt the small, tight nipple stiffening beneath his hand. Emma gasped and began to breathe unsteadily and Leo thrust his tongue deep into her mouth and took her taut nipple between his fingers, lengthening it, pinching it until she moaned.

There was something deliciously wanton about a woman with her clothing open. Emma lay on the sofa with her head tilted back, exposing her white throat, and the fronts of her blouse were pushed back to show her tender breasts naked above the lacy scrap of her bra. For a moment Leo thought of holding her down and just doing it to her, parting her thighs with a jerk of his knee and then sheathing himself within her to the root in a single thrust. But that was not what pleased him. It was the gentle urging of seduction that made him feel powerful. Instead he lowered his head to her breasts and began to suck and lap against her nipples until the coral flesh engorged, even the areolae stood out proudly from the white skin of the breasts. One of his hands was free, and with it he began to lift Emma's skirt.

'Leo,' she whimpered, 'don't,' and for a moment her hands fastened on his upper arms and pushed as if she would push him away from her. But he sucked harder at one proud nipple and Emma's protests died away into a groan of pleasure.

As always, she was wearing hold-ups and panties that were no more than a scrap of flimsy lace. As Leo's hand moved up over her slender thighs she sighed and her legs moved apart almost of themselves. The crotch of her panties was already warm and damp with readiness. Leo stroked his finger over the taut fabric and she shivered and moaned with pleasure.

With the ease of long practice Leo slid one finger below the lace panties and at once found the tiny stiff pearl of Emma's clitoris, already engorged and begging his attention. He stroked at it and sucked harder at her nipple and she began to cry out and move her hips regularly.

How many orgasms would he give her before he took her? How many times would he make her cry out before he parted those soft, damp lips and pushed his way between them? She seemed already to be nearly there, shuddering and whimpering as he caressed her secret flesh with gentle, deliberate precision. Leo traced his finger along the soft moist folds of her labia, probed for an instant at the entrance to her tight, virgin tunnel, then returned to the little proud bead of flesh at the front of her sex and stroked and stroked it until Emma arched and tensed against his hand, crying out with little sweet sounds as her first climax took her.

Leo lifted his head from her breast. She opened her big blue eyes and looked up at him, astonished and breathing fast.'Good?' he asked softly.

'Oh, Leo, I – '

'I've got a special treat for you tonight,' Leo said. 'I'm going to make you come another way.'

'How?' asked Emma, opening her eyes even wider.

'Here,' Leo said, pushing her skirt up around her hips, 'down with the panties.'

'No,' Emma said, fighting against the alcohol that coursed through her blood, 'no, Leo, I won't let you.'

'Don't worry!' he reassured her. 'I'm going to use my mouth on you.'

Emma was suddenly very still, breathing quickly as she looked at him. She was tempted. Her little pink tongue ran quickly around her lips, moistening them. 'Your mouth,' she said softly.

'You'll love it.' Leo took hold of the edges of her panties and rolled them down her thighs to her ankles. 'Put your ankles over my shoulders,' he suggested, kneeling at her feet. 'Then I can get at you.'

'Oh,' Emma whispered, 'that's so dirty. Oh, I don't believe it.' But she lifted her thighs and rested them on his shoulders as he had asked.

The whole of her tight, tender sex was exposed to him, beautiful, delicious, gleaming with honey-smelling juice. The curls of fine fur were pale brown and the hole was small, delicately made, asking for him to caress it. Her labia and clitoris were swollen from her earlier orgasm and when he leant forward and touched his tongue to the little pink pearl Emma shivered from head to foot and let out a wavering cry. 'Oh God, oh that's amazing, oh, Leo, Leo.'

Very gently, very diligently, Leo lapped at her. His tongue was strong and skilled and he flickered the tip against her, then flashed the whole blade across her quivering flesh until she moaned aloud. Emma writhed on the cushions of the sofa, entirely overtaken by pleasure, and Leo continued to serve her with his mouth until she was pushing her slender hips up towards his face, desperate for him to lick her harder, to take her to the heights of pleasure with his tongue and lips. He obeyed her, aroused to fever pitch by her delicious responsiveness and by the knowledge that in only a few minutes he would be the first man ever to plunge his penis into that fragrant, trembling flesh.

'Leo,' Emma wailed, 'oh, Leo, I'm coming. Please, please don't stop.' And her slight body bucked and shuddered against him as her orgasm possessed her utterly.

Leo knelt between her thighs, not moving, hardly breathing. For long moments Emma was still, and then she let out a long, long sigh and relaxed. Leo reached down and opened his trousers, releasing his massively engorged cock from its prison of cotton. He thought she might detect the rustle of the packet as he opened a condom, but he moved his tongue gently against her and she moaned with resurgence of pleasure.

He was ready. All that remained now was to make sure that she could not resist him. In his pocket was one of Tess's long silk scarves, ready tied into a loop. He reached up behind his head, felt for Emma's slender ankles, and fastened the loop of silk tightly around them.

'Leo?' Emma said in a voice that was suddenly puzzled and anxious. Leo smiled to himself and lifted himself over her. Her tied ankles were hooked around his neck, opening her to him so wantonly, so helplessly, that he shook with arousal. Her eyes were open too, startled pools of blue. 'Leo!' she said, trying to struggle.

'Emma,' Leo said softly. 'I've given you an orgasm with my fingers, and I've given you one with my mouth, and now I'm going to give you one with my cock.' He felt huge, smooth and strong and powerful, bigger than he had been in his life and ripe with seed. He lodged the swollen, shining head of his cock between the lips of Emma's wet sex and leant towards her.

'No,' Emma moaned. Her little hands were flat on his chest, trying to push him away from her. 'Leo, no.'

'Yes,' Leo whispered. This was not the time for mercy, and the very mercilessness of it aroused him so strongly that he shuddered. He thrust a little and felt resistance. Her maidenhead, her virginity, waiting for him, and his thick stiff cock was there, ready to take it.

'Please, please,' Emma moaned. She writhed beneath him, trying to escape, but her tender body was fixed beneath him like a nail prepared for the blow of the hammer. 'Leo, Leo, oh God.'

'Oh, Emma,' Leo gasped, and he clenched his buttocks and thrust and thrust, slow and strong, until at last her maidenhead gave way and his penis entered her, penetrating her completely, sliding up and up into her tight, sweet sex until it was all hidden.

Emma's blue eyes opened very wide and she stared up into Leo's face. 'Oh, my God,' she whispered, stunned with disbelief and pleasure, 'oh, my God.'

'Feel me,' Leo whispered. 'Feel me inside you, Emma. My cock's right up inside you, buried inside you. Feel it.' He withdrew a little and thrust again and Emma gasped as if she could not breathe. 'Feel how deep it is, Emma.'

'Oh,' Emma moaned again, 'Leo, I can't . . .'

Leo withdrew almost entirely and then let his weight bear him down on top of Emma's small slender body, driving him within her until he was embedded to the neck of her womb. Emma cried out and twisted her head on the cushions. Leo ran his hands down her body and took her small, firm buttocks in his hands, lifting them, opening her to him even wider, and she cried out again.

'Emma,' he hissed, and he thrust again, a long, slow, juicy thrust. Emma groaned. He put his mouth on hers and kissed her and as he kissed her he slid his thick shaft out and in again and felt her lips flinch and her tongue shudder as he penetrated her utterly.

He took her relentlessly, without his usual gentleness, lunging into her with frantic energy until his body slapped against hers and her cries became shrill and trembling. He was determined that she would come, and his hands were everywhere, tugging at her taut nipples, caressing her white shoulders, pulling apart the cheeks of her bottom and even stimulating the delicate ring of her anus until at last her body responded and she began to cry out in rhythm with his urgent thrusting.

'That's it,' he gasped, shafting her with delirious strength. 'That's it. Come, Emma, come now, come now,' and as if obeying his order Emma's body twisted beneath him and her eyes rolled back and her lips parted. Her tight sex spasmed about his plunging cock, gripping feverishly at the thick glistening rod that ravished her, and Leo roared aloud and flung back his head as his balls tightened and twitched with the spurting of his eager seed.

Tess rested her chin in her hand and shook her head disbelievingly. 'What then?'

Leo grinned. His bruised voice was hoarse, but he wanted to tell her everything. 'I picked her up with my cock still in her and carried her to the bedroom. When you've wanted a woman as long as I've wanted her you can get it up as often as a thirteen-year-old. By that stage I think she'd forgotten everything except pleasure. She even used her mouth on me, and she's always sworn she would never, ever do that. And I remember she knelt on the bed with her face on the sheets and her lovely bottom stuck in the air and I took her from behind. I lasted for ever that time, by the time I came she was slumped forward and I was beating myself into her like – like a battering ram. And when I'd finished she sort of subsided, like a pricked balloon. It looked so incredibly voluptuous, Tess, I can't tell you, I just wanted to do it to her again and again. And she liked it when I was rough. I know I'm not imagining things. At one point I – I put my finger in her arse while I was doing it to her, right up inside her arse, and she came screaming. She liked it, I know she did.'

'But she was sorry in the morning,' Tess said ruefully.

'You win some, you lose some.' Leo looked up at the

blue sky with a far away expression. 'Christ, though, it was worth it. To see that little doll's face change when she felt my prick sliding up inside her. It was worth it.'

There was a long silence. Then Tess said in a very small voice, 'Did you like doing it to her more than you did with me?'

Leo frowned, apparently surprised. Then a very tender smile lifted the corners of his mouth. 'Tess,' he said, 'what can I tell you? I'll never sleep with Emma again, she made that clear this morning, and to be honest, I don't care. I wanted to take her cherry, not have an affair with her. With you – well, we stayed together for months. It wasn't the same at all. We were in love for a while, weren't we?'

'I suppose we were,' Tess said, feeling a pang of nostalgic regret.

'Do you love Tony?' Leo asked, suddenly sounding stiff and awkward.

Tess looked into his face for some time before replying. At last she said, 'No. No, I don't love him. Sometimes I don't even particularly like him.'

'He's such a sexist bastard,' Leo said angrily. 'Why does he get away with it?'

'And Emma's such a little prick teaser,' Tess answered. 'Why does she get away with it?'

'She didn't last night,' Leo grinned. Then he shook his head. 'And the wages of sin is death: at least as far as this production is concerned. Come on, Tess: time we went to give James the bad news.'

Act Four, Scene One

The theatre, Green Park

'OK,' called the voice of the stage manager, 'places for the bar scene. We've just got time for the Act Two opening, folks. Places, everyone.'

'So,' said Tony in a low voice, 'we're on for tonight?'

Say no, Tess thought. *Say no, Tony, I don't want to go back to your flat again. Why don't you come over to my place, just for once? Just for once? And I don't want to be your sex slave, I've had enough. Just say it.* But Tess looked up into Tony's hot dark eyes and heard her own voice saying, 'All right, Tony, sure. Straight after rehearsal.'

'Good. You know I'm not around for a couple of days. I'd miss you if I had to go without for three nights.'

Tess heard her cue and pulled free from Tony's possessive hand. 'I'm on,' she said quickly. He let her go and she ran onto the stage for the gypsy dance that opened the act.

The costumes were nearly ready and Tess was wearing her second best outfit to get used to the way she needed to move in it. She liked it a lot. All the girls liked their costumes, except Emma, who seemed to be displeased by everything at the moment. She was not at rehearsal today, since Micaela wasn't in the acts on the schedule, and Tess was frankly relieved. Since breaking up with

Leo, Emma had been spending even more of her time flirting with Tony, playing up to him in a simpering little-girl kind of way which set Tess's teeth on edge and made her want to scream.

The costume designer had been very careful to take the physical shape of the singers into account when putting the clothes together. So Jeannette, who was as slender as a wand, wore tight, tight Capri pants that clung to every inch of her taut buttocks and a short Lycra top that showed off her athletic frame and her high pointed breasts. Catherine had a sort of flounced gypsy outfit that exaggerated her already generous curves. And Tess wore a skintight skirt split to the thigh on one side, scarlet heels, and a tight, low-cut, uplifting bustier that set out her splendid bosom as if on a shop counter. The first time she had appeared in it the stage hands had greeted it with cheers and a chorus of wolf whistles. As a costume it restricted her movements somewhat, reducing her gypsy dance to a sort of circumscribed gyration on the spot, but it was without doubt the sexiest thing that she had ever been asked to wear on stage. At the beginning of rehearsals she would have felt uncomfortable in it, but not now.

> *The dance's rhythm draws them on,* she sang,
> *Burning, crazy, mad with passion,*
> *They are drunk with joy, wild with passion,*
> *Sweetly ravished by the gypsy's song!*

The dancers joined her and Jeannette and Catherine on stage and whirled around her as she stood with her hands thrust skyward and her hips swivelling to the rhythm of the dance, closing her eyes as she tried to capture a sense of power, the sense of power that had filled her when she dreamed of the mermaid. But she could not find it. All she could think of was how Tony had demanded what he wanted of her, and she had submitted to him.

The dance crashed to its end. For a moment there was

a tense silence where the applause should have been. Then from the auditorium Adam's aristocratic voice said, 'Hold everything, darlings. There's someone arrived you have to meet.'

'The new Escamillo,' Jeannette whispered in Tess's ear. They stood side by side, wondering what would appear. It had been hard for James to find a replacement. He had picked some young unknown, a Canadian baritone whose only appearance in England to date had been in a televised singing competition, which he hadn't won. They knew his name, Richard Shaeffer, but they didn't know any more.

'Ladies and gentlemen,' said James's voice off stage, 'let me introduce you to our new Escamillo, Richard. He's been studying the production for three days and he joins rehearsals tomorrow. I know you'll all be pleased to see how well the costume fits him.'

Cast and stage hands laughed as James came onto the brightly lit stage, his arm on the elbow of a lean, dark young man dressed already as Escamillo, the TV star, Carmen's last and fatal love.

Tess sensed Jeannette's jaw dropping, but she couldn't take her eyes from the new arrival. He was wearing Leo's costume, which was made mostly of black and silver Lycra and concealed nothing about him, but there was no similarity between him and Leo. Chalk and cheese. The new Escamillo was a little taller than Leo, which made him just over six foot, and where Leo had been growing distinctly soft edged he had the build of an athlete. His strong shoulders were wide and a fine chest tapered beautifully to a narrow waist and hips with the pencilled muscles of a runner.

'Hi, everyone,' said the new arrival in a voice which sounded charmingly modest. 'Good to see you. Richard Shaeffer.'

He had a really attractive voice, warm and caressing with a rough edge to it like plush. Tess tore her eyes from his body and looked at his face. Handsome, with soft dark hair in rough curls like a lion's mane, a narrow nose, fine-cut, flaring nostrils, a mouth that was far too sensual to belong to a man, and wide-set, bright eyes that were an intriguing mix of green and brown and starred with long, dark lashes.

'Richard,' said James, 'meet our Carmen, Tess Challoner.'

'Hi,' said Richard again, holding out his hand. It was warm and dry and his grip was surprisingly strong. 'I'm really pleased to meet you, Tess. Wow, you sounded fabulous on stage just then. That's real power you've got in your voice.'

'Thank you,' said Tess, spellbound by his handsomeness and his simple, direct, modest manner.

He smiled at her. 'You look great too, of course, but hey, get these costumes, aren't they something? I feel like a character out of *Blade Runner*.'

'You look good too,' Tess heard herself saying. She was looking into his eyes, and she knew that her eyes were telling him that she thought he was beautiful and that instantly, viscerally, she had liked him.

'Thanks. Won't matter if I can't sing a note though, will it?' he said with a smile. His eyes looked straight into hers, making her midriff melt. 'I'm really looking forward to working with you,' he said. 'I've been working hard to learn the moves, but I'll have to rely on you a lot, with only a few days before the performance. I'm shit scared, believe me.'

His honesty disarmed her completely. 'Anything I can do,' she said, 'just ask.'

'Jeannette Baldwin, Catherine Gibbs.' James was continuing with the introductions. 'And Tony Varguez is lurking here somewhere. Ah there you are, Tony. Meet our new Escamillo, Richard Shaeffer.'

'It's an honour to meet you,' said Richard, and his face matched his words. 'I've got so many of your recordings.'

478

'Good to meet you too, Dick,' said Tony, with a smile that looked more like a snarl.

'Richard,' Richard said, wincing slightly.

'Well,' said James, 'that's enough for tonight. Richard, I'm glad you could make it this evening. You're coming back with Adam and me, we'll go over more of the production details with you. Everyone else, you know Tony can't be with us tomorrow, so we'll concentrate on the openings to Acts Two and Four. Usual time, see you then.'

'Tess,' Richard said, turning quickly to meet her eyes, 'it really was good to meet you. I'm looking forward to tomorrow.' Then James's hand was on his arm, steering him away. He looked over his shoulder at Tess as he went and smiled and waved at her.

'Wow,' said Jeannette in a smothered voice, but before Tess could respond Tony was there beside her, reaching out to catch hold of her elbow with one strong hand. 'Home,' he grated through his teeth. 'Now.'

What did he think she was, some little wifey? Tess swung to face him, bristling with anger and ready for a fight. But the sheer fury that she saw in Tony's eyes struck her dumb. He kept hold of her arm and towed her through the staring cast, out from the bounds of the temporary theatre and into the park.

She had got control of her shock by the time they reached Piccadilly. 'Christ,' she exclaimed, 'Tony, for God's sake, I'm still wearing my costume –'

'One word,' Tony said, swinging on her with venom, 'and I'll rip your costume off you here and now.'

His face showed that he meant it. Tess flinched unconsciously away from him, afraid of his vehemence and the sheer physical threat in the way he loomed over her. He flagged down a taxi and pulled Tess into it after him.

The taxi drove along Piccadilly and from Piccadilly Circus up Shaftesbury Avenue towards Seven Dials. Tony sat absolutely silent, his jaw set hard. A muscle twisted beside his mouth, over and over again. The traffic was bad and the journey took a long time. Tess cleared her throat, took a deep breath, made all the preparations for speaking, but in the end she was afraid. She remembered what Catherine had said, that Tony had once hit the woman who was his lover. He looked now as if he might hit her. He looked sullen and dangerous and she did not dare to speak to him.

They drew up outside the flat. Without a word Tony got out, paid the driver, held the door for Tess and escorted her into the lift. His courtesy was exaggerated and served only to make her even more uncomfortable. As the lift slid silently up to the penthouse he began to breathe deeply, as if he was preparing himself.

The moment they were inside the flat he turned on her. 'So,' he said thinly, 'what do you think of our new baritone?'

Tess shook her head before she answered. His jealousy was obvious and stupid and it made her angry, but he had right on his side, too. She had thought Richard attractive instantly and she must have showed it. That was improper, when Tony was openly her lover. He had reason to be jealous. In a voice which shook, although she fought to keep it calm, she said, 'Tony, listen. You don't need to – '

'I asked you a question,' Tony snapped. 'I asked you what you thought of him. Answer me!'

'I thought he was – ' Tess extended her hands, helpless. How could she say the right thing in such a situation? 'Very – nice,' she finished lamely.

'*Nice?*' Tony repeated, with infinite scorn. 'Nice? You bloody English are all the same! What does *nice* mean now? It means you want to fuck him!'

'How dare you!' Tess shouted, jumping forward, really incensed. She raised her hand as if she was going to slap Tony's cheek, but he caught hold of her wrist and held it tightly, glaring at her. 'Let go of me, you bastard,' she shouted. 'You bastard! How dare you?'

'How dare I?' Tony's lips drew back from his teeth in

480

a snarl of rage. 'Because you're my woman, that's why, you bitch! Did you really think I'd let you go drooling over some new man the moment he shows his face on the stage?'

'You don't own me!' Tess cried, trying to pull free. 'You don't own me! Let go of me!'

For a moment they stood poised, balanced against each other, staring into each other's eyes. Tony's face was tight with passion, his black hair disordered and falling over his high brow, his nostrils flaring, his black eyes glittering with rage and jealousy. His cruel lips twitched as if he would speak, but for long moments he said nothing.

Then, quite suddenly, his face changed. It was still taut with jealousy, but the anger was gone, replaced by vivid, ferocious lust. 'Christ,' he hissed, 'you're beautiful, Tess.'

'Don't,' Tess said, still pulling against his grasp.

'You don't want some other man,' Tony said, more quietly now. 'I know it. You just do it to drive me mad, don't you? You just love making me jealous. Little witch, little witch, it works every time.' And he pulled her towards him and caught her face in his hand and dropped his mouth onto hers with such strength that she could not resist him, just stood passive and whimpering beneath his fervent kisses. She was angry and afraid, but she could not restrain her instinctive, physical response. Her breath came faster and her body tautened, seeking the pressure of his strong limbs against her.

When at last he lifted his mouth from hers she tried to pull away. She was still angry, she couldn't bear being treated like a possession. In a smothered, urgent voice she said, 'Tony, don't behave like this. I didn't do anything on purpose. I don't like it when you're jealous. I – '

'You didn't?' He had his hand on her face, holding her still so that he could look down at her with his snapping

481

black eyes. 'You didn't do it on purpose? You mean you really – wanted him?'

'No,' Tess protested hopelessly.

But Tony's hand tightened on her chin, gripping so hard that it hurt. 'Listen to me,' he said, and now his voice was thick with cold anger. It made Tess shiver. 'Listen to me, Tess. Keep your hands off him. If you go near him, you'll wish you had never been born.'

'Tony – '

'I can make you a success, Tess,' Tony hissed, 'or I can wreck you. Understand me? Nobody wants a young singer without looks these days, do they?'

'What?' Tess gasped, hardly believing what she heard.

'In here,' Tony said, dragging her after him into the bedroom. He flung her across the bed so hard that she fell sprawling. While she recovered herself he opened the drawer of the bedside table and drew out a small object. As Tess came upright, floundering and opening her mouth to protest, he held it out towards her and suddenly, before her eyes, a bright, steel blade sprang out, glistening with sharpness.

'You know what this is, don't you,' Tony said. 'It's a flick knife, isn't it. Just like the fakes we use for the duel, huh? But there's a difference, Tess.' He took a step towards her and Tess scrabbled across the bed away from him, gasping, her eyes fixed on the gleaming blade. 'This one's real, ' Tony said. 'Real and sharp. Wouldn't it be a shame if I got the real one and the fake mixed up? Wouldn't it be a shame if I – injured you? An industrial accident, if you like?'

He looked angry enough, crazy enough to do it. Tess slipped down from the far side of the bed and retreated until her back was against the wall and still he came on. She swallowed hard and said, 'Tony, don't be a fool. You can't do this. You can't behave like this.'

He was standing before her, the knife held at the length of his arm. It didn't look remotely like the fake. The blade was blue at the edges and faintly oily, horribly businesslike. 'Promise,' he said, 'that you won't go near Richard Shaeffer, except on stage.'

'Tony – '

'Promise!'

This isn't happening, Tess thought. I'm standing in a flat in Covent Garden and a Mediterranean maniac is threatening me with a knife. It's not happening.

But it was happening, and she was afraid. Sarah had been right to see danger in the cards. At last she said, 'All right! All right, I promise!' and covered her face with her hands, because as well as fear she felt horribly ashamed of having given in.

Tony straightened and folded the blade back into the flick knife. It vanished as if it had not existed and Tess took a long breath of relief. 'Good,' he said. 'That's good. Now, Tess, I'm going to remind you just why it is you don't want any man other than me.'

'You're not going to touch me,' Tess said quickly, full of anger now that her cause for fear had gone. She moved quickly to push past Tony and make her escape, but he reached out almost lazily and caught hold of her arm.

'Come here,' he said, pulling her to him.

She fought him, trying to scratch him, to hit him, anything to get him to take his hands off her. But he ignored her blows and at last got hold of both her wrists in one strong hand and wrestled her to the bed. 'Fight me,' he hissed, leaning over her and staring down into her furious eyes. 'That's it, fight me. Fight, Tess. It makes you look so gorgeous. Fight me before I fuck you.'

'You're not going to fuck me,' Tess protested, doing her best to knee him where it hurt. But her tight skirt prevented her and Tony laughed and lowered his body onto her with an abruptness that made her gasp with shock and sudden consciousness of his strength and the hard eagerness of his muscled body. 'No,' she said again, 'I won't – '

One of Tony's strong hands thrust inside her bustier,

catching hold of her breast and squeezing so hard that she cried out. Pain, but pleasure too. And his body was thrusting against her, so heavy and powerful, holding her down. No, she thought furiously, I won't let him do this to me, I won't.

But his hand squeezed her breast again, forcing the nipple into stiff readiness and then bruising it with the ferociousness of his caresses, and as she struggled and arched her body against him, trying to resist, he gave a cry and pressed his mouth to hers in a kiss that seemed to suck out her soul.

Tess could not tell when her desperate resistance changed, sliding seamlessly into equally desperate compliance. Suddenly the tense spring of her spine was pushing against him not to try to throw him off but to encourage him to press against her harder, her mouth was searching his not to bite him but to draw his kisses to her ever deeper, her hands were knotted in his glossy black hair not to hurt him but to hold his lips more firmly on hers. His furious assault did not change, no tenderness crept into it, and her response matched it, equally vehement, avid and lustful, wanting to feel him beating her into submission with the blows of his strong penis.

He did not trust her. One hand still held her wrists, pinioning them above her head. With the other Tony dragged up her tight skirt, rucking it around her waist. He caught hold of her panties and ripped them off with a curse, then thrust his knee between her thighs and jerked them apart. His glans nestled between the lips of her sex, hot and smooth, ready. She could sense the power of his cock behind it, swollen-shafted, hard as a piece of bone.

There was a silence. They stared into each other's eyes, tense with hatred and anger and desire. Then Tony snarled and drove himself into Tess as if he was splitting a tree with a wedge, and her white throat twisted and she screamed with bitter pleasure. Her nails raked his back and she lifted her head and set her teeth into his bare throat and he roared and took her harder still, beating his body against hers as if he could conquer her and possess her with the simple power of his thrusts. She pulled at his hair and writhed under him and cried out, 'Bastard, bastard, bastard!' and he laughed and spread her wrists wide and held her still as he rammed his thick strong cock deeper and deeper into her with every stroke.

'Bastard,' Tess wailed again, heaving her hips up to meet him, offering the soft mound of her sex to his impassioned lunges, grunting like a beast as he sheathed himself to the hilt inside her with every jolt of his fevered body. She had not expected pleasure, and it took her by surprise. 'Oh Christ,' she cried, jerking up towards him in amazement and delicious agony, 'oh Christ, I'm coming, I'm coming ...' And then her eyes rolled back and her whole body was twisting and flopping beneath him like a landed fish, helpless, spasmodic movements that convulsed her from head to foot, her breasts juddering as he snarled and let go of her wrists to clutch her buttocks tightly in his fists and hold her still to receive his final desperate thrusts. When she felt his cock pulse and twitch inside her she dug her fingers deep into his scalp as if she would hold him there for ever, as if she wanted nothing more than to be the eternal receptacle of his vivid, furious lust.

He fell forward onto her and lay still for a moment, his weight smothering her. She lay very still, feeling the shuddering echoes of her orgasm pulsing through her, gradually fading. As her thoughts cleared she realised that although he had given her pleasure her feelings to him had changed. She detested the way he behaved to her. She felt as though she stood on a great cliff. With only a tiny push she would fall forward and spiral down through the clouds and cry out as she fell that she hated Antonio Varguez.

Say something awful, she thought. Make it easy for me.

But Tony rubbed his cheek against the skin of her breast like a big satisfied cat. 'Beautiful Tess,' he whispered, kissing her. 'Gorgeous Tess.' And she couldn't summon the energy to be angry with him when he was kind and attentive.

'Come on,' Tony said. 'Let's get into the bed, hmm? Kiss and make up?'

He helped her undress and smooth out her crumpled costume, then slipped with her beneath the sheets and drew her into his arms. Suddenly Tess remembered how on their first night together he had held her in his embrace all night, and she had felt so warm and safe. Was she being ungrateful, absurd?

Tony's breath stirred against her ear as he laughed. 'Don't know why I'm worrying,' he said softly. 'Dick's gone home with James and Adam, hasn't he? He's probably just another bum-boy. The woods are full of them.'

The following day Tess arrived a little late for rehearsal. Tony had found her again in the kitchen and as always the sight of her being domestic had acted as a direct stimulant to his sexual nerve endings. He had pressed her up against the wall of the kitchen and taken her there, roughly, brutally, without preliminaries, muttering Spanish obscenities beneath his breath. Then he had said, 'Remember, Tess. I'm back on Monday. And if I think you've done anything with Richard Shaeffer that I wouldn't approve of, you'll be sorry.'

And so Tess arrived subdued and unhappy, feeling bullied and manipulated. She wished she had told Tony to fuck off and die. But it wasn't that easy.

They were rehearsing Act Two from where they had left off the previous night. Tess looked around when she arrived, rather dispiritedly, in case Richard should be there, but he was not to be seen. The day was clammy and hot, threatening thunder. Yellow clouds veiled the sun. Tess shifted from foot to foot, flapping her shirt to try to encourage some cool air to move inside it.

'He's changing,' said a voice in her ear, making her jump.

'Catherine!' Tess turned, clutching her pounding heart. 'Who's changing?'

'Richard Shaeffer, of course. You were looking for him, weren't you?' Catherine grinned. 'Like every other woman in the cast.'

'No,' Tess's denial didn't sound convincing.

'Right,' called Adam's voice from the auditorium, 'number thirteen, entrance of Escamillo. On stage, everyone! Places!'

Tess took up her spot with Jeannette and Catherine, right at the front of the stage by the proscenium arch. She was intrigued. What sort of a performer would the young Canadian turn out to be? She had met singers before who were personally charming, and had been disappointed to find them insipid on stage.

Insipid. Dan had said she was insipid in bed. Was she still? Tony didn't think so. He thought she was gorgeous, he wanted her every time. Was that why she could not bear to leave him? Because, for all his faults, he made her feel eminently desirable, everything Dan had told her she was not?

Julian crashed the opening chords on the piano and the chorus burst into song. Carmen and her friends were supposed to look curious and excited, and all three of them were.

The piano launched into the introduction to Escamillo's aria and the scenery and crowd parted to reveal Richard, wearing his amazing black and silver costume with a helmet not unlike a Roman centurion's and high, black boots. Tess almost recoiled. He looked relaxed despite the cloying heat, and he moved forward like a panther, like a leopard on a leash, conveying in his movements a sense of controlled ferocity that made her spine tingle. Yesterday his hazel eyes had been warm and cheerful, but when he turned and looked at her for the first time in the character of Escamillo a shock went through her from her nape to her ankles. He looked powerful, virile, dangerous – and yet, behind the sense of physical strength, there was a warmness in his eyes, in his voice, that suggested a vast capacity to love and be loved, a selflessness that was utterly lacking in Tony's macho egotism.

He was looking at her as if he thought she was beautiful. Of course he is, Tess told herself desperately, that's what James has told him to do. It doesn't mean anything, he's acting. And yet as her eyes met his she felt her blood leaping with a surge of response so strong, so gut-wrenching, that she almost staggered. She wanted him more than anything she had ever seen, more than Dan, more than Tony, more than Julian, more than her success.

Richard was a professional to his fingertips. He delivered the aria very competently and the rehearsal ran straight on. Escamillo advanced across the stage towards Carmen, his eyes fixed on hers.

Sweetheart, he said, *I'd like to know your name. Next time I appear, I want to mention you.*

Me? Carmen responded. Tess's excitement, her pleasure were only half acting. *It's Carmen. Carmencita. You choose which you like.*

And suppose I said that I loved you?

You'd be wasting your time, said Carmen, looking deep into vivid sparkling eyes. *I'm not free right now.*

Not very promising, said Escamillo, *but I can wait and hope.*

Anyone can wait . . . and hope is sweet.

The act ran on, but for Tess it was as if a light had been switched off when Richard made his exit. She was glad that Tony wasn't there. She didn't feel that she could have put any emotion at all into Carmen's eager reunion with Don José.

When Adam called, 'OK, principals, thank you, that's all for today. Chorus on stage please for technical,' Tess stood in the wings not knowing what to do. Go home, said a little voice in her brain. Just go home and walk on the Heath until you're tired, then go to bed.

'Tess,' said Jeannette beside her, 'are you all right?'

'Fine,' Tess said, looking up with an artificial smile.

'Want to come home with us?' Jeannette asked encouragingly. 'Emma's out with some friends, Bob and Stefan are coming round this evening, I know Charlie would come too if you liked.'

Tess shook her head. 'No thanks.'

She stood for a while in the auditorium, alone, watching the lights going up and down and the stage hands crawling about the gantries to ensure that everything was just so. The chorus stood on the stage like sheep under the hot lights, fanning themselves and chatting to each other. Tess noticed in the front row the two she had seen making love at first rehearsal, Tom and Gina. They both saw this production as their big break. Lying half-naked on stage, simulating sex for an audience of prurient middle-aged opera-goers! Christ, Tess thought, there's no business like show business.

'Do you always watch technical rehearsal?' asked a warm transatlantic voice behind her. 'Or don't you have any paint to watch drying right now?'

Tess spun round and found herself looking into Richard Shaeffer's changing hazel eyes. He had changed out of his tight sweaty costume and now wore loose, soft stone-coloured chinos and a fine-gauge T-shirt that showed off the shape of his broad, elegantly muscled shoulders. Tess swallowed, feeling tongue-tied, like a fourteen-year-old. 'I – ' she faltered. 'Nothing better to do, I suppose.'

'If you've got nothing better to do,' Richard said with a smile, 'how about showing a poor hapless stranger how London fits together?' He gestured towards the edge of the park. 'They've got me a room at the Ritz.

Great, huh? But so far I've gone there and walked here and ventured up and down Piccadilly a bit. I got as far as Fortnum & Mason last night, daring stuff! But I don't know where to start.'

'Haven't you been here before?' Tess asked, genuinely surprised.

He shook his head. His soft, dark, curly hair fell into his eyes and he pushed it back with a graceful, unconscious gesture. 'No, not to stay. I came through when I was in England before, but just in a taxi. If you're not busy, could you?'

How could she refuse? Tess smiled and shrugged. 'I'd be glad to. What d'you want to see? Art? Architecture?'

'Listen,' said Richard, smiling more widely, 'you're talking to a boy from Saskatchewan. I have a family who live in the middle of nowhere. You know what I really want to do? I want to go somewhere cool and have something to eat and buy my sister a present.'

'Really?'

'Really. Where should we go, Harrods?'

Tess pursed her lips, considering. She was considering whether she should go at all as well as where they should go. But after all, he was a stranger, and she was a native of London, and it was no more than one singer should do for another under the circumstances. It didn't have to mean anything, did it?

'Well,' she said, 'we could go to Covent Garden, or the Kings Road, but they'd be bloody hot in this weather. How about walking across the park to Harvey Nichols?'

'To Harvey whom?'

'Harvey Nicks. It's a great shop, and the café has a balcony and it's seriously trendy.'

'Lead the way!'

They walked together across Green Park to the corner of Piccadilly and then through the network of tunnels at Hyde Park Corner into Hyde Park itself. Tess led them by devious routes, taking in the Serpentine, the statue of

Peter Pan, anything to allow her to saunter along beside Richard, talking to him.

Talking with him. It was so unlike talking to – being talked at *by* Tony. Richard seemed to be well educated and well read and he was certainly intelligent, but he seemed just as interested in what Tess had to say as what he was saying. They talked mainly about the production, about James's ideas and the designer's conceptions, about working with the conductor, Benedetto Corial, a flamboyant young Venetian who was also making his London debut with this production. They talked about music in general too, and found that their opinions and attitudes were sufficiently different to provoke stimulating debate, but not so far apart that they would annoy each other.

At last they arrived at Harvey Nichols and fought their way through the crowded ground floor and up through the increasingly rarefied air of three floors of expensive fashion to the exalted heights of the living area and further beyond to the food hall and café.

'Well,' said Richard slowly, looking from side to side, 'this is a bit different from Fortnum & Mason.'

'See here,' said Tess, 'here's the cook book of the most trendy restaurant in London right now. Italian cooking, basically. And look here, a whole rack of nothing but oils and vinegars. The best bred salad dressings start here.'

'How does this compare to Harrods?'

'Oh, we'll go there in a minute. They're completely different, Harrods is all solid and reliable and this is, ah, self-consciously chic. Have you seen *Absolutely Fabulous?*'

Richard shook his head, looking blank. 'Heard of it. Isn't it a TV show?'

'I couldn't possibly explain,' Tess said with a smile. She stretched to see over a small woman in an extraordinary hat. 'Hey look, no queue for the café. Come on, let's go.'

They were fortunate enough to get a table by the door

to the balcony, where the fresh air wafted pleasantly past them. A dappy young waiter brought the menu, which they studied in silence.

Presently, Richard said, 'What's aïoli? Isn't it garlic mayonnaise?' Tess nodded and he asked rather plaintively, 'So why serve it with chips? Wouldn't ketchup do?'

'And balsamic vinegar with everything,' Tess said. 'But it's nice food, Richard, honestly.'

All through their light, perfectly presented, rather expensive meal they continued to talk and Tess found herself unable to concentrate on the seriously trendy people coming and going. Richard watched the people, and she watched Richard.

This is infatuation, she told herself. You only want him because he's forbidden. You can't possibly feel like this about someone you've only known for a day.

But every time she opened her mouth she felt that she was at risk of saying something out of place, something about how attractive she found him, how much she enjoyed his company, how much she would like to – to make love to him . . .

Richard leant forward and lowered his voice. 'Table beside us,' he whispered. 'Check it out.'

Tess turned her head as if she were looking through the window and let her eyes rest on a couple. The man was a good looking 45 or so, with a Caribbean tan and very expensive, very casual clothes. The woman might have been thirty, but it was hard to tell under the make-up. Her hair was the shade of platinum blonde that comes from an expensive hairdresser. Her long legs were clad in glossy dark mink tights and her very short skirt and the jacket that skimmed her slender, perfectly proportioned body were black and edged with white trimming with tiny diamanté chips that glittered. She wore high strappy sandals that would have crippled Tess in five minutes and while her companion was munching his way through the most substantial dish on the menu, complete with chips and aïoli, she was toying with a small green salad and a mineral water.

'Trophy wife?' Richard mouthed at Tess. She looked at the woman's left hand and raised her eyebrows at the huge, square diamond she saw there above a plain, white gold band. She shrugged.

'They haven't exchanged a word in twenty minutes,' Richard said beneath his breath, shaking his head. 'I don't get it. What do they see in each other if they've got nothing to talk about?'

Tess looked at him, amazed. She almost said that Tony would love to have that sort of woman, then closed her lips tightly and shook her head, feeling wretched. She liked Richard as much as any man she could remember, felt she had a huge amount in common with him, thought him exceptionally attractive and would be pleased to share his bed. But if she did . . . If she did, she could imagine Tony's anger. And, possibly, his revenge.

'Tess?' Richard asked. 'Are you OK?'

'Sure. Fine.' Tess managed a smile which she knew would look artificial. 'Shall we, er, go and find your sister's present?'

Like many foreigners Richard wanted to send his sister something typically English, and although both of them agreed it was dull, they settled on a pretty ribbed cashmere sweater. 'Very suitable for Canadian winters,' Richard said. Tess was impressed by the fact that he not only knew his sister's size, but also what colour would suit her.

They walked out onto the street and recoiled from the intense, sweltering heat. 'Jesus,' Richard said, 'I thought England was supposed to be cold. Is there any water around here?'

'There's boats on the Serpentine,' Tess said, and then before she could control herself she had run on, 'but it's the place that does it, being in the centre of London, I mean. If we went out to where I live, out to Hampstead, on the Heath it wouldn't be half so hot.'

'What's Hampstead?' Richard asked.

'It's, a suburb, I suppose. It's quite expensive and smart,' Tess explained. And then felt constrained to add, 'My flat used to belong to my grandmother.'

'Wow!' said Richard, obviously impressed by this evidence of English history. 'That's pretty cool. I'd love to see it. Hampstead, I mean,' he added hastily, as if trying to change the subject.

Tess looked into his brilliant eyes. A slight flush coloured his high cheekbones. Perhaps it was embarrass-ment at a near miss, perhaps it was just the heat. She wanted him so much that her abdomen ached with the heavy weight of desire. How could she have got herself into this situation?

But it couldn't hurt just to go and look, could it? 'If you can stand the tube,' she heard herself saying, 'we could be there in half an hour.'

The tube was purgatory, like the seventh circle of Hell, hot and noisy and crowded with rush hour travellers. Tess and Richard were pushed apart and she almost lost him at King's Cross where they changed to the Northern line. They barely exchanged a word until they were out of the lift at Hampstead, drawing in great breaths of warm, sticky air.

All through the journey Tess had been arguing with herself, trying to suppress her growing attraction for Richard. She wanted him, but she was afraid of Tony. It wasn't until she felt her feet on her own home ground that some of Carmen's strength and stubbornness rushed into her and made her say, 'Would you like to come back to my flat and have a drink before we go and look round the Heath?'

They stood in the street, commuters whirling round them, and Richard looked into her eyes. She watched his expressions, surprise, shock, delight, anxiety. 'I'd love to,' he said at last, began to say something else and hesitated. At last it made itself heard. 'Tess, excuse me if I'm talking out of turn. But Emma Ridley told me that you were, er, in a relationship with Antonio Varguez: with Tony. I don't want to put a spanner in the works, cause problems, you know what I mean?'

Now's your chance, said Tess's cowardice. Back off. But she thought of Sarah's words: *you have to take control.* And she thought of Carmen saying to Don José, *I don't love you any more: it's over.* Aloud she said, 'I have been seeing him. But, but it's over. It's over now.' Richard still looked uncertain. His bright eyes narrowed as if he wanted to see through her, to look to the bottom of her soul. 'Will you come back to my flat?' she asked, and she knew she was asking him to her bed.

His expression showed that he understood her. 'Yes,' he said simply.

They walked side by side along the sweltering streets, not hurrying, both of them looking straight ahead. Tess's pulse beat hard in her temples and her throat was taut with excitement. All the research she had done should have been a good grounding for this deliberate admission of lust, but it was not. It was no help, because this time her heart was involved.

She sneaked a sidelong glance at Richard and found that he was looking at her. She stopped moving, startled and embarrassed, as if she had been caught doing something wicked. For a long moment they looked into each other's eyes. Richard's tender, sensuous lips were parted and over the noise of the traffic she could hear his breath whispering between them. She was riveted by the beauty of his face, the warmth of his breathing lips. Very slowly she lifted one hand as if she would touch his mouth. It felt as though she were pushing her fingers through thick treacle. At last her fingertips just brushed his cheek, and as she touched him he gasped her name and closed his eyes as he reached for her, pulling her to him as blindly as a drowning swimmer seeking safety. Her other hand caught at his hair, felt its softness, and then his lips were on hers and they were locked together, devouring each other, smothering under the weight of their desire.

Every nerve, every muscle of Tess's body strained to draw him closer to her, to squeeze him within her until her bones were his bones and his flesh was her flesh. His tongue quivered in her mouth. When at last he lifted his lips from hers she whispered, 'Richard, I want you so much,' and she was not afraid of his reaction. She knew he felt the same way.

'Christ,' he hissed, 'come on, Tess, come on, take us home, or we'll have to do it in the street and shock all these respectable people.'

Tess laughed and caught his hand and they ran together along the street towards the small, tree-lined avenue where Tess's house was. The key leapt from her bag to her fingers, the door was open and they were racing up the stairs and through the inner door into the cool, airy lightness of the flat.

Richard didn't even seem to see it. He stopped inside the door and stood still, panting. Tess slammed the door and caught again at his hand and drew him after her through the drawing room to the bedroom. She went to the window and flung it wide open, then drew the curtains. For a moment she rested her forehead against the heavy fabric. Then she turned and looked into Richard's eyes.

'Tess,' he said softly, 'I want you too.' And he put his hands to his T-shirt and with one quick movement stripped it off.

His torso was as beautiful as she had known it would be, pale, golden skin, smooth and fresh. His muscles were well developed, but not too prominent. He looked like a healthy young man who earns his living in the open air, natural, not created. There was a long white scar on one shoulder, old and faded, a teenager's scar. His flat belly lifted and fell, his singer's diaphragm working hard to suck in air, to control his breathing. He stood very still with the T-shirt held in both hands, looking into Tess's eyes.

Slowly she unbuttoned her shirt and let it fall behind her. She walked across the room to him and reached up her lips to kiss him again, and as their tongues met and caressed her hands went to the button of his chinos and he reached for her skirt. Tess pushed down the waistband of his trousers and then caught her breath in rapture as she felt how soft and warm his skin was, faintly beaded with sweat from the heat, slick beneath her exploring fingers. She could smell the scent of his body, complex and musky and intoxicating. For a moment they wriggled in ungainly eagerness, like a pair of snakes trying to mate and shed their skins at the same time. Then the last garment was discarded and they were naked, their bodies pressing together, closely as twining creepers. His penis shuddered against her belly, hot and dry and hard as wood. She moaned with a sudden upsurge of lust and pulled herself free and dropped to her knees before him, reaching up to take hold of him and draw down the glistening head of his splendid shaft to within reach of her wet lips.

'Jesus,' Richard groaned as Tess extended her tongue and flickered the tip of it against the taut shining dome that crested his rigid phallus. 'Oh Jesus, God, Tess.' And as if taking pity on him she opened her lips and let first the tip, then the head, then the thick pillar of his flesh enter her mouth. She wanted to take all of him and moaned in disappointment when she could harbour only a few inches of that proud, splendid rod in her throat. With her hands she caressed the tight orbs of his beautiful buttocks, squeezing them, digging her nails into the tender skin, and she let her wet lips slide slowly, lasciviously up and down his quivering penis.

'Tess,' Richard whispered, and his strong long-fingered hands suddenly caught at the thick mass of her tumbled dark-red hair. He pulled her up and back, drawing her into his arms. 'Tess, Tess, not just me, not just me.'

Clutching each other, shaking with desire, they swayed together to the bed and fell onto it. The warm breeze through the window made their skin glisten with perspiration and their limbs alternately stuck and slithered across each other, slippery with need.

Tess had not had her fill of his wonderful cock. She wanted to taste it again, to feel it moving within her mouth, swelling and tightening with the waiting seed. She began to slide down his damp body, kissing the hollow of his shoulder, sucking one of his flat male nipples until it stood up just as hers would have done, rubbing her cheek against the delicious hardness marking the edge of his rib cage. But he murmured in protest, reaching out for her. 'Let me,' he breathed. 'Let me do something for you too.'

She knew what he meant. Briefly, like the last flare of a sunset, she remembered how it had felt to be shy, to be afraid of showing herself to her lover. She had not dared, with Dan, to do this same thing, to offer her sex to his mouth as she caressed his penis with her lips. But the memory only added piquancy to the eager desire she now felt. With a smothered cry she turned her body over him and pressed her face between his thighs, kissing and licking the hot, swollen shaft of his cock, loving it. Her legs were parted, her knees planted on either side of his face, and she rejoiced to feel his eyes resting like a touch on her secret centre, opening her, knowing her.

She drew the head of his cock into her mouth, moaning with the joy of feeling him stirring in her throat. He groaned: beneath her his taut body vibrated with the deep sound of his pleasure. Then he reached up and his hands took hold of her white buttocks, pulling them down towards his mouth, spreading her. Tess's closed eyes tightened, waiting to feel his tongue and lips there, there where she burned with need for him.

First she felt his hair, soft against her thighs, and then

at last his lips upon her. His mouth embraced her sex, warm and yielding, and she gasped with expectation. Her mouth moved faster on his throbbing cock. But he did not use his tongue, and after a moment she hesitated, suddenly anxious.

Then, without warning, Richard drew in a long breath and let it out in a deep, vibrating hum. The sound startled Tess, and then she pulled her lips away from his penis because she was crying out with sudden, shocked pleasure. His whole mouth, his warm, wet mouth, was quivering against her sex, a deep elemental vibration that made her shudder with delight. The sensation was so intense, so unexpected, that she could not keep her balance. She fell to one side and Richard moved with her, his lips pressed between her open legs, playing out his expert breath in long, shivering whispers of music that thrilled through her body as if he had tapped her spinal cord. He moved a little to bring his cock within reach of her mouth and she opened her lips blindly to admit him, but she could not concentrate on sucking him. She lay on her side, moaning with helpless ecstasy as his humming lips impelled her towards orgasm, and he thrust his taut penis gently in and out of her unresisting mouth.

The moving shaft of his flesh gagged her, holding in her sounds of pleasure. Richard continued to hum, and now as he did so he began very gently to touch her with his tongue, moving it with infinite delicacy against the engorged, quivering bud of her clitoris. Tess cried out past the gag of his thrusting cock and arched her body helplessly and Richard held on tightly to her soft haunches and began to lick her harder and harder, sweeping strokes of his strong tongue that lifted her to the height of bliss in seconds. Her hips jerked against his mouth and her lips slackened, allowing his rigid penis to slide deep into her throat as she hung in momentary eternity, burnt and frozen by orgasm.

Then he was moving, turning, until he was lying

beside her and looking into her face. She opened her heavy eyelids and whispered, 'Richard.'

'Tess, Tess.' He pressed close to her, raising one hand to weigh her breast, stroking the nipple so that she sighed with resurgence of joy. He had not come yet, and his cock was thick and strong, feverishly swollen, his balls drawn snugly up beneath his body, heavy with lust. He gently caught hold of her knee with one hand and lifted her leg over his thigh and then moved between them and positioned the head of his penis at her entrance.

Then he waited. He met her eyes again and smiled a little. Tess let out a long breath of yearning and murmured, 'Yes, Richard, yes. Now.'

And at her words he thrust and the whole of his long, thick cock slid up within her, penetrating her with gentle deliberacy, remorseless as the root of a tree which can split the rock. When he was sheathed inside her he paused, waiting, looking into her eyes. She gave a little eager gasp and tugged at his tight buttocks, wanting him to take her, and he began to move.

So slow, so deep, like the currents of the deepest ocean stirring inside her. For a while she watched his face, watched the sensations changing his expression as he drove his body deeply into her, his eyes narrowing and his nostrils flaring and his lips drawing away from his teeth almost as if he were in pain. But then the pleasure was too much, and she closed her eyes and tightened her hands on his haunches and felt his fingers closing on hers in answer and immersed herself in the rapture of his possession, letting her hips sway towards his thrusting penis like the waves of the sea. She imagined herself as a chest of treasure cast up on a sandy beach, its timbers weakened by the roaring ocean. The winds rise and soon the chest is pounded by waves, great arching waves of enormous power that toss it from side to side and beat it down upon the unforgiving sand, curling up above it higher and higher, falling upon it with merciless force until at last it shudders and yields and bursts asunder and everything it holds is thrown up and spilt into the foaming sea, starring the wilderness of white with gems and gold, littering the sand with tumbled pearls.

Through the red mists of her second orgasm she sensed him crying out, holding her, shuddering as he spent himself within her. His hands on her flanks held as tight as claws. After a long moment of stillness the tension broke and they relaxed, holding each other, looking into each other's eyes with faces of wonder and disbelief.

The curtains stirred and flapped, driven away from the window by a sudden fierce gust. Tess and Richard moved a little apart and sat up, holding each other, looking out at the blackening sky.

'It's going to thunder,' Richard said, and as if in answer a low rumble shuddered across the roofs. 'I love thunderstorms.'

Tess felt light-headed with bliss. She wasn't ready to sleep. 'So do I,' she said, trying to shake her heavy hair off the nape of her neck. 'What do you say, do you want to go for a walk in it?'

Richard stared at her, shook his head disbelievingly, then grinned. 'You're off your head,' he said. 'Why the hell not?'

She lent him an old baggy sweatshirt, because the wind was suddenly cold, and they tumbled down the stairs of the flat and ran hand in hand towards the Heath. They were like lovers, laughing, kissing, pointing up at the sky when quick lightning flared in one part or another.

'This is amazing!' Richard exclaimed as Tess led him to her favourite dell. 'It's like the country, not like a park. It's wonderful.'

'I love it,' Tess said. 'Especially now, in the rain, when there's nobody here.'

'Nobody except us,' he said, and kissed her.

501

Above them lightning split the sky and suddenly the rain was falling, huge drops like steel-headed nails, falling so thickly they drew vertical lines across the landscape. Richard and Tess gasped and retreated automatically beneath the thick canopy of an oak tree.

'It's dangerous to stand under trees in a lightning storm,' Tess said suddenly, looking around from side to side. 'We could be hit by lightning.'

The sky lit again with brilliance and the thunder roared. Momentarily blinded, Tess closed her eyes. When she opened them again she was looking into Richard's face. What she saw there took her breath away.

'I've already been hit by lightning,' Richard whispered. He looked desperate, driven, like a lost soul. 'I'm scorched,' he said softly. 'Scorched and still burning.'

His lips fell upon hers as if her mouth was the cool stream that would quench his scalding thirst. He pressed her back against the rough bark of the oak tree and kissed her with feverish eagerness, trembling as he touched her. His hands thrust inside her shirt and found her breasts and began to stroke them with such fervent gentleness that Tess moaned aloud and spread her hands flat upon the tree's broad trunk, her fingers digging into the twisted grooves of the bark. Richard jerked up her shirt and sweater and bared her naked breasts and the cold rain fell upon them, startling her nipples into stiff points of hardness and trickling in transparent rivulets down the silky white crease. He bent his head and kissed her breasts, sucking the points until they swelled and blossomed and she whimpered and closed her eyes. Then he pushed up her skirt and pressed close to her and she felt his penis naked against the naked skin of her belly, hard and burning, and without a thought, without a sound she parted her thighs and opened herself to him and he penetrated her.

This time it was not gentle, but furious, filling her with pleasure as brilliant as the lightning that flashed above them, as piercing as the cold rain that stung their bare skin and soaked their clothes, as deep as the thunder that shook them where they stood. The harsh bark of the tree scraped against her naked buttocks and her head snapped to and fro as he thrust himself into her so fiercely that the sound of flesh meeting flesh was clear over the steady hiss of the rain. He held her breasts tightly in his hands, closing his fingers on her tormented nipples, and as he took her he looked down to see his golden body entering her white one, the thick rod of his flesh sliding up inside her until it was sheathed to the root and then withdrawing, gleaming with her juices, only to lunge again.

The rain ran down her face and his. When their lips met they tasted the rain, fresh with thunder. He beat his body against her with astonishing power, all the lean strength of his muscles intent on that one movement, and as he thrust she felt the claws of climax beginning to grip her, shaking her until she would have fallen but that she was impaled on the strong shaft that worked to and fro within her clasping sex. 'Richard,' she gasped, 'Richard,' and above them a huge fork of lightning speared the sky and the thunder grasped them and shook them until they fell together to the wet earth, shuddering bodies joined in ecstasy, twitching still with the aftershocks of orgasm as if the lightning animated their lifeless limbs.

Act Four, Scene Two

The Hampstead flat

*B*irdsong and traffic noise competed to wake Tess up. She lay still for a moment, stretching, looking at the bar of sunlight laid like a ruler across the white ceiling and savouring the delicious ache of her limbs.

After returning to the flat they had made love again, and again, all evening, wrapped in a sensual ecstasy as deep as winter, as glorious as spring. Richard was tirelessly and endlessly inventive, finding one new way after another to bring Tess to orgasm, and when sheer exhaustion denied her another climax he laughed at her and pushed her to the floor and held her there as he took her for his own pleasure, the simple direct masculine pleasure of possession, thrusting into her with feverish energy until he twisted and shuddered in the grip of his urgent release and she moaned beneath him with the delirious bliss of total, rapturous submission.

The memory alone made Tess ready for more. She yawned and licked her lips and lifted herself on one elbow, looking down at Richard asleep beside her.

He did not have Dan's classical perfection or Tony's dark Mediterranean glamour, but his sleeping face revealed everything about him that she delighted in, in his character as well as his body. Lips so finely cut, so sensual, that just to see them was to imagine them kissing, licking and caressing. Sharp, narrow nose and cheekbones, making him look lean and fierce as a prowling wolf, and soft tumbling dark curls which her fingers longed to disarray even further. And those wide-set eyes, shielded now by his heavy, long-lashed eyelids, which only had to open to bathe her in glittering warmth like sunlight reflecting from a forest pool.

He turned in his sleep, flinging one arm up above his head and taking a deep, slow breath. Tess gently caught hold of the single crumpled sheet that had covered them and drew it away, revealing his nakedness. His body was lear. and strong as a predator's, muscled and taut, ready even in his sleep to leap up and seize its prey. Blue veins were etched finely onto the lightly tanned skin of his forearms and throat, moving faintly with the hidden power of his pulsing heart.

Once upon a time, Tess thought, I didn't dare to wake my lover. But that was before Carmen. She leant slowly towards him and let her lips hover above his mouth. She knew he would wake, and he did, stirring very slightly before his eyelids flickered and opened.

She smiled into his face. 'The problem with going to bed with a handsome prince,' she said, 'is the risk that when you kiss him in the morning he will turn into a beautiful frog.'

Very gently she set her lips on his, tasting him, savouring him. He closed his eyes and lay very still, allowing her to control the kiss. Then, when she lifted her mouth from his, he croaked softly, 'Ribbit,' and smiled at her.

Then he reached up and drew her down to him, pressing her body beneath his so that their naked flesh clung from breast to ankle. They kissed as if they wanted to become one creature, fusing together gradually, first skin, then muscle, then bone, finally the soft pulsing organs of their bodies, lungs and brains and thumping hearts melting one into another, mingling and welding in a conjunction of oneness until their souls, too, were united.

'Richard,' Tess whispered into his breathing mouth. 'Richard.' And he groaned and strained her closer to him and his hot, stiff cock moved between her parted thighs, prodding with its blind eye as if seeking its way. She opened her legs wider, offering herself to him, yearning for him to sheathe himself within the aching cleft of her sex. The smooth, dry head of his penis pressed against her, soft as sueded silk, hard as bronze, and then it entered her, filling the empty hollowness within her, sealing their union, completing her.

The soft walls of her vagina and the delicate flesh of her labia were tender and bruised from the last night's endless love-making, and a spurt of exquisite pain filled her as his loins nestled closely against hers. The sharp bones of his lean hips fitted into the hollows of her thighs as exactly as an egg in the cup. At the same moment their hands sought each other's haunches, drawing themselves yet closer together, striving for the ultimate contact.

'Oh,' she moaned in delicious agony and blissful fear, feeling him so deep within her that another hair's-breadth of penetration would impale her very essence. 'Oh God, Richard, be gentle.'

'I have to be cruel to be kind,' he whispered, and he held her still to receive the first surging blow of his body. She cried out in desperation, writhing like an animal dying on the spear as he took her with a slow deliberate power that reduced her to nothingness, to a moaning wreck, a helpless captive of his remorseless phallus.

There was pain. Every soft tissue of her sex was swollen and sensitive, complaining shrilly as it felt itself again invaded, stretched, wrenched open and possessed. For a few moments the pain obliterated the pleasure, like the dark disc of the moon covering the sun at the point of total eclipse. But even at that point of pain the glow of ecstasy surrounded her like the sun's corona, visible only then, only then when its white heart was shielded, arching from the surface of her pleasure into the dark unfamiliar reaches of space, leaping sprays of liquid flame that curved from her sex to her limbs, from her limbs to her brain. And then Richard held her more firmly and slid his thick, rigid penis faster and faster in and out of her quivering flesh, and as he took her, thrusting his hard cock with feverish urgency into the yielding centre of her body, the obscuring shadow of her pain moved aside like the moon to reveal the blazing core of bliss, dismissing the aurorae with its brilliance, blinding her with the molten conflagration of climax.

She clung to him, listening to his slowly pounding heart. Its steady, strong double thump measured words that filled her brain but which she was not yet ready to utter. *I love you. Love you. Love you.*

His cheek rested on her hair and his eyelashes fluttered against her skin. 'Tess. Did I hurt you?' He touched the inside of her thigh, very gently. 'You're bruised. I'm so sorry. Are you all right?'

'Yes. No. It doesn't matter, it's all right. Oh, Richard – ' and she lifted her face to his, wanting still to feel his lips on hers.

The telephone rang. Tess stiffened and tried to ignore it, but she couldn't. As the answering machine clicked she reached over and seized the receiver and said huskily, 'Hello?'

'Hello Tess?' said a honey-sweet voice. Tess screwed up her face in distaste as she recognised the dulcet tones of Emma Ridley. 'Sorry to bother you, but James called me. He's looking for Richard, apparently he didn't go back to the hotel last night and James is worried.'

'What time is it?' Tess asked blankly.

'It's nearly half past eleven,' said Emma. 'You don't know where Richard has gone, do you? Gina told me that she saw him going off with you after rehearsal yesterday.'

Tess held the receiver at a little distance from her ear,

thinking fast. That little bitch! James wasn't pursuing Richard, he wouldn't, it was the weekend. Richard knew his schedule, and besides, he needed time to recover from travelling. Emma was just indulging her own prurient curiosity. But she was chummy with Tony, too. If she had guessed what had happened, she would as usual broadcast it far and wide, and she would certainly tell Tony. It would at least mean that Tess didn't need to break the news to Tony herself.

'Tess?' said Emma's voice. 'Tess?'

'Yes,' Tess said quickly. 'Sorry, Emma. Yes, Richard's here, actually.' Beside her Richard straightened up in bed, looking shocked, and Tess shushed him. 'Yes, I showed him around London yesterday for a bit and then we went up to Hampstead and then it was rather late for him to be going home, so he stopped here. Shall I get him to ring James?' That'll call your bluff, she thought.

'Oh,' said Emma quickly, 'no, no, no need, I'll just let him know that everything's OK, I think he was just checking up.'

I think you were just checking up, Tess thought sourly. 'Right then. 'Bye.'

She put down the telephone. 'That was our little bush telegraph,' she said to Richard. 'Emma Ridley on line. Everyone in the cast will know about this first thing Monday morning, Richard. I hope you're ready for it.'

'Why,' Richard asked innocently, 'is it a problem?' His brows drew down over his eyes, making them glitter. 'Tess, will you be in trouble? Is Tony – '

'Don't worry,' Tess said with more confidence than she felt. 'I'll handle Tony.'

Richard smiled at her, leant forward and kissed her. 'If you say so,' he said, 'I'll believe you.' He stroked his hand gently through her hair and looked into her face, then touched his fingers to her lips. 'Stay here,' he said, 'keep yourself comfortable. I'll bring you breakfast in bed.'

Tess lay sprawled on the crumpled sheets, her limbs

blissfully relaxed, looking up at the sunlight crawling across the ceiling and listening to the little comforting domestic sounds emerging from the kitchen. The clink of crockery, water running, then Richard's footsteps in the living room. His face at the bedroom door, grinning. 'Hey,' he said, 'there's one thing you Brits have sorted out, and that's making tea. Just tell me, why don't we have electric kettles on the other side of the Atlantic?'

'Search me,' Tess said, with a smile and a shrug.

'Mind you,' Richard added, 'you seem to be a bit short of food. I'll see what I can do, though. Earl Grey all right for you, or would you prefer,' he adopted an accent vaguely reminiscent of John Gielgud, 'English Breakfast?'

'Earl Grey,' said Tess, with a sigh of simple pleasure. 'Please.'

He was actually making tea for her. A man was making her tea in the morning! Even Leo, who was not proud, had been far too dozy on first waking up to stagger out to the kitchen and switch on the kettle, and as for Dan and Tony . . .

After a little while the warmth of the room and the warm slick sensation of her love-juices trickling gently between her thighs lulled her into a doze. At once she began to dream, an odd, confused, disturbing sequence of images that were both erotic and frightening. She was a slave, stripped naked for sale, and the man who dragged back her shoulders to show off her breasts and forced her thighs apart to show her moist secret flesh to the silent sweating purchasers was Richard. Then she was waiting for her flight in the airport departure lounge, plastic bags of duty free goodies clustering around her feet, and suddenly James and Adam were standing before her, hand in hand, and Adam said, 'Right, now everyone watch this demonstration,' and as all the travellers got to their feet and clustered around Tess felt her clothes evaporate like smoke and she was naked and ashamed and Adam opened his fly and took out his cock, huge, gnarled, like the stump of a tree, as big as Jeannette had said, and he said to her, 'Turn round, bend over,' and she tried to protest but there was nothing she could do. Adam's fingers were diving between her legs to anoint her arse with her juices and then he spat in her crease and it was cold and it tickled –

'Tess,' whispered Richard's voice in her ear. 'Hey, wake up. It's nearly noon. Wake up.'

She opened her eyes. He was sitting beside her on the bed, holding a mug of tea towards her. His naked body glowed pale gold in the sunlight and his eyes glittered as he smiled at her. She whimpered gratefully and took the mug and buried her face in it, inhaling the fragrant steam.

'Now,' said Richard, 'breakfast, that was tricky. So I thought I'd just do something simple, you know, something delicious . . .'

He brought out his other hand from behind his back. In it he was holding a large tub of Häagen Dazs ice cream and a spoon.

'Ice cream?' Tess asked, astonished. 'For breakfast?'

'Not just ice cream,' Richard smiled. '*Real* ice cream. Sexy ice cream. Didn't they run an advertising campaign here that suggested the best thing you could do to this stuff was find interesting ways to melt it?'

Tess finished the tea, set down her mug and regarded the tub of ice cream soberly. 'Fudge ripple,' she said softly, 'my favourite.'

'Yeah? Well, I should hope so, in your icebox.' Richard said, holding the tub towards her. 'Here you go. Eat it straight out of the carton if you like, or maybe, ah,' he put it into her hands and stretched out on the bed along one of the bars of sunlight, 'maybe you could think of a more unusual receptacle?'

Tess bit her lip, then laughed. 'Receptacle?' she repeated, looking admiringly at the flat, lean planes of

510

Richard's prone body. 'Richard, just tell me one place I can put it, apart from your navel.'

'How about here?' Richard suggested, pointing to the delicate hollow of his throat. 'Or here?' The curve of his shoulder. 'Hey, use your imagination.'

'I could imagine a banana split,' Tess said, sliding one hand down the smooth warm skin of Richard's body towards his flat stomach. He smiled at her and between his legs the soft curl of his resting penis stirred and began almost imperceptibly to thicken. He leant back into the pillows and closed his bright eyes.

For a moment Tess knelt beside him, considering. Then she dipped the spoon into the ice cream and lifted it to her mouth. The delicious, sweet taste spread slowly across her tongue. A drop fell from the spoon onto her naked breast and she jumped at the sudden cold. 'Won't the, ah, the temperature put you off?' she asked hesitantly. 'I thought men had an optimum operating temperature, you know, they need to be warm.'

Richard's lazy eyelids opened and he raised his eyebrows at her. 'Maybe, maybe not. You never know till you try.'

'Well,' said Tess, 'OK. Here goes.' And she let a small spoonful of ice cream fall delicately into the hollow of Richard's smooth, muscular shoulder.

'Ah,' Richard breathed. His whole body tensed, then relaxed. Between his legs his cock continued to grow. Now it was almost at its full splendid length, although it was still soft as dough. Tess leant slowly forward and extended her tongue and licked the cold melting ice cream from Richard's tanned skin.

She hadn't expected to be able to taste him, but she could, a subtle, salty counterpoint to the sweet main theme of the vanilla and fudge ice cream. A pale thread of melted cream slipped down towards his nipple and she smiled and caught it up on her tongue and Richard's breath hissed through his teeth.

Another spoonful, this time in the centre of his chest,

511

just on the flat, bony plate of his sternum. It was so delicious and his reactions were so arousing that Tess began to become artistic. With her tongue she swirled the ice cream out to surround his nipples, smiling as they tautened just as hers would have done. Her own breasts ached with an echo of Richard's pleasure. She dug the spoon in again and let the soft, cold substance fall onto his stomach, just below his navel.

'Christ,' Richard breathed. His cock was fully hard now, lying tautly along his abdomen, a glistening pillar of flesh. Tess licked all around it, but didn't touch it. He moaned with faint protest and the shining head of his cock lifted towards her lips all by itself, as if it were desperate to seek the soft haven of her mouth.

'Banana split,' Tess whispered, and dropped the next spoonful directly onto the head of Richard's cock. He cried out and his back arched in protest: then his cry was stifled as Tess leant further forward and gently, deliberately drew him into her mouth, swirling her tongue around the hot shaft to clean it of dribbles of cream.

'Oh,' she said, surfacing, 'that's delicious. Oh, God, I can taste your come, and me, and you, and it's gorgeous.'

The next spoonful fell onto his taut updrawn balls. Tess laughed as she burrowed to retrieve it, pushing her face in between his legs, getting ice cream on her nose, in her eyebrows, in her hair. Sweet trickles ran down the insides of his thighs and between the cheeks of his taut arse. 'Open your legs,' Tess mumbled.

'Oh, Jesus,' Richard moaned, but he obeyed her. She thrust her tongue closely between his spread thighs, caressing the delicate skin behind his balls, just beginning to probe at his crack, and he whimpered and shivered. For a moment she thought of licking him there, forcing her tongue into him, but she didn't want to startle him. So she moved back up his body and with delight and relief opened her lips to accept his taut, straining cock into her mouth.

She would gladly have sucked him until he came, but

Richard had different ideas. 'Hold on,' he said through his teeth, lifting himself from the pillows to catch hold of her tousled hair and lift her gently away from him. 'Hold on, Tess. Your turn.'

He positioned her on her knees, leaning backwards, her weight supported on her arms. Thus arranged her breasts thrust forward, lustful and eager. She let her head fall back and closed her eyes, waiting with a shiver of delight for what she knew was coming, the delicious coldness of the ice cream caressing her taut, aching nipples. Her breasts felt tender and swollen, desperate for his soft mouth upon them to soothe them and torment them further.

Richard dug the spoon into the tub of ice cream and without a word dropped a small mound of it onto Tess's left breast, then at once plunged his mouth down and sucked and sucked until she writhed and spread her knees wide apart as if she wanted him to take her now, at once, slide his hot, thick cock right up inside her as his warm mouth worshipped her straining nipple. He laughed at her wantonness, but he did not take her, only anointed her other breast and sucked at it until it too was swollen and engorged with fevered lust that the cold liquid could not soothe, only increase.

Then he made her lie face down on the bed, her head pillowed in her arms, her face hidden. She wriggled where she lay, anxiously anticipating the chill kiss of the ice cream. Where would it fall? Shoulders, neck, spine, buttocks?

He took her entirely by surprise, dropping a little liquid gob into the hollow of one knee. She squeaked with shock, then the sound changed to a moan of incredulous ecstasy as she felt his warm, soft tongue there, caressing the delicate skin, moving up a little to stroke the inside of her thigh. He parted her legs and gradually moved upwards, trickling the slowly melting ice cream further and further up her thighs until she thought she would scream with pleasure and frustration.

Her whole body shivered and her tight, hard nipples rubbed against the sheet, sending quick barbs of bliss through her.

Then he let one spoonful fall directly into the crease of her buttocks. She cried out in surprise and anticipation of ecstasy. She had done it to Tony, but despite Jeannette's promise it had never been done to her and she wanted –

'Oh God,' she moaned as she felt his tongue there, probing between her cheeks, slithering delicately along the length of her crease. It found the puckered ring of her anus, touched it, circled it and moved on. Tess heaved with disappointment and whimpered helplessly, then cried out again as another spoonful of chilly ice cream landed on the spot.

'Jesus,' hissed Richard's eager voice, 'Jeez, Tess, you have a beautiful ass. Christ, it's gorgeous. It's edible.' And she felt his face there again, pressing between her cheeks, and this time there was no hesitation. His warm, wet, strong tongue collected the chilly melting liquid, conveyed it to the tight flower of her anus and gently, gradually thrust its way inside. Tess shut her eyes tightly and lifted her buttocks towards him, eager, wanting more. His hands were on her thighs, on the insides of her thighs, moving up, moving closer, almost touching her, and as his tongue penetrated her delicate forbidden passage his hands found her sex and began to stimulate her, touching her clitoris, stroking her labia, sliding inside her. First one finger, then two, moved slowly and strongly in and out, in and out of her wet sex.

'Richard,' Tess moaned, 'Richard, Richard, oh God that's amazing,' and as the warm point of his tongue tenderly rimmed the satin flesh of her anus and his fingers drove into her sex she began to shudder and tense as the strong claws of climax gripped her and shook her and left her gasping. He did not wait, but laid his body directly on top of hers, so that his skin pressed against her all down her, and he spread her thighs wide apart and without a word he pressed the searing tip of his cock against her sex and entered her. She cried out with shock and delight, because in this position he seemed to penetrate her incredibly deeply and the strange angle of his stiff cock sliding deep within her bruised, tender vagina was almost unbearably stimulating. At once he began to move, quick urgent thrusts that made her white flesh shake as his body struck hers, and after only a few minutes he started to groan and shudder and he took hold of her hips and pulled them up towards him so that he could shaft her even harder, fill her even more, drive himself into her like a nail into an oaken beam.

'Oh Christ,' he cried out. His breath was hot on her neck and his warm skin slid over hers on a glistening sheen of sweat and cream. 'Christ, Tess, I'm coming, I'm coming, oh God your ass is so beautiful – ' and then he was there, snarling with the urgent power of his release within her.

He was hers for what was left of Saturday. They slowly staggered to their feet, committed the wrecked sheets to the washing machine and then crawled to soak their sticky, weary limbs in a hot and entirely necessary bath. Bathing gave them the opportunity for further leisurely sensual exploration of each other's bodies, after which they went out to walk on the Heath.

Every leaf and blade of grass was glittering with raindrops and the paths steamed as the bright warm sun sucked last night's storm back into the sky. They walked hand in hand, hardly talking, and Tess let her fingers gradually familiarise themselves with the shape of his hand, the big square palm, long fingers, wide flat nails, until she would have known that hand among a million others.

Then back in the afternoon to the flat and out onto the secluded roof terrace, where Richard covered Tess's

515

naked body with his own to protect her from the hot sunlight that might otherwise scald her white skin.

On Sunday Richard had to work. He went to the theatre to meet the fight director and commit all the stage fights to memory and Tess went too to watch. She took keen pleasure in seeing Richard learning his moves, his strong agile body flexing and twisting like an athlete's. The main fight was between Richard's character Escamillo and Don José. Although Escamillo is the better fighter he slips on the garbage-strewn streets and loses his weapon, leaving him at José's mercy and enabling Carmen to intervene to save him. It was a spectacular piece of theatre, quick and vicious as a real knife fight must be. Richard learnt the moves fast and then went through the whole thing with the fight director standing in for Tony as Don José. Although Tess had seen the action built up piece by piece and she knew that at no time was Richard in any danger, he acted so well that when at the end he lost his knife and stood helpless she felt her heart pounding with fear for him.

Monday's rehearsal was a full run through, but without the conductor. The singers would just mutter their notes, saving their voices for the dress rehearsals and first night later in the week. Tess arrived alone, since Richard had gone back to the hotel that morning to sort out some business, and she realised that she was afraid of what Tony might do when he knew that she had broken her promise. She was late on purpose and her luck was in, Tony was already on stage. She stood in the wings waiting for her entry and watching his face. He looked and moved as if he were containing tremendous rage, and it was no surprise to Tess when Emma brushed past her as she made her exit and whispered archly, 'Think you're in for a bit of a storm today, Tess darling.'

She had to admit that Tony was a professional. When they were on stage together he acted his part perfectly, and in the face of his concentration Tess found it surprisingly easy to become Carmen, falling in lust with Don

José at first sight. At the end of Act One she fled the stage, hoping to avoid Tony entirely, and took refuge in the dressing room she shared with Emma, one of a number of well-appointed Portakabins.

She had hardly caught her breath when in her mirror she saw movement behind her. She looked up quickly, sure that it would be Tony, but it was Richard, leaning against the doorframe and smiling his warm, slightly lopsided smile.

'Hi,' he said. 'I was out front. You were great. This is a hell of a production.'

'Thanks,' Tess said, turning and walking straight into his open arms. 'Thanks, Richard. If it had been for real I thought I might have cracked my top note, I was so nervous.'

'Nervous? Why?' He held her more tightly. 'You don't need – '

'Act Two is about to start,' said a silky, tautly controlled voice with a Spanish accent. 'Don't you think you should be on stage, *signora la diva?*'

Tess pulled away from Richard, cold with apprehension, and looked up into Tony's bleak, furious face. His cruel mouth was twisted with anger. She bit her lip and took a quick breath, but before she could speak he had turned his back on her and stalked away.

'What's bugging him?' Richard asked, raising his eyebrows. 'I thought you said you two were finished.'

'We are,' Tess said, with a guilty sense that she had not been entirely honest. Well, they were certainly finished now. She thought that Tony's expression and behaviour had made that abundantly clear.

Act Two went well, without a hitch. At the end of the act Carmen and Don José embraced before they left the stage. Tess was ready for a half-hearted stage clinch, but Tony surprised her. He caught her into his arms as if they had been in the bedroom, knotted his strong fingers into her mane of tousled hair and dragged back her head with such violence that she gasped. Then he pressed his mouth onto hers with feverish urgency and despite herself she felt her body responding, jerked into arousal by the darting thrust of Tony's hot, eager tongue. The curtain fell and she tried to pull free, but Tony would not release her. She groaned with a potent mixture of fear and shame and sheer excitement as he kissed her so forcefully that her breath lurched and fluttered and the soft flesh between her legs tautened involuntarily.

At last she tore herself away. 'No,' she protested in a fierce hiss, 'Tony, don't.'

'You bitch,' Tony whispered into her face. 'You lying bitch, Tess. You'll be crawling on your knees to me for forgiveness.'

Was he going to play the irrational jealous lover till the end? Couldn't he see that it was over? She couldn't see any point in arguing, and so she pushed her hands through her hair and stalked away across the stage without looking back.

They ran on straight into the next act. Tess moved as if sleepwalking through the ensemble that opened the act and then stood off stage, watching in the wings as the action flowed on towards the duel between Escamillo and Don José. She could not speak to Richard, he was on the other side of the stage waiting for his entrance. Though she could see him, his face revealed that he was concentrating totally on the action and she did not want to interrupt him. She felt an extraordinary sense of dislocation, total confusion. The sensual paradise of her weekend with Richard had begun to be obscured in her mind by the ferocious erotic passion of Tony's kiss. She knew that between her legs she was wet. Why was her body so treacherous? She was sure that she was in love with Richard, so why was there anything left in her to respond to Tony's possessive, macho posturing?

Perhaps, said her intellect, this is the price you pay for understanding Carmen. She desires two men at once, she wants Escamillo while she is still in love with José. Why should you be any different? Why shouldn't you want Tony and be in love with Richard at the same time? You can't deny that Tony was exciting in bed.

She couldn't deny it. She thought of the incredible things he had done to her, tying her up, almost choking her with his thick penis, dining off her naked breasts, using her anus for his pleasure with almost greater frequency than her sex, treating her as if every orifice of her body were provided purely for his convenience, for his use. And in the process, giving her orgasms of a violence and ferocity that she never before experienced.

And yet the weekend with Richard had been, not just different, but better. There were a lot of similarities between the way each man made love and the way he conversed. But Tony had to be in control, he always had to have things his way, while Richard had the confidence to accept her ideas, to allow her to lead on occasion as well as follow.

Once, she remembered, on Sunday, when she was sucking Richard's cock, greedily laving its proud, glossy head with her tongue and lips, she had parted his legs and pushed her hand between them and felt between the cheeks of his bottom, letting her spittle trickle down the shaft of his cock to provide lubrication, and gently, firmly pushed the tip of her index finger into his quivering arsehole. He cried out and the tight rim of his sphincter contracted so fiercely that her finger was almost expelled, but she persisted, pushing further, deeper into him until her whole finger was buried in his secret crevice and he was moaning desperately with pleasure and shock and disbelief. Tony would never have allowed it. He always wanted to be in control and he had even stopped her from using her tongue on him when the pleasure became too extreme, but Richard trusted her with his body. He had pleasured her thus, and he would let her pleasure him. And as she sucked and sucked at his throbbing penis, she slowly, deliberately thrust her finger in and out, fucking his anus, shuddering with arousal at the thought of what she was doing to him, and after only half a dozen thrusts he writhed and yelled and his cock exploded damply within her mouth, flooding her eager throat with his slippery seed.

And when he had recovered and his phallus was erect again she had turned her back on him and looked archly at him over her shoulder and with her hands opened her backside to him, offering him that tight puckered hole, wanting to feel him opening her, stretching her. Tony had always demanded this route to pleasure from her according to his whim, ignoring her preferences, and it gave her piercing satisfaction to be able to offer it to her lover. Richard had been startled, she remembered his expression, but he had not refused her, just fallen on her and lodged the staring tip of his cock in her crease and thrust and thrust until he penetrated her and groaned aloud with the sensation of her secret passage gripping his ravenous cock like a velvet gauntlet.

Give and take, mutual bliss, offering pleasure as well as having it thrust upon her. Tess shivered and wrapped her arms tightly across her chest, lost in erotic daydreams.

'Wow,' said a voice behind her, 'he moves well, doesn't he?'

Tess jumped and turned to look into Jeannette's huge, liquid eyes, then glanced onto the stage. The duel was just beginning: Tony and Richard, knives in their hands, were stalking around each other like a pair of dogs before a fight. She nodded and Jeannette grinned. 'You didn't waste any time,' she said softly. 'Straight into his knickers. What was he like, Tess? Any good? Was he as kinky as Tony?'

'Yes. And no,' Tess replied unhelpfully. She didn't feel in the mood to indulge Jeannette's curiosity.

'I think you had us all fooled,' Jeannette went on. 'Pretending to be Miss Innocent. First you fuck Tony ragged and now you jump straight into bed with Richard. I can't keep up with you.'

'I don't believe that for a minute,' Tess murmured. She was watching the knives and frowning. Tony's knife looked different from Richard's: longer, wider bladed, a slightly different colour.

'Hey, guess what,' said Jeannette. 'Julian came back home with us last night. Emma was out, she didn't say where, I think she'd gone round to find Tony and tell him all about you and Richard. Anyway, it was just us and Julian, and . . .'

She continued to talk, but in Tess's ears her voice faded and became no more than a sound. Tess stood perfectly still, hardly breathing, as she realised what was different about Tony's knife.

It was real.

She could not be wrong. That blue, oily, wavering gleam of sharpness reflecting from the blade was unmistakeable. Tony was lashing out at Richard with vicious, rapid thrusts, almost reaching him, almost slashing his face.

Oh my God, she whispered to herself over and over again, *oh my God, the real knife. He's gone mad, he's going to kill him, he . . .*

Richard stumbled on cue and dropped his stage fake and Tony pounced, kicking the fallen weapon halfway across the stage out of his opponent's reach. Richard drew back, bravely upright, unaware that the blade he faced was real and deadly.

Whether or not it had been in the script Tess would have done what she now did, which was to launch herself onto the stage and grab Tony by the arm, fighting with all her strength against his iron wrist until he cursed and dropped the knife and stared at her gaping with surprise.

With a superhuman effort Tess remembered her line. *Hey, José, stop! have you gone crazy?* And she stooped and picked up the flick knife and tried to make the blade retract. It slipped in her hand and she gasped with pain and looked at a little cut in the ball of her thumb, slowly welling a bead of blood.

Tony swore in Spanish and snatched the knife from her hand. His eyes were dark pools of fury outlined in staring white. For a moment he was very still. Then, without warning, he hit her in the face.

It wasn't a particularly hard blow, but it was so unexpected that Tess staggered. In the auditorium James jumped to his feet with a cry of surprise and Richard saw at once the difference between a stage slap and the real thing. He leapt forward to catch Tess by the shoulders and hold her up, whispering anxiously in her ear. Then he lifted his head and stared at Tony, bristling with rage, and shouted, 'Son of a *bitch!*'

Julian stopped playing and everything ground to a halt, cast and crew and director all staring at the tableau on stage. Tony raised himself on his toes as if he would jump at Richard and without hesitation Tess shook herself free of Richard's grasp and stepped between them, her hands extended to keep them apart. They stared at each other, as tense and ready as beasts waiting to pounce, and Tess kept her position, hands outstretched, daring them to pass her, daring them to fight. At last Richard snarled and took a step back and the tension slackened slightly. Tess lowered her hands. For a few seconds she was still so angry that she couldn't speak. Then she said very slowly, 'That's it, Tony. That is it.' He tried to interrupt her, to shout her down, but she continued to speak with an icy determination that in the end silenced him. 'It's over. From now on I speak to you only on stage.'

'Tess – ' Tony said furiously.

'You've got no choice,' Tess said in a cold deadly undertone which reached Tony's ears alone. 'You've got no choice, unless you want me to tell everybody what you're hiding.' She looked pointedly at the pocket of Tony's jeans, where the flick knife made a barely discernible bulge.

'You bitch,' Tony whispered.

Tess shook her head, stalked to the front of the stage and called out to James in the auditorium, 'James, I want to go straight on to the next scene.'

'What the hell is going on?' James demanded, hands braced angrily on the front of the scaffolding that supported the stage.

'It doesn't matter,' Tess said coldly. 'It doesn't have to concern you. Let's go straight on.'

James stared up at her, frowning. He looked beyond her to where Tony stood, simmering with hate and jealousy, glowering first at Tess, then at Richard. At last the director raised his eyebrows and said with a shrug, 'All right, Tess. As you wish.'

Tess was as good as her word. On stage she was coolly professional, but offstage she refused to speak to Tony or even to acknowledge his presence. The rest of the cast were confused, but she never revealed the danger Richard had been in, not even to Richard himself. After a while people saw that she had finished with Tony and was now with Richard and they assumed that the whole thing had been a sordid lovers' quarrel enacted on the open stage, a typical manifestation of artistic temperament.

At first Tony pursued her whenever Richard was not with her, trying to assault her verbally if not physically, but she was immovable. Eventually Tony seemed to be in a state of such incoherent jealousy that he could not even express himself to her any more, and to her relief he left her alone. She was afraid that he might follow her away from the theatre, make her life a misery outside rehearsals as well as within them, but he did not do so. Perhaps he was ashamed to. Tess didn't know and she didn't care.

For a little while she worried about Tony's anger. Sarah had predicted danger, and she had been right. But hadn't the danger been to Richard, not to Tess? Did that mean that something else would happen, that Tony had not yet worked out all of his jealous rage?

But quite soon she forgot her fear and forgot even to think about Tony and what he might do. Outside rehearsals other things were on her mind.

Richard was on her mind. Every night he returned with her to the Hampstead flat and they made love. He was tireless, sensual, inventive, a delight. Nothing was beyond their joint imagination. They enjoyed each other in bed, in the bath, on the living room floor, on the roof terrace under a dome of neon glow crowned by hanging stars like little lanterns.

They even scandalised the ghosts of the nursery by making love on Tess's beloved rocking-horse. Richard sat on the saddle and Tess straddled him and lowered herself slowly until she was impaled on his throbbing penis and they could wrap their arms around each other, enfolded, breast to breast, mouth to mouth. Then Richard tensed his back and made a gentle thrusting motion and Tess moaned with pleasure as his penis stirred deep inside her and the horse began to rock, creaking gently, its deliberate movement like the waves of the sea, increasing the delicious sensations that filled them both. Richard's iron-hard penis stayed quite still within Tess's hungry silken sex, but as the horse rocked to and fro, to and fro, it felt to Tess as if he were penetrating her over and over again, filling her, and the constant pressure of her engorged, shivering clitoris against his hard, lean body drew her into such a height of ecstasy that she leant back in his embrace, eyes closed, lips parted, her vulnerable white throat helplessly offered to his predatory mouth. She moaned in desperate bliss, slack and shuddering as her climax blossomed inside her and went on and on and on until she hung in his arms, limp and sated, dimly sensing the pulsing surge of his cock embedded deep, deep in her tender flesh.

She loved him. She loved him more than she had ever loved a man. Her affection for Leo and her passionate

524

crush on Dan seemed in retrospect no more than a teenager's flights of fancy. She thought, she believed that he felt the same, but she couldn't be certain, because neither of them spoke of it.

Neither of them dared. He was Canadian, she was English. Both of them were just beginning careers that could take them all over the world, Munich one day, Rome the next, Paris, London, Milan: never in the same place at the same time. And wouldn't he want to try to make his living on the other side of the Atlantic, in New York and San Francisco and Montreal, while she would prefer to work in Europe? The logistics of the situation defeated Tess every time she thought of them. So she did not dare to admit to Richard that she loved him, because she was afraid of the pain that she would feel when they were separated. Deep down she knew that whether she spoke or not the pain would still be there, but something irrational, something superstitious, prevented her still from admitting that she was in love.

The day before the first dress rehearsal the orchestra gathered in the theatre to practise the music where it would be heard. There was no production rehearsal that day, but Tess went anyway and stood on the stage, listening to the sound of the orchestra in the dense gloom behind the lowered curtain. She was worried that the different sound quality of the orchestra would prevent her from singing in tune and she stood with her head lowered and her middle fingers resting below her ears, listening intently.

The weather was still warm, and Tess was wearing a light button-through cotton dress, flat sandals and no bra. A temporary theatre, created out of scaffolding and planks like a Meccano model, does not benefit from luxuries like air conditioning, and while the auditorium was open at the sides and caught the breeze, backstage it was hot.

The orchestra played through the overture twice and

then launched into some of the main production numbers. They were good, very good. Now they were playing Escamillo's theme, his showpiece aria. Tess closed her eyes and immersed herself in the music, imagining Richard's rich, baritone voice singing the words, imagining his taut muscular body drawing in deep breaths and playing them slowly out with the line of the song. She could not conceive anything more beautiful than his body when it made that fabulous sound, an instrument perfectly under control and yet expressing such passion, such emotion, that Tess thought she would rise from her grave to listen to it.

Thinking about Richard made her think of sex. She couldn't help it. Whenever he was near her she wanted him, and she knew that he felt the same. She remembered seeing Tom and Gina making love at that first rehearsal, Gina pressed against the wall and moaning rapturously as Tom slid his erect penis deep within her. She hadn't been able to understand how anyone could couple in a public place. But she had changed since then. She knew that if Richard was with her now she would clasp him close and pull him down on top of her and open her thighs and gasp as he entered her with his wonderful, thick cock. They would do it there, on the stage, rolling to and fro entranced by the sensations that their bodies were sharing, and they would press their lips together in fervent kisses to smother their moans as he thrust himself ever deeper into her wet, willing flesh.

Suddenly she heard a footstep behind her on the stage. Richard! She turned, smiling in welcome, and froze as she saw that it was not Richard at all, but Tony.

After a second she turned to run off the stage, but Tony sprang after her and caught her by the arm. She whirled to face him, fighting against his grip, but he was strong. After a moment she stopped struggling, trying to seem calm. 'Let me go,' she said softly. 'Tony, let me go.'

The orchestra launched into one of the entr'actes, a fast exciting Spanish dance. Tony held on to Tess's arm, squeezing it so hard that he hurt her, and for a moment did not reply. His black eyes were narrowed into mere glittering slits and his thin cruel lips were slightly parted, showing his white teeth. He looked dangerous.

'Let me go,' Tess said again. She was afraid. Her heart was pounding and the breath shook in her lungs. Tony held her eyes, then slowly, deliberately ran his gaze down her body from head to foot. It felt to Tess as if he had stripped her of her clothes and was touching her, running his cold hand over her naked flesh. She turned her head away and murmured protestingly, 'Tony – '

'You two-timing bitch,' he whispered at last. 'Just waiting for me to turn my back so you could jump into bed with Mr Canadian Perfect.' She swung around and glared at him, furious, and he laughed softly into her face. 'Is he a nice boy in bed, Tess? Squeaky clean? I bet he doesn't realise what a dirty girl you are under that cool English exterior. I bet he hasn't done what I did to you. Wouldn't be nice, would it? Does he stick to straightforward fucking? Him on top? Or maybe he'll go as far as letting you sit on his cock? What's his cock like, Tess? Clean cut as the rest of him?'

'Shut up,' Tess hissed, tugging again to free her arm. 'Shut up, Tony. I don't belong to you. It's none of your business. Fuck off and leave me alone.'

'Don't tell me to fuck off,' Tony snarled, and he jerked her towards him and caught hold of her other arm. 'Don't you dare, you bitch. I'll show you – '

'There's a whole fucking *orchestra* out there,' Tess said furiously into Tony's face. 'All I have to do is raise my voice – '

'Oh, no, you won't,' Tony breathed, and he dropped her arms and caught hold of her by the hair and drove his mouth down onto hers and kissed her, silencing her with his lips. She moaned in protest and struggled, tearing at his black glossy hair with her hands, bracing her body against his, but she could not free herself. Tony's strong tongue twisted within her mouth, forcing the breath from her, and his lips bruised her with their fierce demand.

She tried again to free herself, but he was strong, stronger than she was. His big body was hot and hard and she sensed rather than felt the quivering readiness of his cock, trapped erect and gleaming inside his jeans. She knew that if she couldn't get away from him he would have her then and there, on the stage.

Her body remembered the delicious power of Tony's penis and softened with eagerness, but her mind rebelled. She did not belong to him, he had no right. Her heart was given to Richard. She wanted to be faithful, and she fought against Tony's strong hands and against her own desire, forcing her body to struggle and writhe, trying to break free from his remorseless grip, attempting to subdue the hot lust that burned in her limbs. Tony grasped a handful of her hair so tightly that she flinched and kept his mouth pressed on hers, locking in her moans of protest. He hooked one ankle around her calf and jerked, pulling her off balance, and they fell together to the dirty grey vinyl that covered the stage.

Within seconds he was on top of her, resting the whole weight of his body on her, expelling the breath from her so that even if his mouth had lifted from hers she would not have been able to scream. His knee drove between her legs, parting them with a vicious jerk. He caught her flailing wrists and held them above her head with one hand as with the other he began to unfasten the buttons of her dress, revealing her white body.

Tess moaned and writhed, but she was helpless. She hoped that someone in the orchestra might hear the sounds of their struggle, but the music was growing louder and louder, beating in her ears, and she knew it was hopeless. She had played games of force with Tony often enough to realise that now there was no chance for her to escape. He meant to have her, and he would take her at his pleasure.

Her dress was open. Tony hissed with delight as his

strong hand explored her naked breasts. He lifted his mouth from hers for a moment, watching her carefully in case she drew breath to scream, and his black eyes were glinting with dark amusement as well as with arousal. 'No bra, Tess?' he whispered. 'I might almost think you were expecting me.'

'You bastard,' Tess replied through her teeth. 'I hate you.'

'Shut up,' Tony said, and gagged her once more with his lips.

With one hand he unfastened his jeans and pushed them open. Tess felt his cock against her inner thigh, hard and scalding as red-hot iron. The delicate flesh between her legs was wet, melting with readiness. Even though she hated him, her sex wanted to feel him inside her.

There was nothing she could do, and she knew it. He's a jealous idiot, she thought, and I hate him, but I might as well enjoy this. He's going to do it to me whether I enjoy it or not. She strained up against him, eyes tightly shut, waiting.

And it was there, the glossy head and thick shaft of his cock pressing against the damp willing lips of her sex, parting them, penetrating her. His mouth lifted from hers as he gasped with the sudden desperate pleasure of possessing her and Tess bared her teeth and hissed, 'Oh *fuck*,' and then reached up and pressed her mouth to Tony's neck, biting his olive skin, worrying at his flesh as if she wanted to eat him alive.

'Bitch,' Tony whispered as she bit him harder still. His hands were on her wrists, pinioning her beneath him, and his hot breath ruffled her hair. His body smelt of sharp sweat and sexual excitement and his buried shaft throbbed inside her. 'Bitch,' he whispered again. 'Sharp teeth, you bitch.'

He pulled away from her, dragging his strong throat out of reach of her teeth. Tess writhed in protest, trying to reach up to him, but he held her down. Their bodies were joined, linked by the thick bolt of his penis driven into the socket of her sex, and they stared at each other with lust and hatred. 'Fuck me,' Tess hissed over the growing roar of the orchestra. 'You bastard, fuck me.'

'Don't worry,' he told her, but he did not move. He stared down at her, his eyes glowing under the black bars of his brows. 'Christ, look at you. You slut. You're gasping for it. What a whore.'

'You –' Tess protested, struggling with rage.

'A whore, yes, a whore. You couldn't be faithful to me and now you aren't going to be faithful to him. I wish him joy of you.'

Rage made Tess shudder. She hated Tony for doing this to her, for making her unfaithful to Richard, and she hated him even more because it was giving her pleasure. She wanted to hurt him, to make him suffer for what he had done to her, and she thought she knew how she could do it. The muscles of her sex clenched and spasmed around Tony's invading penis and he gasped.

'You don't know anything,' she said. 'Do you think it was just him? Listen, listen to me. While you were seeing me I had other men. Lots of them.' How many? She frowned in concentration, thinking back. Julian. Dean. Charlie and Bob and Stefan, one after another and all together. Tony was staring at her as if he didn't believe what he had heard and she smiled ferociously as she saw the success of her stratagem. 'Three of them all at the same time, once,' she told him with bitter satisfaction.

'You're lying!' Tony's body jerked with unconscious reaction, driving the thick stem of his cock into her even more deeply, so that she gasped.

'No,' she said, when her breathing had steadied.

Tony's face contracted in a sudden spasm of jealous rage and he snarled something in Spanish and forced his mouth down onto Tess's as if he would gag her, prevent her from saying more. He released her wrists and his hands grasped at her breasts, clutching them tightly. She

530

moaned with reaction and he began to move inside her, fierce direct thrusts that shook her whole body. His tongue darted within her mouth and his hips beat against her as he shafted her. He was shuddering with excitement and Tess too felt herself possessed by manic arousal. The sound of the orchestra surged in their ears like the sea and unconsciously the rhythm of their fucking matched it, pounding on and on towards the final crashing chords that announced the death of Carmen and the end of the opera. The music drowned out their animal cries of pleasure. As she approached her orgasm Tess thought that the curtain separating them from the musicians began to rise, revealing her to an auditorium suddenly full of people, hundreds of people sitting in intense silence watching as she and Tony rutted like animals on the bare stage. Her naked body was pinned beneath him, her legs wrapped around his waist so that the whole of the audience could see the thick rod of his cock driving into her, sliding again and again into the soft heart of her sex until she could bear no more and the wall of avid eyes witnessed her writhing and crying out in the throes of her delirious climax.

The orchestra was silent, the curtain was in place. Tess returned to herself, shuddering. Deep inside her Tony's cock was still twitching with lascivious remnants of pleasure. She heard the voice of Benedetto Corial, the conductor. 'Very good, not bad at all. But at the climax there I want even more passion. Give it everything you've got. Too much is never enough.'

Tony was looking down into her face. Drops of sweat coursed down his high cheekbones and his dark throat. 'You lied,' he hissed softly. 'Tell me you lied.'

She pulled away from him, wincing as his softened cock slid out of her, and staggered slightly as she got to her feet. Slowly she began to fasten the buttons on her dress. When she was restored to decency she shook back her hair then lifted her head and looked coolly at Tony and said, 'No, I wasn't lying. It was all true.' She thought back to the early days of rehearsals and remembered her afternoons of libidinous luxury with Jeannette and Catherine and smiled slightly, a secretive smile. 'In some ways, you could say I haven't told you the half of it.'

'I don't believe it,' Tony whispered. 'While you were seeing me?'

His anger left her quite unmoved. Her body was sated and her heart untouched. This is how it feels to be Carmen, she thought to herself. I have had my pleasure, and now I don't give a damn about him. I'm ready to go back to the man I love. And I'll tell him what happened today, I'll tell him everything.

Tony pursued her to the edge of the stage. 'Listen!' he called after her. 'Listen, do you think only women can play that game? I fucked Emma Ridley on Sunday, I've fucked her every night this week, what do you think of that?'

Tess turned and looked at him. 'Good luck to you. What's she like?'

For a moment Tony did not reply, as if Tess's calmness had surprised him. Then he said lewdly, 'A dirty little bitch,' as if he thought it might make Tess jealous.

'You seem to like turning your women into dirty little bitches,' Tess remarked. 'I wouldn't usually approve, but in Emma's case I think you're probably made for each other. Enjoy her, Tony.'

Tony frowned angrily then tried again. His voice was increasingly desperate. 'How about if I tell your precious Richard what happened just now? What if I tell him that you let me fuck you? That I made you come? I'm a better lover than him, aren't I? You know I am!'

'No,' Tess said simply, 'you're not. And don't think you'll break us up by telling him about this: I'll tell him myself. Not all men are jealous maniacs like you, Tony.' She straightened her shoulders and said firmly, 'Goodbye,' and as the orchestra launched again into the final number she turned her back and walked away.

Finale

The opening night

They sent a car to pick Tess up from the flat and take her to the theatre. In some ways this did not seem sensible, since it was a Friday evening and the traffic was appalling, but at least it meant that Tess would arrive rested and calm, without exposure to the rigours of the Northern line at rush hour.

At least, that was the theory. But as Tess sat in the back of the car, her head tilted up to stare blankly at the ceiling, she wished fervently that she were travelling on the tube, surrounded by its sound and fury and by infinite numbers of strangers. She could have watched their faces and tried to pretend to herself that some of them were as unhappy as she was.

She had told Richard at once what had happened between her and Tony, explained how she had felt and asked for his forgiveness. He hadn't been angry with her, but he had been distressed. After a long silence he had taken a deep breath, then said, very gently, 'Tess, everything is happening too fast, isn't it? I'm under quite a lot of pressure already, you know, having to step into this role at short notice, and I think that things are getting a bit heavy, a bit complicated right now. So why

533

don't we just, ah, ease off for the moment? For the rest of the rehearsals?'

'But I want to see you,' she had protested. 'I don't want anything to change. I – ' She had been going to tell him that she loved him, but he was slowly shaking his head and her voice faltered.

'I'm not saying this is permanent,' Richard said, still very gently. 'I just think I need to concentrate during the remainder of rehearsals. I can't cope with you, and the production, and on top of everything Tony Varguez hovering around like Otello in the background. Let's just take a break, Tess. I can't cope with all of this.'

And since then she had seen him only at rehearsal, and he had been very proper, as if they had never made love, as if she had never seen him groan in the clutch of ecstasy or stir and wake in the morning, as if he had never pressed her up against the trunk of a tree and forced himself inside her while rain drenched their shivering skin and thunder and lightning shook their very souls. He was quiet and studious and when they were on stage he had kissed her as if they were strangers, in the approved drama school method that looked passionate and in fact was utterly impersonal. And Emma, eager as ever to report someone else's misfortune, had told everyone that Tess and Richard had broken up and that now Tess was on her own because she, Emma, was now firmly attached to the wonderful Tony Varguez.

So after all her work, after her striving to understand Carmen and learning to cope with Tony's sexist dominance, she had lost the man she really cared about. Was this the conflict, the challenge, the danger that Sarah had seen in the cards? Was this what happened when a woman tried to take control of her own life? If so, Tess thought, she wished she had never taken the part, let alone tried to master the character of the wilful gypsy.

The car dropped her at the entrance to the park nearest to the theatre and she made her way slowly across the parched, dusty grass. A trio of mallards whirred in front of her, heading towards the pond in St James's park. She watched them fly into the distance and sighed.

At the entrance to the enclosure which was acting as back stage she saw Leo waiting, looking around for her. He was holding an enormous bunch of orange and yellow lilies. His face brightened as she approached and he hurried towards her, holding out one hand. 'Hi,' he said. 'I knew you weren't here yet. I wanted to wish you luck.'

'Thanks, Leo,' Tess said, really touched.

She took the flowers from him and was bending to sniff them when he said warningly, 'Watch out, lily pollen stains. You don't want to go on with a yellow streak on your face.'

'Then I'll kiss you instead,' Tess said, lifting her lips expectantly. Leo smiled and gave her a soft, gentle kiss. When he drew back she said, 'How are you, Leo? How's the voice?'

'It'll be fine in a week or two. I had a lesson yesterday,' Leo assured her. 'How about you? You look pale. Are you all right? Are you scared?'

Tess considered the question, then laughed ruefully. 'To tell you the truth, Leo, no,' she said. 'No, not scared. I've got other things on my mind.'

'It's not that bastard Varguez, is it?' demanded Leo. 'Jesus, Tess, you should have dropped him by now. He was never any good for you. He – '

'No,' Tess lied, shaking her head. 'Look, Leo, I ought to go and get ready. Do you want to come backstage?'

'No, no, I won't bother you. I'm going to go and get a bite to eat and then come back to watch the performance. I'll sit behind the *Sunday Times* critic and talk loudly about how brilliant it is. And then I'll cheer. You'll hear me, Tess. I promise.'

Tess reached up again to kiss him on the cheek, then went through the little gate that pretended to be the stage door with the lilies in her arm. Other members of the cast and crew were hurrying purposefully about, and they all spoke to her as she passed them, wishing her luck.

She walked slowly up to the Portakabin that acted as dressing room for her and Emma. The door was shut. Outside someone had propped a big bucket of water, and it was full of bunch after bunch of flowers. This was usual before a show began, but Tess bent down to look at them in case any were for her. There were several bunches for Emma – no surprises there – and a massive garland of hot house blooms for Tess from her agent, Michael. He always sent her half of Kew Gardens on the first night.

And there, at the bottom, almost crushed by the other flowers, was a single white rose in a curl of cellophane. Tess lifted it and saw that the card was addressed to her. She frowned and opened it.

Good luck, Tess, said the tiny card. *Let's start again. R.*

Tess put one hand to her throat. Her heart beat strong and fast beneath her palm. For a long time she stood looking at the note, reading its six short words over and over again. Huge relief, huge happiness began to well up inside her. Then suddenly she thought that it was a joke, that someone was playing a cruel trick on her: Emma and Tony, perhaps.

But it was Richard's writing, she was sure of it. She clutched the flower closely to her, scenting its perfume, and tears of joy began to squeeze from beneath her closed eyelids. She wouldn't be able to talk to Richard until after the performance, but now she had nothing to fear. She kissed the rose and held it against her breast as she put her hand to the door of the dressing room and entered.

And stopped in her tracks. In the middle of the floor stood Antonio Varguez, panting with pleasure, and before him knelt Emma Ridley as if in worship, her rosy lips fastened tightly around the dark pillar of his erect penis. As Tess came in Emma rolled her eyes and squeaked with protest and tried to pull away, but Tony's hands were buried in her curling dark-blonde hair and he held her head still and thrust his swollen cock harder into her mouth as if her attempts to escape only aroused him more.

'Jesus,' Tess said, and she turned to flee. But before she could get out of the door Tony was there, pulling her into the dressing room, slamming the door and turning the key in the lock.

'Get out of here, Tony,' Tess panted. She was shivering with shock and anger. 'Get out. I have to get ready. Just get out.'

Tony shook his head and slipped the key into his pocket. 'I think not,' he said. 'I haven't finished yet. If you remember, Tess darling, it's Emma who's on first, not you. So if she's got time to suck me off, I'm sure that you've got time to watch.' He turned back to Emma, who was still kneeling on the floor looking up at him like a spaniel at its master. Her big blue eyes were very wide open and her lips looked swollen and tender. The skin of her delicate throat was flushed. 'Right, Emma,' Tony said, taking his cock in his hand and lifting it again towards her mouth. 'Open up. More.'

Emma's eyes flashed up to Tess. 'I can't,' she whispered. 'Not with her – with her watching.'

Tony leant unhurriedly forward and spoke very quietly into Emma's face. 'Emma, are you being *disobedient?*'

'Oh no,' Emma said hastily, 'no, no, Tony, no.' And although her eyes glanced anxiously again at Tess she made no more demur, but stretched up her soft lips and opened them and drew the broad shelving tip of Tony's penis into her mouth.

'Ah,' Tony breathed, thrusting gently with his hips until nearly the whole of his shaft was buried between Emma's trembling lips. 'Ah, that's good. Good girl, Emma. Now lick it, lick it, just beneath the tip, you know where I like it,' and Emma moaned in acquiescence and

537

her cheeks hollowed as she obediently went to work with her tongue.

Tess felt behind her for the door handle and shook at it, but it was securely fastened. She didn't want to watch, but she found her eyes drawn inexorably back to the scene before her, little virginal Emma Ridley whimpering as Tony slowly shoved his thick rigid cock in and out of her willing, compliant mouth. What would Leo say if he could see this? He had guessed, he had known what Emma was like beneath the surface. He had said to Tess, *She just needs someone to master her.* How right he had been.

'See this, Tess?' Tony said softly. His breath was hissing as Emma worked on him. 'See what you're missing? And I hear you haven't been getting any satisfaction from Mr Canadian Perfect, either. Gone off you, has he, since our little escapade on stage?'

Tess tightened her lips and said nothing. The thornless stem of Richard's rose pressed against her fingers, calming her. Richard had forgiven her, he wanted to begin again, and it wasn't within Tony's power to hurt her any more.

But it was within his power to arouse her. As she watched him taking Emma's mouth she felt her bowels churning with need, readying her against her will for sex. She leant back against the door, breathing quickly. Tony's penis moved faster and faster in and out of Emma's mouth. Its thick stem was shining with her saliva and dark veins pulsed on its silken surface. Tony was panting now and his fingers were clutching hard at Emma's hair. He was within moments of orgasm. Tess expected him to thrust deeper between Emma's lips and force her to swallow his come. But Tony suddenly with a jerk freed himself from the velvet grip of Emma's mouth and groaned as at the same moment his cock twitched and spasmed and began to spurt in thick, milky jets. His semen fell onto Emma's face, onto her eyelids and cheek, and trickled down towards her gasping mouth. Tess thought she would flinch or protest, but she did not, just extended her little, pink, pointed tongue to catch the creamy trickle as it crept down towards her jaw.

Tony still held Emma by the hair. He pulled back her head and gestured at her face. 'See?' he told Tess fiercely. 'I said she was a dirty girl, didn't I. Aren't you a dirty girl, Emma?'

'Yes,' Emma moaned, catching up another drop of semen and running her tongue around her lips in lascivious delight. 'Oh, yes, Tony.'

'What happens to dirty girls?' Tony hissed. He spoke to Emma, but he was holding Tess's eyes, staring at her with an expression of cold deliberate challenge.

'They're punished, Tony,' Emma whimpered, rubbing herself against Tony's legs like a cat. 'Punished.'

'Get up,' Tony commanded, and Emma got to her feet. For a moment she stood still, her head bowed as if in shame and her hair hanging around her face. Then she looked up at Tess and their eyes met. Emma's face was rapt, transfigured, as if she were already on the point of orgasm, and Tess frowned in mystified horror.

'Open your blouse,' Tony said, and without a murmur Emma obeyed him. The white cotton parted to reveal her little, high breasts, the small, tight nipples already swollen with desire. 'Now touch your nipples,' Tony said, and Emma closed her eyes and sighed and lifted her hands. Her fingers caressed the points of her breasts, flickering gently over the taut peaks until the areolae swelled as if someone had sucked them.

'Good,' Tony said. 'Now lift your skirt. Show Tess your pretty little pussy.'

Emma's huge eyes opened, wide and glittering. She looked as if she was about to cry. 'I don't want to,' she whispered.

'You don't want to?' Tony repeated disbelievingly.

He jumped forward and caught hold of Emma's skirt and wrenched it up. Beneath it she was naked, and Tess gasped with shock and put her hand to her mouth. Emma's pubic mound was shaven, smooth and hairless as the tender flesh of her pale thigh. Emma moaned and lay back in Tony's arm, shivering with delicious shame as he pulled her legs apart and showed Tess the naked moist folds of her sex, damp and pink as the tumbled petals of a rain-soaked peony.

'Look,' Tony said. 'See what she's done? Taken all the hairs off her little honey pot just to please her master. Doesn't that look pretty?'

Tess wasn't sure whether it looked pretty or peculiar, but it certainly looked arousing. Tony dragged Emma's slender thighs wider apart and put his hand on the pale flesh of her hip. His dark olive skin made a pleasing contrast with her ivory whiteness. 'Let's see if she's ready,' he said to Tess, smiling cruelly.

His hand moved slowly across to Emma's naked mound and down it to where the cleft of her sex began, to where the delicate bud of her clitoris just showed between the labia that were swelling and flushing with desire. Emma sighed as his finger brushed across the epicentre of her pleasure and her legs parted even further, inviting his invasion. Tony smiled again and without a word thrust two fingers deep into Emma's sex, withdrew them gleaming with her juice, sniffed and licked at them approvingly, then replaced his fingers and began to move them in and out.

My God, Tess thought, gazing at Emma as if hypnotised. My God, she's actually going to come. And indeed Emma's body was heaving and tensing in rapture. Her little hands were opening and closing helplessly and her nipples were swollen and erect. Tony plunged another finger into her and flickered his thumb over her engorged tender clitoris and Emma's body shimmered like a reflection in broken water and she let out a high, wavering cry of ecstasy as she succumbed to orgasm.

'Isn't she a dirty girl?' Tony hissed as he supported the still twitching body of Emma on one strong arm.

'Fancy that, Tess, letting me masturbate her right in front of you. Making her come with somebody else watching, just imagine. Could you do that? I bet you couldn't. What a dirty little girl. So now she has to be punished.' He licked his glistening fingers and then took hold of Emma's rapturous face. 'Bend over,' he told her.

Obediently Emma bent, her hair hanging around her face, her breasts dangling. Tony heaved up her skirt around her slender rounded haunches and presented her bare buttocks to Tess's eyes. Between the white moons of her arse Emma's sex was pink and soft and gleaming with desire. Looking at her Tess suddenly realised how a man must feel when in the grip of dominating lust. She would have loved to have taken something long and thick and hard and driven it deep into Emma's moist willingness and made her cry out with shock and pleasure.

'Now,' Tony breathed, and with one strong hand he slapped Emma's bare behind, a sharp slap that left the imprint of his hand red on her white flesh. Emma moaned and trembled and Tony slapped her again and again, paying attention to each perfect buttock, spanking with a regular motion until Emma's round white arse was glowing pink and she was wriggling in his grasp.

Tony's cock was hard again, thrusting forward eagerly from the open fly of his trousers. He rubbed at it, checking its readiness, then without a word, slipped a condom over his length and positioned the glossy head between the lips of Emma's sex, caught hold of her white hips and pulled her violently back onto him. His thick penis slid quickly up into her wet vagina, burying itself entirely, and Tess gasped and bit her lip. She remembered vividly how it had felt when Tony had done that to her, how he had bruised the tender flesh of her haunches with his ferocious grip.

He was looking at her now over Emma's bowed body, watching her reactions as he drove himself time after time into the hot centre of Emma's naked sex. 'Don't you wish,' he gasped between thrusts, 'don't you wish I was doing this to you, Tess? Don't you? Don't you?'

Tess swallowed hard and shook her head. Richard's rose was held tightly between her tingling fingers, like a talisman. Tony snarled as he saw her denial and thrust harder, making Emma grunt and gasp as he shafted her.

'Tony,' Emma whimpered. Her hanging hair swung to and fro as Tony beat his body against her with the ferocity of his attack. 'Oh, Tony please, oh yes, my lord, please, please. Harder, harder. Oh God, God.' She staggered and would have fallen, but Tony's strong grasp held her up. Limp as a doll she hung from his hands and her body began to shudder in the grip of another orgasm. As she quaked and moaned Tony withdrew his prick from her sex and lodged it against her tight puckered rear hole and forced his way into her arse, invading her and stretching her until she cried out and writhed in his grip. One strong thrust, two, three, and suddenly Tony was gasping and his hands on Emma's haunches were like claws as he climaxed inside her.

After only a few seconds he withdrew and let Emma fall to a quivering heap on the floor. He turned and faced Tess, smiling slightly. 'Feeling jealous, Tess?' he asked.

'You must be joking,' Tess said. She was proud of the fact that her voice was steady. As she lifted her head with a jerk of scorn she caught sight of herself in the mirror on her dressing table and her eyes narrowed in amazement, because her face showed nothing but smouldering anger and fervent lust. It was the expression that she had tried to adopt, all those weeks ago when she stood before the mirror in her bedroom with Dan asleep in the bed behind her, and which had eluded her.

Tony frowned. He seemed for the first time to see the rose in her hands and without warning he stepped forward and snatched it from her. She cried out in protest and grabbed it back, but not before he had scanned the note attached to it. He turned to look at Tess with anger and disbelief, and she slapped his face.

'Get out of here,' she said, 'or I'll shout for help, Tony, I swear.'

The shape of her hand flared on his cheek like the mark of Cain. Tony's cruel lips drew back from his teeth. He was shaking, shuddering with emotion: fury, rage, jealousy, lust, all of them together. He looked more than half mad. 'You,' he said very softly, 'have made me look a fool, Tess. You'll be sorry, I swear. You'll be sorry you ever set eyes on me.'

Suddenly a chill of fear gripped Tess. To be forced to watch Tony screwing the guts out of Emma had been pleasantly arousing and mildly absurd, but now the expression on his face terrified her. She drew away from him instinctively, clutching the rose protectively to her breast. He gave her one long, cold stare, drew the key from his pocket and unlocked the door.

It opened to reveal the assistant stage manager, looking harassed. Tony brushed past him without a glance and stalked away.

'Ten minutes to curtain up,' the ASM said. 'Emma, are you ready?'

'Oh, God,' Emma exclaimed, jumping up from the floor and reaching out for her costume.

That performance was the most extraordinary experience of Tess's life. From the moment she walked onto the stage she felt as if something had bound the audience with a silken thread and placed the end in her hand. She had total control of them: they were enraptured, spellbound. They loved Carmen, they wanted her, just as José did, just as Escamillo did.

In the first act, when she was on stage with Tony, her hatred for him emerged as an electric current of lust that flowed almost visibly between them. She knew that he was desiring her even as he sang, that his fingers itched to touch her, that his lips burned to kiss her, that even on stage his cock was hard for her. She tormented him, teased him, played him as an angler plays a fish, as a cat plays with a mouse. How could little submissive Micaela compete with her, with Carmen, who possessed the stage and every man upon it with her blazing certainty, with the knowledge that she was desirable?

'You're red hot tonight,' Jeannette whispered in her ear before they went on for Act Two. 'What's got into you? They're eating out of your hand.'

Tess said nothing, just smiled. It was true. She had never in her life felt more powerful. It was as if everyone who looked at her was her captive, as if hers was truly the voice of the mermaid, the siren's song that held all who heard it in chains of adamant.

She did not see Richard until he entered as Escamillo, and then according to the production as planned he did not see her until nearly the end of his aria. When he looked at her his eyes were burning with love and desire and she knew that her response showed in her face. Their glances blazed across the stage, searing the air with passion. Tess wondered if he could tell that the rose he had given her was next to her skin, pressed within her bustier, its silken petals lying against the silken flesh of her breast.

At the interval the audience clapped and stamped. Behind the scenes the cast and crew milled about, excited, but superstitiously avoiding any comments about how well the show was going. Tess hurried to Richard's dressing room, hoping to see him alone, but it was full of people, other members of the cast changing, Richard's agent, two journalists from music magazines and one from Radio 3, and she turned away with a frustrated sigh.

Julian was standing before her, his pale face glowing with excitement. 'Tess,' he said, 'I've been down with the orchestra, I've been watching. It's marvellous, it's amazing, I can't believe how well it's going. You're fabulous.'

His blue eyes were fixed on her face. She smiled at him, remembering how she had seduced him, how she had opened the buttons on her skirt and shown him the naked skin of her white thighs. His expression showed that he knew that she was remembering and that he remembered too, that he was still enslaved to her. She reached out and touched his cheek, just touched it, and then walked past him.

She had no time after changing her costume to do anything other than run back to her position for Act Three. The ensemble passed fleetingly, like a dream, and then Emma was onstage singing Micaela's stunning second aria, so beautifully and with such grace and power that the audience's sighs of delight were audible in the wings. Then Tony and Richard were onstage, singing the duet that led up to their fight, and Tess stood staring onto the stage clenching her fists in fear in case Tony should choose again to take matters into his own hands.

But he did not. The fight passed off exactly as planned, and the gnawing apprehension in the pit of Tess's stomach began to fade. She fell effortlessly into Carmen's character, and when Tony as José seized her shoulders and exclaimed desperately, *I'll keep you, damn you, damn you, you are mine, I'll force you if I have to! I'll never let you go, I'll never leave you, never!* she lifted her head and stared into his eyes and laughed a mocking, silent laugh that revealed the depth of the scorn she felt for him.

At the beginning of Act Four Tess stood in the wings beside Richard, looking up at him. Neither of them spoke, they did not need to. Their love showed in their eyes, in their radiant faces. Tess was half aware of Tony standing behind her, waiting for his entrance later in the act, watching her with dark brooding anger naked in his eyes, and knowing he was there made her feelings for Richard all the sweeter. Then they walked on to the stage together, Carmen and Escamillo arriving at the studio to a rapturous ticker-tape welcome. Tess reached up and caught Richard's face between her hands and drew it down towards hers and they kissed, a passionate, unrehearsed kiss that made the watching audience shudder with voyeuristic delight and shook them both with the depths of desire that it stirred in them. Richard put one hand to Tess's breast and squeezed it as they kissed and she arched her body against him, racked with desire for him. If he had wanted it she would have submitted to him now, now on the stage, before the eyes of the world. She would have opened the heart of her body to him and received him within her with rapture. He did not require of her that she submit herself, but still her lust filled her and overran with longing. And she could sense Tony's hot, dark eyes watching her from the shadows of the wings, and she smiled bitterly to think of the pain she was causing him.

Now Escamillo was gone and Carmen was alone onstage, waiting for her final, fated rendezvous with Don José. Tony entered slowly, his eyes fixed on Tess's face, and as they began to sing it seemed to Tess that the separate threads of her real life and the life of Carmen twisted and knotted inextricably together, so that suddenly she *was* Carmen and everything that was happening on stage was real.

I know that this is the end, Carmen told José. *I know you mean to kill me. But whether I live or die, no, no, no, I will not give myself to you!*

That man in there, José demanded, *he's your new lover! You won't go to him, Carmen, you'll come with me, I swear!*

Let me go, Don José, I'll never go with you!

Do you love him? Tony's face was black with jealous rage. He drew out the flick knife from his pocket and touched the clasp. The blade sprang free, glittering in the lights of the stage. He held it towards her, and his hand was shaking. *Do you love him? Tell me!*

The blade gleamed blue and oily. Tess suddenly shuddered. Was it, could it be the real knife? Did he mean to kill her? Had Sarah seen death in her cards, but kept it a secret?

For a second she wanted to scream and flee. But how could she? She was Carmen, and she feared nothing. *Yes,* she sang, flinging back her head proudly and staring into Tony's maddened, white-ringed eyes. *Yes, and if it kills me I'll say again, I love him!*

The knife shivered in Tony's hand. Reflections leaped from the blade. *For the last time,* hissed José, *you bitch, will you come with me?*

It was her last chance. She was afraid, terrified, certain that in a moment he would leap on her and she would feel a real knife tearing at her flesh. But she shook her head violently and pressed her hand to her bustier, where the white rose lay next to her skin. *No. No!*

Die then, you bitch! José screamed, and flung himself on her. Tess flung open her arms as if receiving her lover, waiting for the blow. It came: but it was only the slight thump of the stage fake, the blade retracting the instant it touched her body. She fell to the ground and writhed and jerked as James had shown her, but as she 'died' she fought sternly against the urge to laugh. Tony had not dared to do it. She was the winner now, in every way. She had nothing more to fear from Antonio Varguez.

At last she lay still. Twelve bars to go, and then the curtain would fall. Tony dropped to his knees beside her, wracked with staged remorse, and then it was over and the audience burst into a storm of cheers even as the orchestra blared out the final chords.

Then everything seemed to happen in slow motion. The curtain calls went on for ever. A wall of faces, a wall of sound as the audience stamped and clapped and roared their approval and flung flowers onto the stage and called for her again and again. Tony's claque of female fans were there in force, but their rapturous cries were drowned by the cheers that the rest of the audience raised for Tess. She saw Leo standing up in the auditorium, clapping and yelling, risking his barely healed voice with his shouts. She caught his eye and he grinned broadly and pointed at the man sitting in front of him and mouthed, '*Sunday Times!*'

When at last she was allowed offstage her agent Michael was waiting for her in the wings and with him was a man Tess recognised with a shock as the director of Opera Shop, a small company famous for its innovative, commercially successful and sometimes scandalous productions, which were as popular with Channel 4 and BBC 2 as with the theatres.

'Tess,' Michael said, 'I don't have to tell you how amazing you were. Look who's here to meet you: Jeremy Tate.'

'Hi,' said the director, smiling libidinously at Tess. His casting methods were infamous. 'I was seriously impressed, Tess. We have a lot to talk about. Can we do lunch soon?'

'Sounds great, Jeremy,' said Michael. 'And there's lots of other things Tess and I need to talk about, right now. Tess, if you can, the sooner the better. Can you – '

'Michael,' Tess said huskily, 'I need to change, I need to – ' and she broke away and ran through the cool evening air towards her dressing room. Emma was probably in there, but she didn't care. She had to get away from all these people and hurry through the time that would pass until she could see Richard again. People called out to her with congratulations and praise, but she hardly heard them. Jeannette and Catherine were there, pressing forward to take her hands and kiss her on the cheek, but she couldn't make herself talk to them. She pulled herself away and pressed on.

She passed Emma standing in the open air, chatting and laughing cheerfully to a group of colleagues. Her part had gone well too, and it never does a singer harm to be involved in a truly successful production. She caught Tess's eye and grinned broadly and blew her a kiss. 'Great show, Tess!' she called out. 'Imagine what the rest of the run will be like!'

Tess smiled feebly back at Emma, then looked around for Richard, but he was nowhere to be seen. Nor was

Tony. She ran the few paces to her dressing room and pulled the door open and leapt inside.

It was dark within the little, boxy room. Tess closed the door and turned the key, then reached up to the light switch.

A strong hand closed over hers and pulled her fingers from the switch. She stifled a scream, certain that it was Tony lurking there in the gloom to wreak his final revenge on her. She tore herself away and fumbled for the key, but before she could open the door the hand closed on her shoulder and a soft, warm voice said reassuringly, 'Tess, darling, it's me.'

'Richard!' She turned to him as swiftly as breathing and flung herself into his arms. His lean, hard body pressed against hers and he enfolded her in his embrace, holding her so tightly that the air sighed from her lungs. Without a thought their lips found each other and they stood enraptured, kissing with fervent eagerness.

'Richard,' Tess said when she could speak, 'I love you.'

'Christ, Tess,' Richard whispered. His low voice caressed her ear. 'I've been going mad without you. I can't stand not having you. You looked so amazing tonight, I wanted you all night. Jesus, I thought the whole audience would see my hard on in these pants. I've got to have you. Now, Tess.'

'Yes,' she whispered. The unquestioning admiration of hundreds of people had left her already sensitised. She was wet and ready, and his passionate words inflamed her. Her hands went to his haunches, pushing down the tight Lycra of his costume. His cock sprang free, quivering with excitement. His hands fumbled with her skirt, trying to push it up around her waist. Its tightness defeated him and he struggled with the zip and grunted with success as it whined open. Soon the skirt was off and the bustier followed it and the corpse of the rose fell to the floor.

'You wore it,' Richard breathed.

'Next to my heart,' Tess murmured, and she reached

out for him. There were no preliminaries, she needed none. She lay back on the cold floor and pulled him down on top of her and parted her legs and he lay on top of her, crushing her with his wonderful male weight, and with one strong thrust he sheathed himself within her to the hilt and she gasped with the hot, dark pleasure of being penetrated.

'Tess,' Richard moaned, 'Tess, Tess, I love you.' He was shaking with need. He clutched her, his fingers twined in her hair. They lay together, mouth to mouth, and the silken fist of her sex grasped strongly at his thick cock as it slid deep within her. She held him tightly, her fingers exploring the strong muscles of his arms, his shoulders, his lean, flexible spine. His head twisted from side to side with bliss and she reached up to bite and suck at his vulnerable throat. He groaned with pleasure and rolled over, pulling her on top of him.

Tess let out a long cry and leant back, thrusting forward her taut swollen breasts. In an instant his hands were on them, fondling, squeezing, tugging at the hard pink tips until shivering flames of pleasure ran through her body like brilliant fish through murky water. She rose and fell on his throbbing cock, moaning with joy as she impaled herself over and over again. She grasped his strong thighs with her hands and arched her body to accept him within her, deeper and deeper, and as his powerful penis surged to and fro in the velvet tunnel of her sex she thought of a statue she had once seen of a female saint in ecstasy, glistening white marble that breathed as if the stone were flesh. The saint's hand was on her breast, squeezing it through her clothes, and her lips were soft and parted and you could almost see her eyelids fluttering as she was possessed and overcome by heavenly rapture. The cause of her ecstasy was a spear which a stern angel drove into her side. Tess pictured the angel with Richard's face, that perfect beauty imbued with heavenly rigour, and the angel's sharp spear was his thrusting, fervid penis. And as she imagined and felt that remorseless spear penetrating her, violating the temple of her flesh with its bitter-sweet sharpness, the saint's ecstasy began to rise within her own body. She jerked and cried out and began to writhe with the desperate buffeting of her orgasm, and as she collapsed in the throes of climax Richard rolled her onto her side and then onto her back and began to thrust wildly into her, ravishing her, taking her with such fervent power that her orgasm seemed to be infinitely prolonged, infinitely consuming. When at last he cried out and his cock spasmed inside her she lay beneath his shaking body quite still, utterly vanquished, his and only his.

'Tess,' Richard whispered into her ear, 'I love you.'

Someone tried the door, then knocked on it. 'Tess!' It was Michael's voice. 'Tess, are you OK? Are you coming?'

Tess began to laugh. She laughed Richard right out of her body and held him tightly against her as she chuckled. 'I certainly am, Michael,' she called back. 'I'll be right out. Shan't be long.'

They clung together in the gloom, breathing each other's breath. She was naked and hot and his hand passed slowly over her shimmering skin, reacquainting itself with the complex curves of her body.

'Guess what,' Richard said softly.

'What?'

'I've got an offer,' he said. 'ENO want me as a company principal. English National Opera, Jesus! My agent's going to work on it. It would mean, ah, staying in England for quite a while, a year maybe, maybe more.'

'That's marvellous, Richard,' Tess said emphatically. 'It's wonderful. What do they want you to play?'

Richard smiled nervously, suddenly overcome by modesty. 'Don Giovanni. Can you believe it?'

'Don Giovanni?' Tess thought of how Tony would feel when he discovered that his hated rival had landed the part he most desired. 'Richard, that's amazing. I'm so pleased for you.'

'My agent has to do some negotiating, and I have to think about it, but you're right, as an offer it's pretty amazing. I had a lucky day when James chose me to sub for Leo.' His eyebrows contracted suddenly and his eyes glittered. 'I don't mean just for my career, either.'

There was a short silence. Then Tess asked quietly, 'Will you accept?' Her whole world hung on the answer.

He kissed her lips. 'If you love me,' he said, 'I'll accept.'

She held him more tightly and laid her head on his shoulder. 'I love you,' she said softly.

'Then I'll accept.' He kissed her again. Then he said slowly, 'I love you, Tess. I've never met a woman like you. You're strong, you're independent, and you're so goddam sexy I could go crazy just looking at you.' His arms tightened around her and the lashes of his closed eyes brushed her cheek. His lean, strong body pressed against her. 'I love you,' he whispered again.

For long moments they lay together, touching, kissing, exchanging love. Tess closed her eyes, savouring the joy that filled her whole body. Her future lay before her as bright as the dawn, and Richard glowed in the heavens like her morning star.

Then Richard lifted his head and against the faint light through the windows of the dressing room Tess saw him look at the door.

'Well, Tess,' he said, 'the overture's finished and the audience is waiting. Time to go on stage.'

They got up, preparing to face the world together. Tess hesitated and murmured with a frown, 'I wonder what the critics will say?'

He smiled down at her. 'Hey, who cares? Come on, Tess. Let's go.'

And, hand in hand, they went.

What the critics said:

'Exhilarating ... thrilling singing and a riveting production ... electric performances from new English star Tess Challoner and Canadian unknown Richard Shaeffer ...' *Financial Times*

'I felt Tess Challoner's definitive Carmen had taken the measure of every man she encountered ...' *The Daily Telegraph*

'Opera as you've never seen it!' *Daily Mail*

'The man behind me certainly seemed to be enjoying it ...' *The Sunday Times*

'Live sex on stage!' *Today*

THE END

Ace of Hearts
Lisette Allen

Chapter One

*T*he late afternoon sun poured in through the high windows, burnishing the bare oak floorboards of the spacious attic room. From the narrow London street below came the muffled clatter of carriage wheels on cobbles, and the shrill cries of street sellers. But up here, the only sound that mattered was the delicately lethal kiss of the two rapier blades that gleamed like slivers of light in the still air.

In a sudden flurry of movement, the shafts of steel shuddered together then fell, sighing, apart. The two opponents, solitary occupants of the room, circled one another warily. One was fair, the other one dark; their features were concealed by the wire face masks they wore. Both were clad in open-necked silk shirts that were tucked into slim-fitting buckskin knee breeches. The room echoed to the soft tread of their stockinged feet on the polished oak boards as they moved gracefully, assessing one another. There was a sudden hiss of indrawn breath as the fair one's arm whipped up; blades clashed gratingly, to be followed by a moment's fierce, sinew-straining tension as both strove for mastery. Then the dark-haired man gave ground and let his blade slide gently aside. The slither of steel died away in the silent room and he said thoughtfully, 'Your riposte was good. You improve every time we meet.'

His opponent's fair head bowed slightly in acknowledgement of the compliment. 'My thanks, Signor Valsino. That is my intention.' Then the two blades tapped once more in salute, and once more the stockinged feet tensed and stepped sideways in their purposeful dance. Muscles flexed and rippled beneath thin silk shirts that were damp with perspiration; the room seemed charged with the energy of vital combat.

Suddenly the slighter of the two, the fair one whose face was all but obscured by the mysterious wire mask, lunged forward to deliver a lightning thrust in tierce, with arm held high and silk sleeve falling back to expose a slender yet sinewed wrist. The dark-haired man whipped up his blade in retaliation, the muscles of his forearm ribbed and hard. There was a scuffle of blades in forte, a sparking clash of metal as the rapiers jarred and adhered, to be followed by a final, deadly struggle as each combatant tried to force the other aside. A soft hiss of expelled breath was followed by a sharp clatter of steel as the fair fencer's rapier flew in a silvery arc through the air, landing with ringing finality on the oak floor.

The dark-haired man's sword flashed in for the kill, his rapier point jabbing with deadly accuracy at his vanquished opponent's heaving ribs. The moment seemed to hang suspended in the bright, thin air. Then the victor laughed. Lowering his sword, he pulled off his wire mask and tossed it onto one of the striped satin settees that lined the long wall. He lifted his sword in mock salute and said, in a musical, slightly foreign voice, 'You prove yourself a worthy opponent, my dear.'

The fair-haired combatant pulled off her mask as well and shook her long tresses out of the narrow black ribbon that restrained them. Once free, her hair clustered in thick curls round her slender shoulders, honey-gold in the spring sunshine. 'I will be a truly worthy opponent for you, Signor Valsino, when I beat you. I strive, as always, for perfection.'

Her voice was low and melodious and sent shivers down his spine, just as if he were stroking a fine rapier blade. He stood watching her in frank admiration, drinking in the pale gold silk of her cheeks and throat, lightly sheened with perspiration after her exertion. He noted her slender but deceptively strong shoulders and arms that wielded the rapier with such skill, and saw how the sinuous folds of her silk shirt clung to the contours of her body, reminding him, with a familiar, stabbing ache, that beneath the cool silk were firm, high breasts crested with darkly tantalising nipples, as luscious as peaches ripened in the warm Italian sun. And as she stood there, with her hands poised boyishly on her leather breeched hips, he realised that he wanted her now, badly.

He said, 'You seem quite perfect as you are to me, Signorina Marisa.'

She gazed coolly back at him with her devastating blue eyes. She must have seen the blatant desire in his dark gaze, but she deliberately chose to misunderstand him, because she said breezily, 'My father taught me well. You told me that yourself, the first time I came to you for tuition.'

He stirred, conscious that he was still staring at her rather besottedly, and said, 'Your father must have been skilled in the art of swordplay. He's instructed you in all the moves of someone tutored by the Angelos themselves. Fencing was a pastime of his?'

She chuckled, a richly beguiling sound that drove him wild, and ran her hand through her thick, honey-blonde hair. 'You could say it was a necessity, Signor Valsino, rather than a pastime. You see, my father was forever fighting his way out of debt. Either that, or escaping from the people he'd cheated at the gaming tables.'

As she spoke, she was moving with unconscious grace towards the ewer of water that adorned a polished mahogany stand near the marble fireplace. She poured the cold water into a bowl, then she dampened a linen towel and bathed her face and wrists with sensuous pleasure. 'Together,' she went on, 'we travelled round half the capitals of Europe. Inevitably in rather a hurry.'

'An unusual education for a girl.'

'It had its advantages.'

He smiled, his arms folded across his chest, taking pleasure in just watching her. She'd unfastened the top buttons of her shirt so that she could draw the moistened towel across the delicate skin of her throat, and he could see the gleam of her naked shoulder in the shaft of slanting sunlight, could see the warm beginning of the heartstopping swell of her breasts.

He dragged his dark eyes back to her face, watching her as she threw back her head in unselfconscious delight at the caress of the cold water. Her long thick hair cascaded down her back, drawing his gaze down to the handspan slenderness of her waist, to the sensual swell of her tight, firm buttocks in her clinging boy's breeches. He ached for her, and was conscious, again, of the impelling heat at his groin.

Carefully he turned towards a small gilt table set between two French settees where a decanter and two glass goblets had been left, and said lightly, 'You'll take a glass of wine with me before you leave, Signorina Marisa? My next pupil isn't due for an hour.'

She had been letting her eyes drift idly along the display of illustrious visiting cards and invitations set along the marble mantelshelf, evidence that David Valsino numbered the elite of London society amongst his clients. But at his suggestion she turned from them and smiled.

'Wine. Why not?' And without waiting for further encouragement, she flung herself cat-like amongst the plump silk cushions of the nearest settee and rolled onto her back, her head pillowed by her arms, her stockinged legs stretched out luxuriantly.

David Valsino brought her a brimming goblet of the rather good hock. She pulled herself up, leaning her elbow on the padded silk arm of the couch, and drank it all down with evident enjoyment. He watched the slight rippling of the muscles in her slender throat as she eased her thirst and he reached to refill her glass. He waited for her to drink again, then took the glass from her hand and

560

replaced it on the small gilt table. Lowering himself with easy grace onto the tapestry footstool at her side, he took her hand and began to kiss her wrist. Slowly he pressed his mouth along the soft, blue-veined whiteness of her inner arm, at the same time easing back her silk cuff with his sinuous brown fingers. His eyes were dark and burning.

She ran her other hand through his black, curling hair and leaned back against her cushions with a contented little sigh. 'Dear David. It's good to be back in London.'

David Valsino, exclusive fencing master to some of the richest men in London and discreet lover of many of their wives, felt his heart lurch like a boy's. 'We've missed you, *carissima*, these last few weeks. Where have you been?'

She relaxed contentedly on the beautiful Louis Quinze settee. 'I've been living in luxury. In the country.' She wrinkled her face exquisitely.

'And the country bored you, my dear?' said David, still stroking her wrist with his fingertips.

'Not as much as I expected. I can always find some kind of entertainment.' She laughed. 'But my companion bored me excessively. He was very rich, and very stupid.'

David Valsino grinned, his teeth white and even in the sunbrowned perfection of his face. 'Most women of my acquaintance would say that was the perfect combination.'

'Not for me.' She reached languidly for her wine and drank again, savouring the sweet, rich liquid. 'Though I miss his wealth, I could do with some money of my own.'

'Couldn't we all?' said David lightly.

She turned suddenly towards him, resting her hand on his forearm. 'David, you've got lots of rich clients, haven't you? Won't you introduce me to some of them?'

'You want to seduce them, *carissima*?'

She shook her head, smiling. 'Not unless they're very, very eligible. You know how fastidious I am, David. No, I want to win their money. I want to be invited to those discreet, fabulously wealthy parties of theirs, where the gaming goes on all night, and they think nothing of wagering thousands of guineas on the turn of a single card.'

Her blue eyes were glittering, her voice husky. He said, 'My dear, I know of your reputation. I can't possibly introduce you to my patrons, because you'd fleece them all within a week.'

She pouted a little, trailing her fingers down his forearm. 'You're accusing me of cheating, Signor Valsino?'

He laughed. 'Oh, no, Marisa. You're far too clever for that. But I have heard that you have the most incredible luck. Save it for the gaming hells of Leicester Street that you and your friends frequent, eh?'

Her eyes became shuttered. There was a silence, and then, to his relief, those wonderful blue eyes glinted mischievously as she smiled up at him from beneath the thick veil of her lashes. 'Ah, well. An hour before your next pupil, you say, Signor Valsino?'

He caught his breath, then said smoothly, 'A whole hour, *carissima*.'

'And what shall we do with that hour, signor?'

His eyes darkened in anticipation. Her shirt clung damply to her skin where she'd washed herself, and he could see the dark ripeness of her nipples thrusting against the silk. He swallowed and said, 'You are the one with the ideas, Signorina Marisa.'

She smiled deliciously. 'That's true. Well, then. In view of your recent, scandalous comments about my prowess, shall we have a game of cards?'

'As I've said, everyone knows of your luck in any kind of contest, Signorina. You are bound to win.'

She clapped her hands. 'Then let it be dice. And if you provide them yourself, then how can I possibly have the advantage?'

He hesitated, then nodded. 'But what shall we play for?'

She looked at him directly with an enticingly mischievous expression in her eyes. 'Why, the winner can have exactly what he, or she, desires.'

He felt a throb of excitement. 'I still feel you are bound to win.'

'Ah,' she murmured, leaning closer to him, her finger-tips trailing along the soft dark hairs on the back of his hand. 'But if we both want the same thing, then that's no problem, is it? No problem at all.'

He got up, his dark eyes smoky with desire, and walked slowly across to the inlaid walnut bureau in the corner of the room. He took his time in unlocking it, because he was only too aware that his fingers were trembling with excitement and he didn't want her to notice it. As he searched for the dice, trying to appear casual and in control, he swiftly ran through everything he could remember about Marisa Brooke.

She'd arrived in London last summer, after travelling round the continent for many years with her father. He'd gathered that it was her father's unexpected death in Vienna that had precipitated her return; but Marisa spoke little of her past.

When she'd first made contact with David through a mutual acquaintance and asked him for lessons in fenc-ing, he'd resigned himself to a mildly entertaining session with yet another spoiled society beauty who would be anxious to toss the rapiers aside as soon as possible and engage him in another sort of rather more intimate physical combat. David Valsino had no false modesty about his reputation in fashionable circles. Women found his dark Italian good looks and lithe, graceful body intensely appealing. His discretion was an added bonus.

But when Marisa Brooke arrived on his doorstep, he realised immediately that she was quite different. He judged her to be around 23, or 24. She looked younger, because of her slender build and innocent face, but she had all the quiet self-confidence of a mature woman. She'd brought foils of her own, which he'd checked over; they were a trifle overlong for his taste, but they were wonderfully balanced. In addition, she had her own face mask, made according to the original design introduced by La Boissiere 35 years ago. 'It belonged to my father,' she'd explained simply in her low, musical voice when he admired the way the wires had been oiled and cherished.

She was also, he'd realised at that very first meeting, one of the most exciting women he'd ever met. At first, he'd thought her face to be utterly angelic; it was heart-shaped, exquisite, with a delicate tip-tilted nose and huge, thickly lashed eyes of cornflower blue, comp-lemented by a full, enticing mouth that had a tendency to part in delicious invitation whenever she smiled.

Angelic. That was what he'd thought, when she'd first come to the door of his discreet residence just off St James's Street, asking him if he really was the best fencing master in all of London.

He'd realised extremely quickly that 'angelic' was not quite the right word to describe Marisa Brooke. He realised that when she first slipped her hands down his breeches, coolly and deliberately, then bent down to taste him, as if he were some fine wine.

They'd had several encounters since then, and they were always memorable. She told him little about herself, and he asked few questions, but he gleaned that she made some sort of living amongst the gaming dens with which the back streets of London teemed. Occasionally, he knew, she allowed herself to be patronised by some rich, besotted admirer, but these affairs never lasted long. David knew that it was always Marisa whose ardour cooled first. Not many men succeeded in holding her interest.

He found the dice at last in their little leather box and walked back towards her, bending to place them on the little gilt table by the settee. As he did so, Marisa leaned forward to pick them up, and her loose silk shirt fell apart to afford him a devastating glimpse of her rosy-tipped breasts. It was done deliberately, he was quite sure. He swallowed hard, conscious of the rearing hardness at his loins. Dear God, but she was utterly bewitching.

Marisa Brooke, watching him discreetly from beneath her thick lashes, let the dice click in her palm like old friends and smiled secretly to herself. David Valsino was very sure of himself, as always. But, though he didn't realise it, she, Marisa, was the one in charge.

Her body was still supple and warm from the fencing. Surreptitiously she'd allowed herself to become progressively aroused as the duel progressed: the lithe, fluid movements of combat, the muscular grace of her opponent, her own taut prowess as her body's balance was gracefully expressed in the very tip of her dancing rapier, never failed to excite her. And what happened next was up to her.

She tipped the two dice into their little leather box and assessed her partner thoughtfully. David Valsino was not tall, but he was beautifully made, with wide shoulders and slim, muscular hips; just as she liked her men, even if he was somewhat arrogant. His face was darkly handsome, in a way calculated to make simpering Englishwomen melt; his skin was smooth and warm, and gilded to a light bronze by the sun of his homeland. By way of contrast, she knew that his thighs and chest were lightly matted with silky black hair, which intensified to a thick, wiry nest of delight at his loins. As she fondled the dice, she remembered their first meeting with a little quiver of amusement. He'd been desperate for her, but was uncertain about making the first move. When Marisa had slid her hand down his slim-fitting breeches, her blue eyes wide with lethal innocence, he'd cried out hoarsely in surprise. She herself had been forced to admit privately to a pleasurable sense of shock when she'd felt the size of the hard, hot shaft of his erect manhood thrusting agonisingly against her teasing fingertips. After that, she and the fencing master had proceeded rapidly to a most satisfactory mutual pleasuring, the first of several.

There was a rather promising swell at the fencing

master's loins now, if Marisa was not mistaken. Her eyes glinted at the thought of that excitingly eager penis, sturdy and endearingly long in erection, pushing urgently at the placket of his breeches. He sat calmly before her on his stool, with the little gilt table between them, his elbows resting on his parted thighs. She knew that he would be quite sure of triumph, one way or another.

Marisa leaned forward confidentially and said, 'Let's keep it simple, shall we? Best of three?'

He nodded. 'Whatever you say, *carissima*. You first.'

She cast a three and a four. When David reached silently for the ivory cubes, Marisa felt her nipples harden against her soft silk shirt as she watched his lean brown fingers fondling the dice, and imagined those same fingers caressing her full breasts. She was aware of a pleasant stirring of sensuality, a sweet promise of pleasure that could all too soon flare into a primitive carnality that the handsome Italian would be all too ready to assuage. He was calmly confident that he would win, and she was equally confident that she would.

He threw two fives. Trying to keep the gloating tone out of his voice, he said, 'What did you say we were playing for?'

Her shadowed blue eyes glittered. 'Winner to decide.'

'Anything?'

'Anything.'

David swallowed. Outside, the sun was starting to fade, and cool shadows stretched across the lofty room. A dust-specked shaft of light fell across the marble mantel, with its enticing array of invitation cards. Marisa let her eyes rest just for a moment on one larger than the others, importantly edged with gilt. In the street below, there was a noisy altercation between two carriages fighting for space, but the raucous oaths of the drivers seemed a world away. Marisa reached lazily across the table to place her hand on David's hard thigh, and felt him tense as her fingers travelled slowly upwards. She paused tantalisingly just before she came to the place where his taut breeches strained across the thick stem of his phallus, and she saw the colour rush to his face. Marisa smiled, and took the dice box. Perhaps she should let him win after all. She knew very well what he would claim as his reward, and the idea was far from repugnant to her. She knew from experience that his fingers were gentle yet knowing, his body firm and sweet, while his penis was an exquisitely lengthy weapon that he wielded as skilfully as any rapier.

She leaned forward to make her cast, aware that the secret flesh at the juncture of her thighs, which was gently yet insistently caressed by her tight breeches, was liquid with need. She longed to feel his hands cupping the fulness of her hot breasts, longed to feel his delicious mouth tugging at her tight nipples as her secret self opened up like a nectared flower to the dark thrust of his penis.

She trickled the dice out. Five and six. She saw the brief flicker of anguish on David's face and stopped him gently with her hand as he reached out for the box.

'There's no hurry,' she said softly, sliding the dice back in. 'Do you know, I've a fancy for some more wine.'

When he came back with two full glasses in his hands, she saw the shock in his face as he realised that she was lying back casually on the settee with her shirt unbuttoned, while her hands lovingly cradled her small but full breasts. He swallowed hard.

'Your drink,' he said in rather a hoarse voice.

'Thank you,' said Marisa charmingly. She was examining her thrusting nipples intently with her fingers, knowing that her self-absorbed caresses would make his already swollen penis rear in agonised need. 'Your throw, I think, David.'

With a low groan, he seated himself and emptied out the dice. A two and a one.

'Oh, bad luck! Last throw to decide,' said Marisa sweetly. 'This is so exciting, I can hardly bear it. Come and sit beside me, David.'

He ran his hand somewhat distractedly through his

dark, curly hair and did as he was told. She nestled against him, still sipping her wine, with her pouting breasts deliciously exposed. He longed to caress them, but her cool self-possession disconcerted him.

She slanted a mischievous look up at him and murmured, 'Still as hotly primed as ever, David? How is Lady Morency? Does she still pay you to pleasure her? Does she still like to crouch on all fours for you, and call you her mighty stallion?'

He preened himself, just a little, and laughed dismissively. 'Lady Morency became rather a nuisance, so I cancelled our engagements for a while. But I'm busy enough, yes.'

'I'm not surprised. I've missed you, David. I've really missed you.' And before David could move, she'd twisted round to bend over his lap and was starting to unbutton his breeches. Within moments she'd freed his penis so that it sprang out, darkly engorged. David laughed a little weakly.

'Marisa, we've not finished the game yet. But of course, *carissima*, if you can't wait . . .'

She smiled. 'Poor David. It must be so trying to have women so desperate for you. How delicious you are. We'll return to the game in a moment, shall we?'

As she spoke, she let her fingers flicker along the dark stem of his rearing phallus. It trembled and strained towards her, and David's breathing became ragged. Marisa, her delicate tongue just protruding from her parted lips, positioned herself with great concentration so that her pink-crested breasts hovered just above the angrily swelling tip of his penis. Then she lowered herself and rubbed her nipples lightly against the velvety glans.

David clutched at her shoulders with a groan and pulled her face towards him to kiss her hungrily. She responded for one tantalising moment, her mouth yielding and her tongue flicking coolly against his. Then, almost regretfully, she pulled herself away.

'Rather a wild thrust in prime, that, wouldn't you say,

Signor Valsino? What did you tell me about fencing, on my very first lesson? "Know your opponent's weakness." '

'Dear God. Marisa, you witch!'

She laughed merrily and turned back to the dice. 'My throw, I think.'

A five and a six again. She smiled at him, letting her eyes drift down to his swaying penis as it thrust up hungrily from his open breeches.

He said, a little tightly, 'Is it really worth my throwing, Marisa? After all, we both want the same thing, don't we?'

'Possibly.' She reached for the little leather box and gave it a light kiss before passing it to him. 'Your throw.'

He shrugged, and made his cast. A three and a two.

'Well. So much for the dice,' he said dismissively, and turned swiftly towards her, his hot eyes lapping up the sight of her naked breasts pouting enticingly from between the parted folds of her silk shirt.

She put out her hands gently to stop him touching her. 'We had a bargain, Signor Valsino. And I won, remember?'

'Yes. Of course I do. But surely, this is exactly what you wanted, isn't it, Marisa?' he said, caressing her with urgent certainty.

She sighed and let her gaze linger on his quivering penis. Then, to his horror, she began to slowly button up her shirt. 'Not exactly, no, pleasant though it would be. You see, there's something I want rather more.'

'What do you want, God damn it?'

She stood up and walked casually across to the fireplace. 'I want this, David.'

And she reached for the large, gilt-edged invitation that took pride of place amongst the assorted cards and letters on the marble mantelshelf.

There was a moment's aghast silence, and then he exploded. 'But that's my card for a masked ridotto at Vauxhall tonight. Why in hell do you want that?'

She stroked the thick, creamy card with her fingers, almost purring. 'Because it looks rich and discreet. No names, no identity. Just this little mark of the ace of spades in the corner. A masked ridotto at Vauxhall, you say; it's ideal for me, David. Will there be card play, do you think?'

David stood up, his handsome face dark with annoyance and disappointment. He started to rearrange his clothing, and his penis throbbed angrily as he forced it back inside his breeches.

'Undoubtedly,' he said bitterly. 'So that's it. You want to make a fool of some other unwary punter, just as you've made a fool of me.'

She walked to where he stood and reached up to draw a finger softly down his lean, smooth-shaven cheek. 'Now don't be like that, David darling. I did ask you earlier if you'd introduce me to some of your wealthy friends, but you refused. Then I caught sight of that invitation, and decided I'd have to take matters into my own hands. After all, it was a fair contest, wasn't it?'

'I don't know,' he muttered. He'd heard all the rumours, that Mistress Brooke had a range of impossibly devilish tricks that enabled her to gull the entire world at faro and hazard without a flicker of her innocent blue eyes.

'But I couldn't possibly have cheated, David. After all, they were your dice. And you did agree when we started that I could have whatever I wanted.'

'I thought,' he said stormily, 'that you wanted me!'

'Then let that be a lesson to you,' said Marisa Brooke softly. 'Of course, I adore you, but just now, I want this invitation rather more. A masked ridotto! No-one will recognise me. The whole affair will be delightfully *incognito.'*

David said, through gritted teeth, 'I could tell the host that my invitation was stolen. I could warn him not to let you in.'

'Oh, David. That would be most ungenerous of you. By the way, who is the Ace of Spades? Is he rich and stupid?'

She was laughing at him, mocking him. He replied stiffly,

'Surely you'd rather that the identity of your host was a surprise, Marisa. You like surprises, don't you?'

Her husky laughter tinkled around the darkening room. 'Yes. Yes, I do like surprises. Dear David, you are still my friend, aren't you? You're not really angry with me, just because I want to win lots of lovely money off a crowd of drunken, aristocratic fools who are only to eager to lose it all anyway.'

He struggled, then laughed ruefully at her deliciously expressive face. 'I'm not angry. Just incredibly disappointed,' he said frankly. 'Dear God, Marisa, you must be the most tantalising woman in London.'

'In that case our next meeting should be something for you to look forward to,' she smiled. She'd walked across to the doorway and was pulling on her supple leather boots.

'Perhaps we can play piquet next time,' said David, following her. 'I'm quite good at that. I might even win.'

'Don't count on it,' Marisa laughed. She was easing on her long, silk-lined greatcoat, cut to look like a man's, and then she pulled on her curly-brimmed hat, tucking her hair up into its crown so that she looked like some exquisite blond youth. She reached up to kiss him affectionately on the cheek. Then, without waiting for his footman to show her out, she ran lightly down the stairs.

'Enjoy yourself tonight,' called out David suddenly, but he wasn't sure she'd heard him.

Marisa paused for a moment on the pavement outside the row of tall stuccoed houses where David lived. The sun was setting now behind the rooftops; the grey light of the London dusk softened the hard outlines of the busy street. A fruitseller went by, singing out her wares. Marisa bought an apple, and bit contentedly into its crisp, juicy flesh.

As usual, she'd got exactly what she wanted. She glanced up affectionately at the high windows of the lofty room where Signor Valsino gave his expensive private fencing lessons. Dear David. She'd almost given way to temptation and pleasured herself with him, against all her resolve; the rapier-play had excited her, as it always did, and he was exceptionally handsome.

But he was also rather conceited. And from the moment she'd caught sight of that mysterious invitation from the Ace of Spades, displayed so enticingly on his mantelshelf, she'd wanted it badly, so she'd played to win. The exquisite thrill of uncertainty as she'd substituted her own weighted dice just before each of her own throws sent the blood racing through her veins. In fact, it was almost as exciting as the proximity of David's warm, virile body.

She'd heard once of a man who'd orgasmed at his moment of triumph in a low-class gaming hell in Southampton Street. She'd laughed when she heard of it, but secretly she could understand. Poor David wouldn't understand. He'd not suspected her of cheating at all, and that was part of the joy. He never had the slightest idea that each of her daringly intimate caresses was intended to distract him, while she dexterously replaced his innocent dice with the pair she always carried in a tiny secret pocket in her breeches, the pair that were weighted so that they never gave any result but a five and a six.

Marisa was gifted with luck and skill, a lethal combination. She considered that it had been a successful afternoon, but it could have been better. Her body told her so as it twinged softly with regret at what might have been. She frowned as she finished the apple and tossed the core into the gutter, only too aware that her secret feminine parts were still moist and swollen, still anticipating the delicious caress of David Valsino's serviceable penis. But she'd been right to turn him down on this occasion. Sex was without a doubt the supreme pleasure, but as with all pleasures, Marisa's greatest strength was that she could take it or leave it, depending on how it fitted in with her plans.

Today, David had been oversure of her. And besides, from the moment she'd seen that invitation beckoning her from his mantelpiece, she'd wanted it badly. With a quickening of her pulses she reached into the silk-clad inner pocket of her coat and drew out the gilt-edged card with its intriguing instruction to admit the bearer to a masked ridotto at Vauxhall Pleasure Gardens that very evening. There would be supper, dancing and cards, and from what she knew of such occasions, all the guests would be expected to remain anonymous, not revealing their names unless requested by their host, the ace of spades himself.

The Ace of Spades. Probably some fat, aging old roué, a contemporary of the Prince Regent, Marisa told herself dismissively. But at least he and his guests would be rich, and she could win lots of money off them and depart swiftly into the crowds at Vauxhall, with no-one being any the wiser as to her identity. No-one would even guess she wasn't a genuine guest, unless, of course, the ace of spades himself challenged her.

She shivered deliciously as she contemplated her evening, feeling as though she was on the verge of some exciting new world, where absolute discretion was the unstated rule, and not an eyelid flickered as fortunes were won or lost at the turn of a card. Where the winnings might be so great that she would never have to play again.

Her thoughts were interrupted as an open chaise, coming from the direction of St James's Square, edged rather too close to the kerb in order to avoid a milkman's dray. Marisa jumped swiftly back out of the way, at the same time instinctively assessing the fine equipage. The chaise was of bottle green, with glittering brass lamps and high yellow wheels. It was drawn by two handsome chestnuts, and its driver was swathed in a many caped greatcoat of fine broadcloth and a tall crowned hat. He handled his spirited team with consummate skill, avoiding the big dray with inches to spare.

And then, she realised that he was drawing up outside

David's house. She felt a moment's unease, then shrugged. Another of David's rich clients, no doubt. She turned to walk on, away from the splendid vehicle, but she pulled up in surprise as the driver's peremptory voice followed her down the street.

'Here, boy. A shilling for you to hold my horses.'

Marisa whirled round to see that the man in the fine green chaise had swung himself down from the box and gone to his horses' heads. She said darkly, 'Are you by any chance speaking to me?'

He didn't even look at her. He was too busy attending to his horses as they restlessly champed at their bits. 'I am indeed. Be quick about it, will you?'

Marisa caught her breath. He hadn't realised she was a woman. No fault there, as she knew she looked very much like a youth with her man's greatcoat concealing her feminine curves and her wide-brimmed hat hiding her long hair. But she burned with indignation at the arrogance of him. Why, he hadn't even bothered to look at her as he issued his command. She said, with slow deliberation, 'I think you've made a mistake. No-one pays me to do anything.'

His face jerked towards her at that, his attention drawn at last from his precious horses, and Marisa had the satisfaction of seeing a pair of world-weary grey eyes open rather wide as he realised his mistaken assumption as to her sex. 'Really?' he murmured in a silkily cultured voice.·'You surprise me. I should think that quite a few people would pay a small fortune to see you out of those clothes.'

She caught her breath, and gazed calmly up at him. '*You* certainly couldn't afford it.'

'You think not?' His wide, thin mouth mocked her. 'In my experience, everyone – but everyone – has their price.'

He'd taken off his high-crowned hat, and laid it on the driver's seat of his chaise. Marisa, her practised eyes assessing him narrowly, took in the fashionably short dark hair that was cut in a Bedford crop, the pristine

574

folds of his white lawn cravat, and the luxurious shine of his top-boots that gleamed beneath the sweeping folds of his coat. An aristocrat, thought Marisa grimly, in his early thirties, awash with money and self-importance. Rich, powerful and utterly arrogant.

'How very sad for you,' she said sweetly, 'that you have to pay for your pleasures. But of course, I can understand it. After all, no self-respecting female would come to someone like you of her own accord, now, would she?'

The cold perfection of his haughty features seemed chiselled in ice. 'And what exactly do you mean by that, Ganymede?' he said softly.

Ganymede, the boy beloved of the gods, a kind of bisexual concubine. How dare he address her thus? Marisa's mind crept tantalisingly over all the backstreet cant she knew by way of revenge, but she rejected it all as being too subtle a form of insult. Instead she said pityingly, 'I mean, of course, that it's quite evident that you must have a very small penis.'

His face seemed to blaze. Then his eyes flickered over her thoughtfully. 'Well, I do believe I should horsewhip you for that,' he said in the same level, silky voice.

'Ah. You enjoy that kind of thing, do you?' said Marisa in wide-eyed innocence. 'Do you pay for that as well? There are some women in a house in Vere Street, most discreet, I believe, who'll not charge you overmuch.'

The man's hand was tightening ominously on his riding crop just as the big door of David Valsino's house flew open and a flustered footman came hurrying out.

'Lord Delsingham,' the footman uttered in distress. 'A thousand pardons, my lord, that no-one was here to greet you. Signor Valsino is expecting you, of course. If you would care to go inside, my lord, a groom will take your carriage to the stables round the back.'

Marisa stood transfixed. Lord James Delsingham, one of the richest, most fashionable men in London. She felt rather faint.

Delsingham was saying coolly, 'No need for the stables. My visit is only a short one. Tell the groom to walk the horses up and down until I return – with care, you understand, or believe me, there'll be the devil to pay.'

'Yes, my lord. This way, my lord.'

Lord Delsingham turned to go up the steps to David's house. Then, seeing Marisa still standing there transfixed, his mouth twisted in unexpected acknowledgement, and she felt a sudden wild racing of her pulses.

'Remember, my sweet Ganymede,' he said softly. 'Everyone has their price.'

Marisa pulled herself together. 'I told you before,' she said stoutly. 'Nobody pays me to do anything, my lord!'

'A pity,' he murmured, his narrowed grey eyes raking her. 'My imagination runs riot at the sight of you in those breeches. And the thought of you out of them is quite devastating.'

Hissing, she lunged forward while at the same time whipping back her hand to strike him across the cheek, but he caught her arm effortlessly to parry her blow, and even as she gasped in surprise, he bent his dark head to plant a kiss on the inside of her wrist. As she struggled to free herself, he parted his lips to let his tongue trail insolently along the delicate veined skin, and she felt the wicked warmth of his caress burning her, melting her insides. She couldn't move. She couldn't speak.

He straightened up, still holding her hand. He seemed to tower over her. 'I'll wager,' he said thoughtfully, 'that mine is the best offer you'll get all day, Ganymede. And by the way, you are quite wrong about my physique.'

With that, he smiled coldly and let her go.

Marisa watched rather weakly as he strode up the steps to David's front door, his beautiful long coat swirling behind him. She made an obscene gesture after his retreating back, but he was sublimely unaware of it. 'Hell and damnation,' she muttered angrily.

Her good mood was quite, quite broken. Before, she'd felt in charge, even triumphant after the success of her encounter with David. But now this insolent aristocrat, with his jeering mockery, had quite subdued her spirits.

Lord James Delsingham, she knew, was one of the richest men in London. He was also, Marisa was quite sure, the type of man who would be a hard, selfish lover, taking his pleasure with little regard for the feelings of the woman he was with. Cold, powerful, arrogant. She had a sudden fleeting vision of him in bed, with that hard, muscled body naked and aroused, and she shivered and shut her eyes. The tiny, insolent caress of his lips and tongue had disturbed her senses in a way that David's more obvious approaches had quite failed to do.

Well, damn him, she wouldn't let him spoil her day. She set off at a brisk pace towards Pall Mall, looking forward to the bright, candlelit shop windows that would brighten her journey home as dusk fell. Feeling almost calm again, she searched for the invitation in her pocket and stroked it. The cold, silken feel of the thick card against her fingertips soothed her. Tonight, she would be going to Vauxhall Pleasure Gardens, where amongst the lamplit shrubberies, rich and poor, pickpockets and the highest in the land, would mingle with one another in normally unheard-of freedom. The occasion would suit her purpose very well indeed.

At the thought of that tiny but elegant ace of spades emblazoned mysteriously in one corner of the card, she felt a little shiver of excitement that put Lord Delsingham almost completely from her mind. But not quite.

After David Valsino had heard Marisa's light footsteps retreating down the staircase to his front door, he'd slumped back rather despairingly on the settee. The silk cushions still smelled tantalisingly of her hair and her skin, driving him wild.

He remembered again the first time they'd met, one day last summer. She'd taken him completely unawares when, just as he was putting his precious rapiers away, she'd sunk to her knees at his feet and carefully released his penis. It was already engorged, inevitable in her exquisite presence, and she'd smiled at it happily, approvingly. Then she'd licked him quite deliciously, running her tongue around his swollen glans and driving him demented as her moist lips glided up and down his straining shaft. That had been their first meeting, and he was still just as helpless in her presence. And now she'd fooled him yet again with that infernal dice game, and stolen his invitation as well. All in all, he'd been utterly routed.

As soon as the big front door banged shut behind her, he surreptitiously released his painfully engorged genitals and began to caress himself. Damn her, with her infernal teasing. She'd utterly bewitched him, and there would be no peace for him until the fire in his loins was extinguished. Lying back tensely against the cushions, he pumped his foreskin up and down the bone-hard core of his penis with swift skill until he ejaculated. And at the very extremity of his pleasure he imagined he heard Marisa's light, melodious laugh, almost as if she knew what he'd been reduced to, damn her.

Then he heard the front door again, and he sprang guiltily to his feet as he heard slow, steady masculine footsteps coming up the stairs. Swiftly wiping himself with his handkerchief, he struggled to rearrange his clothing, and had only just succeeded when his footman knocked at the door. 'Lord Delsingham, Signor Valsino.'

Delsingham. Damn. He'd almost forgotten that they had a rapier practice arranged for this hour. And then Delsingham was in the room, imperiously sweeping past the hovering footman as David stammered out, 'My lord. You are a little earlier than I expected.'

Delsingham's cold grey eyes assessed the fencing master's somewhat dishevelled appearance with amusement. David wondered despairingly if the room smelled of sex.

'No matter,' said his lordship evenly. 'I can tell I've taken you by surprise. I've just called by to postpone my rapier session with you until another time. I find myself somewhat pressed. I have certain preparations to set in order for this evening.'

'Certainly, my lord. Whatever you wish.'

Delsingham was lazily scanning the room. 'If I didn't

know better, Valsino, I'd say you'd just had some woman up here. You are coming tonight, aren't you? I don't see my invitation on your mantelpiece.'

'T-tonight, my lord?' stammered David.

'For a fencing master,' drawled Delsingham, 'you seem somewhat slow witted today. To my masked ridotto at Vauxhall, of course.'

'Of course, my lord! The invitation is – is downstairs, in my front parlour. How many guests have you invited?'

Delsingham shrugged, his wide, powerful shoulders rippling beneath the fine cloth of his greatcoat. Taller than David, he was unusually fit for a man of his height. He had considerable skill with the foils, and David normally enjoyed their encounters. But not today.

Delsingham said carelessly, 'I'm not sure of the exact numbers. Fifty or sixty, I think.'

In that case, thought David, with a sigh of relief, he won't even know if everyone's there, especially if all his guests are in masquerade, and he won't notice Marisa's there instead of me. 'I look forward to tonight, my lord,' he said aloud.

'Good. So do I.' Again Delsingham smiled, that wide, thin-lipped smile that made him look even more dangerous than usual. 'Well, I'll leave you to carry on with whatever it was I interrupted.'

Then, thank goodness, he was gone. A few moments later David heard the sound of his chaise drawing away down the street, and wondered if perhaps Delsingham had passed Marisa earlier. He wondered what Marisa would say when she found out that the ace of spades whose invitation had so intrigued her was in fact one of the richest men in London.

David supposed he ought to have warned her, but he was damned if he would. After all, it was a subtle kind of revenge, to let her go unprotected into the lion's den. If any man could sort out Marisa Brooke, he reflected ruefully, then it was James, Lord Delsingham.

Chapter Two

Marisa was almost home. As she made her way purposefully through the labyrinth of narrow streets that lay behind the Strand, she felt her spirits rise inexorably in spite of the gathering darkness. Here the shabby houses pressed in on one another in crowded disarray, a world away from the spacious residences of the area where David lived. But as the lamplighter did his rounds, there was an air of vitality, of things about to happen amongst the crowds who passed between the low taverns and gaming hells that clustered in this quarter of London. Already the noise of music and laughter came from lighted doorways, and as Marisa passed Bob Derry's notorious cider cellar on the corner of Maiden Lane and Half-Moon Alley, a bunch of drunken young bucks spilled out noisily, their purses no doubt considerably lighter than when they went in. Realising that Marisa wasn't a boy, as they'd first assumed, they gaped at her with lecherous eyes, but she merely laughed at them and carried on, her long coat swinging jauntily around her calves, her boots sturdy and comfortable as she walked swiftly on towards Covent Garden, where an unsavoury collection of wine booths and tumbledown shacks now mocked Inigo Jones's beautiful square and piazza.

Her pace quickening, she turned at last down a narrow alleyway where scruffy urchins played with broken skittles outside an ill-lit local tavern, and here she came to a halt. The Blue Bell was popularly known as The Finish, because it was open all night, and harboured drunken punters who'd been kicked out of everywhere else. Marisa was fond of it. Pushing open the battered door, she made her way along the grimy passage that led past the tap room, breathing in the familiar strong odours of beer and tobacco smoke.

She didn't pass unnoticed. At a nearby table, she observed the flash of cards and the gleam of coins changing hands. She paused as someone called out to her, 'Marisa! Marisa, darling, you'll join us for a game?'

She turned, grinning. 'And play with your marked cards? Not tonight. I'm on my way out again soon. I have higher stakes in mind.'

'Then we wish you luck,' came the friendly response. Marisa, who'd moved into rooms above the inn some months ago and used it as her base, had quickly become a favourite with all the Blue Bell's patrons. They'd been suspicious of her at first, and then they'd tried to fleece her. But she'd calmly beaten them all hollow at cards one night, and then coolly tongue-lashed a drunkard who tried to kiss her, until he crept from the crowded tap room for ever. After that, she had quickly become a firm favourite, almost a kind of talisman for the patrons of the inn.

She picked up a lighted tallow candle and hurried quickly up the narrow, twisting staircase to her rooms, feeling in her pocket for the key. The door creaked open into the darkness and she stepped inside, setting her candlestick down on the battered oak table against the wall. Then she stiffened.

Instantly, she knew beyond doubt that there was someone else in her apartment. A soft light came from the bedroom door, which was slightly ajar, and she could hear the secretive murmur of voices. She frowned and moved lightly across to a chest of drawers, opening it silently and drawing out a gleaming flintlock pocket pistol, her only tangible legacy from her father, who'd also shown her how to use it. If there were intruders, then she would deal with them. Easing off her big coat and laying it across a chair, she walked quietly towards the half-open bedroom door, relishing the warm, smooth walnut grain of the pistol against her palm, and stole a look inside.

The light came from one solitary oil lamp flickering on a small table in the corner of the bedchamber. She rarely used this room, because she found it oppressive and preferred to sleep on the comfortable day-bed in the small front chamber that she laughingly referred to as her parlour. This room was filled with heavy oak furniture and dark faded draperies dating from the last century, when the inn was a relatively respectable posting-house and the chamber was used for overnight guests. Tonight, Marisa realised as she fastidiously wrinkled her tip-tilted nose, the fusty smell was stronger than ever; in fact, the room reeked of sex. Her cornflower-blue eyes opened wide and, holding her breath, she edged further inside.

In the far corner of the room was a solid four-poster draped with threadbare silk hangings that almost concealed the interior of the bed from her view. But it was quite evident that behind the hangings, two people were moving in the unmistakable preliminaries to copulation. Marisa, frowning, moved silently sideways so she could see them, and her finger caressed the trigger of her pistol.

A man was sprawled back on the bed, moaning aloud. He was a servant, to judge by his coarse homespun shirt and baggy breeches, and his clothes were fairly insignificant anyway, mused Marisa wryly, since they were almost off him, thanks to the endeavours of the plump young woman who knelt on the bed beside him. Her long dark curls tumbled loosely round her shoulders as she dipped her head to flicker her tongue enticingly round the man's exposed, fully-erect penis, and in response the man was arching his hips distractedly towards the woman's mouth, reaching out for her generous breasts as they spilled from her bodice, his fingers squeezing avidly on the dark crimson teats.

Marisa's delicate blonde eyebrows lifted. The man was undeniably well made, she decided. His member certainly matched his big, muscular frame. In fact, it was of mouthwatering proportions, meaty and gnarled and stout enough to satisfy the most lascivious of women. His dark-haired companion was evidently of the same opinion, because she was uttering little whimpers of delight as she released the man's engorged shaft from her teasing lips and dangled her ripe breasts against his sturdy, thrusting phallus. The man clutched convulsively at her mane of loose brown curls and groaned aloud at her lewd caresses.

Marisa considered it a pity to interrupt them at this point in the proceedings. Feeling suddenly generous, she settled herself quietly in a big, carved oak chair in a shadowy corner by the door and watched them contemplatively.

The couple were still quite unaware of her presence, and were anyway quite beyond caring, which Marisa found rather endearing. The woman had rolled over onto her back, pulling her legs apart so that her full skirts fell away to reveal the dark serge stockings that were gartered just above her knees. The man grunted aloud and the perspiration stood out on his brow as he hurriedly knelt between her plump, fleshy thighs and gripped his hugely throbbing penis in his fist, pulling down his breeches with his other hand so that Marisa was given a shameless view of his muscular, hairy buttocks.

Marisa let out a little sigh as the man tenderly fondled the woman's lush secret parts with his swollen purple rod, liberally adorning its tip with musky female juices. Then, as the woman scrabbled desperately at his broad shoulders and clasped her trembling calves round his waist, he held his breath, and slid himself slowly into her. 'Now, then, my darling,' he was muttering hoarsely, 'easy does it, now.'

Marisa felt a reluctant stab of desire as her own nipples tightened hungrily at the sight. She wished it was her. She wished she was experiencing that fine, manly shaft sliding roughly up inside her, pleasuring her already moist vagina with delicious thrusts. Her hand stole to her aching breasts, caressing their fulness beneath the silk of her shirt until her nipples were hard as stones; then she pulled her hand away.

No. Better by far to be the one in charge, to be coolly aloof. She always chose her men carefully, and this muscle-bound peasant wasn't for her. But in spite of her resolve a soft flush rose in her cheeks. As she leaned forward slightly to get a better view, her tight buckskin breeches seemed to caress her moist, swollen labia, and she felt the ridged seam at her crotch pressing relentlessly against her heated clitoris, the sweet kernel of all her pleasure. She bit softly on her full lower lip and stroked the warm wood of her pistol, frowning as she watched.

The woman was on the very brink of her extremity, tearing at the man's broad shoulders with her hands and bouncing fiercely on the brocade covers of the bed as she gasped aloud. 'Dearest John! That's what I want; give it to me, give it to me now. Let me feel your fine fat prick deep inside me. Oh, yes . . .'

The man was certainly doing his best, thought Marisa wryly. His muscular bottom was pounding away dementedly, and his face was dark with the approaching onslaught of rapture. They were both nearly there. Marisa looked forward to seeing the looks on their faces when they realised they had an audience. Then she stopped thinking, because the man had withdrawn almost completely, preparing himself for a final, mighty assault. Marisa's pulse quickened helplessly as she caught a mouthwatering glimpse of his massive penis, its gnarled purple length sleekly coated with the woman's juices. As he slowly drove it back in between her fleshy lips the woman writhed and squirmed beneath him in delight, and Marisa felt an ominous tightening at her own belly, felt a warm, liquid melting between her thighs. Suddenly

584

she could imagine all too vividly what it would be like to enfold that mighty rod within her own silken flesh.

She closed her eyes tightly, fighting down her arousal as the couple on the bed bucked in frantic ecstasy, making the faded silk hangings ripple and sway as they shouted aloud in the extremity of their pleasure. But Marisa soon realised that closing her eyes was a mistake. Because, inexplicably, she was suddenly assailed by a vision of the man who had insulted her outside David's house. She saw his arrogant, aristocratic face with its chillingly handsome features, saw the cold mockery in his grey eyes as he murmured, like a wicked promise, 'I assure you, you are quite wrong about my physique.'

Lord Delsingham. Helplessly she remembered the wicked feel of his flickering tongue against her inner wrist, and imagined that same velvety tongue dancing between her swollen labia, parting them, finding her exquisitely engorged clitoris and bringing her, with long, rasping strokes, to the very brink of orgasm. At the same time she rocked forwards helplessly in her chair, so that the tight seam of her breeches pressed insistently between her thighs at all her most secret parts. She ground her fingers down helplessly against her clitoris, pressing herself through the leather into a sweet, hard little climax, and her body leaped and quivered silently as she imagined Lord Delsingham smiling triumphantly down at her with his beautiful, devilish grey eyes.

Utterly shaken, she drew herself dazedly back into the present, her body still flushed and trembling as the couple on the bed shuddered finally to their release and then collapsed in exhaustion.

Marisa let them lie there for one minute on the rumpled bedcovers, their bodies sheened with perspiration. Then, recovering her composure, she got up and sauntered across the room, holding her pistol lightly in her right hand.

The man saw her first. He practically fell off the bed in alarm, and as he started to fumble with his disarrayed clothes his face was dark with consternation. The woman whipped round and gasped when she saw Marisa.

Marisa put her hand on her hip as she surveyed them. Then she said calmly, 'Lucy. Dearest Lucy, if you're going to continue as my maid, or companion, or whatever you wish to call yourself, then you really will have to learn to control your lascivious impulses. Who is it this time?'

The young woman, pulling her skirts down and her bodice up, slipped hastily from the bed and bobbed a hasty curtsey. Her pretty face was flushed with embarrassment. 'Oh, Mistress Brooke! Don't be cross with me, please don't. I thought you wouldn't be back till much, much later. I was just tidying your rooms, you see, and then I saw John the new coachman cleaning the harness out in the back yard, and – and – '

Marisa said sternly, 'You have been very wicked, to pleasure yourselves so lewdly in my private rooms.'

Lucy's hot brown eyes gleamed with excitement. 'Will – will you punish us, Mistress Brooke?'

Marisa considered. 'Perhaps.'

Lucy's tongue flicked across her lips as Marisa went on, 'But not now. I have to go out very soon, Lucy, and I need you to help me get ready.' She turned to the coachman, who'd dressed himself hastily and was gazing in fascination at her slender, boyish figure. 'As for you, John,' she said softly, 'you'd better get back to your duties, hadn't you? I assume you weren't hired by the landlord solely to pleasure the women of the house, in spite of the generous size of your manhood.' She fingered her pistol gently. 'And if you've any thoughts of pleasuring me, then you'd better think again. You see, I prefer a little finesse in my men.'

He blushed and looked alarmed. 'Yes, Mistress Brooke. I'm truly sorry!'

She gestured silently towards the door, through which he made a hasty exit, and moments later Marisa heard him thudding clumsily downstairs.

Marisa and Lucy burst out laughing and fell into one another's arms.

'Oh, Marisa,' giggled Lucy, 'dearest Marisa, he couldn't take his eyes off you, with your tight breeches and boots and that lovely silk shirt that gives just a glimpse of your breasts. You look absolutely delicious, my dear, and that pistol is a wonderful touch. It was all so exciting.' She sighed. 'I only wish you'd come to join us instead of just watching.'

'I did consider it,' admitted Marisa, her blue eyes glinting as she threw herself on the big bed and lay back against the pillows, her hands behind her head. She grinned at Lucy. 'He looked extremely well endowed.'

Lucy's brown eyes shone. 'Indeed, he is. He's rather slow-witted, but his penis is quite delicious, my dear, so hard and rampant, and he seems to be able to go on for hours. You would have loved him.' She sighed happily and drew herself cosily up on the bed beside her friend. 'But of course, you have more self-control than me.'

I didn't have a moment ago, thought Marisa with a twinge of shame as she recollected her brief, excruciating moment of pleasure. But already Lucy was chattering on, saying happily, 'Marisa, you said you had to get ready to go out shortly. Yet you mentioned nothing about it this morning. Where are you going?'

Marisa went quickly into the other room to fetch the invitation from her coat pocket. She had few secrets from Lucy, who had become her ally and her friend on almost her first night in London. Lucy had been fleeing from the watch, after rather clumsily picking a stout gentleman's pocket as he emerged from the theatre in Drury Lane. Marisa, quickly assessing her plight, had hissed to the panic-stricken girl to hide in a doorway behind some winecasks, and had then told the constables that the young woman they were after had tried to pick her pocket too and had run off into the seedy depths of Martlet Court. Lucy, emerging from her hiding place when all was clear, had vowed eternal gratitude; and Marisa, taking a sudden liking to the girl's mischievous

587

brown eyes and merry face, had taken her into her employ as servant, companion or whatever the occasion required.

Now, with the embossed card in her hand, she returned to the bedchamber and climbed back onto the high bed. 'Look, Lucy. Look what I've got here.'

Lucy scanned the card eagerly. 'Who's it from?'

'I've really no idea. And that's all part of the fun, don't you think?'

'But – how did you get it?'

'No more questions, now, Lucy. It would take far too long to explain. But I'm going, and that's all that matters.'

Lucy sighed longingly. 'A masked ridotto – at Vauxhall. How very exciting! But you must be in costume, Marisa, what will you go as?'

'Why, I'll go as a 'bridle cull' – a female highwayman, of course. I'll wear my black riding habit and a tricorne hat. After all,' she smiled wickedly, 'they'll no doubt consider me a thief by the time I've stripped them of all their lovely guineas.' She leaned forward a little, her smooth brow puckering, and said more seriously, 'I need a lot of money, Lucy. Really a lot. The trouble is that people round here are starting to know me. They suspect me of trickery, and are wary of playing deep if I'm at the table. I need to win so much that I don't have to play again for a long, long time.'

'But they'll never catch you cheating – you're far too clever for that.'

'I certainly hope so. But anyone who wins steadily is always suspected of some sort of trickery; it's only natural. And last week, at that private card party I went to in Hertford Street, Sir Peregrine Thickett was muttering darkly to anyone who would listen about innocent-looking females who weren't what they seemed. He'd just lost 200 guineas to me, you see.'

Lucy frowned fiercely and put her arm around her friend's shoulder. 'Oh, Sir Peregrine, I remember him. He's nothing but a fat, foppish fool. I was talking to his coachman once, and he told me that Sir Peregrine likes nothing better than to invite some plump young serving maid to his bedroom and make her pretend to be his nurse.'

Marisa wrinkled her tip-tilted nose in distaste. 'No!'

'But yes,' Lucy smothered a giggle. 'Whenever his wife's out of the house, he calls his favourite maid up to his room. He makes her unlace her bodice so he can suck at her titties, and she reaches into his breeches to fondle him till he grows nice and hard, and tells him he's a naughty boy. Then he crouches on the floor in front of her, grovelling, and she has to smack his bare bottom until he goes very red in the face and calls out, "Please, nursie, please don't smack me," but she beats him harder and harder until he spurts out all over the floor.'

'Gods,' said Marisa disgustedly. 'And to think that earlier that night, before I won all that money off him, he was offering me 50 guineas a month and a house of my own if I would become his mistress.'

'Nursie, nursie,' crowed Lucy, and they both exploded with laughter.

Eventually Marisa went on, more seriously, 'Anyway, Lucy, Sir Peregrine was cross when I turned him down, and after that I could see he was watching me very closely each time I dealt. He couldn't see anything, of course.'

Lucy breathed in awe, 'Had you bent the cards?'

'Used the Kingston Bridge trick, you mean? No, they were all watching too closely for that. But I employed this little toy, very discreetly.' As she spoke she pulled a small gold ring off the little finger of her left hand, twisting it to show Lucy how it contained a tiny, retractable steel pin that could be hooked out with the flick of a fingernail.

'It's wonderful,' said Lucy. 'So you use that little pin to prick certain cards?'

'Yes. Just at the very edge, and then I can feel with my fingertips as I deal. A man in Drury Lane made it for me, and it's been worth every penny.'

'So you'll wear the ring tonight? At Vauxhall Pleasure Gardens?'

'Certainly.' Marisa smiled demurely. 'It should go well with my highwayman's outfit, don't you think?'

Lucy leaned back on the pillows, sighing with satisfaction. 'Oh, Marisa, you are lucky. I went to Vauxhall last spring, it was beautiful, like fairyland, with hundreds of lanterns lighting up the trees as darkness fell, and people dancing in the pavilions, and fine lords and ladies strolling up and down the avenues.'

'And tricksters, and knaves, and females of the very lowest kind lurking in the woodland walks,' said Marisa, swinging her legs to the floor and getting to her feet. 'Just the right kind of place for me, don't you think? Come on, Lucy, it's time for me to get ready.'

Lucy, still in a happy dream, nodded and pulled herself reluctantly up. Then she suddenly clapped her hand to her mouth. 'I almost forgot – a letter arrived for you while you were out. I put it over there, on that chest of drawers – it looks rather important.'

Marisa went to pick it up, turning it over slowly in her hands before opening it. The spidery, close lines of writing were little more than a blur to her. She'd always admitted, laughingly, that the one thing that frightened her was a lawyer's letter. She scanned it slowly, feeling the familiar regret that the rather unusual education she'd received hadn't equipped her to deal with such things. She hated these long, awkward words that leaped up from the page at her and mocked her with their incomprehensibility.

'It's from my attorney,' she said slowly, running her finger tortuously along each line. 'Mr Giles, of Bedford Street. He handled all my father's finances, or perhaps I should say all of his debts. I think – ' and she pored impatiently over the last sentence, 'I think he's saying that he wants to see me at my earliest convenience, about some sort of bequest.'

Lucy frowned. 'A bequest? What can it mean?'

Marisa shrugged and tossed the letter into the fire.

'That yet more of my father's debts have come to light, no doubt. That's the only kind of inheritance I'm ever likely to come into.'

Lucy had already lost interest and was looking longingly at the invitation instead. 'The Ace of Spades,' she was murmuring happily. 'How really, truly exciting, not to know who he is. He might be some rich, powerful lord, Marisa. You'll ensnare him tonight with your bewitching beauty, and his noble heart will be yours forever.'

'I'd rather have his money than his noble heart, thanks,' responded Marisa dryly as she picked up a silver hairbrush from the dressing table and started to draw it through her thick, luxuriant locks. 'In my experience, most members of the nobility are fatuous, incompetent fools.'

But then suddenly, she remembered Lord Delsingham. As she gazed at her candlelit reflection in the mirror, her blue eyes seemed to grow hazy with desire. She remembered the way his aristocratic face had been alive with intelligent irony as he bent to caress her wrist in that subtly insulting way. Lord Delsingham, she was quite sure, was neither fatuous nor incompetent at anything.

Her preparations all complete, Marisa set off in a hackney carriage across Westminster Bridge to Vauxhall at nine that evening, with Lucy as her maid and John playing the part of her strapping manservant. Never having visited Vauxhall before, Marisa had gone prepared to be unimpressed, but as she showed her invitation at the gate and entered the gardens at last, she caught her breath in wonder. As Lucy had promised, it was like entering an enchanted world, a world illuminated by hundreds of golden lanterns strung between the lines of trees, with leafy walks winding enticingly away into the· darkness. Half hidden by foliage, elaborate pagodas and secret bowers glimmered enticingly in the distance, while above the noise of the crowds that milled excitedly round the main walks could be heard the sweet, liquid notes of groups of musicians playing in the shady groves.

The sky above them was studded with stars; the evening air was still and warm. 'Just perfect,' declared Lucy happily, 'for Vauxhall!' They stood for a moment, taking it all in as the other visitors to the gardens swept past them. Quite a number of them were in masquerade, or all-concealing dominos; Marisa wondered which of them were in the Ace of Spade's party, and she felt a frisson of excitement as she wondered if he himself was here yet. Lucy was in a desperate hurry to reach the main pavilion, where the invitation had instructed them to gather; but Marisa wanted to take her time. With a sigh of satisfaction she smoothed down her elegant, severely cut black riding habit with its short, tight-fitting jacket and full skirt, and adjusted her neat black tricorne at a rakish angle over her blonde, piled-up curls. Her pistol was tucked in at her waist, together with her money-purse, and the upper part of her face was concealed by a black velvet mask. She was aware of a number of men glancing at her with open admiration in their eyes, and she smiled coolly, feeling herself to be the epitome of an elegant, discreet lady of fashion.

She had come a long way, she decided. A long way since the wild, rollicking journeys from one city of Europe to another as her careless, charming father, a former cavalry officer who had gambled away his pay and run from his regiment in disgrace, concentrated his considerable energies on evading his creditors and escaping from former gaming companions who suspected him, quite rightly, of cheating them.

The youthful Marisa, utterly devoted to her handsome father, had assumed that there was no other way to live. She'd picked up an education – of sorts – from the various women who sometimes joined their entourage, the women her father referred to as governesses. But Marisa quickly realised that these governesses were there to attend to her father rather than herself, hence her haphazard inadequacy in such basic skills as reading and writing. Of far more use to her than the education offered to her by these governesses were the skills she learned from her father. He was a fine swordsman, and taught her all that he knew about fencing without making any allowances for her sex. He also taught her how to shoot and ride, and introduced her to the art of gaming, of knowing when to take a risk not only with cards and dice, but also with life.

Unlike her father, Marisa usually won. She learned from his mistakes. Her combination of a cool, natural intelligence together with her stunning, innocent-looking beauty, which inevitably distracted her male opponents, made her a formidable opponent in any kind of game.

She'd learned the pleasures of the opposite sex from a charming young Polish cavalryman called Frederic, who'd introduced her most sweetly to the delicious sensations of her own body one night when she and her father were staying at a roadside inn on their way to Hanover. Her father was deep in vingt-et-un in the coffee room below when the handsome Polish cavalryman, with whom she'd made a whispered assignation earlier, had romantically climbed up the balcony to the window of the room she shared with her governess. Marisa felt quite dizzy with power as he speedily undressed her and adored her body with his mouth and lips and tongue.

At first, when he'd drawn out his penis, she'd been startled, because it looked so hot and angry and huge. But he'd continued to caress her gently, stroking his big, calloused horseman's hands over her pouting breasts, and encouraging her to touch him down there. She'd gasped with shock, because his flesh quivered at her touch and throbbed angrily against her tremulous palm, but it felt lovely as well, velvety and powerful and strong, and she ached with an indescribable longing that melted her insides. When he finally laid her gently on her little bed and sheathed himself inside her, she'd gasped and gone very still.

'I am hurting you, darling?' Frederic had said in his husky Polish accent.

'Oh, no.' Marisa had sighed happily, running her fingers over his lovely strong shoulder muscles. 'Far from it. Oh, very far from it.'

He'd caressed her skilfully with his hands, gently thrusting with his silken penis and stroking the tender nub of her clitoris until she'd arched herself dizzily towards him, feeling the sweetest ripples of ecstasy surge through her melting flesh as his bone-hard member eased away her tight virginity. Then she'd exploded, rubbing her small breasts against his hard chest, extracting every last, delicious ounce of rapture from his pulsing rod as he pleasured her into oblivion.

They'd been disturbed at that point by a gentle knocking at the door. They flew apart, Marisa giggling as she pulled the sheets up to her chin and Frederic cursing as he struggled to fasten up his tight cavalryman's breeches.

'Frederic,' a soft feminine voice called. 'Frederic, my dearest, are you there?'

It was Isobel, Marisa's latest governess. Marisa, with a quick look at the handsome Frederic's guilty face, realised instantly that the plump, pretty Isobel was also in receipt of the Polish officer's favours. Pointing quickly to the open window, Marisa hissed, 'Out!' and Frederic fled, scrambling over the balcony. Then, with a sheet draped carelessly around herself so that her flushed, still swollen breasts were just peeping over the top, she walked slowly to the door and opened it. Isobel, an insipid brunette who was some ten years older than Marisa and had often chided her tartly for various minor misdemeanours, stood there with her jaw dropping open stupidly at the sight of Marisa's near nakedness.

'Were you looking for Frederic?' enquired Marisa sweetly.

'Why, yes. We – we had some business to discuss.'

'He has already settled that business. With me.' Marisa smiled secretively. 'I wouldn't bother him again if I were you, Isobel. He told me that you are a shrivelled, passionless spinster, and that he would rather have a good bottle of claret for company than you.'

Isobel fled with a smothered cry of distress, and neither Marisa nor her father ever saw her again. Frederic secretly visited Marisa the next day, bringing her flowers and begging her to meet him again, but Marisa had coldly dismissed him, saying that she had taken a sudden unaccountable dislike to Polish cavalrymen. She'd smiled as he rode off, having listened impatiently as he declared himself to be quite heartbroken, and she relished her moment of power, the power of being in charge. She decided then that she was never, ever going to relinquish that power to anyone.

She'd been sad when her father died unexpectedly just over a year ago, soon after Napoleon had been finally defeated at Waterloo, but she'd not wasted time in grieving, resolving instead to return to London, a city forbidden to Captain Brooke because of his desertion from his regiment. London was undoubtedly the capital of Europe, awash with pleasure-seekers and gamblers now that the long European war was finally at an end. And here, Marisa was convinced she would finally find her destiny.

She was brought abruptly back to the present by Lucy's excited chatter. 'Over there,' Lucy was pointing happily, 'that's where the tightrope walkers will perform. There may even be fireworks later. And down here is the grand pavilion, where the dancing takes place.'

'And the card rooms?' queried Marisa, suddenly alert again.

'There are several private card rooms leading off the pavilion. But Marisa, how will you know which party to join, when you don't even know who your host is?'

Marisa laughed, suddenly feeling calmly confident. 'I would imagine that the Ace of Spades will make quite certain that his guests can find him.'

She was right, of course. She had scarcely entered the brilliantly lit rotunda, where sets of people glittering in silks and satins danced to the lively music, when a liveried footman moved discreetly towards her. Glancing decorously at the invitation which she held in her hand, he indicated the curtained doors of a private room. 'Please to proceed this way, my lady.' And then Marisa noticed that his cream silk waistcoat was embroidered with tiny black spades.

Her heart fluttered unaccountably, but her voice was cool as she turned to dismiss Lucy and John. 'Be near at hand in case I need you,' she said softly. Then, as the footman held open the big door, she walked slowly into the room, conscious of many masked pairs of eyes upon her as bowed heads were lifted from their study of the green baize gaming tables, and cards were held delicately poised in mid-play.

She was late. And by being late, she'd made herself conspicuous; not a good start. But she outfaced them all, men and women, young and old in their assorted costumes and disguises, reminding herself that anonymity was the unspoken rule at a discreet affair such as this, and that no-one would dare to challenge her if she only brazened it out. She looked round disdainfully, handing her hat and gloves to the footman, and felt a secret shiver of excitement as she sensed the men assessing her slim figure in her tightly cut black riding habit with open greed, while the women's eyes glittered with jealousy behind their masks. Was the Ace of Spades here yet? Which one was he? Somehow she imagined him to be mysterious, powerful, utterly irresistible.

The room settled slowly back into play. Everyone was seated, except for the hovering groom-porters who sternly called out the odds and provided fresh packs of cards as required. Marisa paused, wondering whether to join the hazard table, or try her luck at the faro bank.

She jumped as she felt a hand touching her arm. A light, amused male voice drawled in her ear, 'You must forgive them, my dear, for staring at you so when you first came in. But I rather think they were unsure whether you had come to play cards with them, or to rob them. Your costume is quite divine, by the way.'

Marisa whipped round. She was confronted by a man: a tall, formidable man in an enveloping black domino and mask, though in spite of that mask she would have known those alert grey eyes, that cultured, mocking voice anywhere in the world. They belonged to Lord Delsingham, the man who had been so hatefully insulting to her earlier that day.

She hoped desperately that he wouldn't be able to recognise her in her mask, but that hope was swiftly dismissed as his mouth curled in sudden amusement and he said, in a more intimate tone, 'Well, well, fair Ganymede. Fancy seeing you here.'

'It is no more surprising, my lord,' snapped Marisa, 'than for me to see you here. But then, I suppose you think that your money gains you entry everywhere.'

His eyes glinted. 'What a pleasure it is to have the chance to exchange sweet compliments with you once again. You have an invitation to this little entertainment?'

Marisa felt herself colour. 'Of course I have!'

'How very intriguing.'

'Have you?' she said hotly, stung by his disbelieving tone.

'In a manner of speaking, yes, I suppose I have. Let me offer you a glass of champagne. And then, fair Ganymede, you must come and join me at the hazard table.'

She lifted her chin defiantly as he handed her a crystal glass of champagne. 'Actually, I prefer cards to dice.'

He shrugged his wide shoulders. 'As you please. Perhaps you will honour me with a game of piquet later.'

Marisa smiled sweetly. 'If I do, you will regret it, my lord. I must warn you that I'm rather good.' Then she swiftly turned her back on him and headed for the twenty-guinea hazard table, just to annoy him.

Once seated at the circular table, she played a quiet, steady game so as not to draw attention to herself, losing an insubstantial sum that caused no comment, and giving herself time to recover from the unpleasant shock of Delsingham's presence here. As the dice box moved steadily round, she assessed the room quickly, seeing how the punters' tokens were accumulating at the faro-bank, and how they were betting heavily at the vingt-et-un table. Deep play indeed, just as she'd hoped. She felt a quiver of excitement as she breathed in the heady atmosphere of risk and tension. And then, slowly and carefully, she began to win. She knew she had no hope of using her weighted dice here, because it was too risky in this expert, watchful company, but nevertheless she concentrated on using all the subtle techniques for casting the dice that her father had taught her, placing the cubes nonchalantly in the box and just trickling them out with a deceptive flick of her wrist so that they fell exactly as she wanted. If she used the trick sparingly, then no-one would suspect, and even if they did, they wouldn't have a shred of evidence against her.

She was starting to win. Carefully she piled her guinea tokens in the little mahogany stand that a manservant had placed beside her, with its rimmed cavity for holding her champagne glass. The click of the dice thrilled her; she waited her next turn with excitement as the groom-porters impassively intoned the odds.

Then she looked up and saw Lord Delsingham watching her, his grey eyes steely behind his black mask. She felt a tiny shiver of fear assail her, and something else – a sharp, febrile stab of desire. Helplessly she remembered his challenging caress earlier that day, and remembered her wicked fantasy about him making love to her with his delicious mouth and tongue. A sudden, awful thought struck her. What if he were the Ace of Spades?

No. Impossible. If he was the host, then he would have known immediately that she was not an invited guest, and would have had her thrown out bodily. But he was still watching her, and it unsettled her badly. It was her turn to play. She coloured beneath her mask, and threw so clumsily that one of the dice landed on the floor. She saw Lord Delsingham murmur to a groom-porter, who hurried to pick it up. In the darkened gaming hells, a dropped die was a well-known opportunity to cheat, but there was no earthly chance for substitution in this watchful company, thought Marisa somewhat faintly.

Shortly afterwards Delsingham left with some other

guests for the supper boxes and Marisa, feeling more relaxed, moved across to the faro bank. Her choice of numbers was good; her guinea tokens continued to accumulate satisfactorily. And then her concentration was broken as a cluster of new arrivals burst into the room, their voices loud with the champagne they'd consumed. Marisa, placing her token carefully on a seven, tried to ignore them. But she jumped when a shrill male voice called out, 'That woman there with the blonde hair, the one in the highwayman's rig. She's a cheat, a vicious little cheat! I'd recognise her anywhere.'

Marisa spun round to see a plump, foppish man dressed in a scarlet domino. Sir Peregrine. She felt rather faint. An elderly man who had been sitting beside her and watching her play with an appreciative eye got to his feet and said, 'That is rather a grave accusation, Sir Peregrine.'

'Grave it might be, but it's true, by God!'

Marisa laughed shortly. 'Prove it.'

'I most certainly will. Last time I played with you, madam, you trounced me so roundly that after you'd left I picked up the discards and checked them. And I found a tiny mark at the corner of each picture, made with a pin.'

There was a hiss of indrawn breath around the room. The liveried groom-porters had moved to stand in menacing fashion on either side of Marisa. Somehow she forced herself to stay calm, although the little gold ring on her finger seemed to burn her.

'I challenge you', she said, 'to discover any such mark on the cards here.'

Sir Peregrine hesitated then lunged forwards. 'Her ring,' he shouted. 'Look at that ring. I remember how she fingered that little trinket all the time we were at play. Examine it, will you? If she's innocent, she'll make no objection to that.'

Marisa did have objections – plenty of them. Springing quickly to her feet so her fragile gilt chair fell backwards, she kicked at the nearest groom-porter's stockinged shins extremely hard with her pointed little boot. He howled with pain and stumbled backwards, crashing into several astonished guests. Before anyone realised what was happening, Marisa had charged for the door to the ballroom, pushing her way between the startled dancers and out into the clear night air.

Damn, damn, damn. Of all the ill luck. She cursed stupid, fat Sir Peregrine, who was so hopeless at cards that on the night he spoke of she hadn't really needed to cheat at all to relieve him of his guineas. She cursed the Ace of Spades, whoever he was, for inviting such a stupid booby to his card party. Her one consolation was that the hateful Lord Delsingham hadn't been there to witness her humiliation.

She heard shouts behind her and set off down a narrow path towards a Japanese pagoda, conscious of passers-by turning to gape at her as she flew past them, her hair streaming out behind her as her lovely little hat tumbled to the ground. In no time at all, the whole place would be on the alert for her. No good trying to get out through the main gates again. No good relying on John and Lucy, who were no doubt engrossed with each other in some dark corner. They had the brains of a pea between the two of them, with all their mental activity concentrated in their loins.

'There she is,' someone yelled. 'Stop her!'

Marisa plunged down yet another twisting path, the now hateful, coloured lanterns winking at her, the fiddlers in their cocked hats seeming to mock her as they played their jaunty music in the leafy glades. Two young, drunken bucks ogled her and tried to block her path, but she stunned them with a vicious stream of invective and ran on, her heart pounding against her ribs, until at last she became aware that the lights and the crowds seemed to have faded away. She pulled up, her chest heaving, and tore off her mask. She was in a wild, obviously unfrequented part of the gardens, where the tangle of undergrowth and the untamed trees told her that she must be on the very edge of open countryside. Somehow,

600

she must get out of here. If Sir Peregrine caught her, he'd hand her over to the magistrates, and with no-one to speak up for her, that could mean a hefty fine she could ill afford, or possibly even prison. It seemed as if her luck was running out at last.

Suddenly she heard a menacing rustle in the bushes behind her. She whirled round to see two young, roughly dressed men grinning at her, openly assessing her fine clothes. Marisa's stomach lurched. Footpads, thieves. Fool that she was, she'd quite forgotten that the Pleasure Gardens were a notorious attraction for the very lowest sort of criminal, on the lookout for easy pickings.

Well, she wouldn't be anyone's easy pickings. She turned to run, but they caught her without difficulty, even though she struggled and kicked out at them. If only they knew, thought Marisa disgustedly, that she was in just as much danger from the authorities as they were.

Chapter Three

The two men dragged her along a narrow, overgrown path that was in utter darkness, laughing at her attempts to escape. At last she saw the flickering glow of a fire, in a leafy clearing. They came to a halt there, with each man gripping her arm securely, and she saw that another man sat cross-legged by the fire with two blowsily dressed girls lying on the ground beside him. The remnants of a meal lay about them, and some empty wine bottles. The man by the fire was still drinking from an almost full bottle, but he put it down when he saw them.

'Well, well,' he said softly, getting to his feet. 'Caleb, Tom. What have you brought me?'

He had dark, curly hair, and a gold ring glinted in his ear. They were gypsies, realised Marisa suddenly, vagabond gypsies on the prowl.

'We found her, Seth,' said one of the men, the bearded one. 'Found her skulking in the bushes.'

The man Seth walked slowly towards the captive Marisa and drew his brown finger down her cheek while the women watched hotly from the fireside. Marisa felt a sudden quiver of awareness as he touched her. His smooth, hard-boned face was tanned nut-brown from the sun. He was young, with a lithe, muscular body that was clad simply in a loose, open-necked white shirt and corduroy breeches that were tucked into soft leather boots, and his dark eyes seemed to glitter with sensual awareness as they assessed her slender figure in her severely cut, black riding habit.

Then his hand slipped to her shoulder, and Marisa spat at him. He looked surprised for a moment, then drew out his handkerchief and brushed the moisture away from his jaw. 'A spirited little beauty,' he laughed softly. 'Calm yourself, my pigeon. We'll do you no harm. All we want are your money and your jewels.'

Marisa glared at him defiantly, remembering her abandoned winnings in the card room with acute regret. 'I've nothing, you brute!'

For answer, he lifted up her hand and pulled off her precious little gold ring, which he silently pocketed. Then he ran his hands softly beneath her tight-fitting jacket and over the silk shirt she wore beneath it. Her small breasts tingled suddenly as his palm brushed them, and she caught her breath, not knowing if the intimacy was deliberate or not. And then, he found her pistol. 'This looks worth a good guinea or two,' he said appreciatively, weighing it in his strong hands.

Marisa lunged to retrieve it, twisting free of her captors. 'Give it back to me.'

'I might consider it,' he said. 'But what are you going to offer us in exchange, fine lady?'

Marisa caught her breath. There was something about the way he looked at her that made her feel strangely excited. A game. A challenge.

The women were watching her from the fireside. There was a young slim one with long dark hair, and a slightly older one, a plump, brazen beauty with loose red curls and a low-cut lace bodice that exposed the upper portion of her full breasts enticingly as she rested her chin in her hands and gazed up at Marisa.

'I like her fine clothes, Seth,' the woman said enviously. 'Let's play for her clothes.'

The bearded man, who'd seized hold of Marisa's arm

again, laughed aloud. 'Aye. Rowena's right. Let's play for her clothes, and then for her. I've a fancy for a little sport, and it's a long time since we had such a fine, aristocratic wench on our hands.'

Marisa felt a momentary spasm of fear. Then she met the eyes of the dark-haired man Seth, and realised that he was saluting her in challenge, as if they were opponents before a duel. She drawled coolly, 'I hate to disappoint you all, but I'm no aristocrat.'

Seth said, 'Anyone out looking for you?'

She smiled up at him. 'I sincerely hope not,' she said, and he laughed. She could hear the faint strain of violins, ghostly in the distance, but the Pleasure Gardens seemed a hundred miles away to her just then.

'I want her clothes,' drawled the redheaded Rowena petulantly, getting up and coming over to lean her head coquettishly against Seth's shoulder. Marisa realised she was rather drunk; they probably all were. 'Make her give us her fancy clothes, Seth darling!'

Marisa gazed at Seth. 'If you tell these men to unhand me,' she said evenly, 'I'll take them off myself.'

There was a hiss of surprise from the others, but Seth nodded thoughtfully and the men released her. Slowly, in the hypnotised, heavy silence of that little wooded clearing, Marisa started to ease off her beautiful riding habit, feeling unaccountably excited as their hungry eyes devoured her. The odds were stacked against her this time, but she was used to that. Her eyes rested briefly on her father's pistol, which the man Seth had laid on the grass beside the fire. She would get that back very soon, she promised herself silently.

Seth took her jacket and skirt from her, and then her silk shirt. She stood there demurely in her chemise and tight-laced corset and stockings, feeling how the cool, night air made her nipples surge and stiffen against the crisp, white cotton. She tossed her head so that her loose, golden curls tumbled around her bare shoulders. She could see that the big bearded man, Caleb, who'd moved back into the shadows to watch her, was rubbing surreptitiously at his groin. She was playing a dangerous game, she reminded herself. But at least, this way, she stood a chance. She felt the familiar, nerve-tingling excitement of pitting her wits against the odds. Then the bearded man stepped forward, his genitals an ominous bulge against the tight crotch of his breeches. 'Let's dice for her, Seth,' he said, his voice coarse with lust. 'The man with the highest throw gets to have the wench.'

But Seth, with a dangerous smile playing around his beautifully curved mouth, held up his hand in restraint. 'Hold, Caleb.' He turned to Marisa. 'What do you say to that?'

Marisa shrugged her deliciously bare shoulders. 'I think', she said, 'that you're all disappointingly devoid of imagination. You really want just one person to win, so that all the rest are losers?'

'Then what do you suggest?' said the man Caleb roughly.

'Have you ever heard of the game King's Pleasure?' queried Marisa demurely.

They shook their heads, all of them hanging on her every word, even the young, dark-haired woman who still sprawled lazily by the fire.

'You play it with cards,' said Marisa Brooke. 'You've got some cards?' She smoothed down her simple white chemise over the narrow, boned corset that encased her ribs and thrust her breasts upwards, revelling in the gypsies' avid attention. 'All you have to do is pick two cards in turn. Ace is high. And the winner of each round can order any other player to do anything. Anything at all.'

'Anything at all?' echoed the redheaded Rowena incredulously, still raptly stroking Marisa's discarded riding habit. The other woman had got to her feet as well and was listening open mouthed.

'Exactly,' said Marisa softly. 'But only one command can be given at a time, so as to make the game last, and give everyone a chance.'

There was a moment's tense silence as they considered

her proposition. Caleb and the younger man, Tom, who had been silent up to now, seemed to be muttering together in consultation. Marisa went on in her low, musical voice, 'Of course, I'm bound to lose, because there's only one of me, and you'll all be playing against me.'

Seth, their leader, was watching her carefully. He was nice, thought Marisa with a sudden shiver of delight. He had a strongly made, sinewy body and a mobile, striking face, with high cheekbones that somehow added to the exotic allure of his rough mop of curling, dark hair and his gypsy earring. 'You're quite sure about this?' he asked Marisa softly.

Rowena was watching Seth angrily. Marisa realised that Seth must be Rowena's man, and the redhead was fiercely jealous of Marisa. Something to watch out for there.

'Of course she's sure, Seth,' Rowena hissed out. 'Can't you see she's nothing but a high-class whore?'

Marisa said cuttingly, 'I'm neither high-class nor a whore. Nobody buys me with their money, which I'm quite sure is more than can be said for you.' Rowena swore aloud, but Seth restrained her as Marisa went on calmly, 'However, I am fond of a wager. Shall we play?'

They settled themselves round the fire, and a pack of worn cards was brought out. In spite of her apparent calm, Marisa's heart was thumping so loudly that she was sure they must hear it. She tried to steady herself, because the stakes were too high for her to make any mistakes.

Seth dealt. They each drew two cards, and the bearded man Caleb won the first round. He drew a deep breath and gazed hotly at Marisa. Then he said gruffly, 'I want you to pull that fancy garment of yours right down to your waist and show us your ladylike titties.' He leaned hungrily across the circle towards her. 'And then I want to play with them, and suck them, and – ' Seth struck him back brutally with the back of his hand so that the older man groaned with pain.

'One thing at a time, Caleb, remember?' Seth said flatly. He turned to Marisa, his dark eyes quite calm. 'You heard, I think, what he said.'

Marisa met his gaze steadily. He was different, this one. Quite, quite different. She suddenly imagined him without his clothes, sunbrowned, muscular, lithe. His penis, she knew, would be deliciously smooth and lengthy, and he would smile as he pleasured her. Keeping her eyes locked with his, she calmly pulled her thin-strapped chemise down to her waist. Underneath it she wore a short, tightly laced corset that encased her ribcage, its upper rim cunningly shaped and boned to push up her naked breasts. She felt her exposed nipples tighten rosily in the cool night air, and heard a hiss of appreciation from her audience. She saw that the third man, Tom, was watching with desperate intensity, his silky brown hair falling across his flushed, beardless face as he gazed at her. Another one who couldn't wait to get his hands on her. She felt a fierce lick of excitement at her belly and allowed herself, just for a moment, to fantasise about having all three of them, all three sturdy, rampant cocks only too eager to pleasure her in any way she wished. She pulled her attention back to the game with an effort. This time, she must win. The pack lay loosely beside Caleb, ready to be shuffled and re-dealt. As she slipped her own card casually back into it, she checked that no-one was watching her. Then she splayed the cards rapidly and managed, within the blinking of an eye, to mark the corners of two kings and an ace with her sharp thumbnail. 'Sauter la coupe,' her father had called that particular little trick.

In the flickering firelight, none of them seemed to notice how piercingly she scanned the fan of cards that was offered to her. The pack was badly scuffed and worn, but even so within seconds she'd caught sight of her own familiar tiny marks. Two kings: that should do.

And it did. She'd won. When they'd all drawn and thrown back their cards in disgust, she turned to the woman Rowena and pointed towards Tom. She said silkily, 'I want you to pleasure him, Rowena. With your mouth.'

A flicker of astonishment crossed the woman's plump, lascivious face. 'Now?'

Marisa smiled sweetly. 'Yes, indeed. Do it now. And here, so that everyone can see you.'

The man Caleb laughed, jealous. 'You chose the right one there, didn't you? Sucking cocks is a favourite occupation of Rowena's. Only usually she gets paid for it.'

'And deservedly so, Caleb,' said Rowena, shooting him a fiery glance.

Tom was already shivering with excitement. Rowena swaggered around the hushed circle towards him, her hips swaying enticingly, her breasts peeping curvaceously above her lace bodice. The stillness was painfully intense as she slowly sank to her knees before him and worked to release his penis from his breeches. It was already erect, but Marisa saw that even so it was small and white and slender; a boy's weapon rather than a man's. Nevertheless Rowena took it in her mouth with evident satisfaction, licking and teasing with her pink little tongue. Tom came almost immediately, groaning as he spurted his seed into her hot mouth, but Rowena, instead of abandoning him, started work on him again, nipping and teasing with her salacious lips until his cock started to grow once more. Excellent, thought Marisa quickly, she's going to make it last. And the others were watching with glittering eyes. So far, so good. She let her eyes rest just for a moment on her precious pistol, lying on the ground almost within her reach.

Seth won next. Marisa felt a dark flicker of excitement as his gypsy's gaze roved her vulnerable body, and then he said to her quietly, 'Your breasts are exquisite. They must give you great pleasure. I would like to see you fondle them yourself.'

Marisa met his gaze steadily and started to run her palms over her upthrust breasts until they ached with sweet fullness. She imagined Seth's beautiful mouth paying homage to her nipples, and they stiffened hungrily against her fingers. 'Like this?' she murmured.

He leaned back against a low tree stump, quite relaxed, his shirt gleaming whitely in the firelight against the smooth brown of his face. 'Exactly.' He smiled, and Marisa, imagining how his beautiful cock must be stirring and thickening as he watched her lewd behaviour, swallowed hard.

Underneath her outer calm, she was seething with desire. She was desperately excited by the gypsies' hot enjoyment of her bare flesh, by the atmosphere of open sexual hunger that filled this secret firelit glade. She could hear the soft moans of the youth Tom as Rowena tortured his slender penis exquisitely with her hot mouth, while Seth, lovely, dangerous-looking Seth, was just watching her, a small smile playing around his lips. She found his smile the most exciting thing of all. She kept her eyes deliberately on his face as she played with her nipples, twisting them and sending delicious little shafts of pleasure-pain shooting through her body. But inevitably her eyes slid down to his groin, where beneath his skintight breeches she could see the wicked promise of a fine, thick rod of swollen flesh pushing against the confines of the straining fabric.

Licking her lips, she shifted her stockinged thighs beneath her chemise, feeling her labia swell and moisten. She had to stay in control, because this was one game she had to win, and strategy, as ever, was all-important. She knew that she could quite easily win every draw of the cards by marking more and more of the pictures each time she slipped her cards back into the pile, but the gypsies might lose their easy-going good humour if they suspected they were being duped. And yet it was essential for her to win just one more time if her plan was to succeed.

She drew a king and an ace. Her father would have been proud of her. Now it was her turn to give instructions, and she must do something about the bearded one, Caleb, because he was the one most likely to turn nasty if he didn't get some sort of satisfaction very soon. She leaned towards him, her pert breasts pouting enticingly above her tight-laced white corset, her nipples tawny as wine in the glow of the fire. 'Do you know, Caleb,' she breathed, 'I have a real fancy to see your cock in action.'

He grunted and lurched towards her hotly but she laughed and slipped to one side. 'Not with me, my fine stallion,' she said archly, 'at least, not yet.' She pointed at the dark-haired girl by the fire, who had so far stayed silent but was eagerly watching every move. 'I'm sure you're well primed already, Caleb. Use your weapon on her, will you? Then I can watch, and I'll know what I've got to look forward to, won't I?'

He grinned avidly. 'Oh, you can look forward to this, my fine lady,' he breathed. 'Imagine being pleasured by this mighty weapon, eh?' And without hesitation he pulled out his penis and began to stroke it fondly.

Marisa felt her breath catch in her throat. Caleb's phallus was already hotly engorged, but his loving caresses made it swell to an even greater size. It was a great, purple-headed monster that strained upwards from his breeches, swaying hungrily. She felt her moist secret parts twitch and run with juices as she imagined that thick, veined shaft sliding up between her own hungry sex-lips and pleasuring her into delicious oblivion with each virile thrust. Her nipples tightened painfully, tugging at her breasts, and with a supreme effort she tried to ignore the sweet, pulsing ache at her body's core. She couldn't afford to indulge herself yet, it wasn't part of her plan. And anyway, the dark-haired woman had already moved in on Caleb with burning eagerness. She stood on tiptoe to whisper in his ear, giggling, then she dropped swiftly to the ground on all fours, casting a mischievous glance behind her.

With a low growl, Caleb pulled up her crimson skirt and lace-edged petticoat to expose her ripe, flaring bottom. Kneeling behind her, he gripped his lengthy penis in his hand and lunged towards her, prodding hungrily towards the lush folds of her vulva. The woman was hot for him; her body's nectar anointed him lasciviously, and he drew back for a moment, using his palm to slide the glistening moisture up and down his quivering shaft, muttering hotly to himself. Then, with a great cry of satisfaction, he gripped her bottom and slid himself into her, inch by delicious inch. The woman moaned softly and writhed in delight as he impaled her, playing hungrily with her own nipples to heighten her ecstasy.

Caleb hissed, 'Steady now, my little beauty. No rush.' He drew himself out, very slowly, so the woman whimpered out her loss and thrust back towards him, but Caleb was taking his time. He gazed down, openly admiring his own meaty weapon as it nudged at her buttocks. Marisa was unable to drag her eyes away from the sight of it, and she moistened her lips as she caught a glimpse of his hairy balls swaying at the root of his glistening shaft. She shivered as she watched him slowly slide himself back inside the girl, wishing that it was her being ravished by that delicious weapon. Then she dragged her eyes away with an effort to quickly assess the rest of the little group.

Rowena was still playing with Tom's slender cock, reducing him to a helpless, quivering mass with her tormenting caresses. Tom had orgasmed violently yet again, his seed spilling on the soft ground, but still Rowena would not let him go. Now she was stroking his small, firm buttocks, pulling them apart and sliding her finger tormentingly into his tight anal crevice so that he was groaning with excitement. So, thought Marisa. They were busy for a while yet. Only Seth to deal with. She would have to win one more time, and hope that he didn't suspect.

Seth drew a king and a ten. She found it difficult to discern her marks, because Seth was watching her, and he was the most dangerous, the most handsome of them all. She wanted him badly, which affected her concentration, but she won, with a carefully drawn queen and ace. Seth watched her all the time, his dark eyes inscrutable, and she thought desperately, He knows! He knows that I've tricked them all. But she had to continue brazenly with her game. She had no alternative. Leaning towards him huskily, she whispered, 'Seth. You know what I'd really like?'

He shook his head, his eyes glinting. 'Tell me.'

She slid her hand along his forearm, pushing back his loose sleeve. His sinewy skin was brown from the sun, and lightly sprinkled with silky dark hairs. 'Seth,' she whispered, 'I'd like to see your lovely penis. And then, just to start with, I'd like you to rub it against my breasts. That drives me wild, really wild.'

He gazed at her stiffened nipples as they poked out from above her corset, but his face was still cool and impassive, which worried her. He was nobody's fool. Then she glanced at his groin, and saw the thick knot of his penis straining against the fabric of his breeches, and felt much happier. He was just as easily manipulated as the rest of them. She crouched over him and reached carefully to unfasten his breeches and draw out his cock. It was lovely, just as she'd imagined it, long and hard and silky. Her hand trembled as she caressed it with her cool palm, feeling its heat burning into her; on a sudden impulse she dipped her head and tasted it, wrapping her tongue round its swollen head and sliding her parted lips down over the sturdy flesh. She felt him shudder as his penis swelled yet further and thrust against the back of her mouth. Then gently, still not saying anything, the gypsy withdrew himself and laid her down on the soft turf, kissing her exposed breasts with his long, expert tongue until they were slick with his mouth's moisture. Marisa moaned softly, running her fingers through the tangle of his silky dark curls, aware that he was shifting himself slightly in order to position his velvety penis just above her swollen breasts. He circled her nipples with its smooth glans, each in turn, while gazing intently at her face.

Marisa wanted to climax there and then. The delicious sensations arrowed down to her womb, and gathered hotly in her throbbing clitoris. She wanted to pull him down onto her, to thrash wildly against him until she felt his delicious shaft sliding deep into her vagina so she could clutch at it with her quivering inner muscles and pleasure herself with it until the waves of longed-for rapture rolled through her. Her honeyed vulva spasmed with tension as she desperately ground her thighs together. She could see the whiteness of his teeth in his dark face as he smiled down at her, deliberately teasing her aching nipples with the smooth head of his penis, making sure that she could see every inch of the long, thick shaft as he slowly rubbed it only inches from her face.

Marisa gritted her teeth and reached out with cold deliberation to caress the heavy sac of his testicles, stroking and pinching the hairy flesh and letting her fingers slide round behind into the musky cleft of his buttocks. Seth groaned aloud and convulsed almost instantly into orgasm. He threw his head back in despair as his lengthy penis started to twitch sweetly against Marisa's taut breasts and his semen spurted out in hot, delicious bursts.

Marisa felt the sticky heat of it on her nipples and rolled away from under him. Then she jumped to her feet and swiftly picked up her discarded clothes and her precious pistol.

He was groaning softly on the ground, pumping himself to expel the last trickle of his semen, too engulfed in the throes of pleasure to move. And the others were certainly beyond caring, noted Marisa swiftly, seeing how they were still avidly pleasuring themselves in the shadows. 'Sorry, Seth,' she whispered. 'Hope you enjoyed it.' And then she ran, twisting through the trees and bushes until the firelit glade was far behind her.

After a few minutes, she paused behind some trees to pull on her clothes and get back her breath. She was genuinely sorry to have duped Seth, but she had more important things on her mind than pleasure, such as how to get out of this damned place. She had no idea where she was, or what to do next, but on coming across a narrow path between the bushes, she decided to take a chance and follow it, every sense alert for the gypsies' pursuit.

Too late, she realised she'd made a mistake. This path was leading her back towards the lights, and the crowds, and danger. On turning a corner, she found herself suddenly amongst a crowd of revellers, and almost instantly she heard a man cry out, 'There she is. There's the blonde wench who gulled Sir Peregrine. Catch her!'

And then they were all around her: men, women, servants, even a man brandishing a violin, all of them screaming at her and blocking her escape until she wanted to put her hands over her ears and shut them all out. 'That's her,' they yelled in chorus. 'She's nothing but a vile little cheat. Take her to the magistrates!'

Marisa's mind whirled with desperate plans, but she was totally surrounded by her captors, and this time even she had to admit that it looked as if she was finished. Damn that mysterious invitation from the Ace of Spades, whoever he was. Damn stupid Sir Peregrine. Damn them all.

Then a new yet somehow familiar male voice broke in on the cacophony, saying coolly, 'Is there some problem here?'

The crowd seemed to part at the sound of that voice, giving Marisa space to breathe. 'Why, yes, my lord,' someone called out eagerly. 'This is the wench who cheated Sir Peregrine, remember?'

'There has, I think, been some mistake,' said the unseen man. 'This wench, as you call her, is with me.'

'But, my lord!'

'You heard me.' The authoritative voice was colder now. 'The lady is mine. If Sir Peregrine has any problem regarding her behaviour, then he can sort it out with me.'

The mob fell away from her, and at last she was able to see the man who spoke. Still trembling with defiance and fear, she gazed up at the painfully familiar figure of Lord James Delsingham, who had removed his black cloak and mask to reveal the undoubted sartorial perfection of a superbly cut coat of grey, superfine wool worn over tight-fitting cream breeches and gleaming black hessians.

He gripped her arm. 'Take your hands off me,' she hissed, but his fingers tightened painfully around her wrist.

'Come, my dear. My carriage awaits, and I rather think it's high time we left the pleasures of Vauxhall, don't you?' he said, in a loud, clear voice that was as brittle as ice. 'Believe me, I can't hold them off for ever,' he added curtly in a lower voice. And with steely purpose he escorted her through the gaping crowd.

'Damn you, what are you playing at?' demanded Marisa, stumbling along beside his tall figure but still struggling to pull her arm away. 'You expect me to go anywhere with you?'

Looking straight ahead, he said, 'They're still following us, my Ganymede. And I feel quite sure that they will follow us at a respectful distance all the way to my carriage. Try to look pleased to be with me, will you?'

'You must be mad to interfere,' she said scornfully. 'Didn't you hear that Sir Peregrine has threatened to set the magistrates on me? You'll only get yourself into trouble for getting involved with me.'

He was steering her relentlessly along the thronged path towards the exit. 'I hardly think so, my dear. I fancy my station in life is a little higher than that.' He smiled gently down at her. 'And while you're under my protection, you are quite immune from further provocation, believe me.'

Marisa dug her heels angrily into the gravel path, bringing him to a halt. 'Under your protection? Let me assure you, I need no-one's protection, my lord.'

'Is that so? Well, we're almost at the exit.' He pointed calmly at the tall redbrick building which housed the official entrance gates. 'Since you insist you can look after yourself, prehaps you'd rather I left you to make your own way out.'

She hesitated, knowing very well that they might have been alerted at the gates to look out for her. On her own, she had no chance. Almost fiercely she thrust her arm once more through his as he escorted her out towards the line of waiting carriages while he continued conversationally, 'I assume you'll deign to take a lift in my carriage? Or would that offend your principles too?'

She had no money at all for a hackney, and he must know it. 'I'll take a lift, but only across the river. After that, I can walk.'

He gazed down calmly at her defiant expression. 'You look remarkably beautiful when you're angry, Ganymede. I take it you've not enjoyed your sojourn in Vauxhall Gardens?'

'I wish I'd never, ever come to this vile place. I wish I'd never even heard of that detestable card party.'

'Presumably,' he said with interest, 'you inveigled your way inside in the hope of duping yet another poor gull like Sir Peregrine, and making off with your winnings.'

'I didn't inveigle my way in. I had an invitation, from the Ace of Spades himself. Damn you, why are you laughing at me?'

He stopped by a beautiful, black glossy carriage, with a coat of arms emblazoned on the door. 'Perhaps,' he chuckled softly down at her, 'because I happen to be the Ace of Spades.'

Marisa gazed up at him blankly, feeling as if a bottomless pit was opening up beneath her feet. 'Then – then why didn't you say something?' she whispered. 'Why didn't you have me thrown out when you first saw me amongst your guests?'

Four liveried manservants were waiting impassively by the carriage for Lord Delsingham's command, but, ignoring them, he said to Marisa, 'I suppose I wanted to see what game you were playing. I felt a certain curiosity about you, you see. And I also wanted to know how the devil you contrived to get into my private party when I'd not invited you.' Marisa started to speak, but he held up his hand quickly. 'No. Don't tell me yet. I'm sure the story of how you obtained your invitation is quite fascinating, but we've no time for it now.'

One of the manservants was silently holding open the carriage door. Marisa tensed, looking round wildly for escape, but Delsingham murmured in her ear, 'Better get in, my dear, before Sir Peregrine arrives. Am I really such a vile prospect?'

Marisa gazed up into his shadowed face, feeling dizzy with danger and excitement and the heady arousal of her encounter with the gypsies. Lord Delsingham, the Ace of Spades, was most definitely not a vile prospect. In fact, he was quite spectacularly handsome, but she wasn't going to let him know that. She said angrily, 'I don't appear to have much choice, do I?'

'Correct,' he acknowledged, his steely grey eyes glinting. Then he handed her up into his carriage, nodding curtly to the driver up on the box who was holding the four beautiful greys in check. Lord Delsingham stepped up behind her. The door closed and Marisa settled down rather faintly against the thickly padded velvet upholstery, her heart beating wildly.

Then suddenly, she heard the pounding of heavy feet outside, and several fists banged roughly on the door. Delsingham opened it so swiftly that it slammed into someone's face. 'The next knave to damage my paintwork will be horsewhipped,' he said. 'What is it?'

Marisa saw the men grovelling as they recognised him. 'My lord. Begging your pardon, but we are officers of the law – Sir Peregrine sent us after you. He accuses the wench in your carriage of cheating him.'

'Is that so?' drawled Lord James Delsingham. 'Then I'm afraid Sir Peregrine is going to be disappointed, because the girl stays with me. I also have business with her, as you see.' And before Marisa could even guess at his intention, he'd drawn her purposefully into his arms, quite heedless of his audience. There were muttered murmurs of 'Yes, my lord. Some mistake, my lord,' and the carriage door thudded shut as the horses strained at their harness and slowly started to pull away.

Marisa pushed fiercely at his wide shoulders, striving desperately to twist her face away, but his powerful arms tightened around her and he murmured, 'They're still watching us, Ganymede. Let's make it convincing, shall we?' and before she could draw breath to reply his mouth closed over hers in a kiss.

At the touch of his lips, something happened to her and her already overwrought senses exploded, out of control. Suddenly she was oblivious to everything except the exquisite movement of his strong mouth on her lips, the delicate flicker of his tongue against her silken, sensitive skin. His kiss intensified; she gave a little whimper, and her hands wound round the back of his neck, her fingers running through his thick black hair as his arms tightened around her and crushed her aching breasts against the hard wall of his chest. There was a dark, agonised yearning at the very core of her being that longed to be assuaged, and as the carriage pulled steadily away, her tongue entwined deliciously with his, drawing him hungrily into her. 'Steady, my sweet,' he murmured softly in her ear. 'We have time enough.' But as his fingers parted her little velvet jacket and silk shirt, and his mouth trailed lingering kisses over the soft swell of her breasts, Marisa moaned with need and pulled him towards her desperately.

With careful strength, he laid her along the soft cushions of the seat and steadily pulled down her chemise to expose her tautly straining nipples. He gazed at them silently, and Marisa caught her breath at the dark hunger in his eyes. Then, very gently, he ran his strong hand up her stockinged thigh beneath her skirt. She trembled violently as his big, strong hands met her melting flesh, and he caressed her there subtly, cupping her with his palm, drawing his long finger between her lushly nectared, flesh folds. She arched against him with a soft cry, almost ready to take her satisfaction from his probing finger, so desperate was she.

'Well, well,' he murmured as his finger did its seductive work, sending shivers of wanton desire shooting through her. 'What games have you been playing in the garden of pleasures tonight, my Ganymede?'

Marisa gasped as the pad of his finger brushed her throbbing clitoris. 'I've had enough of games, damn you. Take me. Take me, now.'

He was still watching her face, his eyes glinting as he said, 'But I thought you didn't have a very high opinion of my amatory skills. Earlier today you made a certain inference about my physique. Remember?'

Marisa groaned. Her eyes slid helplessly down towards his hips, where she could see how his slim-fitting cream breeches were straining across the mouth-watering bulge at his crotch. She replied archly, 'I'm sure you've got a sufficiently high opinion of yourself for both of us.'

He shifted her hips gently to the edge of the seat and eased her legs apart, kneeling on the floor between her thighs. 'Then you will have to decide if that opinion is well-founded, won't you?' he said gently.

He pushed her skirt back up around her waist and dipped his dark head to lick her. His tongue was long and rasping; he stiffened it cunningly and parted her labia with sweet strength as his hands fondled her stockinged thighs. Marisa clutched at his head, pressing his face down against her hungrily, but he was very careful not to bring her to orgasm.

He lifted his face, and she closed her eyes in disappointment. 'I wonder,' he said softly, 'what is your opinion of me now? Have you had enough?'

The gentle motion of the coach forced her to steady herself by hanging onto the leather straps that were fastened into the panelling. 'Bastard,' she hissed through gritted teeth, knowing that her exposed flesh was wantonly pulsing only inches from his face. 'Bastard.'

He smiled, his white teeth glinting in the darkness. 'Tell me what you want and I'll oblige. I'm a man of my word,' he added helpfully.

Marisa sucked in a long, shuddering breath. She would die if he didn't release her soon from this exquisite torment. 'I want you to push your cock into me, damn you,' she cried out at last. 'Now! Whatever its size,' she added ungraciously.

He obliged. As she gripped onto the leather straps to brace herself against the jolting of the coach over the rough road, she saw him reach down to the fastening of his breeches and draw out a long, darkly rigid penis that made her catch her breath in excitement. She felt the swollen petals of flesh between her thighs quiver and trickle with fresh moisture at the proximity of it. His face tense with control, he gripped his shaft carefully and stroked her labia with its velvety blunt tip until she arched towards him, her body shimmering with need. Then he slid his exquisite length deeply into her honeyed recesses as he crouched between her splayed legs, reaching with his hands to cup and fondle her breasts as they spilled hungrily out above the tight confinement of her corset.

Marisa was on the brink of orgasm already. She hung desperately onto the straps as the coach bumped its way along the rutted lane that took them away from Vauxhall towards Westminster Bridge, while he pleasured her slowly and sweetly, his face taut with concentration. She shivered with the warm, intense pleasure of it as he drove the firm length of his exquisite penis deep within her, and she groaned as he withdrew, only to be submerged in utter bliss as she felt him return. She held back for as long as she possibly could, hovering on the very edge of ecstasy. But then his hand slipped down to tangle in the moist, blonde curls that adorned her heated love-mound and his forefinger started to wickedly brush round her swollen clitoris. She gasped aloud and bucked against him as the searing pleasure invaded every nerve-ending. He was good, damn him. So good. Smiling in dark satisfaction, he began to drive himself into her, faster and faster. She glanced down and caught the thrilling sight of his lengthy shaft gliding slickly between her hungry labia. Then his mouth dipped to caress her swollen breasts, sucking and pulling at them with his

620

thin, sensual lips and gently nipping at the hard, dark buds with his teeth. Marisa held her breath as she teetered on the very edge of the abyss. Then she began to throw herself wildly against him, shouting aloud as the fiery waves of pleasure started to engulf her, until nothing existed except the white-hot frenzy of her orgasm as she strained against the straps that supported her and bucked frantically against the exquisite rod of flesh that impaled her.

He drove himself silently to his own powerful orgasm a moment later, and she felt a renewed onslaught of delight as his lengthy penis spasmed deep within her. He lay, just for a moment, with his dark head lying against her breasts, and she felt a sudden tenderness, an unexpected longing to stroke the soft thickness of his hair. But then he drew himself up to sit on the padded seat a little way from her and began, quite calmly, to readjust his clothing. 'Delicious,' he murmured, his appraising eyes flickering over her lush nakedness. 'Quite delicious.'

Marisa's body was still purring with pleasure. She would have liked to curl into his arms, to feel his lips on her hair, her cheek, as she recovered from her rapture. But with those words he seemed to be distancing himself. He sounded like some connoisseur of fine wines, damn him. Any minute now, he would tell her how much she was worth. Swiftly pulling her own clothes back into some semblance of decency, she arranged herself with cold elegance on the seat, and gazed calmly up at his too perfect profile.

'So, my Lord Delsingham. You said earlier that you were curious about me. Is your curiosity sated?'

He smiled lazily down at her, a dark glint in his eyes. 'If curiosity is a kind of appetite, my dear, then I would say that it has been whetted, rather than satisfied. A brief taste of something exquisite makes the hunger for it all the sharper, wouldn't you say?'

Marisa gazed up at him, all wide-eyed innocence. David Valsino would have warned Lord Delsingham to be wary of that look. Pushing back her blonde curls, she purred, 'Perhaps it depends, my lord, on the kind of repast you're used to.'

Delsingham smiled and leaned back against the velvet cushions, stretching out his long, booted legs and brushing a speck of dust from his breeches. He said, 'A full night of pleasure should suit us both, I think. I've ordered my coachman to drive us back to my house in Cavendish Square. There, my dear, you'll get a chance to savour the entire feast.'

Oh, will I? thought Marisa grimly. And you don't even deign to ask me! He was just as conceited, just as impossibly arrogant as the rest of them. She felt a twinge of disappointment, because he'd been such a delicious partner. But there was no time now for regrets.

His arm had moved casually round her shoulder; he'd rested one booted foot carelessly on the seat opposite, and was gazing out of the window. 'We're just coming up to Whitehall,' he announced with satisfaction. 'It won't take us long to get to Cavendish Square.'

Marisa snuggled up to him, her cornflower-blue eyes soft with adoration. 'You're so kind, Lord Delsingham. But,' and she paused innocently, 'how did you know that I wanted to come back to your house, when you didn't even ask me?'

He laughed, his strong hand caressing her shoulder through the fabric of her jacket. 'I have yet to sustain a refusal from any female, Mistress Brooke,' he said.

Marisa patted his thigh lightly as the carriage pulled up in a sudden flurry of traffic close by the King's Mews. 'My dear Lord Delsingham,' she said kindly. 'If you had troubled to get to know me just a little better, you would soon find out that I am not like any other female in existence. In fact, I am the exception to every rule ever made.'

And with that, she jumped lightly to her feet, flung open the door of the carriage, and sprang out into the late-night crowds that were milling along Cockspur Street from the clubs and gaming dens of St James.

'Marisa,' he jumped out after her, with a furious instruction to the coachman to hold the horses. 'Marisa, wait, damn you. Marisa!'

But she evaded him with ease, darting and twisting amongst the crowds until his voice was quite lost.

So much for you, Delsingham, she thought defiantly. But at the same time she was conscious of a twinge of regret, because he really had been a delicious lover, equipped with a devastating body and the finesse to match his looks. If it weren't for his hateful arrogance, he really would rank as an ace amongst the pack.

Nevertheless, it was only a slight twinge. After all, she'd taken her pleasure with him, a fine way to end the evening, and she'd also, during that last, cosy little embrace, taken his lordship's rather fine gold watch. Patting it softly as she slipped it into the pocket of her skirt, she set off briskly for home.

Marisa knew the minute she came within sight of the Blue Bell that something was wrong. Maiden Lane itself was crowded as usual with the late-night revellers who habituated the area's notorious gaming hells and taverns; they staggered along arm-in-arm, much the worse for wear after too much rack-punch and cheap claret. Ripe for plucking, as Lucy would say. But there seemed to be a curious stillness around the narrow courtyard of the Blue Bell. A few candles guttered dimly in the grimy windows, but the front door was firmly closed.

Marisa stood on the corner of the street, frowning, all her instincts warning her of danger. Then suddenly an arm tugged at her, and she turned round to see Lucy, looking distraught and dishevelled.

'Oh, Marisa, thank goodness I caught you in time. You mustn't go anywhere near the Blue Bell – it's been raided!'

Marisa felt her heart miss a beat. 'Raided? By the watch?'

Lucy was panting in distress. 'They said they were officers of the law, but they looked more like robbers to

623

me. John and I came back here just over an hour ago, because we couldn't find you anywhere at Vauxhall, and thought you might have come back home. We got back just in time to see it all. Those brutes were throwing people out onto the street, while they searched the place from top to bottom.'

Lucy's plump, pretty face was stained with tears. Marisa took her hand and said, 'But why, Lucy? Why the Blue Bell? I know there's some illicit gaming – but there are dozens of worse dens around here!'

Lucy gazed at her tearfully. 'It sounds as if they were looking for you, Marisa. You see, that's not all: apparently there were a couple of strangers round earlier this evening, soon after we'd gone out, asking about you. The taproom regulars sent them packing, of course, but they said they didn't like the look of them.'

Marisa's heart seemed to stop. A private vendetta; this was bad news. Who'd put the curs onto her? Lord Delsingham? No: he'd barely have had time to discover that his fine watch was missing, let alone arrange his revenge. Anyway, she doubted if a man of his standing would want to admit to the world that he'd been gulled by a light-skirt. Sir Peregrine? Now, that was more likely. The plump fool was turning out to be quite venomous. He could well have sent a couple of spies to track down her lodgings, even as he pursued her so relentlessly in Vauxhall Gardens. She said evenly, 'It's not the end of the world, Lucy. It should all have blown over by tomorrow.'

'We can stay at my sister's,' said Lucy valiantly through her tears, and Marisa nodded, though her spirits sank at the thought of the noisy, child-filled poverty of Lucy's sister's house in a narrow little alley off Drury Lane.

'That will be fine,' she said. 'Then tomorrow I can collect my things from my rooms, and we'll find somewhere else to live.'

'But they've taken everything, Miss Marisa,' wailed

Lucy in fresh distress. 'Your clothes, your papers – everything.'

Damn, damn, damn. They'd certainly been viciously thorough, too thorough for the stupid Sir Peregrine. Pehaps this was Delsingham's doing after all, his way of taking revenge for the insults she'd offered him this morning. Tonight she seemed to have lost rather a lot, one way or another. Thank goodness for Delsingham's watch, at any rate. Tomorrow she'd take it to a pawn-broker in Clare Market who would ask no questions, and the money from that should keep her going for a while.

Then suddenly she remembered the letter from her notary, Mr Giles, which she'd thrown into the fire earlier that evening. At least the thieves hadn't been able to get their dirty fingers on that. Some sort of bequest, the notary had said. If there was anything she needed now, it was a bequest. Some money, or jewellery? Or yet more notices of debt? She couldn't believe that it was anything of importance, but even so she resolved to go and see Mr Giles first thing in the morning, before her unknown enemy struck again.

Mr Giles was only too pleased to see Marisa, and after some preliminary pleasantries he imparted some news that made her frown in disbelief. For a moment there was no sound except the ticking of the old clock on the dusty mantelshelf of the notary's shabby little office.

'A house?' she repeated incredulously. 'And some money?'

'Yes, indeed, my dear.' Mr Montague Giles leaned back in his aged leather chair and knotted his fingers on the desk before him. 'A rather substantial house, in fact: a little remote, you understand, in the wilds of Hampshire, but a pleasant enough situation, I believe, with nigh on a hundred acres of parkland. And the money that comes with it is not inconsiderable.' He coughed lightly, shuf-fling the papers on his desk. 'A sum of 20,000 guineas, to be exact.'

Marisa felt rather lightheaded, 'Left to my father, you say? But why?'

Montague Giles's, small dark eyes twinkled behind his pince-nez. 'It appears that the owner of the property, Lady Emily Ormond, was an elderly widow, whom your father, er, befriended some years ago when she was taking the waters in Baden. Your father continued to keep in touch with her. Their last meeting, apparently, was in Paris. You don't remember her?'

Marisa shook her head, trying to suppress the urge to laugh. Her father had always had a winning way with older women. There had been hundreds of Lady Emily Ormonds in his life, utterly besotted by his gallant cavalry bearing and his extravagant manners. But, miracle of miracles, this one was rich.

Montague Giles continued, 'She died just over a year ago, predeceasing your father by some two months. It has taken her lawyers some time to track down the beneficiary, namely, yourself. Needless to say, the terms of the will have caused some stir amongst Lady Emily's family.'

'I rather suppose they would,' said Marisa a little breathlessly. 'Who should have inherited the property?'

He shifted his papers, peering through his pince-nez. 'A nephew, I believe, Sir Julian Ormond, but of course there is nothing he can do to contest the will. It's all perfectly sound.'

Marisa nodded, still scarcely able to take it all in. A house. Money. She couldn't believe it. 'Mr Giles, when can I take possession?'

He spread his hands. 'As soon as you like, my dear Miss Brooke. The house is quite vacant. There are some formalities to be concluded, but with your permission, I can handle them easily. Would you like to read through the documents while I order you a dish of tea?'

Marisa glanced at the papers he passed across his desk and felt the familiar sinking feeling at the sight of all that close, spidery writing. She pushed them back. 'You can handle all that, can't you, Mr Giles? And as for the tea, well, I really think that I'd rather have a brandy.'

'Then brandy it shall be. Anything you wish, my dear Miss Brooke, anything at all.'

Delicious words. 'I also think,' Marisa went on slowly, 'that I should like to travel there as soon as possible. I'll perhaps take a day or two to make some suitable purchases here in London, and then I want to take up residence immediately. Will that be possible, Mr Giles?'

He poured them both a generous glass of brandy and lifted his in salutation. 'With your money, my dear,' he said, 'anything will be possible. Anything at all.'

'Oh, good,' said Marisa. She raised her glass, a mischievous smile playing round her lips. 'Let's drink to my inheritance, Mr Giles. And to whatever pleasures might be in store.'

Chapter Four

*I*t was evening and the warm dusk was just starting to enfold the wooded landscape as the big hired chaise, laden with trunks and bandboxes, left the dusty main road and turned in through the high wrought-iron gates. Birds twittered in alarm in the big chestnut trees and a squirrel scampered away towards a distant stand of beeches as the carriage swept up the long drive and pulled to a halt at last in front of the wide, stone steps that led up to the imposing entrance of Melbray Manor. The carriage door opened almost before the horses had stopped, and Lucy jumped out, gazing all around her, breathless with excitement. Marisa followed her more slowly, smoothing down her elegant brown silk travelling pelisse and adjusting her fashionable straw bonnet, newly acquired from Madame Thanier, exclusive Bond Street modiste.

Marisa's expression was outwardly calm and composed as she assessed her new inheritance in the fading light of the velvety spring evening, but in reality her heart was thumping with excitement. Melbray Manor was beautiful, more beautiful even than she had dared to hope. It was a substantial country residence, mellowed by the years so it seemed to blend in with the beautiful mature parkland that surrounded it. Built of honey-coloured stone, its multitude of ornate mullioned windows glinted brightly in the setting sun, while masses of yellow roses half-smothered the weathered stone pillars on either side of the imposing front door, spilling their lush petals across the courtyard. In the warm, still air, their scent was bewitching.

Marisa stood there, gazing silently up at it all. Mr Giles had told her how many bedrooms there were, how many reception rooms, but she'd forgotten the details. 'A gentleman's residence,' he'd said almost apologetically. 'Nothing terribly grand, I'm afraid. There are several far more imposing and palatial homes in that particular neighbourhood.' Then he'd proceeded to tell her about the kitchens and the cellars, and the storerooms and the stables, but she'd not really taken it all in, and anyway it didn't matter. To her, used to cheap lodging houses and rooms above shabby inns, it was palatial indeed. With this house and the money she'd inherited, every one of her dreams could be made reality now. Such delights in store. She drew in a deep breath as she gazed up at the magnificent chestnuts that lined the sweeping driveway, their creamy candles of blossom glimmering like the lamps at Vauxhall in the gathering dusk. All hers. It was so wonderful that she almost laughed aloud. And the best of it was that no-one here would ever, ever guess that she'd clawed her way up to all this, cheating at cards and dice, duping stupid old men, and picking pockets in the teeming back streets of London.

John the coachman, whom she and Lucy had persuaded with very little difficulty to leave the Blue Bell for good, had swung himself down from the driver's seat of the hired chaise and was starting to unharness the horses. They'd travelled post, calling at Esher and Guildford for changes so as to make the best possible speed, and stopping for a wonderful lunch of cold salmon and chilled hock in the private dining room of The Travellers' Rest on the road to Farnham. It had all been wickedly expensive, but as Marisa had casually pulled out the guineas to pay for it all she'd been overwhelmed by the delightful thought that cost was of no consequence now. Mr Giles had given her more than enough money from her inheritance to set herself up quite nicely – until the finalities were completed, he explained.

'You're sure you'll be all right going there straight-away?' he'd asked her yesterday as he gave her the keys, looking just a little anxious. 'The house has been closed up for some time, you know, ever since Lady Emily died. I really don't know what sort of condition it's in.'

Marisa had laughed. 'Dear Mr Giles. For me, it's utter luxury just to be assured of a roof over my head, believe me.'

How her father would have loved it all, she thought regretfully as she gazed up at the beautiful house. Captain Brooke would have played the role of wealthy country gentleman with as much courage and style as he brought to every other role in his crowded life. Drawing a deep breath, she took the big iron key from her reticule and moved with a rustle of silk towards the wide, shallow stone steps that led up to the imposing entrance.

Then she froze as the big oak doors swung open, and a man came out of the house and down the steps towards her, a well-dressed, elegant man with swept-back fair hair and a concerned expression on his refined face.

'Miss Brooke?' he said quickly. 'Please forgive me if I startled you. My name is Ormond, Sir Julian Ormond. I'm Lady Emily's nephew. You are Miss Brooke, I take it?'

'Yes, I am,' replied Marisa, warily holding out her gloved hand as the man bowed low over it. Dear heaven, she thought rather faintly, what was he doing here?

Straightening up, Ormond smiled down at her. 'You'll be wondering what I was doing in the house,' he went on. 'The truth is, Miss Brooke, I've been keeping a bit of an eye on the place. My aunt died some time ago, as you'll know, and there's been no-one to look after the house except me.'

'You live nearby?' queried Marisa rather sharply. This really was an unexpected complication.

'Yes, indeed. I have a place of my own: Greenfallow Park, just the other side of Crayhampton. So, you see, it's been no trouble to me to look after the old place from time to time, send my men over to tidy the grounds up a little, and so on. Now you're here, I won't need to, of course. But please, if there's any way at all I can help, then do feel free to call on me.'

Too good to be true, thought Marisa narrowly. She'd deprived him of his rightful inheritance, and here he was, offering her his help. She gazed up at him with her deceptively wide blue eyes, quickly trying to assess him. 'Thank you,' she said, still wary. 'I'll certainly remember your kind offer.'

He bowed again. 'I sincerely hope you will. And by way of a welcoming gesture, you'll find a cold repast laid out for you in the dining room, Miss Brooke. I do hope you don't mind, but I took the liberty of bringing over some food for you which my own cook has prepared. You see, I suspected you might be tired and hungry after your journey.'

Marisa nodded her thanks, feeling really mystified now. Nobody, in her experience, did something for nothing. What was Ormond after? 'You are very kind.'

'Not at all,' he responded. 'After all, we're going to be neighbours. I hope we'll meet again very soon.' Just then a mounted groom rode out of the shadows by the stable wing, leading another horse forward, a big, stocky grey. Ormond swung himself into the saddle and gathered up the reins. 'You enjoy riding, Miss Brooke?' he said quickly, seeing her watching him. 'You have horses of your own?'

'I love riding,' she acknowledged, then improvised quickly, 'But of course my horses will take a little time to arrive.'

'I have a sweet-tempered mare in my stables that you might enjoy. She could do with some regular exercise. I'll send her over with my groom tomorrow, if you like.' Before she could even think of a reply, he nodded briefly, saying, 'Welcome to Melbray Manor, Miss Brooke,' and set off at a spirited trot down the driveway, his groom riding at his heels.

Lucy was watching him from Marisa's side as he disappeared round the curve of the sweeping drive. 'Something odd about that one,' she pronounced. 'A bit too smooth, if you ask me.'

'As long as he hasn't poisoned the food,' said Marisa lightly. 'I don't feel inclined to make any decisions at all about Sir Julian Ormond, except to be grateful for something to eat. I'm starving. Let's go inside and see what he's left for us.'

Ormond had left them a repast fit for a king: cold baked ham and chicken, vegetable terrines, and tiny tartlets of apricots and strawberries, along with several bottles of delicious white wine. Marisa and Lucy ate hungrily, then piled their plates with fruit and filled their glasses and wandered round exclaiming in delight over everything, while John got on with stabling the horses. The house, though shrouded in dustsheets of brown holland, was spacious and beautifully furnished. On the first floor were ten bedrooms, which Lucy counted excitedly, darting through door after door, while the ground floor contained several oak-panelled reception rooms with lovely full-length windows, crammed with old carved furniture and tapestry wall-hangings. The main reception hall, from which the oak staircase led upwards in a wide, sweeping curve, was adorned with stags' heads and faded oil portraits and ancient weapons. Gaping at it all from the foot of the stairs, Lucy drank down her third brimming glass of wine and turned to Marisa rather breathlessly. 'You'll need plenty of servants to look after a place like this.'

Marisa looked thoughtful. 'We certainly need servants, Lucy. But we'll have to choose them carefully.'

Lucy refilled both their glasses with the cool, pale wine. 'Young, strong and virile, you mean?' she breathed, her brown eyes lighting up.

Marisa laughed. 'I was thinking more in terms of discretion, dear Lucy! If I'm going to fit into local society, then there must be no hint of scandal.' She grinned wickedly. 'At least, not for a while. But you're right. We will find ourselves the most exquisitely endowed servants in all of Hampshire.'

John, who'd been tucking into a hearty cold meal by himself in the kitchen after seeing to the horses, reappeared at this point to ask gruffly if there were any more jobs to be done. Marisa set him to pushing back the big shutters, drawing off dustsheets and lighting candles to bring the old manor to life. As he worked, silent as ever, Marisa curled into the corner of a big, brocade-covered settee at the foot of the stairs and watched him surreptitiously, thinking that at least she'd made a good choice there. He looked big and strong in his corduroy breeches, with the brown leather jerkin that he wore over his white linen shirt emphasizing the brawny width of his shoulders; the candlelight flickered on his tanned face, on his sun-streaked brown hair as he moved stolidly around the room. Marisa suddenly remembered the sight of him pleasuring Lucy in her little bedchamber above the Blue Bell, vividly recalling the mouth-watering sight of his sturdily erect penis, and she felt her pulse quickening. Lucy, who had sat down beside her with yet another glass of wine in her hand, was obviously thinking along the same lines, because she pushed back her dark, loose curls from her slightly flushed face and said, a little breathlessly, 'If we get more manservants, John will be terribly jealous of them.'

'Oh, we'll hire maids as well, and John can join in,' said Marisa airily and the two of them giggled together, feeling more than a little inebriated as they watched John bringing in some logs to lay in the huge inglenook fireplace in the corner of the vast hall.

Lucy lifted up her glass a little unsteadily. 'To Sir Julian Ormond,' she pronounced. 'May he continue to provide us with food and wine – especially the wine.'

Marisa said thoughtfully, 'It certainly is exceedingly generous of him, considering I've deprived him of his inheritance. I wonder what his motive is.'

'He's probably planning to marry you and get his aunt's money back that way,' giggled Lucy, hiccuping slightly. 'Though come to think of it, he doesn't look the marrying kind to me.'

'Whatever do you mean?'

Lucy shrugged; her gown was slipping a little from her plump shoulders. 'Oh, I don't know. He was smooth enough to look at, with his fine clothes and fancy speech – proper gentry and all that – but there was just something about him.' She frowned, but was distracted as John came into the hall again, carrying a basket of logs whose weight made the muscles of his shoulders and upper arms bunch unmistakably beneath his shirt sleeves. Lucy gazed at him and licked her lips. 'Now, there's a fine man. You must try him, Marisa – he's delicious, he really is. He's so strong and sturdy, and he seems able to last for ever.'

Marisa sipped thoughtfully at her wine as she curled up amongst the cushions that were strewn across the big settee. She remembered again how she'd seen John's hot, hungry penis giving such pleasure to the whimpering Lucy, and felt the warm flesh between her thighs start to swell and throb warningly. Turning to Lucy she said coolly, 'I'm not at all sure that he's my type.'

Lucy giggled. 'Depends what you want. He's like an animal: no finesse, no conversation, just good simple pleasure, and that's why he's so valuable. He really wants you, Marisa – haven't you noticed how he's always watching you? Look, he's excited now, because he knows we're talking about him!'

They nestled close to each other on the big settee, giggling and whispering, and John glanced round at them suspiciously, the sweat beading on his wide brow from carrying in all those heavy logs, which he'd coaxed at last into glimmering flames. And Marisa saw, with a sudden dryness in her throat, that what Lucy said was true, because there was already a thick, knotted bulge at his groin, where his stalwart penis swelled and strained against his tight cord breeches. Marisa suddenly realised that after the excitement and tensions of the day, with the wine singing through her body, what she needed now was sex, sex with a strong, willing man who wouldn't make life awkward. And perhaps the pleasure was there for the taking.

The candles John had lit gleamed smokily in the wall sconces, casting a golden, flickering light across the high-beamed hall and making shadows across the stone-flagged floor. John stood there uncertainly, until Marisa called out clearly, 'John. Come over here, will you?'

He walked across the hall with an anxious face, his heavy boots clumping on the flagstones. His erection seemed, if anything, to have grown more noticeable.

'Is there anything else you want me to do, my lady?' he said in his soft, burred voice. 'Just tell me if there is. I'll work all night if you want me to.'

Marisa moistened her lips and leaned forward. She'd taken off her travelling pelisse earlier, and was wearing a demure-looking gown of delicate rose crêpe with long, tight sleeves and a little lace fichu at the neck, a most suitable travelling dress for a lady of gentle birth. But if she loosened the lacings on the bodice, and removed the fichu, and leaned forward, as she was doing now, the gown was very far from demure.

John's eyes fastened dazedly on her high, small breasts as she eased them free of her bodice, with their soft, pink nipples just peeping over the edge, and the dark colour rushed to his face. Marisa saw the unmistakable stirring at his groin and said huskily, 'I don't think you'll have to work all night. But you'll certainly have to be ready for some fairly vigorous exertions. Take out your penis, John, and show it to me.'

Lucy gasped at her side, her brown eyes wide as saucers. John stammered out, agonised with shame, 'But my lady . . .'

Marisa liked him calling her 'my lady.' That, she decided, was what all her servants would call her. 'It's all right, John,' she said calmly, her hands moving thoughtfully over her own provocatively upthrust

635

breasts as she enjoyed the sensations she was arousing in her tingling nipples. 'No need to be ashamed of your virility. Unfasten your breeches, and release your penis.'

He did so with big, trembling hands, and Marisa felt her insides palpitate with lust. A mighty weapon indeed, fat and lengthy, and rearing like a live thing towards her, its bulbous head throbbing and purple. She felt her vulva tingle deliciously at the thought of sliding herself up and down on that beautifully engorged pillar of flesh. She smiled sweetly up at him through her thick lashes, aware of his hot eyes feasting on her naked breasts. 'Do you like my breasts, John?' she asked him gently. 'Would you like to lick and suck at my nipples, and rub your mighty cock against them?'

He lurched towards her, his stiff penis swaying grotesquely. 'Oh, my lady . . .'

She frowned dangerously, crossing her hands across her breasts. 'Restrain yourself, John. Learn some control. And then – ' and she let her angelic face soften again, and ran her hands slowly through her blonde ringlets, 'and then, who knows what I might permit?'

She leaned back languorously on the settee so that her breasts bobbed out pertly above her loosened bodice. Then, letting her knees spread just a little apart, she gently started to draw up the long skirt of her gown until the hem rested across her slender thighs, showing her little laced-up leather boots and her pale silk stockings gartered just above the knee. He stood transfixed, the single eye of his helplessly rampant penis weeping with frustration as he fought not to grab hold of his hot member in his big fist. Marisa saw how his face was contorted as he watched her fingers trail slowly up her leg towards the dark, secret place at the apex of her thighs. She laughed and moved her hand away, watching him all the time. Then she sucked slowly at her finger, sliding her moist lips up and down it suggestively. John groaned aloud.

Marisa said carelessly, her blue eyes gleaming, 'I can see you've got a good cock, John, but that's not always enough, is it? Lucy says you can last a long time, and I want to find out if that's true.' She leaned forward and went on in a husky voice, 'John, I want you to pleasure Lucy with your lips and tongue. If you do so satisfactorily, then I might decide to use you for my own pleasure. Do you understand?'

With a happy little cry, Lucy jumped from the settee and ran to settle herself in a small velvet chair nearby, where she could spread her legs apart and display her nest of curly dark hair to John's lust-crazed view. With an eager growl, he knelt in front of her, pulling her dark-stockinged thighs apart still wider so that Marisa could see the plump pink flesh folds of Lucy's sex, dripping with moisture, desperately craving attention. And John certainly gave her that attention, lapping and licking as eagerly as some thirsty dog at water, drawing his long, rasping tongue happily up and down between her parted labia and rubbing his nose against her clitoris. Then he began to make short, sharp tongue-thrusts deep inside Lucy's hungry vagina until she clutched at his shoulders, beating him with her clenched fists and crying aloud, 'That's it. Yes, John – right up me – oh, yes, yes!'

Marisa leaned back against the settee and sipped at her wine, frowning slightly at the dark eroticism of the candlelit scene. She could see John's ravening penis quivering between his thighs as he worked, and she continued to play lightly with herself, drawing her finger tenderly along the ridge of her throbbing clitoris and imagining the big serving man's rough tongue attending to her own hungry vulva. She could see how his heavy, hairy balls swayed between his buttocks as he worked on Lucy and wriggled his long, snakelike tongue deep inside her. She felt her own hard, keen excitement curling and gathering in the pit of her womb as the stem of her swollen pleasure bud hardened and burned against her delicate finger. With her other hand she fondled her own breasts, feeling the stone-hard nipples pouting hungrily. Nearly there – oh, nearly there. But she would save herself. She needed a good, stout male shaft to slide inside her and pleasure her moist inner flesh, to give her that final, rapturous relief.

Lucy was finished. Even as she sighed out her last shiver of bliss beneath the onslaught of John's tongue, Marisa called out sharply, 'John. Over here.'

He staggered to his feet, his breeches round his hairy thighs, his quivering penis purple with engorgement as it stood up stiffly from the thick, coarse mat of hair at his belly and loins. Marisa, her eyes shadowed with lust, gazed up at him and breathed, 'Now, John. I think it's my turn, don't you?'

He towered over her as she lay back on the settee, his penis throbbing hungrily, and Marisa drew up her skirts, teasingly splaying her thighs for him. With a throaty cry of lust he lowered his hips between her legs and started to thrust eagerly until the swollen, pulsing knob of his mighty shaft pushed its way between her soaking sex-lips and slid slowly, deeply into her aching flesh. With a gasp of rapture Marisa squeezed her inner muscles tightly around his bone-hard phallus and lifted her stockinged legs to lock them around his waist. John, uttering a husky growl, dipped his head to guzzle and suck at her distended nipples, and she felt his bristle-shadowed cheek rubbing deliciously against the soft mounds of her breasts. She shut her eyes, conscious of nothing but the throbbing force of his massive male member driving into her, ravishing her with a sweet, solid thoroughness that made her feel quite delirious with pleasure. She lifted her hips to meet him, grinding herself avidly against him in an effort to bring sharp release to her agonised clitoris, his big tongue snaked and circled at her stiffened teats, pulling them out with his lips and rolling them from side to side, and she gasped aloud, rigid with tension, almost there.

Then, with an indrawn hiss, he drew himself almost out of her, and went very still. She gazed down at his shadowy loins, her eyes hot with fascination. His penis was long and dark and thick, its base encircled by thickly curling black hair, its stalwart stem glistening with her bodily juices. She lifted herself towards him, feeling herself to be hovering on the agonised brink of rapture. Then he began to drive himself into her with strong, vigorous strokes that penetrated the very last of her self-control. Arching her hips, she writhed deliciously against him as the oncoming rapture gathered tightly in her womb, and as he continued to thrust, she reached down to touch her soaking clitoris and soared into great, engulfing spasms of pleasure that racked her whole body.

She felt him explode deep, deep within her, felt his penis twitch and spasm as he groaned in the ecstasy of release, and she lay very still, breathing in the musky male smell of him as the afterwaves of orgasm rolled sweetly through her sated flesh. A ten in the pack, she mused. No finesse, but incredibly well-endowed. Definitely a ten ... 'Good, John,' she whispered, stroking his sweat-streaked thick hair back from his face. 'Very good.'

He lifted his head, quite dazed from his exertions. 'You are pleased with me, my lady?'

'Oh, yes.' She sighed contentedly, stretching out with her hands behind her head, and a happy smile split his suntanned face.

'You're going to let me stay here?'

'Indeed I am. In fact,' Marisa went on softly, 'I think that I shall make you my butler. Melbray Manor ought to have a butler; it's a very important post, John. Would you like that?'

His eyes glittered. 'Oh, yes, my lady.'

Marisa smiled languorously, then began to straighten out her dishevelled clothes. Lucy, who to judge by her flushed face and bright eyes had just teased herself with her finger to yet another intense little orgasm as she watched them, was leaning forward eagerly in her velvet chair. 'And me, Marisa darling? What shall I be?'

Marisa smiled at her, her thick-lashed blue eyes still hazy with satisfied lust. 'You, dear Lucy, can be my personal maid, and my companion in pleasure.'

Lucy sighed happily and went to pour herself yet

another glass of Sir Julian Ormond's fine wine, bringing the bottle over to Marisa.

'I'm hungry,' said Marisa suddenly. 'Let's go and finish off Ormond's food.'

They sat laughing together in the big kitchen, where the whitewashed walls gleamed with copper pots that softly reflected the warm candlelight. They ate chicken and ham pies off silver plates, while John, who saw himself already as the butler of the household, served them eagerly. Lucy was by now quite merrily tipsy, and John, who'd been helping himself to some ancient port he'd found, was almost as inebriated. Soon the pair of them had moved into a shadowy corner, with Lucy kissing him hungrily and running her hands all over his stalwart body.

Marisa sat and watched them thoughtfully, her mind reeling with plans. She wanted servants, fine clothes, a stable full of horses, her own carriage, but above all she wanted to be in control of everything, so she would never be at anyone's mercy, ever again. No-one would ever laugh at her for being poor, or try to take advantage of her. Not that anyone ever had, except for one man.

She found that she was thinking, rather intensely, of Lord James Delsingham. Damn him, he had been an ace indeed, the only one she'd ever known: a truly spectacular lover. A sleek, beautiful thoroughbred, compared to whom John was nothing but a sturdy if serviceable carthorse.

Seeing that John and Lucy were grappling noisily in the corner, she rose silently and made her way slowly up the broad, sweeping staircase. She and Lucy had been busy earlier that evening, finding linen for the beds. She'd left the casement window open in the spacious chamber she'd chosen for herself, and the warm night air was soft on her flushed cheek as she leant on the sill and gazed out into the silent, moonlit beauty of the rolling acres of parkland that surrounded the house. For a moment she thought she saw something moving in the shrubbery beyond the stables, and she stiffened with instinctive fear, suddenly remembering the vicious raid on her rooms in London. It was probably nothing but a breeze stirring the foliage she told herself, smiling at her own stupid nervousness. Everything was going to be wonderful here. But she did feel more than a fleeting regret that the most spectacular man she'd ever encountered was now well beyond her reach, and she would never see him again.

Out in the darkness beyond the walled shrubbery, the man on horseback saw the candles going out one by one in the windows of Melbray Manor, and as he watched his eyes were cold and bleak. When the blonde-haired woman leant out of the first floor window, he moved his horse back quickly into the dark shadows, waiting until she closed the window, gazing impassively until finally her light went out as well.

'Make the most of it all, Marisa Brooke,' he said softly to himself. Then he swung his horse's head around, and guided it swiftly away into the blackness of the enveloping woodland.

Marisa was awakened the next morning by warm sunlight flooding through the heavy curtains. For a moment she lay wondering where she was, unsettled by the silence. What had happened to the clamour of the street sellers and hawkers, the rumbling of iron wheels on cobbles, the barking of the hungry dogs in nearby Maiden Lane?

Then she remembered, and pulled herself up against her luxurious feather pillows, letting her eyes feast on the silken hangings of her beautiful mahogany bed, on the delicate rose-covered paper on the walls and the exquisite walnut furniture that was arranged around the spacious room. Hers, all hers. She drew a deep breath of satisfaction. Then she realised that she'd overslept. Outside the birds were singing and the sun was hot against the front of the house. Quickly she threw off the bedcovers and ran to the window, dressed only in her cotton shift, to tug back the heavy drapes and fling the casement wide open.

Her eyes widened when she saw that down below her in the sunny courtyard was a beautiful chestnut mare, fully harnessed and saddled, her head held by an anxious looking young groom who gazed around him uncertainly. She remembered in a blinding flash that last night Sir Julian Ormond had promised to send her over a horse, and she'd quite forgotten. Wondering with a stab of guilt just how long the young groom had been waiting there, she hurriedly dressed herself in her plainly cut, dark, cloth riding habit and pulled on her little leather boots. Then she ran a silver-backed brush through her disordered blonde curls and tied them back with a black velvet ribbon, quickly checking her reflection in a long cheval glass before running down the stairs and struggling to heave back the big bolts on the heavy front door. Where, she muttered to herself, was John? Probably snoring in Lucy's arms in some rumpled bed, utterly sated on wine and sex, damn him. Soon she would have to get the two of them into order. Swearing under her breath, she got the door open at last and stepped out blinking into the bright sunshine.

If the groom was surprised to see the lady of Melbray Manor herself opening the front door, then he made a valiant effort to conceal it, though he was obviously overwhelmed by the sight of Marisa herself.

'Sir Julian Ormond sent me, my lady,' he stammered out, his eyes dazzled by her blonde, petite figure, set off to devastating effect by her black riding habit with its long, elegantly cut skirt and tight-waisted little jacket. 'He promised you this mare yesterday, I believe.'

Marisa bestowed on him one of her most charming smiles, and saw him melt. 'How very kind,' she breathed. 'Thank him from me, won't you?'

'I will, my lady.' Eagerly he handed over the reins. 'She's a spirited ride, but she has a lovely temper. As you see, my master's already had her saddled and tacked up.

He says if there's anything else you need, then just send over to him.'

Marisa took the mare's bridle and fondled her silky nose. 'She's beautiful. Tell him that I'm extremely grateful.'

The groom, still blushing and by now utterly smitten, touched his forelock and moved away bashfully to mount his own big horse and ride off down the drive.

Marisa watched till he was out of sight, then turned to her new acquisition. 'Well, my beauty,' she breathed, running her hand down the mare's warm, sleek neck. 'Our neighbour Ormond certainly seems to be a surprisingly generous friend. I wonder why?'

The mare whickered softly and rubbed at Marisa's hand, eager for titbits, and Marisa felt her heart thrill at the sight of her lovely, clean lines, her muscular flanks and elegantly arched neck. Knowing she should have waited, or at least told Lucy or John where she was going, she nevertheless decided to take her out straight away; the prospect of a morning ride through her very own property was quite irresistible. Gently murmuring to the mare to soothe her high-bred restlessness, she led her across to the old stone mounting block in the corner of the yard and eased herself up into the side-saddle, bringing one leg round the pommel and neatly adjusting her skirt. She much preferred to ride astride, but even so it was wonderful to be on horseback again. She felt the mare move sweetly beneath her as she gathered up the reins and set her in motion. The sun was warm on her face and the air moved lightly against her cheek as she circled the gardens and headed for a wide, grassy ride that led between the trees towards a distant stand of oaks.

She still couldn't believe that all of this was hers. There was no other dwelling in sight: just the endless green turf stretching through the cool woods, and the blue sky on the horizon. Carefully, feeling the mare's willing eagerness through the tips of her fingers as they caressed the reins, she eased her into a gliding canter. To feel the soft breeze in her face, to feel the beautiful horse gather and stretch in glorious rhythm beneath her, was wonderful. Within a few minutes, Melbray Manor was out of sight, and apart from the curlews that wheeled over the distant downs, she was the only living figure in the landscape. Once, she thought she heard hooves behind her, and she pulled in to listen, but there was nothing except the melodious sound of the birds in the trees, and the ripple of the little stream that ran nearby. Her path lay across the stream; she negotiated it carefully, then brought her horse up to speed again and cantered on, her hair streaming out behind her.

And then, with unexpected abruptness, she felt the saddle lurching to one side beneath her. Gasping, Marisa clutched at the reins, but the mare, panicking at the sudden shifting of the weight on her back, shied and reared up with a fierce whinny. Marisa grabbed for her mane, but her fingers slid through it helplessly. She felt herself fly through the air, and as her head and shoulders hit the ground with a thump, she felt shooting sparks of pain, followed by absolute blackness.

Some moments later, she opened her eyes slowly to feel strong male arms cradling her and something cold and cool being pressed to her forehead.

'Marisa,' a strangely familiar voice was saying urgently. 'Marisa, are you all right?'

She nestled instinctively into the man's shoulder, feeling safe and warm. Her head still throbbed with pain, but the coldness at her temples was wonderfully soothing. 'Yes,' she replied dazedly, 'yes, I'm all right, but my head aches abominably . . .' She opened her eyes, but the overhead sun sparkling between the trees all but blinded her, and she shut them again. 'What happened?'

'You fell off your horse,' the unseen man was saying thoughtfully as he continued to dab the wet, cold muslin of his handkerchief against her forehead. 'And it must have been quite a knock to keep you silent for such a long time. My dear Miss Brooke, you've not insulted me yet, nor stolen anything. I really feel quite anxious about you.'

Marisa sat bolt upright at that, and the pain shot through her head again. With sheer disbelief, she gazed up into a pair of amused grey eyes that glinted with sparks of gold. Delsingham – Lord James Delsingham. 'Hell and damnation! What are you doing here?' she gasped.

He chuckled, but kept his arm around her shoulders. 'Now, that's more like it, my fair Ganymede. For a moment, I was beginning to think that the fall had done you irreparable damage. In answer to your question, I'm here because this just happens to be my land. But what are you doing here? I'd like to think you were paying a courtesy call to return my pocket watch, but that seems just a little too much to hope.'

She heard the gasp of her own indrawn breath. 'Your land? But it can't be.'

'Really? Why not?'

'Because,' declared Marisa heatedly, 'it's mine!'

For a moment, she had the minor satisfaction of seeing Lord Delsingham look blankly amazed, then he put his hand to his forehead and said, very slowly, 'Melbray Manor. You're the new owner of Melbray Manor. Dear God, I don't believe it.' And he began to laugh, very softly. 'No, don't tell me, sweet Marisa. You won it at cards, didn't you? Either that, or you lifted the title deeds from someone's pocket, or you blackmailed some elderly, besotted lover into giving it to you. Come on, now, which was it?'

She sat up rather abruptly, pushing him away. 'You'll just have to believe it, I'm afraid, because it is mine! It was bequeathed to my father, and now it's come to me. Whatever made you think this was your land, Lord Delsingham? Or are you just in the habit of claiming everything you set eyes on?'

Delsingham said carefully, 'I live at Fairfields, which is further down the valley. My land, Marisa, adjoins yours. The boundary between our properties,' and he lifted his hand to point, 'is that little stream back there, and you've crossed it. The land on which you chose to fall off your horse, sweet Marisa, is mine.'

She gazed up at him, still a little faint from the shock of her fall, her heart stupidly pounding. Oh, no. So Lord James Delsingham was her neighbour. And he knew her for what she was, a gambler, a trickster, a thief . . .

She snapped, 'I didn't fall off. I never fall off!'

He was getting to his feet, calmly brushing bits of grass from his beautiful grey riding coat and breeches. 'Is that your usual method of dismounting, then?'

'No,' retorted Marisa, following his example and pulling herself upright. 'It was the saddle – ' She broke off suddenly, remembering. There had been something wrong with the saddle. And where was her horse? It had been a mistake to get up so quickly; her head swam again and he put his arm round her, steadying her, but she pushed him away, saying tensely, 'My mare – was she injured?'

'I caught your horse,' he said quietly. 'She's fine; she's tethered beside mine, over by that tree. And you were right about the saddle. It came off just after you did. It's just there.' She glanced at where he was pointing, and saw the horses, and the big leather side-saddle lying arched on the grass. He went on, almost casually, 'Who saddled up that horse for you, Marisa?'

She said defensively, 'Sir Julian Ormond's groom brought her over ready saddled this morning.'

He looked astonished. 'Ormond?'

'Yes,' Marisa retorted hotly. 'He welcomed me last night, and offered to send over one of his horses for me until I could get my own.'

He looked as if he were about to say something, then he seemed to change his mind, remarking simply, 'I should be a little wary of Ormond, if I were you.'

'He's been most courteous. He brought me food, and wine, and offered his help in any way I wanted.'

Delsingham said kindly, 'He obviously doesn't know

you yet, if he thinks you need help. Where is my watch, Marisa?'

She felt herself colour faintly, then met his penetrating gaze with defiance. 'Who knows? One of the fences in Clare Market took it from me; it could be anywhere by now. Anyway, it's all you deserved, for your arrogant presumption in just expecting me to come back with you to your house for the night.'

He started to laugh, his hands resting on his hips. 'You would have enjoyed yourself,' he said.

Marisa swallowed. She had no doubt at all of that. He was still just as devastating as she remembered, his figure tall and wide shouldered in his beautifully cut dark grey riding coat, with his cropped dark hair slightly ruffled by the warm breeze. Her eyes slid surreptitiously down to his long, hard thighs, encased in tight buckskin breeches and high riding boots. She remembered how deliciously he'd pleasured her that night in his carriage, and she felt her head swim again and was only too aware that her breasts were tingling uncomfortably against the tight jacket of her riding habit.

She tossed her loose hair back and said scornfully, 'I find you quite amazingly arrogant. But then, I suppose someone as rich as you finds it hard to believe that not every woman is just waiting to fall into bed with you.'

'I don't invite every woman, by any means,' he said evenly. 'I'm actually quite fastidious.'

'And so am I. Now, if you'll excuse me, I think it's time for me to go.' And she turned to march quickly towards her waiting mare, bending to pick up the side-saddle that lay on the grass nearby.

It was impossibly heavy. Gritting her teeth, she looped her arms beneath it and struggled to pull it up, while Delsingham, curse him, was just standing there watching her with his arms folded across his chest, and that maddening smile still twisting his damnably handsome face.

Then she remembered. He'd told her the saddle was broken. She dropped it with a thud and a curse. He said calmly, 'Oh, by the way, I did fix it for you earlier. One of the girth buckles had come adrift. I replaced it with one of mine, while you were recovering from your fall.' Marisa stared at him, speechless. He said, encouragingly, 'Aren't you going to thank me? You really need to learn some manners, sweet Marisa, if you're going to be mistress of Melbray Manor.'

She clenched her fists at her sides. 'I need no tuition from you about how to conduct myself.'

'I think you do,' he said regretfully. 'For example, Marisa, real ladies don't go galloping about the country-side without a groom in attendance.'

'I haven't got a groom yet. I've not had time to appoint all the servants I need, but I will. I've got money enough for anything.'

He laughed, leaning his back against a tree, his arms still folded. 'Another mistake, my dear. Real ladies don't talk about how much money they've got. Somehow, I don't think Hampshire society is quite ready for you. What's it worth, sweet Marisa, not to tell all your fine new neighbours that you're a thieving little card-sharp from the back streets of London?'

Enough. The rage swelling in her heart, Marisa, quick as lightning, darted for the hateful man's riding crop where it lay on the ground near his feet, and lunged to strike him in a fluid, graceful movement that David Valsino would have been proud of.

But he was quick too. He parried the blow just in time with his forearm, and trapped her hand as she struggled out blindly. 'Steady, steady,' he murmured, grasping her arms easily in his strong hands and holding her firm as she twisted and writhed in his grasp. 'You seem to forget that I hold all the aces here. I know all about you, you see, and I could quite spoil all your little plans. What are they exactly, I wonder? Do you plan to cheat the local gentry at cards? Rob them of their silver and jewels, perhaps? Or maybe find yourself a rich, rich husband who'll oblige you in your every whim?'

Marisa sagged in his arms, her head bowed in defeat,

utterly silent. He frowned and relaxed his grip a little. 'Marisa? It's not like you to take a rebuke so quietly. Are you all right, Marisa?'

The minute she felt his strong grip loosen, she drew back her little booted foot and kicked him hard on the calf. His boots were sturdy, but so were hers, and she'd caught him just on the tenderest part of his leg, where the shin bone was close to the skin. As he swore vigorously and staggered back, she turned and ran desperately for her horse, stooping once more to pick up the saddle. Now that she knew it was mended, she must be able to get it back on, she must . . .

But she didn't even get to lift it from the ground. Delsingham was behind her, grabbing her by the waist. She lashed out blindly, but she lost her balance and the next thing she knew, she was sprawling face down across the arch of the saddle with its warm leather curves pressing up into her belly and ribcage. Her enemy was instantly behind her, kneeling over her, breathing hard. She could feel the substantial weight of him pressing against her back, could feel his warmth against her cheek.

'Let me go,' she hissed out, struggling desperately. 'Damn you, Delsingham, let me go!' She tried to twist round, to see her tormentor, but he'd imprisoned her quite firmly, kneeling over her as she sprawled helplessly across the steep curve of the saddle. 'Sweet Marisa,' he was saying tenderly, 'you really are quite adorable when you're angry.'

And then she realised, to her horror, that he was doing something with the stirrup leathers; he'd twisted them round her wrists, and was binding them swiftly to the pommel, tightening the straps by gradual but definite degrees so she was quite unable to pull them free. She hissed aloud and tried to twist round to face him, but she couldn't even manage that. Her long curls streamed across the saddle to the ground, blinding her: she could smell the well-oiled leather, and the grassy turf close to her face, while the steeply rounded curve of the saddle across which she lay arched her body up towards her captor. Her knees just touched the ground where the saddle rested; her buttocks were clenched high, and the underswell of her breasts was caressed through her clothing by the warm, smooth leather. She almost sobbed aloud, so trapped did she feel. What was he planning to do? She could hear him moving gently behind her, but had no idea what was going on. Would he leave her here, or perhaps beat her for her attack on him? She suddenly remembered his ominous words to her at their first, fateful meeting outside David Valsino's house, when she'd insulted him so rashly, 'I should take a horsewhip to you for that, sweet Ganymede. Some day, perhaps I will . . .'

She shivered at her helplessness. Her nipples sprang into taut life, and she felt the soft folds of flesh between her thighs pulse and tingle. What was her enemy going to do to her?

She didn't have to wait long to find out. She felt the sudden kiss of cool fresh air on her sensitised flesh as he carefully lifted up her heavy riding skirt and flimsy silk chemise to expose her bottom. She shuddered with shame as his hands slid softly over her upraised buttocks, and again she tugged desperately at the straps that bound her hands firmly to the heavy saddle. Then she gasped aloud as she felt his fingers slide down her thighs, as far as the delicate ribbon garters that held her silk stockings just above her knees, and slowly, with infinite tenderness, he eased her legs apart, and she felt all the hot, naked shame of knowing that he would be feasting his eyes on the dark, glistening flesh of her exposed femininity. Even though she couldn't see him, she could picture him gazing down at her. She could also imagine only too well the powerful stirring of his magnificent manhood, and the shaming moisture of arousal trickled anew down her thighs. Oh, but she wanted him, wanted him desperately.

His finger trailed up her thigh and brushed lightly against her silky folds, sliding in their nectar. She gasped and clenched her teeth to hold back the moan of need. He was saying thoughtfully, 'You obviously enjoy horse riding very much. Considering your low opinion of me, I really can't imagine what else can have aroused you so.'

'Certainly not you,' she hissed out. Then she moaned again as his finger slid down her juicy cleft and thrust, very gently, into her warm vagina.

'Are you quite sure?' he enquired.

She pushed back against him, unable to help herself, longing to feel more of him caressing her so wickedly, but he slowly withdrew his finger, and she slumped across the saddle in burning disappointment and shame. 'Damn you,' she muttered against her arm, the tears of shame starting to burn at the back of her eyelids.

And then she gasped, and couldn't even think of saying any more, because his warm, firm hands had clasped the creamy globes of her bottom, and were kneading and pulling gently at her sun-warmed flesh. She was aware that he was kneeling behind her, nudging her legs even further apart. And then she felt the glorious, velvety kiss of his erect penis nudging gently between her thighs and probing at her honeyed cleft, gradually easing its way with blissful skill between her swollen labia. For a moment he paused, and she groaned aloud and pushed her buttocks back against him helplessly, picturing that proud, lengthy phallus poised so deliciously at the entrance to her yearning vagina. Then she heard the hiss of his indrawn breath as he prepared himself for entry, and she realised, with a shudder of excitement, that he was every bit as fiercely aroused as she was. She held her breath, until, with incredible, measured power, he mounted her at last, sliding his exquisite length slowly into her aching vulva from behind and holding it there, very still.

She let her flesh palpitate all around him, relishing every second of the bliss of having him filling her, impaling her on his hot, bone-hard shaft. Then he began to move, very slowly. He was still kneeling on the ground behind her, tenderly gripping her buttocks as he pleasured her, powerfully driving his strong phallus in and out as Marisa, bound helplessly over the saddle in front of him, gasped out in shameful delight. Oh, but he was delicious. His penis was so firm, so lengthy, so controlled. She began to whimper aloud as he leaned into her, feeling his flat, hard belly against her buttocks and his heavy balls swinging against the backs of her thighs, while his hand slid slowly but surely up her stockinged thigh, reaching round to stroke her heated mound and delicately circle her fiercely throbbing clitoris as he continued to ravish her slowly, beautifully.

She pulled and strained in her excitement at the leather straps that bound her, throwing back her head and biting her lip. His hand moved forward to slip under her tight jacket, feeling its way under her bodice to grasp and squeeze at her stiffened nipples, twisting them gently until the darts of exquisite pleasure-pain shot down to join the fierce, demanding heat of her clitoris. Marisa writhed ecstatically beneath his body as he covered her, thrusting herself back with hungry jerks to engulf his massive penis, almost swooning with delight at the sensations aroused by the solid, lengthy shaft of flesh sliding gently but firmly inside her honeyed vagina, caressing her trembling inner core with such consummate skill that she was already whimpering and crying out his name as the hot sun beat down through the dappled shade of the trees. At last, just when she thought she would scream out with longing, his strong, teasing finger brushed lightly but persistently against her quivering bud of pleasure, and she bucked helplessly as the pleasure began, raising her bottom to him in wild abandon as he began to thrust faster, deeper. His hand pressed harder against her clitoris, and she toppled over the edge into wave after wave of excruciating pleasure, rubbing her nipples against the oiled leather of the saddle beneath her, clutching her inner muscles tightly around his delicious shaft of flesh and crying aloud all through her endless, luscious climax. Sighing, she collapsed face down across the sweat-sheened leather, dimly aware that he too was losing his iron control at last. She felt him clutching at her bottom cheeks and pounding into her until his mighty rod twitched and pulsed in release at her very core. Then he leant his cheek against her back and reached to softly stroke her aching, swollen breasts, and all she could hear was the sound of their two horses unconcernedly cropping the grass nearby.

Exquisite, thought Marisa dazedly, quite exquisite. And wholly dangerous. Whatever happened, she mustn't ever let him know how wonderful a lover he was.

Gently, he pulled down her skirt to cover her nakedness and Marisa felt a pang of extreme regret as his warm body moved away from hers, because she'd have liked him to hold her, to kiss her tenderly. Then the cold leather straps biting into her wrists brought her back to reality. How dare he treat her like some back-street slattern? Her hands were still tethered, but she managed somehow to twist her head round and face him, her blue eyes suspiciously wide and innocent.

'Well,' she said, surveying him almost with pity as he readjusted his clothes, 'it seems, my Lord Delsingham, as if I was right on our first encounter.'

His grey eyes narrowed warningly as he smoothed down his coat. 'And what exactly do you mean by that, Ganymede?'

'I mean,' Marisa said kindly, 'that you've just proved to me yet again that no self-respecting female would come to you of her own accord. You've already told me that you're willing to pay for pleasure, and now you've shown me that where money fails, you'll take what you want by force.'

His thin, sensual mouth curled slightly. 'Be careful, sweet Marisa. You enjoyed yourself rather thoroughly, I think.'

She said scornfully, wrenching at the straps, 'You think I'd have let you do all that to me willingly, my lord?'

He bent gracefully on one knee to unstrap her with his long, dextrous fingers. 'I think,' he said, 'that you are rather proud, and I simply made it somewhat easier for you to accept my advances. You can protest as much as you like now that it's over, but you can't deny that you enjoyed it.'

Her hands were free. She struggled to haul herself up from the saddle and stood there before him, still dizzy with pleasure. Then she pushed her hopelesssly tangled hair back from her face and smoothed down her crumpled skirt and hissed, 'It must be wonderful to have such a high opinion of yourself. What a shame your physique and skills don't match it.'

He laughed. 'So we're playing games now, are we, Marisa? You like it that way?' He tilted his head a little to one side, assessing her dishevelled figure with mocking eyes. 'We'll come to an agreement then, since you profess you won't come to me willingly. You give me what I want, and I'll promise in return not to give you away to your respectable new neighbours. I won't tell them that the new mistress of Melbray Manor is no lady.'

She caught her breath at the enormity of his suggestion, and yet she felt the excitement curl through her entrails at the silky promise in his voice. 'If I were a man, Lord Delsingham, I'd call you out.'

He calmly strapped her heavy saddle onto her horse's back, then turned back towards her, his grey eyes dancing. 'What an enchanting idea. A duel at dawn – swords or pistols?' He laughed aloud. 'Such a pity you're not a man – in some ways, that is.' His eyes lingered on her breasts beneath her little buttoned-up jacket, and she felt hot again in a sudden shameful rekindling of desire.

'Some day,' she said shakily, 'some day, Lord Delsingham, you will receive my challenge, I assure you.' She scrambled up into the high saddle and gathered up the reins to pull away from him, her face tight with chagrin, but he held onto the bridle a moment longer.

'Marisa,' he said, his voice suddenly more serious as he gazed up at her. 'One thing you ought to know. That saddle strap was bound to break some time during your ride; there was scarcely an inch of sound leather at the buckle.'

She scanned him coldly. 'Then it was an unfortunate accident.'

'No accident,' he said curtly. 'The strap had been cut. Be careful, Marisa.'

She felt a sudden cold chill as the sun went behind a cloud. It was a lie. He was deliberately trying to frighten her. 'I'm quite used to looking after myself, Lord Delsingham, believe me,' she retorted, and turned her horse's head sharply back towards Melbray Manor.

Chapter Five

*L*ater that same morning, Sir Julian Ormond, nephew to Lady Emily, was disturbed by a tentative knock at the door of the anteroom to his bedchamber. He pulled himself up quickly, gathering his exquisite brocade dressing robe around himself and girding it at the waist. The two half-naked, tousle-haired gypsy girls he'd met the day before at the fair started to get up too, but he beckoned them back.

'Stay here,' he said curtly. 'And say nothing.' He let his eyes linger on them, just for a moment. They were a couple of sluts, but ripe and willing enough, especially the plump one with billowing red hair and mischievous green eyes. She looked as if she would enjoy anything. He smoothed his dressing gown over his slim hips, hoping the loose folds would conceal his erection, and went out into the anteroom to answer the knock. It was almost noon. The sun beat down outside, but here in the private quarters of Greenfallow Park the heavy damask drapes were all drawn, and the air was dark and stifling.

He opened the big mahogany door. It was the young groom, the one he'd ordered to take the mare across to Melbray Manor earlier. The man looked pale and anxious, not a good sign. 'Well?' Ormond questioned him softly.

The groom swallowed. 'I took the horse to her, sir, just as you instructed. The woman set off immediately, by herself, and I followed her at a safe distance like you said. She never saw me, I swear it.'

'And?' Ormond's voice was smooth, dangerous.

'She rode onto Lord Delsingham's land, sir, just across Trickett Brook, and it was over there that the strap broke. She was cantering, and she took a nasty tumble and had all the breath knocked from her.'

'So. You moved in, I take it?'

'N-no, sir,' stammered the nervous groom. 'I couldn't, because Lord Delsingham himself turned up. The last I saw, he was bathing the woman's head with water from the stream. I thought I'd better make myself scarce, in case there were some of his men around.'

Sir Julian Ormond had gone very still. A shaft of sunlight from the corridor outside caught his smooth fair hair; his eyes were pale and cold. 'So,' he said thoughtfully. 'Rather a waste of time, then, wouldn't you say?'

The groom shrugged his shoulders, his relief only too apparent because his master didn't seem particularly angry. 'I suppose so, sir. Better luck next time, perhaps – '

And then he broke off, because Ormond suddenly struck him hard across the cheek with his well-manicured fingers. The groom cried out and twisted to one side to avoid the follow-up, but Ormond had quickly grasped one of the riding whips that stood in the stand by the door and began to systematically beat him across the back and shoulders. The groom cowered, driven to his knees by the sheer force of the blows, trying to protect his face and head with his hands. He was wearing a sleeveless leather jerkin which protected him from any real damage, but even so he trembled as the lash snaked down across his shoulders again and again.

At last Ormond seemed to tire. He stepped back and said in a low, vicious voice, 'Get out of my sight.' The groom, half sobbing, scurried out and shut the big door behind him, leaving the room in heavy darkness once more.

Ormond stood there for a moment, forcing his breathing to slow down. He could feel his penis thrusting hot and urgent against the folds of his rich brocade robe. He rubbed it slowly, slipping his hand under his robe to caress the hard, silken length before returning to the curtained darkness of his bedchamber, where the air was thick with the cheap, potent scent of the gypsy girls.

Marisa Brooke had fortune on her side, it seemed. His eyes narrowed in thought as he turned back, and then he saw that the door of his bedchamber was ajar, and that the two gypsy girls had been peeping out, watching him all the time.

Their eyes were alight. The redheaded one said softly, 'We were interrupted, I think, my lord,' and he suddenly wanted them badly. They moved quickly aside as he swept back into the bedchamber and eased himself onto his huge curtained bed, letting his robe fall back from his slim but muscular body so they could see that he was fully erect. 'We were indeed interrupted. Carry on,' he said tersely.

The gypsy girls moved in on him eagerly, their imitation jewellery tinkling and the cheap, musky scent that they used wafting through the dark, airless room. The plump redhead was on his left, and the smaller, dark-haired one called Matty on his right. Both wore blowsy, full-skirted gowns in bright colours, with gaudy laces and ribbons. They'd unlaced their bodices earlier so he could feast on the sight of their lusciously naked, sun-browned breasts, and now the dark haired one was bending to take him in her mouth while the other one just watched him, teasing at her dark brown nipples with her fingers and running her tongue along her lips.

His penis strained hot and hungry beneath the girl's tongue as she avidly licked and sucked at the hardened flesh, and his testicles ached. She started to rub at the base of his engorged shaft with eager fingers and he felt the pressure building black and hard at his temples as her eager mouth danced and glided along his straining shaft.

Then the redheaded woman, the one that first caught his eye at the fair yesterday, glanced at her friend's ardent efforts, and turned to look through the open door into the anteroom, where the leather whip lay discarded on the floor. She wandered slowly out to pick it up, then came back and stood by the bed, fingering the lash meaningfully. Matty stopped what she was doing, leaving the man's cock sticking red and angry into the air, and Ormond's breath caught raggedly in his throat. His penis twitched; a fresh drop of moisture glistened at the tip of the swollen glans.

'You'd like a touch of this, my fine lord?' said the redhead softly, licking her pouting lips with her tongue as she fingered the leather lash and drew the handle meaningfully across her own lushly exposed breasts.

Ormond swallowed, his penis jerking helplessly now as it thrust up from the circle of fine, blond hair at his loins. He grated out, 'Yes. Yes, damn you.'

Rowena stood beside the bed, and used the whip to raise her own full skirt teasingly so that he could see the tops of her dark serge stockings. Then she lifted the hem even higher with the solid whip handle and slid its smooth tip between the tops of her plump white thighs, drawing it to and fro against her exposed vulva and closing her eyes in pleasure. The dark-haired one climbed onto the bed by Ormond's feet and lay on her front, her chin in her hands, watching her friend avidly. Then, suddenly, the redhead moved, flicking out the long lash so that it curled across Ormond's taut belly, just inches from the waving stem of his angry penis. He cried out in a despairing mixture of pleasure and pain. She bent over him so her ripe breasts dangled near his face, drawing the silky lash round his bulging testicles and pulling very lightly so the plump, hair-covered globes were slightly lifted from his body. He moaned softly as she tugged at the lash and it slowly came free again.

She stood there, watching him. 'On your knees, now, my lord,' she said huskily, her voice a whisper of promise. 'Matty, pull off his lordship's fine gown, will you? I've a fancy that this is what he's really after.'

Ormond slid off the bed, trembling in spite of the warmth of the room, feeling weak with desire and excitement. Wordlessly he crouched on all fours on the floor, feeling the harsh wool of the carpet scratching against his hands and his knees, and the girl Matty slipped off his dressing robe and crouched behind him, fondling the twin globes of his tight, small buttocks.

'There you are, my lord,' she whispered happily. 'Aren't you a pretty picture, now? He's all yours, Rowena dear.' And she lowered her head to gaze avidly at his yearning red penis as it thrust hungrily up against his tense belly.

It was then that Rowena struck. Standing with her legs planted firmly apart just behind him, her full breasts quivering as she moved, she used the silky lash to caress and sting alternately, to bring the heated blood to his pale taut skin, and Ormond pressed his cheek against the floor and closed his eyes. Then Matty, nodding in silent communication with her friend, slipped lithely beneath him and started to lick avidly again at his stiff, ravening member, sliding her moist lips up and down as far as the silky coronal of pale pubic hair, while Rowena, with a little smile on her rapt face, reversed the whip and started to probe at his tight buttocks with the tip of the smooth leather handle.

Ormond groaned aloud as he felt that intimate, insistent caress at his dark, secret cleft, and Rowena dropped swiftly to her knees behind him so that she could make a more accurate assault, pulling apart his bottom-cheeks and stroking thoughtfully with her fingers at the tight anal aperture. There was some balsam oil on the dressing table. She got up quickly to fetch it and kneeled down again, anointing her fingers with it and probing gently with each digit until they slipped in past the tight collar of muscle. Ormond shuddered, and Rowena, pulling out her fingers and quickly rubbing oil onto the whip handle, started to slide the thick, rounded handle into the puckered little opening, feeling him quiver and convulse around it as she invaded him, slipping it lazily in and out while the man shuddered with torment.

'This is what you wanted all along, isn't it, my fine and fancy gentleman?' muttered Rowena under her breath, her green eyes glittering. 'I knew it as soon as I saw you yesterday at the fair, with all your grand clothes and haughty manners. All high and mighty, you pretend to be, but I've met your type before. Go ahead, Matty.'

And Matty, still crouching beneath Ormond's bowed, quivering body, nodded eagerly and renewed her efforts, sucking and licking at the man's hot, straining penis until it was thrusting helplessly at the back of her throat. He arched his back desperately as Rowena continued to pleasure him with the oiled whip handle, and clenched his buttocks so tightly round it that she thought it would break. Then he cried out, and he was spurting hotly, juicily into Matty's mouth, his hips thrusting furiously, his refined face contorted with degrading pleasure. Matty swallowed hungrily, running her fingers around his throbbing testicles, enjoying the salty taste of him and relishing his helpless spasms as his semen spurted forth.

At last, he was finished. As Rowena silently withdrew the whip handle from his quivering buttocks, he drew himself up, his face pale and expressionless, and pulled on his discarded bed robe. A strange one, thought Rowena. Handsome enough in a cool, refined sort of way, but obsessive, and maybe cruel.

She and Matty waited silently as he went over to a drawer and pulled out some coins. He was controlling his breathing with difficulty. At last he said, 'There's work for you both here, of various kinds, in the kitchens and around the house. I'll inform the housekeeper that you're staying for a while.'

They took the coins he offered and bobbed dutifully. 'Yes, my lord.'

'And now,' he went on softly, 'you can get out. And remember. If there's any hint of trouble – any theft, any spying, any gypsy mischief – then you'll regret it, believe me.' He turned towards the open bottle of wine that stood on the mahogany bedside table, and started to pour himself a glass. Matty and Rowena curtseyed and hurried out into the corridor, half blinded by the noon sunlight after the artificial darkness of the bedchamber. 'Easy money,' gloated Matty.

'I'm not so sure.' Rowena pocketed the coins and began to slowly tidy up her clothes. 'He's a strange one, and no mistake. And I don't know about you, Matty, but I'm real desperate to feel a good man's cock up me after all that messing about.' She grimaced as she eased her full, sensitive breasts back into her tight bodice, tugging the fabric over her large, brown nipples. 'I wonder – why did our fine new master beat that groom?'

Matty shrugged carelessly. 'Sounds as if he was after someone, arranging some sort of accident. Nasty. Nothing to do with us, anyway.' She was much more interested in gazing about her. They were on the first-floor landing of Sir Julian Ormond's fine country house, and she loved the elegant finery of the place, with its richly gleaming furniture and all the fine gilt mirrors that reflected the glittering chandeliers. 'We'll do as he says,' Matty went on, 'and find this housekeeper, and do whatever we're supposed to do. I quite fancy staying in this big house for a while. Then later perhaps this evening, we can slip out and find the men.' She giggled meaningfully. 'Reckon Caleb and Seth'll be ready to give us what we want, Rowena, even if our fancy new master ain't up to a good straightforward pleasuring. Wonder if Seth's any nearer to finding that woman he's after? He seemed dead sure she was somewhere in these parts. Got word from other travellers, he said.'

Rowena's plump, pretty face flushed suddenly beneath her red curls. 'I still don't see why he's so desperate to find her.'

'Said he'd got a trinket of hers, didn't he? A gold ring, or something. Tells everyone he's going to give it back to her, but if you ask me, the real reason for getting us to trail all this way after her is that our randy young Seth is hot for her!' She chuckled.

But Rowena snapped, 'Then he'll soon find out that she's just a high-class whore, won't he, for all her innocent, blue eyes and pretty, golden hair and fancy manners. He'll regret the days he laid eyes on that bitch, you mark my words.'

Matty was going to say something, but then she saw the rage in Rowena's green eyes and thought better of it.

They reported duly to the housekeeper, a thin, tight-lipped woman who was no doubt well-used to her master's ways and made no comment as she found them two demure maids' gowns to wear, with little white aprons, and showed them to the two small, sparsely furnished attic bedchambers they would occupy. Then she set them to cleaning silver in the big back kitchen.

'No thieving, mind,' she said tartly. 'Your new master has his own ways of dealing with those who try to do him out of anything that's rightly his.'

Matty and Rowena exchanged expressive looks. 'I'll bet he has,' whispered Matty, thinking of the unfortunate groom cowering on the anteroom floor beneath Ormond's heated blows.

They got their tasks done quickly and efficiently during the course of the afternoon, to the dour surprise of the housekeeper. There was no sign of Ormond, and no-one noticed when the two women disappeared up to the attic to relieve themselves surreptitiously of the rather urgent sexual excitement that had been burning in them since the session in Ormond's bedchamber earlier.

'Not as good as feeling a real man's cock up me,' gasped Rowena, lying back on her narrow little bed as Matty fondled her full breasts and started to pull up her skirts, 'but I'll burst if I don't have some pleasure now. That's it, Matty, love. Run your tongue up and down me, stick it up me. Oh, I'm so hot and wet, I think I'll die . . .' And she gurgled with pleasure as Matty's long, thin tongue pleasured her, running up and down the plump, fleshy groove between her thighs and wriggling about

663

just inside her lush vulva. Rowena came quickly, panting and thrusting against Matty's face. Then it was Matty's turn, and this time Rowena pleasured her friend with her fingers, knowing exactly how to tease her soaking little pleasure bud with just the right amount of pressure, while using her other hand to stroke gently at her sex-lips and slide two, then three fingers deep inside, moving them about so Matty could clutch hard at them and bear down on them as she shuddered her way to a sharp, fierce little orgasm. They lay together for a while afterwards, flushed and sated, giggling quietly about what they'd do with Caleb and Seth and Tom that night. Then they washed and went downstairs to eat their tea of rather stale bread and slices of thin ham in the servants' kitchen. The other servants regarded them disdainfully, but Matty and Rowena didn't care.

They were just going to lay the fire in the dining room, as they'd been ordered, when they heard the clatter of horses' hooves, and the sound of a carriage pulling up at the front of the house. Rowena, ever curious, ran quickly to the nearest window to gaze out.

'Who is it?' called out Matty, who was on her knees laying kindling in the big grate. 'Some more fancy gents?' She chuckled. 'D'you think Ormond will be requiring our services again tonight, Rowena?'

But Rowena, by the big window, had gone very still. Stepping out of the carriage was a lady, a beautiful, slender lady in an elegant pelisse of darkest blue velvet, with a matching bonnet adorned with curling feathers set fashionably on her stunningly fair curls. She alighted gracefully, with her big manservant handing her respectfully down the steps. Then, after gazing around her assessingly for a moment, the lady headed towards the big front door and knocked on it decisively with her little riding crop.

'Well,' breathed Rowena, 'I'll be damned. It's her, Matty – the fancy little whore who duped us all at Vauxhall Gardens that night. The one Seth's chasing round the country after, more fool he. And would you believe, the bitch is acting like the finest lady in all the county.' She crossed her arms over her ample bosom and smiled grimly. 'Well, my proud lady. Here's two of us who know all about you. We remember how you enjoyed baring your ladylike titties and getting our fine Seth to cream all over them with his lovely big cock before you decided to beat a hasty retreat. Somehow I don't think you'd like us telling anyone round here about all that.'

Marisa stood alone on the sweeping steps of Sir Julian Ormond's imposing mansion and glanced down quickly at her velvet pelisse and elegant little boots, flicking an imaginary speck of dust from her York tan gloves. This was her first neighbourly call, and she looked right for the part, didn't she? No-one, surely, would ever guess that she wasn't born into the role of a fine lady, no matter how much the hateful Lord Delsingham might tease her about her humble origins.

A groom had come to help John with the horses, and now they were being led away round to the stable yard. Marisa gazed around with practised eyes as she waited for someone to answer the door, admiring the elegant Palladian facade. Everything about this residence spoke of easy, accustomed wealth; presumably Ormond didn't miss his aunt's legacy too much. She grinned to herself. Of course he didn't, or he wouldn't be so affable to her, Marisa, who'd inherited what he must surely have expected to acquire for himself. She hoped he was at home, because she wanted to thank him personally for the loan of the mare, and the visit also gave her a discreet chance to learn a little more about him. She wouldn't bother mentioning to him the fact that she'd taken a heavy tumble, because after all it was only an accident. Delsingham had just been trying to frighten her with his talk of deliberate damage to the saddle straps.

In fact, when she'd got in that morning from her unexpectedly eventful ride and eased herself into a deliciously scented bathtub, she'd even found herself wondering darkly if somehow Delsingham himself had arranged the accident. It wouldn't surprise her in the least, because the loathsome man seemed capable of anything. And it certainly seemed strange that he was so near at hand at the time of her fall, perfectly positioned to take advantage of her, damn him! She felt the colour warming her cheeks at the memory, and her body tingled suddenly in a renewal of sensation as she remembered how gloriously he'd pleasured her from behind as she'd lain trapped across that dreaded saddle. Well, it would be the very last time he tormented her like that. And yet, the fact that he knew exactly who she was gave him a hateful hold over her.

All of a sudden, the big front door jerked open to reveal a sour-faced housekeeper dressed all in black. 'Yes?'

Marisa, deciding immediately that she was an old witch, gave her her sweetest smile. 'Is Sir Julian Ormond at home? Pray tell him that Mistress Brooke of Melbray Manor wishes to see him.'

The woman gave a grudging curtsey, and hurried off. Marisa pulled a face at her back, and waited. Then, to her relief, she saw Ormond walking quickly across the big, tiled hallway towards her. His eyes seemed to flicker a little in surprise, and then he smiled.

'My dear Miss Brooke,' he said smoothly, reaching out to take her hand and bowing over it, 'how are you? Are you finding Melbray Manor to your liking? Please, come into the front sitting room and I will order some tea for us.'

It was very pleasant, reflected Marisa as she followed him along the hallway, to be greeted so courteously. He certainly knew his manners, unlike Lord Delsingham, and his refined, elegant welcome made her spirits rise. To be sure, the dark-haired, youthful-looking little housemaid who brought in the tray of dainty scones along with the tea looked at her a little oddly from beneath her lace cap, and for a moment Marisa could have sworn that there was something familiar about her, but then the maid had gone, and she was able to concentrate on her host. He was exquisitely dressed, in a dove-coloured coat and buff pantaloons; his silky white cravat was arranged with discreet perfection, and his smooth fair hair was immaculately swept back from his handsome, almost delicate features.

'Everything is wonderful, thank you,' she responded from the comfort of the little velvet armchair he'd shown her to, as she sipped carefully at her tea with her little finger crooked out. 'The food last night was quite delicious, and the mare your groom brought over this morning is a delight to ride.'

Was she mistaken, or did a sudden shadow cross his bland face? He put down his tea rather quickly and said, 'You've had no problems with her, then?'

'None whatsoever,' lied Marisa, pushing aside the shameful memory of her fall. She didn't want him thinking she was an incompetent horsewoman.

'I'm so glad. Keep her for as long as you wish, and if there's anything else I can do to help, please let me know.'

Marisa smiled prettily in thanks. Lord Delsingham had said that Ormond was no gentleman, but how wrong he was! Delsingham was just bitter and twisted, because Ormond's generosity showed him, Delsingham, up in such a bad light.

'You're very kind,' she responded. 'It will take me a little while to get settled in, but I'm sure I'll manage. I need to purchase so many things: household goods, clothes, horses, a carriage or two . . .'

He said quickly, 'You'll find, I think, that the tradesmen in Crayhampton will be able to provide everything you require – no need to go as far as Winchester. Before you leave, I'll ask my housekeeper to give you a list of reputable suppliers.'

'Thank you. You really are very obliging.'

'Think nothing of it, my dear Miss Brooke.' He hesitated a moment, taking a pinch of snuff from a little laquered box with his exquisitely manicured fingers. 'There is something else I might be able to help you with. You can tell me, of course, to mind my own business.

But I understand that you have been left a considerable amount of money by my aunt. You have probably already made arrangements to invest it, but if I can assist you in any way, please let me know. It must be very difficult for you to cope with these things now that your father is no longer alive, and I have considerable experience of such matters, so please do consult me if you are wondering how best to invest it.'

Marisa stiffened. No-one was getting their hands on all her wonderful money. But then, suddenly, she remembered the arrogant Lord Delsingham saying, 'I shouldn't trust Ormond, if I were you,' and she bridled at the memory of his autocratic tone.

'I've made no plans for investment as yet,' she said, 'but I might well be glad of your advice some time in the future.' She put her teacup down and rose gracefully to her feet. 'I must be going now. There's so much for me to do. But soon, I hope to be in a position to do a little modest entertaining, and I should be delighted if you would come and visit me.'

'I can think of nothing I'd like better,' he responded warmly as he escorted her to the door. 'I'm sure that the whole neighbourhood will be eager to welcome you, Miss Brooke.'

John was waiting, with the carriage. Ormond handed her up respectfully, and she turned to give him a little wave as John clicked on the horses and the carriage swung away down the wide drive. Lord Delsingham, she decided, was jealous and spiteful to speak ill of Sir Julian Ormond. It might be a good idea to make a particular friend of Ormond and take the advice he was offering, just to spite her tormentor Delsingham and show him that she could look after herself quite adequately.

As the carriage rolled out through the high gates, she remembered the little dark-haired maid with a sudden feeling of unease, but dismissed the memory quickly. Her mind was playing tricks on her. How could she possibly have met her before?

* * *

Sir Julian Ormond, standing by a tall, silk-draped window, watched the carriage disappear from sight with expressionless eyes. Then he went over to the walnut bureau in the corner and opened it, brushing his hands mechanically across the dockets of paper that lay inside.

They were all unpaid bills. His debts were such that he didn't even dare contemplate them. Soon, this house would have to go. It had been mortgaged up to the hilt years ago, on the expectation of his aunt's fortune.

He looked out of the window once more, but Marisa Brooke's carriage had long since disappeared from view. His slender, well-manicured hand tightened round the sheaves of bills one last time, then he locked up the bureau and went to tug quickly at the bell-pull by the door.

The little dark-haired maid came in, the one with the soft lips and tongue. She bobbed demurely, but he still caught the greedy glitter in her eyes. 'You wanted me, my lord?'

He shut the door. 'Yes.' His voice shook slightly.

He told her to get on her hands and knees on the floor, and he took her quickly. She was slim and almost boyish from behind, with tight, pert bottom-cheeks. She squealed and shuddered with delight as he roughly threw up her skirts and entered her from behind, pulling her buttocks apart as he thrust into her. She cried out with pleasure as he slid his stiffened penis home into her moist, tight depths, and she writhed back to meet him as he slowly withdrew then drove himself in again. The gypsy girl was hot for him. She was starting to climax already, jumping about with pleasure and sighing as she felt his slim, throbbing shaft impale her. Gripping her buttocks, gritting his teeth, he drove himself quickly to his own harsh release, pulling out his ravening penis just at the last moment and rubbing it swiftly across her ripe bottom as his semen spurted out across her creamy flesh.

When he was quite spent the girl drew herself up quickly, readjusting her crumpled black gown and pulling her lace cap back onto her disordered curls. By the time she'd done that, he was standing by the empty hearth with one arm stretched casually along the carved mantelshelf, watching her coldly.

'Will that be all, sir?' said Matty primly.

'For the time being, yes. You may go.'

She bobbed a curtsey, then picked up the tea tray and left. A find, these two gypsy girls, thought Ormond, a fortunate find, the redheaded one with the mischievous ideas especially. But he mustn't allow them to distract him from his main task, which was, somehow, to deal with Marisa Brooke.

That night, Rowena and Matty crept out of the house under cover of darkness, letting themselves out through the kitchen door round at the back. Giggling furtively, they hurried round by the stables and ran on light feet through the wooded, silent gardens of Greenfallow Park, while the moon gleamed down on them through the dark foliage of the trees.

It took them half an hour to reach the gypsy camp, which was on the common land down near the river. There were several gypsy families there, who'd all come to the Crayhampton fair to sell horses and trinkets, and tell fortunes, and hopefully dupe as many locals as possible out of their money before they moved on. Seth had decided to set their painted caravan some distance from the others, in a pretty clearing surrounded by alders and willow, and as Matty and Rowena drew near, they could see Seth and Caleb sitting cross-legged by the fire, drinking wine and talking in soft voices.

Rowena dropped to the grass beside them with a little sigh, spreading out her skirts around herself. 'Let's have the wine, then, Caleb, while there's some left. Where's Tom?'

Caleb grinned. 'Found himself a girl of his own at last. Swaggering about like he's the only man in the world to have found a use for his cock. Enjoying working for your fancy gentleman, are you?'

670

Matty laughed. 'He's as dirty as they come, Caleb, gent or not. Wicked, he is! Beat one of his grooms this morning, and his prick stood out all red and angry. Rowena and I could see he wanted some of the same himself. So I took his lively weapon in my mouth and tongued him, and Rowena whipped his bottom, real hard.'

Seth smiled. Caleb drew nearer to Matty, his arm slipping round her shoulders so he could fondle her breasts through her tightly laced bodice. 'Like it, did he? Did he have a good cock on him, then, this gent of yours?'

Matty ran her hand along his brawny thigh. 'Nothing as good as yours, Caleb my sweet. It was thin and red, and waved about desperately while Rowena was beating him. Then she slid the end of the whip handle into his tight little arse, and moved it in and out a bit, and he gasped and moaned so much I could hardly keep his prick in my mouth.'

Caleb's face was suddenly dark with desire. He fondled Matty's breasts more roughly as she talked, pulling them free of her gown and bending to nuzzle at their pouting crests with his bearded mouth. Matty arched against him, stroking his groin where his penis was already bulging, and whispering into his ear. 'Take me, stick it into me, Caleb, do. I'm that desperate for a real man, for a big, hard cock up inside me.'

Caleb grunted, and together they rolled into the shadows beyond the caravan, where Matty scrabbled with his breeches and pulled out his big, meaty shaft longingly. 'Ah, that feels good, Caleb. So good.' She lay quickly on her back, parting her legs for him and lifting her knees, groaning in delight as he stroked her unfurling sex with the bulbous tip of his phallus and then began to slide the thick shaft of it between her juicy flesh-lips, inch by glorious inch.

Seth and Rowena watched them, enjoying their open lust. Rowena leaned back against Seth's shoulder, her eyes green and catlike in the firelight, and took another

671

long pull at the rough red wine, feeling it arouse her excited body still further. She gazed up at Seth possessively, drinking in his dark curls and high Romany cheekbones. He had a beautiful face and body, and he knew how to pleasure a woman better than anyone she knew, with his sensitive gypsy fingers and his lovely, long cock. 'Any nearer to finding your fine lady, Seth?' she enquired casually.

He paused. 'Not yet. But some of the hired hands were gossiping at the fair today. They were saying that there's a new lady come to live hereabouts. No-one seems to know where she's come from, except that she's young, and very beautiful. I'd like to find out more about her.'

Rowena ran her hand possessively along his forearm, excited by the feel of the silky dark hair that roughened his warm brown skin. 'You're not still hot for her, Seth, are you?' she murmured. 'You don't want her more than me, do you?'

'Sweetheart,' laughed Seth, kissing her forehead, 'at this very moment, I couldn't want anyone more than you, I assure you.'

Rowena smoothed her hand avidly across his crotch, realising that the flesh of his penis was already hard and swollen. She unfastened him with feverish haste and unbuttoned her own bodice. His erect penis jutted towards her from the dark hair at the base of his belly, and with a little moan she bent to rub her heavy, swollen breasts against it. As the velvety tip of his pulsing rod brushed her dark brown nipples, she licked her lips in anticipation, feeling the hard tightness gathering at the pit of her stomach and the moisture seeping already from the lushly tingling flesh at the juncture of her thighs. The muffled sounds of Caleb and Matty pleasuring one another nearby excited her wildly, with Matty's little whimpers rising higher and higher as Caleb lifted her hips with his hands and drove her demented with the length of his big, gnarled cock. Rowena stole a glance at them, noting that Matty was already shuddering in the throes of orgasm as Caleb slowly drove himself in and out of her. Then she saw with a thrill of fascination that Caleb had drawn out his great, glistening shaft and was rubbing it avidly all over Matty's breasts. Suddenly he gave a hoarse shout and started to spurt in great gouts all over her, his penis twitching with delight while his heavy, rounded balls grazed her tender belly.

With a little cry, Rowena urged Seth back onto the ground and sat astride his hips, pulling up her own skirt to her waist. She spread her thighs wide and stroked her own swollen labia with her fingers, tenderly drawing out the sweet, seeping nectar that coated the dark-pink petals of flesh and letting her thumb just brush the yearning little stem of her clitoris. Seth smiled up at her lazily, his hands pillowing his head, his lovely, long cock rearing upwards in anticipation. She lowered herself carefully onto him, gasping aloud as she felt the fatly rounded tip of his manhood pushing her apart, nudging its way in, sliding into her hungry vagina and filling her with delicious male power. Wriggling her hips voluptuously, she took in the whole of his lengthy shaft, relishing every rapturous inch of him and whimpering softly in delight.

He was all hers. Rowena began to ride him fast, playing with her own heavy breasts and pulling at her distended brown teats, relishing the hard, sweet delight that filled her as his sturdy member caressed the very core of her femininity. Soon, she was almost at the brink. She squeezed tightly on him with her pleasure-engorged inner muscles, and held herself very still, her head thrown back, trembling in anticipation. Tenderly Seth reached with one hand to caresss her soaking pleasure bud, and she throbbed into fiery orgasm as he started to drive himself powerfully, steadily from beneath her.

'Seth,' she gasped, 'stick it into me, Seth. Yes, oh, yes . . .'

The throbs of pleasure beat their way through her almost violently as she trembled and bucked above him, feeling his delicious pillar of flesh ravishing her as she convulsed around him. At last she was sated, though his erect cock still caressed her tenderly, begging for more attention. Rowena, slipping herself off him with a little sigh, bent her head to take as much as she could of him into her mouth, sliding her lips up and down, excited anew by the taste of her own musky juices on the silken stem, running her tongue round his straining glans and fondling his tight balls with her hand until at last his juices gushed hotly against the back of her throat and she felt his lithe body convulse with pleasure.

Afterwards she lay with her head against his chest, stroking the silky, muscle-padded flesh beneath his shirt. Her Seth, all hers.

She lifted herself up suddenly on one arm and gazed at him, seeing how his curling dark hair fell away from his sleepy, suntanned face. She said, 'You wouldn't get to like this fancy lady more than me, would you, Seth?'

He reached out to touch her cheek. 'Jealous, Rowena?'

'You know she's no good for you, Seth. She's not like us – she's dangerous. But,' and she hesitated, 'if I told you I knew where she was, would you be pleased with me?'

He was quickly alert then, pulling himself up and gazing intently at her. 'You know where she is, Rowena?'

'Better than that,' she announced triumphantly. 'I've seen her.'

And she told him about Marisa's visit to Greenfallow Park. 'Remember she's just a high-class whore, Seth,' she finished warningly. 'No better than Matty and me.'

He kissed her soundly, but his face was thoughtful. 'Nobody could be better than you, my sweet. You're staying the night here?'

Before she could reply they were joined by Matty, who'd crawled across to the fire, leaving Caleb snoring. Greedily she drank the last of the wine. 'No fear!' she laughed, picking up the conversation. 'We're going back to our fine gentleman. I've already earned two gold pieces for doing little more than talk dirty to him.'

Rowena hesitated, just a moment, then said, 'Yes, we're going back. It's nice to sleep on feather beds and be able to pinch plenty of good food and wine for a while. But we'll join you here again tomorrow night, Seth.' Seth kissed her, and she added quickly, 'You'll still be here tomorrow, won't you?'

'Of course,' he said lightly. 'Where else would I be?'

Chapter Six

A few days later, Marisa received her very first invitation.

Her eyes narrowed in calculation as she read it through slowly, word by tortuous word. She remembered Lord Delsingham's mocking laugh as he'd said, 'Somehow, my sweet, I don't think country society is quite ready for you.' Well, this prompt missive was decisive proof that he was wrong. The invitation was to Southland Grange, the home of Sir Andrew and Lady Blockley some five miles away, and it was hand delivered with some ceremony by a mounted manservant. Lucy put the gilded card proudly on the mantelpiece in the drawing room.

'Your first invitation into grand society, Marisa,' she breathed. 'How exciting!'

Marisa shrugged carelessly. 'It will be nothing of importance, Lucy. Just a few sets of country dances, and a cold supper, and old ladies playing casino and whist at a penny a point – no doubt exceedingly dull.'

But nevertheless she felt a secret frisson of pleasure. It didn't matter if the evening was as dull as ditchwater; she was on her way. She'd spent several enthralling days exploring Melbray Manor, interspersed with shopping trips to Crayhampton to order stocks of Naples soap, rolls of silk, and finest hock at thirty shillings the dozen;

in fact, all the luxuries she'd always longed for. Now she was ready to meet her new neighbours. She grinned, wondering mischievously if they were ready for Marisa Brooke.

Early on the evening of the party she took a leisurely bath, rubbing her pale gold skin with subtly scented oils until it was soft and perfumed. Then she washed and brushed her long, honey-blonde curls until they glittered in the brilliant candlelight of her room, and prepared to dress. She'd decided, after much thought, to wear the most daring of her purchases from Madame Thanier's exclusive establishment in Bond Street, an elegant ivory muslin gown with a high waist and short puffed sleeves. The sleeves and low *décolletage* of the gown were adorned with pale pink satin ribbons, and Lucy, after studying Marisa thoughtfully, found another, wider length of matching ribbon to tie round the high waistline, just below her breasts. After slipping her small feet into a dainty pair of pink shoes, and pulling on some white satin gloves that clung like a second skin as far as her elbows, Marisa gazed critically at herself in the long cheval glass.

The white muslin sheath clung beguilingly to her slender figure, making her look younger than her 23 years. So much the better. Lucy, with her customary deftness, had arranged her fair curls into luxuriant ringlets, and piled them high in a pink satin bandeau, and by the time she had draped her flimsy silk shawl in a darker shade of rose-pink elegantly over her gloved arms, Marisa decided that she looked exactly like one of the beautiful, rich ladies of fashion who visited the theatre in the Haymarket, or the opera at Covent Garden, before heading back to some grand party in Mayfair. Her new neighbours, she smiled to herself, would never guess that she was adept at mains of hazard in the dingy backrooms of the Blue Bell, or at elbowing her way past the noisy, disreputable taverns of Covent Garden dressed in buckskin breeches and a big man's coat, matching oath for oath with all the gulls and tricksters who teemed in the narrow London alleys.

Then suddenly, as she turned in front of the mirror, the memory of Lord Delsingham's laughing sneer echoed in her ears: 'You, Marisa? A fine lady?' She clenched her small gloved fists. She would show him. Oh, yes. She wondered suddenly if he would be there tonight, and the colour mounted slowly in her cheeks at the thought of confronting him once more.

The Blockleys' house was a big, sprawling, ivy-clad grange, originally an Elizabethan farmhouse. Sir Andrew, a prosperous gentleman farmer with a stout figure and port-reddened cheeks, came warmly to the door to greet her, with his equally plump wife at his side, her grey curls enclosed in a purple silk turban that matched the colour of her dress. It was Sir Andrew himself who eagerly drew Marisa into the large, firelit hall to introduce her to his other guests. Marisa saw the male guests' eyes light up at the sight of her, while their womenfolk watched her warily.

'New little lady at Melbray Manor, Miss Marisa Brooke,' beamed Sir Andrew. 'Enchanting, eh? Know you'll all give her a warm welcome this evening.'

Marisa heard a woman just behind her whisper in an excruciatingly clear voice to her neighbour, 'My dear. Just look at that skimpy dress. Did you ever see anything so vulgar?'

She felt the colour rush hotly to her cheeks, and looked quickly around to meet the acidic gaze of a tall, thin brunette, perhaps the same age as herself, who was wearing a modest, high-necked gown of dark blue silk with long, narrow sleeves and a little muslin ruff. She gazed at Marisa almost pityingly. Marisa felt her blood churn with rage, and opened her mouth to make some angry retort. But then, as the rest of the female guests gathered together and began one by one to remove their little capes and pelisses, Marisa began to realise, with a steadily sinking heart, that she was indeed dressed far more skimpily than any of the others. No wonder the men gazed at her plunging neckline with such interest. Hell and damnation, she thought bitterly, the women here were dressed more like nuns than women of wealth and breeding.

She felt her heart thumping, but held her head high in defiance as she stood there all alone. The men didn't dare to speak to her, while the women eyed her surreptitiously and whispered viciously about her behind raised hands, encouraged by the poisonous brunette. Then suddenly kind Lady Blockley, who seemed oblivious to the gossip, was at her side again, handing her a glass of ratafia.

'Now, my dear Miss Brooke,' she said, 'I do hope you don't find cards too, too boring, because I want you to join me for a rubber of whist. A penny a point, my dear. Can you bear it, do you think?'

Marisa laughed, feeling suddenly happy again. What did she care for the gossips? 'I'll join you with the greatest of pleasure, Lady Blockley.'

'You do play whist, I take it, my dear?'

'A little,' Marisa replied, her blue eyes sparkling. 'Are you to be my partner, Lady Blockley?'

'Oh, no,' said the older woman, gleefully taking her arm. 'We have someone else for you, someone you'll like very much. Come and see.'

Marisa's heart sank again. No doubt they'd found her some hopelessly dull-witted clod of a partner. What a good job they were only playing for a penny a point.

Lady Blockley was already enthusiastically guiding her into the card parlour, where groups of guests were happily playing casino at the green baize tables. Still chattering aimlessly, Lady Blockley wove her way between the players towards her husband Sir Andrew, who was deep in conversation with a tall, dark-haired man whose back was to Marisa. Her heart lurched suddenly. Oh, no. It couldn't be . . .

It was. Sir Andrew's companion turned round slowly, as if relishing the moment, and Marisa saw that it was indeed the hateful Lord Delsingham. She caught her breath, and glared up at him with flashing eyes. No doubt he would laugh at the way she was dressed as well, just like the rest of these obnoxious people. She braced herself for his put-down.

He took her hand, his grey eyes dancing vividly in the sober refinement of his handsome face. 'Mistress Brooke,' he drawled. 'What an exceedingly pleasant surprise.' He bowed low over Marisa's fingers and she felt quite faint at the brush of his warm lips on the back of her hand. He grinned secretly at her as he straightened up, like a wolf eyeing its helpless prey. She returned his gaze furiously, waiting for him to make some jeering remark about her stupidly flimsy attire, but all he said was, 'You look quite divine, my dear.'

Marisa laughed shortly, aware that Sir Andrew and his wife were fussily seating themselves at the nearby card table and leaving them in momentary privacy. 'I look ridiculously out of place,' she replied in a cutting voice, 'and you know it, my lord. There's no need for you to sharpen your sarcasm on me.'

There was a pause as he gazed steadily down at her. Then he said quietly, 'I mean what I said, Marisa. You're the only truly lovely woman in the room. The rest of them have about as much elegance as a gaggle of farmers' wives on their way to market.'

Caught unawares by his compliment, she was aware of her heart fluttering rather strangely. The colour flooded to her face, and she tossed back her head, unaccountably disturbed. 'I think I almost prefer it, my Lord Delsingham, when you're hateful to me,' she said almost shakily.

He grinned. 'Oh, I can manage that as well, believe me. You're joining us for whist? How absolutely delightful. I have a feeling you will teach us all a thing or two, Miss Brooke.'

He started to pull out a chair for her, but she put her hand on his arm and said in a voice that was still tense, 'Just one thing. If you're going to give me away, Lord Delsingham, and tell everyone about my former life, then

I would prefer that you did so now, rather than endure an evening's charade.'

'Give you away?' he replied innocently. 'Now why should I do that, Mistress Brooke, when you and I have such a delightful arrangement?'

She felt her stomach lurch at the reminder. Damn him, he looked utterly desirable in his dark grey coat and slim breeches, with his exquisitely arranged cravat emphasizing the lean, aristocratic lines of his face. An ace indeed. He was gesturing her towards her chair, but she stood behind it and said defiantly, 'Pray, don't think you shall have it all your own way, my lord, with your talk of arrangements! It didn't take me very long to receive my first invitation into polite society, did it? Even though you assured me that I would never be accepted here.'

He smiled gently. 'Oh, you were bound to be accepted, my dear. You see, it was I who suggested to Sir Andrew that he invite you.'

Marisa gaped at him, speechless with rage. The pleasure that had lit her like a warm glow since she received her precious invitation was suddenly like cold ashes in the pit of her stomach.

'I think,' he went on smoothly, pointing delicately towards the vacant chair, 'that Sir Andrew and his good lady are ready for play.'

'So am I,' she said meaningfully. 'Oh, believe me, so am I.'

She played like a novice, deliberately throwing away her highest cards when he was winning and wasting point after point. Delsingham raised his eyebrows but said nothing; his little pile of coins diminished rapidly along with hers, and she wished, viciously, that they were guineas. He wouldn't want to be her partner again for a long, long time, that was for sure.

And then the Blockleys, having gleefully won several rubbers, rose apologetically to their feet and said they really must go to the dining hall to check that everything was in order for supper. Would Lord Delsingham and

Miss Brooke mind terribly if Mistress Caroline Henshawe and her husband Richard took their place in the game?

It was too late to object anyway, because the couple in question were already on their way over, and Marisa saw to her dismay that Caroline Henshawe was the tall brunette who'd made such disparaging remarks about her gown. Mistress Henshawe sat quickly next to Delsingham, resting her hand intimately on his arm and smiling up at him; only then did she turn to Marisa and say with honeyed venom, 'You must let me introduce you to my dressmaker in Winchester, Miss Brooke. I gather you only came into your fortune recently. It must be difficult to adjust to new-found wealth. If I can give you any advice, I will gladly do so.'

Marisa gritted her teeth, gazing pointedly at her opponent's dark, high-necked gown. Then she said, 'Oh, but I wouldn't dream of asking for your advice. You see, Mistress Henshawe, where I come from, it is by no means considered usual to dress for a party as if one were about to enter a nunnery.'

Caroline Henshawe looked a little pale, apart from the spots of anger that burned on her beautifully elegant high cheekbones. Delsingham intercepted smoothly, 'Well, now. I think we should raise the stakes a little, don't you? This looks like being an interesting game.'

Richard Henshawe, a plump, nondescript man who was already rather drunk, came alive at that and said, 'Hey? What's that you say? Capital idea, Delsingham. Five shillings a point, d'you think?' And play began.

Marisa wanted to win this game. She wanted to humiliate Caroline Henshawe, who looked down her long aristocratic nose at her as if she'd crawled out of the gutter. And to make matters worse, the hateful woman was coolly possessive about Delsingham, touching him at every opportunity and smiling at him with obnoxious familiarity. So engrossed was Marisa in her resentment of her opponent that it took her some time to realise that Delsingham was watching her, Marisa, with a strange intensity as he examined his cards. And then he said, quite inconsequentially as he sorted his hand, 'How warm the weather is at present. I wonder if the sunshine will last.'

Richard Henshawe mumbled something banal back, but Marisa, whose turn it was to lead, gazed at him transfixed, her heart suddenly beating rather fast. Why would he make such a trivial, boring remark? Unless . . . He was looking at her again; she thought she saw him nod imperceptibly. 'How warm,' he'd said. H for heart . . .

She led with a low heart, the four, and he won the trick for them with the ace, following with a king. Her pulse started to race. Was she mistaken? Was it just a coincidence? He played skilfully, winning trick after trick. Then it was Marisa's lead, and as she hesitated, he said thoughtfully, 'Supper should be ready soon, I think. But we've time for a few more minutes' play.'

Marisa led with a seven of spades, knowing that the highest cards in that suit had already gone, and Delsingham won with a knave. She was right; he was using one of the oldest and simplest tactics for cheating at whist, prefacing his remark with the letter of the suit he wanted her to play. Simple but effective; together with their mutual card-counting skills and total recall of what had been played, they were devastating partners. Suddenly feeling happy and confident, Marisa met his eyes and saw them sparkle in answer. Suppressing her smile, Marisa lowered her eyelashes demurely to her cards, and together they continued like two conspirators to roundly trounce Caroline Henshawe and her husband and deprive them of a not insubstantial sum of money before supper. Marisa felt the old, familiar elation of successful trickery. Lord Delsingham was a superbly subtle player, and together they were unbeatable.

At last Caroline Henshawe stood up, her elegant face tight and frosty. 'Time for us to get some supper, I think, Richard,' she told her bemused, half-inebriated husband. Then she turned with an icy smile on Marisa. 'Well, Miss Brooke,' she drawled. 'You're certainly successful at cards, aren't you? I wonder where you learned so well.

I'd almost suspect you of hiding the cards somewhere about your person, except,' and her eyes raked Marisa's flimsy muslin dress with scorn, 'there isn't really anywhere to conceal them, is there?'

With that, she turned to go. Marisa hissed and started after her, hands clenched into fists, but Lord Delsingham's fingers bit into her gloved arm.

'Leave her be,' he said quietly. 'Her husband is a drunken, impotent boor. Mistress Caroline, I believe, finds consolation by taking her pleasure with servants. You'll find some way soon to get your own back on her, I'm quite sure.'

Marisa said through gritted teeth, 'I'm going to find a way now, this minute.'

He chuckled. 'Isn't winning 50 guineas off her enough?'

She turned to gaze levelly up at him. 'No. Five hundred guineas wouldn't be enough. You meant what you said? That she's addicted to serving men?'

'I did indeed.' His dark eyebrows gathered. 'Dear Marisa, what are you plotting now?'

'Something I'm quite capable of managing on my own, thank you.'

'I'm sure you are, and that's the trouble.' His eyes danced. 'By the way, you play a marvellous game of whist.'

She flashed a brilliant smile back up at him. 'So do you, my lord,' she replied quickly, then hurried off with the cold light of determination in her eyes to find John the coachman.

Caroline Henshawe wandered slowly out into the private, walled gardens of Southlands Grange to get away from her boring husband, whom she'd left with a full plate of food in the dining hall. She brought her brimming glass of wine with her, knowing that she'd already drunk enough to set her blood racing with dark thoughts and make her judgement a little suspect, but she was past caring. She was hot and angry at the memory of that half-clad little blonde bitch who'd somehow cheated her at cards and made a fool of her. And sitting next to Delsingham had made her fatally aroused, even watching his strong, graceful hands as they expertly dealt the cards had made her feel quite weak. She'd surreptitiously pressed her knee against his well-muscled thigh beneath the table, but he'd pretended not to notice.

That little blonde newcomer, with her big, innocent blue eyes and disgusting dress, was making a play for him; of that she was quite certain. The slut might even have bedded him already.

The soft night breeze was cooling on her hot cheeks as she wandered into the clipped yew gardens. Her body was burning, on edge at the thought of Delsingham and that slut. How had they managed to win so easily? She'd seen the looks they exchanged, knowing, intimate looks. She imagined Delsingham pleasuring the little bitch, taking her roughly from behind with his beautiful lengthy penis darkly erect, and she felt faint with need. At this moment she wanted nothing more than a man, a sturdy, well-endowed, virile man.

She drank down the rest of her wine, feeling a little unsteady. She must have consumed the best part of a bottle. She would have to be careful, or her eyes would be bloodshot, and people would know.

'Now, then.' A man's voice, rough, uncultured, exciting, came from the shadows somewhere behind her. 'Were you out here looking for something by any chance, Mistress Henshawe?'

She turned with a little gasp, her hand to her mouth. A man was walking slowly between the high, clipped yew hedges towards her, a big, stocky man with sun-streaked brown hair, dressed like a servant in his leather jerkin and coarse knee breeches. His linen shirt was open at the neck, and she could see the enticing gleam of his bronzed chest; he looked young, muscular, fit. He was grinning as he walked slowly towards her, and his thumbs were locked loosely into the waistband of his breeches. He stopped when he was a few feet away, and she saw with stunned disbelief that he was starting to rub slowly, meaningfully at himself through the thick fabric of his clothing. She let out a little scream and leaned faintly back against the wall, only too aware of the outline of his knotted penis moving, swelling as he touched himself. He must be huge, she thought weakly, rough and brutal and huge. She opened her mouth to scream again, but then she stopped, because he was unbuttoning himself now, and as she gazed breathlessly at his busy fingers, he parted his breeches and drew out his thickly erect penis. Immediately it sprang towards her, jerking with hungry life.

Caroline shut her eyes and opened them again, quite unable to look anywhere except his groin. His shaft was long and thick and meaty, gnarled with veins, the purple tip glistening with moisture. He continued to rub it luxuriantly as it reared from the nest of hair below his belly. She felt her breasts tingle and ache in response as her nipples peaked, and was aware of a sudden trickle of moisture between her thighs.

'Well, now. Is this what you want, my beauty?' the man said, grinning.

She swallowed hard, her hand at her throat. 'Oh, yes,' she whispered. 'Yes, yes.'

There was a little summerhouse in the garden, perhaps twenty yards away from them, set in the middle of the scented rosebeds. As Caroline moved towards the man, the door of the summerhouse opened very quietly and a slender, shadowy figure slipped quickly inside, but Caroline Henshawe was too entranced by her mysterious admirer to notice.

The shadowy figure belonged to Marisa Brooke. Marisa knelt carefully on the cushioned window seat of the little circular summerhouse and leant her elbows on the sill, gazing out raptly into the moonlit garden. The air was thick with the scent of roses, and she breathed in deeply, realising that she had a perfect view of everything. So far, her plan had worked brilliantly.

After leaving Lord Delsingham, she'd gone quickly to find John, who was in the back kitchen drinking Sir Andrew's potent ale with the other coachmen. She'd drawn him to one side and whispered to him to follow the haughty Henshawe woman everywhere she went until he had a chance to get her on her own. And things had worked out beautifully, even better than Marisa had dared to hope, because the woman had not only obligingly wandered out into the garden, but was also, it seemed, in a pleasant state of drunkenness. John had seized his chance with admirable style, and now Mistress Henshawe looked as if she couldn't wait to get her dainty hands on his stalwart great prick as he meaningfully rubbed at its exposed bulk. Marisa didn't blame her. His penis was already massively engorged, and as he gently stroked the foreskin up and down, the glans seemed to swell yet further, and Marisa saw the beading of moisture at its glossy, bulbous tip.

She felt the familiar tightening in her abdomen, felt her nipples stiffening and poking provocatively at the thin muslin of her bodice, and knew it wasn't just the cool night air making them tingle so. John was playing his part so well, she fancied taking him herself.

She drew a deep breath and pressed her cheek against the cool glass of the little summerhouse, noting that John, still grinning, was putting his big hands on Caroline's thin, aristocratic shoulders, then letting his fingers slip downwards so he was roughly fondling her tiny breasts through the thin silk of her high-necked gown. Caroline grabbed his hands, grinding his calloused palms against the hard nubs of her nipples, her face dazed with greedy lust. 'Oh, take me,' she gasped, 'take me now, you big, rough peasant.'

John clutched her to him and kissed her hard, his big tongue thrusting and delving into her open mouth as she lay back dizzily in his arms. Quickly he unlaced her bodice, tugging it away so he could dip his head to lick hungrily at her exposed teats. Though her breasts were small, her nipples were long and stiff, and he was able to push them from side to side with his rasping tongue, while at the same time clutching at her hips and grinding her against his upright penis; her hands slipped tremblingly towards it as it thrust hard against her. 'So big,' she whispered, 'so fine. Oh, let me taste it, please let me taste your big, fat prick . . .' And before Marisa's startled gaze Caroline dropped to her knees, clutching at John's heavy, bulging testicles and leaning forward to lick avidly at his fiercely jutting penis.

John too looked startled, and not displeased. As Caroline struggled to take as much as she could into her eager mouth, he gripped at her shoulders and started to thrust his hips against her mouth, his eyes glazed with lust as her lips slid up and down his glistening shaft. He drew a rasping breath and whispered hoarsely, 'Well, now, my lady. How would you like to feel my big, fine cock up inside you, eh? I'll give you a right good pleasuring, I swear. I last a real long time, I do.'

Mistress Caroline Henshawe, her scarlet tipped breasts gleaming in the moonlight, removed her mouth lingeringly from his throbbing appendage and breathed, 'Yes. Oh, yes.'

John put his hands on his hips, and his penis quivered and swayed with a life of its own. 'How do you like it then, wench?' he grated out.

'I – I'd like you to lick me first, with your big, rasping tongue. And then I want you to do it to me quickly, strongly. And – ' she licked her lips, pale with excitement – 'I want you to call me rude names while you're doing it.'

John laughed huskily. 'So you like to talk dirty, eh, my fine lady?' He stroked his meaty penis meaningfully; it glistened with her saliva. 'Fair enough. So do I.' Still chuckling, he lowered her to the smooth turf of the little hedged garden, pushing back her silk skirts. She'd already parted her thighs, and was eagerly pulling his face down towards her. John grunted in approval, and started to lick thoroughly between her legs as she wriggled and moaned in ecstasy. Marisa sighed a little as she leant on the windowsill, wishing it was her feeling his strong, thick tongue probing between her own heated flesh folds, finding the sensitive nub of her little pleasure bud. Her hand strayed to her swollen breasts, slipping beneath the low muslin bodice to cup them and stroke them tenderly, trying to assuage the ache but only succeeding in starting a more fiery surge of desire deep within her loins.

And then, too late, she felt the sudden whisper of fresh air on her cheek as the little summerhouse door opened quietly behind her, and a strong masculine hand covered her mouth, stifling her instinctive cry of alarm. At the same time, an all-too familiar voice was saying dryly in her ear, 'Miss Brooke, you really are very wicked, you know.'

Delsingham's voice, Delsingham's hand. Hell and damnation. But then the words of indignation died in her throat, because his hands had slipped inside her bodice and were on her breasts, deliciously cooling and firm as they stroked the smooth, swollen flesh, lightly teasing her protruding nipples until the sharp tongues of desire flew meltingly down to the base of her belly, making her moan and shift her thighs together, only too aware of how her secret sexual parts were slick and slippery with her need.

He was nuzzling at the back of her neck with his warm, dry mouth as she kneeled helplessly against the window seat with her back to him. She felt the sudden dart of his tongue, wickedly licking and caressing her neck until she shuddered helplessly, arching back to press her slender, muslin-clad figure against his tense, powerful body. Then she gasped as she suddenly felt cool air on her thighs and buttocks. He was lifting her flimsy skirt high, gently caressing her bottom, sliding her stockinged thighs tenderly apart as he knelt behind her on the window seat while continuing to kiss the nape of her neck. And then, as she caught her breath and pressed her cheek blindly against the window, she felt the most glorious sensation of all – the firm, purposeful nudge of his beautiful, strong

689

penis slipping between her thighs and probing purposefully between her juicy folds of flesh, stroking its way
between the lushly nectared petals of her labia before
slowly, deliciously insinuating itself into her yearning
vulva.

She ground herself back against him, enfolding him,
wanting more and more of him. 'Oh!' she gasped aloud,
gripping the window ledge and writhing helplessly
around on the delicious impalement. His hands reached
round to tighten on her nipples, sending renewed spasms
of exquisite pain-pleasure shuddering through her
exposed body.

'Is this what you were after?' he murmured against the
lobe of her ear, thrusting gently but firmly as inch by
delicious inch he eased his thick, powerful penis deep
inside her.

'Yes,' gasped Marisa despairingly. 'Oh, yes. But wait a
moment, please. I want to see them, out in the garden.'

'A little voyeur,' he murmured, his hands still teasing
her rosy buds. 'Very well. I can wait, if you can.'

Marisa was really not at all sure that she could wait,
but she had to watch, she had to be able to concentrate,
to make sure that her plan was working. Desperately she
strained to look out of the window into the moonlit
garden, conscious of Delsingham's hands still lightly
cupping her breasts, of his strongly erect penis pulsing
gently deep inside her vagina, knowing that all she really
wanted to do was to lean back into his arms, and let him
pleasure her into oblivion.

Frantically she pushed his hands away from her
breasts. 'Watch!' she hissed.

John, good loyal John, had mistress Caroline Henshawe
on all fours now amongst the lavender bushes. He was
kneeling behind her and grinning from ear to ear, gripping her firmly by her slender buttocks as he ravished
her with his fine sturdy shaft. Marisa, dry mouthed,
could see the great meaty length of his member sliding
in and out; it was dark and glossy with feminine juices,
and John's face was going red with pleasure as he

pumped away, his hairy balls swinging between his thighs as he worked. Caroline was thrusting back against him to take as much as she could into herself, her face flushed and her eyes glazed as she moaned out in her refined voice, 'That's it, stick it up me, please. You big, rough stallion. What a wonderful, wonderful penis you have!'

'Enjoying it, wench?' John grinned back. 'Bet you've not had one as good as this for a while, eh?'

Marisa felt her own musky juices flowing freely, anointing Delsingham's shaft anew as he held himself very still inside her. She clutched convulsively with her inner muscles on his lovely bone-hard penis, unable to control her trembling excitement at the lewd sight of John pleasuring the haughty Caroline Henshawe so vigorously. She heard Delsingham chuckle softly in her ear, saying 'Control yourself, sweet Marisa, or all this will be over rather quickly.'

She bit her lip in mortification as he mocked her, trying to fight the dizzying lust that surged through her body just at the sound of his beautiful, husky voice. Then, at last, what she'd been waiting for started to happen. Suddenly the shadowy garden beyond the little summerhouse seemed to be alive with figures moving towards the copulating couple from the tree-filled darkness, with Lucy, wonderful Lucy, leading them all, perhaps seven or eight of them. They moved quickly, silently in the moonlight, as if following some pre-arranged plan, which, knowing Lucy, no doubt they were.

First of all a man stooped in front of Caroline's head so that he was kneeling in front of her crouching figure. Swiftly he drew out his penis and rubbed it quickly into stiffness, then as Caroline gasped in delight at the sight he thrust it into her mouth and she sucked greedily. Two giggling maidservants reached below her to toy with her long, dark nipples while another couple lay on the ground close by and started to engage in eager copulation just in front of her. Lucy watched with her hands on her plump hips, grinning.

Suddenly, John renewed his stalwart attentions, driving his sturdy, long penis deep between Caroline's bottom cheeks. The two women lay on the ground so they could suckle at her breasts, while the man kneeling in front of her steadily slid his cock in and out of her mouth, groaning as she avidly licked it. Another man masturbated just beside her, pumping away at his engorged shaft with glazed eyes and shouting out as his seed started to spurt against Caroline's face. Another woman had slipped behind the thrusting John, and was reaching between his muscular thighs to stroke his heavy balls as they tightened with excitement. And Caroline Henshawe, taken to the very extremity of degradation, was starting to have the fiercest orgasm of her life. She sucked avidly at the man's cock in her mouth as his seed spurted to the back of her throat, while John, at the brink himself as the woman behind him stroked and fondled his velvety balls, continued to pound away at her with deep, ravishing thrusts. Caroline cried out and trembled convulsively as she felt the women beneath her tugging at her distended nipples with their greedy mouths, her whole body awash with rioting sensations as they all moved in on her, while John gritted his teeth and started to climax with a great roar of pleasure.

And Marisa too felt her last resistance ebb away as Delsingham's strong, gentle fingers renewed their assault on her incredibly sensitised breasts, and his rampant penis began to move slowly, deliciously within her very core.

'You are delightfully wicked, Mistress Marisa,' he murmured in her ear as the moonlit orgy continued unabated outside, 'and I think it's time now for your punishment. Don't you?'

Marisa leaned back against him, feeling his broad chest pressing against her back and aware of his powerful thighs moving in controlled rhythm as he splayed her legs even further so that she could enfold every inch of his thick, lengthy shaft. Oh, but he was magnificent. An ace indeed. She closed her eyes as she felt his knowing hand slip down to touch her soaking, exposed clitoris and she began to gasp, feeling her abdomen tighten with dark, sweet pleasure around his thrusting penis. At the same time his other hand squeezed and pulled at her pouting nipples, and she threw back her head, feeling him tenderly kissing her tousled hair, her neck, her shoulders. Then she was driving herself hard against him, impaling herself anew as the rapture burst upon her exquisitely tormented body and the warm, blissful waves of pleasure rolled through her as he continued to ravish her with slow, incomparable strokes. Only when he'd drawn every last drop of excruciating pleasure from her shuddering body did he pull her hard against him and thrust deeply, harshly, to find his own release. She heard his rasping breath, and felt his iron-hard penis spasming deep inside her, and she shuddered again in a warm renewal of pleasure. In the silence that followed he held her tenderly, his lips just brushing the nape of her neck, his body cradling hers so that she could feel the strong, steady beating of his heart. Bliss, she thought rather dazedly, utter sensual bliss.

Then he murmured in a low voice, 'I think your little pageant is almost over, my Ganymede. Mistress Henshawe is just starting to come to her senses.'

Marisa opened her eyes rather dizzily and saw that Caroline Henshawe was staggering to her feet, her gown torn and rumpled, while all around her stood the grinning band of servants led by John and the brilliant Lucy, whose arms were folded in satisfaction. Caroline Henshawe looked suddenly aghast, as if only just realising what she'd actually taken part in; her hand flew to her mouth as she stifled a little cry, and John, grinning, said, 'Was I good enough for you then, Mistress Henshawe? Any time you need a fine, sturdy man, just let me know.'

And Caroline Henshawe, looking round rather wildly at them all, let out a strangled sob and fled back towards the house.

Marisa giggled. Lord Delsingham, stroking her disarrayed curls, said, 'That was very naughty of you, sweet Ganymede. I take it you arranged it all?'

'Yes,' Marisa laughed rather breathlessly. 'I spoke earlier to John and Lucy, and they made plans with a few other servants. I couldn't believe it when she came out on her own into the gardens. It was just perfect.'

She'd turned round as she was talking to meet his eyes; she caught her breath as Delsingham, gazing down at her, said quietly, 'Yes. It was, wasn't it?'

She went very still, conscious of his dark, burning gaze that was somehow strangely intent. Suddenly feeling shy, she started to pull her disarrayed bodice up over her breasts, the colour still warm in her cheeks. He drew himself up abruptly, dispelling the strange mood that had fallen over them, and held out his arm to her.

'Perhaps we should return to the house now, Mistress Brooke. How I enjoyed our demure walk through the gardens. Shall we go and partake of some supper?'

'With the greatest of pleasure, my lord,' Marisa responded lightly, and they walked back companionably through the now-silent gardens towards the house to rejoin the other guests, as if they'd partaken of nothing more than a moonlit stroll.

And then, just as they were entering the big, crowded dining-hall, where hams and pies and all kinds of succulent delicacies were spread out on the large oak table, Marisa saw that Sir Julian Ormond was there, engaged in earnest conversation with Lady Blockley. His pale blue eyes seemed to flicker a little as he saw her enter the room with Delsingham. For some reason Marisa hesitated, then she moved quickly towards his elegant figure with Delsingham following more slowly.

'Why, Sir Julian!' she exclaimed. 'I didn't realise you would be here.'

He bowed to her, smiling. 'The pleasure is all mine at seeing you,' he said. Then he acknowledged Delsingham.

The two men bowed stiffly, and Delsingham said, with unmistakable coolness, 'Your servant, Ormond.' He turned to Marisa. 'I regret that I must leave now, Miss

Brooke. It's later than I realised.' Marisa gazed up at him in perplexity, aware of a sense of crushing disappointment at his abrupt announcement. Then he smiled, and said quietly, so that only she could hear it, 'I enjoyed our moonlight stroll.'

Before she could say anything he was gone, his tall figure cutting a swathe through the crowded, noisy room. Marisa, pulling herself together, turned back to Ormond.

'How pleasant to see you here,' she said brightly, hoping that Lord Delsingham would look back and see that she wasn't put out in the slightest by his abrupt departure.

Ormond bowed his smooth fair head. 'And you, Mistress Brooke. You look enchanting.' His cool eyes flickered over her lightly clad figure, making Marisa uneasy, as if he somehow guessed about her and Delsingham, out in the garden. But of course, he couldn't have any idea, could he? They chatted inconsequentially for a little while, with Ormond giving her advice on buying a closed carriage, and where to get someone to replace a slight leak in the stable roof. 'And remember,' he added, 'if you ever need any help with your financial affairs, I'll be only too glad to oblige.'

'Thank you. You've been more than kind.'

He hesitated. 'If you truly regard me as a friend, then I hope you will forgive me for being so personal. But I couldn't help noticing that Lord Delsingham was paying quite a lot of attention to you earlier. You do realise, of course, that he has rather a reputation?'

'I'd be disappointed if he didn't,' Marisa said lightly.

Ormond's eyes narrowed as he poured her more wine and handed her back her glass. But he said nothing else about Delsingham, and shortly afterwards, Sir Andrew Blockley came over to claim her as his partner for another game of whist. She took great care to play rather badly, so that Sir Andrew was able to give her lots of avuncular advice and pat her shoulder fondly in consolation at having lost. Then it was time for the dancing sets to be drawn up, and Marisa, who could fling an Irish reel with the best of them in the Old Cider Cellar in Maiden Lane but knew nothing of the intricate steps of the gavotte or the minuet, quickly made her excuses and left.

John drove them home, and the cool night air was fresh on their faces as Lucy and Marisa sat side by side in the open carriage. Lucy was chuckling softly at the recollection of Caroline Henshawe's humiliation out in the gardens.

'I declare, she couldn't speak for excitement when she saw us all moving in on her,' grinned Lucy. 'And John, you were wonderful, to keep her on the brink for so long, giving us all time to come out and join you.'

John, sitting up on the box, blushed proudly in the darkness. 'I know my duty, I hope.'

'You performed admirably, John,' said Marisa, but her mind was elsewhere. She was thinking, rather too much for her own peace of mind, of Lord Delsingham.

Marisa half expected Delsingham to call on her during the next few days, and one morning, when she was disturbed by the clatter of a horse's hooves in the yard, she hurried downstairs from her chamber, hoping that it might be him. She was aware of a rather unsettling sensation of disappointment when she heard John open the door, not to Delsingham, but to Sir Julian Ormond – on a neighbourly visit, he said.

Marisa, who was fortunately dressed most demurely in a high-necked morning gown of dove-coloured silk, received him in the sunlit drawing room, and Lucy served them neatly with coffee and little cakes. Ormond had brought lots of papers and other documents, and he began to talk to her about investments.

'You did say', he reminded her earnestly, 'that you would be glad of my advice regarding your finances, Miss Brooke.'

Marisa stiffened warily. Her money was hers, and hers alone, besides which, she hoped very much that he wouldn't expect her to read anything, because she didn't want him to realise how ill-equipped she was to deal with formal documents. She began to feel nervous, but Ormond, settling himself elegantly into the chair she offered him, had already started to talk.

'They say that wool and iron are bound to take off in a general revival of trade now that the war in Europe is over,' he told her. 'My adviser in the City, who's a three-star East India man, has put fifty thousand pounds of his own money into the woollen industry.'

Marisa listened with an effort, finding herself distracted by the sun glinting on the yellow roses that nodded against the outer casements. A three star East India man? What on earth did Ormond mean? He was talking about another world, a world she didn't understand. 'Perhaps,' she said abstractedly, 'I'd better discuss it with my attorney, Mr Giles, when next I'm in London.'

Ormond laughed dismissively, drawing out his laquered snuff box and taking an elegant pinch. 'My dear Miss Brooke. I mean no disrespect, but do you really think a backstreet attorney could know more about such matters than my friends in the City?'

Marisa gazed at him coolly, not liking his patronising tone. 'Lord James Delsingham also offered to advise me. I might just discuss your proposal with him.'

Ormond's brow lifted in surprise, and he looked concerned as he started to gather up the papers he'd strewn across the small inlaid table. 'But Lord Delsingham won't be in the neighbourhood for some time. Didn't he tell you he was going away?'

Marisa felt her fingers tighten on the arms of her velvet-upholstered chair. 'No doubt he did. But I don't remember exactly.'

'He's gone to Bath,' continued Ormond smoothly, 'to visit Lady Henrietta. You did know, of course, that Delsingham is engaged to be married?'

Marisa felt rather as she had done when footpads came upon her one dark night in Drury Lane and struck her a blow on the head with a cudgel before running off with her purse. With a supreme effort, she sipped calmly at her little china dish of coffee, but it tasted sour on her tongue. 'Of course I knew about it,' she lied calmly. 'He told me all about her, actually. She sounds quite charming.'

'I'm glad he's told you about her,' Ormond said quickly, his smooth forehead furrowed in concern. 'Lady Henrietta is in Bath at the moment, taking the waters. She comes from a very well-bred family, you know, and has connections with the highest in the land. I've heard that she's extremely beautiful and accomplished.'

What in? thought Marisa viciously. Sex? Sword-play? Card sharping? Oh, no. Lady Henrietta was probably accomplished in playing the piano, and dancing the minuet, and painting delicate water-colours, all the insipid arts that were reckoned to be important in a future bride. Well. She took a deep breath, and smiled brightly at Ormond's concerned face as she toyed with her coffee cup. Of course a man like Delsingham would be engaged. He was wealthy, titled, and handsome, and had no doubt had all the eligible brides in the land chasing him for years. And she, Marisa, had no intention of marrying anyone, ever, so why did this news shake her so badly? She struggled to pull herself together, realising that Ormond was still talking suavely as he sharpened the quill pen to which he'd helped himself from her little bureau.

'Delsingham has gone to Bath to discuss their impending marriage, I believe. I would assume her parents are eager for the nuptials to proceed as soon as possible. Delsingham is quite a catch, after all, despite his – ' and he coughed gently, 'despite his reputation for having rather liberally sown his wild oats.' He leant forward earnestly. 'Miss Brooke, I really would advise you to take advantage of this investment opportunity. My friend in the City tells me that within a week or so, all the options will be taken up. There will never be a chance like this again.'

Marisa hardly heard him. She felt dazed. Damn Delsingham. And he had had the gall to warn her against Ormond, when he himself was playing a double game.

'I'm sorry?' she said quickly. 'What did you say I have to do?'

Ormond pushed the quill pen and ink towards her quickly. 'Just sign here, my dear Miss Brooke,' he said softly. 'Unless, of course, you want to read through it all first?'

Marisa shook her head quickly, the familiar panic washing through her at the sight of all those lines of print. 'No. No, that won't be necessary.'

'Then just sign. And later, of course, you will need to instruct your bank. I'll help you with that as well if you like.'

Marisa picked up the pen distractedly. She didn't want to think any more about stocks and shares and the East India company. All she could think of was Delsingham, and how stupidly eager she had been for his advances that night in the little summerhouse. Well, it was the last time ever, because no-one made a fool of her and got away with it. She scribbled her name quickly, and didn't notice how Sir Julian Ormond seemed to let out a little sigh of relief as he drew the papers back towards him.

Chapter Seven

The next few days dragged badly for Marisa. The weather had changed at last, and she awoke each morning to see a solid, drenching curtain of rain outside her window that seemed to engulf all the surrounding areas of parkland and turn the former sylvan landscape into a monotonous, dank prison of dripping greenery. The house itself seemed empty, cold and damp, and even though she ordered John to light fires everywhere, his attempts did little to relieve the gloom. Marisa wandered restlessly around her rural domain, unable to settle to anything. The furnishings seemed heavy and dark to her. The oak panelling that had glowed so welcomingly on her first evening here now seemed oppressive and old-fashioned.

She found herself thinking longingly of London. She missed the noise, the crowds and the dirt of the place, missed the coarse cries of the pedlars and the crossing sweepers, and she missed her dissolute friends from the Blue Bell.

Then suddenly the rain stopped at last, and the sun broke through, sparkling on the leafy trees and lawns, bringing the old house to life again as it poured through the diamond panes of the old, mullioned windows. Several rolls of exciting new dress fabrics that she'd ordered arrived, and Marisa, bored with moping, decided that Lord James Delsingham was nothing but a conceited fraud, and not worth spending her valuable time on. Lucy further helped to restore her temper by telling her some of the tales she'd picked up from the other servants on the night of the Blockleys' ball. Marisa was particularly amused by Lucy's account of a popular dancing master from Crayhampton, who was apparently a great favourite with the local gentlewomen in spite of his miniature stature. 'He can scarcely be five foot tall, ' giggled Lucy. 'His name is Monsieur Gaston – he claims to be French, you see. And his favourite saying is, "Little dogs have long tails." '

Marisa grinned. 'I do believe I could do with some dancing lessons, Lucy. I wonder where he is to be found.' Then she noticed that Lucy was blushing, and she said accusingly, 'Lucy, I have a strong suspicion that you have already met Monsieur Gaston. Well, is it true? Is the diminutive gentleman's reputation well-founded?'

Lucy giggled. 'Indeed, it is. I encountered him the other day in Crayhampton, when I bumped into Jenny, Lady Blockley's maid, on her afternoon off. We called at Monsieur Gaston's apartments in the High Street, and, my dear, I have never seen such a small gentleman, and so well hung! When Jenny asked him about his private parts, he showed us willingly, and the sight of his great long shaft and heavy balls made me feel quite faint.'

'And?' said Marisa narrowly.

'Well,' went on Lucy rather breathlessly, 'Jenny shrieked and vowed that she failed to see how any woman could enfold such a massive weapon. But Monsieur Gaston showed us this delightful little accessory he has, a cunningly formed wooden chair with an aperture in the middle on which the lady seeking to pleasure herself with him can sit astride, quite demurely. Jenny obediently placed herself as she told him, and Monsieur Gaston wriggled beneath her. At first, he tongued her through the secret hole, until poor Jenny was quite red in the face with pleasure, and then I saw him grip his mighty purple weapon and slide it up through the aperture in the chair, and Jenny, feeling his hardened flesh slip into her eager lips, went quite, quite silent.' Lucy swallowed hard, her own eyes bright with lust. 'She bounced herself into a state of extreme pleasure, of course, and the arrangement seemed to work very well.' She stopped, and lowered her eyes demurely.

Marisa said dryly, 'And you, of course, Lucy, left at this point?'

Lucy grinned wickedly up at her. 'Oh, no, Mistress Marisa. After witnessing such a fervent pleasuring, you can imagine that I too wished to take my turn on Monsieur Gaston's fine pleasuring couch, and he pumped his mighty staff into me until I was faint with pleasure. We galloped a fine gavotte together, I tell you.' She dimpled. 'And Jenny tells me that he has many more intricate dances in which he instructs his students.'

Marisa laughed, and after that, believing her spirits to be quite restored, she arranged to go into Crayhampton herself, not to meet with Monsieur Gaston, as Lucy teasingly suggested, but for a leisurely dress fitting at the fashionable milliner's in the High Street. She also spent a small fortune on silk shawls, and fans, and dainty slippers for dancing, along with parcels full of stockings and lace and all sorts of other fripperies. Afterwards, she visited the carriage-makers that had been recommended by Sir Julian Ormond, and purchased a fine travelling coach with handsome navy blue paintwork and beautiful velvet upholstery. It had only recently been built, she was assured, for a gentleman of the very highest quality, who had unfortunately lost a fortune at gambling.

'Cards, you know,' confided the carriage-maker to Marisa in hushed tones. 'Dear me. Such a dreadful curse of our times, Miss Brooke.'

'Indeed,' agreed Marisa rather breathlessly, running her hands over the beautiful brass adornments of the carriage with sensual delight. She would have a riding habit made to match her new carriage, she decided; navy-blue velvet would set off her blonde colouring

702

exquisitely. After that, she went to dine at the Bull and Crown, feasting in the private room with Lucy off pheasant, and strawberries and cream, and a wickedly expensive claret that was like velvet on the tongue. By the time John drove them back in the new carriage, it was early evening, with the sun slanting low over the fresh green countryside. Marisa and Lucy, reclining back against the padded velvet of the upholstery, were surrounded by exciting parcels and packages and hat boxes, and Marisa, feeling her spirits surge, decided that she had quite got over Lord Delsingham. So he had a fiancée, more fool him, she thought derisively. Lady Henrietta was probably prim, demure, and virginal, and altogether utterly boring, even if she did come from one of the best families in the land. Well, if Delsingham decided to come to her, Marisa, for a little light relief, then she would treat him with the contempt he deserved.

The sun had almost set behind the trees when they got back to Melbray Manor at last. Marisa and Lucy started on a fresh bottle of wine and, settling themselves in the cosy front parlour, gleefully began to open all the parcels. Marisa tried on a new white muslin gown, with fashionably long, close-fitting sleeves and a jonquil coloured overtunic of fringed satin, while Lucy pirouetted around in a flimsy dress of almost transparent cream tulle with little puff sleeves, draping a long silk shawl in kingfisher blue dramatically around her arms. 'Do you think Monsieur Gaston would approve of me in this?' she grinned mischievously.

'I think he'd prefer you out of it,' said Marisa, helping herself to more wine.

John lit the candles and laid a fire to ward off the evening chill, watching them all the while with an eager eye as they examined all their new finery. No doubt he anticipated more entertainment later. And then, suddenly, they heard the big knocker being rattled against the front door, startling them all into guilty silence.

John, whom Marisa had equipped with smart formal livery as befitted his role as her personal manservant, went to open the door as Marisa and Lucy, both quite tipsy by now, quickly tried to gather up the flimsy gowns and shawls and undergarments that were scattered around the parlour. But they were too late, because in came three women, all demurely dressed in grey shawls and gowns and bonnets, their prim faces bright with visiting smiles. To do them credit, they hesitated only slightly when they saw the empty bottles and glasses, and the discarded clothing strewn about the candlelit parlour. Then the foremost one, a big, strongly made, middle-aged woman in a severely cut riding habit, stepped forward brightly, holding out her hand.

'My dear Miss Brooke, I do hope we haven't called at an awkward time. Just a neighbourly visit, you know? My friends here and I organise a few small functions around the parish. Cynthia here is the churchwarden's wife. We hold sewing groups, musical afternoons, charitable works and so on, and we wondered if you might be interested in joining us.'

Marisa shot a fiery look at Lucy, who was desperately trying to stifle a giggle as she stood there half-naked in her flimsy tulle gown. Then she stepped forward to return the rather firm handshake, feeling decidedly inebriated.

'How – how very pleasant of you to call,' she replied a little faintly. 'Do please sit down. Can I offer you some refreshments? Tea, perhaps?'

'We haven't got any tea,' hissed Lucy in her ear.

Marisa gestured rather helplessly towards the scattered wine bottles. 'Some wine, then, ladies?'

There was a deathly silence. Then one of the three women, who was thin and bespectacled with her brown hair drawn back in a bun, said rather breathlessly, 'I would love some wine. I only ever get a glass at Christmas, at my brother's. With the goose, you know,' she added rather sadly.

'And there's the communion wine,' said Cynthia the churchwarden's wife darkly. She was plump and quite pretty, with faded fair hair peeping out from beneath her grey silk bonnet. 'But my husband always locks it away. He says it's to stop the servants drinking it, but I know it's because he doesn't want me to enjoy myself.'

Lucy was already handing out glasses, and filling them with the remnants of the dry white wine she and Marisa had been drinking. The women tasted it avidly, their faces bright with excitement. The tall one in the riding habit drank hers down in one go and turned confidingly to Marisa.

'We saw you at Sir Andrew Blockley's house the other week,' she confessed. 'Saw that some of the women were a bit frosty to you. They're like that round here with newcomers. But we thought, now, there's someone who'll liven things up around here.'

The thin shy one with the brown hair pulled back in a bun drank her wine reverently. 'Oh, I do hope so.' she whispered, gazing at Marisa.

Marisa took a deep breath. Then she turned to John, who'd been standing impassively by the doorway. 'John,' she said quickly, 'I think we bought some champagne today, didn't we? Bring it in, will you?' She turned back with a winning smile to her visitors. 'I think we ought to make one another's acquaintance in style.'

John bowed and turned to go. Marisa had fitted him out in a short, close-fitting beige jacket in the military style, so that his high-waisted, slim breeches emphasized his muscular buttocks and strong legs quite deliciously. As he went, Marisa noted that three avid pairs of female eyes were most definitely fastened on his retreating backside, and her mind began to run riot.

The bottle of champagne was opened, and then another, and soon their visitors were extremely inebriated. Marisa, watching the three women pityingly, decided that they probably hadn't had so much fun in years. They told her all about their insipid village scandals, and the servant problem, and the attempt at amateur theatricals last winter that had resulted in the new curate running off with the squire's flighty younger daughter. Hannah, the big woman in the riding habit who'd first introduced herself, turned out to be passionate about hunting. She was married to the local magistrate, Sir Henry Davenport, whom she spoke of with dismissive scorn.

As John piled up the logs on the fire and drew the curtains across the windows, the candlelit room grew cosy and warm, and the women giggled like girls as they drank more and more of the champagne. The one with the bun, Emily, looked quite young and pretty as her brown hair slipped slightly from its pins, and Marisa felt so sorry for them, with their drab lives in which a glass of champagne was a rare treat, that she longed to liven up their evening somehow. Then she saw how Cynthia and Emily were enviously fingering the new clothes that she and Lucy had unwrapped so haphazardly.

'Go on,' she urged, laughing. 'Try them on. They'll come to no harm. Choose what you fancy, and try it.'

John thoughtfully retreated to the hall, and in no time at all they were all parading around in clouds of muslin and tulle, under the encouraging guidance of Marisa and Lucy. Cynthia, the churchwarden's wife, thoroughly drunk and with her fair curls in disarray round her plump shoulders, paraded round in a calf-length silk chemise and pale stockings; the thin, brown-haired Emily, whom Marisa assumed was a spinster, undressed rapidly and rather dizzily tried on a lovely brocade dressing robe embroidered with Chinese motifs, while Hannah, the magistrate's wife, who was rather too big for most of the garments, wore her own stiff-boned corset under a long, floating tulle wrap. When the women got onto the subject of men, Marisa and Lucy's eyes met in bright speculation. Cynthia had draped herself across a velvet settee and was downing her champagne straight from the bottle, in between complaining about her strait-laced husband in a rather slurred voice. 'He regards sex as a marital duty, you see. He doesn't like me to move, and he doesn't like me to see him. Just think, girls,' and she giggled, rather hysterically, 'I've never, ever in my life seen an erect penis!'

Hannah the huntswoman snorted as she lay back in a big carved chair, her tulle wrap falling apart so they could see her big, billowing breasts above the line of her buckram corset. 'You want to see my husband's? Blink, and you'd miss it. And it's all over so quickly; a quick push and a grunt, girls, and he's finished. What a fuss about nothing. How I'd love to spend some time with a real man!' She looked assessingly towards John, who had wandered in again to pour out champagne when needed. Marisa and Lucy caught that look, and their eyes met conspiratorially.

Emily, the little spinster, was quite pink from the unaccustomed champagne. Her rather pretty brown hair had fallen loose from its bun and lay around her shoulders, and her dainty voice was a little unsteady as she knelt on the rug before the fire, stroking the thick brocade of her embroidered dressing robe. 'They say', she whispered, 'that Lord James Delsingham is a wonderful lover. They say that if you spend one night in his arms, you'll experience utter bliss.'

Marisa froze, but Hannah laughed aloud. 'Poor Emily. Aspiring rather high there, aren't you, m'dear, seeing as you've never been ridden by a man in your life? Delsingham's rather out of your sphere, Emily, though I've heard similar stories myself.'

'One can dream, Hannah,' said the pink-faced Emily, with a certain amount of dignity; the others laughed at her, teasing her. Such was the noise and chatter that none of them heard the fresh knocking at the door, except for the alert John. He went to answer it, then came back quickly and murmured to Marisa, 'Some men to see you, my lady. Say they know you.'

Marisa, glad to get away from the talk about Delsingham, moved quickly out into the shadowy hallway and stopped in amazement. 'Seth!' she gasped out in delight.

It was indeed Seth, the gypsy from Vauxhall Gardens, standing there in the doorway and gazing at her, with his dark curls, his golden earring and his warm brown eyes. Just behind him she could see big, bearded Caleb, with shy, youthful Tom grinning at her bashfully. Seth smiled, his teeth white in his suntanned face.

'I've brought you this little trinket,' he said, holding out her precious gold ring.

'Thank you, oh, thank you,' breathed Marisa, taking it happily. 'But how did you find me, Seth?'

'We Romanies have our ways,' he replied quietly, folding his arms across his chest as he gazed down at her. He was wearing a loose, white cotton shirt tucked into tight cord breeches, and a short sleeveless jerkin. Beneath his loosely tied red neckerchief his shirt was unbuttoned, and she could see a heart-stopping triangle of bare brown skin. She remembered the feel of his lithe body, the silky sensation of his beautiful cock caressing her breasts, and the champagne sang deliciously in her blood. She suddenly wanted him very much. 'I also heard,' he went on, his dark eyes holding her thick-lashed blue ones, 'that the beautiful new mistress of Melbray Manor might be in the way of wanting some reliable manservants. There's myself, of course, and Caleb, who's big and strong as an ox, and Tom, who's young but learns quickly.' His eyes twinkled. 'We'll work round the estate, or the gardens, or stables – anything you want.' He paused meaningfully, his eyes resting on her beautiful gown, drinking in the sight of her. 'Anything at all.'

Marisa was aware of a breathless hush in the room behind her, and realised that Lucy and her three visitors had moved out silently into the hall to absorb the unexpected sight of the three handsome, stalwart gypsies. She gestured towards the fire-lit parlour and said huskily, 'Come in, Seth, Caleb, Tom. I do believe I have work for you already.'

Her three female vistors were suddenly shy, trying desperately to draw their disarrayed garments around themselves, but Marisa could tell by the way they looked at the young, virile gypsies exactly what they were thinking of as the champagne they'd consumed raced around their fevered blood. She went slowly round the

708

room to blow out all but two of the candles. Darkness, she knew, was a friend to decadence.

'Ladies,' she said softly into the breathless hush that surrounded her, 'I wish to propose a game.' She was aware of Seth's beautiful mouth twisting in a mocking smile, but she turned to him quickly and murmured, 'No cheating this time, I promise.' He bowed his head in acknowledgement, and her flesh tingled as she once more remembered his lovely, long cock rubbing yearningly across her breasts. No cheating, but she'd make sure she had Seth tonight, one way or another. She went across to the little walnut bureau in the corner to fetch two dice while the women watched her, quite breathless with anticipation.

'We're going to have an auction,' said Marisa. 'Here we have four lovely men: Seth, Caleb, Tom, and of course John. All my manservants, and all under orders to give you exactly what you want.' She paused, allowing time for the frisson of unspeakable excitement to ripple round her guests. Then she went on, 'Yes, an auction, ladies. Only instead of paying for these lovely men, we'll dice for them.'

'Four men, five women,' pointed out Seth quietly.

She smiled back at him. 'I can wait. For a little while.'

Someone coughed nervously, and Emily, the shy spinster, looked ready to faint. But then the inimitable Lucy sprang forward eagerly to take the ivory dice from Marisa's hand, and John went round filling up their glasses, fetching more for the gypsies, and they were away. Marisa curled up on the velvet settee beside the fire, smoothing her clinging muslin gown around her legs, and surveyed them all contentedly, quite happy to watch and wait for a while. She sipped her cold champagne and relaxed.

Lucy, wonderful, exuberant Lucy, her plump breasts already falling out of her low-cut bodice, made Tom stand up first. He grinned sheepishly at the women, who gazed on him in silent excitement; he looked endearingly sweet, with his soft brown hair and slender, wiry body.

They all threw, and Emily won. She was so drunk from the unaccustomed wine that she almost fainted with delight, having no idea at all what to do, but Tom carefully removed her spectacles, unpinned the remaining strands of her hair, and kissed her gently. Her long brocade robe fell back, exposing a slender, surprisingly youthful body with small but firm breasts. She just wanted the young gypsy to kiss her, but Tom, who obviously found her appealingly pretty, had other ideas, and lowered his head to gently kiss her bosom, letting his tongue flick over her soft pink nipples until they stood out stiffly at his caress. She went very still, then clutched his face hard against her breasts. 'Oh,' Emily gasped aloud. 'Oh, nobody's ever done that before. How wicked. My God, how very, very wicked – please, don't stop.' Tom mouthed her for a few moments more as she shuddered and gasped. Then he took her hand, and pressed it against his groin, so she could feel his hardening flesh stir beneath his breeches. The colour rushed to her face, and she started to pull his clothes off frantically.

Cynthia the churchwarden's wife won John, and she was ecstatic. She made him take his clothes off slowly, providing a delicious erotic spectacle for the rest of them, because John stripped with calm, self-confident ease, knowing that his muscle-bound body was a treat for any woman. When he slid his breeches down, Cynthia leant forward, breathless with delight, her eyes fastened on his thick, lengthy penis which was already stirring with promise as it hung down between his thighs. She pressed her hands to her burning cheeks in delight. 'A man,' she crowed, 'a real, live man. Oh, let me get my hands and mouth on you, you beauty.' She dropped to her knees in front of him, stroking his penis with fluttering fingers, and then, as John's mighty rod surged into its full glory, she reached to kiss it, avidly tasting and licking its thick, veined length so that John had to brace himself against her ministrations. Gasping with pleasure at the taste of him, she began to frantically pull off her thin chemise so she was clad in nothing but her pale silk stockings, exposing all of her plump, fair body to him. She rose on her knees a little, gripping his springy cock and rubbing it against her heavy breasts, cushioning his shaft between her nipples as John fought for control. 'Oh, you lovely man. What a beautiful cock. How I love the feel of it against my tits.'

Caleb and Seth were still to be played for. Marisa, reclining on her settee, forced herself to stay calm and not to join in, though she couldn't stop herself from becoming rapidly aroused as she watched the others in their decadent play. Tom, who had lowered Emily onto the rug in a dark corner of the room, was gently easing his slender cock between the woman's thighs, caressing her and encouraging her; she was breathless with delight as the tip of his penis slipped into her, making little moaning sounds and running her hands all over his supple, naked back and buttocks. John, less subtle, had roughly turned Cynthia the churchwarden's wife onto all fours and was grunting with pleasure as he ravished her plump, quivering bottom.

Caleb was up for the taking next. Lucy threw two fives for him and so did Hannah, the horse-riding magistrate's wife. Lucy gazed at Caleb's strong, virile figure with hot eyes and said to Hannah, 'Well, now. He looks as if he's got a fine meaty prick on him, doesn't he? Let's see if he can manage both of us.'

Laughing and giggling, the two women flung off the remainder of their clothes and then began on the willing Caleb, tussling him to the floor and stripping him, laughing as they exposed his huge purple appendage already thrusting blindly from his hairy loins. Hannah gasped with delight at the sight of him, while Lucy, cried out, 'Oh, I love men with beards. Pleasure me, gypsy, pleasure me with your hot tongue.' Quickly she sat on his face, wriggling about with her swollen vulva pressed against his mouth until his lips and tongue found her hardened nub of pleasure and he greedily started to lap away. Lucy threw back her head in delight and played with her own plump breasts, drawing out her long nipples and thrusting avidly at his face with her hips as his long, stiff tongue drove between her fleshy labia. Caleb grunted, thrusting high up into her juicy vagina and then wriggling about until she shouted with pleasure.

Hannah the horsewoman jumped astride his hips, her powerful thighs flung apart and her buttocks towards Lucy's face. She shouted aloud in delight as she lowered herself carefully and felt his ravening, gnarled penis impaling her eager flesh. She bounced up and down, hissing out her delight at the feel of that great, stiffened shaft sliding up inside her, shouting out, 'Now, that's what I call a real man. Stick it up me, Caleb, you wonderful boy; drive it all into me – oh, yes, yes.' And she bounced about deliriously on his rampant penis, reaching with eager fingers to stroke at the fat, hairy sac of his semen-filled balls.

Marisa bit on her soft lower lip as she watched them, her body quickening with desire. They were all eagerly pleasuring one another, heedless of the rest of the company. Tom was showing the flushed spinster Emily how to lick his cock, while John was making the churchwarden's wife masturbate him. She was eagerly rubbing his foreskin up and down while he whispered rude words in her ear. Caleb, meanwhile, was keeping his two women happy with amazing vigour. Lucy was already flushed and breathless with the pleasure of his big, skilful tongue lapping hungrily at her secret parts, while Hannah was lifting herself high on the thick, throbbing stem of his penis then pounding down again, rubbing voraciously at her own clitoris as her fierce orgasm started to envelop her.

Marisa swallowed, feeling her own secret flesh to be moist and pulsing. Her breasts were a warm, throbbing ache beneath her muslin dress, and her nipples were tight and painful. The tension was building up inexorably in her body, and she was desperate for release. Suddenly she saw that Seth was moving towards her in the candlelit shadows. He poured out a fresh glass of cooling champagne and handed it to her, then poured out some for himself, and sat beside her on the velvet settee.

She smiled at him, liking him. 'You weren't angry with me that night in Vauxhall Gardens, were you, Seth?' she said. 'For running away?'

'No, I wasn't angry,' he said quietly. 'In fact, I thought you were quite wonderful. That was why I decided to find you again.' Gently he put his arm round her, and slipped his hand inside her low-cut bodice so that Marisa gasped in delight at the feel of his strong, cool fingers against her swollen flesh. Carefully easing her breasts out of the constricting garment, he turned her towards him so he could use both his hands to cup them and soothe the swelling globes. With the ball of his thumb, he gently rolled her straining pink nipples, and a languorous tremor ran through her.

'I'm glad you did,' she whispered, her blue eyes shadowy with desire and her lips tremulous as she thought of his kiss. 'I was sorry to have to leave, believe me.'

'I think we have unfinished business, you and I,' he said, his lean brown fingers tightening round her rosy nipples.

She leant back then against the settee, her eyes half closed in pleasure, and she let him touch her and kiss her and lick her all over as he eased off all her flimsy clothing except her stockings and the delicate, lacy corset she wore beneath her breasts. He took off his clothes too, and she gasped aloud at the beautiful silken texture of his sun-browned, firm body. Pulling him towards her, she rubbed her eager breasts against the hard muscular wall of his chest and shuddered as she felt the meaningful rasp of his powerful, hair-roughened thighs against her stockinged legs.

He laid her back on the cushioned settee and lifted her knees high, then crouched between them so he could lick at her nectared labia, parting the petal-soft folds with his tongue and trailing its tip lightly along her urgently throbbing clitoris. She could see his lengthy penis straining with dark promise at his groin. She moaned aloud and drew her sharp fingernails along his rippling shoulder muscles, unable to conceal her need. Sensing her urgency, he moved upwards again to kiss her, his tanned, handsome face all wet with her juices. He whispered dark Romany words to her that she couldn't understand but could guess at, and she shivered with delight as she felt the long, hot rod of his pulsing manhood rubbing insistently against her taut stomach.

At last, he lifted himself over her, and was in her, slipping deliciously between her parted, swollen sex-lips. His phallus was strong and silky and satisfying, just as she'd known it would be, and better. She clutched her inner muscles tightly round him, relishing the male thickness within her, and wrapped her legs around him as he drove deeper and deeper inside her with gentle yet devastating thrusts. She felt the hard, sweet pleasure gathering in her womb, and as that great, stiff rod of flesh expertly ravished her inner core, Marisa gasped and arched herself desperately to meet him, feeling how her clitoris was pressed and rolled against the base of his shaft. Then she was there, at the pinnacle, and she shimmered into a febrile dance of ecstasy as he drove faster and faster and convulsed with a hoarse shout deep within her spasming loins.

She felt his long penis continuing to twitch inside her and sighed contentedly, still quivering with the aftermath of rapture. Good, so good. His lips were still nuzzling lazily at her sated breasts; her body was fused to his with a light sheen of perspiration. She stroked the dark curls at the nape of his neck and uttered a sigh of sheer bliss.

Slowly, with amusement, she began to realise that the other occupants of the room were still busy. Several more bottles of champagne had been emptied, and all her guests were now thoroughly drunk. Emily, totally naked, was eager to show off her new-found skills, and was going round the room, avid to taste all the men's penises. Tom had initiated her well, and she looked pink-cheeked and pretty with her shiny brown hair tumbling round her shoulders. Hannah had harnessed up Caleb with his own leather belt, buckling it around his chest and under his armpits, and now she was gleefully riding astride him as he crawled round the room on all fours. With an eager yelp, Emily spotted his long, thick cock dangling between his legs as he moved, and she wriggled beneath him, licking at it avidly until it started to surge and grow with fresh vigour. Hannah slapped at his rump while Emily sucked, urging him on. Cynthia was leaning back against the wall with glazed eyes, and muttering, 'Yes, faster, damn you, faster,' as John thrust himself hard into her, and Lucy and Tom were writhing happily on the rug before the glowing fire, as Tom rubbed himself urgently and spurted his hot seed all over Lucy's bouncing breasts.

Seth was watching them all too, and laughing softly under his breath. 'Your new neighbours?'

'My new neighbours. They came to invite me to join their sewing group. The country is full of surprises.' Marisa stroked his shoulder gently. Glancing down at his hips, she saw that his penis, still thick and firm, lay heavily against his thighs, beneath it the twin globes of his testicles looked velvety, vulnerable, exquisite. He looked as if he would be ready for more quite soon. She gazed up at him steadily. 'You'll stay?'

'I'll stay, and gladly.' He put his hand over hers, caressing it. 'But only for a while. Gypsies never stay long in the same place.'

'Of course.' Marisa smiled. 'Neither do I.' Then she remembered something, and said, 'At Vauxhall, Seth, you had two women with you. Where are they?'

'Oh, they're nearby.' He reached out and began to lazily pull on his shirt and breeches. 'They're working for some fancy gentleman over the other side of the valley. He sounds rather twisted, but he pays them well, and they're enjoying themselves.'

Marisa lifted her delicate eyebrows and cupped her chin in her hands. 'Really? How very intriguing. I didn't realise there was anyone as interesting as that around here.' Her eyes roved round the room. 'But obviously I was mistaken.'

Seth laughed. 'As you say, the country is full of surprises.' He poured them both more wine, and Marisa nestled against his arm, feeling relaxed and happy.

At long last their female guests left, rather dazedly vowing eternal friendship to their new neighbour Marisa. John, whose powers of recuperation were considerable, offered to drive them back. There were comfortable servants' quarters at the back of the house, and Lucy, giggling over her role of housekeeper, showed the gypsies to their sleeping quarters, though Marisa guessed that Caleb would probably be vigorously enjoying the pleasures of Lucy's bed before too long. She herself toyed with the idea of inviting Seth to her own bedchamber, thinking that it would be comforting to sleep with a man's arms around her, and Seth was nice. But she decided against it, partly because she needed time to think, but mainly because it was one of her rules not to commit herself too much. One could get too used to sharing a bed. Marisa liked to limit her liaisons with men to the purely physical, to sexual satisfaction only. Anything else led to trouble. She needed time to be herself, time to stretch out and think and dream.

So she went up to her rose-scented chamber alone, and washed herself luxuriously with the ewer of warm water Lucy had thoughtfully remembered to bring up for her. She slipped on her filmy lawn nightgown, then knelt on the velvet-padded window seat, drawing back the heavy curtains and gazing out at the moonlit gardens and the wooded parkland beyond.

Tonight had been fun. At least three of her new neighbours were glad she was here, and she knew that they would never breathe a word of their adventure to anyone, least of all their inadequate husbands. She was willing to wager that they would be stealing back to Melbray Manor for more of the same very soon.

Somewhere out in the darkness an owl cried out, and she shivered suddenly at the melancholy sound, wrapping her arms across her still-sensitive breasts. Seth was a beautiful, considerate lover, well above her minimum of ten. He was possibly even a king. But he wasn't an ace, like Delsingham.

She frowned. Too bad. When he came back – if he came back – after visiting his simpering, aristocratic fiancée, she would refuse even to see him, let alone allow him to tempt her into intimacy again.

Out there in the gardens, just beyond the shrubbery, she thought she saw something move. Stupid, of course. Probably just some small animal, or even the breeze moving the bushes. But she felt suddenly cold, and turned quickly to climb into her big four-poster bed, where she fell into a deep, languorous sleep.

With Seth, Tom and Caleb joining the household at Melbray Manor, Marisa began to feel really in charge of her wonderful inheritance. During the long summer days, the men worked hard, reclaiming the overgrown gardens, felling storm-damaged timber and repairing the walls and fences that secured the parkland while their bodies grew sinewed and bronzed in the sun. Lucy was quite besotted with them, so Marisa salved John's slightly dented pride by putting him in charge of the stables, which now housed two fine bay carriage horses and a big sturdy hunter for John, in addition to the beautiful mare that Ormond had insisted she keep. Lucy, meanwhile, dressed with alacrity in her pretty housemaid's outfit and took in a couple of girls from the village, who walked over for a few hours each day to clean and sweep and do the washing, as well as working in the kitchen to help Lucy fill the ovens and pantries with all sorts of good food.

Marisa dressed like a fine lady, outwardly demure, though her cornflower-blue eyes sparkled from Seth's tender lovemaking. She paid sociable morning calls on her new-found friends, Hannah, Cynthia and Emily, and received visitors herself. Sir Julian Ormond called round occasionally, making brief enquiries as to how she was faring, and offering helpful suggestions as to the management of her land. She transferred some of her substantial capital in order to honour the promising investment he'd made for her, and he assured her he'd let her know more soon about some of the profitable shares a banker friend in the City had whispered to him about.

Ormond was never anything but polite and courteous, but as he left one day, Lucy pronounced darkly, 'I don't trust that one. There's something strange about him; he's too smooth by far.'

Marisa laughed, stubbornly pushing her own doubts to the back of her mind, because in accepting Ormond's help she was resolutely defying Lord Delsingham, and that was all that mattered to her. 'Dear Lucy, your imagination's running riot. You must be getting bored with country living.'

Lucy grinned at her, her brown eyes very bright. 'Me, bored? Oh, no, miss Marisa. I've never been less bored in my life.'

Lucy and Caleb seemed pretty well besotted with each other. Lucy couldn't get enough of the big, bearded gypsy, and Marisa wondered briefly if John would be jealous, but then she found him one day in the butler's pantry, leaning back against the table with the two giggling village maids on their knees before him, taking it in turns to stroke and lick his throbbing member, exclaiming happily over its size and vigour. After that Marisa stopped worrying about him. And of course she herself had Seth, who was a tender and virile companion. Often in the evenings they would drink wine in front of the log fire in the parlour, just the two of them, or sometimes they played cards, and Marisa showed him how her little ring worked. In turn, Seth told her about Romany ways, and the places he'd visited, and showed her just a little of what he could read in the cards.

She lay beside him one evening on the thick rug before the fire, watching his slim brown fingers as he thoughtfully dealt and turned over the three cards that he'd teasingly said were supposed to reveal her fortune.

'This is your first card, Marisa,' he said. 'The ace of hearts, symbol of wealth, and love.'

She laughed, her blue eyes glinting with pleasure. 'How true. And the next one. Turn over the next one, Seth.'

His face darkened slightly, and he hesitated. Marisa pushed his hand away from the card, and saw the knave of diamonds. 'What does it mean?' she said quickly.

'It means you have a hidden enemy, Marisa.'

'What nonsense!' she laughed. His Romany eyes rested on her thoughtfully, and then he turned over the third and final card.

The ace of spades. She felt the colour rise slowly in her cheeks as he fingered the card. 'The third card stands for the man in your life,' Seth said. 'Do you know who it is?'

'Of course not,' she said a little shakily. 'After all, it's all nonsense, Seth, isn't it?'

He kissed her tenderly, and they made love in front of the fire, but she was aware all the time of the discarded cards on the floor beside her, mocking her.

Chapter Eight

When Rowena heard that the gypsies had moved into Melbray Manor, she felt the hot rage burning up inside her. She'd sneaked out of Ormond's house one night and headed for the gypsy encampment on her own, hoping for a good few hours of pleasure with Seth, but when the other gypsies told her where he and the others had gone, the thought of him rutting with the cunning blonde whore made her feel quite sick.

She'd headed back for Greenfallow Park in a daze, and entered, as she usually did, by the back staircase, but she must have been careless, because she was only halfway up the stairs when she realised that Ormond himself was there, blocking her way. He was gazing at her with that cold, vicious look that made her stomach leap with fear.

'Where have you been?' he said softly.

'Out!' Rowena retorted defiantly, tossing back her loose red locks as his eyes raked her gaudy gypsy finery. 'I couldn't sleep, see? So I went out for some fresh air. It's strange for us Romanies, to be sleeping under a roof all the time.'

He'd reached out to grip her arm, not hurting her, but the warning was there, in his fingertips. 'I hope,' he said curtly, 'that you're not thinking of stealing anything. You see, I don't like people who take what's mine.'

'Of course not,' she replied quickly, her heart suddenly pounding in fear, because in fact she and Matty had a tidy little store of trinkets and silver hidden under their mattresses. 'You can trust us gypsies, my lord, you know you can.'

'Really?' His lip curled. Rowena, in a sudden moment of wild defiance, blurted out, 'Why not, my lord? After all, that fine lady at Melbray Manor trusts everything to a band of gypsies. Why, she even has them in her bed.'

There was a sudden, sharp silence, and a look appeared in his cold, smooth face that made her shiver. 'What are you saying?'

His hands gripped her more tightly now, but Rowena lifted her head defiantly. 'Didn't you know, my lord? That fine Marisa Brooke is taking her pleasure with a band of gypsies.'

He seized her wrist then, and pulled her quickly up to his private rooms. Rowena stumbled after him, her mind racing. He was livid with rage. Why? Somewhere, here, there must be a chance for revenge. Once in his bedchamber, he let her go of her arm, and she sank to the floor with her shoulders against his heavily draped bed, her green eyes smouldering up at him, waiting. He stood over her, his breathing jerky. 'If you're lying . . .'

She licked her lips. 'Oh, no, my fine lord. I'm not lying. Ask anybody.' She saw then that his pale eyes had fastened on her luscious, lace-covered breasts. Slowly, deliberately, she started to pull down her blouse, revealing the ripe globes to his hot gaze. 'It seems that Mistress Brooke enjoys being mounted by the gypsy men. Doubtless they've got real long cocks, like gypsies do, and no doubt they know lots of secret little tricks that the fine ladies love, like sucking at them and tickling their bottoms and whispering dirty Romany words.'

Still fondling her breasts until the long brown nipples stood out stiffly, she saw how Ormond's face had gone quite white in the shadows. She reached up to stroke one hand along his thigh and saw the unmistakable knot of hard flesh where his breeches were drawn tight across his groin. Oh, yes. There was mischief to be made out of this, somehow.

'And that slut, the lady at Melbray Manor,' she whispered, 'I bet she just begs them for it. She sounds real fancy, but she's just a high-class whore. I can just see her, as she crouches on all fours and pleads with one of them to slide his fine big cock up her, while she plays with the other two, and sucks them off, and gets them to spurt their hot seed all over her.'

Ormond was shaking now. 'No. It's not true.'

Rowena reached up, her eyes glittering, and gently unfastened his breeches. He groaned aloud as his slender, angry penis jerked free, and tenderly she started to rub it.

'Oh, it's true,' sighed Rowena. 'Me and Matty, we've seen these gypsies in action, you see. Real dirty, they are. You'd like to see them at her, wouldn't you?' Raising herself a little, she dreamily rubbed his quivering shaft against her overflowing bosom, catching the tip of it along her hard brown nipples. 'Just imagine: three of them, all fucking her, all playing with her fine titties, sticking their mighty cocks up her dark little bottom hole. The one she's chosen as her favourite, he's got a lovely thick, silky cock – bet you'd like to feel him up your tight arse, wouldn't you, my lord? He'd do it, too, if you paid him enough – he'd pleasure you real good.'

Her lips fastened suddenly over Ormond's thrusting member, licking salaciously as he shuddered and gripped her bare shoulders. At the same time, she was thinking furiously. Money, she thought, that was behind it all. That blonde slut Marisa must have paid the gypsies really well, otherwise her fine Seth would never, ever have gone with her. She must have paid him lots of gold to ravish her dainty arse, damn her.

'She's a slut,' Rowena gasped aloud, pulling her face away from Ormond's rampant weapon and starting to fiercely caress his tight balls. 'A filthy slut, who needs endless pleasuring. Just think of her, my lord, in her fine silks and satins, writhing around on a lovely gypsy prick as it dances and leaps inside her – oh!'

She broke off because Ormond was starting to climax furiously beneath her ministrations. Clasping her heavy breasts swiftly around his jerking shaft, she caressed him tenderly as his semen spurted hotly over her quivering nipples. He gasped aloud, calling out her name as the sweat beaded on his forehead, and then, when he'd finished, he said in a low voice, 'You're sure about this?'

'About the gypsies and Marisa Brooke? Oh, yes,' said Rowena bitterly, gazing up at his drained face. 'It's true all right.'

'This is too much. She must be stopped.' He seemed, for a moment, to have forgotten that Rowena was there. She crouched silently at his feet, letting his seed trickle coldly down her bare flesh. Then he drew himself up and said sharply, 'Enough. Get out of here.'

She scurried back quickly to her own room, the one she shared with Matty, half exultant and half afraid.

A few days after Seth had drawn the cards for her, Marisa was frightened badly. She'd been out riding by herself through the parkland a couple of miles from the house, close to the boundary with Delsingham's land. She'd just forded the little stream, when the silence of the hot August afternoon was shattered by the crash of a nearby gun. The rooks rose clamouring in protest from the trees overhead, and Marisa's horse reared, nearly throwing her; she clutched wildly at its mane, and then she heard the clatter of another horse's hooves whirling to a stop just beside her. Seth was there sliding off his little pony and yelling out, 'Marisa, Get down. For God's sake, get down!'

He was pulling her so roughly off her horse that she tumbled gasping to the ground and lay there in his arms, all the breath knocked from her body as her mare cantered wildly off and Seth's little pony whinnied in alarm. Another shot rang out, this time whistling just above her head; she felt the breeze of it against her hair.

723

Absolute silence followed. She lay stunned and trembling. Seth soothed her as he would a frightened colt. 'There, there, my lovely one. It's all right, now. It's all right.'

She drew herself up, her blue eyes wide and dazed in the whiteness of her face. 'Someone was trying to shoot me, Seth.'

He frowned, looking anxious, but then he said quickly, 'Nonsense. Just some crazy poacher, perhaps. I'll send Tom and Caleb through the woods to hunt him down, but first I'm going to take you back to our home. You're shaking. And, Marisa, you must promise me. Don't ever ride out on your own again, without me or John or Caleb with you. Do you give me your word?'

'Yes,' she whispered rather faintly as Seth whistled back her terrified horse and soothed it with expert hands and voice before calmly helping her back into the saddle. She suddenly remembered the other accident, when she'd fallen from her horse. Delsingham had said the strap was cut, and she'd laughed at him, but she didn't feel like laughing now. She remembered, too, the cards that Seth had drawn for her, and the gypsy's disturbing silence as he turned over the knave of diamonds. A hidden enemy, he'd said.

Dear God, Marisa thought rather dizzily, I've faced the gambling dens and brothels of backstreet London, and I've outfaced gangs of Covent Garden ruffians, but I've never, ever been as scared as I am now!

She took Seth's advice seriously, and two days later, when she rode over to a nearby farm to order some supplies of corn, Seth himself accompanied her. The farmer promised to provide exactly what she wanted, and at a good price, so after drinking a glass apiece of his wife's creamy, home-brewed ale, Marisa and Seth set off for home in the late afternoon sunshine. The trees were heavy with summer foliage, and the air was scented with the fragrance of hedgerow flowers. Distant cattle grazed contentedly in the drowsy heat, and swallows swooped low over the river, chasing the clouds of dancing gnats.

Seth started to sing some gypsy songs as they rode along, in his own tongue. He had a sweet, mellow voice, and Marisa listened, entranced. When he had finished she grinned at him and responded by singing an extremely licentious lyric about a young lady who used to frequent certain bordellos in Leicester Fields. They laughed together, taking it in turns to make up more and more outrageous verses as their horses ambled along the dry, dusty track that led through the woods towards Melbray Manor.

Their singing was abruptly interrupted by the sound of horses crashing through the undergrowth alongside the track. Seth's hand was on his pistol. He hissed out, 'Marisa, ride for your life!'

He was too late, because four big, roughly dressed men on horseback had already surrounded them and were pointing guns at their heads, while one of them, a ginger-haired man with a cruel face, was saying to Seth, 'Just drop that pistol of yours, gypsy scum. Don't try anything, or you'll be dead, and so will this fine whore of yours.'

Seth hissed out, and urged his horse suddenly forwards towards the man who spoke, but another of the ruffians rode up beside him and struck him on the back of the head with the barrel of his gun, and Seth fell heavily from his horse.

Marisa let out a low cry, controlling her own frightened mare with difficulty. The men looked coarse and brutal; they wore rough, tattered clothing, and their hats were pulled low over their faces. Two of them dismounted quickly and hurried towards the groaning Seth as he lay on the ground, while the other two made their way purposefully towards Marisa and dragged her struggling from her horse. She lashed them verbally with a stream of vicious invective and tried to hit them with her riding whip, but one of them pulled it easily off her and laughed.

'Fancy you knowing such words, darling, and you so innocent-looking too. Just keep nice and quiet, now, and you'll come to no harm.'

'Then let me go, damn you!' hissed Marisa, still struggling fiercely as the two of them pinioned her. 'What do you want – jewels, money? I've not got much on me, but you're welcome to it. Just let me and my manservant go.' She was conscious that her hat had slipped off, and her blonde curls were tumbling around her face as she pleaded with them. They stared at her, their eyes hot on her breasts, which were outlined by the tight jacket of her riding habit. One of them said, 'We don't want your money or your fancy jewels, Miss Brooke. Hold that gypsy tight, Varley, won't you?'

No ordinary footpads these. They knew who she was, and they wanted something. Marisa began to feel really frightened.

Seth was struggling too, but to no avail. The man with the ginger hair, whom the other had addressed as Varley, pinioned the gypsy's arms roughly behind him, laughing to Marisa, 'Your manservant, eh, my lady? Is that what you call him? He's your filthy gypsy lover. You let him share your bed, don't you? Has he got a fine, stalwart cock on him, then, as well as a handsome face? Do they do things differently, the Romanies? I've heard they've got lots of fancy little tricks to keep their ladies happy in bed. Has he shown you them?'

Marisa had gone quite white as she saw how the man twisted Seth's arms behind his back, forcing him to the ground on all fours. Seth's face was gaunt with pain.

'Let him go, you filthy cowards,' she breathed. 'He's a better man than any of you.'

Varley, who seemed to be the gang's leader, laughed unpleasantly. 'You think so? Perhaps we'll try him out. And maybe by the time we've finished with him, you won't be quite so hot for him, my fine lady. He's a horse thief, aren't you, pretty lad?' His brutal grip tightened on Seth's arms. 'People are hanged for less. A vicious horse thief, who's been taking his pleasure a bit too freely. We've orders to punish him so he doesn't dare to show his Romany face in these parts ever again.'

'Whose orders?' cried out Marisa, but the man just laughed. Seth's face was white as they dragged him along and tied him face down against the sturdy stump of a recently felled oak, securing him with thick rope one of them produced so that he was kneeling over the tree with his cheek laid helplessly against the smoothly-sawn surface. Marisa struggled again with the two men who held her, and wondered if there was any trick she could employ, but they were big and muscular, too formidable by far for any of her ruses. She felt sick with unknown fear for poor Seth; something terrible was going to happen to him, she knew. She said, as steadily as she could, 'If you release him and let him go unharmed, then I'll make sure you get a lot of money, I promise you. I'll pay you in gold for his safety.'

They laughed. Varley mocked her. 'My, my, he does mean a lot to you, doesn't he? But we're already being paid, thank you kindly. Paid more than enough, eh, lads?'

Marisa moistened her dry lips. 'Paid to do what?'

Varley laughed again. 'Watch, and find out. Our orders were pretty clear, so we'll do it with great care, believe me. Maybe you'll enjoy it.'

Marisa felt sick at the cruel mockery in the ruffian Varley's words. The warm, earthy depths of the forest that had earlier been so tranquil suddenly seemed full of menace. The light breeze had dropped, making the air almost suffocating, and even the birds had stopped singing. Varley was starting to rip Seth's clothes from his pinioned body, tearing off his shirt so that the gypsy's tautly muscled brown back was exposed, every sinew stretched by the ropes that bound his arms and wrists to the gnarled roots on the other side of the stump. When Varley pulled out an ugly knife, Marisa felt the blood drain from her face, and then realised that he was using

727

it to cut at the belt of Seth's cord breeches, ripping them away from his kneeling body so that the gypsy's tight, smooth buttocks were exposed to the leering gaze of the men. Someone laughed, and muttered something to Varley; Varley nodded and started to pull off his own leather belt, stroking it meaningfully.

'Know what we do with gypsy horse thieves round here, pretty lad?' he said softly to Seth. 'We leather their arses, just gently, you understand. Just a warning. And you know what we do with gypsies who are bold enough to pleasure our womenfolk with their dark Romany cocks? We teach them a different kind of lesson, lad; one you might even enjoy. The lady's watching you, gypsy. Let's see what kind of performance you put on for her this time, shall we?'

And, his face grimly intent, he drew back the leather belt and started to swing it across Seth's bared bottom-cheeks.

Marisa cried out as the leather landed on Seth's firm, tender flesh, and felt sick as she saw the red weal spring up across his beautiful body. She saw him shudder in his bonds, not so much with pain, because they weren't aiming to hurt him physically, but with the degradation of it. His head was bent against the stump of the tree; his arms were outstretched, and bound at the wrists. She could see that his eyes were shut; his face set tense against the kiss of the belt as it sang through the air, again and again. His buttocks were taut and reddened. Between them was exposed the dark, shadowy cleft, lightly kissed with tendrils of body hair, and she could glimpse the tender pink bag of his testicles dangling helplessly between his thighs.

And then the man called Varley paused, letting the belt dangle heavily in his hands. He laughed unpleasantly and said, 'Enjoying it, lad? Is this something your fancy lady likes to do to you?' He nodded to one of his grim-faced companions. 'Loosen his bonds a little and turn him round. Let our lady get a good look at him.'

The other man did exactly as he was bid, leaving Seth's

arms bound but twisting him round roughly at the hips. Varley had ripped the gypsy's breeches down to his knees, and as Seth's body was forced round, Marisa saw with a stab of shock that his penis was already darkly turgid, stirring with secret excitement as it hung down between his thighs. The man who'd turned him saw it too. He laughed unpleasantly and gripped Seth's member in his big fist, rubbing it up and down with coarse skill. Marisa, scarcely breathing, saw poor Seth's face twist away in agony as his penis swelled inexorably and stiffened in pleasure at that lewd caress.

'No,' breathed Marisa, 'no.' The men holding her tightened their grip on her arms, and one of them said, 'Be quiet, and enjoy it, my lady, or we'll make things worse for him, mark my words. Besides, can't you see the pretty gypsy lad's enjoying himself?'

Marisa bowed her head in despair, still straining silently against the men who held her in their rough grip. But at the same time, she felt a dark wave of shameful, degrading desire wash through her as she saw that what they said was true, that Seth, poor Seth, was indeed aroused by that vile man's attentions, that his beautiful, lengthy penis was continuing to thicken and stiffen into helpless erection as the man brusquely stroked it up and down, pulling the foreskin along the bone-hard stem while grasping with his other hand at Seth's velvety testicles until the fully engorged shaft was rearing up hungrily beneath his rough but accurate ministrations. Marisa glimpsed the angry, dark plum at its tip that continued to swell and redden, and she felt the soft flesh at the juncture of her own thighs quiver at the thought of that hot, hungry penis sliding up inside her. Even here, in front of these hateful men, the idea excited her desperately. Her breasts ached remorselessly, her nipples were like heavy stones dragging at the swollen creamy flesh that surrounded them. She was unable to pull her eyes from his helplessly quivering rod as his tormentor stroked him, soothed him.

'There. Enjoying that, my lad, aren't you? No wonder

the fine lady's so fond of you; it's a pretty toy you've got there. Pays you well, does she? Makes it worth your while?'

Another man laughed and called out, 'How much do you gypsies charge the ladies for a good fuck behind the hedges, eh?'

Seth's eyes flashed as the man crudely fondled his penis. Suddenly he lifted his head and said clearly to his tormentors, 'Try asking your own womenfolk. They'll know the price well enough.'

The men drew back from him with a swift hiss of anger, and Marisa, gazing in despair, saw the ginger-haired one, Varley, step forward threateningly. He said, 'You shouldn't have said that, gypsy boy, about our women. Oh, no.' And while Marisa watched, her throat dry with horror, he grimly unfastened his own rough breeches and drew out his own penis from its bush of wiry red hair. She saw, with fascinated revulsion, that it was already jutting fiercely upwards, throbbing with arousal. He too, it seemed, had been enjoying Seth's humiliation. He fondled his penis himself, lovingly stroking the thick shaft until the veins stood out. Then he said suddenly, 'Turn him back round. Make sure he's secure.'

The other men quickly did as they were told, tightening the rope round Seth's wrists to force him into submission. And then Marisa saw Varley spit calmly into his palm and anoint his own penis with saliva, rubbing it lovingly until it was engorged with blood, a dark and angry shaft. Then he knelt behind the pinioned Seth and gripped the gypsy's tight bottom-cheeks, fondling and stroking roughly and pulling them apart until his anal aperture was just visible, a tiny, pouting bud. With a grin, Varley leant forward, gripping his own penis meaningfully as he gently prodded and probed between Seth's cheeks. Marisa gasped and tried to break free, but one of the men holding her said, 'No, my pretty. He's enjoying it. See how the gypsy's cock quivers anew.'

Marisa watched dry mouthed as Varley's penis slipped at last into the tight aperture. She saw, too, because her captors made sure she could see it; how Seth's erection throbbed and beat against his own belly at the fresh stimulation, saw how the gypsy threw his head back, his mouth contorted as the dark, forbidden pleasure of penetration assailed him. Varley, his penis gripped by the gypsy's tight anal ring, began to move slowly, carefully between Seth's muscled buttocks, and the other men watched with hot excitement as Varley murmured lovingly between thrusts, 'You're enjoying this, aren't you, my fine gypsy lad? Enjoying being mounted by a good, strong man, enjoying feeling my mighty cock in your tight little hole . . .'

And as his penis slowly slid in and out of Seth's exposed bottom cheeks, Marisa felt the hot waves of despairing excitement flood her own body. She longed to throw herself beneath Seth, to take his beautiful, straining penis with her lips and tongue, and feel his tormented shaft thrusting to sensual oblivion deep within her mouth until his seed was all spent and his agonised face was bathed in bliss. But the men tightened their grip on her, their faces dark with lust as they watched their leader take his pleasure. 'Enjoying it, lady?' whispered one of them softly. She threw her head back in defiance, her lips pressed tightly shut, determined not to let them see how shamefully aroused she was by the animal lust being displayed before her eyes.

Varley, still thrusting with keen pleasure, was near the point of release. His face was dark as he drew out his glistening, meaty penis with slow relish before avidly driving himself back in. Seth was gasping as he crouched, the sweat beading his forehead, his own penis darkly distended. Varley's rough companion suddenly dropped to his knees beside him, laughing crudely. 'Nearly ready, gypsy lad? Let's give you something to really remember us by, shall we?' and as Varley pounded faster and faster into him from behind, the other man gripped the gypsy's straining phallus and swiftly squeezed and pumped at the distended flesh until Seth gasped harshly and his semen started to squirt in dark, shameful rapture. The

731

man behind him suddenly pulled out his penis and orgasmed between Seth's clenched thighs in his own frenzy of lust, his hips thrusting frantically, and Marisa, unable to help herself, felt a violent, helpless spasming at her own core as her body went into involuntary climax. She did her very best to hold herself rigid, squeezing down on her throbbing womb and praying that the men who held her were too hotly aroused themselves by the playing out of the lewd scene before them to notice her secret, despairing ecstasy.

Silence fell. The air seemed hot and heavy. Seth's head was bowed in agony after the sweet pleasure of release. Varley got slowly to his feet, fastening up his breeches as he did so, his face still flushed. 'Let's go,' he snapped to his men. 'I think we've taught the gypsy a lesson he won't forget for a while. And as for you, lady,' and he turned to Marisa, 'let's see if you fancy him so much after seeing what he really enjoys, eh? It's well known that the gypsies will do anything for a penny or two, like letting the gentry stick their cocks up their tight Romany arses. Folks round here don't like ladies who rut with gypsies. Find someone of your own kind to take your pleasure with in future.'

'A filthy animal like you, you mean?' said Marisa with blazing eyes, her body still trembling from the secret, shameful explosion that had taken her by storm.

'Oh, lady,' said Varley, fingering his groin as he fastened his breeches, 'I wish we could teach you a lesson as well.' His hot eyes were on Marisa's panting breasts. 'But that wasn't in our instructions, much as you would have enjoyed our attentions.' He grinned. 'Let's go, lads. We've done as we were bid.'

Quickly they went to their horses and mounted up, galloping off into the dark cover of the woods. As the hoof-beats died away, Marisa ran over to Seth and frantically untied the bonds that still held his wrists. He got quickly to his feet, pulling at his torn clothes to cover his body. She saw that his face was drawn with tension

732

as he said quickly, 'You're all right, Marisa? They didn't hurt you?'

'No. They didn't touch me, except to force me to watch. Oh, Seth, the things they did to you – we must report it to someone.'

He laughed bitterly, his face set and tight. 'You think the magistrates would be interested? As those brutes were at pains to point out, it could have been worse, much worse. Gypsies are supposed to put up with anything, remember? And do you really want them looking into your past, Marisa?'

She was silent, knowing he was right.

'And did you hear what they said?' he went on. 'Someone was paying them to do what they did; they were under instructions from someone.'

'Who could hate you so much, Seth?' she said with a shiver, reaching up to stroke his cheek.

He took her hand, and replied grimly, 'No, you've got it wrong, Marisa. You see, it's not me they hate, but you.'

They rode back together in silence in the low, sultry heat that carried the promise of a thunderstorm. As they dismounted in the stable yard, Lucy came rushing out anxiously with the news that one of the local magistrates, Sir Henry Davenport, the husband of Marisa's new-found friend Hannah, had ridden round that afternoon to ask sternly if there were gypsies living at the house.

'I told him there were, Marisa,' Lucy cried out, twisting her hands and glancing apologetically at Seth. 'Because it seemed to me as if Sir Henry knew all about them anyway. I said they were here quite rightfully, because they were employed by you.'

'It's all right, Lucy,' said Marisa soothingly as she dismounted, though her heart was beating uncomfortably fast. 'What else did he say?'

'He said – he said as how there'd been horse thieving in the district, and the local landowners were complaining that the cows had stopped giving milk. Last night a mare lost her foal over at the Blockleys' place, and folk are saying the gypsies are putting a curse on the neighbourhood. The magistrate said it was best that you all leave, Seth, before local folk take matters into their own hands.'

Seth stood steadily beside Marisa as he listened. 'I'm not going anywhere,' he said. 'Neither are Caleb and Tom. You need us here, Marisa.'

Marisa turned quickly to him. 'Seth, you must go. It's not safe for you here. It sounds as if Sir Henry was trying to warn you. Please listen to him.'

Seth put his hands on her shoulders, gazing into her troubled blue eyes. 'Marisa, it's you, not me, who's in danger. I told you that before. Remember the gunshots, the riding accident you told me about when your saddle leather was cut – and now this. I'm not going anywhere.'

There was a heavy silence, then Marisa said shakily, 'Then you're dismissed. All three of you.'

His hands dropped to his sides. 'What?'

'You heard me,' said Marisa, gazing defiantly up into his shocked face. 'I want you off my land by sunset, Seth. I'll pay you well for what you've done for me.'

His face grew dark and stormy. 'I don't want your damned money.'

'And I don't want you to stay,' she shouted back, 'and perhaps be killed next time. Do you think I want to see you punished again, as you were this afternoon?'

He was silent, his dark eyes blazing. She shook her head slightly and her lip trembled as she gazed up at him. 'Seth, Seth. You must go, please. I can look after myself. I still have John to protect me.'

He lifted his shoulders in a tiny shrug. 'Very well. Since you're the one in charge, we'll go. But remember, Marisa, we'll be around if you ever need us.'

He went to find the others, and they packed their few belongings and loaded them on their ponies. Marisa watched them go from the drawing-room window, gazing after them until they disappeared behind the sweeping curve of the chestnut-lined drive. The sky had grown unnaturally dark. She could hear the distant, ominous rumble of thunder, and she suddenly felt alone and frightened. And yet she knew, somehow, that she'd done the only thing possible. Seth had been right; his dreadful humiliation that afternoon was because of her. The cards had correctly foretold that she had a secret enemy, and she couldn't bear to put Seth further at risk. Who was it? Who hated her so much that he'd punish Seth in such a degrading way? She remembered the darkly erotic scene out there in the silent woods, with Seth desperately climaxing beneath the ministrations of the two big, coarse men, and she shivered, aware of her own shameful arousal still stirring at the pit of her belly.

She hardly slept that night. The next morning she arose unrefreshed and heavy-eyed, already missing the comforting presence of the gypsies, and when Sir Julian Ormond called round, she was quiet and abstracted. He bought her good news, he said, about her investments, but she found it difficult to concentrate on what he said. After glancing at the papers he showed her, and feeling the old familiar helplessness start to overwhelm her at the sight of all those tortuous words, Marisa quickly agreed to place yet more of her capital in his hands, and was glad to see him go.

Time seemed to pass slowly, as if she were waiting for something, or someone. She wandered restlessly around the big, empty house, and wondered about going back to London, if only for a short stay. She missed her friends in Maiden Lane; she missed the vivid taproom ruffians of the Blue Bell, and she missed the quiet sophistication of friends like David Valsino. Soon, she resolved, she would return to the city. But why not now, why not today? She shivered. She wasn't waiting for Delsingham, was she? If so, then she would be waiting a very, very long time.

Rowena, on hearing that Seth and the others had left Melbray Manor at last, hurried from Ormond's house late one night without Matty and sneaked over to the gypsy encampment, where the three men had taken up their old place again. Seth seemed strangely distant, though Rowena did everything she could do get his attention, even offering to spend the whole night with him.

'There's no need,' he said. 'You have to get back to your fine master, don't you? Or you'll lose your post.'

'He won't notice I'm gone,' she said defiantly. 'Besides, Seth, it's you I want. I've really missed you.'

She bent to fondle him, pulling out his somnolent penis and licking it until it grew into stiffness. He responded then and gripped her head, thrusting violently against the back of her throat while she used all the tricks she knew to tease and excite his throbbing shaft. He was lovely, her Seth. His penis. was so manly and long and straight, and his balls were velvety hard, bursting with hot seed, a delight to touch. While she was working on him, Caleb came up and took her from behind, and she could tell that Seth was excited by the sight of her being so crudely pleasured by Caleb's big, meaty prick, because his own strong penis grew even longer and harder, so she had to take the remaining inches of it in her saliva-moistened palm and caress him that way while her tongue danced around his swelling tip. It was wonderful, to be pleasuring Seth so and feeling his body stiffen and jerk as he finally lost control and shot his seed into her mouth with a great gasping cry, while from behind Caleb's mighty penis was ravishing her thoroughly, its ridged thickness sliding steadily in and out of her juicy sex-lips. Rubbing her breasts avidly against Seth's face, she pushed her dark brown nipples right into his mouth and moaned happily into orgasm while Caleb thrust away dementedly behind her and came with a great shout of satisfaction, his heavy balls bouncing against her buttocks.

Caleb left, and Rowena stayed with Seth, wanting badly to sleep in his arms, because he still seemed cold somehow.

'You don't still love the blonde bitch at Melbray Manor, do you, Seth?' she murmured sleepily, snuggling against him as they lay on a blanket in the shelter of the caravan.

'You don't still think about her? She'll have found herself a new lover by now; hot for sex, she was, anyone could see that. No doubt she's found some fine lord to pleasure her fancy arse, and give her lots of money as well. That's why she got rid of you, my love. Now she's a great lady, she thinks you're not good enough for her.'

Seth turned suddenly, gripping her by the arms so hard that she was frightened. 'Shut up, Rowena,' he said. 'You know nothing about her. Marisa Brooke is brave and honourable, and I'd go back to her any time, believe me. So don't push your luck. You're good company, and you know how to pleasure a man well, but so do lots of women. So keep your mouth shut, unless you want me to kick you out.'

Rowena was silent then, but her green eyes glittered with hatred as she thought of Marisa. So Seth was still besotted with the fancy bitch, was he? She'd have to do something about that. The rage burned steadily within her. She decided not to spend all night with Seth after all.

It was John, doing his usual slow rounds of the house before locking up at midnight, who first saw the flicker of embryo flames glinting from the direction of the stable block. Then he smelled the acrid smoke and roared out in alarm, rushing towards the pump in the courtyard, and Marisa and Lucy, who had been talking lazily over a late night bottle of wine in the drawing-room, ran out to help him, hurling bucket after bucket on the smouldering hay while the horses stamped and whinnied in alarm. Smoke-blackened and soaked, the three of them soothed the panic-stricken horses into placidity again and gazed at one another silently.

'You were just in time, John,' Marisa said quietly. 'That straw had only just caught. A few minutes later, and we wouldn't have been able to do anything to stop the whole stable block going up in flames.'

John was rubbing his hand slowly through his soot-blackened hair, his face puzzled and anxious. 'I don't understand it, my lady. I never take a light near the stables, never, not even a lantern, in case a spark should drop on the straw. Somebody must have slipped in here and lit it deliberately.'

Lucy gave a little whimper of terror, and Marisa, who'd already come to that unpleasant conclusion herself, felt the cold renewal of the fear that she'd been trying for so long to put to the back of her mind. They checked that the horses were all right, and were just preparing to go back inside when Marisa's eye was caught by something on the ground. Bending to pick it up instinctively, she saw that it was a tiny bundle of twigs, carefully tied with twine. Just right, she thought rather dazedly, for lighting a fire.

Lucy saw what she was holding and grabbed it from her with a little cry. 'That's elder wood, Miss Marisa. The gypsies say that to burn it brings the Devil into the house. It's like a curse on the place.'

Marisa said calmly, 'Nonsense, Lucy. That's just old superstition, and you know it.' But Lucy was still shivering, and as she hurled the tiny, sinister bundle of twigs into the darkness, Marisa suddenly remembered Seth's quietly ominous words: 'It's not me they hate, Marisa, but you.' Who hated her? Who was her secret enemy?

It was well past midnight when Rowena got back to Greenfallow Park. She could tell by the absence of his carriage that Ormond was out late, but then he often was, drinking or gambling with his fancy friends somewhere in the neighbourhood. She tiptoed up the stairs, seeing with a sigh of relief that everything was in darkness, and tumbled wearily into her little bed, after glancing quickly across at Matty to see that she was asleep and gently snoring.

Several hours later, while it was still dark, she awoke with a cry of alarm as the bedroom door softly opened, and then she gave a sob of fear as someone stepped into the room. Ormond. Damn him, but he was back late, and he looked as if he'd been drinking. He also looked as if he wanted something from her, and she knew what that might be. She raised herself quickly, wishing she'd washed the smoke stains from her face and hands, and tried a sultry smile.

'What's your pleasure, my lord?' she whispered enticingly, keeping her voice low so as not to wake Matty.

He was in a hurry. His face tight with urgency, he pulled down his breeches, and pushed her head down onto his slender, straining cock, making her take him in her mouth. She enjoyed this, and was good at it, enjoying her feeling of power over him, and imagining the familiar tension on his pale, agonised face as he drove his rampant penis between her lush lips.

Then, suddenly, he pulled himself out, and gripped her wrists, turning her hands over to inspect them. They were dirty from charred kindling. He touched his finger against the smoke stains on her cheek and hissed softly, 'Where have you been, gypsy slut?'

'Nowhere,' she stammered. 'I – I was just laying the fires for tomorrow, and I was that tired, my lord, I forgot to wash properly.'

'Liar,' he said, still gripping her wrists. 'There's been a fire over at Melbray Manor tonight. It was you that started it, wasn't it? It was you . . .'

Rowena began to whimper. 'Don't report me to the magistrates sir, please. Don't – they'll hang me, for sure.'

He slid his hand beneath her nightgown and took her brown nipple between forefinger and thumb, pinching slightly so she moaned with delicious arousal, her eyes travelling greedily to his still-throbbing penis. 'I won't report you to the magistrates. But you've made a mistake, Rowena.'

She gazed at him speechlessly, not understanding.

'Yes,' he went on, 'you've made a mistake. It's Marisa Brooke who must be destroyed. But not Melbray Manor – you understand?'

No. She didn't understand at all. But it looked as if he wasn't going to report her, as if he was almost pleased with her.

She watched his set face, half horrified, half fascinated as he slowly gripped his slender shaft and pushed it towards her heavy breasts. 'Melbray Manor is special, Rowena,' he went on softly. 'It's mine. And I want that bitch out of it.'

His penis was angry and hot against her cool flesh. Rowena smothered a low cry of fear as he gripped her shoulders. Then swiftly he turned her over, so she was crouching on all fours on her tiny bed in the darkness. Her body began to beat with the dark throb of arousal as she felt him thrust his stiffened shaft avidly, desperately between her lush thighs. He lasted only a moment before he pulled himself out and started to cream over her buttocks with a groan of despair. As soon as Rowena felt him jerk and spasm against her sensitised flesh, she began to desperately rub her long, brown nipples against the rough wool of her bedspread, at the same time reaching down with one hand to rub hungrily at her soaking clitoris. Immediately she felt the excitement gather in her loins, and she rose to silent orgasm as the last of his seed spurted voraciously over her bottom-cheeks. His ominous words rang through her as she shuddered in the very throes of climax.

So Marisa Brooke had another enemy, and a dangerous one at that.

Chapter Nine

*A*fter the fire, Marisa herself went round late every night with John, making sure that all the doors and windows were secure. She knew she needed more men-servants, but she wasn't sure who to trust, and mean-while, even though she chided herself for being stupid, the feeling that she was being watched grew more and more intense.

Then she remembered that there was a gun-room at the back of the house, approached by a small staircase that led up from the main, first-floor gallery. She'd scarcely been in it, except to lay her precious foils up there when she first arrived, but after the incident of the fire she decided to explore it more carefully, finding the keys to the dusty glass-fronted cases and meticulously examining the contents. They contained mostly old sporting guns, heavy and slow, but she also made the discovery of a pair of silver-mounted flintlock pistols, which she carefully cleaned and oiled, making sure that the powder and balls were nearby and that both John and Lucy knew how to use them. She also still had her father's pocket pistol, which she started to keep by her bedside at night. Some-one was trying to drive her away from her inheritance, and of one thing she was certain; they wouldn't succeed. Returning to London wasn't an option now.

One afternoon, when John and Lucy had driven into Crayhampton for household supplies, Marisa felt a sudden urge to take her rapiers out and feel their familiar suppleness in her hands once more. It was late August, and although the heat of summer still lingered, the sky was dark and lowering with the promise of heavy rain later. Shivering a little, Marisa lit a candle against the unaccustomed afternoon gloom and went up to her bedchamber, where she swiftly changed into tight buckskin breeches and a man's silk shirt that felt cool and free against her warm breasts. She pulled her loose blonde curls back into a black velvet ribbon, and slipped her silk-stockinged calves into the soft, leather top boots that she'd had specially made for her in Bedford Row. In the easy garb of a man, she immediately felt more confident, more in charge. Picking up her father's pistol from her bedside table, she took her candle in the other hand and hurried up the narrow flight of stairs to the gun-room.

This was a spare, masculine room, with a high ceiling and tall windows. The floor was of bare wood, while the whitewashed walls were adorned with nothing but rows of metal hooks for the storing of old-fashioned weaponry and harness. There were no other furnishings except for the gun cabinets, a big oak table in the centre of the room, and an old carved settle set beneath the window. The air was redolent with the distinctive aromas of smoke-stained panelling and oil and gunpowder. Carefully she set down her flickering candle on the oak table, glad of its light because the sky was now almost black and the heavy raindrops were already beginning to beat against the leaded windowpanes.

Eagerly she unlocked the case that contained her precious rapiers and examined them critically, balancing the familiar metallic weight in her hand. She tried a few delicate moves, letting the blade become part of her again, feeling her supple body seem to come to life as the blade danced in the shadows. Carefully she balanced her weight on her slender hips, feeling her wrist sinews tingling as she straightened her arm, imagining that

David Valsino was there watching her and murmuring curt words of encouragement. 'Speed and accuracy, Miss Brooke.'

'There's no replacement for speed and accuracy!' she laughed aloud, throwing her weight onto her left foot to make a straight thrust. 'Prepare for the *en garde!*'

And then, above the drumming sound of the raindrops against the window-panes, she suddenly heard something else, the sound of a door opening and shutting quietly somewhere down below. A shiver of alarm trickled like ice down her spine, and then, to her horror, she heard the sound of footsteps, slow, steady, deliberate, climbing up the narrow stairs to the gun-room. Marisa stood transfixed, the fine hairs prickling at the back of her neck. Someone was coming up here. And that someone was neither Lucy nor John, because she would have recognised their footsteps immediately. Whoever it was was getting nearer now; the big oak door was slowly opening. With a little sob, she quickly positioned herself with her foil outstretched, her arm poised, ready.

The door opened wide, and Lord James Delsingham stood there, filling the doorway. His brows arched, just a little, when he saw her in her man's garb with her blade held ready. Then he murmured, 'Well, Ganymede. I'm glad you're so pleased to see me. Is this how you usually welcome your guests?'

Marisa caught her breath, conscious that her outstretched arm was beginning to tremble. 'Guests are invited,' she said in a low voice. 'Who let you in?'

'Nobody. I let myself in; the door was unlocked, you see. You really should be more careful, Ganymede.' He wandered over to where the other foil lay on the oak table and picked it up thoughtfully. 'A trifle overlong, aren't they? And the hilt is somewhat heavy; however, that's a matter of opinion. You play with these toys?'

After her earlier shock at his intrusion, Marisa found herself growing more and more enraged at his calm possessiveness. 'Try me and see if I play, Lord Delsingham.'

He turned to face her. He was wearing a loose but superbly cut grey coat over his ruffled silk shirt; his close-fitting nankeen breeches were tucked into glossy black hessians, and he looked effortlessly graceful. His cropped hair was black from the rain, emphasizing his dangerous good looks. She felt a little weak, because she'd forgotten how physically devastating he was, six foot of hard-packed muscle and bone that made her own slender feminine frame seem quite diminutive. He responded to her fevered challenge by saying carelessly, 'You're serious? I must warn you: I have some skill in fencing.'

'No, I must warn you, my lord,' she said through gritted teeth. 'So do I,'

He stroked the blade he was holding carefully, feeling its edge with the ball of his thumb. 'Well,' he said, 'since you're obviously not going to put your rapier down until someone disarms you, I suppose I'd better oblige.' And he eased off his coat, unwittingly displaying his tall, wide-shouldered frame to perfection. Marisa hated him, wondering if he'd done it deliberately to weaken her, then realised that he'd done it quite unselfconsciously, because he was without any kind of peacock, male arrogance. Staring at him without realising it, she suddenly caught the laughing mockery in his eyes as he waited for her to recollect herself, and she felt the blind rage spill through her again. Carefully she rolled up her shirt sleeves, then she hissed venomously, 'Prepare for the *en garde*, my lord!' and their swords flashed in brief, hostile salute.

Delsingham was good; she realised that quickly. She'd hoped his size would be a disadvantage, but he was surprisingly speedy and graceful for so tall a man. But she was good too, well taught, with quick reactions and plenty of courage, and her much smaller size enabled her to move deftly to avoid his blade. Even so, after a few moments she was brought to realise that she had perhaps met her match, and he didn't seem to be even trying particularly hard, damn him! She lunged forward suddenly on her right foot, delivering a lightning thrust in tierce that she hoped would catch him unawares, but he parried and countered with a scuffling of blades, saying, 'A good try, Ganymede. But it's too well known a trick; try something different. And remember to play from your wrist, not your shoulder.'

Marisa gritted her teeth, her breathing by now coming quick and hard. She could see the sinewy muscles of Delsingham's forearm rippling in readiness, could sense the wily, skilled strength that informed every shift of his glittering blade, and suddenly she wanted more than anything in life to beat him, to humiliate him. Swiftly shifting her balance, she attempted a flanconnade, but just at that moment Delsingham disengaged, giving way with the point of his blade, so that Marisa's foil spun glittering from her grip and landed with a clatter on the bare floorboards.

Marisa hissed out an oath as she grabbed for her fallen blade. Delsingham leaned calmly against the big oak table, examining his hilt, and saying, 'Gently, now, my dear. Your flanconnade was premature, you know. Try a little more subtlety next time. You really are quite a capable opponent – for a woman, that is.'

Marisa lifted her reclaimed rapier threateningly. By now her hair was falling from its ribbon, and she could feel the perspiration wet on her palms. 'Damn you, Delsingham, don't patronise me.'

'Patronise you? I wouldn't dare. Play on, my dear.'

Marisa gasped another oath and lunged again, clumsily. Her hilt was slippery with sweat, and as her foible was raked by Delsingham's forte, she realised, in a flash of instinctive alarm, that the protective button had slipped from her point, so that her blade was naked, lethal. Delsingham saw it too. Parrying with cool precision, he took a step backwards and said quickly,

'Draw back your blade, Marisa. Your point is uncovered.'

But Marisa was wild with rage and humiliation. Crying out, 'What does it matter, when I've come nowhere near you anyway?' she began to press him steadily backwards towards the door, intoxicated with her advantage at last, feinting and thrusting with her arm muscles stiff and outstretched. She saw a flicker of real concern cross his hard face as he slowly gave way, concentrating solely on his defence against her whipping, deadly blade. She saw the light perspiration sheening his clean-shaven jaw, saw the play of the powerful muscles beneath his thin silk shirt as their blades grated and jarred.

'Come to your senses, Marisa,' he snapped, as the point of her blade caught at his shirt just below his armpit and a ragged tear exposed his gleaming, muscle-padded ribcage. Marisa paused, breathing hard, secretly aghast at the dangerous folly she was indulging in. Another half inch and she'd have caught his flesh, drawn blood. And she was endangering herself, because now she could see that he was no longer lazily detached, but was cold, angry, purposeful. Suddenly he whipped up his point deliberately against her forte so that his own protective button flew off. He said between gritted teeth, 'So we're playing that kind of game, are we?' and there was a dazzling glitter of steel and a sliding of his booted feet sideways as his blade caught in the thin silk of her shirt and split the fabric from shoulder to waist, so that her left breast was completely exposed. 'A hit,' he said.

Marisa drew in a deep, shuddering breath, feeling the cool air kissing her pink nipple as it protruded shockingly from the torn fabric. 'You – you could have killed me,' she gasped.

Delsingham smiled, a dangerous, lupine smile. 'Oh, no,' he said softly. 'If I wanted to kill you, then I would, believe me. Are you ready to disarm yet?'

'No, damn you!'

'Very well. If this is how you want to play, then so be it.'

Their blades clashed once more. His point glittered in the shadowy candlelight, slithering lethally down her forte. Marisa wrenched it free with a little sob of indrawn breath, but not before he'd caught at her billowing sleeve with his blade and ripped it almost away. Her upper half virtually naked, she gritted her teeth and lunged forward on her right foot, delivering a lightning thrust in carte. There was a scuffle of blades and she lunged again, her point catching in his loose shirt just an inch above his breeches. She whipped it away, slicing a foot-long scar through the silk, so she could see the flat, hard muscle of his belly tensing as he moved. He swore softly under his breath as they disengaged, and, with his blade lowered and his eyes all the time on Marisa, he deliberately ripped away the last remnants of his torn shirt. Marisa watched him, breathing hard, feeling her heart thudding against her ribs, and not just with exertion. He was magnificent, this beautiful, half-naked male animal who stood before her in the darkening gun room. Her whole world seemed to have narrowed down to a breathtaking vision of those wide, powerful shoulders that tapered enticingly down to his sinuous hips. Inevitably her eyes flickered towards the all too evident bulge of masculinity at his groin, confined into a hard, challenging knot by the tightness of his breeches, and she felt quite faint.

By now her own shirt was in tatters from Delsingham's subtle play, and damp with perspiration. Her upper body was all but naked now, like his. She could feel his eyes on her breasts as they thrust out high and provocative from between the remnants of her slashed shirt. Beneath his dark, purposeful gaze she could feel their pink crests stiffening involuntarily, but the sight didn't put him off his stroke, damn him, as his own body put her off hers. Apparently quite impervious to her near nudity, he was moving again already, and their swords rang together with wrist-bruising ferocity, scraping fiercely before the inevitable disengagement. Delsingham was beginning now to press the attack, but still Marisa fought on more and more wildly, her slim wrist numb from the jarring blows, until she knew with despair that she was tiring, making mistakes. She was also more than a little distracted by the sight of Delsingham's naked torso, and by the sight of his powerful muscles sliding and coiling beneath his perspiration-sheened skin. She backed up further, her eyes on his dangerously exposed blade, knowing with despair that the wall was only a few feet behind her. Already she could smell the musky, virile heat of her opponent's body as he relentlessly pressed on with his attack. No escape. The end must be near, she thought desperately.

He made a sudden feint, and she parried a fraction of a second too late. It was what he'd been waiting for, and his point flashed in under her guard. She tried to counter his attack, but he was bearing her wrist irresistibly upwards until she thought that the delicate bones would snap with the strain, and then, in blind despair, she felt her foil spin away from her aching hand and heard it land with a sickening crash on the floorboards.

She leant back against the wall to steady herself, her legs trembling and her fists clenched, trying to conceal her wild panting. Delsingham was still advancing on her slowly, his sword outstretched. He seemed to tower above her, and his body looked lithe and dangerous.

'The disarm, I think, Miss Brooke.You concede victory?' he said softly.

Her blue eyes blazed up at him. 'No. You took advantage of me. You cheated.'

'How?' he frowned, tossing his blade with a clatter to the floor. He was only inches away from her now. Her eyes were on a level with his. chest, and as she gazed helplessly at the enticing curves of gleaming male muscle, the fierce desire licked at her stomach, dragging away the last of her strength. 'By – by distracting me,' she retorted helplessly.

He laughed. He leant slightly forward, resting his hands against the oak-panelled wall on either side of her head so that his wrists were just above her shoulders, while his slate-hard eyes devoured the sight of her small, pouting breasts as they rose and fell rapidly beneath the tattered remnants of her shirt. 'Am I to take it, then, that you don't consider yourself to be a distraction, Miss Brooke?'

Feeling quite faint with wanting him, scarcely able to stand, she tossed back her blonde head defiantly. 'Obviously I'm not a distraction,' she snapped back sharply, 'as you seem able to disregard me quite easily, for weeks on end.'

His grin showed his even white teeth. 'So you've missed me, sweet Marisa?'

'Of course not.'

There was a silence. 'I've missed you,' he said.

She caught her breath. 'What?'

'I've missed you,' he repeated. He was gazing down at her; she could see the golden sparks dancing in his intense grey eyes. 'Oh, my dear, how delicious you are when you're angry.'

And before she could think of escaping, he'd cupped her face gently in his hands, and bent his head to kiss her. His mouth was firm and warm and strong as it persuaded her tremulous lips to part. Then he drew his tongue lightly, caressingly along the line of their parting, and took possession of her, his teeth nipping gently at her silken inner lip, his tongue moving wickedly to ravish her moist inner place with cool masculine intent. Marisa shuddered, feeling her own tongue entwining helplessly with his as his hands slipped round her shoulders, pulling her firmly against him so that her breasts were pressed against his naked chest. She could feel the hardness at his loins nudging with increasing urgency against her slender hips as she arched with instinctive longing towards him.

As if sensing her surrender, he gave a low sigh of triumph, and Marisa froze suddenly. How dare he! How dare he leave her for weeks, without a word, to go and visit the woman they said he was going to marry, only to return, and think he could take her, casually repossess her, just as if she was nothing, just some slut of a backstreet girl whom he could carelessly discard until he felt the need to sate his restless loins on her again. No-one treated her, Marisa Brooke, like that – no-one.

Well, there wasn't much time to prove her point.

Delsingham's breathing was growing heavier, slower as he pressed intimate kisses against her face and throat. His hand had slid from her shoulder to fondle her breast, rubbing at the nipple, and sending shivering darts of longing down to her abdomen. Fighting back her own betraying lust, Marisa stretched her hand behind his back, reaching towards the oak table on which her father's pistol lay. She fumbled for a moment or two, her senses in disarray from his caresses, but at last her fingers fastened round its familiar cold smoothness. She lifted it up, and flexed her wrist to press the pistol's muzzle against his naked back.

His mouth moved away from her throat in stark surprise at the kiss of cold metal against his ribs. 'Marisa?'

'Get away from me,' she said.

He twisted a little, then saw the pistol and laughed. 'Sweet Marisa, what joke is this? You want a duel with pistols now?'

'No,' she replied evenly. She drew the pistol close to her body and pointed it steadily at his chest. 'I want to remind you that this is my house and my property, Delsingham, and I'm not some cheap little doxy you can come to visit whenever you can't think of anyone else to sate your lust on.'

He put his hand out defensively. 'Marisa – '

She cocked the pistol. 'I'm warning you, my lord. I know how to use this toy. Another useful lesson my father taught me.' She fingered the pistol thoughtfully. 'An unfair advantage, strictly speaking, but as you're twice as heavy and powerful as I am, I think I deserve a little assistance, don't you?'

His body was poised and still. 'What are you going to to with me?' he said quietly, watching the gun.

Marisa shrugged. 'I suppose I could just ask you to leave. And yet . . .' Her blue eyes glinted wickedly. 'I'd like you to know how it feels, I think. How it feels to be used, as if you were just some cheap, impulsive purchase, and then discarded without a thought.'

And then, as she paused, she heard the voices down below. Lucy and John were back. Her wide blue eyes gleamed maliciously: oh, perfect timing. Keeping her gun pointed on Delsingham, she backed towards the doorway to call out to them, and immediately they came up the stairs, still chattering and laughing together. When they saw Marisa's state of undress, and saw Delsingham pinned against the wall, they fell silent, and Lucy's eyes grew suddenly hot with lust as they alighted on his superb torso.

'Lucy,' said Marisa silkily, 'as you see, we have a surprise visitor. He wasn't invited, Lucy. So we're going to teach him a little lesson, about manners.'

Lucy licked her lips. 'Beautiful,' she murmured, still gazing at Delsingham, her eyes flickering from his starkly muscled chest down to the skintight breeches that covered his well-muscled thighs. 'Quite beautiful. What are we going to do with him, Marisa?'

Marisa gestured to the corner of the gun-room, where the leather harness and belts that were used to store the old weaponry were slung on iron hooks. 'You're going to tie him up, so he can't move. John, help her.' Delsingham made an involuntary move towards the door, but Marisa levelled the gun at him. 'Oh, no,' she said softly. 'You're not going anywhere, my lord.'

Delsingham's face was still as Lucy and John advanced towards him, but he remained silent. Marisa felt herself quicken with excitement as she watched them spreadeagle his arms, and carefully secure each of his wrists to the wall by twisting the supple leather harness around the hooks until the sinews of his shoulders stood out like steel cords. With a surge of power she saw that his arousal had, if anything, increased; the bulge of his genitals against the tight crotch of his breeches was unmistakable.

Still levelling the gun at him, she said steadily, 'I'm going to make you beg me for release, Delsingham. You're a bit too used to people begging you for the favour of your rather splendid cock, my lord, but now you can feel what it's like to wait in humble silence, to be tormented until you can't stand it any more.'

He said nothing but just watched her, a pinioned, silent prisoner who nevertheless dominated the shadowy room with his breathtaking male beauty. Lucy couldn't drag her eyes from him, but John was watching Marisa, his hot eyes feasting on her naked breasts and her loose blonde hair curling round her slender shoulders as she lounged casually on the window seat with her pistol in her hand. Outside, the rain was drumming down coldly against the leaded glass panes, but in here the warm air was tense and expectant.

Marisa was conscious of an insistent beat of excitement throbbing at her own loins. She wasn't quite sure what was going to happen yet, but she knew it was going to be good. And then Lucy came sidling up to her. 'Please. Oh, please, Marisa. I've got an idea.' She whispered carefully in Marisa's ear so Delsingham couldn't hear, and Marisa smiled grimly. 'Go ahead,' she said. 'Do whatever you like.'

Delsingham knew. He could tell, she knew, what he was in for. He kept himself very still in his bonds, but she saw a muscle pulse in his lean jaw. Her eyes slid downwards to the delicious knot of male flesh at his groin, somehow obscenely prominent against the backdrop of his slender, snakelike male hips. The greatest humiliation for him would be that he would enjoy everything they did to him. Lucy would make quite sure of that.

Marisa settled herself back against the window ledge, her booted legs slightly apart, her arms folded across her naked breasts. There was no need for the gun now, because he was trapped. The rain beat down outside as the afternoon light faded, and the solitary candle guttered warningly. The room was filled with the pungent scents of oak, resin, and gunpowder, and the strong musk of heated sexual arousal.

Lucy knew what to do only too well. She sidled across to the spreadeagled man, pulling coquettishly at her own tight bodice and slipping out her full breasts to cup them lusciously in her hands. As she drew near to Delsingham Marisa saw a tremor run through his lean, pinioned frame. Lucy, mimicking the enticements of a Covent Garden flower girl to perfection, jiggled her breasts inches from his face and simpered, 'Well, my fine gent. You're a handsome specimen and no mistake. Like the look of my rosy teats, do you? Like a taste?' She rubbed her breasts mockingly against the hard wall of his chest until her nipples hardened with excitement. He shuddered involuntarily, his eyes half closed, and Lucy, seeing it, laughed. 'I think you do like me, my lord. Let's see what's happening to your beautiful cock, shall we? But first, I think you'd like to take a better look at me.' And with a mischievous smile, she slithered completely out of her dress, letting it rustle to the floor, and stood there clad only in her laced white corset and her silk stockings.

Lucy was plump but shapely. The corset, which was cunningly stiffened with buckram to push her full breasts up and apart, was laced tightly down the front, and came to a point just above the enticing dark curls of her pubic hair. Her thighs were round and creamy above her garters, and her bare bottom-cheeks below the tightly waisted corset were deliciously dimpled. Marisa heard John's grunt of excitement from the shadows as Lucy paraded slowly before the helpless Lord Delsingham, the heels of her little laced-up ankle boots clacking on the floorboards.

'Like what you see?' taunted Lucy to her prisoner. 'Like to stick your cock up me, would you?' Still Delsingham was silent. With a wicked chuckle, Lucy dropped to her knees and began to work at the placket of his breeches. Then she gave a gasp of delight.

His penis sprang out fully erect, and Marisa, watching, fought hard against the desperate renewal of desire between her thighs at the sight of that long, thick member, duskily pulsing with power. Lucy stepped back, breathless with excitement at the sight of the superbly built man standing there pinioned, his arms stretched wide and taut as his lengthy, purple-tipped shaft thrust up helplessly from the hair-roughened pouch of his testicles. Ready for the taking, thought Marisa, wildly imagining that beautiful length of flesh sliding deep within her own melting core.

Lucy, regaining her breath, gave a gurgle of delight. 'Oh, it's beautiful! So long, so thick. Let me taste you and lick you; let me feel your mighty cock in my mouth.' And Delsingham closed his eyes as Lucy's vigorous pink tongue darted out and encircled him. Marisa watched, eyes narrowed, as Lucy slid her full lips avidly over the throbbing muscle of his penis and slid up and down the silky rod with little crooning noises, her hands caressing his flat, taut belly and his seed-filled balls.

Then John, who had been standing silently in the shadows with his fists clenched at his sides and his breath coming in ragged bursts, suddenly moved. Marisa, a little dizzy from the sight of Lucy pleasuring Delsingham's shaft, was about to shout to him, to order him back, but then she realised what he intended, and she went very still.

John had knelt behind Lucy and was grunting as he clumsily pulled his thick penis out of his rough breeches. He pumped it quickly into fulness, and then, while Lucy continued to caress Delsingham avidly with her mouth, John grabbed her plump bottom-cheeks where they flared out beneath her tight corset, pulling them apart and thrusting blindly between her thighs until his cock was anointed with the creamy nectar that flowed between her pink sex-lips. Then, pulling back with a groan, his purple member moving and thrusting with a life of its own, he began to prod blindly at the dark cleft between her buttocks, until the glistening tip of his penis found the tiny pink rosebud of her secret entrance and slipped eagerly up into that tightly collared hole.

Lucy cried out in delight as John tenderly started to ravish her, carefully sliding his thick shaft deeper and deeper between her fiercely clenching bottom-cheeks. In a frenzy of delight, she licked and mouthed avidly at Delsingham's straining phallus, grunting out her pleasure in time to John's manly thrusts. By now Delsingham's head was pressed back helplessly against the wall, and his thin, sensual mouth was compressed against the onslaught of rapture as Lucy's wicked tongue snaked up and down the lengthy, rigid shaft of flesh that jutted fiercely from his loins.

Marisa felt faint as she watched them. In the shadowy candlelight, she could see Delsingham's beautiful silken cock sliding in and out of Lucy's greedy mouth; she could see John's muscular, hairy buttocks pounding away at Lucy's rear, his ballocks swaying against her as the fat, purple stem of his cock eagerly pleasured the gasping Lucy. Marisa longed to join in. Her breasts were painfully tight, the nipples tugging like fiery cords at her abodomen, while the moisture seeped wantonly from her swollen labia. She wanted Delsingham's beautiful, captive body so much; she wanted to kiss his agonised face, to take his cock into her aching core, and run her hands over his straining, sinewed torso, to feel the glory of his orgasm exploding all through his beautiful body.

But there was no time. John was shouting out hoarsely now, reaching round to fumble with Lucy's heavy breasts as he pumped faster and faster. Lucy, with a cry of joy, wriggled back against him, relishing every inch of his glistening fat rod as it penetrated her so deliciously. At the same time she continued to rub at Delsingham's saliva-slick penis with eager hands and fingers, and Marisa saw her prisoner go helplessly rigid as his magnificent penis spasmed into orgasm, sending milky jets of semen gushing over Lucy's plump breasts. Lucy, in the throes of climax herself, rubbed frenziedly against his twitching glans, delighting in the floods of hot seed spilling across her engorged nipples, clutching at his tight, thick testicles as the dark pleasure convulsed his powerful body. John, too, was spent at last, and they were all still. Delsingham, his arms still pinioned high to the wall, stood with his head bowed, while Lucy subsided with a contented sigh to the floor, and John knelt beside her, slowly lapping their prisoner's copious semen off her now soft pink nipples with his long, rough tongue.

Marisa felt suddenly tired and drained. The solitary candle had gone out, and outside it was almost dark, with lowering clouds obscuring the last of the daylight. Walking slowly across the room, she said flatly, 'That's all for now, Lucy, John. You can go.' They nodded their heads and scurried off, pulling their clothes around them as they went, their faces still flushed with exertion. As their footsteps faded away down the stairs, Marisa moved across to Delsingham and began to unstrap his wrists. She concentrated steadfastly on her task, avoiding his gaze, and avoiding too the sight of his now-soft phallus as it hung, still thick and lengthy even in detumescence, against the silken-haired skin of his inner thigh.

'You can go too,' she said shortly as the last of his bonds came free.

He began to rub his wrists gently, bringing back the circulation. Marisa trembled, realising that even now, now that she'd humiliated him, she still wanted him as badly as ever. She'd hoped to make him appear lustful and degraded and stupid as her two servants played with him, but instead he'd been magnificent, and the memory of his hard, silken penis spasming with a life of its own across Lucy's swollen breasts still made her feel faint with longing. She wanted to stroke him into arousal again, wanted to take him for herself, to feel his virile shaft tenderly caressing her, filling her, urging her into the realms of sweet, sensual delight she knew he was so superbly capable of providing.

A fantasy. She'd driven him away now for good, and wasn't that what she wanted? She went slowly to pick up the rapiers and started putting them away in their case. 'You heard me,' she repeated tersely, not looking at him. 'You can go.'

But he was walking up behind her. She could hear the soft fall of his leather boots on the floorboards as he came nearer. He put his hand on the rapier case, and said, quite calmly, 'Why, Marisa?'

She twisted round sharply at his words. 'Why what?'

'Why all that charade?' he said softly, his eyes assessing her. 'Why do you hate me so much, when I thought we were friends?'

She laughed scornfully, planting her hands on her slender hips. 'Friends? I thought you would have described me more as some kind of free whore. Someone you could just come to when you felt like a quick bit of fun. Well, you can't! And maybe the memory of that,' and she nodded sharply at the discarded leather straps on the floor, 'will remind you that you can't just go off to visit the woman you're going to marry and then come back to me!'

'The woman I'm going to marry?' he said. 'What do you mean?'

Marisa caught her breath. 'And now you're trying to deny it. How truly pitiful. I mean Lady Henrietta, of course, who I believe is taking the waters in Bath.'

Delsingham gripped her shoulders, his fingers burning her flesh through the tattered remnants of her shirt. His breeches, still unfastened, were clinging by some miracle to his lean hips; his exposed genitals in their nest of soft dark hair were a threatening reminder of his all too potent masculinity, though he himself seemed calmly indifferent to his nakedness. 'Who told you', he said, in a dangerously quiet voice, 'that I was going to marry Lady Henrietta?'

Marisa tried furiously to twist away from his strong grasp, but failed. 'What does it matter who told me, you bully?'

His fingers tightened painfully around her narrow shoulders; his dark eyes burned her. 'It matters,' he said, 'because it's a lie. There was talk, once, of an alliance between her family and mine, but I never took it any further. I'm not engaged to marry anyone, Marisa.'

She gazed up at him, stunned. 'Then – where have you been all this time?'

'Minding my own business,' he said curtly, 'but I can see that I should have been here, minding yours. What's all this I hear about gypsies, and bullets that just miss you, and fires in the night?'

'How do you know?'

'I have my methods,' he replied grimly.

Again she tried to struggle free of him. 'I don't see that any of it matters to you, Lord Delsingham.'

He shook her. 'It matters because you matter to me, Marisa, damn you! Maddening as you are, I find you quite, quite irresistible, as you can see all too clearly for yourself.'

Her eyes dropped once more to his groin, and widened. Her heart was hammering wildly, but she did her best to sneer up at him coldly in response. 'I can see that your powers of recuperation are quite remarkable, my lord, but so are those of a rutting stag. Am I supposed to be impressed?'

'No,' he said, his eyes narrow slits, his voice husky with restrained desire. 'No, but you're supposed to kiss me, damn you.'

'And you,' she replied angrily, 'are supposed to ask me.'

His breath was coming short and hard now: she could see the hot desire burning in his dark gaze. His hands slipped to her breasts, cupping them, twisting at her throbbing nipples. 'When', he said slowly, his eyes glinting, 'did you ever have any time for men who asked you, Marisa?'

She gasped as the fierce arousal leapt through her body at his touch. 'Never,' she said, with a sudden, tiny ripple of laughter. 'Oh, never,' and with a growl of masculine victory he started to cover her face and breasts with burning kisses.

'A hit?' he said softly.

'Oh, yes,' she murmured breathlessly. 'A veritable hit, my lord . . .' And she sighed aloud with delight as his tongue circled and flicked at her tight pink nipples.

He drew himself away, just for a moment, in order to

lay her carefully back against the big oak table, pillowing her hips and shoulders with cushions he pulled almost savagely from the window seat. Then, desperate for the renewal of his touch, Marisa helped him to ease her buckskin breeches from her hips, slipping them completely away so that he could pull her slender thighs wide apart as they dangled over the edge of the table. She knew that her lush, crinkled feminine flesh was already honeyed with moisture. He ran his fingers teasingly through the pale down of her pubic mound, and let the ball of his thumb separate her darkly engorged labia, spreading them like petals and pushing up gently into her yearning sex with his fingers until she cried out and almost climaxed against him. He let his hand slide away, keeping her teetering deliciously on the brink, straining in exquisite torture, and desperately she reached out to feel for his beautiful, thick penis, guiding its solid length towards her churning hips. He laughed gently, saying, 'Patience, little one,' but Marisa had forgotten the meaning of patience, and as he carefully parted her sex lips and slid the swollen head of his dark shaft into her honeyed passage, she clasped him to her, thrusting her yearning breasts against his warm, wet mouth and clamping her hands round the firm globes of his buttocks, gasping with joy as she felt that beautiful, solid shaft of male flesh slowly driving into her. She arched frantically up to meet him and, sensing that she was well past the point of no return, he reached down carefully with one hand to savour her glistening clitoris as it thrust out hungrily from her parted flesh folds, while continuing to drive his lengthy penis deep within her, and pleasuring her into such a wanton frenzy of lust that her splayed thighs trembled and jerked. She clasped him to her, feeling all that delicious length ravishing her, again and again, until nothing else existed but the sweet, hard pleasure of his penis. She cried out his name, engulfed by the white hot explosion that was rippling out in great, sensual waves from her very core.

He drove himself powerfully into her as he too reached

his climax. She stroked his heaving shoulders as he lay against her breast, feeling her womb still pulsing slowly and sweetly around him.

Afterwards he kissed her very tenderly and helped her to her feet. She leaned dizzily against the table, trying to push her disordered blonde curls back from her face. Her hand strayed to the discarded rapiers. 'I rather think', she said a little distractedly, 'that you were the victor in that particular bout, Lord Delsingham.'

They ate alone that evening in the vast dining room, with a log fire blazing in the great hearth and extravagant branches of candles glittering on the fine crystal and silver plate. They'd ransacked the pantry like children, piling up huge platefuls of cold ham and pickled salmon and Lucy's delicious veal pasties; there were peaches, too, from the glasshouse, and late raspberries, washed down with delicious goblets of claret from the cellar. Marisa felt deliciously lightheaded and carefree, until Delsingham sat back and said, 'And now, Marisa, I think it's time you told me exactly what's been going on while I've been away. Don't you?'

She told him reluctantly about her feeling of being watched all the time, and the shots that just missed her, and the fire, although in reality she just wanted to forget about it all. He listened silently and sipped at his wine, showing no reaction until she mentioned the incident with Seth. She didn't tell him everything, but she told him that they'd beaten the gypsy brutally, apparently on someone's orders, and at that his expression grew hard.

'You've no idea who arranged it?'

She shrugged carelessly, trying to seem unconcerned, though the memory of Seth's terrible punishment still made her cold with fear. 'I assumed at first that it must be someone who doesn't like me being here at Melbray Manor. But then, the other night, I remembered that something happened in London, before I even heard about my inheritance.'

He refilled her glass. 'Tell me,' he said.

So she told him about the raid on the Blue Bell, explaining how at first everyone thought it was the magistrates, making one of their forlorn gestures against the illegal gaming dens that infested that part of London, only now they knew that it wasn't, because her attorney Mr Giles had made discreet enquiries, and the magistrates knew nothing about it.

Delsingham frowned, listening to her carefully. 'A private vendetta, then.'

'So it would seem, especially as my rooms bore the brunt of the raid. They stole or destroyed nearly everything. Not that I had much,' she addded wryly.

He said, 'It could well be the same person who's trying to frighten you off here, though I suppose it's always possible you have more than one enemy. You're taking care of yourself, Marisa? Not going out by yourself, and locking up well at night?'

She nodded. 'Yes, I keep my pistol with me all the time. And of course I've got John and Lucy, who are alert and quick witted. It's not as if I've never faced danger before. But – ' and her eyes shadowed suddenly, 'I feel frightened this time, because I feel as if somebody hates me.'

'What, you, frightened?' He touched her cheek gently. 'The girl I first met striding around London in her breeches and greatcoat, exchanging coarse insults with coachmen and defying the world?'

She smiled back, but her eyes were still troubled. 'This is different, James. You see, in London I knew who my enemies were.'

He reached out his hand and put it calmly over hers. 'Then it seems as if perhaps you need a little help from me.'

She drew her hand back quickly. 'I can manage. I can look after myself: I've always had to in the past!'

'I know. But Marisa, let me help you this time. Let me stay with you for a little while, and perhaps together we can track your enemy down.'

She hesitated. The idea was desperately tempting. She imagined sleeping with his arms around her, knowing that he would make her feel safe and exquisitely cherished. But it was one of her rules, to take her pleasure where she pleased, but to sleep alone.

As if guessing her thoughts, he said quietly, 'I'm not asking you for any sort of commitment, Marisa. Neither of us want to lose our independence; we both know that. But I would like to be with you for a while, because I think we can offer each other company, and pleasure.'

She glanced up at him mischievously, her resistance broken. 'Pleasure? Again?'

His mouth twisted into a grin. 'Most definitely. Remember what you said earlier about my powers of recuperation?'

She laughed, feeling suddenly very happy. He got to his feet and swung her up into his arms as if she weighed nothing, then he carried her up the wide staircase to her chamber. There he laid her gently on the bed, then drew the curtains and bolted the door and turned back to her, smiling in the darkness.

Chapter Ten

*T*he bright, lush greens of early summer turned into the heavy ripeness of late August. As the corn turned gold in the fields under gentian-blue skies, and the birds grew silent in the dusty heat, Marisa felt lazy and voluptuous, as if she, too, was ripening in the hot sun.

Lord James Delsingham stayed with her most nights at Melbray Manor. Marisa filled the house with lushly scented roses from the garden, and dressed in flimsy, sprigged muslins and little straw bonnets trimmed with pastel ribbons. When he wasn't there, because of course he had his own, much larger estate and tenant farms to see to, she sat dreaming in the sun, or wandered aimlessly through the cool shrubberies of the garden, thinking of him. He'd sent some of his own men over to work on her land, and, he said, to keep an eye on her. The feeling of being cherished and protected was quite new to Marisa, and she revelled in it.

At night they would make love passionately, and afterwards Marisa would lie on the crisp linen bedsheets with the casements thrown open to the cool night air, gazing at him as he slept. Often he would wake up and turn to her, smiling lazily, and draw her into his arms to kiss her and make love to her all over again. It was a

dream-like summer, and Marisa shut the future resolutely from her mind.

During the long, hot afternoons Delsingham taught her
to drive his high phaeton. They laughed together as she
learned, but she was an apt pupil, and soon she was
bowling capably along the leafy lanes of the neighbourhood in the fast, sporty vehicle, showing off the new,
dark-blue riding habit she'd had made, which she wore
with a ruffled silk shirt and a little velvet hat with
sweeping feathers. Delsingham was a member of the
Four Horse Club, and renowned as a whip, so when he
quietly praised her deft handling of his team she felt a
secret burst of pride.

From time to time they were invited separately to
social events in the neighbourhood, and they greeted one
another with cool politeness, taking pleasure in concealing the intensity of their relationship from their neighbours. Later, alone together, they would laugh at the
absurdities of their fellow guests, and Delsingham would
chide Marisa for the way so many besotted male guests
trailed around after her.

'Their wives hate me,' laughed Marisa. It was another
hot, breathless night. They were lying together on her big
four-poster bed, with Marisa clad in the flimsiest cream
silk wrap and pale stockings, while Delsingham, who
had undressed down to his breeches, pulled himself up
from the pillows and poured them both chilled champagne. He had filled the little brick-built ice-house in her
garden with ice from his own store, and the cold,
sparkling wine was one of her greatest pleasures.

He handed her a glass, and watched her as she sipped
happily at it. 'Their wives hate you because you're
beautiful and clever.'

Marisa gazed at him. 'They also hate me because I've
got you.'

The champagne was cool and delicious, and she drank
it with relish, feeling the heady bubbles stinging against
the roof of her mouth. Then slowly, deliberately, she
leant across his groin, letting her hair and breasts brush

his hard belly. She unfastened his breeches to cup his already stirring penis in her hands, then slowly she drew her tongue across the dark, wrinkled pouch of his balls, taking them one by one into her mouth and sucking at the tender globes. He gasped, and wickedly she moved her mouth along the silken shaft of his veined phallus, loving the way it sprang and stiffened beneath her caress. He leant back with a little shudder against the pillows, his hands behind his head, his eyes tightly closed in the intensity of his pleasure. Marisa, lifting herself, sipped more of the champagne, then took him immediately in her mouth so that the cold sharpness of the wine cooled his hot penis and made him groan aloud with delight. Tantalisingly she repeated her ministrations, sipping at the champagne to cool her velvety lips and tongue then sliding her mouth up the silky pole of his flesh, feeling it thicken and swell inexorably, grazing the back of her throat, until at last he clutched his hands in her hair and she felt him start to thrust urgently against the back of her throat. Quickly she slid her fingers round his hips to cup his taut, muscular buttocks, then she eased one finger into his tight anal crevice, teasing rhythmically at the quivering little hole while her lips continued to suck on his thrusting penis. He began to shudder in violent ecstasy at the dual assault, and at last she felt his whole body go rigid as he started to spurt his hot seed into her mouth. She swallowed avidly, relishing his ecstasy, loving the movements of his shadowy, convulsing body. He was hers, all hers.

Moments later he laid her gently back against the silk bedspread to reciprocate with his own tongue, driving it deep within her soaking cleft and moving it about with gentle thrusting movements so that she melted with liquid desire, while at the same time he rubbed his high-bridged nose against her throbbing clitoris. She cried out his name urgently and arched into a fierce climax, parting her thighs as wide as she could and grinding her vulva against his delicious tongue and lips, sobbing aloud as he steadfastly extracted every last ounce of pleasure from her trembling body.

Afterwards he poured them more champagne, and Marisa nestled contentedly into the crook of his shoulder, murmuring sleepily, 'You're the ace in the pack, James. Have I told you that? The only one I've ever come across.'

He laughed. 'And are aces high or low?'

'High, of course. That was why I stole that invitation with the ace of spades in the corner. It intrigued me.'

'And I didn't disappoint?'

'Oh, no.' She curled up her smooth, slender legs against his powerfully-muscled thighs, loving the way they caressed her. 'Not at all.'

His arm tightened round her. There was a pause, then he said, 'Marisa. There's something I want to say to you.'

His voice was suddenly serious. Something constricted round her heart like a cold fist, and instantly she was quite sober. He was going to tell her that it was over. Pleasure, no commitment, that was their mutual bargain. Their summer idyll couldn't last for ever.

And didn't she know it already? From the moment she'd met him, she'd known he was wildly beyond her reach. In spite of her inheritance, she, Marisa Brooke, the daughter of a shiftless army deserter, could never belong in his world. She fought down the sudden sick feeling rising in her throat. 'Neither of us want to lose our independence,' he'd warned her. She should never have allowed her to feel like this about anyone, never.

She turned to him with light, laughing eyes, and drawled lazily, 'Dear James, you sound very serious all of a sudden. What is there to be serious about? This is a delicious summer interlude. We both know that very soon it will be over.'

He frowned. 'Marisa, I have to go away for a few days, into Winchester, on business. There are some things we should discuss – '

She pressed her finger lightly against his mouth. 'Let's not shadow the end with discussions and declarations, shall we? I'd much, much rather you kissed me than talked to me.'

Still he hesitated, his dark eyes sombre, but then he kissed her, and they didn't talk any more.

Delsingham had said that he would be back from Winchester in a few days, and Marisa, trying hard to pretend that his absence meant absolutely nothing to her, went out riding by herself in defiance of his instruction that she must never go out alone. By now the days were growing noticably shorter; there was a heavy dew on the lawns in the morning, and the horse chestnuts that lined the sweeping drive were revealing more than a hint of burnished gold amongst their heavy green foliage.

She rode as far as the beech woods, and was just turning her mare slowly back when she caught a glimpse of a shadowy movement in the trees. Her horse shied in alarm, and she struggled to control it, her heart in her mouth, as a man moved quickly out into the open. 'Seth! It's you.' She breathed a sigh of relief as she recognised the gypsy, conscious that her heart was hammering madly.

'Marisa,' he said quickly. 'I'm sorry to have startled you.'

She guided her horse nearer to him and he stroked its neck, calming it with his usual magical skill with horses. 'How wonderful to see you, Seth,' Marisa said warmly. 'How are you?'

'Well enough.' His face seemed strangely closed. 'But I've something to tell you. It's about Lord Delsingham.'

Marisa caught her breath. Something in the way the gypsy said his name warned her that Seth felt no kindness towards Delsingham.

'Yes?' she said quickly. 'What about him?'

He gazed up at her. 'I know how things are between you and him, Marisa. Reckon everyone does in these parts. But I just thought you ought to know that he was seen a couple of days ago, talking to that man with the ginger hair – the man called Varley. You remember him, Marisa?'

Marisa's fingers tightened round her reins. She felt rather dizzy and sick. How could she forget? 'You're trying to tell me that Lord Delsingham was talking to the man who attacked you, Seth?'

He held her gaze steadily. 'Aye, that's right. They were seen together at the fair up Winchester way, two days ago.'

Marisa shook her head, bewildered. 'Perhaps it was just a coincidence, a chance word, Seth.'

'Lord Delsingham gave him money, Miss Marisa. The two of them were seen whispering together for several minutes, then Delsingham passed the ruffian gold. It's the truth. We gypsies have our ways of knowing everything. I thought you ought to know.' He nodded his head and moved to go. Marisa called out rather wildly, 'Wait, Seth, wait! What is it you're trying to say?'

He turned back, gazing up at her steadily. 'I'm trying to say nothing, Marisa, just telling you the facts. Reckon you can draw your own conclusions just as well as me. You'll know well enough that there's some of the gentry who wouldn't relish the idea of a gypsy man taking pleasure with a lady they'd a mind to. Take care.'

Then he went, vanishing like a shadow into the woodland. Marisa couldn't have thought of any words to keep him.

Normally Marisa would have thought nothing of Delsingham's absence, and would simply have busied herself in different kinds of pleasure around her lovely home, always with the awareness at the back of her mind that on his return there would be a delicious reunion. But now she worried all the time, with dark, unstated fears at the back of her mind.

She found it impossible to believe that Lord Delsingham had anything to do with poor Seth's dreadful degradation. But why had he been talking to that hateful man Varley? She remembered Delsingham's frown of concentration when she'd told him just a little about the vile assault on Seth; she remembered how very little he'd said about it, though he questioned her thoroughly about all the other incidents that had worried her. And she suddenly remembered how he'd come quietly and unannounced into her house that afternoon when she was trying out her foils in the gun-room. Had he thought the house was empty? If so, what was he planning?

Suspicion came as second nature to Marisa. She'd found, during her eventful life, that it was a lot safer than trusting people. She suddenly looked at the men that Delsingham had sent over to work on her estate, with a view, he'd said, to keeping an eye on the place as well. They were quiet and self-contained, sleeping in the stable quarters instead of in the main house, and even Lucy couldn't coax a smile from them. Once, Marisa got back early from her morning ride and found one of them coming out of her study, where she kept all her papers and business documents. He'd looked embarrassed, and said he was looking for Lucy, but Marisa knew he was lying. Suddenly, instead of feeling protected by the presence of Delsingham's men, she began to feel spied on, trapped.

Then one afternoon, while Delsingham was still away, Sir Julian Ormond called by to say he was going away for a while. He asked her to sign several papers that were connected, he said, with her latest investment, and Marisa, feeling the familiar panic at the sight of all those close-written words, signed them quickly. Ormond took them back and said after a moment's hesitation, 'Is Lord Delsingham here, Marisa?'

'No,' said Marisa with apparent unconcern. 'He's away for a few days. He had to go up to Winchester on business, I believe.'

Ormond seemed to hesitate. He paced the room a little, and the sun that shone through the tall windows sparkled on the immaculate lace that spilled forth at his neck and wrists. He turned back to her suddenly. 'Marisa, I hate to see you hurt. Delsingham is rather notorious, you know, with regard to women.'

Marisa felt her breath catch in her throat. Then she said, 'A little while ago, you told me he was engaged, but that was untrue.'

Ormond moved forward then stopped, his hand on the back of a chair. 'Only because Delsingham broke it off, a short while ago. Lady Henrietta's family were devastated. London is apparently still ringing with the scandal. Delsingham is very attractive to women, I believe. You really should be wary of him, Marisa.'

Marisa said coldly, 'Is there anything else, or have you just come to regale me with country tattle?'

His face seemed to close up. 'I just want you to be careful, Marisa. You do realise, don't you, that Delsingham has nothing at all to gain by marrying you? He already has enormous wealth, and would only marry for the sake of some connection with one of the highest or most influential families in the land.'

Marisa suddenly moved towards the window, turning back to him with a brittle smile. 'I really must inform you, sir, that I have no intention of marrying anyone, ever. I do appreciate your assistance in managing my finances, but I require no advice whatsoever in the matter of my private life. And now, if you please, I see that the groom is bringing your horse round to the front door. Thank you for your concern, but I consider that my friendship with Delsingham has nothing at all to do with you.'

Ormond bowed his head, and a muscle flickered in his tense jaw. 'Of course. But there is one more thing. I am reluctant to mention it, but I really think you ought to know that Lord Delsingham has made arrangements for an investigation into your financial affairs.'

Marisa, white lipped, took a step forward. 'What?'

'It's true, I'm afraid. I received a quiet word from Newmans, the London bankers who have charge of some of your money, that he's been trying to pry into your investments. Unless – ' and he looked at her sharply, 'unless I've made a mistake, and he had your permission to do so.'

Marisa felt dazed, suddenly remembering how she'd caught one of Delsingham's men in her study. 'No. No, he certainly didn't . . .' She moved over to the window so her back was to him, not wanting to be under his anxious scrutiny any longer. When she'd composed herself, she turned back to him. 'Thank you for your visit, Sir Julian. I shan't detain you any longer. Just one thing before you go: I find myself in need of a little of my capital. Could you arrange for some of my investments to be sold, say to the value of two thousand pounds?'

He seemed to hesitate, then said smoothly, 'Of course. But it might take a week or two. Leave it with me.'

He went at last, leaving her feeling restless and unhappy. Later that morning, she summoned the man-servants who had been sent to her by Lord Delsingham, and she dismissed them all.

Late one evening, Lord Delsingham returned. Marisa, who was half-heartedly gossiping with Lucy in the drawing room, heard the clatter of his horse's hooves in the courtyard, and her heart started to thump uncontrollably.

Lucy ran to the windows and pulled back the heavy drapes. 'It's Lord Delsingham,' she cried out happily. 'All by himself. John's out there taking his horse.'

Marisa, getting to her feet, said quietly, 'Perhaps you'll open the door to him, Lucy. I'll see him in here.'

Lucy rushed out eagerly, and a few moments later Lord James Delsingham strode in, his high-crowned hat in his hand.

'Marisa,' he said swiftly. 'Are you all right? I expected to see some of my men here, but John tells me they've all gone. Why? Has something happened?'

Marisa stood very still in front of the fire. She wore a gown of palest green tulle, and her fair curls were bound up loosely in a green satin bandeau. She folded her hands in front of her. 'I sent them away,' she said.

His brow darkened. 'Why? They were there to protect you, Marisa, as well as to work for you. Why did you tell them to go?'

She held her head high to met his burning gaze. 'I need to be independent, James. I need to know what's going on around me. I don't like to be surrounded by someone else's spies.'

He stepped forward angrily. 'Spies?'

'Yes – spies! I – I can't afford to trust anyone. Can't you see that?'

He said in a low voice, 'You don't even trust me, Marisa?'

She shook her head. 'Least of all you. And I think you know why.'

He moved swiftly towards her and gripped her shoulders until his fingers bit into the pale, filmy fabric of her gown, and his face blazed down on hers as he cried out, 'No, I don't know why. Tell me, damn you.'

She held herself rigid in his arms and said, 'You've been investigating my affairs, haven't you?'

He went suddenly still. 'How do you know?'

Marisa felt the onslaught of real despair then, because he hadn't even tried to deny that he'd written to her bankers and set his men to spy around her house. 'Does it matter?' she breathed.

He said heavily, 'No, I don't suppose it does. If you don't trust me enough even to want to talk about it, then there's nothing more to be said at all. And if you trust that crook Ormond with your money, then you deserve everything you've got coming to you.'

Her throat was burning with unshed tears, because she'd never seen him look so angry. 'Why should I trust you,' she breathed, 'when you were seen at Winchester fair, talking to that man who attacked Seth so vilely? How do you explain that?'

He took a deep breath and said through gritted teeth, 'Ever since you told me of it, I've been trying to track down the people who were responsible for that outrage, trying to find out who paid them to do it. You're still in danger, Marisa – don't you realise?'

She shook her head, her face white with distress. 'How can I believe you? You were seen giving money to that vile man. How do I know that you weren't the one who paid him for what he did? I learnt long ago that I can't afford to trust anyone, anyone at all. Can't you see that?'

Slowly he let his hands drop to his sides. His face was harsh and drained as he gazed down at her. At last he said, 'Marisa. If you trusted no-one else, ever, you could have trusted me. Remember that. But I don't stay to argue my case with anyone. I'm going. You've made it quite clear that you value your stubborn independence more than my friendship. You know where to find me if you change your mind.'

He turned and went out, and she heard the big front door thudding behind him. As his horse's hooves clattered away down the drive, Marisa was left standing there white faced, her eyes burning and dry. She wouldn't cry, she told herself fiercely. She wouldn't.

Rowena was back with the gypsies again, and she was glad. Ormond had told her he was going away for a while, to London, so she and Matty were no longer required in his household. Rowena had a feeling it was something to do with Ormond's vendetta against Marisa Brooke, and she was delighted. He'd given her gold too, and she pretended to be sorry to leave, but really it was good to be back with her friends, to be sitting here beside the fire on this warm, still night with the stars out overhead, and the gossip of the other Romanies a distant, comforting murmur. Seth was away buying horses, and his absence disappointed her, but Caleb was here. She sat by the fire with him drinking lots of rough wine, and scornfully told him about Ormond's cold, aristocratic ways, and his fondness for being humiliated. Caleb growled and took her hand, making her feel the hefty bulge at his groin. 'You need a real man, girl, don't you?'

'Oh, I do that, Caleb,' she laughed, nuzzling against him. 'I need to feel your big, fine cock up inside me.'

He bent to kiss her roughly, but just then one of the mean, skinny lurchers that encircled the gypsy camp began to bark suddenly. Caleb pulled away, annoyed. 'What's that dog rowing about, blast him?' He went off to investigate, and came back a few moments later, grinning.

'There's a mighty fine gentleman loitering over beyond the trees. Says he has a fancy for a hot gypsy wench.' Caleb opened his clenched fist, letting her see the gleam of a gold coin in his hand. 'He also says there's more where that came from.'

Rowena got hurriedly to her feet, smoothing down her full crimson skirts and swinging her hips. 'Well, now. And what does this fine gent want me to do?'

'Why, tell his fortune, of course,' chuckled Caleb, and patted her behind affectionately as she moved off towards the trees, an anticipatory smile on her face and a nearly full bottle of wine in her hand.

A fine gent. Rowena wondered suddenly if it was Ormond, come back from London, but no, Caleb knew him by sight and would have told her.

She caught her breath when she saw the man standing in the shadow of a clump of birches. A fine gent indeed: tall and handsome as could be, with long, fine legs in those tight breeches and boots, and a ruffled white shirt and cream silk waistcoat that showed off his lovely broad shoulders. Rowena licked her lips. Then she drew nearer, and she realised who it was: Lord James Delsingham, owner of Fairfields, the biggest place hereabouts, and the one they said the fine ladies went wild for, especially Miss Marisa Brooke.

Well, well. And he'd come looking for her. She, Rowena, would certainly give him something to remember. She moved her shoulders slightly so that her smocked blouse slipped down to reveal the creamy upper swell of her breasts in the moonlight, while her nipples were like dark berries, just visible beneath the wispy

774

fabric. She said in her husky voice, 'You wanted me, my lord?'

He gazed down at her, his beautiful mouth curving in a glimmer of a smile. 'Try persuading me,' he said softly.

She sidled up to him, her lips pouting provocatively, and reached up to draw one finger down his lovely lean cheek. Then she pulled lightly at her blouse again, so that it slipped to show all of her breasts, with the tawny nipples already tingling and stiffening. She rubbed them gently against his silk shirt, feeling the long protuberances drag from side to side against his hard male chest in delicious arousal. Reaching up with one hand, still clutching her wine bottle in the other, she pulled his dark head down and kissed him languorously, reaching and probing with her pink tongue and letting its tip flicker in the intimate recesses of his lovely mouth. She gasped when she felt him respond, felt his powerful long tongue thrusting back and entwining with hers, probing in a divine pretence of copulation as he slipped his hands round her back and pulled her towards him.

Rowena gasped at the pressure of his narrow hips, where the exquisite bulge of his hardening genitals was all too obvious through the fine wool of his smooth-fitting breeches. She pulled away a little to get her breath, gazing up at him with glittering green eyes, devouring him. 'Let's go over there, my lord,' she whispered. 'I know a little clearing where we'll be nice and private – as private as you could wish.'

He nodded, and she led him to a moonlit dell in the woods, where the mossy turf was studded with buttercups. She sank down onto the grass, drawing him with her, feeling desperately excited at his proximity, and while he settled himself she took a deep swig of the wine she still held, feeling it race through her blood. Then she handed it to him, enjoying watching the muscles of his throat as he swallowed. Beautiful, she thought dreamily as she gazed at his perfect profile, the most beautiful man I've ever seen. No wonder they say the women run wild for him. She thought suddenly of Marisa Brooke, and her eyes grew hard.

Well, she decided triumphantly, he must have tired of Miss Marisa Brooke, mustn't he? And she, Rowena, would give him something to remember. She reached for his hand to place it on her hot, swollen breasts, and he stroked them softly, pulling at her nipples. Gasping as the tawny crests sprang out at his touch, she let her thighs fall apart beneath her full skirt, feeling the cool night air whispering against the lush folds of her vulva. A sudden fierce spasm of desire shook her and the moisture trickled down her thighs as she anticipated the feel of his beautiful, strong penis.

He was watching her, assessing her as he pulled and teased lazily at her dark, throbbing teats. 'Well, mister,' she gasped a little faintly, 'are you going to get on with it, or what?'

He laughed. 'What a hot little gypsy girl you are.'

With a muttered curse of impatience, she ran her hands up his lovely strong thighs and began to struggle with the fastening of his fancy breeches. At last his cock sprang out, already dark and rigid, and she licked her lips and moaned as she caressed its silky, long shaft with trembling fingers. 'Please, mister,' she whispered, 'take me now! Stick your lovely juicy cock into me. You needn't pay me anything at all. I just want to feel you inside me . . .'

He arched himself over her, and she reached to touch his penis with impatient fingers, pulling back her full skirts with her other hand and rubbing avidly at her own swollen labia. Then she stretched out her thighs and opened herself to him, longing for the penetration of that throbbing, engorged shaft; her pleasure bud was a stiff little rod of tingling sensation, yearning to be caressed. She moaned out as she felt the smooth, rounded glans nudge at her glistening sex-lips, and raked at his shoulders, but he caught her hands, pushing them back to the ground above her head, and kneeling between her thighs, pinioning her as his long, stiffened penis danced just a fraction of an inch away from her soft-petalled vulva. Rowena cried out in longing, trying to lift her hips to meet him and enfold him, but he was powerful, even more powerful than she'd realised, and she was trapped. 'Please, mister,' she begged, her eyes hot, 'don't keep me waiting. Please, stick it up me . . .'

His grey eyes suddenly seemed hard and dangerous, and she noticed how tiny gold sparks seemed to flicker in them, like flames. He said, in a low, clear voice,

'You'll have what you want in a moment, gypsy girl. But first, I want you to tell me a few things.'

Rowena blinked dizzily, trapped beneath his weight, her hands pinioned. There was something inhuman about this one. What other man, with a great, throbbing cock poised just above her parted legs, would want to talk, for God's sake? A little frightened, she said, 'Depends on what you want to know, doesn't it?'

His mouth a thin compressed line, he lowered his snakelike hips, letting his lovely bone-hard cock slide just an inch into her moist, soft flesh. She gasped with delight, clutching at him with her inner muscles, and her gasp turned into a sob of disappointment as he slowly withdrew. He watched her reactions, and said softly 'Tell me a little about Sir Julian Ormond.'

Rowena's eyes flashed defensively. 'Not much to tell,' she said scornfully. 'Oh!' She gasped in delight as his quivering, beautifully controlled phallus nudged again between her silken sex-lips.

'I'm not too interested in the intimate details,' he said, 'but I would like to know what interest Ormond has in Marisa Brooke.'

'How should I know?'

His hands were tight around her wrists. 'I think you know quite a lot.'

'Well, he has her watched, has his men spying on her. Nothing wrong in that, is there?'

'Why?' His voice was hard.

Rowena was suddenly frightened of him. She guessed he knew everything anyway. Why was he asking her?

She went on hurriedly, 'He hates her, of course, because he reckons that the house and everything should have been his. But he seems to think he'll have her out of there quickly enough.'

Delsingham's hands tightened again warningly. 'How? How will he get her out?'

'Cause all her money's gone, or something like that.' Delsingham seemed to swear softly under his breath. Rowena muttered sulkily, 'Are you going to do it to me, or not? Can't wait for ever.'

He ground his penis slowly into her, and lowered his head to her breasts, using his strong tongue to flick her long, straining nipples to and fro. The fierce delight shot straight down to her throbbing clitoris, as if he was actually tonguing that little stem of flesh, teasing it with his teeth, sucking on it with his hot wet mouth. At the same time the sweet length of his penis slid into her, filling her aching void, and she flushed and shuddered against him. 'Oh, yes! Yes, that's better, my beauty – fuck me now, harder, please, I'm nearly there . . .'

He slid out and poised himself above her as she gasped with loss and writhed her hips beneath him.

'And the fire?' he said meditatively. 'The fire that was deliberately started in the stable block at Melbray Manor?'

'He said he'd kill me if I ever told.'

Delsingham moved himself into her again, just parting her puffy, glistening labia, and thrust gently, teasingly in and out of her. She strained towards him, desperate to pull him inside herself as the beautiful, shimmering sensations of fulfilment hovered just out of reach. She lifted her head and saw his penis thrusting wickedly above the fiery nest of her pubic hair, its shaft dark and thick and long. Oh, if only he'd pound into her. If only he'd drive his delicious cock deep within her, so she could fasten herself round it, and feel the blissful waves of release pour through her . . .

'Tell me,' he whispered softly.

'Why, one of Ormond's men started it, of course,' she

778

lied frantically. 'He wanted to frighten her, to drive her away. It was the same with the broken saddle, and the same with what those men did to Seth.'

'Did you know what they were going to do to Seth?'

'No. I told that bastard Ormond that Seth was with Marisa, because I hated her, but I didn't want them to hurt him. Please, mister, do it to me, let me feel your lovely cock sliding into me . . .'

'Why do you hate Marisa Brooke?'

'Because she's a whore, a filthy little whore pretending to be a fine lady. She gambled with us gypsies at Vauxhall, for sex, that was where she first put her spell on Seth. Loved it all, she did, getting us to play games, making fools of us all. She bared her titties, and let my Seth cream all over them. She's a fancy slut!' Rowena got one of her hands free at last, and grabbed for his hips in desperation. The memory of the fierce pleasuring in Vauxhall Gardens that night, as Caleb took her from behind and the others sported lasciviously around her, had brought her almost to the brink. 'Are you going to punish me now, mister? Don't be angry with me, will you? You've got such a beautiful cock.'

Delsingham said, 'I have my own ways of punishing people,' and then, slowly, unbelievably, he began to get to his feet. Rowena lay there, naked and shivering, her face incredulous as he carefully eased his still-rigid penis back into his breeches and rearranged his clothing.

'What the hell are you playing at?' she demanded angrily. 'You promised me money.'

He casually tossed a gold sovereign; it landed close by her head. 'There you are. Easy money for you, I should say.' And he turned and started to go.

'Damn you!' she called after him. 'Damn you, you're as perverted as Ormond.'

He laughed back over his shoulder. 'Dear God, I sincerely hope not.'

Caleb was waiting a few yards away in the shadows, spying on them, hungrily rubbing at his swollen penis beneath his breeches as he watched their sex-play. Now he was bewildered, because the fine lord had seemed to have changed his mind, and was coming towards him as if he'd known all the time that he was there. Caleb flushed angrily as the man stopped and said, 'Enjoying yourself? I hope so, because you're needed rather urgently over there.' He nodded back towards where Rowena lay, then strolled on. Caleb glared at him suspiciously and hurried down to the little glade.

'That was mighty quick,' he said to Rowena suspiciously. 'Did he pay you?'

Rowena hissed, 'Yes, he paid me, damn him, and that was about all. Quickly, Caleb . . .' Even as he crouched beside her, she was pushing her hand inside his breeches, pulling out his meaty cock and pumping it into full hardness. Grunting with surprised pleasure, Caleb leaped astride her and began to thrust vigorously, feeling Rowena climaxing almost instantly beneath him as she writhed her hips against his big, stalwart penis. Caleb came too, driving himself hard, swept away by her feverish excitement.

'So much for the fine gentry,' he grunted in satisfaction as his lengthy shaft spasmed repeatedly inside her. 'What you needed was a real man up you, eh, my beauty?'

Rowena said bitterly, 'Caleb, you're a clumsy great fool.' She pushed him off, and went to wash herself in the cool little stream that ran nearby. He lay there in the darkness shaking his head, his eyes blank with puzzlement.

Some days later, Marisa stood in the cool oak-panelled hall of Melbray Manor, breathing in the now familiar aroma of the old tapestry hangings, the carved wooden furniture and the dark, smoke-stained oil paintings that were relics of a previous age. From the open door, mingling subtly with the scent of beeswax and wood, came the fragrance of late summer roses and lavender, and she could hear the faint sounds of singing in the distance as Lucy cheerfully polished the copper pots and pans in the old, stoneflagged kitchen. She rested her hand on the carved balustrade and remembered how Delsingham had carried her up the wide oak staircase on that first night they spent together, laughing as she pretended to struggle and protest, silencing her at last with his all too devastating kisses in the shadowy, silk-hung stillness of her bedroom.

Well. That was all over. And now it was necessary for her to pay a visit to her bank in Crayhampton. Several bills were pressing, and Ormond, her adviser, was away from home, having forgotten, it seemed, to provide her with the money she'd asked him for. Letting John drive the carriage, she called in at the offices of Smith and Tavitt, her bankers in the High Street, and enquired discreetly about getting access to the investments Ormond had made for her. She felt nervous, because anything to do with official transactions sent her mind into a state of helpless inadequacy.

The banker checked through the sheaf of papers she silently handed him, and when he'd finished his face was grave. 'You've been badly advised, I'm afraid, Miss Brooke. These shares have collapsed. It's been a bad time for the manufacturing industries. Now the war is over, foreign competition has undermined the trade badly.'

Marisa's fingers tightened round her little velvet reticule, not quite taking it in. 'And my investments in the shipping venture? Are they accessible, Mr Tavitt?'

His earnest grey head jerked up at that, and he leafed through the papers again. 'I have no record of them here. You put your money into shipping? My dear Miss Brooke, I fear that your investments have been catastrophic. You have other capital elsewhere, I hope?'

Other capital? Somewhere outside in the street a dog barked, breaking the heavy silence. 'Why, yes,' Marisa lied, knowing full well that she hadn't. Her own voice sounded strangely distant in her ears. The room seemed to be ebbing and swaying around her. Her money, all her money, gone.

'I'm glad to hear it,' said Mr Tavitt concernedly.

'And of course,' went on Marisa rather breathlessly, 'I

have the house and the land. I could always raise money on them. That's what people do, isn't it?'

Edward Tavitt leaned forward across his desk, his thin, kindly face really anxious now. 'But my dear Miss Brooke, the house and land are already mortgaged up to the hilt.' He pushed a document towards her. 'It's all here. You must have realised that, surely? You signed the papers for that transaction only the other day. Sir Julian Ormond brought them in, saying that you needed the money rather quickly, so you'd asked him to see to it all for you. I was surprised at the time, but I assumed you knew what you were doing.'

Marisa tried to look calm as the rows of incomprehensible words spun once more before her eyes, though she felt ill with shock. 'So you gave Ormond access to the money?'

'Of course. After all, you'd signed the additional papers giving him power as your sole executor. Miss Brooke, is anything wrong? You look quite pale, my dear. Can I fetch you anything? A glass of cordial, perhaps, or some tea?'

Marisa had risen to her feet, controlling herself with a supreme effort, though she knew her face must be quite white. Brandy, perhaps, a rather strong brandy. 'No, I'm fine, thank you. I'm sorry to have troubled you, Mr Tavitt. Everything is quite in order, I assure you. Good day to you.'

She made her way down the narrow stairs in a state of numbness and stood for a moment on the crowded pavement, trembling with cold in spite of the warm sun.

Everything – everything gone. She'd let Ormond dupe her, wilfully trusting him against all Delsingham's advice; in fact, she'd befriended him initially just to spite Lord Delsingham. She'd been too proud, too vulnerable in her own weakness to ask anyone for advice about the papers Ormond was asking her to sign; too proud to admit to anyone that she couldn't even make out half the words, let alone understand them.

Stunned, she rejoined John and Lucy, who were waiting by her carriage, and told John to drive her home. It was no easy task to weave through the narrow streets of Crayhampton, because it was market day, and the pavements were thronged. She gazed silently out of the window, all the figures and faces just a blur to her, until suddenly she stiffened, because she'd caught sight of two young women watching her with bold eyes as her carriage rolled slowly by. They were gypsies to judge by their gaudy dress, one of them slight and dark haired, and the other with flowing red curls. As Marisa met her eyes, the red head's voluptuous mouth twisted in open contempt.

Lucy's hand was suddenly on her shoulder. 'Look, Marisa. Those are the two gypsy girls that Ormond kept for his private pleasure. He's dismissed them now, they say.' She laughed, recalling the vivid servants' gossip she'd heard. 'They were too much for him, I should think.'

The carriage was moving on, but Marisa turned back, her eyes still held by the beautiful gypsy girl's venomous gaze. She knew her, knew them both. Then she remembered the gypsies at Vauxhall. Redheaded Rowena had belonged to Seth. No wonder she was looking at Marisa as if she hated her.

And Lucy's casual words were slowly turning in her whirling mind. Rowena and Ormond: the woman quite open in her jealous hatred, the man quiet, deadly, venomous. Suddenly she remembered the sinister little bunch of elder twigs she'd found by the stables after the fire: a gypsy's curse, Lucy had said. Well, the fire had failed, but together they'd finally finished her off. Ormond, her secret enemy, had made an utter fool of her, ruined her. He'd certainly got his revenge on her for inheriting what he believed should have been his. And she couldn't even accuse him of treachery, couldn't report him for fraud and theft, because after all she'd signed everything he'd put in front of her. He would only have to produce those papers to destroy her case against him completely.

783

When they arrived back she went slowly up to her lovely silk-hung bedroom and began to carefully pack the few belongings she'd originally brought with her from London. As she worked, she had just one burning idea in her mind, driving away everything else.

She would go back to where she belonged, to where she understood the rules and wasn't anybody's fool. And then, she would use every trick she knew to make Melbray Manor totally hers again.

Chapter Eleven

*I*n the upstairs chamber of his elegant house in Park Place, David Valsino reflected ruefully that Lady Georgina Morency was being more than usually demanding this evening. Fortunately he didn't really mind. Although in her late thirties, and rather inclined to plumpness, Lady Georgina was still exceptionally beautiful, and, what was more, exceedingly rich. Her elderly financier husband indulged her besottedly, paying David vast sums for his wife's particular whim – her fencing lessons. Today, they hadn't even got the rapiers out before Lady Georgina had jumped on her tutor, avidly struggling with the buttons of his silk breeches and pulling out his thick, dusky penis. She'd encouraged him swiftly to erection, and bounced about on top of him, coming almost immediately. Now, she seemed to be eager for another bout, but David, lying back against the settee where they'd been exchanging kisses, laughed rather helplessly. 'There's time enough, Lady Georgina.'

'Oh, no, there isn't,' she replied, her eyes fastening greedily on his freshly stirring erection. 'An hour with you is never time enough.' She adored the handsome Italian fencing master. She dreamed every night of his lithe, compact body; of his beautiful bronzed skin with the light matting of hair on his chest, his superbly muscled legs, the dense bush of black hair at the base of his belly from where his lovely instrument of pleasure swelled and grew so willingly. At night, when her elderly husband was asleep and snoring, full up with over-rich food and too much port, she'd pretend that David was with her, and she'd rub herself with hard and hungry fingers, desperately imagining the lovely silken caress of the Italian fencing master's fine shaft inside her as she shuddered into solitary orgasm.

She'd been looking forward to this session all week, and she was going to make the most of it. She eased off her bodice, letting her plump but still firm breasts pout provocatively above her corset, feeling how her stiffening nipples tugged at the creamy skin of her bosom. 'Now,' she crooned, stroking the erect length of David's dark veined weapon and admiring the velvety globes of his testicles, 'now, give me something to really remember, Signor Valsino . . .'

Then the door to the upstairs chamber opened, and the sudden draught blew out all the candles. Georgina gave a little cry of dismay. She dreaded the thought of someone spying on them. Her husband was fiercely jealous. If he knew of these encounters, she would be banished to the country for sure. David too sprang up, a hiss of anger on his lips, while Georgina, her heart thumping beneath her lush breasts, watched faintly from the settee as a beautiful blonde youth stepped inside the room.

It was almost completely dark in here without the candles, but she could just discern by the dim glow of the street lamp through the window that the intruder wore a long, loose greatcoat over his shirt and breeches, and his blond hair was cropped short beneath a wide-brimmed hat that shadowed his fair, smooth-shaven face. She could also see that in his hand the youth carried a pistol, and it was pointed straight at them. Georgina heard David Valsino let out a hiss of breath, then he went very still.

'Don't let me interrupt you,' said the newcomer in a low, husky voice. 'Carry on.'

Valsino said, 'You must be joking.'

The pistol lifted fractionally. 'Oh, no. I never joke about such things. Do proceed. I hate to interrupt urgent matters. Both of you on the floor, I think, and then I can see you properly.'

Georgina was beside herself with mingled shame and excitement. David, grim faced, reached to touch her arm. Miraculously he still had an erection, which swayed ominously as he said to her quickly, 'Better do as he says. Kneel on the floor, Georgina.'

Georgina gasped, 'He's going to watch us?'

'Unless you want me to argue with that pistol, he's going to watch us, yes. Kneel on the floor, and let me deal with things.'

And suddenly, Georgina was deliciously excited. She crouched rather breathlessly, and shuddered with shame as David lifted her skirts, knowing that the beautiful blond intruder would be watching her firm, ripe buttocks, would be seeing how her heavy breasts hung helplessly, brushing against the floor. Her excitement continued to mount relentlessly as she felt David's strong penis nudging between her thighs, dipping itself in the silky, silvery moisture that seeped from the soft folds of flesh between her legs. Then she heard the youth's voice, light and cool and confident.

'Tell your fencing master what to do to you, Lady Georgina. Tell him exactly what to do.'

Georgina swallowed hard. She was frightened and ashamed, but she was also more aroused than she'd ever been in her life. David whispered urgently in her ear, 'Do as he says. Remember, he's got a gun, and he looks as if he knows how to use it.'

'I'm waiting,' said the voice menacingly from the shadowy pool of darkness by the door.

Georgina cleared her throat, and said rather shakily, 'I – I want you to mount me, David.'

'Louder,' said the voice.

'I want you to mount me,' she cried out desperately. 'I want you to drive your beautiful penis deep inside me. I

787

want you to reach round, David, and play with my breasts, and service me like a mighty stallion, and drive your hot shaft to and fro, and ravish me – oh . . .' She could already feel his lovely, hardened flesh sliding between her pouting labia, burying itself in her moist softness. She shuddered and cried out, gripping herself around him.

'And then?' said came the stranger's soft voice from the doorway.

'I – I want you to squeeze my nipples, and pound into me from behind, while I writhe against you. Then I want you to draw back, and tease me with the tip of your penis, and grip my bottom, and then drive yourself slowly, so slowly, back inside me so I can feel every inch of you . . .' Her voice broke off in a strangled cry of pleasure as David did just that. She could just see the beautiful blond youth leaning casually back against the shadowy door, his big coat hanging loosely to give a glimpse of his lovely, slender figure, but there was nothing casual about the pistol he pointed straight at her in his smooth, elegant hands. Suddenly she wanted him to join in. She wanted to see his lovely Adonis-like face tighten with pleasure, see his slim body melting with rapture, just as hers was. David had gone very still, his penis held steady in her tight love passage, just pulsing gently to remind her he was there. She looked dazedly up at the youth by the door, and whispered, 'Oh, I want you. I want to take you in my mouth while David fucks me. Please . . .'

Georgina heard the hiss of David's exhaled breath behind her and in the silence that followed her heart seemed to stop beating. Then, suddenly, the youth nodded. 'Why not?' he drawled softly, and, thrusting the gun into his pocket, he crossed the floor slowly towards her, and began to unfasten his breeches. Feeling quite faint, Georgina closed her eyes. She had never been so excited in her life. David was still gripping her bottom-cheeks. She could feel his ramrod penis very still inside her juicy love passage, and her inner nectar flowed freely around him. And now the beautiful youth was kneeling before her, reaching with divine skill to play with her hot, leaping nipples, pulling them gently as if he were milking her. She shuddered with rapture as he parted his breeches and she prepared herself to attend to him, knowing he must be as fiercely aroused as she was, as David was.

She felt his hands guiding her head gently towards his loins as he knelt upright in front of her face. And then, the excitement ran through her like a shock wave as she dazedly opened her eyes and saw the lush, crinkled folds of femininity splayed out before her, smelled the sweet scent of womanly arousal wafting towards her from between those slender female thighs, saw the light tangle of blonde down around the throbbing stem of a lustfully exposed clitoris. 'Pleasure me,' said the youth softly.

A woman. An incredibly beautiful, slender young woman, dressed as a man. Georgina's heart gave a great lurch of excitement, and she whispered, 'Who are you?'

The woman was silent, but David, just behind her, was laughing quietly. 'Georgina, my dear,' he said, 'meet Marisa Brooke.'

And then he started to move steadily behind her, filling her, stretching her with his lovely thick penis, and she reached forward in dazed obedience to start tonguing at the soft female flesh that was exposed to her hungry view, feeling how the silken petals parted in welcome, giving her entrance to the dark, honeyed cleft that was the very essence of womanhood. Slowly, deliriously, Georgina ran her tongue up and down those silky folds while Marisa continued to play devastatingly with her nipples and David gripped her buttocks, driving faster and faster from behind. As Marisa squeezed and pulled at her burning teats, Georgina found the other woman's throbbing clitoris, and whipped it with her long pink tongue, slavering at it, feeling it throb and quiver. Then she instinctively fastened her lips round it, and started to suck, hotly, strongly. She felt the exquisite Marisa arch into sudden immobility before crying out and starting to grind her soaking vulva desperately against Georgina's face, coating her with her copious juices. Georgina could feel her open and close like an anemone as the fierce, sweet, pleasure of her orgasm engulfed her, while at the same time David pounded into her from behind, ravishing her with a ferocious strength that sent her own body toppling over the edge. She cried out, 'Oh, yes. Yes! Fuck me, David. Fuck me hard . . .' The pleasure pooled like molten liquid low in her abdomen, and her whole body was wrenched by violent, exquisite convulsions as David's lengthy penis spasmed deep inside her.

David was the first to recover, the first to get up, smiling rather ruefully.

'So you're back, Marisa,' he said.

And Marisa smiled contentedly as she lazily started to fasten up her breeches. She felt at home again now.

Later, when Georgina had left, vowing eternal friendship and making Marisa promise to visit her in her beautiful home in Hanover Square, Marisa leaned back thoughtfully on the little French settee in David Valsino's candle-lit drawing-room and sipped at the goblet of cold Rhenish wine he'd brought for her.

'Where,' she said, 'would a gentleman go if he wanted to win a really large sum of money?'

David leant forward to refill her glass, feeling warm and happy in her presence. Life had been dull without Marisa Brooke. He gathered that she was in some sort of trouble, but he knew her too well to press her for details. 'I take it,' he said, 'that you're not thinking of the reputable clubs in Pall Mall?'

'Oh, no,' she replied scornfully, 'nor the seedy dives in Houndsditch where the butchers' apprentices and the poor city clerks throw away their paltry half-crowns. No, I want real play, David. Deep and dangerous.'

He hesitated, sitting back thoughtfully in his own chair. 'Fashions change in these places, of course. And if they're raided, or if there's any sort of scandal, then they close up pretty quickly. But I did hear, during the summer, that there's a rather notorious club opened up in Albion Place. It caters for jaded aristocrats, mostly younger sons with money to burn who want a taste of danger and excitement. Rumour has it that the Earl of Caterfield's third son won a hundred thousand there one night, and lost it all the next day.'

Marisa nodded. Albion Place. She'd heard of it. It lay in a dark labyrinth of streets somewhere between Whitcomb Street and Leicester Fields. 'What's it called?' she enquired casually.

'It's just known as the Albion, I think, but they keep it very private. Members only, of course, and no women allowed, so you don't stand a chance of getting in, my dear. Anyway,' he added thoughtfully, 'I've heard one or two slightly sinister stories, reports of wild parties and hushed-up scandals. You really don't want anything to do with decadent roués like them, Marisa. Your best bet, if you really want to win some money, is to go to your friends at the Blue Bell and get back into their circle. Either that, or go to some low-class den like the Bedford Arms in Covent Garden.'

Oh, no. She was beyond all that now. Marisa laughed and lifted her glass to drink, eyeing David over the rim. 'Of course I'm aware that places like the Albion are well beyond my reach. I'm just interested, that's all. I like to catch up with the latest scandal.'

'Life in the country's been dull, then?'

'Not exactly,' said Marisa, her blue eyes glinting. 'Sometime I'll tell you all about it. Dear David, you've been such a good friend to me. If I could have a bath, and perhaps a good meal before I go out for the evening, I'd be most grateful.'

David nodded, his eyes straying wistfully over her relaxed, supple figure. Her newly cropped blonde hair added a piquant sexuality to her heart-shaped face, and her slender body looked quite divinely feminine in her shirt and breeches and high leather boots. Lady Georgina had obviously thought so too. He'd been able to watch Marisa's flushed face as she orgasmed beneath Georgina's avidly lapping tongue, and he'd imagined it was Marisa's tightly exquisite loins he'd been thrusting into as he ravished Lady Georgina's plump rear. The memory of that deliciously unexpected threesome was making him grow hard again already. There was no-one quite like Marisa Brooke.

'You'll be back later tonight?' he said hopefully.

She leaned towards him, resting her hand lightly on his thigh. 'I'll see how the evening progresses,' she said.

And with that, he had to be content.

Two hours later, Marisa was busy again. It was just past ten in the evening, and inside the furtive gambling den that nested in a narrow court leading off Drury Lane, there was no sound except the deft slither of cards and the occasional clink of money. A small group of silent onlookers had gathered round one particular table in the far corner, where a final rubber of piquet was being played in the smoky light of some sparse tallow candles stuck into iron holders on the walls. Marisa was one of the players. Feeling well-fed and confident after a generous meal at David's house, she pushed back her tricorne hat and ran her hand through her cropped hair. 'Four in sequence,' she said, calmly surveying her cards. She was winning rather thoroughly, and her opponent, a grizzled veteran of the Peninsular wars, was not happy.

'Your point is good, lad,' he said rather gruffly.

'Very well,' said Marisa. 'Four aces, three kings, and eleven cards played, I think.' The soldier frowned hard at the array of cards which Marisa deftly laid on the wine-stained table. 'I claim repique,' she went on sweetly. 'This time I really think I have you, captain.' The soldier swore coarsely as Marisa reached out to pull a pile of gold coins towards herself and started to get up.

The soldier rasped out, 'Damn you lad, you could at least give me the chance to win some of it back!'

'Oh, no.' Marisa patted her pocket where the coins were. 'This is mine, and now I'm going to find a place where I can win some real money.' Calmly she started to go out through the door, pretending not to notice that everyone else had got up too, their hot eyes fastened on her retreating back, out and up the steps into the comparative gloom of the ill-lit court, where she looked around quickly, and saw more shadowy figures hurrying out of another door to block her exit. She caught her breath sharply. Damn them, but they were quick. They must have been planning to waylay her whether she won or not. She slipped quickly into an empty doorway, and waited resignedly. Soon, the soldier and three of his friends came clattering up the steps after her, all scouring about like hounds after a fox as the others came down the alley to meet them.

'Where is the lad, curse him?' muttered the soldier. 'I want my money back, and then I want him beaten black and blue for his impudence.'

'There,' cried another. 'Just there, in that doorway.'

Marisa slipped her pistol from her pocket and pointed it at them with lethal calmness. 'The first one to come near me gets a bullet in the throat,' she said. 'I mean it, gentlemen. I know how to use this, believe me.'

They hesitated, looking foolishly at one another, none of them wanting to be the first to try her out. Marisa turned with a ringing laugh and ran swiftly on booted feet through the narrow confines of Hartley Court, disappearing easily into the swirling, noisy crowds that surrounded the brothels and wine bothies of Drury Lane.

So far her disguise had worked well. David had smiled at her in reluctant admiration as she left his house earlier that evening. 'Be careful,' he said. 'You make such a pretty lad that all the boy-chasers of Vere Street will be after you.'

'All of them? Well, I'll keep them guessing while I win their money,' promised Marisa. 'Thank you, David. Thank you for everything. I'll see you soon.' With a quick kiss to his cheek, she'd tipped her hat at a jaunty angle and set off into the dark London night, to win back her fortune.

And now, the air of night-time London seemed sweet

and sharp to her nostrils after the leafy, soporific aroma of the Hampshire countryside. Her senses were assailed by the pungent odours of beer and gin and tobacco smoke, by the heavy ripeness of rotting fruit discarded by passing street sellers, by the musky fragrance of the faded prostitutes who lingered in the doorways. And the sounds. The familiar cacophony of the London streets seemed somehow to bring her alive again as she smiled at the coarse cries of passing barrow boys and pimps, and was deafened by the rumbling of heavy cart wheels on the lamplit cobbled streets. She swung jauntily down Drury Lane, conscious that her lovely winnings, just enough to get her into a really serious game, were jingling deep in her coat pocket. Glancing down a dark, unlit passageway, she glimpsed a young sailor vigorously pleasuring a giggling girl as he held her up against the wall, heedless of passers-by. The girl was gasping in delight, her arms clasped frantically round his neck as he pulled up her skirts and thrust into her. The sight excited Marisa, reviving her own sexual appetite, which was already honed by the encounter with Lady Georgina and the thrill of winning at cards.

She thought suddenly of Lord Delsingham, then quickly pushed him to the back of her mind. He'd belonged to another life, another world. Now she was Marisa Brooke again, a child of the London streets. She wore her man's clothes with a swagger, enjoying the sensual feel of the tight breeches enclosing her slender buttocks and the firmness of her high leather boots around her calves.

She took a hackney to the north end of Whitcomb Street, but decided to approach her final destination carefully, on foot, because she didn't know the area well, and here she didn't have any friends to fall back on. Having paid off the cab, she wandered slowly along the lamplit street, wondering how best to get inside somewhere as private, as decadent as this Albion Club. She had no doubt whatsoever that she would succeed. All her confidence, so badly shaken by Ormond's trickery, had come flooding back to her, as if she breathed it in with the familiar sights and smells of London. The streets of this area were alive with the carriages of the gentry, and their attendant hangers-on. She kept in the shadows, watching, waiting her chance.

And then, an elegant closed carriage suddenly pulled up beside her. She saw the coat of arms on the doorway, and her skin tingled with excitement. A man leant out from the window, his face in darkness as he beckoned to her. She sauntered up to the door, her hands in her pockets, her fingers ready on her concealed pistol. The man was young; he had a handsome but weary face, with wine-hazed eyes and lines of gauntness around his mouth that spoke of a life already devoted to dissipation. And he was rich. Marisa gauged quickly that the Mechlin lace at his neck and cuffs was priceless, and in his cravat he wore a glittering diamond pin. Marisa's heart began to thump at the sight of that diamond. She gazed up at him and waited, her mind racing.

'Well, boy,' the man drawled in a smooth, aristocratic voice that was blurred with alcohol. 'You've a pretty face. Not seen you round here before. Come up and keep me company for a few minutes, hey? I'll pay you well.'

Marisa glanced quickly up at the driver on the box, and saw his silent, impassive face as he gazed straight ahead. She would wager all the gold in her pocket that there wouldn't be any interference from that quarter. She drew a deep breath and looked again at the diamond tie pin. Oh, yes, she could deal with this.

'How much?' she said, her blue eyes narrowed in calculation.

The man shook his head, as if he couldn't be bothered. 'Oh, I don't know. A guinea, I suppose. More, if you please me.'·

Marisa pulled open the door to leap nimbly in, and the silent coachman moved the big horses off at a slow pace, no doubt used to his master's ways. Marisa sat on the seat facing the fancy gentleman and saw how he was eyeing her hotly from beneath his heavy, aristocratic lids, while his well-manicured hand was already fondling his own crotch with the lazy intensity of the very drunk. 'Such a pretty boy,' he was murmuring as he gazed at her. 'Come over here and feel my cock, suck it for me, will you? And then – and then – '

But he said no more, because Marisa, her blue eyes glinting, had pulled off her hat and was already on her knees before him, quickly dealing with his buttons and drawing out his penis. He was handsomely made and clean, smelling of silks and satin and lots of money; a pity he was a drunkard, or she would have been tempted to take more time with him, but she had other business on her mind. Skilfully she drew out his penis, which in spite of his arousal was still a little flaccid, thanks to too much liquor, but she knew how to deal with that. She bent her head quickly to wrap her tongue around the succulent glans, teasing him. He groaned aloud and clutched her head against his groin, so she was all but stifled by the male smell of his genitals. His shaft began to stir thickly beneath her lips, but he was taking too long, so she reached with cunning fingertips to scratch lightly at his dark, velvety testicles, feeling them tighten excitingly. Then, as his bottom arched towards her, she slipped one finger further back, tickling at the dark cleft between his buttocks. He cried out in dark pleasure, clutching at her hair, and she felt him stir and thicken remorselessly as she softly sucked him in her mouth. She had him now. He was hard and delicious against her lips as her wicked fingers rasped at his scrotum.

He started to thrust towards her as the big coach rumbled slowly along the cobbled back streets, his handsome, aristocratic face gleaming with perspiration. 'Don't stop,' he moaned as her mouth danced along his straining penis. 'You have such soft, soft lips – don't stop. Take it, take all of it, boy, and suck me, hard.' Marisa obediently did as she was told, enjoying her adventure. She squeezed at his hairy balls, fondling the twin globes almost roughly, and bobbed her head up and down his thick shaft while her tongue drew little circles around the fatly swelling plum of his glans. He groaned aloud, and his hips began to spasm helplessly. Quickly she pulled her head away, crouching back in the corner of the carriage, wary and alert. He shouted out, and began milking himself with his desperate fist, rubbing the foreskin feverishly up and down the iron-hard core as his penis began to twitch and jump. Then his hot seed spurted out over his silk breeches, and he wrenched his head back in a fierce rictus of pleasure.

Marisa tore her eyes away from his wildly spasming cock, grabbed her hat and leapt for the door. Flinging it open, she jumped out and landed lightly on her booted feet as the coach rolled on. She started to walk quickly along the pavement in the opposite direction, whistling under her breath, her blue eyes alight because she had the man's fabulous diamond pin clasped tightly in her hand.

Then her pulse quickened in alarm, because the big coach had pulled to a rumbling stop, and now there were heavy footsteps thudding down the road towards her. A rough voice called out, 'Stop him! Stop the wretch who's just robbed my master.'

Hell and damnation. She'd thought she would have all the time in the world to get away. Marisa started to run, throwing a quick look over her shoulder. She caught a chilling glimpse of the big, burly coachman, who was obviously more alert than she'd given him credit for, hurrying after her, raising the hue and cry. There were more people around than she'd thought, stopping to turn and look, and her pistol was of no use to her here, because if she used it she'd only draw more people in pursuit. Panting for breath, she plunged down a narrow, unevenly paved alley that twisted between dark, over-hanging tenements, then sped desperately on through a labyrinth of unlit lanes until at last it seemed safe to stop and listen. Silence. Perhaps she'd shaken her pursuers off. Then she heard footsteps again, rapidly coming closer, and in the same instant she realised that her way ahead was completely blocked by a high, featureless brick wall.

Marisa spun round, her hands clenched at her sides, breathing hard. The footsteps and the voices were getting nearer. Soon, her pursuers would pass the end of this alley and see her, and she'd be trapped. Looking round sharply, she saw then that there were some dark, unlit steps leading downwards, presumably towards the basement of one of the apparently deserted buildings that backed onto this yard. She flew down them, stumbling a little in the blackness because they were slippery with damp, and finding at their base a heavy door, which was unlocked. Wrenching at the handle, she pulled it open and slammed it behind her, leaning back against it and breathing heavily.

She thought she could hear her pursuers moving around in the yard at the top of the steps, their voices baffled and angry. She had to move on quickly, before they too spotted the steps. Pulling her hat securely over her cropped hair and tugging her big coat collar over her chin, she stepped warily forward into the dark passageway, noting yet another closed door, a few yards further on. She pushed it open carefully a few inches and stopped, catching her breath in surprise.

The building was not deserted after all. Beyond this door, the faint glimmer of distant candlelight revealed to her a wide, spacious corridor with oak-panelled walls and rich Turkey carpets adorning the polished parquet floor. Closed rooms lay to her left and right, and from behind them she thought she could hear the muffled, scarcely discernible sound of cultured male voices, and the light chink of wine glasses.

An adventure. She'd got into the very heart of somewhere exciting and rich and exclusive, a private party, perhaps. Marisa's skin tingled with excitement and her blood raced. She moved along carefully, catlike in the darkness, towards the dim glow of candlelight and the husky sound of masculine voices. An open door lay to her right, revealing an unoccupied card room, with the sealed packs lying temptingly on green baize tables in delightful anticipation of play, though it seemed as if all the players were engaged elsewhere at the moment. Marisa crept forward carefully, her back pressed against the wall in the darkness of the corridor, and soon she saw exactly how they were engaged.

A private club indeed. No wonder nobody had heard her come in.

In the heavily curtained, dimly lit room that opened out in front of her were perhaps a dozen men. Most of them were seated, but some were standing with their backs against the wall, their arms folded impassively. Silent spectators, they looked bored and jaded, and yet the warm air of the room was somehow alive with the intensity of their concentration. Marisa followed their eyes, and understood.

The focus of the watchers' attention was a small, raised dais at the end of the room, lit by several discreetly placed wax candles. On the dais, a woman was leaning forward over a curved chaise longue, clad in a demure silken black gown, but her appearance was far from demure: her skirts had been lifted up round her waist, and her black-stockinged legs were spread wide apart to reveal her naked private parts. Positioned behind her was a big, dark-skinned man in the full silk livery and grey powdered wig of a footman, and Marisa watched in dazed fascination as with the utmost control, with scarcely a flicker of his eyelids, he pleasured the girl in front of all those onlookers. Marisa felt a sudden dryness in her throat as she glimpsed his sleek, lengthy penis sliding in and out purposefully between the woman's plump buttocks. The man was quite impassive as he steadily did his work; the woman was less controlled. As Marisa watched, she desperately pulled her breasts out from her constricting bodice so she could rub her distended nipples hard against the brocade chaise longue, and she groaned aloud with pleasure as she thrust her raised hips back against the man, voraciously matching his sturdy, measured strokes. Marisa felt the sudden assault of her own arousal, and wished it was her sprawled against the cool brocade as the big, stalwart footman serviced her so impeccably with his massive rod, his heavy dark testicles swaying rhythmically against the woman's white buttocks in time with his thrusts. Somehow the strangely quiet audience excited her too. No-one moved, no-one spoke, and although she could scarcely discern their expressions, because most of them had their backs to her as she crouched hidden in the darkness, she knew that in spite of their silence, their self-control, they too would be fiercely aroused, and hungry for sex.

She remembered one night after a drunken, dissolute Bartholomew Fair, when she and Lucy had seen a stalwart but simple youth offering to take a group of women in succession for a guinea a piece. The jeering crowd had laughed at him, saying he'd never last through one woman, let alone several, but he proved them all wrong, and on that hot, debauched night the raucous onlookers were soon baying with excitement as the simple beggar lad, the size of whose appendage was legendary, performed happily in public. The local women had queued up for him, breathless with lust at the sight of his meaty, swaying penis as it thrust eagerly out from his breeches. They climaxed quickly, often almost as soon as he penetrated them, already fully aroused by the drunken decadence of the scene, and the crowd howled its approval as the beggar boy pleasured the women with eager joy. The watching menfolk, spilling out of the taverns at the news of the spectacle, played with themselves openly as they watched, or found groups of more than willing women to take their pleasure with. Marisa and Lucy had watched from the shadows, breathless with excitement. But even that crude display wasn't somehow as exciting as this cold, ritualistic coupling.

The woman in the black silk dress was almost at her extremity. Reaching beneath herself and whimpering, she began to rub hungrily at her juicy cleft, just above where the footman's sturdy great cock impaled her.

Marisa felt her own nipples harden against her loose silk shirt and she shifted her thighs uncomfortably, secretly striving to heighten the gentle assault of the tight seam of her breeches against her delicate, already moistening sex. She licked her dry mouth as she saw the grim-faced footman clutch the wriggling woman's bottom-cheeks, and pull them yet further apart, so his audience could see everything as he drew out his long, swollen penis from her vagina. Then he started to speed up, pounding in deliberately, his buttocks tense. The woman bucked against him as the excruciating pleasure overwhelmed her, and she shouted aloud in the delicious throes of orgasm. Still the footman pumped at her, his strength seemingly inexhaustible, though the sweat beaded on his forehead. Then someone in the audience called out coolly, 'Fifty guineas to see you spill your seed, Matthew.'

The man nodded. With incredible control, he pulled out coolly from the whimpering woman and started to rub his long, glistening shaft with loving hands, making sure that his audience could see every inch of its stunning length as it jutted duskily from his loins. Then he lowered himself slightly to let the swollen tip dance against the woman's still trembling buttocks. Suddenly, just as Marisa thought he was going to go on for ever, he gripped harder and his semen started to jet forth in hot, intense spasms of lust, landing on the woman's creamy bottom-cheeks. She saw him rub his spurting shaft with febrile intensity to and fro across her hips, his balls grazing her buttocks, his face distorted with lust. A sigh seemed to ripple through his rapt audience as the last of his seed trickled out from his mighty, twitching member.

At last, he was finished. Marisa, suddenly realising that her own sharp fingernails were biting into the palms of her clenched hands, heard a cool, disdainful smattering of applause from the audience, and she quickly turned her attention to them, wondering what kind of men they could be.

They were undoubtedly rich. With the ease of years of

practice, she narrowly assessed their beautifully cut clothes, their immaculate, lace-edged cravats, the neatly coiffured precision of their fashionably cut hair. Rich, young and handsome, all of them, perhaps it was a condition of membership. The sort of company, she thought rather bitterly, where Lord Delsingham would feel at home. At the thought of her former lover, she felt a quick, painful spasm of acute need at her loins, and closed her eyes, fighting hard to suppress it. And when she opened them again, she caught her breath in sudden dismay, because there were two big footmen, dressed like the one on the stage, standing just in front of her, and their eyes were hostile and unpleasant as they asssessed her boyish frame. One of them gripped her arm roughly. 'Well, lad?' he grated out. 'Enjoy that, did you?'

Marisa uttered a silent prayer of thanks for the shadowy darkness that engulfed this section of the room as she tried to pull herself free. 'Take your hands off me!' she hissed. But then the other one seized an arm too, so that she struggled helplessly between them, and by now the others had begun to notice the disturbance, and were turning well-bred, cruelly refined faces towards her. Marisa felt her senses quicken as she saw their bored faces flickering with sudden interest. Dangerous play indeed.

One of the men was already coming slowly towards her. He had jet-black hair and a thin mouth, and a long, aristocratic nose. 'Well, well,' he said. 'And what brings you in from the alleys, boy?'

Someone followed him, a plump, foppish looking man who regarded her through his quizzing glass and muttered, 'I told you we should have kept that back door locked, Sebastian. He'll have slunk in that way, mark my words.'

The man he called Sebastian turned round on him icily. 'Sometimes we have to get out of this place in rather a hurry. You know that as well as I. I'm not prepared to take the risk of being arrested, even if you are, you fool.'

He turned back to Marisa and said slowly, unpleasantly, 'I asked you a question. Why are you here?'

Marisa drew a deep breath and lifted her face defiantly to meet his chilling gaze. There was no escape, nothing for it but to somehow bluff her way out, and she'd got out of worse places than this. Her mind working busily, she suddenly remembered the empty card room she'd passed and said coolly, 'Why am I here? Because I heard you played for high stakes, and I've come to join you.'

The man laughed shortly. 'Not just anyone can join us here at the Albion Club, boy. We play for high stakes indeed.'

Marisa's heart pounded. The Albion Club. She'd made it! By the sheerest twist of fortune, she'd made it into the secret, exclusive gaming hell where David Valsino had said the play was deepest in all of London. She felt herself tingle with a new kind of excitement as she lifted her chin and said, 'I play for high stakes too.'

The man took a pinch of snuff from a little laquered box, his coldly handsome face sneering as he ran his cynical gaze up and down her slender form swathed in her loose, long coat. 'I somehow don't think you're quite in our league, boy. What kind of stakes do you have in mind?'

Marisa stared up at him challengingly from beneath the brim of her tricorne hat. 'If you tell these apes of yours to let me go, then I might be able to show you.'

The man Sebastian nodded curtly at the two footmen, who released her with obvious reluctance. Marisa dug deep in her pocket for both the diamond pin and the purse of gold she'd won off the soldier, and as she held them out she saw the onlookers' eyes narrow with greed. 'Here are my stakes, gentlemen. Will they do to start with?'

They could, of course, have robbed her and thrown her out into the street, but amongst gamblers there was an unspoken code of honour, which she rather fervently hoped would prevail here. After a chilling pause, the man Sebastian nodded curtly, and the little group moved silently up a small flight of stairs and through an arched doorway into a small, dimly lit chamber hung with heavy drapes. A single branch of candles glimmered from a round, polished table in the centre of the room, and Marisa felt her senses quickening. So it was going to be dice, not cards. As the men seated themselves round the big table, some of them donned old-fashioned leather guards round their foreheads to protect their eyes from the low glare of the candlelight, and Marisa, pretending to feel a similar discomfort, pulled her hat low over her forehead to shade her face. Silent footmen followed with trays of liquor, as did the women, hovering in the shadows in their black silk gowns, reminding her that gambling was not the only entertainment on offer at the Albion Club. A house of secret pleasures, thought Marisa, for the rich and depraved, and, perhaps, a house where she could replenish her lost fortune . . . Her pulses raced.

They were preparing to play hazard. Calmly she took her seat at the table, pretending nonchalance, but at the same time she slipped her hand into her deep coat pocket, feeling for her own secret dice. Then play began.

When it was her turn to take the box, she called her number out confidently, then cast carelessly and lost her stake. Someone sniggered, and she continued, airily, to lose. But as the stakes increased, and the play grew more intense, she began to employ her weighted dice, and the pile of coins at her side began to grow. The men were drinking too much, a fatal mistake in deep play, because it made you over-confident, and as the casters increased their stakes with remorseless recklessness, she felt the heat of success begin to pour through her blood, bringing its own kind of intoxication. Once, as the footman who acted as groom porter was calling out the odds, she noticed the man Sebastian watching her with narrowed eyes as she prepared to call her main.

'You have some luck in this game, lad,' he said softly.

Marisa shrugged, though the prickles of warning went down her spine like ice. Bad luck indeed that he was sitting next to her. 'Beginner's fortune, sir,' she said lightly as she rattled the box. She let herself lose a few times, and then cautiously began to win again.

The stakes were being raised all the time; some of them were starting to write notes on their banks. The murmured mention of a thousand guineas, the kind of winnings she'd only dreamed of, made her head spin. The box was in front of her now, and they were waiting for her call. Slowly she put her beautiful diamond pin on the table. 'You'll match my stake, gentlemen?'

There were growls of appreciation as those who wished to join the game quickly placed their money before them. 'Eleven,' said Marisa quietly, and rattled the box lovingly before casting the dice on the table. Six and five, the most beautiful numbers she knew. There was a hiss of disappointment from the watchers, but Marisa, ignoring them, began to pull the notes and the money and her precious diamond towards her. At a quick glance, she had at least ten thousand guineas here, small fare indeed compared to the fortunes staked nightly at Watier's or White's, but it was enough, enough to make Melbray Manor hers again.

And then the door opened slowly, letting in a waft of chilly air, and Sir Julian Ormond walked in.

He didn't see her. He sat in a chair against the wall, crossing his legs nonchalantly and taking a glass of wine proffered by one of the obsequious footmen, no doubt aware that any interruption of play would be a grave misdemeanour. But he watched them all, with his pale eyes, and Marisa, bowing her head low over the dice, felt her heart hammer sickly against her ribs. Hell and damnation. He wouldn't recognise her. He couldn't. But the risk was there, nevertheless, and somehow she had to get out of here as soon as possible, with her winnings intact. Play had halted for a moment due to a minor altercation over the odds, and Marisa started, very quietly, to get up. There was an open door, just behind her, in the shadows.

She felt a hand on her arm, restraining her. 'We're

ready to continue,' said Sebastian calmly, handing Marisa the dice. 'Your turn to throw, I believe.'

Damn. Marisa said to him in an undertone, 'In a moment, sir. I was just going to relieve myself. Start without me if you like.'

Sebastian laughed. 'No need to miss any of the action, my dear young sir. There's a pot for pissing in just over there, beneath the sideboard.' He spoke loudly, sneeringly, and they all turned to watch her. Marisa sat down again and took the dice box, cursing Sebastian for staying sober and calculating when the rest of his cronies were almost under the table with wine. 'In a moment, perhaps,' she said diffidently, and prepared to cast. Sebastian said, 'Why, I do believe our brave young gentleman is shy,' and Marisa, shaken by the burst of raucous laughter, substituted clumsily for the first time.

And Sebastian, who had been watching her carefully, reached out and put his hand coldly over her fingers just as she was about to throw.

'Well, well,' he said softly. 'Do you know, I think that our unexpected guest is cheating.'

The whole room fell into deafening silence as the weight of his smooth hand pressed her palm down against the tell-tale dice, and she was icily aware of Ormond looking across the room at her with widening eyes. Hell and damnation indeed. 'Of course I'm not,' Marisa said defiantly. 'How could I be?'

With a knowing half smile, the hateful man Sebastian pulled the dice from under her hand and threw. The little ivory cubes landed on the table with a spine-chilling clatter, showing a six and a five. Everyone had gathered round the hazard table to watch, even the women and the footmen, as Sebastian threw a six and a five again and again, with sickening monotony. At last he palmed Marisa's dice, letting them roll mockingly around in his palm. 'As I said,' he repeated gently, 'you're a little cheat, aren't you?'

Marisa swallowed, silent, her agile mind racing for ways to escape. She could still bluff, could still run for it.

And then Sir Julian Ormond, who'd come quietly up behind her, put his hand on her shoulder and said to the others, 'Oh, she's cheating all right, I assure you. After all, it's what she's done all her life. Didn't any of you fools see through her disguise?'

Someone swore in surprise at his words, then they all turned to look with new eyes at Marisa, who twisted violently in his grip. 'It's you who's the cheat and impostor,' she said to Ormond in a cold, venomous voice, but no-one was listening to her, because Sebastian was reaching across to rip her silk shirt open, and there was a gasp of arousal as her small yet exquisitely feminine breasts were exposed to a dozen hungry pairs of eyes.

'You see?' said Ormond, his voice scornful though his eyes too were hot on Marisa's soft pink nipples. 'Your handsome youth is a woman, you fools. Strip her properly and you'll see.'

Marisa tried to run then, kicking and lashing out like a wild animal, and hissing out vicious invective, but the men held her with strong hands, while the women, giggling and exclaiming, pulled off her remaining clothes with deft fingers until Marisa stood naked before them, her small breasts heaving with exertion. Their hungry eyes feasted on her slender curves, on the golden down that peeped between her thighs. They held her so firmly that she couldn't even struggle. Her mind worked feverishly, twisting and turning to find some way out; but this time she feared, very much, that she'd overplayed her hand at last.

And Sebastian said, 'Well. It looks as if we have some rather novel entertainment in store for tonight, gentlemen.'

Chapter Twelve

David Valsino was disturbed at midnight by the battering at his front door. He was in bed with two beautiful girls, twin sisters of one of his clients: one was nibbling at his erect penis, while the other was crooning over his lithe Italian body and guiding his finger gently but persistently into her vagina. He was just wondering rather dazedly how best to bring them both to simultaneous orgasm when he realised he had a visitor.

He cursed at first, and decided to ignore the violent knocking, because one of the girls was doing something rather naughty to his sensitive testicles with her tongue. Then it suddenly occurred to him that it might be Marisa, and the thought made him pull himself away from those tormenting fingers and lips to reach out for his silk dressing robe. If it was Marisa, then he didn't particularly want his manservant letting her in and betraying the fact that he already had company. The girls protested, clinging to his hands as they twined together deliciously on the bed, their long, dark hair falling over their shoulders, and their faces pouting up at him in disappointment.

'I'll be back in a moment,' he promised, pulling the robe over his aching erection. Then, picking up a candlestick on his way, he hurried downstairs and pulled open the big front door.

It was Lord James Delsingham. The nobleman looked big and formidable in the light of the streetlamp. He was wearing a dusty, many-caped travelling coat, as if he'd just driven a long way, and David could see his phaeton pulled in against the pavement, with his liveried tiger holding the lathered horses with some effort.

'Is she here?' rapped out Delsingham curtly.

'Who?' David, pulling his silk robe around him, made the mistake of trying to appear dazed and innocent.

Delsingham said, 'Marisa Brooke, you fool. I know she spent some time here earlier. Where is she now?'

David, suddenly very alert, said quickly, 'I'm afraid I've really no idea. She has lots of friends in London, as I'm sure you know. She could be with any of them.'

Delsingham had moved closer to David as he talked. Suddenly he was pinning the fencing master against the wall, his strong hands digging into his shoulders. He said softly, 'Don't play games with me, Valsino. I have to find her, and quickly. She could be in danger. There's every chance she's in some sort of gaming den. Have you any idea which one?'

David swallowed. 'There – there was some mention of the private club in Albion Place . . .'

Delsingham's mouth thinned. 'The Albion? Did *you* mention it to her?'

'Yes,' David stammered. 'We were talking of places where the play was deep, and I just happened to mention the name – '

Delsingham pushed him away, so that he sagged back against the wall. 'You'll pay for this,' he said quietly, and turned swiftly back towards his waiting carriage.

David went slowly back upstairs, feeling shaken. Delsingham was a dangerous man to antagonise. He hoped to God that Marisa was all right. Then he shrugged his shoulders. Marisa could survive anything, couldn't she?

Even so, he was worried about her, and it took the twin sisters some time to revive his flagging interest in them.

* * *

809

Marisa lay wary and watchful, struggling to keep all her senses about her. They'd tied her down to a couch with silken cords, the same couch on the raised dais where the young maid had earlier taken such lascivious pleasure from the dusky footman. She could still smell the musky secretions of the woman's perfumed body. She closed her eyes scornfully to shut out the hot, hungry gaze of the onlookers, but inside she felt a secret shiver of fear as they tied her wrists behind her cropped head so that her breasts were thrust provocatively upwards. She almost uttered an instinctive cry of protest as they pulled her legs apart and tied her ankles to the clawed feet of the couch, exposing her naked femininity for all to see, but she knew they'd take pleasure in any show of fear, so she clamped her mouth shut tightly.

Then she heard Ormond saying to Sebastian, 'I know this little slut. She's like a bitch on heat, believe me. Take no notice of her protests. She pretends to be all golden-haired innocence, but she'll rut with anyone if the fancy takes her. For the past few weeks, she's hired a band of gypsies for her private pleasure.'

Marisa gazed at Ormond with scornful deliberation. 'I thought you were the one into secret rutting. It's common knowledge, I believe, that you can't get your rather inadequate penis to stand proud unless someone gives you a beating. Shall I tell them about your two gypsy girls?'

It was a wild thrust, but her taunt struck home. Marisa's mouth curled in sardonic amusement as he clenched his fists, his smooth face quite white with anger, and ordered two of the women to tie a silk scarf round her mouth to silence her.

Then she heard Sebastian murmuring something to the hovering women, and suddenly two of them were crouching beside her, fingering and stroking her pinioned body, pulling at her soft nipples until they sprang into hard, defiant life. She pulled at her bonds in protest, trying to fight down the delicious ripples of pleasure as she felt their hot, wet lips attending to her breasts with consummate feminine skill, and then she went very still, her breath catching in her throat.

Dear God, there was no way she could fight this.

Because now she could feel a pink, pointed female tongue stroking lightly at her swollen labia, skilfully parting her dark petals of flesh as they lay exposed between her outspread legs, and sliding along languorously towards the base of her swollen clitoris. She shuddered at the wicked voluptuousness of the caress as the two women at her breasts tugged and nibbled her distended teats, sending fierce strokes of rapture rushing down to join the dark pool of burning need at her tense womb. As they continued to lick, she felt their fingers as well, cunning, busy fingers, fastening something round her. She felt the kiss of cold leather biting into the soft flesh of her bosom, and looked down to see a skilfully made harness of supple straps encasing each breast and pushing them out with lewd wantonness, the swollen flesh white and creamy as it stood proud from the tight leather. She heard the hiss of indrawn breath around the room, and saw that several of the men down in the shadows of the hall were slowly fondling themselves, rubbing surreptitiously at their distended cocks beneath their clothing as they watched her, their eyes glazed over with lust.

Marisa swore fluently at them and twisted in her bonds, desperately aroused in spite of her resistance. The woman crouching between her tethered legs, sensing her weakness, increased her tender assault on her captive's most secret places, darting and licking as Marisa's juices spilled out, then pointing her tongue and thrusting it as far as she could inside Marisa's honeyed sex, filling it with a rasping sweetness and wriggling it about inside her until Marisa moaned aloud and thrust her harnessed breasts up against the faces of the women who were eagerly tonguing her nipples. In spite of everything she could do to resist she was nearly at the point of delicious, rending orgasm, feeling herself about to split like a ripe fruit as she bore down against the thrusting tongue in her vagina, helplessly grinding the plump kernel of her clitoris against the woman's face. Then she was suddenly aware that Sebastian was whispering in one of the women's ears, and he laughed as he met Marisa's burning eyes. 'Do your work, Susannah,' he said curtly.

Marisa felt the sharp tension ripple through her as the maid, Susannah, came lightly towards her, picking up on her way a long, unused wax candle from a gilt holder on a little satinwood table nearby. Slowly she started to moisten it with a bottle of musky unguent, and all the time her hot eyes were on Marisa's secret parts. Marisa watched, her skin prickling with alertness, and then Susannah leaned across her shoulder and whispered, 'Lift your bottom up.'

Marisa shook her head dazedly. 'What?'

'I said, lift your bottom up, dearie.' The woman grinned. 'I'm not going to hurt you. Oh, no. You're going to enjoy this, believe me.'

Still Marisa resisted instinctively, but with deft fingers Susannah and another woman raised Marisa's slender buttocks and swiftly piled cushions beneath her hips, so her body was arched away from the couch. With a thrill of despair, Marisa realised that now all of her most secret places were exposed to the watching company: the pink, fleshy lips of her vulva, the dark cleft of her pelvic floor, even the tight little rosebud hole of her anus. She licked her dry lips, feeling the leather harness bite gently at her swollen breasts, while Susannah stroked and prodded at her exposed anal orifice with her oiled fingers, caressing the little puckered crevice, loving it, teasing it gently. Slowly she pushed her finger in, and Marisa felt her tight ring of muscle flutter and close around it as her whole body shuddered at the deliciously wicked intrusion.

'That's it, my pretty,' murmured Susannah lovingly. 'You've enjoyed this sort of thing before, I can tell. Like it, don't you? Now for the best part.' And even as she spoke, Marisa felt the slender wax candle ravishing her anus like a phallus. She spasmed instinctively around it, her muscles clenching fiercely as the whole of her lower abdomen began to palpitate with heavy, liquid pleasure at the hard penetration and her breasts in their black leather strapping thrust hungrily for release. Susannah, watching her intently, slid the stem of wax in a little deeper, then withdrew it a fraction, and Marisa gritted her teeth beneath the silk gag. She wouldn't submit to them, she wouldn't. And yet, oh, just the slightest pressure on her burning pleasure bud, and she would topple over the edge into sweet, consuming release. She clenched fiercely at the intrusive candle-stem as the warm waves of degradation washed through her.

Then Sebastian's voice penetrated the velvety blackness in which she lay suspended. 'Enough for the moment,' he said. 'Leave her. At least we know she's ready and waiting for us.'

The women fell away from her, leaving Marisa panting, aroused, open. Her tormentor turned round to look at the hot-faced circle of watchers in the candlelit shadows. 'I think you'll agree, gentlemen,' he said, 'that we need to teach this slattern that nobody tricks us and takes our money.'

The others nodded eagerly. Ormond said coldly, 'What shall we do with the slut then, Sebastian? Take her one at a time?'

Sebastian's voice again, cold and chilling. 'No, I have a better idea. Winner to take all. We'll play for her.'

Marisa lay back on her couch, the room swimming about her. For the first time ever, she was beginning to think that there was no way out.

The table was drawn out, the cards were produced in intense silence and they began to play. Marisa twisted her head on the couch as the cards were dealt for vingt-et-un, trying to glimpse the hands nearest to her, but concentration was difficult with the slender wax phallus seeming to throb like a live thing in the tense passage of her rectum, keeping every one of her senses on edge. Soon, unless some miracle happened, she would be publicly taken, in front of all these people. She pulled in vain at her tight silken bonds. Dear God, there must be some way to get out of here, there must be.

Then the door opened slowly. She turned her head to look, as did everyone else in the room, and her heart seemed to stop as a man came in, tall and formidable in the shadows. She saw his darkly expressive eyes flicker momentarily as they scanned the candlelit room, and then they finally came to rest on her tethered, almost naked body.

Delsingham. Lord James Delsingham. Marisa's eyes blazed with scorn at the realisation that he too belonged with this decadent, debauched set of men. Somehow she'd thought he was different, but then, hadn't she misjudged him all along? For a moment their eyes met and held, but then Delsingham let his bored gaze wander back to the card party, and Marisa saw how Ormond's face flickered with a sudden, intense hatred which he quickly concealed. And then Delsingham drawled, 'Sorry I'm late, gentlemen. I see you've been enjoying yourselves. Any chance of me taking a hand?'

Sebastian gestured smoothly to the empty chair beside him. 'Take a seat, Delsingham. We've only just started.'

Delsingham took off his big coat and eased his tall, athletic frame into the proffered chair. The candlelight burnished his glossy black hair and flickered on the clean-cut lines of his darkly handsome face. Marisa saw with narrowed eyes how the women watched him hungrily, wanting him. 'The stakes, gentlemen?' he enquired lazily, lifting his first card.

Sebastian smiled thinly. 'We're playing with tokens only.' Delsingham raised his eyebrows. Sebastian went on, 'The prize, you see, is rather unusual. The winner gets to enjoy this rather delectable female intruder, whom we caught spying on us earlier.'

Delsingham's eyes flickered once more up to Marisa on the dais. She felt the cords bite into her limbs, felt the harness lewdly pushing out her naked breasts, and hated him for seeing her like this. He said softly, his eyes lingering on the wax phallus protruding from between

814

her uplifted buttocks, 'Well. In that case, I'm definitely glad I arrived in time.'

So he was going to play too, thought Marisa scornfully. He was hateful, hateful. Just as bad as all the rest, only worse, because he pretended to be different.

The cards moved fast. She could see Delsingham clearly. He seemed to pause, very slightly, each time it was his turn, and she saw how his hooded eyes swept the upturned cards with every move. He was counting the cards, she realised narrowly, being only too familiar with that procedure herself. And then she saw something else, something that almost made her forget her predicament and caused her heart to thud slowly, painfully against her ribs. He was wearing her ring, her beautiful gold ring on the little finger of his left hand.

He was using it too. No-one but she would have known it, but from where she lay she could just detect the tiny, almost imperceptible movement as he used the retractable pin to mark the corner of certain cards as they passed through his hands on the deal. Casing the pack wasn't enough for Delsingham; he was really making sure of winning this time. The others were watching him too, hating him for winning so easily, but were unable to detect anything compromising in his steady play. He didn't even bother to lose a few times to confuse his opponents, thought Marisa rather dazedly, as he calmly doubled his stake and displayed an ace and a ten. There was a growl of disappointment from the remaining players as his long, elegant, manicured hands, edged with beautiful Brussels lace that spilled from his cuffs, moved in confidently to pull in the tokens. The other players threw in their cards and scattered their tokens in angry disappointment. He'd won. And his prize was her, Marisa. She held herself very still, hardly breathing.

'She's all yours, damn you, Delsingham,' growled Sebastian, leaning back in his chair, his face drawn with tension. Ormond said nothing, but just watched his enemy with burning, heated eyes.

Delsingham said, 'Here? Now?'

'Those were the terms of play. If you don't want her, someone else will oblige.'

'Oh, I want her,' said Lord James Delsingham. He pushed back his chair and casually strolled across to the dais, his long boots thudding softly on the smooth floorboards. Then he stood looking down at her, his hands on his lean hips, his face expressionless.

'Get on with it, Delsingham,' growled someone from the table, thick-voiced with lust. 'Pleasure the wench, will you? Either that, or let someone else claim her!'

Delsingham stooped to carefully remove the gag from round her mouth, letting his long fingers brush her swollen lips. He had his back to the card table, and she realised that he was deliberately blocking off the other men's view of her face. 'Can you bear it,' he said to her very quietly, 'if we get on with the business in hand here and now?'

Marisa gazed up at him, her eyes burning. 'In front of these animals? I didn't realise your tastes ran to such depravities, Lord Delsingham.'

His mouth thinned. 'They don't,' he said.

'Then get me out of here, damn you.'

He drew a deep breath and said, 'My Ganymede, that's not possible without fulfilling the terms of the game. Our friends over there would feel cheated, and they might cause trouble.'

'They're your friends, not mine. You can deal with them.'

'They're not my friends. And normally I would never set foot in a depraved place such as this.'

Marisa stared at him. 'Then why – '

'I'm here because I was trying to find you, to extricate you from whatever trouble you'd plunged yourself into,' he replied shortly. 'And believe me, I'm regretting it more and more each minute.'

The pack was starting to close in on them. The men's mood was getting restless and ugly. 'Damn you, man,' an onlooker was protesting indignantly. 'Why did you ask to be dealt into the game, if you didn't want the little slut?'

Another man had wandered over to leer at Marisa. 'Perhaps Delsingham can't get it up. Perhaps he ought to let me poke the wench instead.'

Delsingham whipped round at that, and lifted the man who'd just spoken by his high shirt collar, so he couldn't breathe. Then he threw the man aside so that he thudded, dazed, to the floor, and the room fell silent.

Delsingham turned back to Marisa. 'Let's get this over with, Ganymede, shall we? You never know, we might even enjoy ourselves.'

Her eyes narrowed. 'Conceited as ever!' she spat out.

He laughed, 'Of course,' and then he bent to kiss her gently. 'Aren't you glad I won?' Even as he spoke, his hands moved to caress her leather-bound breasts, cupping each globe of constricted flesh while his lips moved to lave at her nipples, his tongue stroking and pulling at both yearning crests until they were hard and stiff.

'What do you think?' she whispered, her eyes suddenly sparkling. And she arched suddenly towards him, heedless of the silken cords tightening relentlessly at her wrists and ankles, melting at his familiar masculine touch, at his scent, as his hard, lithe body pressed against hers.

They had shut everyone else out. His hands continued their delicious work on her breasts as the tight leather harness bit into their swelling flesh. Gently he shifted the silk cushions beneath her hips, lifting them higher, and she felt herself moisten sweetly for him as her thighs fell apart still further. Carefully he moved the slender shaft in her rectum, reminding her anew of its sweet, heavy penetration; she moaned aloud in pleasure at the intimate caress, catching her lip between her teeth to stifle her cry. In the midst of her own excitement, she was dimly aware that he was attending to his own clothing with skilful fingers, finally drawing out his lovely thick penis, which was dusky and already rigid. 'You're ready?' he said very quietly.

'Yes,' muttered Marisa, her eyes on his face, her body melting with exquisite impatience. 'I'm ready. Take me, damn you.'

He arched over her, his substantial frame protecting her from the avid stares of the onlookers. 'That's my intention, my sweet,' he murmured, and she gasped aloud at the wonderful sensation of that thick, lengthy shaft of flesh sliding deep inside her very core. She was doubly filled, her aroused body squeezing and relishing the invasion of her secret flesh. Delsingham rocked gently, moving his powerful member with exquisite skill, and at the same time he drew on her stiffened nipples with his fingers, pulling and rolling at the dark teats and making her gasp as the tingling pleasure-pain shot through her body. Then he clasped her bottom-cheeks up towards him, reminding her of that other, wicked penetration at her rear. She gasped as the heavy sensations rolled through her, but he kissed her to stifle her cries, and proceeded to drive her to sweet distraction with his beautiful firm penis, sliding it deliciously in and out of her quivering flesh until she moaned and bucked wildly against him, shuddering into dark ecstasy as her buttocks clenched around the thin, smooth shaft that penetrated her rear. Gently but strongly he continued to ravish her, his penis a mighty rod of pleasure around which she convulsed and trembled as the languorous waves of bliss crashed through her pinioned body. Harder and harder he drove himself, his tongue darting and tugging at her distended nipples, and she felt his penis plunging at her very heart as his own silent ecstasy consumed him. His hips clenched and jerked above her, and just for a moment his self-control was gone. Marisa felt herself pulsing round his powerful phallus, draining his very essence, holding him deep inside her as the longed-for bliss lapped in slow, caressing waves around her.

She was brought back to stark reality by a slow, calculated burst of clapping from the shadowy figures who surrounded them. Slowly Delsingham raised himself, silently pulling out the invasive wax stem from between her bottom cheeks as he did so and casting it to one side. Marisa shivered, suddenly chilly in the oppressive heat of that richly furnished room. She heard Sebastian's hateful voice saying coldly, 'Well done, Delsingham. The bitch was certainly hot for you; you pleasured her well.'

And then she heard Ormond's voice, cold and snakelike. 'Of course she was hot for him. These two already know each other well. Didn't you realise?'

Delsingham ignored him. He was slowly untying Marisa, his eyes tender as he worked at the cords. He said to her very quietly, so no-one else could hear, 'Your clothes are nearby?'

Marisa nodded: 'Just within reach.'

'Good girl.'

And then Marisa was aware that Ormond was saying in a louder, deadlier drawl now to his companions: 'I tell you, they know each other. This whole thing was set up between them, if you ask me, with Delsingham arriving when he did. The girl is a cheat, and so is Lord Delsingham. You've all been cheated of your pleasure.'

Delsingham swung round to him. 'You want me to tell them about your ideas of pleasure, Ormond? The other day I had a most interesting conversation with one of those gypsy girls you kept closeted in your quarters for a while. Now, she had some tales to tell, believe me.'

Ormond forced a defiant shrug, but Marisa saw the sudden flicker of fear in his pale eyes, and he went silent. So Delsingham knew about the strange alliance between the gypsy girl and Ormond and their plans to destroy her. Had he known about it all the time? Her mind raced, but there was no time for anything now, because at last Delsingham had untied all of her bonds, except the intricately buckled leather harness around her breasts. As Marisa drew herself up on the couch, fighting for alertness, only too aware of the resurgence of menace in the air, he reached to hand her her coat, which lay discarded on the floor beside her, and said very quietly so no-one else could hear, 'Pull this on, then your breeches and boots. And be ready to run.'

'But how – '

'No time for arguments, my sweet. Just do exactly as I say.'

Marisa nodded. Already she could hear the low growling and muttering of protest coming from the crowd of men who were watching. Ormond was silent, white-faced, but she could hear the cold voice of Sebastian rising above them to say clearly, 'You should have left the wench where she is, Delsingham. I've a feeling we were all entitled to try her, just as we originally planned.'

They were advancing towards the couch where she was hurriedly pulling her boots on, their faces mean and ugly with frustrated lust. Marisa felt her heart racing. And then Delsingham, already on his feet and calmly slipping on his own loose greatcoat, reached into his deep pockets and pulled out two pistols. He raised them almost casually, and said, 'I shouldn't try anything, gentlemen, if I were you. I really shouldn't.'

Marisa, hastily buttoning up her coat beside him, murmured calmly, 'I'm ready.'

'Then make for the door,' he rapped out, and as she hurried to open it, he began a slow, measured retreat, walking backwards with his pistols levelled at the thwarted faces of their enemies.

Marisa was already by the door, holding it open, waiting as he retreated towards her with what seemed to be agonising slowness. 'Where now?' she asked tersely.

'Up those stairs behind you,' snapped Delsingham over his shoulder. Marisa nodded and hurried on up, with Delsingham following her. One of the men lurched forward angrily, and Delsingham whipped his pistol towards him. 'I really would enjoy using this, believe me.'

The man fell back, uncertain. They were almost at the top of the stairs. Delsingham said quickly, 'Make for that door down at the end of the corridor, Marisa. It should take us out of this place. Pray God it isn't locked.'

It was. Marisa saw Delsingham's face tighten as he pulled and strained at the handle. She turned sharply and saw the men, led by Sebastian, coming towards them down the shadowy corridor with the greed of approaching victory in their faces. Delsingham whirled round to face them, and said to her, between gritted teeth, 'I might be able to hold them off for a few minutes, while you try to find another exit. Don't worry about me, just run.'

And then Marisa laughed softly. 'No need to be heroic, my dear Lord Delsingham. You see, I think I've got the key.' She fished in her deep coat pocket to pull out a heavy iron key, and with their furious pursuers only yards away, she eased back the lock triumphantly and they plunged into the street outside, slamming the door behind them and locking it from the outside. The rain was pouring down into the silent London street, and with a wide grin, Marisa threw the key over her shoulder, so that it landed with a splash in a puddle. Delsingham was running his hand through his hair, watching her perplexedly. 'How in damnation did you get that key?'

'I picked that oaf of a footman's pocket earlier, when he was manhandling me. He never even noticed,' she announced triumphantly 'They'll have another key, of course, but it might take them a little while to find it.'

'Do you always pick people's pockets?'

'Oh, yes. It's a habit of mine. You see, you never know when it will come in useful.'

Delsingham, his hands on his hips as the rain streamed down his face, began to laugh softly. 'Magnificent, my dear Ganymede. Quite magnificent.'

Marisa grinned back up at him, suddenly feeling very, very happy.

But they didn't get much time. Another door opened somewhere further down the dark lane, and they heard shouts behind them. 'This way. They must be along here somewhere.'

Quickly Delsingham and Marisa began to run through the rain-soaked street, their boots splashing in the puddles. For a moment, Marisa hesitated in dismay as she realised they were in another dead end, but then Delsingham grabbed her hand and pulled her into the warm, hay-scented darkness of a stable, where horses stirred restlessly in the shadows. Somehow he found a wooden ladder up into the hay loft and pushed her up there, following speedily and pulling the ladder up after himself. Marisa, gasping with exertion, lay in the hay, while he put his arm round her protectively and listened at the hatch. 'They've gone on past,' he said. 'We should be all right now.'

'They might call out the constables.'

'I doubt it. When they come to their senses, they'll realise they would be somewhat foolish to draw attention to the rather sordid activities of their club.'

Marisa sat up rather sharply, starting to brush the hay from her face and hair. 'Presumably you too have enjoyed those rather sordid activities, as you call them.'

He shook his head. 'Never. Believe me, I've no fancy to lose a thousand guineas at a sitting. And as I told you, normally the kind of depraved pleasures they offer are rather beyond me. Though not tonight.' His eyes gleamed wickedly as he assessed her slender, rain-bedraggled figure, with her blue eyes wide and strangely vulnerable beneath her close-fitting crop of wet blonde hair. 'You're all right, Ganymede?' he said suddenly, his hands on her narrow shoulders. 'They didn't harm you?'

Marisa smiled a little shakily, then her eyes glittered with familiar mischief. 'No, indeed. They were a bunch of drunken fools, all of them. Though,' and a frown darkened her face, 'I hadn't realised how much Sir Julian Ormond hated me. Do you think he can still cause trouble for me?'

'He's facing complete ruin,' said Delsingham shortly, 'and if he has any sense at all, he'll keep very quiet about his dealings with you.'

'He must have really hated me, from the beginning,' shivered Marisa. 'He must have been responsible for everything: the ransacking of my rooms in London, that fall I took on the horse he lent me, the terrible attack on Seth, even the fire . . .'

'I did try to warn you about him.'

Her eyes glinted with sudden mischief. 'You think I'd take any notice of you? Anyway, I would have dealt with him somehow. Nobody gets the better of me!'

'So I'd observed,' he murmured rather faintly.

'And see. See what I've got here.' Marisa thrust her hands into her deep pockets and pulled out fistfuls of coins, bills, and IOUs, with the beautiful diamond pin glinting on top of the pile.

Delsingham caught his breath. 'I take it you cheated rather expertly?'

'I think they got good value out of me,' she laughed. Then she added regretfully, as she fingered the notes, 'I suppose they'll refuse to honour these, won't they? And the man I stole the diamond from might set up a chase for me.'

Delsingham shook his head, examining her booty. 'No. I don't think any of your victims will dare to dispute their losses in the cold light of day, otherwise we'll threaten to reveal where and how you acquired them. They have much more to lose than you, because some of these men have formidable reputations to keep. You'd be surprised at the exalted positions some of them hold in society. I think they'll stay quiet. And lots of them are so wealthy that they won't miss a few hundred guineas.'

Marisa gazed up at him steadily. 'You make it sound like nothing,' she said. 'But this diamond alone will make sure that I can keep Melbray Manor.'

He smiled down at her, the rain still streaking his dark hair. 'Still want to play the fine lady, Marisa?'

Her face tightened stubbornly. 'Yes, and why not?'

'Why not indeed? I think you're the most wonderful lady I've ever met in my life.'

Marisa stared at him, looking for tell-tale signs of mockery, but there were none. Then, still distracted, she suddenly realised that her coat had fallen apart as she crouched there in the hay, and she remembered that she was wearing nothing underneath but the tight leather harness that the women had fastened round her breasts. Delsingham had just noticed it too. She felt his eyes glide appraisingly over her small, creamy breasts, upthrust and conical in their thin black strapping. She felt a warm tongue of desire assaulting her senses, making her weak; her nipples hardened slowly and shamefully beneath his thoughtful gaze. She wanted him, damn him, wanted him again quite badly, and it unsettled her. She said rather shakily,

'I don't suppose many fine ladies go around dressed like this.'

'True,' he said. 'But most of them would look ridiculous in such attire. Whereas you, my sweet, look quite, quite delicious.'

Marisa moistened her lips. She was suddenly frightened of the power this man had over her. No-one else had ever been able to make her a churning mass of desire just by looking at her. Determined to regain control, she peered down through the hatch in the hayloft a little nervously as the horses down below stirred and whickered. 'I can't hear anything from outside,' she said with a pretence at calmness. 'They must have given up the hunt long ago. I think we ought to go.'

'Oh, no,' he said seriously, drawing her back up beside him. 'They'll still be looking, I'm quite sure of it.'

'Well, then,' she persisted stubbornly, 'even so, perhaps we ought to make a run for it.'

'I think,' he said, 'that we ought to stay.' And he pulled her hand down gently, pressing it against the warm, swelling bulge at his groin. Marisa caught her breath at the feel of that delicious rod of flesh, but she wasn't giving in, not yet.

'Dice for it,' she declared stubbornly. 'Best of three. If you win, we stay. If I win, we go.'

He laughed. 'Oh, no. Dice with you, Miss Brooke? They'll be weighted, crooked, whatever. By the way, did you like the way I used your ring?'

'Yes,' she said impatiently. 'You were almost as good

as me. Look, if you don't want to dice, then we'll toss a coin. Agreed?'

'Agreed,' he said warily.

Marisa pulled a silver coin swiftly from her pocket. 'Tails,' she said.

It was heads. 'We stay,' Delsingham said softly, and Marisa, with a show of reluctance, subsided obediently into his arms.

He kissed her, lapping the rain from her face and throat with his tongue, then entering her mouth with deep, tender strokes that were urgent with passion. He paused to ease off his coat and lay her down on it, dipping his head to caress her wonderfully aching breasts until she was moaning aloud with liquid desire, longing for him to take her with his lovely, silken cock which was already sliding languorously across her taut belly. She struggled to pull off her boots, ripping her breeches down impatiently so she could welcome him into her very heart, and as his wonderful penis slid deep within her, she shivered with rapture, wrapping her arms and legs round him and letting her inner muscles flutter and ripple around that solid shaft of flesh. His strong hand moved lightly down across her belly to tangle in the blond down of her pubis and stroke lightly at the base of her straining little bud of pleasure. She cried aloud, almost on the brink already as the delicious feather-strokes of his fingertip circled and caressed so lightly while his thickly solid penis continued to move slowly, purposefully within her. For a moment, his dark gaze burned into her flushed, melting face. 'Marisa,' he said. Then he started to drive strongly, passionately into her, his hand still lightly caressing her clitoris, his mouth rasping at her straining breasts. She lifted her hips, clutching deliriously round his iron-hard penis with her greedy inner muscles, feeling his moist, velvety mouth rubbing against her breasts and his pointed tongue tugging at her distended teats. She reached down to caress his tight, hard balls as they filled with his seed. With a low growl he drew himself out almost to his extremity, lifting himself so that she could glimpse the darkly masculine root of him, breathtakingly powerful and long, the sleek, veined shaft shiny with the flowing nectar of her inner core. She gasped aloud, writhing her hips, yearning wordlessly for him to possess her, and he smiled and plunged his penis in slowly, inch by delicious inch, stretching her, filling her. Rising with a cry to meet him, her whole body tightened and exploded in dark, wanton rapture as he drove himself to his own harsh, passionate climax.

She lay dazed in his arms, still feeling the gentle spasms of his sated member deep inside her as he kissed her softly. Outside the rain poured down on the cobbles of the dark London street, and she heard the faint cry of the watch in the distance. 'One of the clock, and a fair night.' Languorously she opened her eyes, feeling blissfully content as they lay in the hay-scented darkness. An ace. Quite definitely an ace.

'Marisa,' Delsingham was saying softly, 'Marisa, my precious, it really wasn't like you to misjudge the fall of that coin. You must be losing your touch.'

She smiled up at him, her thick-lashed eyes hazy with calculated pleasure, and showed him the two-headed silver coin she always carried in her pocket. 'I cheated,' she said contentedly, and nestled into his arms.